Through
Phantom Eyes

Through
Phantom Eyes

Volume Five

Christine

by

Theodora Bruns

iUniverse, Inc.
Bloomington

Through Phantom Eyes
Volume Five—Christine

This is a work of fiction. All of the characters, names, incidents, organizations, and dialogue in this novel are either the products of the author's imagination or are used fictitiously.

iUniverse books may be ordered through booksellers or by contacting:

iUniverse
1663 Liberty Drive
Bloomington, IN 47403
www.iuniverse.com
1-800-Authors (1-800-288-4677)

Because of the dynamic nature of the Internet, any web addresses or links contained in this book may have changed since publication and may no longer be valid. The views expressed in this work are solely those of the author and do not necessarily reflect the views of the publisher, and the publisher hereby disclaims any responsibility for them.

Any people depicted in stock imagery provided by Thinkstock are models, and such images are being used for illustrative purposes only.

Certain stock imagery © Thinkstock.

ISBN: 978-1-4759-5474-6 (sc)
ISBN: 978-1-4759-5475-3 (hc)
ISBN: 978-1-4759-5476-0 (ebk)

Printed in the United States of America

iUniverse rev. date: 10/29/2012

Dedication

To the gift of music

Review

Written by

Susan Rueppel, Ph.D.
Energetic Wisdom
Intuition for Empowerment

Through Phantom Eyes—Volume Five—sustains the same non-stop and spellbinding adventure as Bruns' previous volumes. Gripping, suspenseful, and surprising—I couldn't put it down. A gifted writer, Bruns has an impressive grasp of Erik's life and is a master at connecting us with his heart-wrenching emotions and the unexpected twists and turns of his brilliant and often tortured mind. Each volume furthers the fascinating saga of the amazing life of Erik. Always leaves me wanting more.

Cover and Interior Sketch Design
Theodora Bruns
ThroughPhantomEyes. Com

* * *

Cover and Interior Artwork
Judy Sava-Coppola
Savadesign. Com

* * *

Model for Cover Art
Michael Preston
Grandson of Theodora Bruns

* * *

Models for Interior Art
Michael Preston and his wife
Carmen Preston
Grandson and Granddaughter
of Theodora Bruns

Acknowledgments

My eternal gratitude reaches out to those who inspired me and helped me breathe life into this unforeseen work. First and foremost to Erik himself, for, as his lonely existence consumed my thoughts and his mournful pain permeated my heart, my own expressions pleaded for a release from their boundaries. Consequently, without his tragic life so full of love for his music and Christine, my imagination would have remained silent, and I wouldn't have started on this astonishing journey. Therefore, *merci*, Erik.

Next, to Brad Little, whose eloquent voice, along with his amazing musical portrayal of Erik's love, passion, and pain on the stage, unlocked my barren heart. Because of his extraordinary talent, my own passion was aroused in ways previously unknown to me. Brad's awareness of Erik's love for that one exceptional woman, Christine, was what enabled me to spread my awakening heart across the printed page for all to see. I'm forever thankful, Brad.

Then there is Patti, who came into my life quite unexpectedly because of her fascination with Erik's life. Among other things, she helped me keep my fingers on the pulse of those who want to read more about this man known as "The Phantom." Perhaps with trepidation, she courageously spoke her mind and gave me insight. So thank you, Patti, for your time, tender care, and understanding of my special needs.

Also, I send a big thank you to Ann. Her skills in the editing department went far beyond the written word and various punctuation marks. She used her vast knowledge and patiently taught me the proper placement of those words and punctuation marks. I sincerely appreciate the time she spent helping me to become a better writer. I couldn't have gotten where I am today without her.

I would also like to thank Susan, who spent the time and energy to read this volume and then to formulate a review. Hopefully, just a quick glance at her words will help readers determine if they want to follow Erik's journey with me.

In addition, there's my remarkable daughter Debi, who also shares my love for Erik's story. She committed to working long and tedious hours with me to put the finishing touches on every phrase within my labor of love. Thanks to her keen eye, diligence, proofing ability, and patience, I believe the finished product is one that anyone can easily read, understand, and enjoy. She also came to my aid with financial backing. Without it I fear you wouldn't be holding this book in your hands. A mere thank you isn't enough to express my appreciation for all you've done, Deb.

Then there is my sister Janice who also came to my aid and helped finance this project. But what helped me even more were her words of encouragement. In almost every conversation we had she asked how the project was coming along and shared what she liked about the volume she was then reading. So, thank you, Jan, for being such a loving and supportive sister.

Finally, there is my eternal friend and daughter Kelli, who, from the beginning, enthusiastically shared my desire to see Erik with a full and satisfying life. She served as my diligent researcher, patient teacher, gentle critic, knowledgeable literary collaborator, and first fan. She has also added her talents in the public relations department by getting Erik's story in front of those who desire to read more about him. Her self-sacrificing efforts and encouragement over the years stirred my soul and gave me courage—courage that I never knew existed—courage that was an essential element in seeing these novels to their completion. I fear, without her ever-present reassurance, my whimsical ideas about Erik's life would have eventually retreated in a cowardly fashion back into my imagination. There they would be forced to live with the rest of my "happily-ever-after" endings, somewhere in the silent and dark recesses of my fanciful mind. *Merci! Merci beaucoup*, Kelli.

Prologue

It's said that, in the few moments before you die, your entire life passes before your eyes. Well, my entire life had just traveled through my memories, but it had taken me four days to relive it. That is, the part of it before I met Christine—the woman destined to own my heart. With the syringe pressed against my waiting vein, I realized that the moment our paths met, my demise began. In that sense, our meeting was bittersweet.

Oh, Christine, my heart moaned. Why did it have to be this way? Why did I have to see you on that stage and allow you to capture my heart and soul so completely? Why did I allow you to lead me as your senseless slave? Why couldn't you have remained like the rest of the chorus girls I'd seen—faceless? If I hadn't made you my quest or if I'd allowed my curiosity about you to fade along with the stage lights, my life would still be just as it was. I would be living the remainder of my days in my home. I would be as content as I could be, with my music surrounding me.

Why did I pick that moment not to listen to my rational mind? Why did I listen to my wayward heart that was about to lead me down a one-way path? Why couldn't I have remained content, just that once, to silence the moaning of my awakening and lonely heart, instead of allowing you to pluck its ripeness with the splendor of your eyes? Why couldn't we have expressed our unconditional love for each other so we could be one?

"Oh, Christine, why?" I sighed.

There was no answer from her and no use in questioning the events that marred my once-comfortable life. Those events left me all alone, with only a lethal dose of morphine and the grim awareness that it was pulling me toward my impending death.

I glanced over at Christine's emerald pillow and pictured her sleeping there, with her hair spread out over it, resembling spun gold. I missed her presence in my life so much. I missed the sound of her voice in laughter, her smile, and her dark blue eyes each time they sparkled with excitement. I missed her so. How could someone I'd known for such a short time take over so much of my life?

I'd memorized every curve and contour of her face and body, and I wanted to remember everything about her while I still could. That was a beautiful idea, but then I looked down at my reality, the needle as it began to puncture my skin. I clenched my teeth and pushed the needle in further, and then I closed my eyes to that dismal sight and returned to thoughts of the woman I loved.

With my eyes closed and her fragrance surrounding me, I could feel her there with me. I could see her eyes filled with wonder, as they were the first time I'd seen them. It felt as if only moments had passed since I'd spoken her name for the first time. I could still feel my heart race, sending a warm rush through my body.

What was that attraction, that love, that unquenched longing? It was so strong, it caused me to lose my dignity, after I'd sworn not to let anything or anyone take it from me again. What was it that caused me and many men before me to lose our minds? Whatever it was, it made it nearly impossible to tear myself away from her once I'd experienced it. As we stood on that dimly-lit stage, I knew I needed to move further into the shadows, but I couldn't.

I remember trying to catch my breath, while wondering what had happened to me. I remembered watching Meg and that enchanting woman scurry off the stage and into the darkness. Yes, I remember everything about that night—that night when my life began its journey toward its final destination.

Christine

One

Paris, France

February 1881

My days had taken many twists and turns during the 45 years since I began walking life's path, but none of them could compare to what awaited me during one evening in February 1881. The night was cold, with fresh snow covering the cobblestone roads and icicles hanging precariously from the naked trees. I felt the cold as I walked the deserted streets alone, even though I was still hot with anger because of that newspaper article about my midnight rides. It was tiring to watch my every stride just to remain unnoticed, and, with Paris now on the alert, I knew I would have to be even more cautious.

Consequently, I walked quietly through the dark passage beneath the stage, grumbling because of that exasperating reporter. He'd searched for my whereabouts before, and his boldness was becoming troublesome to me. It was bad enough that I had Oded to contend with, but now I had this writer also. Again, I grumbled. Why can't they leave me alone?

Then, to make matters worse and to push my patience beyond its boundary, I heard Buquet's voice. I shook my head, ground my teeth, and turned to leave before I did something I'd regret. But I'd only taken a few steps when he began telling out-and-out lies about me. I growled quietly. How I wanted to give him a piece of my smoldering mind. The final shove to do so came when the girls gasped and cried out. He was enjoying frightening them, and, as I charged back toward their location, I saw red.

Once there, I opened the trap door on the stage just enough to throw verbal assaults at Buquet. When I saw him and heard his fabrications in detail, my pulse quickened even more. So, with narrowed eyes, I waited for the right opening to direct my voice to that foolish man's ears. When it came, I slowly repeated his name—in a deep, threatening tone.

"Buquet!—Buquet!"

Then, from my hidden location, I watched the scene as it unfolded. When he heard his name resound in his head, he twisted in circles, and his eyes bulged as they darted beyond the props and backdrops in a futile search for the mysterious ghost of his imagination. His sloppy mouth gaped open, and he flung his hands over his ears in an attempt to shut out my intimidating voice. He might have momentarily prevented my words from entering through his ears, but he couldn't stop their tone from flooding through his frightened mind.

With delicate hands placed over painted lips, the silly girls in their lavender tutus giggled, perhaps believing Joseph's actions were part of the entertainment. Well, in a way they were—entertainment for me, that is. After all, we were in an edifice designed with enjoyment in mind, so shouldn't one of its builders also receive his due amusement? I believed so. Therefore, I continued to watch the hilarious movements of that superstitious idiot, the one responsible for my displeasure. While I maintained that cold and menacing manner he feared, I struggled desperately to restrain my hysterical laughter.

Once he removed his hands from his ears, I began again. "*Joseph Buquet!* Why do you spread these lies about me? Do you conjure up these falsehoods because of your dull and boring existence? Won't these frivolous girls give you attention without bizarre stories? Aren't you ashamed of yourself? You should be extremely careful, *Joseph Buquet*, or these lies about *my* past could become fulfilled prophecies about *your* future!"

After speaking my mind, I released my control over him. In his attempt at a hasty retreat, he groped backward, stumbled over a prop, and landed with a loud thud on the stage floor. With the color completely drained from his distorted face, he struggled to get to his feet and run away, to where I don't believe he knew or cared. I will forever be amazed at how terrified someone could become at only the sound of my voice.

Instinctively, my hand pressed against my lips to prevent laughter from escaping, but by the time he managed to flee behind backdrops, nothing could have prevented me from expressing my amusement. Watching his desperate plight was better than any comedy script ever written, and, before long, I couldn't suppress my sense of humor any longer. As a result, my booming laughter joined the shrill pitch of the girls' giggles.

Within moments, I became aware that my voice alone was reverberating through the nearly dark house. The ballerinas huddled together, resembling a group of porcelain figurines thrown on a young maiden's bookshelf. They had a death grip on each other in an endeavor to protect themselves from their own over-active imaginations, fueled by the power of my imposing voice. As the last thunderous waves of sound gradually subsided, a chilling silence crept over the stage.

Out of the stillness, a small familiar voice dared to mutter, "It's the Phantom—I know it!"

The familiar voice belonged to little Meg, who began chattering like a frightened baby bird. With a smile and shake of my head, I watched her scurry, with another young chorus girl, behind the dark red stage curtains. Curiosity about what stories she might relate regarding the infamous Paris Opera Ghost gained control, so I quickly and quietly rose up through the trap door. As I made my way into the shadows of the backdrops, I heard another voice.

That sweet, soft, and unfamiliar voice questioned, "The Phantom? Who's the Phantom, Meg?"

Meg responded with the sound of excitement, fright, and intrigue in her voice. "The Phantom is who Joseph calls the Opera Ghost."

"You mean he actually exists?" the new voice asked. "I thought Joseph was only toying with us."

Although scarcely above a whisper, Meg's voice showed the extent of her stimulated emotions as she began her version of the legendary Phantom.

"Yes, he exists! I've seen him! He's extremely tall and always wears a black hat and cloak that flows along behind him. He doesn't have legs, so he glides effortlessly and silently through the corridors and walls—and also through mirrors!"

With another shake of my head, I pondered. I definitely liked Meg's story better than Joseph's. Perhaps she's in the wrong profession. Perhaps she ought to be a mystery writer.

Meg raised her thin arm and looked toward the catwalks hovering high above the stage; then she continued her unbelievable description.

"Sometimes he makes himself invisible, but he can still be heard up there somewhere." Her voice quivered as she looked back at the fledgling dancer. "Then sometimes he can't be heard or seen, but you can somehow feel him all around you."

"Meg, you must be joking! That isn't possible! Anyway, I don't believe in ghost stories," the tiny voice responded, with false bravado and growing fright.

Unknown to me at the time, I was about to become warmed in a way I'd never known before. That night, fate had cornered me and blocked me from riding César, a necessary activity if I were to maintain control of my temper. But then it mercifully granted me one perfect moment. I grasped that moment like a love-starved orphan and used it to catch a glimpse of the most radiant eyes I'd ever seen—and the young woman possessing them.

I, at first, opened my mouth to calm her fears, but, when I saw her clearly, my words stumbled in my throat. I tried a second time, but my vocal cords adamantly refused to obey my simple instructions.

The soft footlights behind her silhouetted her frame like the aura of an angel, and my breath fled completely. As I stared in amazement at her elegance, I was left without intelligent thought or the capacity to leave before I was detected. While they murmured about the Opera Ghost, I dared to move closer, close enough to hear their rapid breathing.

Meg, little-by-little, pulled the heavy curtain back and peeked behind it, not realizing she was looking in the opposite direction from where I then stood. Then a whisper, coming from the angel's glow, broke my dizzying daze.

"Meg, can you see him now?"

Meg replied softly, "No—I don't see him, but I know he's here—I can sense him."

My eyes stayed fixed solely on the new ballerina as she clutched Meg's arm. She was probably about Meg's age, perhaps 20, but, other than that, she was in stark contrast to Meg. Meg's eyes and hair were coal black, and she was much too thin for my liking. I could see clearly every bone in her chest and shoulders.

The new ballerina had thick golden hair that framed her perfect features and then cascaded in curls over her bare shoulders. Only smooth porcelain skin covered her lovely neck and chest, and her face looked so soft, with a petite and slightly upturned nose. Her eyes, wide with anticipation, were like a clear eastern sky at dusk, the deepest blue possible. Her cheeks had a rosy hue while a deep shade of crimson kissed her lips.

Those lips—how full and soft they looked. I recall imagining how it might feel to have them caress mine, but my resourceful imagination didn't come close to the eventual reality.

I'd seen many alluring women during my travels, especially in Persia. The women there had hair as black as ravens' wings and eyes that put the most luxurious polished jadestone to shame. Their smooth olive skin could only be compared to the finest Persian silk. But nothing could compare to the wonder I felt as I gazed at that angelic creature before me.

It might have been her physical appearance that first captured my attention, but what was stirring in me was deeper than any physical attraction—much deeper. Regardless of my intellect and varied experiences in life, I couldn't explain what was happening within my heart and soul.

Who was she? Where did she come from? How long has she been here? Could she sing? Oh, please, my pounding heart whispered, please let her delicate throat carry the sounds of a nightingale—no—the sounds of an angel!

No matter how stunning she might have been, if her voice couldn't match her physical perfection, I couldn't tolerate it. On more than one occasion, I'd had to turn a deaf ear to an attractive woman because of the sound of her speech, let alone the sound of her singing. Even the Opera Populaire's prima donna, Signora Carlotta Guidicelli, had forced me to leave my seat in Box Five during one of my favorite arias because of her squawking. The beauty so close to me right then just had to sing with an excellence to captivate multitudes. Who was she?

I was only faintly aware that most of the girls had scampered away, leaving only Meg and the new ballerina on the stage. After releasing the curtain, Meg turned to the fledgling dancer and resumed her unbelievable tale.

"Every word I've said is true. He even talks to mother in her office. You can ask her if you don't believe me. Sometimes his voice is like thunder, so loud and powerful it makes the scenery shake and the chandelier sway."

As if being choreographed by an invisible director, they both turned and looked at the grand chandelier, cloaked in darkness high above the seats. Slowly, they clutched each other, causing their fingers and arms to resemble intertwined grapevines. At first, they remained perfectly still, and so did I. Then in unison, they turned back and stared into each other's wide eyes. Gradually, the new ballerina released one hand to cover her parted lips and a soft gasp.

"But, at other times," Meg assured her in a calmer tone, "his voice is so soft, so gentle, and so caring—like an angel's voice. Please trust me. It's true, Christine."

Christine! Christine! What a beautiful name for a beautiful young woman.

"*Christine!—Christine!*"

Without thinking, I'd spoken her name aloud, and the two startled ballerinas turned their attention toward me. As they peered into the shadows, they increased their hold on each other and caused me to press my body back against a huge prop and lower the brim of my hat.

They held their grip on each other as Meg started again. "That's him, Christine! He spoke your name. Never have I heard him speak anyone's name in such a way."

Christine began to speak softly, almost trance-like, as she broke her hold on Meg's arms and took a few mindless steps in my direction.

"Meg, his voice is the most enchanting sound I've ever heard. It can't belong to a ghost. It must belong to an angel. He must be an angel. Yes—a magnificent and beautiful angel."

A deafening silence fell over the empty house, allowing the faint hissing of the gas lamps to be heard among the shadows. My heart was beating so loudly that I feared it would unquestionably betray me if I remained there any longer. Therefore, I tried to move further out of sight, but I couldn't persuade my legs to obey that uncomplicated and familiar command. Hence, we stood there only a few paces away from each other, like two granite statues in a shady park.

While she searched for the man behind the voice who'd captivated her senses, I searched to understand the effect her nearness was having on my usual logical and controlled mind. My active curiosity wasn't what controlled my actions that particular evening. There was something about her and the way I felt that I couldn't comprehend.

Directing my voice to stage left, I spoke her name once more, and then I waited for only an instant until she turned away from me. After her sight followed my voice, I had the opportunity to slip further into the darkness. Once behind a curtain, I removed my hat and mask, not wanting my sight to be hindered in any way. I slowly parted the curtain and watched, for one more brief moment, that angelic creature searching for my voice among the curtains of stage left.

Yes—just one more look at the exquisite young woman who adorned my stage. I had to know all about her—this feminine beauty who'd taken control of my lonely heart and soul as none other.

Again, without any control over my actions, I watched her walk slowly toward the shadows of stage left. Then Meg appeared and put her arm around Christine's shoulders. They talked for a moment and then disappeared into the darkness. With a sigh, I released the curtain and stepped back against a pillar, pressing my hot cheek against the cool marble. The moments fled while I pondered, what's happening to me?

I would like to say I had no control over my next actions that night, but I did. I wanted—no I needed—to know more about her. So, against all my better judgment, I replaced my hat and mask and followed her, all the time questioning why I was so reluctant to let her go.

The corridor was almost dark, and I was far enough behind them to stay undetected, but I could still hear Meg chattering about the Opera Ghost, while Christine repeatedly corrected her.

"No, Meg, not a ghost—an angel."

I could tell they were heading for the dressing rooms, and, although I had no idea what I was going to do once we got there, my rebellious heart was drawn toward her. Occasionally, they turned and looked behind them, and my heart skipped a beat as I pressed my body against the wall or into a doorway. During those times, my logical mind told me to stop this insanity before I did something stupid. I knew I needed to go to my home where I belonged, but, as with so many other times in my life when I should have listened to logic, I didn't listen.

Therefore, as they turned one corner after another, I continued to be led by her invisible power. Finally, at the outermost end of the dressing rooms, they stopped in front of a door, unlocked it, and went inside, causing me to stop short and stare in disbelief.

There were over twenty-five hundred doors in the opera house, eighty of them leading into dressing rooms, and only two of them had my specially designed escape routes within them. Both of those rooms were located the farthest away from the stage and all the activity that went on there. Also, they were only used by the least of the ensemble and sometimes by no one at all. I couldn't count the number of times I'd used those mirrors as an easy route to my underground home.

I stood there in the shadows, dumbfounded for a few moments, before my mind spoke to my feet loudly enough to get them to move. Then they moved quickly, and I raced for the passage that led me back to the mirror. I was breathing hard by the time I got within a few meters of it, so I stopped and leaned against the stone wall until my breath caught up with me.

Since I'd hollowed out a few bricks close to the mirror, it was easy to hear in that passage, and I didn't want my accelerated breathing to give me away. As I waited, I smiled with pleasure over the unbelievable chance that my managers had assigned her that room. By the time I reached the mirror, Meg was leaving and giving Christine instructions.

"Hurry, our reservations are for eight."

"I know, Meg, I know. I only need a few minutes to change."

I felt as if I were suffocating, and, while she sat at her dressing table, I struggled to breathe quietly. With the softest smile on her lips, she gazed around her room, and I gazed at her with fascination. The curves of her face were so smooth, and her hands moved so gracefully, twisting the few strands of hair falling over her shoulder. I could have stood there all night watching her do absolutely nothing, but then she chuckled, breaking my trance.

With that slight giggle, she opened a drawer in her table and took out what looked like a lavender diary and matching quill. While writing, she occasionally stopped long enough to push her hair behind her ear, revealing her slender neck. Each time, my eyes closed without command, and I had to remind myself to breathe.

Eventually, she put the quill down and, while still smiling, held the diary close to her chest. After glancing at the clock on her table, she quickly put the diary in the drawer and went to her armoire. As she began humming, she stretched, bending at the waist with her arms over her head. Moving back into a standing position, she stretched one leg and pointed toes above her head. She moved slowly and gracefully, much like a feather gently floating on the breeze.

If I hadn't known better, I would have thought she knew I was watching and was deliberately teasing me. But it was her next action that took my breath away completely. Turning her back to me, she headed for the opposite end of the room and began unfastening her rehearsal clothing, exposing her bare back.

I knew I should turn and not watch any longer, but I couldn't move. It wasn't out of a need to watch her undress; it was out of a need to stay close to her. Over the years, I'd had plenty of opportunities to watch any number of young chorus girls in similar situations by means of that mirror, but I never had. I didn't like pain. My life had been filled with enough of it for many lifetimes. That type of pain, in particular, I treated like the plague.

No, sensual desire wasn't preventing me from moving. Lord knows, my lack of physical contact with a woman was frustrating enough, so I'd never deliberately add to it. No, that wasn't my motivation, but I couldn't explain what my motivation was. I was captivated by her. I didn't want to leave her side, even if a plate of glass did separate us.

I was still arguing with myself over my pure—or not-so-pure—motives when she disappeared behind the curtain that separated her dressing area from the rest of her room. With the sight of her gone, I was able to convince myself that, regardless of my motives, she deserved her privacy. So I turned to leave but managed only a few strides before she started to sing, which automatically stopped me. At that time, my motives were absolutely theatrical and the musician in me closed his eyes and simply listened.

With an overly critical ear, I listened to her sing a piece from the second act of *Romeo et Juliette*. I scrutinized every note and every transition as I waited for her to hit a faulty note, but it never came. Her pitch was perfect. Her timing and control were also perfect, just as perfect as I'd hoped. But, as a frown formed on my brow, I realized her enthusiasm was truly lacking, even painfully so. Her voice sounded so weak and without the force to blow out a candle. I felt disappointed and didn't want to believe she couldn't sing as I'd thought she should. She simply had to be able to sing. She was so flawless in every other way.

I started to walk away again with much disillusionment and frustration replacing my previous captivation, but then I stopped and again listened to her sweet and pure voice. Perhaps, I thought, it wasn't that she lacked expression but that she was frightened and lacked confidence. Yes, that has to be it, I convinced myself.

By the time I'd returned to the mirror, she'd stopped singing and was slipping a long-sleeved, coral dress over her head. When she turned and faced me, I was once more transfixed by her. Mesmerized, I watched her delicate hands as they laced up the front of her bodice and then pressed against her ribs. After a deep breath, she began singing that same piece again. My teeth clenched tightly, my eyes closed, and my head lowered and shook. I wanted to scream. There's no passion, Christine. You must feel the passion in that piece. Confidence! You only lack confidence.

As I watched her, I saw something I hadn't seen before—a frightened child. She reminded me of a fledgling eagle, crouching on the edge of a high precipice and listening to its parents' call in the sky above. Just as that young and inexperienced bird was too frightened to spread its wings and trust in its natural abilities and its parents' care, she was too frightened to express what I knew she was feeling inside. Just fly, I wanted to tell her. Just like the fledgling, spread your wings and fly. If you fall, I'm here to catch you.

I wanted to call out to her, but my fear of frightening her stopped me. Instead, I silently watched, while my heart raced with anxious care for that naive fledgling. Her name made its way to my lips several times and almost escaped its bars, but I continued to fight the urge to tell her to let go and sing—simply sing.

She finally stopped singing, releasing me from my agony. Then she sat in her chair again and began brushing her hair. As before, I watched in fascination as the brush moved through her golden locks, causing me to become envious of its nearness to her.

Then the moment was shattered by a knock on her door. Her call to come in was answered by Meg, and, as if she'd never left, she continued with her chatter about their supper plans. Christine rose to her feet, and, while slipping her cloak over her shoulders, teased Meg.

"Don't be so impatient, Meg. My goodness. You'd think you hadn't eaten in a year."

Within a moment, the lamp was out and they'd started to leave. No! Don't leave! was my silent plea. But the door closed anyway, concealing the light from the lamp in the hallway and the light from her presence. My hand reached out and touched the cold mirror, and, as never before, I felt my silent world press in on me. I was left alone in the familiar darkness, which was no longer my friend.

For nearly 20 years, that darkness had served to conceal me in peaceful solitude, but, right then, that peaceful solitude was replaced with uneasy loneliness. It was at that exact moment that I knew I had to learn more about her. So, with a deep, slow breath, I began my epic quest.

Two

No more vacillating about my desires. I had to act on them. So, as soon as I heard them turn the key in the lock, I opened the mirror and headed for the door, with the intention of following them. I was no sooner at the door that I heard the key in the lock again. Turning quickly, I saw the mirror, my means of escape, close. Turning again, I flew toward the curtains that closed off Christine's dressing area, and I was barely behind them when the door opened. Through the sheer curtains, I saw the faint light from the hallway enter the room, and then I saw Christine move toward her dressing table and lift a necklace from her drawer.

"Would you please clasp this for me, Meg?"

She raised her hair off her neck and turned her back on her complaining friend. Meg grumbled but complied.

"They're going to give our reservations away, Christine. Did we have to come back for your necklace? It doesn't even go with what you're wearing."

"I know, silly," Christine responded as she raised the locket to her lips, placed a delicate kiss on it, and then dropped it inside the bodice of her dress.

Without further ado, they both left, and I again heard the key turn in the lock. I waited a few seconds longer that time to make certain she hadn't forgotten something else. Then I left through her locked door with my own key. I raced down the corridor until I caught up with their chatter, and then I slowly followed and watched as they gaily babbled about something. Their conversation didn't concern me that time; I only wanted to watch Christine for as long as I could. I followed them out the side door and watched from a distance as they approached a coachman.

"Your coach—Mam'selle Giry—Mam'selle Daaé."

Daaé? That name struck a familiar chord. It wasn't one heard every day, but I was too intent on watching Christine to allow my curiosity to have its way. So I gazed on as the coachman took their arms and helped them enter the black brougham. I stood alone in the shadows, mesmerized by the coach's lantern as it moved slowly down Rue Scribe. It got fainter and fainter until the darkness swallowed it up—and Christine along with it. Soon, I could no longer hear the horses' hoofs on the cobblestones.

At first, I walked slowly on my return to my secluded domain, with my thoughts twisting and turning inside my head. I felt such a desperate need to be with her, and, knowing how much encouragement and training her voice needed, I wanted to help her to believe in her potential. That's what my compassionate side told me, but my logical side was telling me to forget about her and her strange power over me. If I didn't, someone could get hurt—more than likely, me. I didn't like either of those feelings, so, like an addict to the needle, I set my sights on my music.

I was in a run by the time I reached the third cellar and out of breath by the time I reached my little boat in the fifth cellar. When I reached my organ, I tried to lose myself in loud and desperate chords, but, after three pieces, I realized my music wasn't going to work its magic on me that night. Somehow, those blue eyes and red lips possessed a stronger magic, making my music, my lifelong companion and protector, impotent.

I got up and paced for a while. How could this happen to me? I always maintain the superior position. I always have the answers. I tried to force my rational mind to gain control, but it appeared her magic had nullified it. I began to feel extremely agitated, which I always would when I lost control of a situation, especially if I didn't understand why I'd lost it in the first place. Once I put my mind to it, I normally wouldn't have that much difficulty regaining my balance, so what I was experiencing wasn't what I was used to. It wasn't me.

Like a storm of locust, questions swarmed around in my mind. How long had she been here? What was she doing here? Where did she go to dine? Where does she live? When will she be back? I needed to find out more about her, but how? I couldn't simply ask one of the stagehands or another ballerina, since no self-respecting ghost would ever think of being that outspoken.

I sat on my piano bench, with my elbows on my knees and running my fingers through my hair. Then, when I pictured her writing at her dressing table, the obvious solution to my predicament hit me, and my head quickly popped up. Without further thought, I charged toward the exit in my music room that led to the third cellar. My destination? Even though I knew I was trespassing on her privacy, I had to read her diary.

Shortly thereafter, I found what I needed, and, with my conscience pricking me only a little, I nervously opened it. I didn't hesitate for a moment in reading it though, blaming my reprehensible action on my insatiable appetite for knowledge about that woman who held me captive.

Her penmanship was impeccable, just as I expected. After reading only my own scribbled hand for so long, hers was most pleasant to behold. Her writings covered the last five months and read like a letter to her father. The first three-quarters of it had been written while she was attending the Paris Conservatory of Music. She was miserable there and felt inadequate. She thought the other artists didn't like her. She wished she could talk to her father and listen to his words of comfort. Several times she told him she was still waiting for her angel. I felt so badly for her, especially on the days when her entries were only a few words.

I'm so unhappy. I'm so sad. I'm so lonely. I miss you so much.

It was apparent that she had a close relationship with her father and missed his presence in her life. I wanted to sit with her and ask her so many questions. But there was no way I could remain the Opera Ghost and have a normal conversation with a beautiful woman at the same time. At least that's what I thought at that moment; therefore, I went back to my reading. Within the next few pages, I got the answer to at least one of my questions, and it made my heart hurt when I read her words.

Even though it's been many years, I still cry each time I run my fingers over your headstone.

Her father had died, and I instantly felt her pain and tears forming in my eyes. The answer to that question only added several more to my list. One of them was about her mother, who wasn't mentioned anywhere in her diary.

The last quarter of her writings covered the last few weeks since she came to the opera house. She spoke about the rehearsals and her feelings about the performances and the people, Meg in particular. She continued to write about her feelings of inadequacy and being so lonely. But then, the sorrow I felt for her turned to anger when I read one passage.

Father, what am I to do? When are you going to send my Angel of Music? How much longer do I have to wait? Is he delaying because I'm not worthy of his instruction? Have I done something wrong? Have I not worked hard enough? I've really tried to do as I'm told, but I feel like such a failure. Please tell me what I've done wrong so I can do better. I know I can't progress and become successful without him. Please, father, please hurry and send my Angel of Music to me.

My eyes narrowed as I thought, another lie told by a person with religious beliefs. At one point, I was getting so angry I almost threw her diary back into the drawer, but then I saw the last passage she wrote under the current day's date.

The voice called to me from the shadows, and it drew me toward it as if I'd lost my personal will. His voice is angelic, breathtaking, captivating, enchanting, and so much more.

I was right. She was just as captivated by my voice as I was by her presence. It was obvious she'd had a hard time finding the right words to describe her feelings about my voice, since she'd scratched out several of them. Yes, I mused, it's hard to describe what we were feeling.

The last words on that page were written in larger bold letters.

Thank you, father. He has come to me. Thank you for sending my Angel of Music to me. Now I can be successful—now I can be happy!

I slowly closed her diary and ran the dangling ribbon bookmark between my fingers. I thought about her words and her feelings for a few moments before I placed her private thoughts back in the drawer. In so doing, my fingers fell against her blue silk scarf, and, after raising it to my face, I took a deep breath of her fragrance—lavender.

With the scarf still against my face, I closed my eyes and pictured her right there where I was sitting, causing an ache to surge through my chest. It was a similar feeling to the ones I'd had when I thought about my father. I missed her. I hadn't even met her, and yet her absence made me feel sorrow. I felt a need to be beside her and touch her hand or her cheek. I needed to talk with her and find out all about her. I wanted to know her innermost thoughts and secret desires, and I wanted to share mine with her.

I took one more deep breath of her fragrance before I replaced her scarf in the drawer and closed it. I turned out her lamp and headed for the mirror. Once inside the total darkness, I listened to the mirror close behind me, and I felt so alone in an unfamiliar way.

I was halfway to the fifth cellar when I couldn't bear the thought of entering my empty home alone, so I turned around and headed for the roof, hoping to find solace there. I walked its perimeter in silence and watched the faint street lamps below me as I had on so many other occasions. But that night, everything was different and would never be the same again. I couldn't get her out of my mind, and the more I thought about her the more confused and frightened I became. I needed her in a way I'd never needed anyone, and I didn't understand why.

I looked up at the multitudes of stars in the night sky and was struck with the alarming realization that I had no control over my life any longer. At that moment, I believed I was being moved through my days in the same way the stars in the heavens were, and I believed I had no more say over what happened to me than those celestial bodies had. I felt as helpless as a pawn being maneuvered around a chessboard, governed by a much larger force. And that thought made my blood flow hot.

What a cruel game You play, my heart protested into the dark sky. If it weren't for Your magnificent creation, I wouldn't believe in Your existence at all. So You're all-intelligent and all-powerful. So You exist. So what of it? You create and then You sit back and watch us like a Caesar at a gladiatorial game. Uncaringly, You watch us stumble and fall and bleed and hurt. It would be better if You hadn't created at all than to create and then do nothing to help Your creation.

Wasn't it bad enough that You made me with this face? Did You have to give me this intelligence along with it? Did You want to see what someone would do with my unusual combination of gifts; a passion for life and music, a superior intellect, the sensuality of any normal, red-blooded man, and this monster's face? Well, are You happy? Do You see what I've become—what I've done? Are my responses to Your cruelty all you expected?

I think not, since You decided to make matters even worse by sending sweet Christine into my life. Are You trying to drive me over the edge of all reason? Was it Your design that I should be moved so deeply by her?

I raised my face and hands to the sky, and screamed, "What do You want from me?"

I lowered my head and slumped back against a granite angel, while my thoughts tore at the depths of my soul. Why now? Why did You do this now when I'd finally reconciled myself to a life of solitude? Why, when I found a place where I could hide from the world? Why did You bring her into my life and awaken all those buried desires? I rose from the stone statue and raced toward the edge of the roof, with my miserable heart questioning my maker.

"Are You having fun yet? I hope so, because I certainly am not! Why? Why?" I cried into the night sky. "Why couldn't You have given me an idiot's mind to go along with my monster's face? Why? Haven't You had enough of moving this particular pawn around Your chessboard yet? Well, I'm tired of being shoved around carelessly. Go ahead and strike me down! Go ahead! Where's Your lightning? Where's Your power? Can't You have a grain of compassion and end it all—right now?"

I dropped to my knees and wept into my shaking hands. I'd just cursed God, and, in so doing, I knew I'd cursed myself.

I didn't move for a long time. It took the icy snow freezing my knees and cooling my heart before I rose to my feet. With my anger vanquished, I descended the stairs slowly, exhausted and drained of all emotional energy. I felt trapped, trapped somewhere between my face and my heart—somewhere between reality and desire.

Once in my home, I automatically went to my organ, hoping again to escape into the notes of *Don Juan Triumphant*. Composing had almost always worked when I needed comfort, no matter what the problem was. I could completely lose myself, but not that night. Nothing I tried was working. I felt so lonely, and I also felt it was only her presence that would quench my thirst. However, I still couldn't understand why. I didn't even know her, and yet the feelings I had for her were stronger than my music. How could that be?

I looked at my watch. It was almost midnight, and on a normal night I could head for César. But that night was far from normal, so, no matter how much I needed him, I knew riding him was out of the question. After that newspaper article about us and the police being on high alert, it was simply too dangerous to take a white horse out at night. I'd never been one to run from danger, but, at that time, my sights were set on solving my problems, not trying to outsmart the police.

I paced through my silent world and was about ready to pull my hair out when the last words in her diary came back to me. It was perfect! It was a script written for us alone and one I couldn't have written better myself. With excitement, I paced faster around my parlor. I ran my fingers over my jaws and chin as I thought of all the possibilities her written words presented.

Thank you, father. He has come to me. Thank you for sending my Angel of Music to me. Now I can be successful—now I can be happy!

With her own words she set our paths in motion; our path to happiness—our destiny. She'd been lonely and sad while waiting for her teacher, her Angel of Music. I could fill all her needs perfectly and she could fill mine. I could be as close to her as I could ever hope to be. We could talk and we could sing together. With the mirror separating us, she would never have to see my frightening appearance, but she could hear my voice that captivated her so. It was perfect!

I could be the parent bird and catch my fledgling if she fell. With my Christine by my side, my heart would soar, and, with her Angel of Music by her side, her voice would soar. Like eagles we would fly high together. I knew it in my mind, and I believed it in my heart.

I wanted to sleep so morning would come quickly and I could search for her. But, as usual, sleep chose to avoid me that night. I tried a warm bath, a glass of brandy, and a good book, all with no results. Therefore, I spent the majority of the night lying on my bed, staring at the ceiling. When I couldn't bear it any longer, I got up and readied myself to perform an act of an entirely different nature. I'd played many parts in my career of deception, but most of them were as far from an angel as the sunrise is from the sunset.

As I climbed the stairs toward her room, my heart pounded in anticipation of seeing her again, and yet I seriously questioned what I was about to do. For the last thirty years, my resolve was to live alone and as far away from the human race as possible. But, as I'd learned on far too many occasions, time had a way of changing attitudes and beliefs. The strongest resolves of yesterday can melt away with tomorrow's sun, if the right time and right set of circumstances intersect.

Well, I must have been standing right in the middle of that intersection, because my resolve of thirty years crumbled at my feet, like a wall of glass when struck with a battering ram. When I watched that girl and heard her voice, my will had been stripped from me. I was drawn to her as I'd never been drawn before. No woman I'd ever encountered had made me feel the way she did. I felt I already knew her and that she was already mine—mine alone.

Shortly, I was behind the mirror with a dimly lit lantern in hand, waiting for the turn of her key in the lock and another look at the woman who had, unknowingly, taken control of my life. While I waited, I began pacing and wrote her Angel of Music's script in my mind. I wanted every word and syllable to be perfect; it had to be as perfect as she was. I had her reaction to his voice also written. I had the entire scene memorized, a scene that would have an audience in tears if it were an opera.

Once I had it just the way I wanted it, I leaned in the corner, counting my breaths to stay calm. Eventually, I sat on the floor with my chin on my knees. Patience was not my strongest trait, but, since I didn't want to miss her appearance, I was willing to wait indefinitely if I had to. That wait lasted for almost three hours before the sound I was waiting for reached me.

I quickly doused my lantern, jumped to my feet, and faced the mirror, all without taking a breath. Then, still breathlessly, I watched as the light from the hallway cast her shadow into the room. While watching her light her wall lamp and lay her wrap over her chair, I desperately wanted to reach out and touch her.

I took a deep, slow breath and tried to relax my shoulders and neck so I could control my voice properly. An angel of music's voice should sound like a soft cello concerto, but I was so tense that I feared my voice would sound more like screechy train wheels on a track. I closed my eyes, stretched my neck, and demanded that I relax before my most important debut. Everything just had to be flawless.

Finally, feeling ready, I opened my eyes and mouth at the same time, preparing to begin. But what I saw stopped me before I could, and I had to turn my back to her quickly. My little speech not only had to sound perfect but it also had to be timed perfectly, and while she was in the middle of changing her clothes was not the proper time. So, once more, I waited.

While waiting, she began warming her voice, and, again, I closed my eyes. The temptation to tell her to relax was easier to resist that time, since I knew I would have plenty of time to instruct her in the days ahead. How that thought thrilled me and confused me at the same time. Why did I have such strong feelings for her?

I wondered, could this be the love that Oded spoke of? Nothing I'd ever experienced could compare to it. It was stronger than any sexual attraction I'd ever known. I'd sworn long ago never to become its slave again, and I never had. What I felt for Christine was much deeper and stronger than those relentless sensations that had driven me blindly toward the emerald eyes of Michaela. It was a world apart from what I felt for Vashti. Those feelings could be dismissed with enough will power, or my music, or a good run with one of my horses.

But this new feeling, which nothing had been able to quench, was penetrating the depths of my very being and maneuvering me, just as a puppeteer maneuvers his marionettes. When I tried to bury it in my music, I found it waiting for me between every note. My usual strong will gave way to it like a willow in a hurricane. During the exertion of running up and down the stairs, it was there with me like the air I breathed. What was that all-encompassing feeling? It had to be love that I felt for her. There was no other explanation.

If it truly was love, was I prepared for such a challenge in my twisted life? If I had to, could I simply dismiss a power that strong and walk away without doing harm, or could the law of averages be made to swing in my favor and have her return my love? Could I make a woman as beautiful as her love me, a deformed recluse?

When I really thought about that possibility, I pictured where I was standing—hiding in my dark and damp passage—and my insecurities crept in. How could she love a man old enough to be her father, a man deformed, a man with such a dark past? I sighed, lowered my head in dejection, and realized that it wasn't possible. I was only kidding myself and heading for a monumental disaster if I pursued her. With that realization, I felt my entire demeanor shrink, and I began to slink back to my hole in the ground where I belonged.

But then Oded's reasoning on that very subject caused me to stop when I recalled it. All the differences in the world could be overcome once love was allowed to grow in one's heart. It only needs nurturing and time. He was right about Vashti. She did love me, despite my age and appearance. The expression in her eyes as I unmasked my gruesome face before her was proof of that fact. But she'd had years to become accustomed to me and know me before that event took place.

Would I be allowed that much time with Christine? Someone like her had to have a dozen suitors at her door. How could I compete with young handsome men? Would it be possible for someone like me, a freak of nature, to have a second chance for a woman to love me?

I felt frightened and confused and powerless. I pressed my hands against my head and told myself to give up my silly schoolboy fantasies. If I pursued Christine, I might be driven out of what was left of my mind. Or perhaps I was already out of my mind for even considering such a possibility.

One more time in my life, I was facing a crossroads, and my heart swung like a swift pendulum within my chest. At one moment, determined, and the next, powerless. My love for her had stripped me of my strength and resolve, but there had to be a way of taking back my self-will and regaining my power and then using it to capture her heart.

The Shah of Persia, and his entire regime, had had no power over me, and yet this small seemingly insignificant person had me on my knees. What was to become of me? I had, for the first time, tasted love's bite, and, for the first time, I was left without a potion to heal its wound. What was to become of Christine and her lonely heart? Could I fill a need for her as she could for me? Could I ever make her love me? Should I dare try?

My head was beginning to ache when my father's words, from so many years in the past, surfaced. Just a matter of minutes before his tragic death, he gave me valuable advice that he wisely knew I would need and that I'd used often.

"Keep your eyes on your goals, Erik, and don't allow anyone or anything, not even yourself, to get in your way."

Then I thought about where I was standing, with his wisdom in my mind instead of my insecurities. I was living in an opera house, just as that ten-year-old child wanted when everyone around him said it wasn't possible. I wanted it bad enough to make it happen, and nothing was able to stop me, not even an international war. Would making Christine fall in love with me also be possible if I put my mind to it—and my heart?

My advanced years had allowed me time to gain wisdom and temperance. My deformity allowed me to be compassionate toward the suffering of others. My being without love for so long made me appreciate its value more than any other man. When I added those qualities to the other attributes my intellect afforded me, I knew I would make a near-perfect husband. But would that be enough?

When I heard her drawer open, I knew she was dressed, so I returned to the mirror. Seeing her again was all I needed to end my argument with myself. She was worth every risk. Even if she refused me and my heart was broken, I had to try. I would never forgive myself if I didn't. So, with renewed determination, I proceeded with my plan.

She was writing in her diary, probably talking to her father about me. It was perfect. I was relaxed and in control, so I again took a deep breath. But the voice that followed wasn't her angel's, it was Meg's.

"Are you ready, Christine?" she asked as she opened the door and stuck her head inside. "We don't want to be late. You know how upset Gabriel gets when he's kept waiting."

"I know. I know," Christine responded while shoving her diary back in the drawer. "Go ahead. I'll be right behind you."

Meg shut the door and I sighed. A missed opportunity. I didn't dare start my act right then or that pest, Meg, could interrupt again.

Christine might have sounded in a hurry but she didn't act it. She actually looked reluctant as she headed for the door and then reached for the handle. Without turning it, she looked back over her shoulder at her reflection in the mirror. It made me feel uneasy—odd, having her look so intently at herself in the mirror, while, from my perspective, it looked like she was looking directly at me. Was she?

I closed my eyes slowly and took a deep breath. When I opened them, she was still there. What was she looking at? What was she thinking? Could she see me? Certainly not, I chastised myself, or she would be screaming. If only I could have her look at me the way she was looking right then and not be frightened—if only.

I'd often heard the expression, *time stood still*, but I'd never experienced it for myself until that moment. With Christine's eyes fixed on the mirror, my heart could pretend she was looking right at me even though my mind knew she wasn't. I watched her with a longing soul, secretly asking her not to leave me alone. I wanted to speak her name. I wanted to keep her there with me forever. I wanted to become her Angel of Music, whom she already had an attachment to. There was so much I wanted to say to her, to help her through her fears, to comfort her in her loss, to encourage her in her voice; there was so much. But I didn't, and, as time stood still, so did I.

Without moving her eyes from the mirror, she turned the handle and moved into the hall. I closed my eyes and lowered my head. She was gone again, and I was alone again.

I believed she was heading for the ballet studio, so that's where I planned to go, but not before I'd read what she'd just written. Not wanting a repeat of the last time I entered her room, I waited before opening the mirror. After making certain the door was locked, I sat in her chair and took out her diary. Her simple writing filled me with hope.

The beautiful voice called my name and permeated my dreams, Papa. Did you send him? Could that angelic voice be my long-awaited Angel of Music?

I sat there, transfixed by her words, and read them over and over. Oh, if I only had a normal face. At no other time in my life did I want one more than then. If I had a nose, I could simply approach her and tutor her in the flesh and make her love me. I closed her book and held it gently in my hands, and then I closed my eyes and let them fill with tears.

It wasn't fair. It just wasn't fair. I wanted to pursue her like any normal man in love. I wanted to send her flowers and ride with her in a coach across the countryside. I wanted to sit and talk with her over a candlelit dinner, with soft music playing in the background. I wanted our voices to harmonize in songs of love. I wanted to sit with her before a fireplace and read to her from a book. I wanted to walk with her on the streets of Paris, and enter shops, and buy her expensive jewels and hats and gloves. I wanted to pamper her as she'd never been pampered before. I wanted to hold her and make her feel safe in my embrace. I wanted her to love me.

If only . . . .

Three

I placed her diary back in the drawer and took a deep breath. Feeling quite sorry for myself, I headed for the mirror and my lonely, dark passageways. I started to reach for the lever but then stopped and looked at my reflection. I removed my cloak and looked intently again. I examined myself from my hair to my shoes. I stepped closer to the mirror and looked at my face, or should I say my mask. After removing my mask, I looked harder. I placed three fingers over my would-be nose and then scrutinized each facial feature.

With the tips of my fingers, I touched my temples, where a few flecks of gray gave away my age. My eyes then traveled to the scar above my right eyebrow and the one on my right cheek that gave away a sad portion of my past. But other than those things, if I had a nose, I wouldn't look that bad. I'd grown into the unusual bone structure I'd had as a child, and even my eyes weren't as sunken as they once were. In addition, with the nutritious food I'd eaten during the last few years, I no longer resembled a skeleton. I looked as fit as any other Parisian man—if only I had a normal face.

But, then, if I had a nose, I wouldn't be living in the bowels of the opera house, and I never would have met Christine. I took another deep breath, replaced my mask and cloak, and then left through the mirror. Regardless of my thinking, the fact remained, I didn't have a nose and therefore I wasn't in the same brotherhood with the rest of the men in Paris.

Within minutes, I was behind the mirror in the ballet studio and there she was, warming up with the rest of the ballerinas. I leaned back against the wall, and, with fascination, watched her every movement. Soon, Gabriel and a pianist came in and the music began. With it, the girls started going through their routines. She was very good, not the best I'd seen, but very good nonetheless. I was completely captivated by her, until Gabriel shouted harshly and broke my trance.

"Mam'selle Daaé! Your lack of attention is disrupting the entire rehearsal. If you can't keep up, then perhaps you should sit out until you can—or maybe you should go home."

I was shocked! What had I missed while in my stupor?

Christine pressed her hands over her face and ran from the room, with Meg right behind her.

"Mam'selle Giry, get back in line!" he shouted.

My confusion first turned to anger, and I glared at Gabriel with a threatening rebuke poised on my lips. But then I glanced at Christine in her flight, and I felt such pity for her that it outweighed my anger. So I turned quickly and headed back to her dressing room, hoping she was heading there also. I was behind the mirror before she entered, and, when she did, my heart broke for her. She was sobbing pitifully and instantly threw herself across her divan, burying her face and tears in a blue pillow.

From the time I was a small child, I was never able to watch a woman cry without feeling completely overtaken with compassion for her. Even when I was angry with my mother, my hardened exterior would crumble when she wept. So to watch and listen to Christine in such need of comfort, I was again overtaken by my own emotions. Therefore, my nicely rehearsed script surrendered to what was in my heart.

"Christine. Don't cry, my child. I'm here," I said softly.

She gasped, and half of her face appeared from behind the pillow. She looked around, guardedly, and whispered, "The voice?"

Then she started breathing rapidly, sat up, curled her legs under herself, and pulled the pillow close to her chest, as if she needed it to protect her heart from any further threats.

Making sure I projected my voice to scatter through the entire room, I continued with the gentlest of tones, "Don't be frightened, Christine. You're safe here with me. I'll protect you now. You're no longer alone."

After several quick breaths, and looking around her room again, she questioned, warily, "Where are you?"

"I'm anywhere you want me to be, my dear, and I'll never be far away from you—ever,"

With wide eyes full of curiosity, she sat up, and asked, "Who are you? Are you the voice that spoke my name last night?"

"Christine, I can be whoever you want me to be. I can be your teacher, your protector, and your friend. I can be your Angel of Music."

"Oh!" she exclaimed, as she bolted to her feet. Her eyes filled instantly with more tears. "Oh!"

With her automatic belief in me, I felt a twinge of guilt over my deception. I was deliberately deceiving her for my own selfish gains, and I felt bad. She was an innocent child, and I was taking advantage of my stolen knowledge about her. She had needs, and I was deliberately using them to trick her just so I could be near her.

For a moment, I wasn't certain I wanted to continue with what I'd started, but it was too late. There was no turning back. My guilt was not sufficient to overpower my own need for her. Besides, I reasoned, if I had a nose I wouldn't be deceiving her. I would approach her in honesty and offer her my helping hand. But, through no fault of my own, I didn't have that necessary facial feature, so, in my eyes, I only had one choice.

"Are you still there?" she asked with concern.

Grinding my teeth and trying to calm my anger over my untruthfulness, I responded softly, "Yes, my child, I'm always here."

Taking a step forward, she began throwing questions at me. "Did you meet my father in Perros? Are you the one who helped him? Are you the one he promised to send to me?"

I was, at first, confused, but an angel wouldn't be confused, so, buying myself time to think, I chose my words carefully. "I've met many people in many places, Christine. You must be more specific."

"My father told me about a man who he believed to be his angel. No, more precisely, an angel of music, because of the sounds he produced with his violin. He came to my father on a beach in Perros at a time when he needed him very much. We had nowhere to live and no money. My father was trying to find a position with the symphony but hadn't yet."

I frowned and studied her face. Then everything fell into place: Perros, Daaé, violin, beach, symphony, Christine. Could it be? I reached out and touched the mirror. What are the chances? It couldn't be the same Christine Daaé, and, yet, it had to be. I'd only been in Perros once as an adult. It had to be, I thought, while picturing the woman on the beach with her hair, like strands of spun gold, being tossed by the sea breeze. I had to shake my head in disbelief when I realized she looked just like her mother. In all sincerity, I focused intently on her next words.

"That man, or angel, who called himself only by the name of Erik, showered my father with many expensive gifts. Those gifts enabled my father to continue his dream of performing with a symphony. Then the angel appeared to him again in a dream and showed him his future as a famous solo violinist. It was that vision that inspired my father, and he did find a position with a symphony and even played solo at times before he returned to Sweden. That's why he was so convinced that the man was his Angel of Music."

I was dumbstruck and without proper words to respond to her, so I remained silent while I stumbled around in my memories.

She took a few steps toward the center of the room and looked all around. "Are you still here?"

"Yes, my dear, I'm still here," was all I could say.

With the frightened voice of a child, she asked, "Why are you so silent? Did I say something wrong?"

"No, Christine, you've said nothing wrong. I'm pleased your father put those gifts to good use."

"He did put them to good use, even the ones he didn't sell. One is a beautiful necklace and the other a wedding ring," she said as she looked at the drawer in her dressing table. "He first gave them to my mother, but, when she died, he wanted me to have them as a remembrance of that special angel. Until the day he died, he believed that angel would come to me someday and teach me how to sing like a songbird. Are you really that same angel, and have you really been sent by my father?"

While she related that story, I felt so strange. My heart felt strange. I looked at her face and then pictured her as that one-year-old, holding that jeweled necklace in her small hands. Then I pictured her the previous day when she placed a delicate kiss on that same necklace. It had served her father's purpose. It had kept her connected to her past and gave her hope to continue without him.

I smiled softly and responded just as softly, "Yes, Christine. I met your father, your mother, and you on the shores of Perros on your first birthday. And, yes, I gave him many gifts. But they were a mere token compared to the other riches your father possessed—your mother and you. And, yes, Christine, I'll teach you how to sing like a songbird. I'll teach you everything you need to know to become great in anyone's eyes. You only need to obey my voice and you'll be the prima donna on any stage."

"Oh!" she exclaimed again. Her fingers covered her mouth, and then she spoke through them. "Do you really think so?"

"I not only think so, I also know so. As long as you're under your Angel's wings, you'll be perfect in every respect."

Her chest rose repeatedly, and her eyes took on the appearance of dreaming. She turned slowly, looking around her dimly lit room. Gradually, her slender fingers found their way to her throat. Her lips parted several times, but she didn't speak, so I patiently waited for her to reveal what was in her heart. The seconds passed silently, and then she finally spoke, almost too softly for me to hear her.

"Am I dreaming? Are you really here? Are you really going to teach me?"

I smiled again at her sweet innocence. "Yes, my dear, and I've already begun teaching you. You now have more confidence in your ability to sing than you did when you first walked in here, do you not?"

She nodded and partially turned around. "Yes, I do, now that you're finally here with me. Thank you. Thank you so much."

Since I wanted to watch her expressions closely, I instructed her, "I want you to look at yourself in the long mirror."

She turned and faced me, and my heart ached so badly. I needed to touch her, but I could only allow my voice to reach out to her. "What do you see in the mirror, my child?"

"Myself," she responded shyly.

"Your reflection is obvious. Now look closer," I ordered. "What else do you see?"

With the slightest frown appearing on her sweet face, she answered, "My dressing room."

Changing my tone from the comforter to the instructor, I tried to reason with her. "That's all true, but there's so much more in your reflection than what you're seeing. Whenever you come into your room, I want you to look into this mirror and see the artist you are. I want you to see what you can be. Now, close your eyes, Christine."

She willingly obeyed my voice and closed her eyes, and, in so doing, she caused me to do the same. After a moment, I took a needed breath and slowly opened my eyes again, studying her face. She was so beautiful and looked so soft. I reached out and touched the mirror, wanting to reach out and touch her, wanting to wrap my arms around her. She might have considered me to be her angel, but, with her golden hair framing her delicate face, she was the one who resembled an angel.

My thoughts were interrupted when she spoke and brought me back to reality.

"Angel, are you still there?"

"Yes, my child. Now keep your eyes closed and tell me, instead of your room, where do you want to see yourself?"

She frowned again, "I don't understand."

"Remember when you were a child and you had a trip planned to go to the beach with your father?"

She nodded. "Yes."

"When you went to bed the night before the trip and closed your eyes, where did you see yourself the next day, and what were you doing there?"

Her face softened and a contented smile appeared. "I saw myself and my father on the beach, running and laughing."

"Didn't you also see yourself picking up broken shells, dusting the sand off them, then holding them up to the sun and watching them shimmer in its light?"

Her eyes popped open. "Why, yes. But how did you know that?"

"I know many things, Christine. Now, close your eyes again and listen to my voice."

Again she obeyed willingly, so I continued. "You saw yourself on that beach down to the smallest details, because you believed, beyond all doubt, that your father would be true to his word and take you there. So I want you to tell me where you want to be in the days ahead so I can help you get there. More than anywhere else in the world, where do you want to be?"

She was silent and then slightly shook her head and responded timidly, "I'm not sure."

I could see my line of reasoning wasn't clear enough to have her follow it, so I directed her thinking. "More than anything else in the world, don't you want to see yourself center stage and in a beautiful gown while singing the pivotal aria in an opera?"

She nodded slightly. "Yes, that would be too wonderful for words. But what I want more than that is to be back in my father's embrace."

Her response took me completely by surprise, and I quickly struggled to find my way back to where I wanted her thoughts to go. "That's by far the noblest quest in anyone's life. A beautiful relationship with those you love and those who love you is assuredly the highest of goals that anyone could reach for. But I'm your Angel of Music, my dear, not an angel of resurrections. While my powers are many and strong, I'm impotent against the forces guarding death's door. Therefore, other than your desire to be with your father again, what would you want most out of *this* life?"

She took a deep breath and nodded while saying, "Just what you said. I want to be a great singer and someday have my voice appreciated."

That might have been what her lips spoke, but, if I hadn't already read her diary, I wouldn't have believed it was her heart's desire. The lack of conviction in her voice was betraying her. Therefore, I lowered my voice and became the strength she needed.

"I'm very near to you right now, Christine, and I barely heard your words. If you want the world to notice your voice then you have to make it heard. So tell me that again, only this time tell me with fervor exactly what you want. Don't be shy. Remember, I already know what's in your heart, so don't be afraid to express its desires to me."

She responded with more strength, but still her voice was weak and unsure. "I want to be center stage singing alone before an audience."

"Remember the beach, Christine. You must believe that I can take you to center stage before you can get there, just as you believed your father would take you to the shores of Perros. Now open your eyes and look at yourself in the mirror again, and tell yourself that you will be center stage."

She opened her eyes and focused on herself in the mirror, but didn't say anything, so I continued to encourage her. "You must believe it, Christine."

She nodded but still didn't respond; in fact, she even looked embarrassed. I was beginning to feel frustration mounting in me, and I was questioning her desire, but then I recalled her continual pleas recorded in her journal. Perhaps she needed a stronger hand, I thought. Therefore, my next words were stronger and almost harsh.

"There are many in this world who are waiting for the chance to have me tutor them. Am I wasting my time on you, Christine? Answer me! Shall I go to them and leave you to ponder your current condition on your own?"

"No!" she nearly screamed. Then her eyes began to fill with tears again as she demanded, "Don't leave me!"

Letting my voice boom across her room, I came back quickly. "Now that's what I call conviction. That's how you need to feel about your ability to perform your music center stage. That's how I want you to speak to yourself in the mirror each time you enter this room. Do you understand me?"

"Yes," she responded.

Unfortunately, her voice had sunk back to its original hiding place, and I wanted to scream. But then I realized I needed time to think through what I was doing, before I did even more damage to that injured soul in need of my tender care.

Therefore, with my voice still strong but also soft, I encouraged her. "I want you to go back to the ballet instructor and prove to him that you have what it takes to be in front of a paying audience."

"Yes. I'll go straight away," she responded, while wiping the remainder of the tears from her cheeks. "I'll do as you say."

I watched her go to the door, but then she stopped and looked around. "When will I meet you again?"

"As long as you're in my house of music, Christine, I'll be close to you. Whenever you wish to speak to me, come to your room. We'll start your voice lessons tomorrow morning at eight o'clock sharp. Now, tell me, my dear, what production are you rehearsing?"

"We're preparing for a gala to be presented 15 March in honor of Messieurs Debienne's and Poligny's retirement."

What! I screamed within myself. My managers are retiring? No! I had just gotten them trained so well. They can't leave!

"Angel? Are you still here?"

Trying to clear my thoughts quickly, I answered her, "Yes, Christine, I'm here and I always will be. We'll start tomorrow morning, and by 15

March you'll be standing center stage in several of your own solo arias. We have much work do, so don't be late."

"Oh," she responded, with her spread fingers pressed under her ribs. "Do you really think I can be ready that soon?"

I smiled at her innocence. "Don't forget—you're speaking to your Angel of Music, and, with him, anything is possible. Now go and prove your worth to Gabriel."

"Yes," she answered with a wide, yet hesitant, smile. Then she turned and was gone from me.

I was left alone again, but, this time, I was filled with hope. Even though a plate of glass separated us, and it was only my voice she knew, she, at least, knew me, and we had our first connection. I felt warm inside in a way that was completely foreign to what I'd known before. That girl did something to me that I was still at a loss for words to describe.

I again followed her to the ballet studio and watched from the mirror. She did show more confidence, not as much as I wanted to see in her, but it was a start. I followed her until she left for the day, and then I returned to my abode with new and hopeful ideas taking over my mind.

I spent another sleepless night in anticipation of our next clandestine encounter. Then, the last few hours before eight o'clock, I again paced in the narrow passage behind her mirror. All night I'd spent in deep thought. How could I help her release the fears that held her in their grip? Something was preventing her from expressing what I believed was inside her, and I needed to find out what it was and release it.

As I waited, I also thought about the face that prevented me from becoming a real man to her. I searched for ways that I could make a mask that might look even more human than the ones I'd already made. I even considered going to a doctor and having a prosthetic nose made, which was a challenge for me on a much different level. Then the moment came when she was once again in front of me, and I could pretend she was looking at me and not at her reflection.

"Close your eyes, Christine," I said calmly, slowly, and deeply. "Listen carefully to my voice and nothing else. Shut out everything else from your mind and listen to my voice alone. Now picture the shores of Perros. Hear the call of the gulls as they glide over your head and then out to sea. Listen to the rhythmic crash of the waves on the rocks, one right after the other.

"Feel the ocean breeze on your face and neck. Without the restraints of heavy clothing, feel the power of the breeze as it flows past your body. Feel it press against you. Feel it as it moves every tendril of hair away from your face. Feel your freedom from all the restraints that bind you. Feel your freedom, Christine. Feel your body turning in circles. Feel the wet sand beneath your feet as you walk along the shoreline. Feel your freedom to run with nothing around you except the gulls and the waves.

"You're alone and vulnerable, but you have no fear, for there's nothing there to harm you. Everything is your friend; the gulls, the waves, and the air are all your friends. No one is there to hurt you, and you're free as never before.

"Take a deep breath of the salty air and hold it inside you. Picture it in your lungs, loosening all the unwanted and stale air of the conservatory. Now, let it out slowly and feel it remove all the restrictive criticism of your former instructors. Again, take a deep breath, and let the salty air heal the wounds of a lifetime. Let it all out, and, with it, release all your fears. Watch the air currents carry them out over the sea. Feel the waves washing against your feet, pulling your concerns out to the deep waters. Picture the waves pounding your fears against the rocks, destroying them completely.

"Now take another breath and listen to my voice as it takes over the sounds of the waves on the rocks. Follow my voice, Christine, wherever it goes. Follow me. There's nothing to hold you back as you follow me. There's no restrictive clothing and no harmful memories of the past. There's only my voice and nothing else around you. My voice is in the waves at your feet, and my voice is in the call of the gulls above you, and my voice is within you in the very air you breathe. Listen to my voice and follow me."

Up to that point, she'd done everything I'd asked of her. She opened and closed her eyes on command. She took breaths when I commanded, and she raised her arms away from her sides, all exactly as I'd instructed. But the real test was yet to come. I sang in a continual soft middle C while gently and firmly encouraging her.

"Follow me, Christine. Take a deep breath, and follow me."

I continued softly with a sustained middle C, and she followed my lead. I increased my volume.

"Follow me, Christine."

While watching her face closely, I started climbing the register, and she followed my every transition.

"Again, Christine. Take a deep breath and follow me."

As her face showed the freedom she was feeling, I smiled through the notes escaping my lips. I kept climbing the register and increasing in volume, while my words continued to encourage her to follow me. Once I reached the top of my register, I told her to continue on her own and she did. I kept encouraging her as she climbed higher and higher. I told her to climb like the gulls and glide on the air, free from all the cares in the world.

She was flawless. She had everything in her that I thought she had and even more. Her voice was exceptional and was only hidden beneath layers of restrictive rules and regulations. Those regulations were laid down by stupid men in their arrogance, just so they could control others with their own preconceived ideas of what was proper.

I watched her face closely as she climbed each note with my instruction. She was exquisite, and the moments were breathtaking. I almost had myself convinced we were alone on the beach and that the musty air inside my passage had turned into the salty breeze. I could actually smell it.

Once I felt she was straining too hard, I stopped her. Then I listened to the room fill with silence, and, in the moments that followed, I felt my heart fill with pride for the woman's voice that had just escaped from the frightened child.

Four

Her chest rose and fell quickly, and I could feel her excitement when she began to realize what she'd done.

"Open your eyes, Christine, and see your world in the light of a new day over which you, and you alone, will be the mistress."

Almost cautiously, her fingers spread across her chest and then slowly to her throat, while her wide eyes searched the room.

"Angel?"

The smile on my lips could be heard in my next words. "Yes, my child."

"Was that me?" her returning timid voice asked.

"Yes, my child."

"Everything was so beautiful there. I wish I could have stayed there forever, with the surf and the birds and the music. I felt safe there. I felt I could do anything there. But I don't feel that way here. I don't feel it was even me singing, now that I'm back in my room. It had to be someone else inside me. It couldn't have been me."

"Why not, Christine? Why not you?"

She stepped back and wrapped her arms around herself. Then her eyes filled with fear. "Because, I've never sung like that before. I must have been imagining someone else on a beach. It couldn't have been me. How could it have been me?" By that time, she'd turned away from me. "Was it you, my angel? Was it you inside of me that I heard and felt?"

"Christine, don't turn away from your reflection. There's nothing to fear. Turn back."

When she did, she looked like a frightened rabbit cornered by a wolf, and I wanted so badly to comfort her in my embrace. But the only comfort I could give her was with my voice. So I spoke, softly and yet firmly.

"Why are you so frightened? Did you not ask for the Angel of Music to visit you and teach you? What did you expect an angel to do—teach you how to be mediocre? Should not the instruction of an angel produce angelic results? You are angelic, and you've just proven that. You must believe that all I did was free you temporarily from the burdens of years at the conservatory, years of being told you couldn't succeed, whether those words were from someone else or from you. The talent is within *you*, Christine. You only needed to set it free, as free as the gulls on the ocean's breeze. Do you believe me?"

With parted lips and wide eyes she shyly nodded. "I want to."

I waited a moment, not certain how far to push her, since I'd just witnessed her fast return to that safe place where harsh criticism was silent. The hands on her dressing table clock told me she had 20 minutes before her ballet rehearsals began, so we started over again.

"We're back on the shores of Perros, Christine. Close your eyes and follow me."

We went through the same routine again. But, again, once she'd conquered every note and then opened her eyes to the reality of her dressing room, she slid back into that comfortable place of non-commitment. Since she was out of time, and I was nearly out of patience, I dismissed her with another word of praise.

"Very well done, Christine. I'll be here when you return."

After she left, I felt exhilarated, yet frustrated and perplexed. I was excited by her natural ability, but I wasn't sure what more I could do to help her realize the special gift she'd been given. Perhaps after enough of our sessions, she'd believe in herself and soar on her own, I tried to convince myself.

However, I had to do more than teach her to believe in her voice; I also had to remove the years of untruths she'd been taught at the conservatory. It looked as if it was going to take all my patience to help her get to where she wanted to be—where *I* wanted her to be.

While walking through my passage toward the rehearsal studio, I had a disturbing thought. While I wanted her to believe in her ability and confidently express herself with her voice, once she did, she would no longer need her angel. She would no longer need *me*. What was I to do then? I shook off that selfish feeling and watched her, and her critical instructor, as she went through her rehearsal routine.

When Gabriel dismissed them, I rushed back to the mirror. If possible, I always wanted my voice to be waiting for her when she entered her dressing room and called for her angel. I wanted her to learn to rely on me and trust me. When she returned, we talked again, and then she left for the remainder of the day until it was time to get into makeup for that night's production.

The next morning before our scheduled lesson, I purchased three red roses and bound them together with a gold metallic ribbon. Once in her dressing room, I placed them in a slender cut-crystal vase and set them on her dressing table. Then I attached a small envelope to the roses, and on it I wrote her name in my best hand. Inside the envelope I put a card with a simple thought written on it: three roses—your past, your present, your future.

I sat in her chair for a moment, running my fingers over the ribbon and thinking of how appropriate the gold was for Christine. Gold was the most precious metal known to man. With its purity and brilliance unmatched by any other substance, it stood alone without competition. Perhaps that's why I'd always been so drawn to it. Perhaps that's why I was so drawn to Christine. To me she was the most precious woman known and stood unmatched in her purity and brilliance.

With a sigh, I returned to the passage behind the mirror and waited for her to appear.

As soon as she entered the room, she turned up her lamp, locked her door, and then, leaning back against it, she asked, "Angel, are you here?"

"I'm always here, my dear," I replied as a warm rush surged through me.

Her pink lips smiled broadly. "I dreamt of you last night. Or was it a dream? Were you there in my room or was I dreaming?"

I wasn't certain how to answer. I'd already told her I would always be with her to protect her from harm, so how could I tell her I wasn't there? And yet, if I started her thinking I would always be there to talk with her, then I was putting myself in a difficult situation. It would be nearly impossible to pull off and still remain an unseen angel.

I thought for a few more moments, prompting her to ask, "My angel, are you still here? Please, speak to me."

"Remember, Christine, I'm your Angel of Music; therefore, the laws I have to obey are written on the notes of music. If I'm to remain in control of my power, I must remain within the walls of music. I'll always be with you, no matter where you go outside the opera house, as long as you keep my voice in your heart. My words are powerful and can go wherever you go, but they're only as powerful as your belief in them. So continue your belief in me, and my voice will always be in your head and heart."

That explanation, while sounding somewhat ambiguous to me, must have pleased her because she smiled and nodded. Next, she spotted the roses on her dressing table and rushed toward them. She bent forward and, with two fingers steadying the stems, placed her nose on the petals. With her eyes closed, she took a deep breath and smiled even broader.

Quickly, she opened the note and, after reading it, frowned slightly before asking, "Angel, do you know who sent these to me?"

My words were strong and sure as I answered, "The one person in your life who cares the most about your happiness."

She glanced over her shoulder. "Who?"

My captivated heart motivated the tone of my voice, which I let speak softly from the roses. "You'll never find anyone else, Christine, who has more interest in you and your life than I—your Angel of Music. Whether that life is your past, your present, or your future, I'll always care the most."

Her sight followed my voice to the roses, and she ran one fingertip gently across a petal. "I should have known my angel sent them."

I sighed at her fragile trust in my every word. "Now face the mirror and tell me—tell yourself—that it's going to be a wonderful day. Say you're going to fill it with splendid thoughts and beautiful music."

Again, she did as I asked, and I spread my hand on the barrier between us and stared into her beautiful blue eyes. I took a deep breath and had to close my eyes for a moment before I could continue. Then I began similarly to the previous day but with additional instructions.

"Today, I want you to feel not only the breeze around you but also me behind you. Spread your arms out to your sides and feel my wings under them, giving them support. Feel my breath and voice." Then I whispered my next word at her ear. "Sing."

With my whispered breath, she jumped and lost her concentration. Quickly, her hand covered her ear, and her wide eyes expressed her shock.

"Please, don't fear my power, Christine. I'm here to help you, not harm you. But I do apologize. I didn't mean to frighten you."

She nodded, guardedly. "That's all right. I just didn't expect to hear you so close. Are you that close to me?"

Now, I had to think fast. "In some ways yes and in some ways no. Angels are much different from mortals, so it's difficult to explain. I only wanted you to feel my power. I want you to be familiar with it so you can use it whenever you need—especially when you sing."

"I see," she responded shyly.

"Let's start over. Face the mirror, hold your arms out from your sides, and follow my voice. Only, this time, I want you to feel the power of my wings around your ribs. They'll give your lungs power."

She responded so flawlessly it made me feel uncomfortable. My entire life I'd been able to control others to one degree or another with my voice and demeanor. But the power I had over Christine was almost supernatural, and it was beginning to frighten me terribly.

My control over each of the others had lasted for only a short time, allowing me to accomplish my purpose. While I had a purpose in my shrouded relationship with Christine, I didn't know how or when to end my deception. I didn't see it lasting only a short time. I didn't see it having an end. I think that's what frightened me the most. I didn't know how I was going to relinquish my power over her.

I wanted her to fall in love with me, the man, but how? To her, I was a powerful angel, not a mortal man. As a man of flesh and blood, how could I remain powerful enough to keep her as my own? In addition, how would she respond when I revealed my sham of playing the angel she held so dear to her heart? Once that lifelong dream was shattered by the reality of my gruesome human nature, what would it do to her delicate heart? I was so frightened. What had I started?

I pushed off those doubts, deciding I could work it out later. For the time being, I needed to concentrate and prepare her for the gala, her chance of a lifetime.

"That was near perfect, Christine. Each time you get stronger and stronger, and your concentration is very good. But it will be more of a challenge to concentrate when you're on stage. There may be things going on backstage or in the audience that you can hear and that will make it harder for you to focus. So, this time when you sing, I'm going to give you some distractions. Do your best not to let them interfere with your concentration."

"I can do it. I've learned how to shut out talk from the other chorus girls. I can do it," she assured me.

"Very well then. Turn around with your back to the mirror this time, then close your eyes." She did as I'd asked. "Now concentrate, and begin your warm up exercises."

She began, and I also began what I feared could be an act with a catastrophe as its final scene. But I couldn't stop. It was as if something was controlling me, just as I was controlling Christine.

"You're on the shores of Perros again, and you can hear the power of the surf as it crashes on the rocks, and you can feel it rumble under your feet."

Having that said, I released the latch to the mirror, allowing it to faintly rumble and open. I was ready to reverse the process quickly if she showed any signs of turning around, but she didn't.

"Now, feel the cool sea breeze as it passes you."

Again I waited for the cool air from the passage to reach her. Since she was holding her focus, I stepped forward, softly, until I was directly behind her. I held her captive by speaking encouraging words, rhythmically. But as soon as I was close enough to smell her fragrance, she was no longer my captive, I was hers, and I couldn't breathe.

Without permission, my fingertips brushed gently against her hair, and I thought I was going to lose control of her and myself completely. I put my lips close to her ear to command her to stay focused, but, instead, I froze on the spot and had to give myself that command.

Somehow, I managed to whisper in her ear, "Imagine you're like one of the gulls, gliding effortlessly on the breeze."

She was reaching the top of her register, so she raised her chin and took a deep breath, revealing her soft neck and décolletage. The temptation to place my lips on her smooth skin was so strong that I knew I'd reached my limitations and had to leave before I actually kissed her. So, quickly, I backed away from her and into the passage. After closing the mirror, I leaned against the wall and tried to calm my rapidly beating heart and labored breathing.

"Oh, Christine," I whispered. "I love you so."

While she'd passed that experiment successfully, I'd failed miserably, and I never attempted it again.

Abruptly, there was a knock on the door and both Christine and I jumped.

"Angel, what should I do?" she whispered.

"Answer the door, my child, but don't betray that I'm here with you."

"Who is it?" she asked while trying to straighten her hair and dress, as if I'd somehow altered her appearance.

"It's me, Meg. May I come in?"

After a deep breath, Christine unlocked and opened the door, and Meg shoved her way in and quickly searched the room with her eyes.

"Who's here with you, Christine?"

"Why—no one," she stammered, while sweeping her hand around the room.

Tilting her head and frowning at Christine, Meg insisted. "But there has to be. I heard a soprano singing as I approached your door."

"Oh, that? That was me. I was exercising my voice."

"Don't play games with me. I know it wasn't you. It was the clearest soprano voice I've ever heard."

"Really?" Christine questioned with a wide smile. Then, while wrapping her fingers around her throat, she questioned more. "Do you really think so?"

Meg moved up close to Christine and looked her directly in the eyes. "Are you telling me the truth?"

Christine nervously nodded as her fingers fidgeted with a tendril of her hair.

"But how? You were perfect. Do you have a tutor?"

Again, Christine only gave a nervous nod in reply.

"Well, I must have his name. I want to be taught by him also. What's his name?" Meg questioned, with far too much enthusiasm.

"Uh . . . uh . . . he . . ." Christine stammered again.

I held my breath while waiting for her answer. She searched the room, and I knew she was waiting for help from me. I would have put a thought in her ear, but Meg was standing so close to her that I feared she would also hear my suggestion. Nonetheless, I was about ready to rescue Christine when she gathered her thoughts on her own.

"I can't give you his name right now. He's very busy and doesn't have the time to tutor another student, but I'll ask him for you anyway."

"Very well, but can you tell me where he lives? Does he live here in Paris?" Meg asked with excitement.

"Sometimes," Christine answered while again looking around the room.

Meg began to ask another question when we were all saved by another chorus girl, Sorelli, charging into the room.

"There you are, Meg. Gabriel wants to see all of us right now."

"But I'm not ready!" Christine exclaimed.

"That doesn't matter," Sorelli insisted. "You have to come with me now."

They all scampered toward the door, but Christine lingered just long enough to whisper, "Goodbye, my Angel," before she shut the door.

We didn't have the opportunity to discuss that encounter until the next day, but, before that happened, I purchased two red roses, replaced the three roses with the two new ones, and again bound them with the gold ribbon. I laid one of the original three roses in front of the vase on her dressing table. Then, with the two old roses in hand, I went to my place behind the mirror and waited.

Again, when she entered, she leaned back against the door and asked, "Angel, are you here?"

We spoke for a while about the cold and the snowfall and then she spotted the one rose out of the vase.

"Oh! How did that happen? The chambermaid! I must reprimand her!"

I was taken aback. That's it! I'd never heard her speak with such spirit. That's what I needed to pull out of her when she sang. But it wasn't the proper time to utilize it, so I explained calmly, "No, my dear, it wasn't the maid who removed the rose. It was I."

"You? My angel? Why would you want to do such a thing?"

"Put the rose back, Christine. The two roses in the vase represent your present and your future. That one rose, separated from the life-sustaining water, represents your past, and you must let it die."

Her frown increased as she laid it down, and I continued, "It will remain there, and, each day, you'll compare it to the other two, which will always be fresh and new. You'll watch the one wither and fade just as your past must. But as long as that one flower remains close to the other two, it will spoil their beauty. Therefore, the day will come when you'll need to dispose of it. When there's no life left in it, when it's black and dry, we'll dispose of it together.

"In the same manner, you're letting your past spoil the beauty of your present and your future. So the day will come when you'll have to dispose of that part of your past that is hurting you. When you do, I'll be there beside you. That's the only way you can experience the beauty of your present and future life."

Her lips parted as she looked at the drooping rose and again ran one fingernail gently across one of its limp petals. "It seems a shame to deliberately let it wilt."

"Yes, my dear, I know. But remove your sight from it and focus on the beauty in the other two roses."

Slightly nodding, she did as I asked, and then I coached her through her lessons until she left for rehearsals. As usual, I stayed close to her the entire day. Then, at the end of it, I once more watched her and Meg exit through the side door and descend the steps. With envy, I watched a driver open his brougham's door for them, and I watched the brougham's light vanish down Rue Scribe, leaving me alone with my thoughts.

That night, in addition to buying two more fresh roses and exchanging them, which I did every night, I began my plans for the gala. I found La Carlotta's scheduled pieces and put them in Christine's dressing room. Then the next morning when she entered, she again leaned back against the door and asked if I was there. I smiled, so thankful to hear her voice and feel her presence.

When she saw the scores lying on her dressing chair, I instantly explained. "They're for you, Christine. They're what we need to start working on before the gala."

As she picked them up and began thumbing through them, she seriously frowned and exclaimed, "No! These are Carlotta's pieces."

"No!" My voice boomed across the room, causing her to jump and drop the scores on the floor. "They're your pieces! Don't doubt me!"

"But how, when she's preparing to sing them?" she asked sheepishly, while kneeling down to pick up the scattered sheets of music.

I answered indignantly, "She can prepare all she wants, but all the preparation in the world won't grant her the voice you have or allow her to take *your* rightful place center stage."

Her frightened voice came up to me from the floor. "Oh, no! I could never do that! Not in place of Carlotta! Not center stage! Not yet!"

"Christine! Why are you here with me? Why are you obeying my voice and doing my bidding?"

"Because," she said softly as she got to her feet, trying to straighten the jumbled papers in her arms.

"Because why, Christine?" I asked powerfully.

She remained silent, with her head down. Then I could see her retreating into that child's hiding place behind her father's coat sleeve, and I couldn't let her go there.

"Why?" I shouted at her.

With a hint of irritation, she responded quickly. "Because I want to sing."

"You can already sing, and you have for years. Remember how Meg described your voice? You're not here because you want to sing. Why are you here, Christine?" She was again silent, so I demanded, "Look at the mirror, and tell me why you're here!"

She turned to face me, and her eyes showed all the fright of a child lost in the woods, so I couldn't help but soften my tone. "Why, Christine? Why did you call for your Angel of Music in the darkness of your room for so many years? Why, Christine?"

She sighed. "Because I needed your help."

"Help to do what, my child?"

"To sing perfectly," she finally admitted.

With those words, she lowered her eyes from the mirror, almost in shame. I gently touched the glass with my fingertips, as if I were stroking her hair.

"And that you shall do. You believed I could teach you or you never would have called for me. Your belief in me was proper, and you need to remember that belief and not question how I will get you to where you want to be. Continue to follow my instructions. Follow me. Will you follow me wherever I lead you, Christine?"

"Yes," was her weak reply as her eyes came back to the mirror.

"Then learn these scores well, because in six weeks time you'll be singing them center stage—with only me by your side."

The next three weeks went well. In fact, since Christine's appearance at the opera house, things had been going so well that I was able to suspend my nightly rides with César without any harm to myself or others. It turned out to be very good timing, considering the number of eyes that were looking for that mysterious midnight rider.

While it was a pleasure to use Christine's tutoring to distract me from the day-to-day affairs of the opera house, I knew it could be perilous to do so entirely. Being ill-prepared for the gala was proof that I was slipping. And I'd almost forgotten about Joseph Buquet stalking me, which put me in a dangerous position. In addition, when I focused on the conversations going on backstage, I realized the rumors about the Opera Ghost had increased measurably. I needed to stay alert, regardless of how I felt about Christine.

Every day I put two fresh roses in her vase, and, as I watched the one lone rose shrivel, I saw new life coming into Christine's spirit. I reminded her daily about the difference in the roses and the difference in her spirit. She was also pleased. She sang, and we sang together. I guided her in the proper inflection and passion for the music she'd be singing the night of the gala, which was from *Romeo et Juliette* and from *Faust,* both full of deep meaning and feeling. As the days passed, I smiled often when I saw her letting go of her fears and inhibitions and becoming one with the characters she'd be portraying.

The only change I didn't see in her was in her performances. While she was part of the chorus, that's all she tried to be, just a part of the chorus and nothing special. That saddened me, because she was special. But, for the time being, I allowed her to remain just another chorus member. It was a safe place for her to be, both for her and for me. Once she reached that place we were working toward and tasted center stage, I could lose her if I hadn't made my true identity known by then. So, safe in her dressing room, filled with our voices, we both remained.

I was so pleased with her progress, and I told her that often. Sometimes I was so filled with gladness that I found it difficult to remain an omnipotent and veiled angel. I wanted desperately to be her friend and squeeze her tightly while congratulating her on her progress. But then, at the end of those three weeks, something unexpected happened to my make-believe world, although it shouldn't have been unexpected. When it happened, almost everything, including our strange relationship, disappeared in an instant.

Five

As usual, she entered the room after the evening performance, leaned back against the door, and asked with excitement in her voice, "Are you here tonight, Angel?"

Her happy mood automatically put me in one as well, so I asked with a smile, "You seem to be in exceptionally good spirits. Tell me, are you that pleased with your performance tonight or are you simply glad to be here with me?"

She sighed, "Well, I'm always glad to be here with you, but tonight something special happened during the performance. I saw someone I once knew sitting in the audience, and I think he must have recognized me because he smiled at me—at me! Oh!" she exclaimed, as she pressed her hands over her heart. "He's making my heart race. I'm so excited! What will I do with myself?"

Words failed me, and I didn't know which emotion was stronger at that moment; anger or pain. But, in either case, my jaws and heart tightened as I watched her turning in circles.

Then, with schoolgirl excitement, and just as if she were speaking to Meg, she asked, "Aren't you terribly happy for me?"

At that question, my words exploded from me with the roar of a thousand cannons. "No! Not at all, you stupid, silly child. How absolutely and utterly stupid could you be? Now I know I'm wasting my time with you. Leave me—you foolish and senseless urchin! Leave me at once!"

I glared at her through the red haze over my eyes. I fumed pure hatred for that friend, whom I didn't even know. My fists were clenching, and I was ready to slam one of them through the mirror. But then I looked closely at Christine's face and realized that, in my anger, I hadn't projected my voice properly. She was looking straight at me, with an expression that told me she suspected where the voice might be coming from. But, at that moment, I didn't care.

She withered right before my eyes, just as that rose had done. In an instant, she slithered back into that frightened child I'd first met weeks in the past. But I was so furious and filled with unfamiliar jealousy that my heart wasn't allowed to play a part in what was happening to her. My jaws began to ache as I ground my teeth with murderous venom and glared down at her. She instantly broke into tears, but my anger, mixed with my fear of losing her, was so great that her tears didn't even begin to penetrate my hardened exterior.

"I'm sorry," she whimpered. "What did I do wrong? Please don't leave me. Please don't send me away."

Huffing, I turned and stormed down the passage, while envisioning my hands wrapped around her *friend's* neck. My heart was so full of animosity that it was unwilling to listen to her pleas. All it could see was that intruder *mysteriously* disappearing.

Under any other circumstances, I couldn't imagine I would do such a hateful thing to Christine. I loved her so much and would have given my life to protect hers. Yet, in an instant, I'd crushed her because of my own insecurities.

I didn't know what to do. I was a novice at that game of love I was playing, and I simply didn't know what my next move should be. I had competition for the first time in my life, and I was unprepared to handle that unthinkable scenario. I'd always been the best at anything and everything I tried to do. I had confidence that I could always outmaneuver and outsmart any opponent on any field of battle.

But the ground I was walking on was new to me, and I realized I was the inferior one in that heart-driven drama I'd become a part of. That person she spoke of, I'm sure, would have a handsome face and not live underground like a mole. How could I possibly spar with that new threat in my life?

I felt completely helpless and with nowhere to turn. There was absolutely no one I could go to for advice. I couldn't go to Oded. He would have a royal heart attack if he even suspected I was deceiving Christine by impersonating her Angel of Music. I shuddered to think of him sinking his daroga teeth into me and ruthlessly tearing me to bits. No, I couldn't go to him for advice on how to contend with my untrained and uncontrolled emotions.

The knowledge I had on the subject of love was limited at best. I'd only begun to learn its mysterious ways when I lost Vashti, and even then it was her heart that was tied up in love—not mine. After that, my tutors were the imaginations of the novelists' or lyricists' words written between the notes on a score. The only thing I knew for certain about the path of love was that it was a delicate and slippery road. Other than that, I was totally ignorant. I felt like a lost child in a foreign land, desperately searching for something familiar to give him stability.

César! He was my stabilizing force, the one source I could turn to for comfort. Not that he could answer my questions about love and jealousy, but he could help me vent my frustration and anger. And that night I didn't even care if I was seen. I needed him, so that's where I headed. I only momentarily gave consideration to any poor souls I might come across in the process of reaching him.

As I rounded the last corner and entered the stable, I saw two grooms working with a horse at the far end of the stalls. So, without taking the time or effort to put them to sleep, I opened César's gate and swung up on his back. Then, with my whispered encouragement, we moved slowly into the first corridor without being seen.

We knew each other well, which was a good thing since I didn't have a halter or lead rope on him. It took only the right word or placement of my hand on his neck for him to know what I wanted him to do, and he willingly obeyed. I might not have been able to take him to the Seine River to work off my anger, but by the time we reached the lake I was already in more control of my temper. Once there, I sat on him, thinking about what I'd just done to poor Christine and what that new situation in my life was going to bring to us both.

I was there with him for several hours, either on his back or sitting beside him, and his closeness did its work completely. Thankfully, I'd calmed down enough to realize I couldn't go looking for my opponent and permanently end his threat to my goal of making Christine love me.

Becoming so angry with her told me two things: first, I needed to control my temper while in her presence. I'd frightened her terribly, and the thought of her tears tore at my heart. I would have apologized right then, but I knew she was gone from the opera house. Second, I knew I had to become a real man of flesh and blood to her. She had to know my feelings for her were more than a teacher's. Also, considering I had competition, I couldn't wait too long before telling her the truth.

But then, I didn't want her concentration disturbed before the gala. She was making good progress, and an upset such as that could destroy all our work. My only option was to put a halt to any relationship she might have with that intruder, at least until the gala, and then I'd have to think of something else.

Once I felt I was in control, I rode César back toward the stable. Before we got there, I heard an argument between the two grooms. They were blaming each other for César's disappearance and felt for sure that one of them was going to get sacked. I'd been so focused on Christine and my new rival that I hadn't thought through the consequences of my actions on those around me. But, at that moment, I felt my problems took priority over their silly jobs, so I didn't feel guilty one bit.

Knowing I couldn't ride him farther, I slid off his back. Then, running my hand under his mane and up around his soft ear for one last touch, I whispered, "You're wanted by many, my friend. Time to go home."

I motioned toward the stable, and he tossed his head, nickered softly, and slowly started walking through the passage. Then I heard excited voices calling his name and exclamations about his ability to unlatch gates. I smiled and began my walk back in the other direction.

My time with César helped me realize I had to maintain both an angelic composure and the stern hand of an instructor if I were to succeed. That's what I could expect from me, but I didn't know what to expect from Christine. What was she thinking after she'd heard her Angel of Music in such a rage?

While I waited for morning and Christine's return, I went to the roof and counted street lights, dogs' barks, stars, and anything else to keep my mind busy. I couldn't allow myself to think that I'd just destroyed everything, or I might have jumped off that roof.

When morning finally came and I was in the passageway behind her mirror, I gasped and my stomach jumped when I heard her key in the lock. As usual, she leaned against the door, and I waited for her to ask if I was there, but she didn't. She lit her wall lamp and then leaned against the door again, cautiously looking around her room. My heart sank when I saw her face. She was terribly frightened and I felt simply horrible. She was even afraid to ask if I was still there, and I knew I had to rescue her from the fear I'd caused.

"Christine," I managed to say, but it wasn't with the controlled strength of her angel that I'd prepared to use. It was the sound of a desperate man in need of forgiveness for the hurt he'd caused the woman he loved.

"Oh!" she whimpered.

Her hands instantly covered her face, her knees went to the floor, and she fell in a heap amid her royal blue cloak. Her shoulders quivered with her sobs, bringing uncontrolled tears to my eyes. I had to fight with all my might not to open the mirror and hold her tightly in my arms.

"Christine, my child, don't cry."

Her head shook, and, without raising it, she lamented, "I was so afraid you would never come back to me. I was so afraid. My father told me that the Angel of Music would not come to those who were bad. I was so afraid."

I closed my eyes and took a deep breath, trying to control my voice. "I apologize for my actions last night. I was wrong. We angels are never to lose control of our feelings. But you must understand that we can feel, just as you do. We have happy times and sad times, and we can also become angry about what we see and hear. But we are always to be in command of those emotions. I lost control last night, so I ask for your forgiveness."

When I finished, she wiped her cheek with the edge of her cloak and looked around the room. "Forgive you? How can I? I'm a mere sinful human. How can I forgive you—a perfect angel? That's not possible. You can do no wrong."

"Yes, we can, and we do. Don't forget the fallen angels of days gone by and their demise. We're not perfect in that regard, and we can fall short of our assigned roles. I fell short last night by becoming angry with you, so please forgive me."

"I can't say those words to my angel—I simply can't," she insisted.

Fearful of her answer, I asked, "Does that mean that you *can't* forgive me?"

"No, it's not that. You did nothing to warrant forgiveness. I committed the wrong, not you."

Oh, my heart was tearing out of my chest. She was so humble. What had I done to her? Her actions were purely innocent and nothing that would upset any *real* angel. She'd done nothing wrong, and I had to help her understand that without jeopardizing my position or my goals.

I couldn't tell her that her actions had made me insanely jealous, for an angel of music would have no interest in her love life, as long as it didn't interfere with her music. And from what I'd seen of her excitement as she'd entered her room the prior night, a love interest would only improve her ability to sing a love song with true and deep passion. How was I to respond after my cruel words spoken in haste?

"Christine, you were innocent of any wrongdoing. You were merely excited over seeing someone you once knew. How could that be wrong? The failure was mine. I should have told you from the start about the conditions under which I could teach you. The only condition I gave you was to listen to my voice, and you've done that perfectly. My voice failed you when I withheld the rest of the conditions."

She rose to her feet and pleaded with renewed hope. "Then, please, tell me them now. Please tell me, so I won't anger you again. I can't bear to hear you angry again."

Lowering the hood of her cloak, she waited for my reply. She was so beautiful, even with her reddened nose and tear-streaked cheeks. The dark blue of her cloak against the gold of her hair only intensified the blue of her eyes. I wanted so badly to hold her in my arms and beg her not only to forgive me but also to love me.

Control, Erik. Control, I demanded. I wanted my words to come out with the strength and compassion of her angel. But I'm afraid the man I was inside, who feared losing her, came through instead.

"I became angry because I saw in an instant that you were throwing away all we'd accomplished. I should have instructed you earlier about your private life and how closely it's related to your success.

"We only have a few weeks remaining before the gala, and you must not let anything or anyone distract you from your work. You must focus intently on what you're doing. You must not go out in the evening with friends and stay up late. It's not good for your health, and it's not good for your concentration. It would be such a shame if you were to work all this time only to be overtaken by an illness at the last moment before your triumph.

"But it's ultimately your life and your choice. If you feel the need to give your heart to a mortal man on this earth instead of to divine music, then there's nothing more your Angel of Music can do for you. If that's your choice, then I must go to the other poor souls who are crying for my help. Is that what you wish me to do, Christine?"

"Oh, no, my angel. No!" she responded quickly. Then her eyes filled with more tears. "Please, don't leave me. I won't do it again, I promise."

Closing my eyes against the pitiful sight, I turned from her and pressed my forehead against the cold wall. What have I done? What was I doing? Was I trying to destroy it all—our hard work, her faithful obedience, and, most of all, her fragile heart?

"Angel, are you still here?"

"Yes," I responded while turning back toward her. "If you still want my instruction, then you must do as I say and never go anywhere other than your home to rest and this opera house to work. Do you agree?"

"Yes, my Angel of Music. I'll do anything you ask. I'm truly sorry. Please, forgive me."

Even though it was difficult for me to say, I knew it was what she needed to hear, so I tried to sound encouraging. "You're forgiven, my precious child. Now, look at yourself in the mirror."

When she turned and faced me, I saw the remains of her tears on her cheeks, and I crumbled completely. Her tears melted what was left of my composure as surely as the noonday sun melts a new-fallen snowflake. Her vision blurred through my tears, and I had to hold my breath to keep her from hearing my moans.

I lowered my head to my hands and fell back against the wall, whispering to myself, "Oh, Christine, I'm so sorry. I love you so. Please, forgive me."

Once I realized what I'd said, and that I hadn't completely concealed my voice, I looked up quickly, while hoping the whispers of my heart hadn't been heard by her. She'd taken a few steps back and was frowning at the mirror. Then when her hand covered her heart, mine quickened.

I was struggling to think my way out of the predicament I'd brought us into, when I saw her lips silently say, "Angel?"

Swallowing hard, I brought my voice back under control and scattered my next words around the room. "It's all right now, Christine. It's over. We can go on from here. Start your warm-up."

She hesitated for a moment, and then, with another word of encouragement from me, she started her vocal exercises. As I watched and listened to her, I had time to recover my composure, and my thoughts turned to my poor Vashti and the strength I then recognized she'd had.

If she'd felt true love for me, I could finally understand what she'd been going through. I knew why she'd dropped that tray, and spilled the tea on me, and ran from me so often when I looked at her or touched her hand. With that understanding, I gained new respect for her that day.

At age 45, I was learning that love can be extremely frightening, as well as confusing. It was even so to me, who'd fought and won battles against the formidable Persian power. In addition, the love I was feeling for Christine was a greater source of fear than anything I'd ever encountered. It stripped me of my power to control my thinking and my conduct.

On more than one occasion, I'd come close to opening the mirror and revealing the true identity of her Angel of Music. Right then, I could see myself falling at her feet and begging her to forgive me and to love me—the man who loved her. I would gladly give everything I had and more just to have her tell me she loved me. But, I didn't, and we survived that day and many more.

As I listened to Christine smoothly transition from one note to another, I thought about that mighty Persian power and Vashti and my struggles with both of them. Then, unwanted images and feelings flashed before me. I felt my heart race and my breaths come in gasps. I stepped forward, and, while studying Christine's face, I placed my palm on the mirror and wrinkled my brow.

"No," I whispered.

What was I thinking? What was I doing? My years of being separated from the affairs of the men above ground must have dulled my senses. I would never forget my time in Persia or my time with Vashti, but somehow I'd forgotten my involvement in her horrible death. How could I forget?

Panic filled my heart when I looked at Christine's perfect face. Then, when I saw what could happen to it, I closed my eyes and turned away from her. I was living under the Paris Opera House for a good reason—to protect others from my curse. Yet, there I was, drawing that innocent beauty into my web of certain devastation.

"No," I whispered again. "Nothing can happen to my Christine."

"Angel, do I practice those pieces now? Angel, are you still here? Oh, no! Angel! Have you left me again?"

It was only the panic in her voice that rescued me from those horrifying visions, and I stumbled over my words while trying to return to the present.

"Yes, my dear, let's practice those pieces now."

After that near breakdown, the days passed without any further traumatic events. I continued to instruct Christine, while making my final arrangements for her most important night. First, I prepared for Carlotta's illness that would unexpectedly overtake her the day of the gala. Second, I designed Christine's gown and gloves for her debut and delivered the sketch and a sample of the desired material to the costume department. Third, I went to the jewelers with another sketch of the jewelry I wanted for her solo performance. In my mind, I could already see the sapphires and diamonds around her neck. I wasn't sure who would be more excited when she opened the box, her or me.

Also, with new managers on the premises, I prepared for another battle to begin. During the night of the gala, I planned to welcome them by allowing them to become a part of a very important experiment. To prepare for that experiment, I made an appointment to see a doctor about a prosthetic nose. I never thought I would do such a thing, but, as I was learning, love can make a man do things he never imagined possible.

Most days, I tried to keep her in her dressing room for as long as I could. If we weren't rehearsing, then we would talk, usually about her childhood. It was during that time that I learned her mother had died when she was six; consequently, she had little recollection of her.

"All I remember is that she was kind, and I liked to feel her hair. It was so silky. She was very beautiful," she said, while dreamily fondling her locket.

"I can attest to her beauty. You look just like her," I replied softly.

She scrunched her face. "Really?" Then, as her face returned to normal, she added to her thought. "That makes me feel warm inside."

When I thought about my own childhood, I offered another comment. "Not having a mother had to be difficult for you."

"Yes," she said, as she looked down at the locket. "But I did have Madame Valerius. She was much older, more like a grandmother, but I called her Mummy anyway. She seemed to like it, and it made me feel good.

She was good friends with my father, and she let us stay in her home in Perros when we were there."

She stopped talking but still looked as if she wanted to say more, so I encouraged her. "Was there something else you wanted to share with me?"

She looked down at her hands in her lap. "Perhaps, but I don't want to anger you."

"You can't anger me by talking about your childhood. Feel free to tell me anything you want," I assured her, since I wanted to know all I could about her.

She hesitated before she went on with her story. "It was during one of those visits that I met Raoul, the friend I told you about. He and his governess were on the beach, and my father called him over to listen to one of his stories. My father loved telling dark stories about the North and to play his violin for anyone who would listen. Raoul and I became friends and did many things together."

"What type of things?" my curiosity questioned.

"Well, for one thing, my father gave both of us violin lessons, and I sang for both of them. I loved to sing. I would set all my dolls in a row and sing for them and Raoul. There was another fun thing we did together," she added with a relaxed smile. "We'd go to all the doors in the village and ask if anyone there knew of any stories about the North. We both loved them. Usually someone who lived there would tell us a story, and I would sing for them as payment."

She had a wonderful, childlike way of expressing herself, and it made my heart happy, so I would try to keep her talking for as long as possible.

"I don't believe I've ever heard any stories about the North. What are they like?"

"One of my favorites was about Little Lotte, a little girl who loved music and stories. Raoul called me Little Lotte often, because I loved the same things as she did."

She giggled and glanced at her reflection in her mirror. Then her smile vanished, and her fingers again felt the locket around her neck.

"But those stories aren't real life. This is real life," she said as she looked around her room. "I stopped believing in those stories of the North when my father died. This is real life. People die and it hurts."

I responded reflectively, "I know, my child. I know it hurts." There was a long pause before I asked another question. "Without your parents, where did you live? Were you put into an orphanage?"

"No, thankfully, I wasn't put in an orphanage. Mummy took me into her home and treated me as a daughter. She saw to it that I got a good education, and she was the one responsible for getting me into the conservatory of music here in Paris. She still takes care of my needs. I live with her, and she is so kind."

Those conversations were enjoyable, and they helped me to understand her better. However, I couldn't keep her in her dressing room all the time, but I could keep her in my sights nearly all the time. Consequently, my obsession over her grew beyond madness, even by my standards.

I watched her with the intensity of a cat focused on a mouse hole. I needed to see if she would stay true to her word and not see that young man, that *presumptuous boy*. Then, if she did, I needed to see my competition. But, more importantly, with my memories of Vashti and my fear that something unthinkable would happen to Christine, I needed to stay near her to protect her.

It wasn't until much later that I realized how foolish I was. My love for her had blinded me to the biggest danger lying in her path—me. So, like the uncontrolled and unthinking fool I was, I followed her day and night.

I watched her as she rehearsed, as she talked to the stagehands, as she questioned the carpenters, as she studied the seamstresses, and as she giggled with Meg. From the catwalks above her, I watched her face closely during the performances, waiting for her eyes to disclose the location of her young suitor.

At the end of the day, I stood in the shadows and watched as she entered a carriage. Then, I was right behind her in another carriage as she traveled to Madame Valerius' home. After all the lights went out, I went back to the opera house and worked on my preparations for the gala and her future beyond it. In addition, I continued to search for more information about her friend. On occasion, I made a quick appearance at Oded's, just to keep him from looking for me.

Before the sun came up, I would be back at Madame Valerius' home, waiting for the lights to come on, and then I would follow her back to the opera house. Needless to say, during those weeks, I seldom slept and never ate a good meal, only a bite of cheese or bread on occasion. In time, my lack of personal care almost cost me my life.

Six

I was fascinated by the activities Christine found interesting, endearing her to me on a much different level. As a result, my love for her grew significantly, more than I'd ever imagined.

There were days when she didn't obey my instructions, but I couldn't be angry with her. On those beautiful sun-lit days, she'd walk home and would usually stroll through the marketplace along the way. I'm sure it warmed both our hearts when she smelled the newly-cut flowers or freshly-baked bread, and even more so when she showed true interest in the shopkeepers. On those days, she always purchased something to take home to Madame Valerius.

About halfway between the market and the elder lady's home was an antique shop. Often Christine would enter and wander around, running her fingers across the old furniture, sculpted picture frames, and porcelain figurines. There was one piece of furniture, a dressing table, that she showed special interest in and always stopped at. Most of the time, she even sat in its chair while letting her mind journey to some unknown destination and her fingers journey across its dark mahogany. It was from the Louis-Philippe period and, unknown to me at that time, would play an important role in my future plans for Christine.

While in the opera house, if she wasn't in her dressing room or rehearsing or chatting with Meg about simple girlish things, she would wander off by herself and enter her own little make-believe world. It was during those times that her true identity emerged, the Christine I grew to cherish.

She regularly spent time meandering through the sets in the third cellar, running her fingers over set pieces, candelabras, paintings, or masks with tender affection. While doing so, she'd hum or softly sing parts of the opera they belonged to.

Watching her helped me to understand how important music was to her. Her eyes expressed the love she had for the theatre and everything that went along with it. Whether she was in front of the audience or all alone with nothing more than a prop in her hands, her devotion couldn't be denied. She reminded me of myself during the days when I could meander through my opera house without the constant fear of being seen. Those were the days before Joseph Buquet arrived.

But the part of her wanderings that endeared her to me the most was when she had contact with others in the house—first of all, the horses. Nearly every day she went to the stable and ran her hands over their faces or laid her head on one of theirs and talked softly to them. Quite often, she'd kiss them on the nose, just as I so often did. To her, it didn't matter if their noses were green with alfalfa or wet with water or both. It never failed to put a smile on my lips when she snuck them sweets. After making certain no one was watching, she'd feed them a cube of sugar and tell them it had to be their little secret.

When she showed César attention, oh, how my heart throbbed. I wanted so badly to whisk her away on him and leave everyone and everything behind. But I could only stand in the shadows and smile, while my heart cried out to her between each beat.

There were times when her actions showed me her true worth, and each time it brought tears to my eyes. On the days when her schedule wasn't too tight, she'd visit different people inside the opera house, like the cobblers, painters, seamstresses, cleaners, and carpenters. She'd talk to them, asking them about their lives, how they'd learned their trade, where they were from, if they had families, what they did when they weren't working, and anything else that popped into her inquisitive head. But it was more than curiosity that motivated her; she had a genuine interest in each of them.

Her conversations with them were always about them and never about her, which was so contrary to the personalities of most of the performers I'd seen. Even among the gypsies, while they cared for all in their group, when it came to other people, they had no interest in them, only in their money. But Christine was so different. She was truly an angel, and, as I listened in on her conversations, my love for her swelled in my heart.

I was quite mesmerized by her and often had to remind myself why I was following her. It wasn't merely for my enjoyment; it was to find out about her childhood friend. I wanted to make certain she followed my instructions precisely and didn't go back on her promise. But I never saw her with any young men.

My stalking periods were like a two-edged sword. They made me feel glad and bad at the same time. I was spying on her privacy with an obsession that would frighten her terribly if I were discovered. In fact, my desperate need to be close to her and protect her even frightened me, but not enough to prevent me from continuing in my pursuit.

I made certain I was at every performance and in a good position to watch her face closely, just in case she spotted her *friend* again. Doing so put me in various positions on the cat walks above the stage. Then, one night it happened. It was during the ballet of the second act when her eyes betrayed her and told me *he* was in the house, her friend and what I feared was going to be my lethal enemy.

From the direction of her glance, it appeared the object of her attention was in one of the boxes in the grand tier, perhaps across from my Box Five. I moved through the maze of ropes swiftly, heading for my box to get a closer look at this presumptuous intruder. Once there, I searched, trying to locate which box he was in, but it wasn't until the closing bows that I spotted it. It was directly across from mine. My eyes narrowed, and I focused harder on the two men who were on their feet and applauding.

One I recognized as Comte Philippe de Chagny. I knew him well by reputation and knew he clung closely to his proper aristocratic upbringing. His family name and wealth dated back to the fourteenth century. Normally, his noble birth and present station would automatically put him on my black list, but he did appear to have a good heart, an unimpeachable history, and flawless manners. Therefore, I rationalized, he would never let his interest in someone like Christine become public.

However, I'd heard it rumored that he spent time with one of the principal dancers, Sorelli. If that were true, then his proper upbringing wouldn't prevent him from giving attention to a woman of a lower station, such as Christine. But then, I recalled Christine's story about her friend having a governess, which would make the man I was focused on too old to fit her description. Therefore, it wasn't the Comte I needed to worry about. It had to be the other man, whom I didn't recognize.

I studied him closely. He was much younger, probably just barely 20, with fair hair and a small mustache. As I looked closer, I could tell it was he who was returning Christine's smile and eye contact. So this is her young friend, I fumed. So this is my rival. At that moment, I felt, as never before, the breath in my chest turn hot with jealousy. That whelp was instantly put in hatred's path, and I pressed my teeth together, allowing my low growl to mix with the roar of the audience.

"You fool! Leave my house at once!"

What I felt right then was so much more volatile than what I'd felt when I first learned about him. It was instant and murderous hatred I felt pulsing through my body with every beat of my jealous heart. Yet I knew absolutely nothing about him, other than that he had Christine's interest. But it wouldn't take me long to find out all I needed to know. From that moment on, I didn't need to follow Christine as closely, since my attention shifted to the young fair-haired boy instead.

As soon as the curtain closed, the young man rushed out of the box, and so did I. I headed for the catwalks above where I knew Christine would be, and I imagined my rival was also heading for her. I spotted her talking with several other ballerinas on the stage, and then I saw him, trying to make his way through the crowded stage toward her. As I maneuvered into a position to watch her expressions, I felt my jaws tighten and my nails press into my palms.

With an extremely large and over-confident smile, he approached her and tapped her on the back of her shoulder. When she turned to face him, his chest rose in a deep breath, and he held out a large bouquet toward her. If possible, his smile broadened even more.

"Christine, your performance was beautiful."

I held my breath, waiting for her response.

At first her eyes widened, but then she simply smiled, took the bouquet from his hands, and said, "Thank you, *Monsieur*, for the compliment and the flowers. They're lovely."

To my delight, without another word, she turned and headed quickly for her dressing room. I lingered on the catwalk only long enough to witness his stunned reaction. He lost his boyish smile, spread his arms out from his sides, and looked completely confused. I almost laughed at his inability to accept her cool reaction.

I took off running toward her room and was barely behind the mirror when her door closed. I was extremely angry because of that arrogant fool and, naturally, jealous, but I couldn't let her know how I felt. Frantically, my mind raced, trying to find the right words to speak.

Before I could find them, she lit her lamp and asked, "Are you here tonight, my Angel?"

I was struggling to control my tone, and, as the light came up, I could see in an instant that she was also trying to hide her feelings. Her cheeks were flushed, almost as red as the roses in her arms. She was completely out of breath, and it appeared she'd just run a foot race. Since I needed time to absorb what had happened before I said something hurtful again, I spoke little.

"Your performance was flawless, but you look extremely tired. I think it's best if we don't visit tonight. You need to go home and rest."

"Yes. I believe you're right. I'll change and go straight away," she replied, with a noticeable sigh of relief.

Adhering to my normal procedure, I followed her to the side steps where *he* was once more waiting for her. He ran up to her with his large boyish grin and began walking beside her. She barely glanced up at him when he opened the carriage door and helped her inside. I believe she thanked him with a polite smile, but then she dismissed him with a wave of her hand, and the carriage moved away.

She was doing exactly what I'd told her to do, and yet, the situation unnerved me. But I didn't contemplate her actions for too long, since I wanted to find out all I could about that new intruder into my private world. That uninvited guest had something that I didn't have and never would have, a history of a relationship with Christine during her happy childhood.

That alone gave him an advantage that increased my apprehension and began to tear down my confidence. I felt threatened in an unfamiliar way, which angered me. Since I knew that type of thinking was bad for my focus, I concentrated on learning more about that insolent boy.

Within a short time, I discovered he was the Vicomte Raoul de Chagny, the younger brother of Comte Philippe de Chagny. Raoul's mother had died giving birth to him, and his father had died when he was 12, which left Raoul in the custody of his older brother Philippe. At the present, he was 21 and had a commission in the Royal Navy. He was in Paris on a six-month furlough, but the disappearance of a ship, the *D'Artois*, had called him back into service prematurely. He was to board the *Reckon* soon and organize an expedition to search for survivors in the Arctic Circle.

I was partially relieved by that information. Not only would he be leaving Paris soon but also his brother, the Comte, was extremely protective of him. Since Philippe had almost raised Raoul, he scrutinized his acquaintances closely. He did, however, bring Raoul to the foyer of the ballet where they socialized with the performers. But I reasoned he would never allow Raoul to become romantically involved with any of the chorus girls, or, at least, that's what I was counting on.

But, in either case, it made me realize I wasn't alone in my attraction to Christine, and I couldn't afford to be complacent about our peculiar relationship. I had to let her know just who I was and what my intentions were toward her. She had to know me, the man, before that handsome young boy could fulfill what I saw in his eyes when he looked at her. He wouldn't be the first prominent and wealthy man to have his way with the feminine gender on the dark side of their gaily-lit world. When I looked at him and believed that was his aim, I hated him even more. I couldn't allow anyone, and especially not a pompous aristocrat, to harm *my* Christine.

From that night on, I was even more watchful over my possession. She wasn't out of my sight for a second during the day, unless Raoul was in the house, and, in that case, I followed him. Because of that, I was eating little and sleeping even less as my obsession with her took over my life completely. I even started talking to her while she was in different parts of the house just to see her smile when she heard my voice. I wanted her to realize that I was always by her side, no matter where she was, and hopefully that would work as a deterrent from any future fraternization with the young de Chagny.

But what lay ahead of us wouldn't be to my liking regardless of what I tried. It seemed as if the three of us were caught in a rip tide and were carried away by its superior strength. At times, it appeared we'd lost our free will and no longer had control over any of our actions.

Raoul followed her after each performance and sometimes after rehearsals. He tried talking to her, but she would ignore him until he went away. I wasn't sure if her actions made me feel any less apprehensive, considering when he walked away she would steal glances at him.

As I sensed my control slipping through my fingers, I felt even more hatred for him. It was bad enough that he was of the wealthy class, which I already loathed, but for him to be trespassing on my domain put him in an extremely precarious position—between me and the only woman I'd ever loved. At another place and time, it would have been easy for me to end his threat to my happiness permanently, but I'd been living a death-free existence for a long time, and I wanted to keep it that way. I liked it that way.

The only saving grace at that point was how quickly the gala was approaching. I knew I needed to concentrate on Christine's lessons, since they were going to stretch our emotional strength to the limit. So I forced most thoughts about my competition to the back of my mind until after her debut performance.

"We only have one week before the gala, Christine, and I believe you're almost ready."

With a slight shake of her head, she replied, "I don't feel ready."

"You underestimate yourself, Christine, and you underestimate your Angel. Now stand before your mirror. I want you to sing the last piece of the night, the prison scene from *Faust*. Only, this time, when you sing it, you'll also be living it."

She turned toward the mirror, and I saw the frightened child I'd seen on so many occasions before, so I spoke softly to her. "Now, close your eyes, my dear."

She closed them, and as if that were her cue to also lift her arms, her arms rose from her sides.

"No, Christine, lower your arms. This time, you're no longer on the shores of Perros, you're in a church in a small village where you live your modest but happy life as a novice, free from the snares of fallen flesh. Then, almost in the blink of an eye, your life changes and you find yourself where there is snow falling and you're cold, colder than you've ever been.

"You think back over the last year and how happy you were when the handsome young man, Faust, swept you off your feet. You feel warmth flood through you at the thought of his name, and you smile inside. You think of how he spoke of love and how safe you felt in his embrace. With your eyes closed, you can feel his touch as he tenderly made love to you, filling your soul with ecstasy.

"You want to stay in that moment forever, but the coldness around you is too biting and brings you to the reality of your pitiful life without him. All you have left of him is a token of his love, his child growing within you. You feel terror when you're persecuted for being a whore. You're left alone with no one to take you and your unborn child into their home, and your fright increases as the days near for your child's birth. You have nowhere to turn for help, and even your own brother curses you to your very face. Then, as he fights to avenge the family's honor, you helplessly watch his struggle against your once-lover, Faust. Ultimately, with horror, you watch your beloved brother fall in a pool of his crimson blood.

"You're despondent, but you still feel a mother's love when you see your son's face for the first time. Sadly though, your respite from the tragedy called your life is momentary and fades as your fear mounts along with the icy cold of winter. You hold the defenseless small life close to you to keep him warm. You give of what little life you have left in you and allow him to suckle your breast. You're so cold and alone as you curl on the ground and press him close to your chest to protect him from the harsh climate—and the even harsher reality of your pathetic life.

"You try to sleep, but there's no rest as you scream at the nightmare of your past, relived by your sleeping mind. Desperately, you run from the demons pursuing you, but there's nowhere to hide. Then you're wakened to your cold existence once more and the realization that you've abandoned your child to the elements of the night. You run to him and then press your lifeless child to your bosom.

"The pain within you is as never before when you look upon the still face of your son, and you no longer care what happens to you. You're powerless against the forces that drag you off to prison, now labeled as not only a whore but also as murderer of your own child. You're empty and all is hopeless as you're led to your execution. Then, with the last of your breath, your soul cries out for divine forgiveness."

I took a moment to study her face closely before I gave her the final instructions. "Now, open your mouth, Christine, and sing Marguerite's prison song; sing Marguerite's lamentations. Sing, Christine! Sing, Marguerite!"

And sing she did. She sang as she'd never sung before, and, as she did, her tears streamed down her cheeks, causing my eyes to moisten. I was so moved by her performance, partially for what she was expressing and partially because I was so proud of her. She'd done it. She'd mastered all I'd been trying to teach her.

As she finished, and the last note faded, she slumped to the floor, completely spent by that perfect and private performance.

Softly, I told her, "That couldn't have been more perfect if it had been sung by the angels themselves. You were flawless in every way, Christine. Your voice has been kissed by God, and, before the gala ends, you'll have Paris kneeling at your feet."

She was laboring for breath, and her hands went to her chest. Then, when she raised her head, I could see she was still crying.

"Christine," I said softly, "wipe your tears and get up." She did as I asked, but the tears didn't stop and her hands were trembling. "Christine, you're no longer Marguerite. You can stop crying now."

Her head shook ever so slightly. "I'm so frightened. I feel like she was inside me. She was so powerful."

I smiled at her. "That's called superb acting, my dear. You've just tasted it, and now center stage belongs to you. Don't be frightened by its power—embrace it."

She took a handkerchief from her drawer and wiped her tears, and I smiled at her continuing innocence. There was such a contrast between her humility and Carlotta's arrogance. I never wanted Christine to sink into that same trap that most stars fall into as their fame climbs. I almost felt bad that I'd started her on that road, which could possibly destroy her sweet sincerity. But then, as I watched her wiping her tears from her rosy cheeks, I simply couldn't picture her ever being anything different than what she was right then, a delicate and modest heart.

"You're ready, Christine, ready for the center of any stage. But you still need my tutoring. I've yet to teach you how to enter that magical place where you can become whatever characters you want without my voice guiding you."

She nodded, and I sent her home to rest. For the rest of the week I took her deeper and deeper into the heart of both Juliette and Marguerite, and each time she was perfect. But, each time, she was completely spent when we were finished and that concerned me. So, the last evening before the gala, I gave her special instructions.

"Tomorrow morning we won't have a lesson, and I don't want you coming in for rehearsals. I want your voice rested. I'll see to it that Gabriel understands why you need your rest. So don't worry. I'll take care of everything for you. Don't return until it's time to get into makeup. I'll be here and help you prepare your voice and your mind for the pieces you'll perform."

She nodded, as she always did, and then I spoke calmly to her. "Now, there's one more act you need to perform this evening. Tonight, you'll appreciate why I told you to leave that one rose out of the vase. Put on your wrap and take that dried rose to the roof. I'll be waiting for you there."

She looked at the dried rose still on her dressing table and asked with a frown, "Why?"

"The time has come," I began, "for you to let go completely of that part of your past that is holding you back. Tonight, you'll watch it disappear—you'll feel it disappear."

She didn't question any further and did exactly what I'd instructed. I followed her to the roof and hid behind the statue of Apollo, watching as she looked around.

"Angel, are you here?"

"Yes, my dear, I'm always here with you. Now, go to the edge of the roof and hold the rose in both your palms over the edge, as if you're offering it as a sacrifice to the stars." She obeyed, and I continued. "Gently, crumble the rose petals between your fingers until they're finely ground."

Again, she obeyed, and I went on with my strange orders. "Now, open your hands and watch the remains of your dead rose drifting to the earth below, vanishing in the mist."

She opened her hands, and I spoke softly at her shoulder. "That's your past, Christine. It's powerless and can no longer harm you. Say goodbye to that part of your past that has held you in its dark prison. You're free now, and you've proven it with the power of your voice. Whenever you hear any doubts creep into your mind, I want you to picture those rose flakes as they are now, gone from sight. Then make those doubts float away—vanish. Do you understand me?"

She nodded slightly. "Yes, my Angel. I'll do as you ask."

"With your past behind you, tomorrow can be a new day, full of music as you've never known before. Go home and rest and prepare for your new life to begin, a new life where you alone will be queen of your destiny."

She turned quickly and looked right where I was, behind Apollo. Had I not thrown my voice properly? Was I too caught up in the emotion of what I was trying to express to her? Had I become careless? Silently, I waited for her to make the first move.

"Are you leaving me now, my Angel? Is this the last of my instruction?" she asked with that same frightened voice I'd become accustomed to. "I'm not ready for you to leave me. Please, don't leave me."

Running my gloved fingers over the cold bronze in front of me, I responded tenderly, "No, my child, I'm not going to leave you." Then the angel and the man struggled within me, before the simple man continued. "I'll never leave you, Christine. I'll walk beside you forever. All you need to do is want me to stay, and ask me to stay, and I'll stay."

When she answered, her voice trembled, "Yes, please, stay by my side. Don't ever leave me."

Closing my eyes and pretending she was actually speaking to me, the man inside the angel's voice, I answered her softly, "Very well then, Christine, that's where I'll remain—by your side—forever."

I laid my head against Apollo's lyre and fought to bring my unsteady emotions under control. I loved her so much and would have given anything to have her say that to me—the man. The deeper I went into my deception, the deeper I was digging my own grave, for, without her, I would surely lose my life in one way or another. While I labored for breath, her words asking me not to leave her flowed through my heart in a steady stream.

Her voice in my mind was taken over by the sound of her steps crunching the snow in front of me, and I looked up in time to see her looking up at the stars. As I studied her perfect face in the moonlight, she spread her arms and held her palms toward the heavens. Then she spoke words that I hadn't expected and that left me momentarily speechless.

"How can I ever express my gratitude to you for all you've taught me? How do you thank an angel with mere words? I wish you were a man of flesh that I could wrap my arms around and thank properly. That I know how to do, but how can I, a mere human, show my appreciation to you, an angel?"

As moisture filled my eyes, I took a step away from Apollo. The man in love took complete control of my actions, and I prepared to unveil myself to her there in the moonlight. What better time would there ever be than right then, when she was so appreciative of what I'd given her? I closed my eyes, took a deep breath, and pictured her arms around me; I felt her arms around me.

My heart pounded, and warmth rushed through me at the thought, but then I felt the pain I would know if she rejected me. I also saw her fear and disappointment take control of her less than 24 hours before the gala. I couldn't do that to her, and, ultimately, I retreated behind Apollo, letting that part of the man who was filled with a lifetime of fears win that battle.

"Angel, are you still here?" she asked.

I quickly swallowed and did all I could to control my tone. "The best way to show your appreciation to an angel is to stay true to the course he helped you begin. Never lose your courage and belief in yourself or in him. That's all he asks. Now, you must go home and rest. I'll be waiting for you tomorrow evening."

She did as I asked, and I followed her until I saw her bedroom light go out. On the brougham ride back to the opera house, I was deep in thought about my Christine. I tried to put aside my personal thoughts and concentrate on the next 24 hours that meant so much to her future success. She'd progressed better than I'd expected, and I felt I'd prepared her as much as anyone could for her debut performance.

My thoughts were still so focused on Christine that the driver of my brougham had to speak to me several times before I responded and got out. Then, as I walked the area above the stage where I would be during her performance, I couldn't get the sound of her voice out of my mind. Her asking me not to leave her played over and over, and, each time, my heart ached for her words to be spoken to me—the man.

As I stood looking down on the stage for one last moment, I pictured my angel, with her golden hair illuminated by the stage lights. I pictured her in the royal blue gown and sapphire jewels I'd personally prepared for her debut. I believe I was smiling the entire time.

I'm not sure if it was because of my fatigue or my concentration on Christine, but, in either case, I lingered there too long. I'd failed to see or hear a man quickly grab the back of my hair with so much force that it sent me back against a beam. My strength returned to me in an instant, and my rage flared, fueled by years of trained reactions. Then I turned on the fool who dared to confront me. My hands were around his neck, and I had him pinned to the same beam he'd had me up against, when I saw who the brainless idiot was—*Buquet.*

My fingers pressed into his throat, and I moved my face closer to his and scowled. Then, instead of showing the fear I expected, he only smiled. His one hand was still gripping my hair, and I prepared for his other hand to grasp my wrist or my fingers, but they didn't. Instead, his free hand ripped my mask from my face, and his expression changed to one too familiar to me.

It was identical to that of the man who'd trapped me in his basement and then sold me, that small frightened boy, to that circus. Instantly, my fury rose to a new height. As I squeezed his throat even harder, my growl of pure rage echoed across the empty stage below us.

"*Buquet*—you've made the worst mistake of your life—*you stupid fool.*"

Then his eyes rolled back and he went limp.

Seven

Fury, fear, and a host of other emotions flooded through me before I could react properly. I first released him, letting him drop hard on the wood boards beneath us. I then knelt down on one knee and wrapped my fingers around his neck again, only that time I was feeling for a pulse. My heart pounded strongly and my lungs strained to pull air in through my tight throat until I felt his heart beating. With my fingers still around his neck, I contemplated his fate. Should I permanently remove that disruptive fool, or do I let him live?

Since the war with Prussia, I'd managed to live without causing someone's death, but was my determination not to take another life stronger than my hatred for that insane man? Fortunately, more for me than for him, the thought that governed my actions right then was wrapped up in Christine. So, with a huff, I removed my hand, grabbed my mask from his fist, and got to my feet.

I looked down at him with scorn. I wasn't going to let him, or anyone else, do anything to mar Christine's debut. I was glaring at him, thinking of what I could do that would threaten him enough to get him to leave me alone. I was about ready to shove him with my foot and send him down a flight of stairs when a stagehand came around a corner, causing me to quickly leave.

I was still fuming once I got to my home, even knocking over a chair and sweeping the table clean of all that sat on it, including a vase full of flowers. I didn't know what to do about Buquet. I had to have him out of the picture before the gala, since it wasn't possible to watch over Christine from the catwalks if I had to be on guard against his meddling. But then, short of killing him, how could I accomplish that feat?

Huffing, I began cleaning up the mess I'd just made, strangely apologizing to the flowers for my behavior. As I picked up my inkbottle and quill, which were also victims of my temper, I knew what I needed to do, so I sat down and wrote my managers one final note.

My Dear Messieurs Debienne and Poligny,

I first want to congratulate you on your forthcoming retirement, but I would be remiss if I didn't express my deep disappointment that I wasn't personally informed of your plans. I thought by now our relationship would have demanded that you consult me before making such a serious and permanent decision. I'll dismiss your ill manners this time, considering, I'm sure, you've been preoccupied with the preparations for the management transfer.

However, I want to remind you that your duties toward me aren't over until after tonight's gala. Since I have only one more request, it shouldn't be too difficult for you to accomplish it before your celebratory dinner.

You have a man in your employ, the chief scene-shifter, Joseph Buquet. He's a bothersome dullard who is continually frightening the chorus and interfering in matters that don't pertain to him. He spreads outlandish lies about me and makes my job of running this establishment more difficult than necessary. All in all, he's a disruptive force that should be discharged. It would be such a shame if your splendid evening were marred because of him.

I strongly suggest that you dismiss him forthwith so I won't be forced to use my own devices and dismiss him in my own unique manner. That would surely put a dark cloud over your last evening in this remarkable building, and I really don't want your memories of our relationship tainted in that fashion.

In closing, I wish you well in your retirement, and I promise to say an extraordinary and final farewell during your special gala dinner.

Respectfully, your omnipotent partner,

OG

I was much calmer once that note was completed, and, if they took my advice, I'd feel even better. Since I was in the writing mood, I wrote a few more notes.

Dear Signora Carlotta Guidicelli,

I'm so sorry to hear about your sudden illness. It's truly a dreadful shame when a singer, such as yourself, has serious throat ailments. But I feel certain you'll recover soon, that is, if you stay in bed and take proper care of yourself.

I know missing the farewell gala's festivities is disappointing, but, after all, it's only one night, whereas, if you don't stay in bed and rest your voice, your condition could become chronic; then you would miss many more splendid nights at the theatre. In fact, you could be absent from my opera house on a regular basis, if you don't heed this experienced colleague's advice.

In closing, I wish you future good health.
Thoughtfully,
OG

Along with that note, I sent her a flower box that contained one long stemmed, but very dead, black rose. I couldn't help but smile when I sealed that note.

My next note was to the chorus master.

My Dear Gabriel,

Regrettably, it's my sad duty to inform you that our dear Carlotta Guidicelli has taken ill and will not be performing at the gala this evening. But don't fret; Mademoiselle Christine Daaé knows the libretto well and will be an excellent replacement for Carlotta. I encourage you to welcome Mademoiselle Daaé with the respect she deserves and use her talent to your benefit. If not, I fear our new managers will be very disappointed when a large segment of tonight's program is missing.
Respectfully, your ultimate artistic director,
OG

Then my last note I sent to my new managers.

My Dear Messieurs Richard and Moncharmin,

First of all, I welcome you both to my home, and I assure you that I'll be just as cooperative and helpful to you as I've been to your predecessors, that is, as long as you follow in their footsteps and execute, in full, your part of our contract. I strongly suggest that, before Messieurs Debienne and Poligny leave for good, you have them explain to you certain clauses regarding the lease of my building. If you do, it will make for a smooth transition and fortify our partnership with the prospect of a bright future.

I sincerely hope this evening will not only be enjoyable but also profitable. I have a personal surprise in store for you tonight. It's one that will tantalize your ears and soothe your eyes. It's one you'll never forget, one that will guarantee your seats are always sold, as long as you use it as intended.

In closing, I want you to know that I'm looking forward to working with you in our shared love of music, and I promise to give you both a personal and unique welcome at the gala dinner tonight. Your benevolent partner,
OG

With tongue in cheek, I sealed that note.

After looking at my floor clock, I realized I barely had enough time to race to all their offices and leave the notes. Consequently, I was soon running through my secret passage between the third and fourth cellars, thankful that I knew it well enough to move quickly without light. My soul filled with excitement over the prospect of what that day's events could bring, and I checked my mental list to be certain I hadn't forgotten anything.

I was somewhere in that thinking mode when I thought I heard a movement in front of me. Since no one else should have known about my private passage, I felt it was probably only the rats again. But with years of instinctive behavior behind me, I automatically released the coil in my hand toward the sound.

That same scenario had occurred more times than I could possibly count, but, since my stabbing by the well, I preferred to act first and search for the cause of the sound later, just as I'd been taught. But the situation that early morning in March was to be much different than the rest, and it set the ghastly tone that pursued me the entire day and the following weeks.

Within that one moment of hearing the sound and releasing the coil, the air was split with a bullet heading my way. I saw the flash from the pistol and felt an excruciating pain grip me at the same time. Through tight jaws, I cried out, and my head and shoulder hit the wall behind me. My left hand reached for the pain in my left thigh and then both my legs gave way. My only thought was, not now, not with Christine counting on me.

I pressed my head back against a stone and listened intently for another sound, but all I heard were my rapid heartbeats and rats' claws close by. Not wanting to give away my location or that I was still alive, I held my breath. I tried to ready another coil, but I was lying on my right side; the side of my cloak that held more lassos. I opted to remain still rather than taking the risk of engaging another bullet that could cause more damage than a leg wound.

As I listened for any movement from my attacker, I pressed my hand hard against my thigh to stave off more bleeding. Shortly, I could feel the all-too-familiar stickiness of my blood seeping between my fingers. The seconds ticked away while I waited for any hint of where my would-be assassin might be. When I couldn't hold my breath any longer, I slowly exhaled, took another silent breath, and listened again. That cycle was repeated several more times while I waited for the shooter to make another move.

When I could feel the warmth from my blood soaking into my right pant leg, I knew I couldn't wait much longer or I wouldn't have the strength to do further battle with my assailant. So, not much after that, I opted to move rather than bleed to death.

First, I cautiously and silently sat up and readied another lasso. Then, while listening and watching in the direction of the blast, I managed to get to my feet and rest my weight on my right leg and the wall. Again I waited and listened, but there was nothing, so I slowly moved along the wall toward my attacker.

Eventually, I could smell a unique mixture of liquor and cheap cologne. Instantly, I thought, Buquet! You stupid fool! If I could smell him, I reasoned, I should be able to hear his breaths, but all was quiet, so I continued to move toward him with a variety of thoughts surging through me. Was he waiting for me? Was he still on his feet? Was he listening for me as I was for him? Was he dead?

After about 15 steps, my foot hit something hard, and I dropped to my knees against the wall, making myself as small a target as possible. Again I waited, but there were no breath sounds, or any sounds at all, so I reached out to feel what I'd touched with my foot, a boot.

Cautiously, I shook it but without response. After a moment of thought, I reached under his pant leg for his ankle and hopefully a pulse, but, this time, he didn't have one. I crept up beside him and felt his neck just to make sure, but, once more, there was no pulse.

"Buquet," I grumbled. "Buquet, I warned you," I sighed. I closed my eyes and lowered my head. "Buquet, you imbecile! You've spoiled everything!"

In anger, I struggled to get to my feet, and then, while leaning against the wall, I lit a match. My head shook when I looked down at the fool. There he lay with my weapon of choice neatly wrapped around his neck and his weapon of choice still clutched in his hand. I closed my eyes again and repeated several times: I tried to warn him—the stupid dead fool—I tried to warn him.

My anger began to rage within me, and, if I'd had two good legs to work with, I would have kicked him ruthlessly. I felt justified in being angry with him; he'd repeatedly refused my warnings, he was the cause of my clean record being broken, I had a serious wound to suffer through and somehow repair, and now his untimely death made it necessary that I take care of his lifeless body on a day when I already had so much to do.

I growled loudly and screamed abuses at him, as if that were going to be of any benefit to either of us. When I'd used up what little strength I had, I forced myself to think clearly. It was obvious I couldn't make it to the manager's office right then and that my first priority was to take care of my injury if I was to function at all. Therefore, I made my way down the stairs to my home where I prepared to remove the bullet.

I stripped my trousers off and sat on the edge of my tub, staring down at my blood dripping into it. I began to shake my head and ask why. Why was there always someone who wanted to end my life? Why couldn't I just live in peace? There was no good answer, other than the fact that I existed, and I was getting quite tired of it. Then my anger turned into hysteria, and I began to laugh uncontrollably.

My out-of-control emotions continued to move from anger, to hysteria, to hurt, until in a burst of anger I slammed my fist against the open wound, releasing a cry of unbelievable agony. That action, though seriously demented and painful, brought me back to the task at hand. On further examination, I realized the bullet had lodged close to my hip joint and much too deep for me to retrieve easily on my own. Reluctantly, I knew I needed help to remove it properly.

One of my tasks for that day was to pick up my prosthetic nose from Doctor Leglise, so, I reasoned, he could remove the bullet for me. But then, to have a nose right away was not a priority for me. All my life, having a nose was of a major importance, but on that particular day it didn't matter. All I wanted was to ensure the evening would be a success for Christine.

Therefore, I made the decision to do everything I needed to do first, and then, if there was time, I would go to the doctor. So I prepared to mend my leg on my own with the help of the morphine I had left over from my last serious injury, my stabbing at the well. I didn't know if it was still potent, but I was going to give it a try anyway.

After giving myself what I thought was enough to dull the pain, I started looking for everything else I would need. I found two long and narrow steel prongs that I sometimes used to help me tune my piano. They would work well as probes. I then found the semicircular needle and heavy thread that I'd used when I made my divan. Lastly, I got my jeweled knife and a new bottle of brandy.

While clenching my teeth, I again sat on the edge of my tub and poured brandy over my leg and instruments. Then, after a deep breath, I began probing for the bullet. After quite a bit of agony, I found it. It had nearly embedded itself in my thighbone, so I knew I had to make a larger incision before I could reach it.

The morphine was helpful, although I couldn't afford to use as much as I really needed to stop the pain altogether. If I did, I wouldn't have the mind to do the work. But then, I was used to pain, and it usually gave me enough anger so I could work through almost anything.

Once the bullet was out, I again poured brandy into the wound, sewed it up in an awkward fashion, and wrapped pieces of torn up bed sheets around it. It was only then that I really began to feel my exhaustion, which, I'm sure, was intensified by the morphine and loss of blood. But my day hadn't even begun, so I pushed aside my desire to lie down and sleep. Instead, I tried to put my priorities in order. I had to deliver the notes to the managers if they were going to have the time to assimilate them before the gala, although the one note about discharging Buquet was now irrelevant.

After tossing that one note on the dead coals in the hearth, I wrote a revised note and attached it to Carlotta's letter and flower box. Since I didn't have the strength or the time to deliver her flowers myself, that note was a request to my managers that her flower box and note should be delivered to her home as soon as possible. Once that was done, I took them and her flower-box up to the managers' office.

They were both there and at their desks, so with the proper words placed in the right usher's ear, the managers were pulled out of their offices. With them gone, I placed the notes on their desks and left without being seen.

Next, I headed for Carlotta's dressing room. If she didn't get my note in time, or if she chose to ignore it, then the amount of quinine I put in her drinking water would make her feel very ill. I felt sure that her chills, fever, headache, and nausea would send her right home for at least a day or two.

By that time, all the morphine had worn off and I was in serious pain, but I still had a very important job to do. Consequently, I headed for Buquet. While looking down at him, I contemplated what to do with his body. I couldn't just leave it there. No one would ever find him, and having to step over him would be a continual annoyance. On top of that, he would begin to smell and that wouldn't do at all.

Having only one good leg to work with, I couldn't dig a hole and bury him, so I decided to take him back down to the third cellar where the props were and present him hanging as if he'd committed suicide. After all, that's just what he'd done by thinking he could end my life. He wasn't the first to commit suicide in that fashion, although I seriously hoped he was the last. The fool, I thought, as I grasped his wrists and began pulling him toward the stairs.

With my leg burning and feeling as if it was ready to break off, I had a hard enough time maneuvering the stairs on my own, but I knew I had to get him to the third cellar before the bulk of the workers arrived for the evening's event. To say it was a difficult and gruesome job would be a gross understatement, but it was finally finished, and I had him hanging with one of the rigging ropes close to a scene from *Rio de Lahore*. He should be found within a day was my thinking.

In order to keep my anger to the fore, and not my remorse and its accompanying depression, I kept thinking about his stupidity. The pain I was in, and knowing he was complicating my day with unnecessary inconveniences, also helped.

Once I was finished, I stayed in the third cellar and gave myself time to think. In addition to needing rest, I still had several things to do. I wanted to make sure that Christine's dress was finished, pick up her jewelry at the jewelers, and check on my managers and their response to my instructions. But my main focus was to make sure that Carlotta wasn't on the premises and that Gabriel was going to call for Christine. Then, if there was time, I could go to the doctor and pick up my nose and get my leg fixed.

Since I was close to the costume department at the time, I went there first and was pleased when I found her dress finished and waiting for her. It turned out to be a beautiful evening gown, with only enough fabric in the bodice to keep within the bounds of French propriety. I had them use the finest royal blue satin for both the dress and the long gloves. I'd designed them both with Christine in mind. As I gazed at it and pictured my blonde Christine in it, I momentarily forgot about the pain in my leg and hip and my fading strength.

I felt a surge of excitement when I thought about Christine on that stage and wearing that dress and jewels. I'd created it all—from the stage, to her gown and jewels, and the supreme jewel, Christine. Along with the excitement, I also felt pride.

After leaving the costume department, I headed for the manager's office, but found no one around. My opened notes were on their desks, and Carlotta's flower box was gone, so I had to assume they'd taken care of that little detail for me. If I'd been in better shape, I would have pursued it further to make certain, but what little strength I'd had to begin that day was all but gone.

Taking that into consideration, I then went to my secret outside door, caught a brougham, and headed for the jewelers. My fingers were shaking and I felt extremely weak as I examined the pieces for any flaws. Thankfully, I found none. I had the clerk put them in a box and wrap it in royal blue paper with a metallic silver ribbon.

With the box in my cloak pocket, I was back in a brougham and headed for Doctor Leglise's office. I tried to relax on the ride there and started massaging my leg. It was then that I realized my black pant leg was once again soaked with blood. I dismissed it, knowing I still had much to do before Christine's appearance in her dressing room.

While I had a chance to relax, I laid my head back and closed my eyes. I was nearly ready to succumb to sleep when the brougham turned onto Rue Tronchet and the doctor's office came into view, ending that short rest period.

When I entered his office, he smiled. "Your prosthetic is ready and waiting for you, Erik."

"Good," I sighed wearily.

While he headed for a box on a bookshelf, I slumped down in a chair, grimacing at my pain. It was only then that I realized just how sick I felt. My breathing was labored, my hands were shaking, and I felt clammy and chilled all over. But it wasn't until Doctor Leglise removed my mask that I realized how much trouble I was in.

"Erik!" he exclaimed. "You look terrible. What's wrong?"

Before I had a chance to answer sarcastically, he laid the back of his fingers against my forehead and then lifted my wrist and felt my pulse.

Frowning, he asked me again, "What's happened to you, Erik? You look as if you're starving to death, and you have a fever."

Over the last few weeks, I'd seen him on several occasions while he helped me make a decision about my prosthetic nose; therefore, I felt I had few secrets from him. So I told him a short version of what had happened.

"It appears my leg got in the way of someone's bullet. But it's been taken care of, so it's fine now."

He gave me that sideways look as he had on many occasions, grabbed my upper arm, pulled me to my feet, led me into the next room, and pushed me down on a cot.

"Lie down, Erik. I'll judge if it's fine or not."

He shoved my shoulder and I easily went down, which caused my head to start spinning.

When he removed the sheet bandages from my leg, his face contorted and he demanded, "What butcher did this to you?" Weakly, I pointed at myself, causing him to shake his head. "Why did you do this? Why didn't you come to me, Erik?"

"I didn't have the time," was my pathetic excuse.

He began reprimanding me the way any respectable doctor would. Then he gave me something to drink, called in his nurse, and started doing something to the wound that I didn't understand or care about at the time.

I closed my eyes and mumbled, "Be quick about what you're doing. I don't have much time to spare."

I heard him chuckle, and then the next thing I knew I opened my eyes to a nearly dark room, with only one small lamp lit low on a table. I gazed around the room, trying to gain my bearings and clear the haze from my mind. When I saw his nurse reading in a chair, I remembered just where I was and why I was there. With anxiety filling my gut, I tried sitting up and then getting to my feet, but my dizzy head and pain forced me to sit back down.

While the nurse told me to stay put and then left the room, I reached for my watch in my vest pocket. I was trying to focus on its small hands when the doctor came in.

"Where do you think you're going, Erik?"

Thinking about Christine alone in her room and panicking when I wasn't there to answer her, I responded curtly, "I told you I didn't have time to spare. Why did you let me sleep that long?" Without giving him time to answer, I took my box from the side table and tried to push past him. "I must leave now. I'll be back soon and pay you what I owe you."

He grabbed my upper arm and easily prevented me from leaving. "You're very ill, Erik. You need rest, good nutrition, and proper care before you can go anywhere."

"Let go of my arm. I promise I'll be back tomorrow if you like."

About that time, his nurse came in the door with a tray of food, I presumed, for me.

He got my attention with his next words. "There might not be a tomorrow for you if you don't stay and let me help you."

I looked at the sincerity in his eyes, shook my head slowly, and said softly, "If I can't keep this one very important appointment, then my tomorrows no longer matter."

Eight

"Then, will you promise me you'll eat and get some rest? And you must keep that wound dry and *you must* come back here tomorrow so I can redress it," Doctor Leglise demanded.

It was the path of least resistance to comply with his demands, and, when I did, he released my arm.

On the ride back to the opera house, I had to concentrate on Christine to keep my thoughts off my pain and fatigue. I put the box on my lap, with absolutely no feelings about it whatsoever. I thought about the prior weeks when I was filled with excitement about finally having a nose, but, right then, it was the last item of importance to me. Christine and her victorious performance were all I cared about.

I felt overwhelmed by the situation Buquet had left me in. I should have been in the house all day to ensure everything went the way I'd planned it, but, instead, I'd spent the most important hours unconscious in a doctor's office. I had no idea if Carlotta got my note or drank my concoction or where she was, and that thought made me apprehensive to a heightened degree.

My actions upon returning to the opera house were sloppy at best. I knew I couldn't maneuver my secret entrance and long passages, so I opted to enter through the *Cour de l'Administration* yard's entrance. I was so intent on staying hidden from the doorkeeper that I failed to see tiny Sorelli, and I bumped right into her, frightening her half to death and sending her off screaming.

It didn't do my heart much good either, and I had to slip into a storage room after that just to catch my breath. I actually felt bad for Sorelli, the poor child. She was so young, only 15, and extremely superstitious. She'd just put a horseshoe on the table in front of the stage-doorkeepers' box for all to touch before going inside. I presume she thought it would protect those who touched it from me. It didn't seem to help her any, since she immediately touched me after touching it. Perhaps she might rethink that particular fallacy, I pondered, as her scream faded and mixed with others.

Once I recovered my breath, I left the room. But I was unable to move with my usual silent swiftness or think clearly enough to take the right passageways the first time or use the proper trap doors. That was especially true once I got closer to the dressing rooms where there were more people bustling around.

It was easier to understand Sorelli's extreme behavior when I heard that Buquet's body had just been found, and that I was blamed for his death. Everyone, especially the chorus girls, were running around and screeching. Then each and every one of them claimed to have seen me floating around in the corridors. Perhaps they did and perhaps they didn't. I really couldn't say at that point.

I hadn't gone very far when I realized I needed to take a moment to reorganize my thinking before I joined them in their insane behavior. So I slipped into a vacant dressing room and leaned against the wall with my eyes closed. Within a few moments, a clatter of excited voices came in my direction. With haste, I put my weight against the door, fearing someone might enter where I was. But no one did. Instead, the group of overwrought chorus girls entered the dressing room across the hall, which was Sorelli's. The door slammed hard, but I could still hear their voices clearly.

"No! I'm telling you the truth," Sorelli insisted.

"But that's not the way Joseph described his head," another girl questioned.

Then Meg joined in with her flare for exaggerated storytelling. "That can only mean one thing—*he* can change his heads the way we change our costumes."

Oh, Meg, I thought, as my head wagged back and forth. Please don't make it any worse than it already is.

I was trying to think my way out of that room, since it didn't have a trapdoor in it, when I heard a strong and demanding voice along with hard knocks on Sorelli's door.

"Girls! Stop this ridiculous behavior and mind your own business." The door opened slowly. "You know he doesn't like to be talked about, so stop this childish lunacy."

That voice belonged to Madame Giry, and, as she began walking away, Jammes asked, "Madame Giry, how do you know he doesn't like to be talked about?"

There was silence for a few moments before Madame Giry answered. "It doesn't matter how I know, but if you keep up your insane chatter it will matter to him—and *you*."

I heard her steps leaving and then the door across the hall shut quietly. I cracked open my door in time to see Madame Giry at the end of the empty hall, so I sent my words of appreciation to her.

"Merci, Madame Giry. I can always count on you to look after my interest. Merci."

She stopped immediately, partially turned, looked in my direction, lowered her head and raised it again, as if to say, you're welcome, and then continued on her way. I took a breath and closed my eyes, enjoying the momentary and relative quiet. Then I left my hiding place and started for Christine's room. When I reached the end of the hall, I heard men's voices coming in my direction, so I moved into the shadows, waiting until they passed.

As they got closer, I heard one of them say, "They've called in the police, so someone should wait for them at the side entrance."

That's all I needed to hear to get my heart pumping faster. That one word, *police*, made me think of Oded, and the thought of him made me think of my lasso. I covered my open mouth with my one hand and then looked down at my other hand, concentrating deeply. Had I removed my lasso from Buquet's neck before I hung him? I couldn't remember. I shook my head, as if that would help shake my memory loose. Think!—Think!

If I hadn't removed it and it was found around that fool's neck, Oded was sure to see it or hear about it. If that happened, then he would know I was involved, and he wouldn't leave one brick untouched until he found my lair. What was I to do? I looked toward the passage leading to Christine and then the passage leading to where Joseph was, and I growled low.

I knew Christine needed me, but there was a lot at stake if my lasso was found. But there was also a lot at stake on Christine's performance. Ultimately, I headed for that dim-witted and troublesome fool. When I was close enough, I could hear men speaking.

". . . no, don't touch him. Leave that for the police."

"It's not as if he'd be more comfortable if we took him down."

"You two, stop gawking at him."

"Come on. Let's go wait for the police."

"Ya. He's not going anywhere."

I listened to their steps move away, and then I moved closer until I could see Buquet's body, alone and still hanging where I'd left him. So I moved as quickly as I could, untied the rope, lowered him down, and had to remove the noose from his neck so I could check for my lasso. Then, there it was, and I was so thankful that my mind was working enough to think of it before it was found by someone else.

With my hands shaking, I was still trying to release my lasso when I heard steps approaching. I believe I was holding my breath until my lasso released and I rushed behind a scenery piece. Again there were men's voices, first gasps and then words.

"I thought you said he was hanging."

"He was, honestly. When we left him, he was hanging right there from that beam."

"The rope must have given way."

"What rope?"

There was silence, and I heard them moving around, so I stepped back farther into a corner. It was then that I realized I still had the rope in my hand, the rope they were looking for. You idiot, I chastised myself.

"Well, I don't see any rope now."

"I bet those chorus girls took it. They were unusually interested in this whole affair."

"Was there any reason why this man would want to take his own life?"

"I don't know. He hadn't been here that long."

"I didn't know him that well."

"Neither did I."

"Do you know if he was hated by anyone?"

About that time, there were many more people appearing and many more questions without answers. I could answer all their questions, but, on that particular day, I was a very quiet ghost. I took all the noise and commotion as my cue to slip away and into one of my passages, where I left the sought-after rope.

Then I faced another decision. I was being pulled toward Christine's room, but I needed to know what Carlotta was doing. After another agonizing debate with myself, I headed for Carlotta's room, hoping I wouldn't find her there. If I did, I honestly didn't know what I'd do. My mind appeared to be in a scrambled state at that time.

Fortunately, she wasn't there, and her pitcher of water was partially gone. If she was the one who drank from it, then she was now very ill. That thought alone gave me enough strength to continue.

Without further ado, I started for Christine's mirror, hoping she wasn't inside her room and frozen in fear because I wasn't there. By the time I reached her mirror, she was almost hysterical, and I instantly tried to calm her.

"Christine, I'm here for you."

"Oh, my angel!" she exclaimed. Quickly, she rose from her dressing chair. "I thought you'd left me to sing on my own."

Her fearful face made me feel extremely bad, but her words about singing alone answered the one question I hadn't been able to answer for myself. Gabriel must have taken my suggestion and put her in Carlotta's place. That was a relief to know.

While trying to breathe normally, I responded, "I would never do that, Christine, and I apologize for my delay."

Then she turned and looked at the mirror, as she had on several occasions when I hadn't projected my voice properly. "What's wrong? You don't sound right. You don't sound like my angel."

How was I going to explain being late or the pain in my voice? It appeared I was caught in my own deception with no way out. While she questioned me, I waited, trying to relax my jaw and throat. As I did, I heard her voice retreating into its former uncertain and frightened condition. Then I swallowed slowly and started my unrehearsed performance to ensure her debut.

"Christine, you need only one thought right now—your performance. I was merely testing you to see if you could do this on your own, but now I see you still need me by your side and that's where I'll be for as long as you need me."

"Do you promise me that?" she came back quickly.

"Yes, that's a promise, my dear."

She sighed and faintly smiled while looking down at her fingers twisting the green ribbons of her dressing gown.

But then her head sprung up, her eyes flashed, and she rebuked me harshly. "How dare you! How could you do this to me now? Why would you do this now, when you have to know how important you are to me? How cruel of you to choose this time to test me. Why now? Why today when everything is going wrong? Poor Joseph. Oh, the horror of Joseph. And the ghost—he's everywhere. How cruel of you. How could you leave me alone—this day of all days?"

She was no longer twisting the ribbons on her gown; she was pulling them so hard that her fingers were turning white. After I recovered from my shock, I had to smile at her. I'd never seen her so angry. If I thought she was beautiful and inviting while enclosed in her soft demeanor, well, what can I say. With her spirited display, my heart began to race, and I wanted nothing more than to grab her in my arms and kiss her passionately. Even to this day, I believe if there hadn't been that mirror separating us, I would have done just that, without thinking about the pain in my leg or my need for the mask.

Before I could respond to her, I had a battle to fight and win, not to remove the shock from my voice but to remove the lust from my heart. During all the time I'd been with her, I hadn't once felt that way toward her. I'd felt love, a deep abiding love, but never lust, and I wasn't certain how to process my feelings or if I wanted to process them. I wanted her in my arms as never before and for an entirely different reason. What was I to do?

That question was answered when I heard her scream at me. "Now you're not going to answer me! What are you trying to do to me?"

When I registered her pain and tears, I became the angel she needed.

"I realize you think what I did was cruel, but, believe me, Christine, I had no choice in the matter. Someday you'll understand and appreciate what I'm doing for you this day and why, even though you can't grasp everything right now.

"I need you to forget what has happened and concentrate on the night ahead of us. I'd like you to step outside your room and count to twenty. Then you need to come back in as if it was for the first time this evening. When you do, we can go through your warm-ups and have a short rehearsal before you get dressed and into makeup."

She was still quite angry with me, and the tightness in her jaw was telling me just how angry she was, so my words had to be convincing and calming.

"Christine, this is your night to shine. You've prepared well, and I know you'll be perfect in every regard. The stage will be yours to command with no interference from anyone."

At those words, she once again turned quickly toward the mirror, which was making me uncomfortable. I suppose it was a normal enough reaction on her part, considering I was always telling her to face the mirror. But there was a look in her eyes that still made me feel anxious.

"How did you know Carlotta was going to take sick today? How could you know that?"

"Don't forget who I am, Christine. I'm your Angel of Music, and it's your voice alone that has been entrusted to me to guide and to protect. So stop questioning how and why, but simply trust me, and I won't let you down. Now stop talking and concentrate. We don't have much time left. Go outside and count to twenty."

She turned slowly and headed for the door and my hand readied on the latch. Just as soon as the door closed, I released the latch and limped inside her room. I placed the blue box on her table right in front of the vase holding the two red roses, and then, as quickly as my leg would allow, I was back behind the mirror and it was closing. Her door opened, and when she walked in, she leaned back against the door and asked if I was there. I actually chuckled, not expecting her to take my words so literally. She looked quickly at the mirror, and, after calling myself stupid, I threw my voice to the opposite end of the room.

"Now, start your warm-up, and let this night of all nights begin."

After only a moment's hesitation, she did as I asked and began her vocal exercises. I only momentarily took her to the beach in Perros, just enough to calm her and help her concentrate. While she was there, I used all the encouraging words I'd been using for weeks with her. I told her I would be right there beside her even though she couldn't see me or hear me. Then I closed my eyes and slumped back against the wall, allowing myself to feel my weakness and my pain, while not giving into it completely.

Once she was warmed up sufficiently, I had her practice only small parts of her pieces, since I wanted her to save her voice for the actual performance. I talked to her for a few minutes about how to take herself into the different characters, and then I released her.

"Call in your wardrobe mistress, and I'll be waiting for you once you're on stage."

As she sat down at her dressing table, she took a nervous and deep breath, and then asked one more time, "Are you sure I'm ready for this?"

I smiled. "You're a star, Christine. You know it, I know it, and in a few hours all of Paris will also know it."

She started to say something else to me, but then she spotted the blue box. She frowned and reached for it, and then looked toward the door behind her. She turned it over a few times and then looked around her table, I think looking for a card. Then she sat motionless and stared at the floor, still with the same frown on her normally smooth brow.

I finally couldn't stand the silence, so I told her, "Open it, Christine. It's for you."

"But . . ." she started to say before I interrupted her.

"Don't question it. Just open it."

Once she removed the lid, she gasped and lifted the necklace and earrings out of the box. Then, with her eyes locked on the sparkling jewels, she asked, "Who gave me these? They're so beautiful. Did the managers do this? Did you see who gave these to me?"

"They came from the same place that the other sapphire necklace you wear came from," I answered softly.

Again she gasped, but that time she looked up and around the room. "You? You gave these to me? But why?"

That was a good question, and, other than the fact that I'd just wanted to give them to her, I had to think a moment for an appropriate answer.

So with a smile on my lips, I simply said, "You deserve them, my dear. You've worked hard all these weeks, and you deserve something special to go with your special night."

I think she must have heard the smile in my voice because she visibly relaxed, nodded, and began thanking me profusely. While wishing I could place those gems around her delicate neck myself, I had a strange feeling.

Up until that moment, her flawed mirror had been my partner, allowing me to come and go in that part of my home with comfort. It had been my friend during the last several weeks in allowing me to come as close as I could to the woman I loved. It allowed me to see her beautiful face up close and to hear the whispers of her heart, but, right then, it became my enemy.

It was the one obstacle standing between Christine and me, the one obstacle preventing me from sweeping her up in my arms and telling her how much I loved her. So, until I could find a sure way around that problem, I had to be patient. Who knows? Perhaps someday I'd be allowed the privilege of holding her in my arms.

"It's getting late, Christine. It's time to call for your wardrobe mistress."

She literally shuddered and took a deep breath. "Are you certain I'm ready for this?"

"I wouldn't be letting you do it if you weren't. I'll be right beside you on that stage. Now go."

I watched her, silently telling her how much I loved her, until her wardrobe mistress arrived with her gown. While she stuttered and stammered over the beauty of her dress, I looked at her through love-struck eyes. I backed away from her mirror and headed for a secluded place where I could rest before the performance began. I would have gone all the way to my home and bathed and dressed properly for her debut, but I had no strength left in me to do so. Therefore, the hard floor of my passage would serve as my bed, and my blood stained clothes would serve as my evening attire for that one night.

An hour later, I was barely aware of the pain in my leg or my cold sweat and chills as I took my place among the ropes and flying scenery above the stage where Christine would be standing. I was so nervous for her. I believe the only other time I'd been that nervous was when I was waiting for the Shah to make his appearance at the palace in Persia so that my performance could begin.

As I watched her take her place in the darkness behind the heavy red curtains, I could feel her anxiety. I wished, beyond all else, that I could absorb her fear into my body, just for that one night. She was so frightened, and we both needed my arms around her to comfort her and calm her fears. But, as usual, all I had to give her was my voice.

Her wardrobe mistress and hair dresser where right beside her, so I couldn't encourage her just yet, which left me to wait, anxiously, for them to leave her alone. Her bare shoulders were taut and her fingers were clutching and pulling nervously at the long satin gloves that covered them.

I could see her eyes darting all around, and I knew she was searching for my voice, but there were still people too close to her for me to comfort her. She might have needed those people for the last touchups, but she didn't need them nearly as much as she needed my voice. Unhappily, I waited for them to leave her side so I could be there for her.

Then I saw the cue given to open the curtains, and her attendants scurried off stage, leaving her alone. As the red velvet began to part, she took several rapid breaths and turned her head, almost as if she was going to bolt.

I instantly spoke softly in her ear, "I'm here, Christine, and there's nothing to fear. Trust me. Take a slow, deep breath and close your eyes for only a moment. Feel the waves at your feet carry your fears away with them."

She did just as I asked, and, as the house fell to silence, the music started—the music to her first solo.

"Now relax your shoulders, Christine, and let your fingers move gently across the delicate petals of a rose. I'm here with you. I'm here in every note. Your Roméo is here and you're my Juliette. Now sing, Juliette."

I saw her shoulders relax, and I laid my whispered voice one last time on her tender neck. "Raise your voice and sing, my angel. Sing for your Angel of Music."

She did it! Just as practiced, just as instructed. I was breathless while listening to every note perfectly executed, every transition effortlessly maneuvered, and every emotion pulled from the depths of her heart. I was so proud of her, and my eyes filled with tears. Then, with the passion that only a man in love knows, my heart filled even more with love for her.

Once I saw she no longer needed my voice, I moved slowly around the rigging above her to capture every angle of her face and form. Her voice filled the house and my soul with her angelic music, and I was once again breathless. She was so beautiful. She was exquisite. Everything about her was wonderful.

Her golden hair once more took on the appearance of a bright halo around the delicate features of her breathtaking face, just as it had the first night I saw her standing almost in that same place. She was an angel in every way. She was my perfect angel that was saving me from my lonely solitude.

I watched as she moved gracefully across the stage, with the soft folds of her skirt flowing fluidly to the floor and out behind her, like a cool refreshing waterfall. The royal blue of her gown did just what I thought it would, causing the blue of her eyes to resemble deep pools of crystal clear water. The silver streaks of metallic thread sparkled throughout her bodice, like thousands of twinkling stars in a night sky. The sapphire heart on the silver chain was perfectly placed, lying close to her smooth cleavage.

Her hands and arms moved gracefully, letting me know how comfortable she was. I thought there was no way I could be more proud of her than I was at that moment, knowing how far she'd come from that frightened child I'd first met. That monumental night seemed like a lifetime ago.

Once I could take my attention away from her, I started watching the audience and it didn't take long to realize they were just as enthralled with her as I was. They were mesmerized, and not one of them was talking or looking around. She had them spellbound. I was so proud, and I wanted to shout from the chandelier—see my Christine, see my angel. But I was a ghost, or an angel, and not a man who could afford to make such a fool of himself by exposing his heart in public.

I was holding my breath and my heart was pounding as she reached, effortlessly, for the last note of her first solo.

There was a hush, and I laid my voice tenderly on her neck. "*Parfait, mon ange. Parfait.*"

I saw her look around only momentarily before the audience exploded with thunderous applause. I moved back farther into the shadows and watched like a proud parent. The moment was nearly perfect. The only sour note came from that young de Chagny, shouting and applauding from his brother's box. You'd think he had a vested interest in her. The arrogant fool.

I tried to ignore his presence and focused only on Christine and her flawless performance. By the time she'd finished with the last piece of the evening, the one from *Faust* that had brought both of us to tears in her dressing room, the entire house was on their feet. And not only the ladies had handkerchiefs pressed against their cheeks but also some of the gentlemen did as well; not to mention me. I was beside myself with pride for her.

Her arms were loaded down with several bouquets of multicolored flowers, while the audience, refusing to release her, continued their thunderous applause. From the shadows on the catwalk, I smiled with unbelievable contentment and watched her through the moisture in my eyes.

But then she collapsed and lay in a pool of royal blue satin and multicolored flowers.

Nine

I jolted forward on the landing above her and cried out her name, but my voice was only one of many that gasped and cried out. My teeth clamped down, as did my fingers on the railing in front of me. What happened? I frantically asked.

Many were around her within seconds and she was lifted up in someone's arms, someone other than me. They headed in the direction of her dressing room, so I was through the maze of ropes, steps, and beams and behind her mirror within seconds, completely forgetting about everything that was wrong with my ailing body.

My hand was on the glass as I watched the room fill with unnecessary people who prevented me from seeing her. She was laid on her divan, and I strained to see or hear something—anything. The only comfort I received was when I saw the house doctor enter the room. Then I heard the words I'd wanted to shout.

"Everyone needs to leave. Mam'selle Daaé needs air. Leave! All of you!"

It was a relief to see everyone start to leave until I saw who was directing them, the Vicomte Raoul de Chagny. He even pushed his own brother, the Comte, and the old managers out of the room. My pleasure turned to anger, which was quickly eased once Christine came into view.

The doctor was beside her, holding her wrist in his hand. I closed my eyes and fought the temptation to rush through the mirror so I could be by her side. I waited, nervously, for the doctor to give some reason for her collapse and for that arrogant boy to get out of our lives.

Finally, all were gone from the room with the exception of the doctor, her maid, and that fair-haired intruder. Christine started to come around, and then the doctor said she'd only fainted from over-exertion. Again, I closed my eyes and breathed a sigh of relief. I opened them when I heard Raoul say her name. He was kneeling beside her and waiting for a response, but I think her unexpected reply surprised both of us.

"Do I know you?"

"It's me, Christine, Raoul. Remember? I'm the one who you sang for along with your dolls. The one who listened with you when your father told us stories about Little Lotte and the dark North."

I hadn't known Christine long, only a matter of weeks, but our association was intimate and on a plane that allowed me to recognize her body language and tone of voice to a heightened degree. So her next actions were clear to me, and I read her with the ease of a child's storybook.

She laughed nervously, and I knew she was acting, and the act was for me, me alone. I could feel my eyes narrow as I glared at both him and her. She had no need to put on an act for either of us, unless she was hiding something. She could simply acknowledge him for the old acquaintance that he was, and then send him on his way. If she were honest, she would do that, but she didn't, and that act bothered me and angered me almost as much as his arrogance and intrusion into our world did.

She continued to fidget nervously, and Raoul continued to try to spark her memory with words about the sea and a scarf. Then I tried to let the love I'd been feeling for her only moments before remove the anger that was growing within me. At that moment, I wasn't sure who I was the angriest with—him or her.

Christine relentlessly insisted that she didn't know the young man, and she spoke like a true diva when she told everyone to get out and leave her alone. The frustrated de Chagny finally gave up and left and so did the doctor, after telling Christine to go straight home and rest. Her maid began giving her compliments on her performance and unfastening her gown, which was my cue to disappear.

I needed to leave anyway. I needed time to rearrange my thoughts. After her superlative performance, which we'd been working toward and eagerly awaiting for weeks, I didn't want my first words to her to be angry ones. But my time away from the mirror didn't work well, mostly because I spotted Raoul hiding in a doorway two doors down from Christine's. He was watching her door closely. Or was he merely waiting?

Was it all a deception that they were both playing against me? Had something happened while I was unconscious in the doctor's office? Was she only waiting for everyone to leave, including me, so she could be escorted out of my home by her young man? Was I just another pawn on another chessboard, being moved around by another set of players?

My anger, combined with my jealousy, caused my head to pound. I headed back to the mirror with my heart beginning to crack open and pour out sheer pain, more so than my leg, so I laced it up quickly with strands of unadulterated anger. With the euphoria of the night now faded and covered with insecurity and distrust, all my body's ills made themselves known, and I felt horrible in every way possible.

I was behind her mirror and glaring at Christine when the maid left the room. Christine went to the door, locked it, and then took her usual position with her back against it.

She smiled and spoke breathlessly. "Angel, are you here with me?"

I was silent while my mind, heart, and tongue battled it out over which words to speak to her first. Were they to be love and pride—or hatred and anger?

She looked around and repeated herself, "Angel, are you here with me?"

I allowed only one, relatively harmless, word to escape through my clenched teeth. "Yes."

She instantly recognized the tone and moved away from the door as her face took on the familiar look of the frightened child. She began to breathe rapidly, while her fingers reached for and started twisting the silk ribbons of her dress. She started moving around the room and glancing quickly in all directions, as if she was trying to find someplace safe to hide. Her lips parted several times in an effort to speak but then quickly closed.

I'm sure she didn't know what to say. There were no safe words to speak and no safe place to hide, because I saw through her deception. There was no way to escape my wrath, and I believe she knew that.

Her hand went to her throat. Then, wrapping her fingers around it, she finally whispered, "Did I sing so poorly that you're angry with me? I tried my best. Please don't be angry, I tried my best."

She sounded and looked so sincere, and I wasn't sure what to feel—anger at her continuing deception, or pride for her excellent acting skills, skills that I'd taught her. Her eyes were wide and her fingers were trembling as she started backing away from the mirror, while I felt my eyes narrow as I stepped closer to the mirror and spoke barely above a whisper, but slowly, coldly, and harshly.

"You're no longer on the stage, *my dear*, so you can stop the act. You underestimate your angel once more, *my dear Christine*. You forget just who taught you that skill you're trying to use on your angel right now. You might be able to convince your young lover with such a display of innocence, but I'm not that easily taken in or entertained by a mere performance filled with hollow words and a shallow heart. Are you now going to slap the face of the author of your success? Have you filled your heart with my voice sufficiently and now wish to carry it away from my home and lay it in the bosom of your lover, giving it to him freely?"

By the time I'd finished my venomous spiel, she'd covered her mouth with her hand and had backed against a wall. But then, after a few moments of staring at the floor, she pulled herself away from the wall and lowered her hand, and her eyes, that previously were filled with hurt, filled with anger.

"Why are you speaking to me this way? What are you accusing me of? You're speaking as if I'm a woman of the streets! Why? You claim to know what's in my heart. Well you obviously don't. If you did, you'd know that I sang for you tonight. I poured out my soul completely this night, and it was so you would be proud of me. How can you treat me this way after all I've tried to do? How can you do this to me?

"What is it you expect from me? I've done everything you've asked me to do—everything. I've pushed aside a friend just because you told me to. I pushed him aside and hurt him just for you. How can you do this to me? What kind of an angel are you, anyway? How can you be so caring one minute and so hateful the next? How can you make me love you one minute and fear you the next? Who are you? What are you?"

We were both breathing hard by the time she was finished venting her frustration, and I was conflicted. She'd either just become the best actress in the world or she was telling me the truth. Had I just made another horrendous blunder or was she taking me along in her deception? If she was telling me the truth, what was I doing? What was I about to do to that beautiful and fragile child with the delicate heart? Or, if she wasn't telling me the truth, what was that devious woman about to do to my tormented and confused heart?

Originally, I thought playing the part of an angel would be simple, especially considering all the other roles I'd performed in my lifetime. But it was turning out to be the hardest performance of my career, and I feared I couldn't keep it up much longer. I wasn't sure how to proceed, so I tried taking a middle ground. As I placed one hand on her mirror, she continued to move around the room while pulling at those same poor, defenseless ribbons on her dress.

My words were still powerful and strong, but I tried to diminish the amount of anger in them as I responded, "To answer your question simply, I'm your teacher and the one that cares the most about your career, but I'm now questioning your sincerity. Do you think you're too good to need my instruction any longer? Is that why you're doing this? Do you wish your Angel of Music to leave you at this time?"

As her fists slammed down to her sides, she answered quickly, "Angel, no! Why would you even think that? What have I done that causes you to speak to me this way?"

Then I let out the reason for my distrust with a commanding resonance. "You toy with the affections of your young lover, and you know that's forbidden."

"No!" she insisted. "He isn't my lover! He's just an old friend—that's all. I think of him as a brother."

"A friend, you say? A brother? Those words he spoke to you didn't sound like the words of *merely* a friend or brother, and that didn't look like the gaze of *only* a friend or a brother when he watched you."

With that, she jumped and turned around several times, as if she was searching for something. From the way she looked, I suspected it was the first time she'd given thought to the idea that I could not only hear her but also see her.

"Where are you?" she demanded. "Show yourself to me."

"Perhaps, in time, Christine. For now, I need to know if you still want my instructions. If you do, then you must not see this young man again or you'll lose all that you've gained. If I leave you, then so will your voice. Do you want that?"

For the first time she didn't respond to my threat with a pleading no. I was shot through with a terrible pain in my chest that rivaled the pain in my leg, with the thought that I was going to lose her despite all my efforts to win her over. I was losing a hold on my reliable power play, and, from the amount of anger I saw rising in her eyes, I wasn't sure what to do without it.

"You can obviously see me, right? Well, then, you have to know that I haven't been seeing Raoul, although, I admit, I've wanted to. I miss him and our talks and walks. I miss having a friend other than Meg. Raoul was with me, and my father, during the happiest parts of my life, and I miss him. I haven't been seeing him because of you, but, from your reaction, it was all for naught, because you're angry with me anyway. So why did I bother to ignore him and hurt him?"

As if I hadn't made a big enough shambles out of the evening, I continued in a direction that was only going to put her anger for me on a straight and secure path.

"He only wants your body, Christine. He cares nothing for your spirit or your soul. He cares nothing for what you truly want, your music. He only came to you once you were on the stage and on your way to fame. Where was he when you were in the depths of despair? Where was he when you cried in this very room all alone? Where was he, Christine, and where was I? Was I not here for you when he was not? He was probably off with some rich debutante. It was only I who was here to help you in your time of need. Remember that, Christine. It was only I, your Angel of Music, who was here. Don't ever forget that or the one who gave you your voice.

"Your father saw the talent that lay within you, and that's why he sent me to you. Are you going to disappoint him and give this all up? Are you not going to fight for your gift? I didn't make your voice blossom only to have you waste it on a flirtatious and spoiled aristocrat who wants to have his way with a beautiful singer.

"You can't have both worlds, Christine. You can't have the common world of a young lover and the heavenly world of an angel's voice. I refuse to keep my spirit in you if you choose the common and ordinary way of life. Do you want to dash the hopes of your father and try to sing without my spirit?"

By then she'd sat down in her chair and was watching her fingers running over those same lavender ribbons. Then she responded softly, "Why do you do this to me? You frighten me, and I'm not sure I want to do this any longer."

My words came back quickly but compassionately. "You're not sure you want to do what? Have beautiful music fill your soul? Music is the only thing that no one can take from you once you have it securely in your heart. It's the only thing that can fill your soul with something bigger than life itself. Do you understand what I'm trying to tell you, Christine? You just experienced what it's like to stand center stage. Do you want to give it all up?"

She shook her head slightly without a verbal response.

"Then you must concentrate solely on your music, Christine. You must love your music more than anything else, and you must love the one who can give it to you more than anyone else—you must love me."

She nodded her head and then raised it, revealing her tear-filled eyes again. Then she spoke softly, "I do love my music, and I do love you. You have to believe me when I tell you that I sang only for you this night. I poured out my soul for only you."

I was torn between extreme feelings, one of glad relief that she was back under my control, and then sad remorse for what I'd had to do to get her there, and finally anger at myself for pushing so hard that she took a step away from me to hold her ground. But, in my stupidity, I couldn't leave it there; I had to push harder.

"Then no more encounters with that young and rich de Chagny. You must quit playing this game with him. You must tell him, outright, that you want nothing to do with him and to leave you alone. You must not play into his hands and end up in his bed. Do you understand me, Christine?"

Then, in an instant and right before my eyes, I saw the death of the frightened young chorus girl I once knew and her resurrection into a strong and determined woman. She took a slow, deliberate breath, rose to her feet, her shoulders went back, and her jaw set before she spoke with defiant conviction in her voice.

"I understand what you're saying, but I disagree. Raoul is not like that. You know nothing about him or his values. He would never treat me as you say. He's kind and good. It's pure cruelty for you to speak about him the way you are when he's not here to defend himself. My father knew Raoul, and he liked him, and I don't believe my father would disapprove of what I want. No, it's more than a want—it's a need."

She took another breath and then told me, without hesitation, the way it was going to be. "In three days it will be the anniversary of my father's death, and tomorrow I'm going to Perros to be with him. I haven't been looking forward to making this trip alone, because I don't like to travel alone. But now I realize what I need to do.

"I'm going to ask Raoul to accompany me there. You claim to know my heart. If that's true, then you know this is something I need to do for myself, and you won't berate me for it or suspect me, or Raoul, of wrongdoing.

"I'm clinging right now onto the kind angel I've known, the one who says he wants what's best for my future and for me. I'm clinging onto his words spoken so softly and gently, and I hope he'll grant me this wish without reprisals."

She stopped for a moment, while she glanced around the room, and I staggered on my feet at the powerful sincerity I'd just heard in the woman's heart.

"I believe my angel to be one of love. I've heard it in his voice often, and my own heart is filled with love for my angel when he speaks to me that way. I can't let myself believe that you would withhold your music from me just because I desire this one thing. I'm going to Perros even if you disapprove and become angry again, because this is something I have to do. Will you withhold your love from me, your music from me, when I do this?"

A few moments earlier I'd felt powerful knowing I had her back under my control, but then within a few seconds our roles were reversed and she had me right where she wanted me, begging for any morsels she might throw in my direction. I crumbled and would have done anything she asked of me. She said she loved me. She said she loved me! It might have been only the angel she loved, but she loved me, and I could refuse her nothing.

With a spirit that revealed the true condition of my heart, I answered her. "I'll refuse you nothing, my dear. You may go to Perros with your friend and with my blessing. However, I'll also go. I'll play for you and your father. I'll raise the bow to the strings at the stroke of midnight and make your heart entranced. I'll fill the trees with the music that he loved, and I'll do it for you, my Christine—my lovely Christine."

That was a turning point in our relationship. Christine never went back to that totally dependent and frightened child I first met. She lost some of her innocence that night. I believe I'd finally pushed her to her breaking point. That, coupled with the power she felt while she poured out her heart on the stage, gave her the strength she needed to leave that frightened young bird in the nest and take to flight. She no longer appeared as a child to me. She was a woman in every respect, a wonderfully strong and passionate woman in full force. And, strangely enough, that power I saw in her only drew me closer to her.

From that point on, our conversations were almost like those of two friends talking by a fireside, and I never again deliberately used against her the power of the position I was playing. That's not to say that I never got angry, but my temper was maintained, and I never allowed myself to hurt her in that way again—well, almost never.

I presume the one word that describes the change I felt for her was respect. I respected her for standing up to me the way she did and putting her priorities in the right order. While I always felt that music was the cure of all cures, she was right, and, without human relationships, music can fall short of providing a fulfilling life. I knew that from my own personal experience.

We talked calmly for some time after that violent outburst. She told me what time she'd be leaving on the train the next day and the hotel she planned to stay in once she got there.

Then I asked her. "What was your father's favorite violin piece?"

With a faraway gaze in her eyes, she replied softly, "'The Resurrection of Lazarus'"

"Then that will be the perfect piece to share with him. It's one of my favorites as well." She nodded, and I added another thought. "I know your father is very proud of you this evening; just as I am. I've never had the privilege of teaching one as phenomenal as you, Christine. No matter how hard I pushed you, you pushed back harder and harder and your spirit rose higher and higher. There's nothing you can't attain with that spirit. You captured the hearts of many this night, including mine. You made this angel, as well as a multitude of other heavenly creatures, cry. You are my own Angel of Music."

And, assuredly, I tried in my strange angel's way to apologize for my conduct—again.

She turned out her lamp and was standing with one arm and hand against the edge of the open door as we prepared to say goodnight. She sighed and laid her cheek against the back of her hand as she gazed at the mirror again with that strange expression. I didn't want to let her go, even though I was barely on my feet by then. In addition, I had a performance of my own that I had to execute before I could rest.

I watched her with only the low light from the corridor lighting her silhouette, and knew I was in trouble on so many fronts. Not only was my health failing but I also knew Raoul was going to be a more serious threat than I'd once thought. And, in my mind, I was already preparing how I could hamper his efforts to be with her in Perros.

But the feeling that threatened me the most was what I was feeling for Christine. After every encounter with that woman, my feelings grew stronger. My very being was somehow intertwined with her, and my soul cried out in a desperate plea to have her in my life. I was frightened as never before.

I talked softly to her, trying not to let her leave me alone, especially considering I felt Raoul was still in the hallway waiting for her. I was close to revealing myself to her right then and there, and in many ways it would be perfect timing. She was strong and not afraid of me.

So as my finger lay over the latch to the mirror, I pictured myself walking into her room without her screaming. I envisioned us sitting on her divan and talking like any normal couple. I saw us walking into that graveyard in Perros together as a couple, where we could visit the graves of our respective fathers.

I was so tempted, but then I was in such bad condition physically. I was sweaty and chilled from the pain and fever. The last two days had been tough on me, and I hadn't been taking care of myself, which meant I was carrying a two-day beard and my clothes were dirty and bloody. On top of that, my prosthetic nose was still in my pocket and not on my face where I wanted it to be when I met her face to face. So, as she said goodnight for the last time, I lowered my hand from the latch, told her to sleep well, and watched the room darken when the door closed.

I moved away from the mirror as fast as my throbbing leg would allow. If Raoul was still in the hall, I needed to see what happened when they met. I also wanted to hamper her effort to have him go to Perros with her, although I didn't know how I was going to accomplish that task.

I wasn't even to the end of my passage when I heard the door to her dressing room open again. So I headed back to the mirror, thinking she must have forgotten something. Before I reached the mirror, I could see the light come up in her room and I automatically smiled with pleasure. But then, as I caught sight of the form moving around in her room, my smile quickly turned to a grimace. It was Raoul.

He was looking around, behind the curtains, behind the divan, and inside her armoire. He was looking everywhere for something or someone. He finally stopped his search and stood still with his back to the door, just as Christine always did. But his reason for doing so was much different; he was trying to prevent me from leaving.

When he started speaking, it was obvious he must have been out in the hall the entire time and heard us talking. He must have heard my voice, a man's voice, and he was jealous. I smiled, again, thinking someone was actually jealous of me, a man without a nose. Then he started questioning me with a tone that would have instantly put him on my bad side if he wasn't already there.

"Where are you? I know you're in here, so stop being a sheepish coward and show yourself. I won't let you out of this room until you do."

At first I almost laughed. As if he could stop me from doing anything. What a joke. But then I felt my eyes narrow with instant loathing for him and his ignorant arrogance. He wanted me to show myself; well, at that moment, that's exactly what I wanted to do, show myself and then wrap my fingers around his insolent throat and escort him out of my house—one way or the other.

My finger again lay over the mirror's latch, and my temptation to open it and end his interference for good became incredibly strong. My left hand was empty, without the coil that I usually held whenever I was threatened. Instead, I felt the tips of my fingers with my thumb, thinking, if I was going to end his intrusion, I wanted to feel his throat under my hands.

It would be so easy, and it would be over before he had a chance to think. I could take him down to the lake and bury him by the well with the rest of the ones buried there. Then there would be no more of his meddling in my plans for Christine. No one would ever think to look for him there. He would simply vanish.

Ten

Yes, it would be so easy. No one would ever know what had happened to him—no one except me, that is.

Up until that day, I'd managed to keep from feeling what I was then feeling. It had been a long time since I'd used my physical skills, instead of my mental skills, to remove threats to my wishes. It had been so long that I thought those feeling might be gone altogether. But, apparently not, according to the way I felt toward Buquet and Raoul. It was then that I realized how easily Raoul brought out the worst in me.

We both stood in the silence for a few more moments, Raoul, looking for the man he'd heard, and me, staring at my newest threat and contemplating his fate. With a hushed sigh, I lowered my hand and watched him. I knew, as badly as I wanted to remove him from my life, I couldn't live with myself or look Christine in the eyes if I did something to hurt her friend. That one act would end any hope I had of a relationship with her. Therefore, it was my love for Christine that saved that young fool's life that night—and many more nights to come.

Once he finished his futile search for my voice, he left and so did I. I followed him through the corridors until a procession of people crossing our path made me stop and seek concealment. It consisted of several police officers and two men carrying Joseph Buquet's body on a stretcher.

I slipped away as they got closer, but not before I heard one of the officers say, "I don't have enough evidence to rule it anything other than a suicide."

I was relieved to hear that declaration, until I heard a group of chorus girls talking as they divided up a rope they'd mistakenly thought had strangled Joseph. For some peculiar reason, they felt it would protect them from "the Persian's wicked eye." I was curious about what they meant by that strange statement, but not enough to stay and listen, considering I still had a lot to do before I could rest. And knowing the girls the way I did, I knew they'd be talking about Buquet's death for many months to come, so I could catch up on their gossip at another time.

Since I'd lost sight of Raoul, I headed for the side entrance where Christine usually found a brougham. But the number of people in the corridors and my physical condition made it difficult to do so quickly. When I finally reached it, there was no sign of that young intruder, so I leaned against a tree trunk, pondering his odd behavior. The conclusion: I had to find out what his carriage and horses looked like so I could spot him on a dark and crowded street if necessary.

I looked at the opera house and groaned, knowing I had to trek all the way down to my home and then back up again. If that evening wasn't offering me such a perfect chance to finish my experiment, I would have simply gone home and slept, but I couldn't pass up an opportunity laid in my lap. Therefore, I was soon filling my tub and stripping off my sweaty and bloody clothes.

As I lowered my stressed body under the water, my wound stung horribly, reminding me about Doctor Leglise's warning to keep it dry. But, regardless of the discomfort or his advice, I had to clean the grime off my body.

Within the hour, I'd bathed, shaved, redressed my wound, and was putting on my fine evening attire. Knowing what lay ahead of me, I gave myself another dose of morphine. Then, with shaking hands and my small shaving mirror, I prepared to attach my nose. But, once it was in place and my reflection looked back at me, I wasn't impressed one bit. In fact, I was horrified.

I instantly went down into my wine cellar where I had a tall section of polished metal that was left over from my mirror chamber. I leaned it against a wine barrel, dusted it off, and then stood back, taking a good look at myself. I looked ghastly, and my head shook in dismay. My clothes, that I'd filled out nicely before Christine arrived, hung on me as if I wasn't even there. My complexion was more pale than usual, and, even though I'd just gotten out of the bath, my skin felt clammy and looked almost slimy.

I visualized the doctor's expression when he looked at me in his office, and then I could understand why he was so appalled. Why, even I grimaced. I didn't know what to think. Perhaps it's only because I'm so ill and have lost so much blood, I tried to convince myself. I didn't want to believe that finally having a nose wasn't going to help my appearance measurably. My entire life I'd believed that having a nose was all I needed. Apparently, I was so wrong.

While still trying to find a logical answer, I thought perhaps I was simply so used to the way I looked in a mask that any other form of concealing my deformity was foreign to me. In either case, I was left feeling miserable, uncomfortable, and uncertain. My face, including my new nose, looked more like a stage prop for a murder scene than a human face. In addition, my substitute nose felt as if it were going to fall off at any time, making me reconsider my experiment.

I felt self-assured and strong in my mask, and it wasn't until that time that I realized just how much confidence it gave me. I knew it wasn't going to fall off, and, given my quick reactions, there was only one person who'd ever been able to remove it from me, and he was dead. I would have postponed my experiment for a time when I felt better, if it weren't for that new challenge in my life—Christine traveling with Raoul to Perros.

Every new encounter made me more desperate to reveal myself to her, and I wanted to have a nose when I did. Especially after Raoul's recent dominating actions in Christine's dressing room, my desperation took on a high note. But, because of my current physical limitations, I gave up on trying to interfere with Christine's efforts to have Raoul accompany her on her trip.

With grave disappointment, I pulled my nose off and went back upstairs where I sat at the first available place, my dining table. Placing my elbows on the table, I held my face in my hands, trying to sort out my feelings. I almost fell asleep sitting there, so I decided to finish with my experiment while I had the chance. I figured I could make any final decisions about the use of my new nose at a later date, perhaps when I was in a better frame of mind and body. Therefore, I reattached my nose, but I put my mask in my coat pocket just in case.

When I felt I looked as good as I could, I painstakingly made my way back up the five flights toward the foyer of the ballet where the gala celebration was to be held. It was already filled with dignitaries, performers, waiters, reporters, members of the business community, and guests who were there to wish my old managers farewell. The long tables covered in white linen were set with silver-trimmed plates, sterling silver flatware, and lavish floral arrangements. The air was filled with talking, laughing, and the clinking of Champagne glasses held up in toasts.

Most in attendance were dressed in evening attire, but there were some members of the *corps de ballet* who were still in their costumes, and I knew why. They'd been too distracted by all the intrigue about Joseph and the Opera Ghost to take the time to change into suitable attire. One was Sorelli, who kept looking down at a speech she held in her hand. Some others also had prepared speeches for both my new and old managers.

I tried to walk without a limp and with my head up, but I felt extremely self-conscious and truly conspicuous without my mask or my passageways to slip into. I knew it was going to be a challenge for me, but, as it turned out, no one seemed to pay any attention to me. However, that wasn't a guarantee that someone hadn't noticed my strange appearance, since the upper-class French had a peculiar way about them.

They rarely let their true feeling show in public. If anything, they'd respond with the opposite of what they were actually feeling or thinking. Being with them in public was like being at a masked ball, always trying to see behind the mask they wore for their true identity. So I felt they wouldn't think of staring at me or pointing me out to their companions, and I was counting on that part of their social graces to remain true, for a while anyway.

With a glass of Champagne in my hand, I walked among them, watching and waiting for any response from them. If nothing else, I figured their eyes would betray them if my appearance was simply too gruesome for them to hold their dignity intact. If they did hold it together, then I'd know I didn't look as bad as I felt. But what I wasn't expecting were their comments about that day's happenings, and that in itself tested my ability to hold the mask of sociability over my face.

"Did you hear about that poor man?"

"Yes. They say it was an accident or a suicide. What do you think?"

"I've never heard of her before, but she sang like a seraph and hit unearthly notes."

"I agree she did tonight, but a few months back she sang like a carrion crow."

I turned to glare at the one responsible for that cruel remark—Meg. How could her best friend say such a thing? I was so glad that Christine wasn't present. She would have been crushed.

Meg glanced around, and I quickly turned around, huffing.

"Where do you think they were hiding this Christine Daaé?"

"Or a better question is, why were they hiding her?"

"Oh my, they found him right under the stage?"

"It will be difficult to get that image out of my head at my next evening at the opera."

"Is Mademoiselle Daaé here? I'd like to meet her."

I again turned and looked at the one responsible. It was the Comte Philippe de Chagny, and, with narrowed eyes, I scrutinized his intentions.

"Shh! Monsieur Mercier asked us not to speak about what happened to Buquet. Tonight is a festive occasion and he doesn't want it ruined."

Too late, Mercier, I thought. Even the acting manager can't remove a skunk's smell with a hushed word.

My experiment was complete, and, while I was feeling better about my appearance, I was feeling absolutely horrible physically. I couldn't stand on my leg any longer, so I began making my way to the stairs. But, before I could get there, all four of my managers entered the foyer at the same time. I was contemplating whether I wanted to put myself through any more pain, when dinner was announced and all started to be seated.

There were two empty seats at the table where my managers were sitting, so I chose one of them as my target. Then, just as if I were an invited guest, I sat down. I had to hold my breath because of my leg, and I could feel sweat rolling down my spine, but I was sufficiently distracted when my old managers began puffing up like strutting peacocks.

"Congratulations, Poligny! It was a splendid gala!" Debienne exclaimed, as he and Poligny tapped their glasses together.

"Congratulations to you also my partner. I believe we've found a new Marguerite tonight," Poligny replied, as he patted his partner on the back.

Then Richard joined in. "Where in the world did you find such a fine jewel?"

"Oh, you mean Mam'selle Daaé?" Debienne rhetorically asked, with an impetuous smile. "We know how to recognize great talent when we see it. That's part of our success. You'll also have to identify that special quality in performers if you want to advance in this business."

"I see," Moncharmin chimed in. "Her voice calms the ear, and her form tantalizes the eye."

There was laughter, and more clinking of the Champagne glasses, and more pats on the back.

I felt my breath turn hot as I thought, as if they had anything to do with Christine's success. The gala was Christine's triumph and mine, not theirs. The arrogant fools! How dare they!

The Opera Populaire would be just another opera house if it weren't for me and the notoriety I'd brought it. They were enjoying my building that had taken my sweat and blood to build, long before they even new it existed, and it was still taking my sweat and blood to manage. And to think they had the audacity to congratulate each other—the idiots! I had the power to take down the entire structure in an instant, and they'd be powerless to prevent me from doing so.

As my heart rate increased, I grumbled deep inside. They didn't find Christine or her voice. I was responsible for the angelic notes that escaped her lips that evening—I and I alone. Those arrogant and presumptuous fools were having too much enjoyment at Christine's and my expense, and I couldn't let them get away with such blatant lies.

I looked around the table at all the aristocrats in their fine clothing and superior attitudes, and not one of them cared about Christine enough to know how sad she was at that moment. They would take credit for her voice, but they wouldn't give her comfort when she shed tears on her father's grave.

I felt compelled to give them a more accurate view of the evening, so I fixed them an angry stare and wrote a quick mental script. I couldn't let them continue with such gaiety at our expense. Therefore, in the same gay tone of voice that they were using, I began.

"Isn't it a shame about poor Buquet? Do you really think it was a accident?"

All looked at me, then at each other, and I think everyone was wondering where I'd come from. But, thanks to their social masks, they wouldn't embarrass themselves or any of the guests by asking who I was. There were a few hushed grumbles as they struggled with their French demeanor to hide their shock. Gradually, you could hear the sound of their forks on their plates as they tried to return to the anticipated jovial evening.

No you don't, I thought. You're not going to ignore my question, so I tried again with a taunt. "Perhaps the *corps de ballet* might be closer to the truth than most would like to think. Perhaps poor Buquet's untimely death was not as much of a tragic accident as one would prefer to believe."

Both Debienne and Poligny responded at the same time, as if cued from the chorus director, "Buquet is dead?"

"Oh, yes. Most assuredly," I responded quickly with another change in tone, one of sarcasm. While rolling the stem of my Champagne glass between my fingers, I held it up in front of me and looked at it. "Just as dead as dead can get. You see, the poor soul seemed to get entangled in ropes close to the set pieces of *Roi de Lahore*—right below the stage itself. Can you imagine that? And on the very day that starts off my new managers' careers.

"But then, it's rather poetic and so opera-like—don't you think? On the one hand we have the bright and brilliant performance of our very own Christine Daaé, inaugurating her future vocation right here on the Opera Populaire's stage." Then shifting the glass to my other hand for emphasis, I continued, "But then, on the other hand, we have the tragic and unexpected sadness of Buquet's demise, which announces his retirement from the catwalks above that stage."

Then I moved the glass back and forth between my hands several times and looked at one shocked pair of eyes to another all the way around the table while I drove in my point.

"After all, isn't that what opera is all about? The scenes change so quickly, going from cheerfulness to sadness with the opening and closing of the red velvet curtains—life and death taken in stride by the actors who are directed by the workings of an author's pen. Ah, yes, opera and true life—not much different, really. Singers follow the notes written in a score, while you mortals walk on a path written by the gods. You see, not much different. Life and opera. Comedy and tragedy at its finest."

Then I raised my glass toward the end of the table where all four of the managers sat. "To all of *my managers* and the true life drama they're either beginning—or ending." Then, looking right at Debienne and then Poligny, I raised my glass more, and added, "As promised—I bid farewell to *my old managers*, who in their wisdom have served me well."

After taking a sip from my glass, I shifted my sight to Richard and Moncharmin, gestured with my Champagne glass, and then finished my act. "And to *my new managers*, who I'm sure will also act wisely and serve me well, thereby ensuring the future success of the world renowned Opera Populaire. As promised—I bid you welcome."

As I took another sip from my glass, there was a hush and then all began speaking at once. They looked at each other in a quandary over who this person was that was speaking in such a hostile way. Since I'd done all I needed to do to spoil their splendid evening, and the experiment with my nose was complete, I decided to leave. I used their confusion to get up and slip back through a door into a dark room, where I collapsed against a wall.

Normally, that type of exertion would be exhilarating to me and give me strength, but, right then, I felt so terrible that all I wanted was to lie down and sleep. After a few moments to regain my breath, I left through another door and started my long trek home. But, once more, all four of my managers crossed my path in haste. They were talking excitedly and heading for their office, so my curiosity overpowered my need for rest, and I headed for the passage behind their office.

I was already waiting for them when they entered, and I smiled when I saw they'd lost their previous and premature gay faces. Poligny gestured for my new managers to have a seat, but they remained standing, watching my old managers move around the office nervously. They all looked from one to the other as if they were waiting for someone to start the conversation that no one wanted to have. Finally, it was Richard who broke the silence.

"Do any of you know who invited that rude man?"

Again, they just looked at each other, and then, one by one, they shook their heads.

Debienne spoke next while looking at the new managers. "I thought he was your guest."

"I would never dream of keeping company with such an ill-mannered man, much less invite him to a festive occasion. I thought he was your guest," Moncharmin replied in true aristocratic style.

In unison, my old managers shook their heads and looked at each other.

Then, as a frown formed on Poligny's brow, he said, almost under his breath, "I've never seen him before, but there was something familiar about him—or was it the words he used? I can't quite put my finger on it."

"Well," Richard huffed, "we need to find out whose guest he was and inform that person not to invite him again. I've never heard such a slicing tongue. The way he said, *my managers,* gave me the chills. And why did he call all of us his managers anyway? He must be involved with the opera's management somehow."

With those words, both Poligny's and Debienne's faces turned white, and, in unison, they lowered themselves into their chairs. My new managers remained standing, watching the strange actions of their predecessors.

Debienne looked at Richard and asked, "You were the closest one to that man. Did you notice anything strange about him, other than his rude behavior? Did you see him talking to anyone in particular? Did you see where he came from or where he went?"

"There was too much going on," Richard began. "Everyone was talking so loudly that I didn't even notice him until he started talking. Then, once everyone started talking again, he was gone that quickly. His appearance was rather peculiar though. His face reminded me of plaster covered with varnish—most unreal—like an opera mask. And his fingers were very long and thin—like an eagle's talons. He appeared to be dressed just as the rest of us though. That's all I noticed about him. Why?"

My old managers again stared at each other, and then Poligny spoke softly to the confused men still on their feet. "You'd better sit down."

They sat down that time, and Debienne reached into his drawer and pulled out the large ring of master-keys to the building, slid them across his desk, and said sternly, "I suggest your first matter of business tomorrow is to have new keys made."

"Why," Moncharmin asked, almost with a chuckle. "Do you suspect this man is a thief?"

My old managers again exchanged serious looks before Poligny answered, "I wish it were as simple as that. But I'm afraid to tell you that you'll be dealing with something far more serious than a thief. I believe the man we all heard and saw tonight was our resident ghost."

Both Richard and Moncharmin laughed aloud, but when their predecessors didn't join in, their natural smiles turned into ones being forced, and the room, once more, fell to silence.

Then Richard asked, "Oh, you mean he's the man who plays the ghosts in your operas. Is that why he looked so strange?"

Poligny responded quickly, while looking thoughtfully at the ring of keys. "If only that were the case, then we could simply discharge him at will. No, I fear the man with the slicing tongue was none other than a real ghost. A ghost who believes this opera house belongs to him, and, now, that you do as well. That's why he referred to you to as *his* managers."

Now my new managers laughed heartily, until Richard tried to speak between bouts of laughter. "That's a good one, Poligny. You almost had me going. I've heard it rumored that you're a jokester, but this time you really went to great lengths to play a game on us. You even disturbed your own gala dinner. Don't you think that's going a bit too far—just to play a prank?"

My old managers again exchanged that look, and I knew they were trying to think of a way to convince the innocent fools of the truth about me and *my* pranks. Shortly, Debienne opened his desk drawer and took out the lease on the building. Turning it to the page containing my additions, he slid it across his desk toward Richard and tapped his knuckles on the red letters. Richard looked at it, read it, and then showed it to his partner. Then they both smiled again and nodded.

"Very clever, Poligny," Richard started. "But this, as well as the note you sent to us, is not going to convince us that we're actually working against a ghost and not two pranksters. Now, if you don't mind," he sarcastically remarked as he took his watch out of his vest pocket, "I don't have the time for any more of this ghost business. I'd like to get back to my dinner."

He got up and headed for the door, while motioning for Moncharmin to accompany him. My old managers also got up and shook their heads at each other. Then Poligny raised his voice and also headed for the door, placing his hand against it.

"We're only trying to help you get started on the right foot, I assure you. You can call this thing whatever you wish. He calls himself OG or the Opera Ghost, while those who've been here a long time call him the lost soul of the commune. The chorus girls call him the Phantom of the Opera. Believe me, it doesn't matter what you think he is or what you choose to call him. If you don't comply with his wishes from the start, you're only asking for a lot of unnecessary trouble. It will be easier on both of you, and your business, if you just do what he asks. Pay him his wages and keep Box Five open for his use. It's really the wisest choice."

Richard, still not a believer, removed Poligny's hand from the door. "You see, you've made too many mistakes in your little play, Poligny. If that were all this entity was asking for, then it would be a simple procedure to have him arrested for his game of extortion whenever he enters Box Five or picks up his money."

"I can see how it would appear to be that simple," Debienne interjected. "But tonight was the first time we've ever seen him. We hear his laughter at times and we get notes from him often, but we've never laid eyes on him before tonight. Neither have the police when we've called them in to investigate. You can even talk to the magistrate about this and read his reports.

"We didn't make this up for you. It's been going on for as long as we've been here. In fact," he said softly as he glanced at his partner, "he's the reason we've decided on an early retirement. We're quite tired of his tyrannical mandates over what he considers his domain, and we'll be glad to be rid of the whole troublesome affair."

My new managers were still skeptical and again chuckled and shook their heads.

"Very well. Have your fun," Moncharmin replied. "But I can assure you that we'll not pay this man 20,000 *francs* a month, and we intend to sell Box Five just as often as we can."

The new managers walked out of the door with Poligny's words following them, "Go ahead and try, but, when it doesn't work, remember our warning."

Poligny and Debienne once more gave each other that look and then followed the other two men back to the foyer of the ballet to finish their party. I started back to my home but then changed my mind, so I also headed back to the party, with Richard's words ringing in my head—*I don't have time for this*. I entered the closest office, and, after locating a pen and some paper, I wrote Richard a note.

Once done, I rendered a server unconscious and dragged him into an empty room. Then, after putting his jacket on, I entered in among the merrymakers again. With a large silver tray raised in one hand, I reached across Richard's chest and removed his dinner plate, along with his pocket watch. Then, while placing his dessert plate in front of him, I slipped my note in his watch pocket. I moved back into a corner behind a bronze sculpture of Pythia and placed my words on Richard's shoulder.

"What time is it?"

Without interrupting the conversation he was having with an attractive woman sitting across the table from him, he reached into his pocket for his watch. But his fingers came out with only the note that he quickly dropped on the table. He frowned and I smiled—let the games begin. He started patting his pockets, getting to his feet to check them all.

Moncharmin looked at the strange antics of his partner and asked, "What's the matter?"

"My watch is missing!" Richard exclaimed.

Instantly, Poligny and Debienne again looked at each other, and then they started looking around the room, not for his watch but for me.

After watching Richard search for his watch for an uncomfortable amount of time, Moncharmin reached for the note. He opened it, and then his mouth dropped open. Slowly, he reached up and laid his hand on Richard's arm, while holding the note up to him. Richard looked down at him without halting his search for his watch, but then he finally stopped looking and reached for the note and read it. He was silent, with his eyes locked on the small piece of paper in his hands. Then, one by one, those around him stopped talking and gave him their attention.

Finally, Debienne asked, "What is it?"

"Just a note," he answered sheepishly.

"What does it say, or is it personal?" Poligny asked.

"I believe you already know what it says, *Monsieur Poligny*. Another very clever trick, masterfully executed. Now where's my watch?"

Richard held out his hand to Poligny, but Poligny only shrugged his shoulders in confusion. "What are you talking about?"

"Give me my watch," Richard demanded as his voice moved up a notch.

All eyes were on Poligny. "I don't have your watch. Have you gone mad? What are you talking about?"

Richard crumpled up the note and tossed it across the table right on top of Poligny's dessert. "For the last time, give me my watch."

Poligny's mouth dropped open and his brow severely wrinkled. Then Debienne, trying to defuse the situation, stood up, reached over and took the piece of crumpled paper from Poligny's plate, and opened it. After reading it, he looked at Poligny with a straight face.

"You'd better read this."

He cautiously, took the note from Debienne's hand and proceeded to read it for all to hear.

My Dear Monsieur Richard,
   You didn't have time to consider the wishes of your Opera Ghost, so now your Opera Ghost has your means of telling time. Take the time to learn of my wishes and comply with them, and then I'll return your timepiece.
Simply,
OG

Eleven

The room fell to silence, and, if it weren't for the sound of the servers removing plates, I would have sworn I could hear my managers' brains working. The silence was immediately broken by Richard's continuing accusations about his watch. Apparently they needed more proof that I was a very real threat to their continued success at the opera house, but I couldn't think about it right then. My main concern at that moment was to get rest and then to be in Perros with Christine.

I closed my weary eyes and laid my forehead against the back of Pythia's robe, taking a deep breath in preparation for my exit. As I turned my head to look around the sculpture for my opportunity to leave, my nose brushed against the bronze and then promptly proceeded to fall off, hitting the statue several times before it came to rest on the marble at my feet.

I was horrified and instantly reached for my mask in my pocket, only to remember that I was in a server's jacket and not my coat. I looked at my nose on the floor, grabbed it up quickly, and tried to replace it, but my face was sweaty and clammy, preventing my nose from adhering to it. My heart began to race before I calmed enough to think my way through my unusual predicament.

This should be quite simple, I thought, especially considering all eyes in the room were still focused on the arguing managers. I only have to hold the tray up in my left hand, place my right hand over my missing nose, lower my head, and walk along the wall on my right side toward the door. It sounded simple in my head, and, thankfully, it was. Soon, I was back in the room where I'd left my coat and mask. The unconscious man I'd also left there was gone, so, once I put on my coat and my trustworthy and comfortable mask, I headed for my home.

I was almost to one of my passages when I heard steps behind me, causing me to slip inside the closest room and wait for them to pass.

But when the man came into view, I quietly grumbled, "Oded! What does he think he's doing?"

He hadn't come for the gala or he would be going in the opposite direction, so what was he doing there? I easily answered my own question.

He'd probably heard about Buquet and had come to do his own investigating. I ground my teeth. I was so tired of him continually suspecting me of everything that went wrong at the opera house; however, he was usually close in his assumptions.

Once he passed me, I started following him. One corner after another he turned, and at each one he paused, watching and listening. I was so frustrated with him and his meddling in my business, but then I wondered if I should confront him and tell him the entire story. I could even show him my wound so he would believe my version of self-defense.

I was considering tapping him on the shoulder, but, by that time, my stomach was very sick, and I knew I needed to lie down, not spend hours convincing him of my innocence. So I decided on a simpler approach.

I wanted him to know that his frequent visits to my home didn't go unnoticed by me, and that I didn't like his constantly searching for my whereabouts. I wanted him to understand how angry he was making me, and that sometimes I wanted to knock off his head. Oded knew me better than any man, so he knew my actions always had a hidden meaning.

With that in mind, I decided to walk up behind him and knock his silly hat off his head. That should send him a clear message without my having to talk to him. If I managed to send his cap in the opposite direction from where I wanted to go, it would give me time to disappear. But, like so many other events that day, it didn't go exactly the way I'd intended.

I was almost in the position to execute my plan when he stopped in front of the stage manager's door and knocked. Swiftly, I moved up behind him with my hand raised in the air and ready to strike. But, before my last step, the door opened abruptly and there stood Gabriel, looking straight at me with his face drained of all color. I jumped back quickly, and so did he. I was safely hidden in the shadows, but poor Gabriel's flight was not as successful.

In his haste to get away, he bumped into several large objects in his office, knocking them to the floor with a loud crash. He even stumbled into his piano so hard that the lid fell down on his arm. Then, while holding his injured limb, he frantically tried to open the side door, only to bang his head on it when it opened. He cried out when he slammed his shoulder against the door frame on his way out. Once he managed to escape that room, he started running.

I glanced at Oded, who was standing in the same spot with his arms spread in utter confusion. I guess once his mind cleared, he started running after Gabriel and calling out for him to wait. Gabriel reached the stairs and began running down them, only to fall when halfway down and tumble the rest of the way, landing in a heap at the feet of two couples.

I was holding my breath until he managed to get to his feet with the help of a chorus girl. Then I took a heated breath when I saw Oded hurrying down the stairs toward him. I knew the conversation that would ensue, and I was glad I couldn't hear it, but I did watch it.

Oded had a good hold on Gabriel's shoulder, and his head was bent down, looking right in Gabriel's eyes. Gabriel was shaking his head and waving his one good arm in the air. Emphatically, he patted the top of his head and his face and then motioned up the stairs, where I was hiding.

As Oded turned around toward the stairs, I pushed myself further back in the shadows. The traumatized Gabriel was still talking, but Oded was only nodding and still watching the top of the stairs. When he released Gabriel's arm and took a step in my direction, I knew it was time for me to leave. I took off quickly toward my closest passage, but it didn't take long before I knew I'd never make it before Oded caught up with me. So I chose the door closest to me to escape behind. Then, with trembling hands, I removed my personal key from my vest pocket and unlocked the door. Once inside, I locked the door and leaned back against it, with the room swirling around my head.

Shortly, I heard Oded's steps almost running through the hall and I held my breath. His steps faded and I breathed again. My head was leaning back against the door and my eyes were shut when I heard his steps again, only slower. Then I heard each door in succession being shaken. I put my hand on the doorknob to make sure it was locked securely. Soon, Oded was at my door and I felt the knob being jostled, first softly and then harder. I was again holding my breath and waiting for that tenacious daroga to tire and leave me alone.

At times, I seriously didn't understand that man. When all others fled from me, as if I was hell's fire, he walked right into that fire without a hint of fear. Why?

When I didn't hear his steps, I slid down the door and sat on the floor, waiting to be sure he wasn't outside somewhere waiting for me to cross his path. I didn't hear his steps again, but I did hear him calling my name.

"Erik! Erik! I know you're here somewhere. Stop being childish and talk to me."

He repeated those words a few more times and then there was nothing, so I continued to wait. Several times I fell asleep while sitting there, only to be awakened by a stabbing pain in my thigh. I was there for over two hours before my anxiety about making that train to Perros outweighed my fear of running into Oded, so I got up and cautiously left.

As I staggered home, I thought over that crazy scene with Gabriel and Oded. At first I was amused, but then I felt angry, and lastly I felt hurt.

Why were people so frightened of me that they'd act so ridiculously? I was only a man. He could have killed himself, and, I'm sure, I'd be blamed for his death. I'd had enough of that night's ludicrous events, so I changed the subject of my thoughts and worked on my next challenge.

I knew from past experience that I would sleep for a long time if I weren't awakened by something, and I couldn't miss that train. Therefore, I had to rig something to wake me, but what? By the time I reached my abode, I was struggling to stay on my feet and breathe at the same time, but I had to make my alarm before I could collapse. Fortunately, it didn't take me too long.

With one of my small clocks and a buzzer from my alarm system on the lake, I made an alarm clock. Then, I went to my room, collapsed on my bed, clothes and all, rolled in my quilt, closed my eyes, and fell asleep instantly, with my alarm clock still in my hand. The next thing I knew, I was in the middle of a horrendous nightmare.

I was lying on the landing with Joseph Buquet, and even though we were both dead, I could see him staring at me with his sickening smile, I could smell his unusual liquor and cologne, and I could feel his fingers still pulling on my hair. I couldn't move away from him, and I couldn't turn my head or close my eyes, so I was forced to watch his dead and smiling face for all eternity.

I could see the pant legs and skirts of the heartless people who nonchalantly walked over us, but I couldn't see who they were. I could hear their cheerful chatter that wouldn't stop for even one moment to mourn our deaths. I wanted to rebuke them strongly for their hardheartedness, but I couldn't speak. I wanted to hide my dead face, without a nose or a mask, so they couldn't gape at me. But I couldn't move—I was frozen in time.

Then I felt something move against my hand—rats! They were eating my fingers, but I couldn't move away from them. I felt my tears swell and roll from my eyes, knowing that without fingers I would never play my piano again.

Then the people walking over us began laughing at us, and they bent down to look right in my face. It was Christine and Raoul, laughing and laughing. I tried to scream at all of them, Christine, Raoul, and the rats, but nothing would come out of my gaping mouth. I tried and tried until, finally, like water surging through a broken dam, I screamed. I was still screaming when Raoul shouted at me to be quiet and started kicking me. It hurt horribly, but I was powerless to stop him. Then he shoved me off the landing, and I fell endlessly into a bottomless pit.

With a start, I woke when I hit the floor; still wrapped in my quilt. My alarm was still in my hand and vibrating my fingers. While laboring for breath, I disconnected the alarm, sat up, began massaging my throbbing leg, and looked toward the light coming from my parlor.

Then I tried to draw the line between my nightmare and my real life. That part of my nightmares/real life relationship was always difficult, since they weren't that different. While removing the tangled quilt from me, I visualized Joseph's face, and I wondered how long it would take for it to leave my nightmares completely, or if it ever would. It had been 35 years since I saw my first victim's blue face, yet he was usually one of my nightly visitors.

After struggling to my feet and limping into the bath, I leaned on the basin, trying to deal with my failing physical and emotional condition at the same time. The horrible and depressing feelings I'd have after a nightmare were sometimes more than I could bear, and my first thoughts went to morphine as an escape.

I began to rationalize that it could help with both problems, but I'd long since learned not to use it as an emotional crutch. If I did, it only made matters worse, so I had to wait until my emotions were under control before I could use it for my physical pain. I took several deep breaths and looked at my tub, and, even though I'd recently taken a bath, I had to take another one. I was once again drenched with sweat and felt dreadful, so under the water I retreated. Although it made my leg hurt worse, it did help me relax and clear my mind of my post-nightmare anxiety.

Once I was out of the bath, I gently patted the area around my wound dry. It wasn't looking good, and it made me remember my promise to Doctor Leglise to go back to see him that day. I knew I couldn't, not if I wanted to make the same train as Christine. So, while putting a clean dressing over my red and hot leg, I made a promise to myself to go back just as soon as I returned from Perros.

While still buttoning my shirt, I went to my music room to get my violin. I had it in my hand and was walking toward the door when I looked at my piano and sighed. The last few weeks I'd been so busy with Christine that I'd seriously neglected my piano, and I missed it. That feeling along with my nightmare made me thankful that I still had fingers to use in such a marvelous way. So I spent the next minutes with my fingers on the keys and enjoying my music.

First my bath and then my music and finally the thought of seeing Christine again left me feeling much better emotionally, so I gave myself more morphine to help me endure that day's activities. Then, with my medical supplies in my violin case, I hailed a brougham and started for the

Montparnasse Train Station. I got there early, hoping I could get the seat I wanted before anyone else boarded, especially Christine and Raoul.

I stepped down out of the brougham carefully, partially because of my leg but mostly because I wanted to stay inconspicuous. I paid the driver and glanced around for any sign of Christine, but I didn't see her. Trying to keep my hat down over my face and my head down, I moved through the people waiting on the platform and through the train office where I bought a ticket. I then went to the train car as quickly as I could, and once inside I took the seat closest to the back door. Once sitting, I again lowered my head and hat, leaving just enough room below its brim to watch the station's platform and the carriages as they pulled up.

I felt extremely relaxed, especially considering what I was doing, and it helped me remain patient while waiting for my golden angel. When she did arrive, she was all in black, as I should have expected, with only a few blond curls escaping her cloak's hood. She first moved around the platform, I presumed looking for her young friend, and, when she didn't find him, she sat on a bench and waited. I also waited as I searched each brougham for any sign of my rival, thinking that was my chance to see what his team and coach looked like.

As I watched each horse pass by, my plans for unveiling myself to Christine started to take shape in earnest. During the times when I watched Christine with César, I'd often thought about how terribly romantic it would be to whisk her away on him. I could picture both of us on his back as he took us to the hills outside Paris. That would be my version of all the happily-ever-after stories, where the fine young and handsome prince takes his beautiful princess away on a white stallion to his shiny castle on a hilltop. While I didn't have all the niceties a fine young prince would have, I did have certain aspects of those stories that I could use much the same.

So I let my fertile imagination take control of my waiting period and formulated my plan. She was already enthralled with my voice, so, once I performed for her at her father's grave, she would be even more so. Therefore, just as soon as we got back to Paris, I would arrange for a special tutoring session with her.

Up until that time, all our sessions had consisted of her doing most of the singing. I only accompanied her to encourage her or to sing the male part of a duet, but at that special time, I would sing alone to her a piece that was just then forming in my mind. It would be composed just for her and just for that occasion. It would be a piece that would reach down deep inside her heart and pull out the woman in her. It would draw her to my voice even more than she'd ever been drawn before.

I was smiling as some of the lyrics and music began swirling in my thoughts. I would pull her into my passage with nothing but the power of my voice, and she would follow me, uninhibited. With only my voice directing her, I would lead her to the end of that passage where César would be waiting in the finest and shiniest black stage tack. With great power, I'd lift her up on his back and then myself, wrapping my arms around her in a protective embrace. I would continue to sing softly words of love as we moved deeper and deeper down toward the lake.

I would be her prince on his white stallion, whisking her away. I wouldn't be taking her to a gleaming castle on the hill but to my shrouded castle by the lake. I would make it sparkle on the inside by buying all the candles and flowers I could find. My home would be as bright and colorful as a noonday meadow, as bright as a castle on a hill.

I would sing to her all the way to my home, even as I rowed her in my boat. I pictured my voice leading us across the water and the mist parting before us. I pictured her in my lantern's light, willingly accompanying me to my home. I pictured her blue eyes wide with amazement at my beautiful home and smiling when she agreed to stay there with me. I pictured her coming to know and love the man behind the voice—the voice that she already loved. It would be perfect there, and we would be perfect together.

I was staring at an empty space on the train platform when I came out of my creative stupor, and I instantly looked for Christine. She was pacing and twisting her black-gloved fingers nervously. She was searching for her fair-haired young man, and I automatically joined her in her search. I pulled out my watch and saw there were only five minutes left until the train was due to depart. I smiled wickedly. Had something detained him—without my interference? How perfectly wonderful, I began to think. Had fate finally decided to deal me a winning hand?

My stomach was anxiously turning as I waited out those last few minutes, hoping he wouldn't show at the last moment. Rejoicing, I heard the final call for 'all aboard' and then Christine entered the car all alone. She took a seat in the middle of the car and on the other side from me, again, just perfect, since I could watch her the entire way.

But my rejoicing hit a sour note when she turned and lowered her hood. There were tears in her eyes, and I recalled her telling me how much she disliked traveling alone. Then I felt bad about my happy state, while, at the same time, glad that I wasn't the one disappointing her or the one who'd prevented her friend from accompanying her.

Since there was nothing I could do to change the situation, I relaxed and leaned back in the corner, gazing at her spun-gold hair. There might as well not been anyone else in the car, because I saw only her. I felt so at peace, which I'm sure was partially due to the morphine once I gave into it, but, also, I was alone with Christine, and I could give her my music at the gravesite without Raoul's intrusion.

I must have drifted off, because I woke when the train jolted and began slowing down. The sun had set, which left the car dimly lit by a lone oil lamp. I instantly looked for Christine, and she was still in the same seat and still without Raoul. I felt sick inside, knowing I'd left her unprotected while I slept, and I vowed not to drift off again.

They announced that we were pulling into a town for a rest stop and would be leaving again in 30 minutes. I lowered my head to hide my mask and let everyone else leave the car before me. I then left and followed Christine to a shop. When she entered, I stayed outside and watched from a distance until she came out and boarded the train again. Once I was back in my seat and we started to pull away, I sighed.

While I felt it was humanly impossible for Raoul to have reached that location before us, I still feared he might. It was just too perfect for him not to be there, so I was waiting for us to be settled in Perros before I'd feel completely comfortable.

We made two more stops, and it was late the next day before we finally neared Perros. When the train started to slow, I got up before anyone else and went to the landing at the back of the car. Then, just before it stopped, I was off of it. I at first wrenched from the pain that shot through my leg and hip, but then moved quickly away and into the shadows while I waited for her to step down. I saw the porter take her hand and help her down, and I sighed deeply, wanting it to be my hand, and no one else's, that steadied her steps.

I followed her to The Rising Sun Inn and then watched from outside on the walk as she checked in and began climbing the stairs. I again followed her to see which room she was placed in; then I went back down and checked in, requesting the room next to hers. Once inside my room, I stood at the wall connecting us and listened for any sounds. I heard her moving around and then there was nothing. I was out in the hall quickly and looked toward her door just as the light under it went out. I smiled. She was going to bed and I could relax.

I spent the night staring at the ceiling and listening for any movement next door, but there was only movement outside in the hall from time to time as others were being checked in. Her room remained quiet.

As I lay there, I fine-tuned my plans for the day when Christine would finally come to understand that I was a man and how much I loved her. When I pictured her in my home and smiling, I realized that, while I'd planned for all the candles and flowers to make it beautiful for her, I hadn't given any thought to her physical comfort. Where would she sleep? Where would she bathe? It would be too awkward if she knew she was sleeping in my bed or bathing in my tub.

With those thoughts, I began making mental changes to my home. I'd purchase the antique furniture she loved so much. I'd buy her scented soaps and candles and new soft towels for her bath and new bed linens and new beautiful paintings and a tapestry for the walls in what would be her bedroom. I would decorate her room with plush bedding and pillows that would make any princess leap for joy. I would fill the armoire in her room with many dresses and wraps and gloves and shoes. I would have to work fast, but I could add another bath for me, a smaller one, off my music room so she could have complete privacy.

By the time the sun was coming up, I had every detail just the way I wanted it, and I had most of the music for our romantic journey written on many pieces of the inn's stationary. I was sitting at the small table in my room, organizing the music, when I heard sounds from her room, so I readied for a day with her. I wished I could be by her side right then, since that day was the anniversary of her father's death, but, as yet, I wouldn't be permitted that privilege.

I waited until I heard her door open and close, and then her steps moved past my door. I left my room and followed her at a discreet distance. After going downstairs, she entered the inn's restaurant and was taken to a table next to the windows. I entered and took a table in the back corner where it was darkest.

I sat with my back to her, but turned just enough so I could glance over my shoulder and watch out for her. She ordered some sweet cakes and hot chocolate. But I was much too nervous to think about eating anything right then, so I simply ordered a *café noir*. I couldn't believe my next thought; I actually wished Raoul were there with her so she wouldn't be eating alone. That was the one thing she didn't want, to be alone, and yet there she was. I was once again thankful that I had nothing to do with his absence or I would have felt truly awful at the sight of her all alone.

Once she was finished eating, she went to the doorman and spoke to him. I was too far away to hear exactly what she said, but I could read her lips enough to know she'd just ordered a carriage. She then walked right past me and back up the stairs. The temptation to step out in front of her and introduce myself was strong, but, instead, I kept repeating: patience, Erik, patience.

I went to my room for my cloak and hat and then left the inn, heading straight for the livery where I rented a horse. After being forced to mount from the right side due to my injured leg, I went back to the inn, but I didn't go inside. Instead, I waited across the street in an alleyway, watching through lightly falling snow for my angel to appear.

Soon the carriage pulled up and Christine came out and entered. I followed the carriage long enough to know she was going to the cemetery, so I took a side road and rode as fast as my leg would permit until I was past the cemetery and up on the hill behind it. I moved to the same spot in a cluster of trees where I'd stood thirty-five years previously, during my father's funeral.

It felt strange to be there like that, waiting and watching for a carriage to approach, just as I'd done that day so long ago. It felt even stranger as her black carriage arrived and she stepped out. My thoughts turned instantly to Gigi in her black attire and gold hair amid the fresh snow and barren trees.

I shook off my memories and concentrated on Christine as she moved through the cold and lifeless tombstones on her way to her father's grave. Then she stopped before a headstone and stood looking down for a long time, without any movement. My heart ached for hers, since I knew exactly what she was feeling. She knelt down, and her head went down also. I wanted so badly to be there beside her, to hold her and comfort her. Perhaps next year, I thought. Perhaps next year.

While she was there, I looked at the surrounding terrain and decided the best place to play my violin for her would be from the top of the church roof. I could be close enough to her to watch her and yet hide behind the cross and steeple. The acoustics would also be the best from that high location, but, with the current condition of my leg, how was I to get up there? I couldn't climb or jump as I normally would. That obstacle would have to be worked out.

After about an hour, she moved toward the church and entered it through the front door. I walked my horse down toward the back of the church and tied him there. It was then that my own black gloved hand went to my mouth in a gasp. Everywhere around me, and especially up against the church, were bones; human bones and skulls, almost buried by the light snow.

I looked around quickly, trying to understand that strange phenomenon. Throughout the entire cemetery, there were some graves that had been unearthed, and my heart jerked, fearing my father's could be one of them. My cloak bellowed out behind me as I tore through the plots on my way to my father's grave. I stopped in front of it, with quick puffs of white air leaving my lips, and then looked down at his stone and grave still in its proper condition. I closed my eyes and lowered my head. I didn't know what I would have done if it were his bones that were piled up against the church, resembling a stonemason's stack. I shuddered at the thought.

I took a deep breath, looked toward the church, and then toward where Christine had been standing. I went there and looked down at her father's grave, also thankful that it hadn't been disturbed. A sick feeling sunk into my chest at the thought of her arriving there and finding her father's bones scattered around the graveyard like so much rubbish.

I felt my brow wrinkle as I looked back at the church and pictured her panicking. My head shook slowly, and I knew for sure if that had happened to her I wouldn't have been able to leave her alone like that. Perfect plans, or no perfect plans, she would have come to know me right then and there, because I would have had to take her in my arms and comfort her.

I hated that she'd seen all that remained of once living men and women. It was disturbing to me, so it had to be disturbing to her. If I'd known the cemetery's condition ahead of time, I would have arrived there much before her and removed the bones so she wouldn't have had to witness such a gruesome sight. But it was too late to do anything about it, so I returned to the back of the church and entered it.

It was dark inside, with the exception of the faint sunlight filtering in through the stained glass windows. It was also quiet as I moved carefully through the shadows. I peered around from behind a pillar until I spotted her in one of the pews close to the front. It was there that I remained for almost an hour before a priest came in.

She talked to him for a moment, and then he started a mass for her father. She stayed a while longer and from there she went back outside and wandered around the different headstones. At each one, she stopped and looked down at it. I wasn't certain what she was doing or thinking, but she was there for almost another hour before the same carriage arrived and she left.

I went back to the horse, back to the stable, and back to the inn. By the time I'd climbed the stairs, made sure Christine was in her room, and gone to my room, my leg had given out on me completely. I'm sorry to say that I was in tears the pain was so bad, so, without any forethought, I took another dose of morphine, but only enough to curb the pain. Too much would put me to sleep, and I wanted to stay awake and listen for Christine if she left her room again.

I lay across the bed and tried to figure out how I was going to get on top of the church roof, but, with the sun setting, my eyelids became heavy and started to close. I was just drifting off when I heard Christine's door open and close, so I was on my feet within a moment. I listened to her light steps and the sound of her skirt rustling as she passed my door, and then I cracked my door open and watched her start down the stairs.

Grabbing my cloak, I followed her once more to the restaurant where she was seated in much the same location as before. I was getting hungry, so when she ordered, so did I. I once again sat so I could observe her over my shoulder and spoke to myself about my need to hurry up the process of letting her know who I really was. I wanted so badly to be sitting there across the table from her and talking with her the way we had through the mirror. I wanted that so badly.

I was in deep thought about the day when that would happen when I heard her exclaim, "Raoul!"

Twelve

I jolted around just in time to see Christine on her feet and heading for my fair-haired enemy. His face lit up with a large smile when he saw her. Removing his hat, he started moving through the sea of tables toward her. They embraced each other, and my teeth clamped down while I glared at them both.

His arrival completely took me by surprise. Once he hadn't appeared on the train, I figured his aristocratic pride had been too severely hurt by Christine's rejection and he wasn't going to show at all, but I was sadly wrong. I was furious with his continual meddling, and my eyes could have burnt holes in his back as they made their way to her table.

Without giving any thought to the consequences, I rose and headed straight for them. They were so engrossed in themselves that they didn't even notice me as I sat at the table right next to theirs, placing my back to them.

If I'd given any thought whatsoever to what I was doing, I never would have taken that chance, but all I could think about was hearing their conversation; I just had to. Although, later when I thought about it, I really didn't need to be so concerned about being noticed, since they would never recognize me for who I was—that is, as long as I remained silent.

By the time I cleared my mind, Raoul was explaining what had happened.

"When I got your note, I dressed immediately and left for the train, but it had already left, so I had to wait for the next one. I'm so sorry you had to travel alone. I know you hate that."

She wasn't alone, you arrogant fool; her angel was with her, I wanted to shout.

"It's all right, Raoul. It's over, and you're here with me now, and you can travel home with me. That's what counts."

He reached across the table and took her hands in his. "Your performance the night of the gala was breathtaking. I was so proud of you. But I don't understand how you could sing the way you did while crying."

I couldn't resist, and I turned enough to see her face briefly, and then I turned back. She was smiling, and her eyes were wide. I instantly recognized that expression. She was trying to find the right words to explain how she felt.

She finally replied, shyly, "Thank you, but I didn't do it on my own. It came from my new teacher."

I closed my eyes and smiled. My precious angel. Still so modest, even after her triumphant debut.

Once the niceties of their meeting were over, Raoul took a stronger hand and became demanding.

"I wanted to talk to you after your performance, and I was really hurt when you turned me away. Why did you treat me that way—as if you didn't even know me? You didn't have to laugh at me and throw me out. You could have been nicer to me after all we've meant to each other."

Almost as if she were telling a secret, she responded softly, "I'm sorry, Raoul. I really wanted to talk with you too, but my teacher had instructed me that I shouldn't."

"Why, Christine? That makes no sense whatsoever."

His tone was harsh, as if he didn't believe her, and it instantly put me on the defensive. But it had the opposite effect on Christine, and, while trying to help him understand, she began telling him what I'd hoped she wouldn't tell anyone until after I'd revealed my true identity to her.

"My father has sent me the Angel of Music, Raoul. Remember? Remember the angel that he said wouldn't visit you if you didn't take your violin lessons seriously? Well, I guess I finally must have been taking my instruction seriously enough, because the angel has visited me."

"Christine, I loved your father and all his stories, but you didn't really believe them—did you?"

"Certainly, I did, Raoul. Didn't you?"

He responded with a harsh, superior attitude, "Well, maybe when we were young, but we're no longer children, Christine. While his stories were entertaining, they were just that—stories."

"You're wrong, because he has visited me and he instructs me every day. That's how I can sing the way I do. If it weren't for him, I would still be just part of the chorus."

"Christine, you made it to the top because of your talent, not because of an imaginary angel. You don't give yourself enough credit."

"No, Raoul, you must believe me. One day I was only a chorus girl. Then I heard his voice, his angelic voice, speak my name. Then, the very next day, he had me sing in my dressing room with his voice in my ear. I sang that day with a strength I'd never known. My room was filled with our voices, and it was so beautiful that I cried and nearly fainted. It was real, Raoul.

"I was on my feet in my dressing room, not at home in my bed and asleep. It was real. And he's been there with me every day since then. That was almost two months ago. He's there with me every day and every day he instructs me, and every day my voice goes somewhere I don't even tell it to go. He tells it to go there and it does his bidding, just as if I had no control over it. It goes almost without me. His voice is so strong that it takes my voice along with his wherever he wants it to go."

"Christine, listen to yourself. You've obviously been working much too hard. It's good you're here and away from the opera house where you can rest for a while. Stay here with me for the week and rest. Then you'll feel better and realize your mind has only been playing tricks on you."

With her voice no longer a whisper, she demanded, "Raoul, no, this is real. I don't need to rest. I feel better than I have in a long time. Why don't you believe me? He instructs me and he sings with me, and he talks with me, giving me advice. And what about the flowers? He sends me flowers, and what about the jewels? The jewelry I wore the night of the gala he sent to me. You had to have seen them. They were real, so he has to be real."

"Christine, why are you making up this absurd story? I know you had a man in your dressing room the night of the gala. You don't have to make up lies. He was the reason you sent me away, so why don't you admit it? Tell me the truth. Who is he?"

"Raoul, how could you?" she responded.

She had that same hurt in her voice that I'd also caused. But considering it was Raoul who was causing her hurt, my uncontrollable temper of forty years took over, and I responded angrily without giving thought to my actions. I rose from my chair, glanced quickly at her hurt expression, and then, with clenched teeth and tight fists, I glared at him.

The voices in the restaurant became a far away subdued rumble, as I looked at the superior aristocratic expression written on Raoul's young and chiseled face. Fortunately, for the young couple, and for me, they were too absorbed in their own heated discussion to even notice my angry posture, but that didn't last for long. I caught their attention when I briskly moved past Raoul, knocking his shoulder and chair with my arm and hip so hard that it sent him and his chair to the floor. I kept going without an apology as he picked himself up and threw crude comments in my direction.

As I moved quickly to the other side of the room, I thought, he needs to be thankful that I have a higher agenda planned for the hours ahead. He needs to be thankful that was all I did to him.

I stood behind a silk screen divider while fuming at Raoul's words, which were hurting *my* sweet and innocent Christine. I was furious with him, but then I became angry with myself, because I wanted to hear their conversion and that was impossible from where I was standing.

I glanced around the screen, and, from the expression on Christine's face, it appeared they'd quickly forgotten the unrefined, cloaked man. She was obviously upset, and I just had to go back. By the time I sat down, Raoul had just apologized and was beginning to question her again. They were both emotionally involved enough not to notice that the clumsy and rude man had returned.

"He sends you things?" Raoul questioned.

"Yes, beautiful things," she responded thoughtfully.

"He sends you things just like any man would?" he repeated.

"Well, I suppose—yes."

"And it was him that I heard in your room after the gala?"

With the child's wonderment, she responded, "Yes. Although I never see him. It's only his voice that fills the room, but sometimes it's right in my ear. He's real Raoul—you must believe me. He's real. I'm not crazy, and I'm not lying to you."

Again there was silence before he responded dictatorially, "I believe you, Christine, but I don't believe he's an angel. I believe he's a man that's playing a trick on you."

"Raoul, why would you want to spoil this for me?"

"I don't want to spoil anything for you, Christine, but you're being deceived by someone clever enough to trick you into believing he's an angel."

Frustrated, Christine tried again. "But why do you continue to insist on this? Why can't you simply believe that he's my Angel of Music? Mummy does, and so does Meg."

By this time, his tone was definitely demeaning. "Because these things just don't happen, Christine. I've seen many desperate men during my tours of duty, desperate men fighting for their lives, and I've seen those same men cry out for divine help, and not once have I seen any of them rescued by an angel. Don't you think someone's life is more important than someone's voice? Why would an angel care more for your voice than someone's life, Christine? Try to think logically about this. The voice you hear and the voice I heard that night was the voice of a man. Maybe a very talented and clever man, but a man just the same and nothing more than that."

"No, Raoul! It's an angel's voice. I've never heard a man's voice like his. It's so gentle and beautiful, and yet, one time, he spoke with such power that it made the large and heavy mirror in my room shake. No man's voice could do that, Raoul—no man's. You heard it yourself. Did it sound like a man's voice to you?"

I visualized Raoul holding her hands as he answered compassionately, "Christine, please listen to me. It was a man's voice I heard, not an angel's. I fear for you. You're so young and naive. For some reason, someone is trying to trick you, and, since it's a man, I suspect he only has his selfish desires in mind. You must stop this instruction now before you get hurt. He only wants one thing from you, and he's using this deceit and your innocence to get it from you."

"Raoul!" she nearly shouted.

Oh, no, I thought. I recognized that tone in her voice. He'd just crossed over the same line that I had. His accusations had just brought out the full force of the protective woman in her.

She sprang from the chair so quickly that she bumped into the back of mine, and then she read him the riot act, much the same as she'd done to me when I'd attacked him. Her skirt was actually against my shoulder and arm as she blasted him, and I nearly lost my composure with her so near to me.

"Raoul, why are you trying to spoil this for me? He's not like that. He's kind and he's helped me gain strength that I never knew I could have. He's strong and yet so gentle, and he would never do anything that would put me in danger or anything such as what you're suggesting.

"In fact, he's done everything to protect me. Even when I'm wandering around the opera house, he watches over me and tells me to have courage and not to be frightened. He's been there for me when no one else could help me. I'm much stronger now, thanks to his help, and now you try to tear him down and take him away from me. No, Raoul, I won't let you do this to me."

She stormed away through the labyrinth of chairs and blue cloth-covered tables. I could have warned him that it was a bad mistake to tear down someone she had faith in, regardless of who it was. I'd learned that the hard way just days earlier. But then, she had faith in everyone, and, as I would one day learn, no one would be allowed to speak badly about anyone around her.

Raoul caught up with her just before she started up the stairs and grabbed her arm. She turned on him, and with a voice that I could hear clear across the room, she rebuked him strongly.

"Leave me alone, Raoul!"

I sat there a moment in surprise over her outward strength and her words of defense for me, and I smiled, knowing he'd just made a huge mistake. Raoul watched her as she climbed the stairs, and then he went to the desk clerk where he stayed for some time. It was obvious to me by their gestures and glances up the stairs what he was doing; he wasn't merely checking in, he was checking on Christine and anyone else who might be with her.

He finally left the clerk and went upstairs, while I set my glass of wine down and followed him. Once I reached the corner to the hallway that went past our rooms, I stopped and carefully looked around the corner. Not to my surprise, I saw Raoul standing right in front of my door. He knocked once and then twice. When there was no answer, he tried to open the door.

He looked down at the knob for a moment and then went to Christine's door where he paused, looked at it, and then went to the next door. He used a key on that door and went in. I groaned, knowing he'd be watching Christine carefully from then on, making it necessary for me to be extra careful.

I went back downstairs and headed for a florist I'd seen earlier. Once there, I purchased two red roses and some gold ribbon. Back in my room, I tied them together and placed them in a glass of water, where they'd wait for their part in my night's performance.

The rest of the evening I stayed lying down across my bed, trying to rest my leg. I even closed my eyes from time to time, but my ears were on high alert, listening for Christine's door or Raoul's voice in her room. I never did hear her door or any voices, but I did hear the heavy footfalls of a man, I'm sure Raoul, in the hall outside my door.

Several times he came to my door and knocked, and each time he tried the knob. Each time that he attempted to meet his unknown opponent, my heart quickened and my jaws tightened. What did he expect to accomplish by sneaking into my room? Other than me, what did he want to find?

I lay there with my fingers clasped behind my head, fighting the urge to let him in and let the games begin, but I didn't, for only one reason; Christine. I wanted nothing whatsoever to mar the solemn occasion of her father's anniversary, so my fingers stayed behind my head and not around his insolent throat.

As far as I was concerned, Raoul had so many strikes against him that he'd never be redeemed in my eyes. He was good looking, young, rich, from a reputable family, he had a sterling reputation, the arrogant attitude of superiority, and, most of all, he had a long established friendship with my Christine. I couldn't have hated anyone more than him. His persistent annoyance for that few hours did serve a good purpose though; it kept me from giving into the morphine and falling asleep.

At eleven o'clock, I put on my hat and cloak and left for the stable with my violin and roses in hand. I hated to leave Christine alone there with Raoul, but if I was going to pull off my performance perfectly, I had to get there well before she arrived.

Once I got to the livery, I called out until the sleepy man I'd met earlier appeared.

"I need a different horse this time," I began.

"Well, I have many. Which one do you want?" he replied with a yawn and a stretch.

"I need an old, dapple-gray gelding, if you have one."

He scratched the top of his bald head and pointed to a stall at the front of the stable. "I have a dapple-gray gelding named Jasper, but he's not that old. He's only five. Will he do?"

While walking toward the horse in question, I asked, "What kind of disposition does he have? Is he gentle? Does he spook easily? Does he talk much?"

The old man looked at me and squinted. "I haven't had any complaints about him, but then I haven't had anyone ask for a horse with those qualities before either. What is it you need him for?"

By then I had the gelding's head against my chest and was rubbing his jaw. I looked at the man and wondered if I should tell him the truth. Since my plan had no room for error, I decided to tell him discreetly.

"I'm going to the cemetery, and I need a horse that will behave and not be noisy. It will be a solemn occasion, and I don't what him talking to me. I might need to stand on his back so I can reach something. Since it's dark, there will be owls that might fly around or other nocturnal creatures scurrying about. Will he stand still and quiet while all this is going on?"

He held his chin in his hand and thought. "Perhaps, but I can't guarantee it. I do have another gelding over there who fits your needs, but he's black. Will he do?"

I shook my head while thinking, no, it has to be a dapple-gray so he can blend in with the snow and shadows. I looked into Jasper's eyes, and then, abruptly, threw my arms over my head, causing my cloak to bellow out, clapped my hands, and shouted. He raised his head and took a step back but didn't say anything, even when a few other horses responded vocally. After a moment, he came back to me and shoved his nose in my chest.

I looked at the livery owner, who had a more startled reaction to my strange behavior than the horse, and said, "He'll do. I'll take Jasper."

I saddled him and left for the cemetery, where I rode him to the back of the church. There, I tied him at the far corner where the roofline was the lowest and the ground level was the highest. Then I went to Daaé's headstone and laid the two roses on top of it. I'd told Christine often that those roses represented her present and her future, and I hoped when she saw them that they would give her courage to look toward her future with confidence and not the pain of her past.

From there, I went back and mounted Jasper. I studied the roofline, calculating the distance between it and my lame limb.

"Well, this is it, Jasper," I whispered. I patted him on the neck and took a deep breath. "Please, stay calm for me."

Cautiously and awkwardly, I stood on his back, talking to him the entire time. Once my balance was solid, I shoved my violin up on the roof, and then I leapt for the roof's edge, landing with my chest on it. From there it wasn't too difficult. I swung my right leg up and then rolled over on my back.

I took a breath and looked down at my faithful mount. "Good boy, Jasper. Splendid job."

Soon, I was across the snow-covered roof and behind the large cross at the highest peak. After sitting down, I tuned my violin and softly played parts of *The Resurrection of Lazarus* in preparation. When I was satisfied with the sound, I tried to relax while I waited for Christine to appear.

The clouds of the day had passed and the moon was bright, so, with the new layer of snow, the entire area was lit almost as brightly as on an overcast day. I looked at my watch, 11:45.

"Not much longer before the curtain rises, Christine," I whispered.

And it wasn't. Within a minute, I heard a carriage approaching, and then it stopped by the front gate of the graveyard. The coachman stepped down and helped her out, and, at the sight of her, I took a deep breath. She was alone—without Raoul. She was cloaked in black, and, as she moved slowly toward her father's grave, she resembled little more than a shadow cast by a cloud.

I was transfixed by her and so thankful that I had her all to myself. A minute or so passed before I heard another coach approaching. Raoul, I first thought. But then another thought sunk into my gut. I looked at Christine and realized the dangerous position she was in, a distraught woman alone and off guard in a deserted cemetery in the middle of the night.

I laid my violin in its case, stood up, took a lasso from my cloak pocket, and prepared for what was to come. The coach stopped on the other side of the cemetery, and I squinted, trying to see through the web of barren trees. A man stepped down, and, once he turned in my direction, I could tell who it was—Raoul.

"No," I growled quietly.

My anger burned instantly. This is our time together, you fool. Go away, I secretly willed him. He started for the gate but then stopped. Instead of entering and following her any further, he went back around the side of the graveyard and began climbing the slope, much the same way I'd done earlier that day. My anger took on a new level when I realized he was spying on her during such a time as that. Just what did he expect her to do in a cemetery and in the middle of the night?

Focus, Erik, focus, I told myself. I didn't want my anger toward him to interfere with my interpretation of her father's favorite piece of music. My anger at times had a way of weaving itself in and out of the notes I played, and I just couldn't let that happen; not that night which was for Christine. I slipped my coil back in my pocket, picked up my violin, closed my eyes, and concentrated on the feel of the instrument in my hands. I took several slow deep breaths, focusing on the muscles in my shoulders and hands, not wanting to transfer their tightness to the strings.

Once I felt more relaxed, I looked for Raoul, who was trying to stay out of Christine's sight behind trees, but he was underestimating me if he thought he was out of my sight. I held my position behind the large cross, where I could see Christine on one side of it and Raoul on the other side, which left me, hopefully, to appear as only a part of the cross from their point of view.

By the time he was situated, Christine had stopped and was kneeling down before her father's grave. I could see her take the roses and hold them first to her face and then to her chest. Then she began looking around. I think I heard her say *angel*, but her whisper was too soft for me to be sure. When she stopped looking around, her head and shoulders went down, and I could tell she was crying. I could literally feel her pain in my chest as I watched her there all alone, once more resembling a lost child.

My heart went out to her, and even though it wasn't in the script, my lips parted. "Don't cry my angel—I'm here with you—You're not alone."

Her head came up, but I couldn't see her face until she removed her hood and looked around again. No work of art had ever been painted that captured the painful beauty of her there, all alone, beside rows of cold and lifeless granite. Her hair took on the appearance of rich liquid gold flowing from a refiner's cup, as it waved softly over her shoulders and down her black cloak. At one point, I held my breath as her gaze passed right over me. Then she lifted her hood back over her head, and her face was once again hidden from me.

I looked at Raoul, hoping he was holding his supposedly secret position, and he was. I wanted to cry out to him and tell him to watch closely the extraordinary connection we had. I wanted him to know the important part I played in her life. But that evening wasn't about me and my competition with Raoul; it was about Christine and her father, so I respectfully held my tongue.

The tranquil and silent moonlit scene awakened with the first stroke of the clock's chime, announcing the end of one day, the beginning of another, and my promise to Christine to commence. The violin was poised under my chin, and I raised the bow and laid it gently across the strings and waited, counting each stroke. 10—11—12. Then, with a deep breath, I closed my eyes and let the first sweet notes of her father's music escape from my Stradivarius, bringing life to the cold air surrounding the lifeless tombstones.

The notes were so breathtaking in the still of the night that I almost forgot where I was and why I was there. After the last note softened and disappeared from that moving, midnight scene, I had to close my eyes tightly to remove the tears before I could focus on Christine. She slowly raised her face and arms to the sky and truly looked like an angel praying. Perhaps she was praying, since her lips were moving, silently.

I was mesmerized by the sight of her until I remembered Raoul on the slope. With a quick glance in his direction, I could see he was still hiding, so my attention returned to Christine. I remained motionless and watched her there for some time before she got up and walked slowly back to her waiting coach.

As I watched it get smaller in the distance, I made the final decision; I couldn't wait any longer to speak with her face to face, person to person, and not angel to angel. I wanted so desperately to touch her hand or her cheek and to smell the fragrance on her and not just on her handkerchief. We would be back in Paris in two days, so that would be the day—the day when my life could start, or, if she rejected me completely, the day my life would end.

Thirteen

When I looked back toward Raoul, he was making his way down the slope toward the side fence. I knelt down and watched him closely while I replaced my violin in its case and my gloves on my nearly frozen fingers. He walked through the cemetery slowly, as if he was looking for someone. He stopped now and then, and he appeared to be listening for something. I believe that something was the one responsible for the angelic music he'd just heard.

I carefully made my way down the back side of the church, but I didn't head for Jasper who was supposed to help me down. I felt he wouldn't let me drop down on top of him without some sort of sound, even if it was only a groan, no matter how gentle he was. So, instead, I lay on the edge of the roof, lowered myself with my arms as far as I could, and then, after holding my breath in preparation for the pain, I let go and landed in the soft snow.

The pain was excruciating, and my legs collapsed under me, but I managed not to cry out. I lay there only long enough for the pain to lessen before I got to my feet, knowing my rival was just on the other side of the church and probably looking for me.

That was one time when my black clothing was not going to help me hide, considering I was surrounded by the bright moonlight reflecting off the white snow. I peeked around the back corner and saw Raoul not far from me, perhaps only twenty meters from the side door of the church. He continued to take a few steps and then stopped and listened.

He even looked closely at the footprints in the snow, my footprints that would lead him toward the back of the church and me. When he started in my direction again, I had to think quickly. Then, after giving a quick apology to the skull lying at my feet, I did the only thing any playful poltergeist would do under the circumstances. I picked it up and rolled it quickly toward him.

That stopped him short, and I could hear him take a quick breath. It had also frightened him, and I smiled. Once he caught himself, he looked in my direction again, and again I rolled another head. That one also caught him by surprise, but I don't believe it frightened him. Therefore, I rolled a few more in rapid succession, which took his sight away from my direction long enough for me to slip in through the side door of the church. Once inside, I waited behind a pillar to see if he was brave enough to follow the skull-rolling shadow inside. Then, lo and behold, I discovered he was.

At that point, I wasn't merely irritated with him; I was also having fun playing with him. Therefore, I continued my little game of ghostly intrigue. When he came in the door and it closed, some of our light was diminished and automatically gave me the advantage. He stood motionless, probably waiting for his eyes to adjust to the darkness, since our only light came in through the stained glass window.

During that time, I slipped past him close enough for him to feel the breeze I created by my movement. He gasped and swung around, looking in all directions, but by then I was behind another pillar. I again waited to see just how brave he was, and he then started to gain a bit of my respect. He had ventured into my domain, the darkness, to seek out who it was that was playing a violin, which meant he wasn't as superstitious as the rest of the ones I'd been around recently.

They all believed me to be some sort of a ghost, or, in Christine's case, an angel. But this young fellow I believe knew or at least suspected that I had a human nature, although I have to admit a strange human nature. I didn't give him too much time to collect his senses before I moved again and then again, from behind one pillar to another.

When I felt he was sufficiently spooked, I moved close to him, close enough to allow my cloak to brush against him. Once more he turned and reached out in all directions, but he didn't gasp. He knew exactly what he was doing, but he still had no idea exactly what he was up against.

I narrowed my eyes and thought; all right, my brave little pursuer, let's see just how brave you really are. I waited until his back was to me and then I quietly moved right up behind him. Then, towering a good head over him, I breathed on the back of his neck. That time, he did gasp and turned quickly to see my black masked face only centimeters away from his. His eyes, at first, widened and his mouth dropped open, but then his eyes rolled back, and he went down.

I couldn't believe what I'd just witnessed. I'd watched many different reactions to my masked face in my long career of frightening people, but never had I had such a response, not even from a woman. He'd fainted at my feet, and, as I looked down at him, I had to laugh aloud while thinking, there lies a mighty naval officer. If he was any representation of France's officers, no wonder she lost the war with Prussia.

Once my amusement was over, I walked to a pillar and waited for him to come around. But when he didn't, I had to think seriously about what was to become of Christine's young de Chagny. Without the protective cloud cover, the night was well below freezing and it could kill.

He might have fainted away before me; however, he looked physically strong enough to withstand the cold until he woke. But if he didn't wake shortly, he could be in serious trouble, so I looked around for a place to put him where he'd be found by the first person coming in. The obvious choice was the altar, so, with his heels in my hands, I dragged him through the pews and laid him on the first step in front of the altar.

I turned and started to leave but then looked back at his vulnerability. I moved back and stood over him, looking down at his fair and handsome face. No wonder Christine was taken with him. He had everything, youth, wealth, respectability, and a good-looking face—complete with a nose. My time of amusement was over, and I was left with the reality that he was a blockade in my quest to capture Christine's heart.

I could end the competition right then with just the right pressure under his handsome jaw. I knelt down and slowly moved my gloved hand to his throat, wrapping my fingers around it and applying pressure. He was even more vulnerable right then than when he was in Christine's dressing room. It would be so easy—so very easy.

No one was around and he was in no position to struggle. I could take my time and do the job so well that no one would ever know it was a murder and not an accidental death due to the elements. It would be so easy. There would be no more interference from him, no more trying to keep them apart, no more fear that he was going to whisk her away before I had a chance to capture her heart completely.

But that freedom would come at a great price. It had been a long time since I'd deliberately caused someone's death. While I was still plagued with guilt over my past actions, they were at least far enough in the past that I could have a measure of peace from them.

I moved my hand from his throat and let it remain on his chest, while picturing Christine's excited glee that evening when she entered her room with news about her friend. It was that happy expression on her face, along with knowing that he was going to spoil everything, that twisted my mind into knots. Ultimately, just as I'd contemplated his fate in Christine's dressing room, it was that look in her eyes that gave me the strength to remove my hand completely from him.

I couldn't do that to Christine. If she was that happy to see him sitting in the audience, then I knew how much pain she'd have at his death, especially, if he died in the very cemetery where her father was laid to rest and on the anniversary of his death, no less. I couldn't do that to my angel. So, once again, it was Christine who saved that *heroic* naval officer's life.

I would fight for the right to have her love me and win her heart, but I couldn't steal it if it didn't belong to me. Therefore, I made only one last statement by folding his arms over his chest, and then I got up and went to the door. Before I closed it, I looked one last time at the young aristocrat lying on the steps to the altar, just like a sacrificial lamb before a pagan god.

By the time I returned Jasper and reached my room at the inn, I was spent, emotionally as well as physically. My leap from the roof of the church hadn't done my leg any good, and once I removed the bandages, I found the stitches had broken loose, leaving the wound open and again bleeding. I redressed it, gave myself another dose of morphine, and lay down. My thoughts turned to Christine, as I listened to a branch scraping against my window. Then, through the movement of the tree, I could hear her soft sobs, and I began to ache all over.

"Christine," I whispered, "don't cry."

Again I wanted to go to her and comfort her. I turned my head and stared at the wall separating us, and then, without thinking about my superb plans for whisking her away on my white stallion, I was on my feet and heading for her door. I gave no thought to anything I was going to say to her. I only knew I couldn't bear being separated from her any longer and the entire act was going to end right then.

My knuckles landed on her door, and, in the semi-darkness, I listened to her steps approaching.

Then, out of nowhere, the little old innkeeper, Madame Mifroid, appeared around the corner, balancing a tray of steaming milk. My instant and automatic reaction was to hide around the corner before she saw me.

The door opened just as the woman stepped in front of it, and Christine, with a white handkerchief in hand, exclaimed, "Why, Madame Mifroid!"

The lady was obviously shocked to have the door open so abruptly, and I heard it in her voice. "Oh, my dear, you're still up. I thought you might like some warm milk to help you sleep."

"Thank you. That does sound good."

"Would you like some company, my dear?"

Christine nodded. "Thank you. I really don't want to be alone right now."

They went inside and the door closed, leaving me alone when I should have been in that room with her to comfort her. Her angel, who knew what she was feeling and what she needed, is who could comfort her, not a strange old woman.

I stood there a moment, looking at her door and feeling so alone. One more time in my life I was left alone with a burst bubble, the bubble that held my position in Christine's life. I went back to my room, lay down, and, while listening to the faint voices from the next room, gave into the euphoric comfort of the morphine and slipped into sleep.

The sun was just rising on The Rising Sun Inn when I got up. After the emotionally draining prior night, I'd decided to rent Jasper again and visit the ocean before Christine woke up. Considering her harrowing day and late night, I figured she would be asleep for some time. So, with my hat and cloak on, I started toward the stairs but stopped when I heard Madame Mifroid give stern orders.

"Get him some blankets! I'll get some hot tea!"

A young man stormed up the stairs and around the corner, heading straight for me. I lowered my head, and he flew past me with hardly any notice. I crept down the stairs until I saw a man help Raoul into a chair in the corner. The young man came running from behind me and then past me with an armload of blankets. I was still trying to catch up when Madame Mifroid set a pot of tea and a teacup in front of Raoul, and the young man wrapped several blankets around my rival's shoulders.

"You'd better go wake Mademoiselle Daaé," Madame Mifroid ordered.

The young man was rushing past me again when I realized Christine would be the next one to pass me, so I moved quickly back into my room. My door was just closing when Christine came out of her room, still wrapping her robe around herself. Down the stairs they went, with Christine asking questions. I moved back down the stairs until I could hear what was being said.

"Oh, Raoul!" Christine exclaimed. "What's happened to you? Oh, my dear God in heaven, your hands are like ice and so are your cheeks. Raoul, what happened?"

Through chattering teeth, he responded, "Your angel is what happened, Christine. I met him and this is the results of his *angelic* nature."

"What! What do you mean?" she asked in confusion.

"You'd better drink that tea while it's hot, young man," Madame Mifroid again ordered.

"Raoul, explain to me what you're talking about."

"I saw him, Christine, and he's no angel. He's just what I thought he was, only worse. He's a man, a monstrous man, and he tried to kill me last night. He's a mad man."

"What?" Christine blurted out.

What! I shouted in my head. The fool! If I'd really tried to kill him, I would have succeeded.

"I was there last night, Christine, at the cemetery."

With Christine's voice moving from surprise to irritation, she threw repeated questions at the shivering young de Chagny.

"You were where? You followed me there? You were spying on me? You don't trust me, is that it? While I was in agony over my father, you were suspecting me of wrongdoing and spying on me?"

"No, Christine, it wasn't that at all. I trust you. I just think you're being taken advantage of, that's all. I wanted to protect you from this diabolical creature that's out to get you for his own pleasure."

"Raoul, not again, please. I don't want to go over this again. I'm not stupid and I'm not crazy. And, furthermore, you don't have to continue your efforts to make me feel worthless."

For the first time I heard true humility in his voice. "Oh, Christine, no. I now understand how you could feel the way you do, believe me. I was also taken captive in that cemetery. For a while, I also believed that your angel was truly an angel. I heard him, Christine, in the cemetery. I heard his music, and you're right, it is angelic. You know how much I respected and appreciated your father's playing, but his pales into nothingness in comparison to what I heard last night. When it first started, I tried to locate its source, but you were so right, it was everywhere and unearthly. It filled the very air I was breathing. I couldn't believe my ears. It was out of this world."

Christine's voice calmed, and became a sweet sound. "Didn't I tell you? And his voice is just the same. It's also unearthly. It's angelic. He has to be an angel."

After a sip of his hot tea, Raoul continued, but his voice had lost its humility, "I thought so also, Christine, and I was planning to go back to the inn and tell you so. But I wanted to visit your father's grave before I did. Then as I was walking through the graveyard, I thought I saw something black, like a shadow, but it didn't have a form like an animal or a human. It was like the shadow cast by a cloud in the moonlight, only much faster. It had moved around the corner behind the church. Then I noticed a man's footprints in the snow leading in that same direction. So I stopped and waited, trying to see in the darkness. Then a human skull rolled toward my feet."

"What?" Christine nearly shouted. "Are you sure?"

"Yes, quite sure, and they kept coming. I could see stacks of them against the wall of the church. At first I thought perhaps a nocturnal animal had started the first one rolling, but then when they kept coming, and all of them were headed straight for me, I began to suspect that it was a reasoning animal that was the culprit."

"What are you saying, Raoul?"

"Christine, there was someone there; some human that was trying to frighten me, and I knew it. While I was dodging the skulls, I saw the shape again as it moved quickly in through the side door of the church, so I followed it. Once inside, I stood still and listened, trying to hear where the shape went, but all was quiet.

"Then without any sound, I saw the shadow again move between two pillars. The shadow kept moving from pillar to pillar for several minutes, and some of the times when it moved, I could feel the air around me also move. Then it moved so close to me that I reached out and touched it. I felt its cloak. Christine, it wasn't a heavenly feeling, it was an earthly one; it was wool, just like my own coat."

"Raoul, it was probably only a vagrant. You know one of their favorite places to sleep at night is in a church."

"No, Christine, it was no vagrant. I'm now convinced it was your so-called angel."

"Raoul, why are you doing this? Why are you using this strange occurrence to work against my beliefs?"

"Oh, Christine, please listen to me. I was ready to accept your beliefs just moments before that all happened, so what I'm telling you has nothing to do with any personal feelings, except for my fear for you. This person is not only clever, but maybe even inhuman in some respects, because I've never seen anything move so fast and silently. In fact, by the time I felt his cloak, he was gone again. He moved so quickly and soundlessly that it was unreal—like he was floating."

Searching wildly for a logical explanation that would protect her angel, Christine rationalized. "Then maybe it was a large animal of some sort, perhaps a bear."

Raoul almost laughed. "A bear? Wearing a wool cloak? I don't think so, Christine, especially after what happened next. I saw him move between pillars one more time and then there was nothing but darkness and silence. Then I felt a warm breath on the back of my neck, and, when I turned quickly out of fright, I saw him clearly for the first time.

"His face was only this far from mine, if you want to call it a face. Under the brim of his hat, where you'd normally expect to see a face, I saw only two golden eyes shining in the darkness—just like a wolf's in the night."

Christine, still not willing to believe her Angel of Music could be the cause of her friend's condition, tried again. "Well, see, that proves it. It was a bear on his hind legs looking at you."

Frustration along with true concern for her showed in Raoul's next words. "Oh, my innocent Christine, no. A bear wearing a cloak and hat?

No, Christine. It wasn't an animal, at least not a four-footed one. I wasn't going to tell you the rest of the story because I'm quite embarrassed to do so, but I can see you need more proof."

"What, Raoul? What's your proof?"

"I was so frightened, Christine. I don't think I've been that frightened in my entire life; no, I know I haven't. As I looked into his eyes looming over me, I could hear my own heart beating in my ears. I really thought I was going to die, Christine. Then . . . then . . . I think I passed out. I don't remember anything else until the priest woke me up. I was . . ."

"That's it, Raoul," Christine interrupted. "It was the priest who frightened you. They wear long robes."

"No, no, no, my sweet Christine. It couldn't have been the priest. A priest can't afford to wear the quality of wool that I felt. Besides, the priest wasn't that tall. This man, who nearly frightened me to death, was a good head taller than me. No, Christine, it wasn't the priest; he was the one who saved me.

"Now, as I was saying, I was lying on the first step to the altar, and I was freezing cold. The priest was asking me all sorts of questions, but I couldn't even remember how I'd gotten there. See, Christine, if it was an animal of some kind, how would it have placed me on the steps to the altar? And why were my hands folded across my chest as if I was holding a lily? You know, the way they put people in their coffins, with their hands over their chests. Whoever it was was trying to tell me something, Christine. He was trying to tell me he wanted me dead."

Clever boy. He'd figured it out. Yes, I wanted him dead, and it was only my love for Christine that saved him, but then it was my love for Christine that put him in harm's way to begin with.

There was silence at the bottom of the stairs until I heard Christine sigh slowly. "I find this all very hard to believe, and I certainly don't believe it has anything to do with my angel. He would have no reason to spend his time trying to frighten you, Raoul, much less want you dead. I'm sure he's much too busy to spend his nights in such folly."

"Oh, my dear Christine. You're so innocent and sweet. You really don't get it, do you?"

"I don't want to talk about this any longer, Raoul. It upsets me, and I don't want to be upset anymore. Please, can we talk about something else?"

There was a silence and then all decided that Raoul needed a hot bath to warm him up. I went back to my room, and, while sitting on the edge of my bed with my face in my hands, I tried to understand what had happened. The night before, I'd been the conqueror. I'd performed something special for Christine. I was there for her, and I felt a closer connection to her than ever. But, right then, it was Raoul who was preparing to spend a day with her. It was his hands she was holding and his cheek she was touching, and where was I? Alone with only my thoughts for company, so what good were any of my efforts of late? No good whatsoever.

The day moved on and they went down to breakfast, and I watched. They spoke softly over a nice meal, and I moaned into my coffee. They made plans for the day and I felt so alone. They wrapped in warm clothes for a romantic walk in the park, and I was already in my same old cloak, hat and gloves, preparing to be tormented more when I followed them.

They walked arm in arm, and I walked alone and watched. They sat on a park bench and looked into each other's eyes, and I sat on a park bench and watched them over the top of my paper. They were together with hearts that were laughing, and I was alone with a heart that was crying. I was miserable, but not nearly as miserable as I was about to be.

Christine looked so beautiful in the bright sunlight, and she looked so happy, so different than what she'd been like in the cemetery. He was good for her, and I could see that in the light of day. He was making her happy, and it hurt my heart. I was losing her, not that I'd ever had her to begin with, but I was losing her, and it hurt deeply. I'd just decided to put myself out of my misery and put myself on the back of a horse and ride away, when Raoul made a serious tactical error.

Fourteen

"He's no angel, Christine. He's the farthest thing from an angel. This is all a trick of a very talented but devious man. He has the skills to teach you, to play beautiful music, and, from what you say, sing just the same. But that doesn't make him an angel. It makes him an extremely dangerous man."

"Raoul, please don't start this again. Don't spoil this day by tearing down my angel."

Raoul lowered his head and looked down at her hand in his. "I never want any of your days to be spoiled, and that's why you need to realize that this entire escapade is a sham—it's not real."

Pulling her hand away from his, she huffed. "Raoul, I don't understand you. Why would you say that? Why do you want to take this away from me?"

Turning on the bench and looking right at her he insisted, "Because someone is tricking you for his own pleasure, and I don't want to see you hurt by him. You're a beautiful woman, Christine. The most beautiful woman I've ever seen, and I know what this man is thinking."

Shaking her head, she frowned at him. "You're so wrong. You don't understand our relationship, and you don't understand him. He would never hurt me. He's kind and gentle when he speaks to me. He only wants to help me, just as my father said he would."

"Oh, Christine, listen to me. Angels don't speak to humans and carry on meaningless conversations."

Angered she rebuked him, "Our conversations aren't meaningless, and angels do speak to humans. They spoke to Abraham and Sarah, and Joseph and Mary, and Jacob, and Elizab . . ."

She was about to list everyone in the Bible when Raoul stopped her. "Christine, stop! We know that, but that was in Bible times. It doesn't happen now—today."

She was on her feet by then and staring down at him. "How do you know that, Raoul? A lot of people say they've spoken to angels, so why shouldn't I? Am I not good enough in your eyes to have that blessing?"

He reached for her hand but she backed away, so he tried softening his words. "Certainly you are, Christine. But it just isn't logical. I tell you, this is a clever trick by a man who wants to have his way with you."

"No!" she protested. "I won't believe you, Raoul. He's not a human man with those types of feelings. He's my perfect angel, and he helps me. You even said so yourself, remember?"

Raoul rose to his feet slowly and again reached for her, but again she pulled away. "Yes, I remember, but that was before I understood the secret nature of his lessons. I tell you, Christine, this is a ruse."

She turned her back on him. "Why do you persist in trying to take this away from me, Raoul? Why don't you want me to be happy?"

He reached out and successfully took her hand. "I do want you to be happy, and that's why I'm warning you to stop this charade before you get hurt."

Pulling her hand out of his, she verbally attacked him. "Oh, you make me so angry. Leave me alone. Go away from here. I don't want to hear any more of what you think. My angel is real, and he's made me happier than I've been since my father's death. Right now that's all I care about. Go back to Paris, Raoul! Go away from here. I wish you'd never come here to spoil this for me. Go away!"

"Christine, listen to me. I can't leave you here alone with this man."

"No! Go away, Raoul! I'm safer here with him than I am with you. At least he makes me happy with his encouraging words and his music. All you've done is spoil everything. You've made this trip a nightmare. Go away!—now!"

He acquiesced and turned, heading back toward the inn. She was so angry with him that she stormed away with her arms folded across her chest. She was coming straight for me on the bench, so I automatically lowered my head and raised the paper higher in front of me. She came so close to me that I could have reached out and touched her, but I didn't. She kept going, heading for a small pond to my right. I looked over the top of my paper and watched her pacing at the water's edge, occasionally pulling at her gloved fingers the way she always did when she was anxious.

My thoughts were twisting in all directions, and I tried to slow them and separate them into some type of order so I could think clearly. Raoul was so right, and I had to have a measure of respect for his intelligence in seeing through my guise. I was just what he thought I was, a man who wanted Christine all to himself. But when I listened to him say the words, they sounded so dark and sinister, and that wasn't how I felt about her. I didn't just want her to lie beside me. I wanted her to walk beside me forever, and therein lay the difference in my truth and his interpretation.

But it wasn't what Raoul thought about me that was important; it was what Christine believed.

As I watched her, I wondered what her reaction was going to be when I revealed the truth to her. I'd just seen what she did to Raoul when he tried to take her angel from her and make him human. What was she going to do to me when I became not only the one to strip her angel from her but also the person who'd been deceiving her all this time? The prior day, I'd wanted to hurry up the process of revealing myself to her, but then, as I watched her, I wasn't sure I was ready for her reaction.

I realized then that I really hadn't thought through my entire ploy when I first started it. I feared it was going to take something more powerful than my angelic voice, quick wit, and genius mind to escape her wrath unscathed once she knew the truth. That was one of the times in my life when I believed what everyone thought about me was true. I was insane for pursuing her. But then, perhaps most men could be considered insane, to one degree or another, once their heart had been taken over by that one special angel in their lives. At that time, I could even recognize that same insanity in my opponent.

Eventually, Christine calmed, and her pacing became a slow stride. I think the ducks she'd been talking to might have helped. She apologized for not having something to feed them and other such comments. But then she started a serious conversation with them, and I listened closer.

"Do you have parents? Are they here with you now? Is that one over there your mother? Is that one your father? Are they still alive or are they now dead? Or do you even know or care? I wish I were a duck like you. Life would be so much simpler. No harsh words. No tears. No losses. Only days spent in peace—floating on the pond, picking at bugs, flying in the clouds, sleeping in the sun. I wish I were one of you."

Then she knelt down and picked up a bright blue duck feather at her feet. Her head went down, and then I heard her sob. No, I thought, don't cry. I couldn't bear it when she cried. I glanced around in all directions, and once I saw we were completely alone, I took a big risk and spoke to her.

After locating a small tree not too far from either of us where I could place my voice, I said softly, "Don't cry, Christine. I'm here."

She jolted to her feet, took a quick breath, and looked at the tree. "Angel?"

"Yes, my dear, it's your angel, and I'm here for you. Don't cry."

Taking a step toward the tree, she said, "I'm so glad you're here. I'm so angry and frightened."

Trying to be her controlled instructor, I spoke. "I know, Christine, but don't listen to the idle talk of unbelievers. They'll only sidetrack you from your goals. Listen to my voice, and I'll continue to instruct you, and you'll continue to capture the world."

Her voice was so beguiling when she defended me. "But did you hear what he said about you? Are you not angered also at his ignorance?"

"I'm always angered by ignorance," I responded, trying not to show the true amount of anger I felt for him. "But I've heard much worse from those with little faith. All they have are words, Christine, that's all, only words. Don't let him or anyone else take from you what I've given you—what you've earned."

"You're right," she said with determination. "I won't talk to him anymore. Even when he says he loves me, I won't listen to him."

I closed my eyes and took a breath, not knowing where to go next after hearing her say those words. But then, somewhere deep inside me, the words of the man I was came forth without any forethought.

"He's not the only one who loves you. I love you very much, my beautiful, Christine. I love everything about you—your angelic voice, your brave spirit, your perfect grace, and your loving heart."

By the time I'd said those non-scripted words, I was no longer hiding behind the paper and it lay on my lap. I looked at her longingly. The morning sun was shining through the barren trees on her golden hair that lay softly over her forest green cloak. Without being told, my heart began to lead me down a dangerous path, and I got to my feet and took a few steps toward her.

I was trying desperately to keep my voice in the tree, which was difficult, considering it wasn't coming from my mind but my heart. "You're a beautiful person, Christine, inside and out. You have no need to cling to the words of love spoken by someone who doesn't understand you or your worth. I love you, Christine, in a way that your young man will never comprehend and you know that, don't you? You can feel it in my voice, can't you? I love you in a heavenly way because you're my beautiful angel—with the angel's voice—the angel's face—the angel's hair—and . . ."

My entire being was aching to hold her close to me, and I fear the tone in my voice was relaying my desires to her. Her shoulders tightened, and she took quick breaths as she stepped back away from the tree. I stopped speaking and also took steps back to the bench and sat down. Raising the paper again, I tried to find a way out of the situation my heart had gotten me into. Therefore, I continued with my words of hidden, earthly love.

". . . and I never want you to forget your worth as a special person, never, Christine. Now relax, and release his hurtful words so you can enjoy the rest of your day here in Perros. Remember the waves at your feet, carrying your cares out to the sea."

I could see her shoulders ease, and she glanced out over the pond. "As always, My Angel, I'll do as you ask, because I know you want me to be happy, and today I want to be happy. Thank you for being here for me. Thank you for your encouraging words. Your being here is such a wonderful surprise and just what I needed. Thank you."

"You're welcome, my dear. Now, when you get back to Paris, I'll have a special surprise waiting for you, a surprise that will open up an entirely new and exciting world for you."

She smiled, scrunched her shoulders, and almost giggled. "I love surprises."

We stayed at the pond for a while longer, talking. We were both relaxed, and I even laid the paper in my lap as I talked to her. But, when she shivered, I suggested she go back to the inn and get warm. She agreed and started back. In so doing, she glanced in my direction and then stopped abruptly, taking a few quick breaths, while her hand went to her chest. I didn't raise the paper or turn my eyes away from her as I should have. Therefore, our eyes met for the first time. I held my breath, waiting for her response, because I hadn't a clue what to do next.

She took a deep breath, nodded, and smiled. I also nodded and smiled, and then she continued on her way. As I watched her walking away from me, I recognized the look on her face; at first it could have been because of my mask, but I think, more than that, she was embarrassed thinking I'd overheard her conversation with a tree. I smiled again and naturally followed her at a safe distance back to the inn. I'd just laid my cloak and hat on my bed when I heard a knock on Christine's door. I cracked mine open just enough to see Raoul on bent knee in front of her door.

I closed my eyes and sighed as she opened the door and he pleaded, "Please, forgive me, Christine. I meant you no harm. I just love you so much, and I fear for you. Please forgive me."

"Oh, Raoul, get up, you silly fool," she said, still with a hint of irritation in her voice.

Without moving from his position, he again pleaded, "Then you forgive me?"

"I forgive you, Raoul, but I'm still mad at you."

He got up and stood in the doorway. Then he continued with his plea, "Please, don't be mad at me. Treat me as a man in love, not as an enemy."

"Oh, Raoul," she said as her voice turned to that of a sweetheart.

I groaned inside with envy and anger for him and for her. I might have considered Raoul intelligent enough to see through my ploys, but when it came to knowing when he was ahead with Christine, and when to keep his mouth shut, he was a brainless idiot. Therefore, when he started talking again, he made another blunder.

"If you want to believe in this angel, then go ahead. I won't try to prevent you ever again."

She quickly flared. "What do you mean, *if* I want to believe in this angel? You still don't understand, do you? It's not as if I want to believe in anything. He's real and he talks with me all the time. He's real. It's not a belief. He knows everything about me, Raoul. He knows about the beach in Perros and my father and his music. He even knows my thoughts and talks to me about things that I haven't mentioned to anyone—not even Meg—not even you. He knows how I feel inside, and no human can do that—no one.

"He cares enough about me to always know where I am and what I'm doing. It doesn't matter where I am, he talks to me. Whether I'm in one of the cellars at the opera house, or in my dressing room, or at the cemetery, or even in that park we were just at. He knew I was there and he talked to me there and gave me comfort that I really needed right then. He's everywhere with me, Raoul, so he has to be real—he is real."

Her voice was raised and she was becoming quite agitated, and Raoul knew he was losing his footing, so he tried to calm her.

"Calm down, Christine. I understand what you're saying, so just calm down. I'm not accusing you of having a weak mind. I believe you. And don't forget, I love you. Oh, Christine," he said softly as he tried another avenue to reach her. "You look so tired. Let me take you away from all of the business at the opera house. You don't have to do this to yourself. I can take care of you. Let me take you on a cruise around the world. Or we can go to any place in the world that you'd like to visit. I'll take you anywhere, just say the word."

"Raoul, you know I can't do that, and I don't want to go away. I do love you, but I also love my music and especially now that I can finally feel it inside. It's wonderful when I sing and I feel my own strength around me, and I feel him all around me. It's such a marvelous feeling when I feel him right here inside my heart."

"Oh, Christine," he said with his voice rising. "Must every conversation always come back to *him*, your so-called angel? Do you love him and your music more than me?"

She didn't fall for that old line and put the blame right back on him. "I thought you said you would do anything to make me happy? Do you call this making me happy? You're downplaying my music, Raoul, and making me sound foolish for the way I feel about it. You don't understand me, but he docs. And he not only understands me but he also supports me in ways that I don't think you'll ever be able to comprehend. And if that makes you angry, then you should just leave."

I saw him appear back out in the hallway with Christine's hand pushing against his chest, but then he stopped, and, after he took a deep breath, he once again apologized.

"Again, I'm sorry. I love you so much, and it hurts to hear you speak of this angel the way you would a man. I guess I'm just jealous of this other man in your life. Even if he's only an angel to you, he's still taking you away from me."

His voice was truly sincere, and it had the effect on her that he wanted. She moved out into the hall and up close to him, placing her hands on his cheeks.

"My Raoul, no one will take me away from you. This is just something I've wanted for so long, and, now that I have it, I don't want to give it up. I don't want to make you mad or lose you. Please, be patient with me, and let me have this one thing in my life while I still can. Please. I don't know how long my angel will stay with me, so I want to be with him for as long as I can."

She stood on her tiptoes and placed a kiss on his lips. Her kiss was so gentle that it wouldn't have harmed a butterfly, but it was also as sharp as a newly forged sword and pierced my heart clear through. I closed my eyes and ground my teeth. When they opened, I saw him lean into her, preparing for a kiss that would have twisted and turned that sword for a sure death.

But she rescued me by placing her hands on his chest and saying, "No, Raoul. Not here. Not now."

He smiled and kissed the back of her hand. I'm sure he felt the conqueror as he reached past her, closed her door, turned her around, and walked with her on his arm toward the stairs. Her spirit was no longer agitated, but mine was more that agitated. She was being so fickle, and it was driving me crazy, or she was being two-faced and it was angering me. I paced for a few moments, trying to understand her, understand if she was being sincere to both of us or deceiving one of us.

Whatever the case, I couldn't stay there any longer. I wanted those moments back when it was only Christine and I at the pond, those moments when our eyes met, those moments that took my breath away. But they were only momentary and were now gone, and I couldn't bear the thought of watching them together any longer. So, after replacing my cloak and hat, I also left the inn without even looking for them. Within a short while, I was once again on Jasper and heading for the sea and, hopefully, some peace of mind.

It was a beautiful sunny day, but Perros was still in its winter season, so the wind coming off the sea was icy. I sat on the driftwood for a while, thinking about my father. I walked out on the jetty, thinking about my childhood. I walked the beach, thinking about the first time I saw Christine as a child right in that same spot. I stood on the ocean property close to the cliff, which was still untouched by man, and thought about my past. After a few hours of meditation, my spirit was warmed but my body was chilled, so I mounted back up and left.

I had several more hours before the train back to Paris was due to leave, and, since I didn't want to look at Christine and Raoul anymore, I decided to visit my father's grave one last time.

Once there, I gazed around at the additional tombstones, attesting to how many more people had died and lay beside my father. Some of the graves had flowers on them in varying degrees of wilting. I looked back at my father's tombstone and gave thought, only momentarily, to putting flowers on his grave. But then I thought better of it. What's the point? Within hours, they'd also be wilting and eventually die, just like my father. So, instead, I ran my fingers over his name, told him I still loved him, and left, with only one more glance at his grave as I passed the gate.

I then took a detour down my old street. I stayed up the street from my old house and looked at it much the way I had the last time I'd been there. That seemed like a million years ago. So much had happened since I started construction on the opera house, especially during the last weeks, with Christine in my life.

As I looked at the house, and felt the memories surface, I couldn't help but think about my sister—and my mother—just as I'd done twenty years earlier. I wondered how they managed without my father. I knew he'd left them financially secure, so that wasn't what I was questioning; it was their emotional stability. My mother was never sure-footed in that department, and I'd often speculated about her. Perhaps she'd remarried, and, with me out of the house and out of her life, had regained what my father had seen in her younger years. Perhaps.

I wondered about Gigi. Along with all the other guilt I had, I still carried guilt because I'd never contacted her over the years. Those were the last words I spoke to that tearful child when I left her room for the last time. I'd promised her I'd contact her soon, but I never did. First, it was because my life was such a mess, and, then, I just didn't know what to say to her after so long a time. Perhaps now that my life resembled a form of order, I should write her and see where she was in her life. Maybe I should go to the door and see if my mother still lived there, and, who knows, maybe Gigi was also there.

Some of my questions were answered when a couple walked out the door and locked it. It wasn't Gigi and it wasn't my mother. Someone else lived there and my questions multiplied. I watched them enter a carriage and leave, and I watched the carriage disappear around the corner. Then I looked back at the house with a strange feeling inside me. Someone else was living in my home, a home I felt I should feel nothing for, but I did. It was the only home I ever knew, such as it was, and it held a strong connection to my father. I felt hurt.

I was being driven by my questions as I looked down the street at Celeste's home. I wondered if she still lived there. The need to find answers to my mounting questions gave me the strength I needed to seek her out. I was impelled to keep going until I found myself standing at her door with my gloved hand made into a fist and ready to knock.

With the knock, I heard her friendly voice respond, "One moment, please."

I smiled, as a flood of pleasant memories associated with her surged through me, and then the door opened. She, at first, took a step back, covered her mouth with her pink hand, her eyes widened, and she shouted my name.

"Erik! Oh, merciful Father in heaven, it's you—Erik."

"Good evening, Celeste," was all I was permitted to get out before she rushed me and wrapped her arms clear around me.

She kept repeating my name as if she was trying to remember it. After only a moment of staunch resistance, I gave in to the feel of human contact and returned her embrace. She'd hardly changed at all. She was still the friendly and smiling Celeste I remembered. Oh, she'd put on a bit of weight and perhaps a few wrinkles, but, other than that, she was pretty much the same. Her hair was still golden, her cheeks still rosy, and her smiling eyes still crystal blue.

She finally backed away from me, looked me up and down, and started chattering like a squirrel defending its nest.

"I can't believe this is really you, Erik. Look at you. My, you turned out nicely. You're so tall, just like your dear father, and so strong also. And your mask, quite an improvement from the one you left here with. And that smile, you still have that incredible smile. And your eyes, still so soft and warm. Yes, you've turned out nicely. You could use some more weight, though, but then you were never a big eater. Actually, you're quite stunning, Erik. But I'd imagine you have all kinds of lady friends telling you that—now, don't you?"

She didn't even give me a chance to respond to her enthusiastic compliments before she started in again, while pulling on my arm. "Oh, where are my manners? Come in, Erik, come in out of the cold and sit down. Here, give me your cloak, and I'll get you some hot tea."

It wasn't until she disappeared into the kitchen that I had a moment to catch up to her words, but then she was back around the corner with a tray containing a teapot, teacups, and a plate of cookies. Then she started in again.

"Sit down, Erik. Now, tell me, what have you been doing with your life. Tell me everything. I want to know everything."

She started pouring the tea and took a breath, which gave me my opportunity to ask my questions. "I really didn't come here to take up your time with my life story. I know how busy you probably are, considering how you're always helping someone, so I'll be brief."

"Nonsense, Erik. There's nothing more important to me right now than to visit with you. Now, tell me, what brings you back to Perros?"

"I'm here on business, and, when I came down the street, I couldn't help but wonder about my old home. I see someone else is living there now. When did my mother sell it?"

The teacup at her lips slowly lowered, and her eyes took on an expression that made me wish I hadn't given into my need to have my questions answered. She took a deep breath as she watched her teacup nestle down in its matching saucer. Her eyes returned to mine, and her lips, which always had a ready smile, were solemn.

"Your mother didn't sell the house, Erik. She died before she had that chance."

Fifteen

I never thought it would hurt so much to hear those words, but then I'd never actually given any thought to hearing them. As a small boy, I feared my father's death to an extreme, but I never considered my mother's death or how I would feel about it. It hurt and I didn't understand why. It hurt inside just as if she'd been a loving mother who'd been with me all those years. The woman who I thought I hated, the woman I swore I hated, died, and I felt an emptiness within me that I couldn't understand.

"Erik—Erik."

I raised my sight from my cup and looked into the compassionate eyes of Celeste. "Yes," I whispered.

"I'm sorry, Erik. You obviously didn't know."

I shrugged my shoulders and shook my head, and then she continued, "I wasn't sure just what you might have heard over the years."

I shook my head slightly and returned my sight to the tea in my hands. "There was no love lost between us, Celeste. You know that. I suppose I assumed everyone would be the same, only older. I never gave any consideration to death, although I should have, considering . . ."

"Considering what?" she asked softly and without the excited flare that had started the conversation.

I looked back up at her innocent and tender eyes. She had no idea who was sitting in her drawing room; no idea at all. She had no way of knowing that at one time I was a skilled assassin, a cold-blooded murderer, and an experienced executioner. If she'd known, then she also would have known that death was somehow always associated with me. I could see in her crystal blue eyes that all she saw was that child prodigy with an angelic voice and a tortured soul.

I took a deep breath and started on just another act in my long career of half-truths. "I should have known there was a possibility of someone dying, considering how long I've been gone."

She held out the small plate of cookies in my direction, and, to be polite, I took one, although eating anything at that time was not on my list of wants.

"What happened, Celeste? How did she die?"

She started to get up and throw another log on the dying fire, so I jumped up, threw the entire cookie in my mouth, and did the job for her.

While stoking the fire, I asked again, "I would like to know what happened, if you don't mind telling me."

"Certainly, Erik. Your question just caught me off guard. I'm sorry."

She poured me more tea and sat down before she started. "You understand, it was a most disturbing time for your mother when your father died and then you left. Poor Anna. She loved you both so much."

I poked the log one more time. "Yes, I saw their love often."

"And you, Erik. She loved you very much. You need to believe that."

"It's all right, Celeste. I reconciled myself to my mother's true feelings a long time ago. There's no need to sugarcoat anything for me."

I sat down and she held her small hand out toward the fire, obviously enjoying its warmth. "I'm not, Erik. Your mother truly loved you, and, once you left, she became obsessed with finding you. I don't think she realized where you were those days leading up to the funeral. I don't think she realized much of anything during that time. But right after the funeral, everything changed.

"She was sitting right where you're sitting now, along with the doctor. I think there were maybe ten of us here, when your mother got up and headed for the door. Then she walked out without a wrap and without saying anything to anyone. We tried to stop her, but she said she had to go get her son. That was the first time she'd mentioned you, and I didn't know how to tell her that you were gone.

"The doctor took over and tried to tell her that you'd left and were on your way to the conservatory in Venice. She said, no, that you were still in Perros, because she could hear your violin and your voice. We tried to reason with her, but she was becoming hysterical, so the doctor said he would go with her and help her find you. Charles and I also went with her back to your house, but, once we reached your gate, she said you weren't in the house. Then she headed down the street toward the cemetery. She kept saying, I think to herself, that she could hear you, while neither the doctor nor Charles nor I could hear anything.

"Trying to keep her calmed, the doctor suggested we look for you with the buggy, so that's what we did. Once we were in the buggy, she kept saying, 'Hear that? That's my Erik. Listen to his voice. Isn't it like an angel's?' That continued until we were about a block away from the cemetery. Then she started calling your name and jumped out of the buggy while it was still rolling.

"She started running, and, once she got past the gate, she ran all over until she stopped at the back fence, still calling your name. We tried to comfort her, but there wasn't much we could do. She insisted you were there and that she'd heard you singing. I felt so bad for her when she kept calling 'Where are you, Erik? Come home.'"

Celeste looked over the top of her teacup at me. "Were you there, Erik?"

I leaned forward, rested my elbows on my knees, and watched my fingers moving against each other. Then, while remembering my mother's plaintive voice that day, I nodded.

With a sigh that expressed her years of unanswered questions, she whispered, "So she did hear you."

I again nodded. "Yes, I was there. I wanted to spend time with my father and play something special for him before I left for good."

She sat with quiet lips for a moment, but her eyes told me she understood. Then she picked up her story where she'd left off.

"That was the start of it. Almost every day she insisted that she heard you singing, playing your violin, or playing the piano. Were you still in Perros during the weeks after that?"

"No," I answered reflectively. "I left Perros shortly after all of you left the cemetery."

Her eyes widened with that new understanding. "You knew she was there?"

I took a deep breath and let it out slowly. "Yes—I saw all of you, and I heard her call to me. It broke what was left of my heart. I came really close to running to her. I could have used her love and embrace right then—although, I always could have used her love and embrace."

"Oh, Erik, that's so sad. Why didn't you go to her?"

I shrugged my shoulders. "I suppose my fear of being locked behind bars was stronger at that time than my need for her love." I took another deep breath, looked into the fire, and spoke in little over a whisper, "I'm sorry I put my mother through that."

"I'm sorry you had to go through so much, Erik. You were only a small boy."

Again, I shrugged my shoulders while thinking about all that had happened to that small boy after that day. I looked back at her, and I wasn't sure what to do next. I wanted to leave and remove myself from all those torturous memories, but something was tying me there. I had a strange need to know what happened to my mother, almost as if I wanted the pain that was swelling in my chest to continue. After a few seconds of silence, she went on.

"We weren't sure if you might still be close to home, and since she was so persistent, we helped her look for you whenever she wanted us to."

"How long did she keep looking for me?"

"Much too long, Erik. It got to the point that she couldn't be left alone. On several occasions, Gigi came to our home, either early in the morning or sometimes in the middle of the night, telling us that her mother was gone. We would quickly dress and go looking for her. It didn't take us long to realize we only needed to look in one place, the cemetery, because that's where she always went, and she always insisted that you were there somewhere, singing. She'd be at the back fence, looking up into the trees, calling your name over and over."

I closed my eyes to the visual image of my poor mother, but it was impossible to close my heart to its emotional response.

Celeste took a sip of her tea, told me to have another cookie, and then continued, "Your mother's health started failing. If she wasn't out looking for you, she was sitting and staring out the back window toward the barn. Or sometimes she'd jump with a start and charge up the stairs saying, 'He's here! He's singing!' Or, if we were up in her room, she'd run to the top of the stairs saying, 'He's playing for me.' Then she'd stand at the railing, looking down at the silent piano. And on many occasions I'd find her in your room, sitting in the middle of the floor with one of your contraptions in her hands.

"She couldn't sleep or eat. Charles and I tried to get her to stay with us in our home, hoping the change in surroundings might help her, but she refused, saying she needed to be there when you got back home. So I started staying with her twenty-four hours a day. Charles even stayed there with us when he wasn't at work.

"I tried everything I could to help her eat. I prepared all her favorite dishes, with a nicely set table and candles. The three of us would sit at the table with her, trying to smile and talk with her. She did try her best to smile and eat, bless her soul, but everything she ate came right back up. She got so thin."

I raised my eyes from my fingers and looked at her watching me with a tender gaze. "It was before sunrise when Gigi came in and woke me for the last time. We again went to the cemetery, but we couldn't find her there, so we widened our search. Remembering how she always insisted you were playing your violin from up among the trees, we looked there next."

She became silent and moved her sight to the fire, and I tried to wait patiently for her to continue, although, at that point, I wasn't sure I wanted to hear the rest of her story. I took a sip of my tea and set the cup down loud enough to be heard, hoping to attract her attention, but her gaze was fixed, perhaps reliving that harrowing time in her life.

She finally took a deep breath and looked back at me. "I never should have left her side that night. I should have sat up with her and not slept. Deep in me, I knew something bad was going to happen that day, although I didn't know what. For days prior, she'd been gaining a hopeful attitude. She would smile at me and say, 'Just three more days, Celeste. Just two more days. Just one more day.'

"She felt certain her search for you would end on that day and she would find you at last. During those days, she cleaned your room from top to bottom. She dusted and swept the floors. She dusted and straightened all your books and experiments. She washed your bed sheets and windows, even though it was snowing outside. She said everything had to be clean for you when you returned."

She again transferred her sight to the fire, and, as tears filled her eyes, she finished her story. "That last day we searched for her was the first of January, Erik—your birthday. We found her in a cluster of trees on the hill behind the cemetery, sitting against one of them. She was in only her nightgown and partially covered with the fresh snow. She was gone and there was nothing the good doctor could do for her."

She stopped speaking and, while her gaze remained on the fire, I tore apart inside. I killed her. I wasn't even there, and I killed her. I was fighting that ache in my jaw that preceded my tears, so I took a drink of my tea, trying to maintain my composure. I was searching, unsuccessfully, through my thoughts to find some kind of a response to her words, but, thankfully, she rescued me and continued speaking.

"She loved you very much, Erik. And while it must be hard for you to hear what happened to her, it should show you how much she loved you."

Unintentionally, my voice sounded somewhat sarcastic when I responded, "You don't think, Celeste, that maybe she was just plagued with guilt for how she treated me?"

She looked at me thoughtfully, got up, and touched my shoulder as she went by me. "Wait here a minute, Erik. There's something you need to see."

She went into her parlor, and, from the other room, made several comments about knowing it was there somewhere. She came back around the corner and handed me a small, green, velvet bag.

"Open it," she said as she laid her hand on my shoulder.

I did as she asked and found a locket, the locket I'd given to my mother.

"Take it out and look inside, Erik. When we found your mother, she had that locket closed in her fist. After your father's funeral, and when we couldn't find you at the cemetery, she started looking for that locket. She found it on your father's dresser, but the chain was missing, so she just held it in her hands. She carried it everywhere with her, until, one day when she couldn't find it again, she went hysterical. After that, I bought her another chain and then she wore it around her neck. I don't think she ever took it off."

The air in the room was still and solemn as I opened the locket. There I found a picture of Gigi, just as anticipated. "I thought there would be a picture of my father along with Gigi's," I remarked.

"Yes, she told me that's what you'd suggested, but she never put his picture there."

I tightened my jaw and started to close the locket when she put her hand on mine. "No, Erik, look closer."

She got up and turned up the light beside me and repeated her instructions. "Look closely."

She pointed to the empty side of the locket, and I turned it in the light, trying to see what she was referring to, and then, there it was. Obviously written with a crude instrument of some sort, and not by a jeweler's precision tool, was one word—Erik.

I could hear my own heart beating as I stared at my name etched in the gold locket, not sure what to make of it. Then I looked up into Celeste's tender eyes.

"She loved you, Erik. She loved you very much. She just had her own problems and didn't know how to show you how much she loved you, but she did. She carried you as close to her heart as she could and in the only way she knew how."

I nodded and looked back at my name, but I still wasn't sure what to feel. I definitely felt pain, but whether it was for her or for me I wasn't sure. I closed the locket, put it back in the bag, and handed it to my gracious hostess.

She held out her hand, but then closed my fingers over the bag. "It's yours, Erik. When we went through your mother's things and packed them in boxes, I tried to give the locket to Gigi, but she said, since you gave it to your mother, you should have it. She kept it for you in her room, believing you would be back soon and she could give it to you. She always knew you would be back someday, and she was right."

I looked down at my closed fist holding the green bag and she went back to her chair. I wasn't capable of making a decision at that time, so I set the bag down next to my tea.

"Thank you, Celeste, for explaining everything to me."

She nodded, but she was still quite solemn. The cheerful face she'd had when I entered her home was nowhere to be found. I was almost afraid to ask her any more questions, but I needed to say something to direct us away from my mother.

"Now, tell me about Gigi. Is she still living close by?" I blurted out like an insensitive imbecile.

The smile almost returned, and she sighed. "Oh, Gigi. That sweet girl. She's living in Madrid now, and I miss her so."

"Madrid? What took her to Madrid?" I asked with honest surprise.

"Well, a young man actually, a very handsome and talented young man by the name of Alfonso, whom she met in Venice."

I was shocked, and it showed in my unrestrained voice. "Venice? Gigi went to Venice? Why Venice?"

"Because some of the best art schools are in Italy," she responded, as if I should have known the answer. "She found one that accepted her in Venice. She became quite good, you know."

"Venice?" I repeated almost under my breath. "Venice?" echoed again from my lips. I felt a serious frown begin as my gaze traveled to the fire. "Venice? She was accepted at a school in Venice?"

"Yes, Erik. Is something wrong?" I couldn't answer. "Erik, what's wrong?"

I quickly looked back at her, with that one word conjuring up decades of agonizing emotional images.

"Nothing really, I suppose. I was only surprised—that's all. You see, a conversation about our plans to move to Venice was the last conversation I had with my father. So . . ." I looked down at the braided rug beneath my feet and gathered my thoughts. "I was just surprised—nothing more."

She moved forward somewhat in her chair and looked at me with questions in her eyes, as well as in the tone of her voice.

"I'm sorry, Erik, sorry you had to go there alone. You did make it to Venice, didn't you? You did make it to the conservatory?"

Taking a sip of my tea to buy time to think, I nodded. Then, with visions of that forsaken child walking aimlessly through the streets of Venice, I answered, "Yes, indeed I did. I found my way to Italy and to Venice and to the conservatory."

She smiled eagerly and leaned back. "I knew you would. I would love to have seen their faces when they heard you. I bet they were surprised to have you walk in with such a talent."

"Yes—you could say that. But, I think, shocked, would be a more appropriate word," I responded, trying to smile and change the subject. "But, tell me, how did Gigi do at the school?"

"Oh, she did wonderfully. She was, and still is, very talented," she responded with such pride. Pointing to the painting over the fireplace, she added, "See that painting? She did that when she was only ten, and it was that painting that won her acceptance to the school. Does any of it look familiar to you?"

I studied the painting that was made mostly of varying shades of gray and white, with highlights of lavender-blue, violet, and light coral. It depicted clouds in the sky and, in the center, almost hidden in the shape of the clouds, was a horse head, and, off to the side and top were a pair of eyes, intense human eyes. It was beautiful, and it did just what any good painting should do; it captivated me, and I stared at it for some time before Celeste repeated her question.

"Does any of it look familiar to you?"

As I looked at it with that question in mind, I realized what she was getting at. "Yes. It's Molly's head, isn't it?"

"That's right, and what about the eyes? Do you recognize them?" she asked with a twinkle in hers.

Squinting a bit, I nodded, "Yes, they're my mother's eyes and most intriguing."

She looked at me with a big smile. "No. They're meant to be *your* eyes. But then you have your mother's eyes, so I'm not surprised you recognized them as hers. You're supposed to be watching over Molly. She got the inspiration for the painting from the times you'd take her out in the pasture with Molly and a blanket. She told me you'd lie on it with her while looking up at the clouds. She said you'd tell her that, if she used her imagination, she could make anything she wanted out of the clouds. She painted that for you, and she was going to give it to you when you returned. She never gave up hope that you'd return, because, as she put it, you promised her you would."

As my guilt mounted, she took a bite of a cookie and went on. "For a long time she waited everyday at the window. I thought the day would never come when she'd stop asking when you were coming home. It broke my heart. She never forgot you or gave up on your coming back. I guess she was right, because here you are."

I remember frowning when she said that, and I felt so guilty. "I know I should have contacted her sooner, but my life was so . . ."

"Busy?" she interjected.

"Well, no . . . well, yes . . ."

I groaned inside, leaned forward again, and pressed my fingertips against my forehead, trying to find words that wouldn't disclose the horrors I was living through during that period when my innocent sister was waiting for me. I looked at Celeste's kind eyes, and a large part of me wanted to let go of what I'd been carrying alone for so long. I wanted to cry and tell her everything that her small genius suffered. I wanted to unburden my heart to her, but I didn't. It might have made me feel better, but she'd already gone through so much because of my family, and I couldn't do that to her. So I told her the only thing I could think of.

"It was a hard time for me, Celeste. I suffered over my father's death for an extremely long time. In fact, I'm still suffering because of his loss. I had to work through a lot of things, and, by then, it had been so long and I figured it didn't matter anymore—I guess."

"I'm sorry you had to suffer so much, Erik. But you're here now, and that's what matters. She's going to be so thrilled when I write her. You should write her. I could give you her address, and you should give me your address so I can give it to her."

I instantly felt like a child caught with his hand in a cookie jar. What address could I possibly give her? The Opera Ghost, care of the Paris Opera House, Fifth Cellar, Paris, France? No, that wouldn't do at all. I felt so deceptive. What was I doing there? I should have known she'd ask me all types of questions that I wouldn't be able to answer.

I tried to smile and nodded. Then I looked at the painting again, trying to change the subject.

"If she painted that when she was ten, she was pulling that vision from a memory at least six years old. She was so young then. How could she remember that much of it to be so accurate?"

"She kept her memories of you alive, Erik. She never forgot you. In fact, there's something else she kept for you."

She set her cup down and headed back to the parlor, while telling me to have another cookie. She came back with a large collection of drawings in a box bound with a yellow silk ribbon. As I looked at them, I recognized most of what she'd drawn. They were Molly, and our house, the cliffs over the ocean, and then there were eyes, several pages of nothing but eyes. I stopped on one of those pages and looked with wonder at her young talent.

"That's you, Erik. She drew that . . . oh . . . it must have been three or four years after you left. She really caught the right expression, don't you think?"

"Yes, indeed," I answered with pride.

She sat on the arm of the sofa beside me and ran her tiny finger over the edge of the page as she added, "I recall asking her how she could remember your eyes so clearly. She said she could never forget them or your smile and laugh. She loved your laugh and said it was the thing she missed the most. That, and your music.

"I believe she missed you more than she missed her father. As the years went by, she couldn't remember that much about him, but she remembered everything about you. She even remembered the last conversation she had with you in her room the night you left. She told me several times it was your words to her that night, about keeping up her drawings, that kept her going at times."

She squeezed my shoulder, got up, and went back to her chair. "I can still see her sitting at that window behind you with her sketchbook. She spent a lot of time there, drawing from memory. I think it was good medicine for her and helped her through the loss of all three members of her family in such a brief period of time. In only three short months, she'd lost her father, her mother, and her brother, who in her eyes was also her best friend. She came to live with us at that time, so she also lost the security of her own room and familiar home. That's a lot for a four-year-old to lose."

Again my jaw began to ache and my eyes to burn. I maneuvered uncomfortably on the sofa, trying to think of some way to change the subject gracefully before my guilt over my selfish and self-centered thoughts during those years made me break completely. I'd never once given any thought to Gigi and how she would be affected during that extremely dark period in my life.

Just to give my hands and mouth something to do while my mind worked on finding my way out of her house, I laid her drawings down, drank my tea in one swallow, and grabbed two cookies. She chuckled at my unusual and abrupt action, and I think she was trying to lighten the mood with her next words.

"But everything worked out well for her in the end. Even though you weren't here physically, your relationship with her while you were here made a large impression on her young heart and gave her courage."

Swallowing the last of the cookie, I responded, "Well, I'm not sure about that, but I am glad she made it to a good art school."

"That was also because of you, Erik. Even though she only wanted to get married and have her own children, we convinced her to wait until she was older and told her it was always a good idea to have a backup in case she was left without a husband the way her mother was. When we talked about additional schooling, Charles and I knew we couldn't afford it. We talked with Gigi about selling your house to pay for it, and she told us the only reason she would let go of the house was because you'd always told her to follow her dream and not let anything stand in her way. And, if that was the only way she could follow it, she would agree."

"I would like to acknowledge those kind words without argument, Celeste, but I can't take credit for them. I was only mimicking my father's words to me. They weren't my thoughts; they were his. I'm sure in time he would have spoken them to her, if he hadn't died first."

She honestly smiled while filling up my teacup again. "Yes, I know you're right about that. Everyone in the town knew what a good father he was, and everyone was so saddened by what happened to your family. It was a good thing that Luca and Peter were sent to prison. I think that helped a lot of people put the horrible events of that winter to rest."

I nearly dropped the teacup from my hands, and my heart began to race as I responded to that unexpected comment. "They sent them to prison? They really did?"

Sixteen

I wanted to say more than that, but I had a lady sitting in my presence, and the words that were swimming around in my mind weren't ones I should speak while in her company. In fact, they were thoughts that shouldn't be shared in any ones company.

"Yes," she replied. "As it turned out, they found someone who witnessed everything, so they knew it was Luca who'd thrown the lantern. And, since Peter was also a part of it, they were both sent to prison. But they didn't spend nearly enough time there to pay for their wicked deed. Luca was killed in prison during a knife fight only three months later, and Peter also died in prison of a fever almost two years after that."

Again my thoughts were not gentlemanly, so, through clenched teeth, I used only a few of them to ask, "And their boys?"

"I don't remember hearing too much about them after that time. I know Franco was sent to a reformatory, I don't remember why, and I don't know what happened to him after that. And Pete Jr., I never heard anything about him, and I never saw him around either."

I was trying frantically to find something uplifting to say to erase those pictures from my mind. Visions of Luca throwing that lantern at my father kept flashing through my thoughts, and I struggled hard for a few moments to clear them and replace them with something more pleasant.

Finally, I blurted out, "I have to be thankful for men like your Charles who came to my sister's rescue. I'm thankful you were there for her, both you and Charles. That was most generous of him to open his home to her. How is Charles?"

The words weren't even out of my mouth when I knew they were the wrong ones, and I instantly feared her answer.

She took a deep breath and exhaled slowly before she answered, "I lost my Charles going on two years now. In fact, it will be two years in just two weeks. Then, only two months after his passing, our good Doctor Faure also passed away. We lost two special men in only two months. It was a sad time for many people in this town. I still miss them both. Naturally, I miss my Charles the most. But we did get to celebrate out fiftieth wedding anniversary first."

"I'm so sorry, Celeste. Charles was always so kind to me, and that kindness helped me. He was a good man."

She smiled softly, nodded, and replied, "Yes, that he was, and I miss him so, especially at night. I have plenty to keep me busy during the day, since there's always someone who's getting married, or having a baby, or who's sick and needs my help. But the nights get depressingly lonely. After having someone to talk to, to eat meals with, and to sleep next to for fifty years, it's extremely hard to be without him."

I would have liked to tell her that I understood her loneliness, feeling I was an expert on that subject, but, then, perhaps I wasn't. I was lonely, but without that same point of reference, whereas she knew what she was missing, which had to multiply her loneliness. It seemed my attempt to keep the conversation uplifting was turning out to be a dismal failure, so I tried taking a safe ground.

"You haven't told me how Gigi ended up in Madrid."

"Well, she was in Venice . . . oh, by the way, Erik, she looked for you often while she was there, but, as you know, she never found you. Did you not stay in Venice long?"

It appeared that attempt also failed, and I thought, how am I going to answer that question? "When did she get there?"

"Well, let's see. She was fourteen when she left here, so that would make the year . . ."

"If she was fourteen when she left then I was twenty. No, I was no longer in Venice at that time. By then I was in Persia."

"Persia? What in the name of God were you doing in Persia?"

I had to smirk at her reaction. "I was commissioned to build the Shah of Persia a palace, so I was there for about five years."

"Oh, my!" she exclaimed as she sat forward and placed her petite hand over her lips. "Erik, that's such a wonderful thing to hear. Oh, my! Your father would have been so proud."

Her excitement over that little bit of news made me smile. "I hope so. While I was building it, the thought of his being proud of me encouraged me to do my best. In fact, my father's words have guided me through all my projects, and the credit for everything I've accomplished goes to him."

"A palace in Persia. I can't believe it. You'll have to take me to see it. I would love to see it, Erik."

I laughed at that, thinking I would never be allowed back in Persia, not unless I was ready to forfeit my life, so I just shrugged it off. "Persia is far away, you know that don't you, Celeste? There are other buildings

I've worked on that are much closer. Perhaps you could see one of them someday."

"Yes, Erik, I know Persia is far away, but I'd love to see it anyway. It must be truly remarkable."

"Well, the Shah was pleased with it, and, since he was the one who paid me for my efforts, I suppose that's what matters." Wanting to get away from the subject of Persia, I tried again. "You still haven't told me how Gigi got to Madrid."

"Like I said, she was in Venice and doing well. I think she was there about three years when she fell in love with a fellow student. Since that was her main desire in life, to be married and have children, it was only a matter of months before they were married. After leaving school, they tried to start a gallery there in Venice. But, as life would have it, she came to be with child.

"It was about that time that Alfonso received an offer of a teaching position in Madrid, which is where he was from. So, under the circumstances, they moved there. They now have three children, all beautiful girls, Erika, Florence, and Anna. Yes, she named her first child after you, Erik. That should tell you how much you meant to her."

I tried to smile and acknowledge what should have been a positive comment, but my thoughts automatically traveled down that road toward Persia and the other child that had the unfortunate distinction of carrying the burden of my name. I could only hope that my sister's child wouldn't maintain my curse along with my name.

"Erik. Erik! Erik! Is something wrong?"

"Uhhh, no," I replied while shaking those old cobwebs out of my mind. "Go on."

"Gigi and Alfonso were finally able to open a gallery just last year. Alfonso is a wonderful and kind man, Erik. I'm sure you'll like him."

I nodded, "I'm sure I will. Perhaps someday I'll travel there and see her. I would love to see her gallery, and it's comforting to know she continued with her dream. Tell me, did she keep up with the piano?"

"Oh, no," she responded with a slight chuckle. "She remembered what you'd taught her and she would play from time to time, but, after you, Erik, all music sounded hollow."

"She should have continued anyway, Celeste. Making music is a wonderful thing to experience."

"Not everyone can play, Erik, not like you. You should know that by now. One of her daughters plays, though. She made sure all three girls had piano lessons. We went to visit her a few years back, and, even though we were there visiting, she wouldn't let them forget about their practicing."

She smiled. "I remember her telling them that they had to practice well because someday their Uncle Erik would want to hear them play."

An uncle. I'd never given any thought to being an uncle. "Are any of them any good?"

"From what I could observe and hear, two of them were doing just what they'd been told and would practice faithfully. But Florence, the middle child, had some talent. Even I could tell she wasn't just doing it because she was told to. After watching your face express your love for music as you played, I could tell she loved what she was doing. But, let's face it, when you eventually hear them, don't be too disappointed because there's only one Erik, and he alone can make the piano speak so perfectly."

I thanked her, I hope graciously, and was trying to find the words to tell her I needed to leave, when her eyes lit up, and she exclaimed, "Erik, I almost forgot! We still have your piano."

She jumped to her feet and grabbed me by the arm before I had a chance to fully digest what she'd said.

Dragging me into her parlor, she burst out, "Look! It's right there."

Sure enough, there it was. I walked to it, and ran my fingers over its top as memories both pleasant and painful swept over me. I could hear the sound of it fill our home. I could see my small fingers stretching over the keys. I could see myself at two sitting by the fireplace listening to my mother play. I saw my father sitting on the bench next to me with his ever-ready smile.

"Erik." Her voice halted my memories mid-stream. "Would you like to have it?"

I was still reeling from the shock of seeing it, so I couldn't even think about answering that question.

I shook my head. "I don't know. Right now, it wouldn't be possible, but maybe in the future. I really don't know."

"Is your home not big enough?" she asked with a tone of surprise.

My mouth was open, but I didn't have a chance to respond before she started again with her exuberance. "Oh, my goodness, Erik, you've told me hardly anything about yourself or where you're living now."

Grabbing my arm again, she led me back by the fire and filled my cup one more time. I was still standing as I took out my watch, and, as usual, I gently ran my finger over the horse heads. Then I checked the time, making sure I wouldn't miss the train.

She looked over at me, set the teapot down, and moved toward me. Evidently, that gesture prompted more questions from my special hostess. She took my hands in hers, and then looked up into my eyes with a certain strange look, and her lips barely moved into a smile. She looked back at my hands and ran her fingers over the back of them. Not wanting to question her peculiar actions, I waited for her to explain herself, while several uncomfortable moments passed in silence.

Finally, she looked back up at me and murmured, "I thought I was looking at your father's hands right then. He had a way of doing that exact same thing with his watch. It's his watch, isn't it?"

I could only nod and take a deep breath.

"And this ring, it's his also, isn't it?" she asked as she ran her eyes and her finger over it.

Again, I could only nod.

Looking intently into my eyes, she smiled. "I thought it was you who'd taken them. You deserved them."

She looked back down and again ran her fingers over mine. Then she spoke with such tenderness you would think she was speaking to a newborn infant.

"Your hands are identical to your fathers, but then you're just like your father. You have his same beautiful smile, and your gestures; it's like watching your father all over again. Even your hair is like his."

With that statement, I raised my eyebrows with a question mark, and again she smiled. "Well, maybe not the color, but definitely the texture and wave, and even the way you have it cut. But those eyes, they're not his. I see your mother in your eyes. The same warm, rich, dark brown—yes, definitely your mother's Spanish eyes."

I was beginning to feel too much like a science specimen and started to tell her I had to leave, but she insisted that I have just one more cup of tea and one more cookie before I left.

"I'm sorry, Erik. I've been jabbering your ear off, and I really want to know what you've been doing all these years. So tell me, what are you doing now? Are you still playing? Oh, that's a silly question; certainly you're still playing. Tell me, what are you doing now?"

How could I tell her I resided as a resident ghost and spent my days conjuring ways to torment people with fiendish delight, and that I receive my pay by extortion? I couldn't tell her that I was pretending to be an angel just so I could steal a woman away from her childhood sweetheart. No, that wouldn't do at all. I couldn't tell her the truth.

I looked at her honest face and knew it was impossible to tell her the facts of what I did for a living, and that made me feel sick through and through. My existence right then was nothing like what Papa had wanted for me, or that she expected of me. I was so glad that he wasn't around to see what I'd done with my life.

I fixed my gaze on the fireplace. I couldn't look her straight in the eye and begin my outlandish lies, not to that most sincere and honest woman. I simply couldn't. I had to tell her something, though, so I told her the closest version of the truth that I could without destroying her happy thoughts about me.

"I'm a teacher, Celeste. I teach voice, and I run an opera company here in France. Right now, I have a student who has great potential. She had her debut just this week, and she's the talk of Paris."

Her eyes widened and she took a deep breath. "That's so exciting to hear, but I'm not surprised. That's exactly what I thought you'd be doing. Do you perform also?"

Thinking that my performances consist of writing notes of threats and frightening chorus girls, I simply answered with my eyes looking down at my hands, "No, I only teach."

"Oh, Erik, that's such a shame. Your voice is one that should not be kept silent."

"You'd think that, wouldn't you?" I said without thinking. Then, to give her what she wanted to hear, I added, "I did travel around the eastern part of Europe and Russia for several years, singing and playing my violin. I made good money doing that, and it was most enjoyable. Right now, I sing mostly for myself and my pupil. But I have some plans on the drawing board, and if all works out well, perhaps I'll be doing more entertaining in the near future."

"Well, that's what I like to hear. And what about composing? Do you still compose?"

Now, with that question I could almost be truthful. "Yes, that I do. I've written many pieces over the years, and right now I'm almost finished with my first opera."

"An opera? Oh, Erik! I'm so proud of you."

Her words were cutting right through me. It might have sounded like something beautiful, but my opera was about a subject that would, I'm sure, make her turn every shade of red and run from the room. And the circumstances under which it was being composed were not romantic in the least. I pictured myself in my dark and lonely home beneath the streets of Paris, being driven by hatred, anger, and loneliness, while she, more than likely, pictured me sitting in a brightly-lit studio in a good neighborhood, with a magnificent shiny black grand piano in front of a large window.

Suddenly, I saw my home, along with my living conditions and everything I thought I had a measure of pride in, in a totally different light. Suddenly, I became everything Raoul suggested I was and more: a sleazy, dark, deranged man with nothing but selfish motives.

Without making eye contact, I tried to answer her without my self-loathing showing through, "It's nothing grandiose, Celeste. Only a simple opera."

"No, Erik, you would never do anything less than grandiose. I'm sure it will be splendid. You must let me know when it's finished and being performed. I must see it. Will you promise me you'll let me know? You have my address. Just let me know."

I promised her, but the sick feeling within me was growing with each of her compliments. I had to get out of there before I exploded.

"I must be going now, Celeste," I said as I got to my feet, put on my cloak, and grabbed my hat. "I have a train to catch back to Paris."

"Oh, my sweet, Erik. It's been so nice to see you again. Thank you for taking the time to visit me. I'm so thankful."

I looked down at her sincere blue eyes and felt like dirt, but she thought me to be a gentleman, so I needed to play the part. I reached for her hand and raised it to my lips, and then I placed a gentle kiss on the back of it.

"Oh, Erik," she giggled.

"Thank you, Celeste. You've always been so kind to me. I've never forgotten all the nice things you said and did for me, and I never will. You're truly the most gracious lady I've ever known."

"Erik, you make me blush."

She took my hands in hers and looked down at them, once more caressing them.

"I watched these hands when they were so small, and I marveled at what they were able to accomplish even then. I knew they would do great things someday, magnificent things, and you haven't disappointed me in the least. I'm so proud of you, Erik, and I know both your mother and your father would also be proud of you if they could see how you've turned out. Take care of these hands, Erik. They're destined to achieve greater accomplishments than I could ever imagine; I just know it."

She looked back up at me. "I know you said you have to catch a train, but do you think you could take just a few more minutes to play me something? I would consider it such a privilege to hear what these hands can do now that they're full-grown. Please, Erik, just one piece."

How could I possibly tell her no? Since I might never see her again, I couldn't tell her no, so I smiled and headed for her parlor while taking off my cloak. I raised the key cover just as I'd done hundreds of times in my childhood, and, once again, the memories flooded through me. I ran my fingers silently over the keys and smiled. I ran my fingers over the keys again, listening for any out-of-tune notes. There were a few, but, knowing

I hadn't the time to tune it, I looked over at Celeste sitting in a wingback chair.

"What would you like to hear?"

Her response came back without hesitation. "'The Blue Danube Waltz' by Strauss."

I nodded and started to play.

Every piano, just like every human or animal, has its own unique voice. All you have to do is listen for it and you can hear it. My old piano was no exception, and, as the first few notes spoke to me, I recognized its voice from years gone by with clarity. Strauss was a great composer, and that particular piece of his was one of my favorites. It almost always managed to make me feel happy and light when I played it. Unfortunately, that day as I played it on my old piano in that dear old friend's parlor, it only multiplied my memories and saddened me beyond control.

I wasn't through the first movement before my eyes began to blur, and, unless I wanted to make a fool of myself by running out of her house in tears, I had to suffer through the pain and finish it for her. I clenched my teeth and swallowed hard, but it didn't help. I looked at the sculpture on top of the piano and couldn't even identify what it was, so I was left with only one option. I closed my eyes tightly, squeezing out the tears and allowed myself to feel the moments to the fullest. I could only hope the inside of my mask would catch the evidence of just how hard it was for me to relive so much of my past, along with the new vision of my current deplorable life.

I sat with my fingers on the keys, waiting for the last notes to fade along with my tears. Once done, and I felt safe to look at her again, I turned to see her in the chair with a handkerchief dabbing the corners of her eyes. I closed the cover, got up, ran my fingers over its edge one last time, took the few steps toward Celeste, and held my hand out to her.

She looked up at me, took my hand, got up, and said, "I don't know what to say, Erik. I knew you had to be better than you were as a child, although I didn't see how. I don't know what to say. You make that instrument cry pure tears. I'll never understand how you do it. It's unbelievable magic."

"Thank you," I replied honestly.

I took her arm and escorted her into the drawing room. But I wasn't to escape just yet. She turned toward me and placed her hand on my chest.

"Erik, I realize I'm probably being just an old pest, but I ask only one more thing. Your voice when you were a child was as none other; it was so angelic. Would you please, before you go, allow me to hear what the man's voice sounds like? You don't have to sing much, just a little, please."

Once more, I couldn't refuse her, but I was hanging onto my emotions by a thin thread. How could I maintain control if I cried again? Then I thought about Christine and the control she had when she sang from *Faust*. She maintained her control, even though her eyes were streaming tears. Could not the teacher practice what he taught? Therefore, taking just a moment to think of something appropriate, I began with Roméo's last lyrics to Juliette. She was watching my eyes as I sang, and I watched her eyes again fill with tears.

When I finished, she shook her head and whispered while wiping her tears, "Never before, and never again, will there be a voice such as yours."

Putting my cloak back on, I stood in front of the door. "Thank you again, Celeste. You've always been so encouraging to me. Your precious heart will surely be one of the blessed."

She picked up the bag with my mother's locket in it and came back to me, placing it in my hand. "You can't forget this."

With a plethora of emotions battling it out within my heart, I again thanked her and placed what I feared was going to be a heartbreaking stumbling block for me in my cloak pocket. She raised her hands to my cheeks and smiled.

"Take care of yourself, my dashing young man. You're a very special person, Erik."

I kissed the back of her hand again, causing her to giggle and lower her head again.

"You also need to take care of yourself, Celeste. You have the most beautiful soul I've ever known. You are, and were, so very kind to me. You're one of the good memories I have of my childhood. You gave me unconditionally the love of the mother I never had. I'll be forever thankful for having you in my life."

She got tears in her eyes once more, and, before I also went back to that place with blurry eyes, I told her goodbye and left her gracious company and her warm home. I was positioning my hat as I walked back to Jasper and wished it were as easy to leave behind the sick feeling I had in the center of my heart as it was to walk out of her door.

All of Celeste's words were a doorway to the truth in my soul. She saw my hands and saw beauty and music. I saw them and saw the blood of all the men who'd taken their last breath beneath them. I stood next to Jasper and looked back at her home. I could see the firelight flickering through the curtains over her window, and I should have felt warmth. I should have felt elated and full of pride after her glowing compliments and high spirits, but I felt just the opposite. I felt despicable, debased, as if I should slither down a dark hole where I belonged.

I mounted Jasper and started slowly toward the stable, with the last remains of the setting sun lighting my way. A cloud cover had replaced the blue of the day's sky, as well as any optimistic thoughts I might have had earlier. The sea breeze had picked up, finding its way through my clothing, and I shivered. But the coldness penetrating me the most was of a different sort, and it passed through my heart like a long, pointed icicle, plummeting to the ground.

I rubbed my hands together for warmth and then looked at my fingers with horror. As far as Celeste was concerned, *those hands* could do no wrong and could only create beautiful music and beautiful buildings. Yet, only one day earlier, *those hands* had nearly taken another man's life right there in her own town.

I took my gloves from my pocket to conceal *those hands* from my sight, but first I touched the spot where Celeste had caressed them. I felt the heavy weight of guilt press down on me in a way that it hadn't done in a very long time. She saw my hands through innocent eyes guided by a perfect heart, but, if she knew the truth, it would surely kill her.

I spread out my fingers, catching the moonlight on the gold band, and closed my eyes to the truth. Celeste saw only my father's good hands, but all I saw were slaves that did the bidding of a wicked heart. I saw them as being more deformed than my face, but not as deformed as my depraved soul.

I quickly put my gloves on, not to protect myself from the crisp air, but to protect myself from any further visual reminder of my past and all the evil *those hands* had done. What happened to *those hands* that at one time knew nothing but good, that created nothing but beauty, whether it was music or a magnificent building? What happened to that child that they belonged to, the child that had so much potential, that child that Celeste still saw in me? What happened to that small innocent child?

Seventeen

When I entered my room in the inn, there was a stream of light coming from a lone gas lamp outside my window. I leaned back against the door and listened to it click as it closed. It was extremely still on the second floor, with nearly everyone in the inn downstairs having a nice meal with a friend or perhaps a lover.

I listened to nothing but my own breathing as I watched that stream of light filter through the thin lace curtains. My leg burned from my ankle to my waist, but the pain that drove me was the pain in my heart, and it was that pain that I needed release from the most.

So I grabbed my vial of morphine, the only power strong enough to remove my torment. I sat on the edge of the bed near the beam of light and tried to fill the syringe. But I was so weak and my hands were shaking so badly that it slipped from my fingers and fell to the floor at my feet. In the process of reaching for them, my spread fingers passed through the ray of light and then they stopped in mid-motion.

My hands were trembling, so I tried to steady them by clenching my fist several times, but each time I opened them and reached again, the tremors returned. I sat there, looking down at my hand, along with my father's gold band, and the syringe just beyond on the floor. I blinked several times as I realized just what I was about to do to myself. I was seeking escape from my emotional pain in a way that I swore I'd never do again.

The last time I tried that type of release, I nearly killed by best friend; what would I be capable of doing this time, with my enemy more than likely just downstairs? That action only intensified my abhorrence of myself, so I slowly got to my feet and backed away without moving my eyes from my supposed helper, lying so innocently on the braided rug.

No escaped my lips as I stared in the silent darkness. I ground my teeth and told myself that, if I was going to take any drug as an escape from my pain, it would be a large enough dose to do it completely. That way, I'd never suffer again, and I'd never be able to create suffering for others ever again. I felt my breaths as they started coming faster and faster, and then I screamed and charged at the defenseless syringe and bottle. Stomping on them repeatedly, I continued to cry out and growl until there was nothing left but shattered pieces of glass sparkling in the lamplight.

Once there were only fractured pieces of my soul left to take back to Paris with me, I grabbed my violin and left. I looked at no one as I limped quickly through the dining room, not caring if Christine and Raoul were there or not. I couldn't sit in the same train car with them; in fact, I couldn't sit in a car with anyone. So I found one filled with cartons of something—I didn't know or care what. I located somewhere to lie down and that's where I stayed the entire ride.

With the winter air flowing through many holes and cracks in the car's walls, I was cold, but I didn't care. What difference did it make if I was cold? I felt it was my punishment for having such a frigid heart.

Once back in Paris, I slithered against the walls and among the shadows as I made my way toward my hole in the ground. I didn't take a brougham; instead, I made myself walk, regardless of the pain in my leg and regardless of the snow falling around me. I was punishing myself severely. I hurt all over, not only physically but more so emotionally. I hurt all over inside and out.

I pushed my little boat hard through the dark mist leading to my self-made prison, which was then like a tropical paradise in comparison to the horrors contained in the dungeon of my soul. Once in my home, I took off my cloak and emptied my pockets of what was left of the medical supplies and my mother's locket.

My poor mother. My poor unhappy mother. Just another casualty in the growing list of souls that have been left damaged or dead in my malignant wake. How many more will there be? How many more will I send to their final resting place before someone stops me and sends me to mine? Perhaps I'd already met the man who could halt my attempts to rid the planet of its inhabitants. Perhaps it was Raoul who had enough courage and enough reason to prevent me from further harm.

I slumped down in a chair and buried my face in my hands, almost enjoying the surges of pain as they shot through my body. I raised my head from my hands and looked at my piano, wanting and needing to play, but that would also be an escape from my torment, so I deprived myself of that as well.

I forced myself to remember all my crimes against humanity until I didn't care about anything anymore. Then I grabbed a bottle of brandy and a glass and headed for the divan where I lay back with a full glass in hand. As I felt the warmth of the first swallow move through my chest, I stared at the mural on the wall and thought about Christine. I knew I would never see her or talk to her again; I would make sure of that. I was releasing her right then to have a normal life, one that Raoul could give her.

I knew she would be in distress as she waited for her angel to return to her, but she would get over it, I reasoned. And with Raoul's help, I didn't think it would take too long—not nearly as long as it would take her to get over her emotional suffering if she were to come to know the real me. So I let her go. I let Christine go. I let my angel go. I let go.

With the glass of brandy in my hand and the pain in my chest mounting with every breath I took, I let her go. I let her slip away as I slipped into a period of deep despair that rivaled any other time in my life. I took a large swallow of my brandy and made myself face the truth about myself and what I'd done with my life.

Celeste's words and looks of sweetness haunted my every thought, and the only positive thought that mixed in with the horrible truth was that she didn't know who her boyish Erik really was. She was blissful with the lie I presented of myself, and that was a blessing. A dashing young man she called me, and Raoul's words for me were a diabolical and selfish man—what a contrast in perceptions.

I wished I could be what Celeste saw in me, but the truth was that Raoul, even though he'd never met me, was closer to the truth about my true nature. Christine was so beautiful and innocent. Raoul was right. She deserved so much more than my deformed body, mind, and heart.

The first glass of brandy went down smoothly and so did the second. After the third one, I no longer bothered with the glass and began drinking straight from the bottle. My eyes became heavy, and I fell asleep. When I woke, the bottle was empty so I headed for another. Time was irrelevant and no longer marked by the movement of the hands on my clocks but by the number of bottles sitting on the table or floor in front of me.

I didn't know how much time was passing and I didn't care. I slipped in and out of consciousness and would wake in a different place around my shrouded castle—my bed, my bathroom floor, with my head down on my dining table, in my boat, under my piano, on the floor by my organ, in my mirror chamber, or in the passage leading to the third cellar. Those are the places I could remember, but I'm sure there were many more locations that I didn't remember.

The only thing consistent about that time was my return to the cupboard and another bottle. I had periodic encounters with my temper as I slammed my fist into some unsuspecting object in my home or wiped the coffee table clean, sending the collection of bottles across the room.

To sleep on and on is all I wanted. I didn't want to think anymore. I didn't want to live anymore, but I was too much of a coward to deliberately end it all. Perhaps if I drank enough, I'd fall asleep and never wake up, I remember thinking. Then the inevitable happened. On one trip to the pantry, I found it empty. Needless to say, I wasn't steady on my feet as I headed for the trap door in the mirror chamber that would lead me to my wine cellar, and the only friend I had right then, another bottle.

My trusty and skilled fingers weren't working well, and it seemed to take a long time to work the spring that released the door, but, once done, I headed down the stairs to my collection of fine wines. My head was spinning, and my legs felt as if each had an anchor attached, which caused me to trip and fall halfway down the wood steps. I hit my head and shoulder hard enough to make me cry out. Then, as I lay there looking up at the faint light coming from the trap door above me, it faded and went out.

I woke, at first not knowing where I was or how long I'd been there. In fact, I had no idea how long I'd been drinking and again I didn't care. But I'd sobered enough for tears to begin forming when my thoughts turned to Christine and my love for her. I repeated her beautiful name over and over as the damp and cold began registering on my unstable senses.

I lay there in the cold cellar, trying to gain some mastery over my tormented mind. What was I doing? I evidently hadn't drunk enough to kill myself, and, within the confusion and haze, I felt an overpowering need to find Christine. I could hear her calling me in the darkness, and I saw her face in tears when I wouldn't answer her pleas to her angel. I saw her pacing in her room and twisting that ribbon on her robe, and I felt horrible. Even while trying to set her free, I was hurting her.

I wondered how long it had been since we returned from Perros, and I wondered if Raoul was successful in his attempts to convince her that I was a disturbed man and not her beautiful Angel of Music. The vision of her standing on her tiptoes and placing that sweet kiss on his waiting lips swam repeatedly through my thoughts. I rolled over on the damp ground, and my senses picked up the smell of the gunpowder surrounding me, again, only adding to the realization of what a demon I was.

I managed to get to my feet, while the barrels of gunpowder and the rows and rows of wine bottles spun around me. I filled my arms with as many bottles as I could hold and headed back up the stairs. Surprisingly, I still had two of them in my hands when I reached the top, while the rest lay broken in the dirt where I'd been lying.

I sat on the sofa and placed the nice, new, full bottles of my comfort on the table beside the empty ones that had numbed me for I didn't know how long. Opening one, I started drinking again. Then I sat there, blinking and trying to focus on the tall clock in the corner. I failed, so my fingers started a clumsy search for my watch, but, once I found it and held it to my ear, it was silent.

"I killed it," I mumbled.

All my timepieces had stopped, and I wondered how many more bottles it would take before time would stop for me. Time? What time was it? I needed to know what time it was, although I didn't know why. I lay down on the divan, and, along with the room swirling around my head, I heard Christine calling for her angel. I needed to know what time it was. I needed to know what day it was.

I staggered to my feet, grabbed my cloak, and headed for my boat, while my hopes that enough liquor would stop my thoughts vanished. I started pushing the pole and moving through the water while looking at the empty seat. Then I envisioned Christine's beautiful form sitting there, as I'd planned. I could hear her angelic voice speak to me, but I was sober enough to know it was only a vision, a painful vision.

The darkness of the lake closed in around me with a deafening quiet, much too quiet. I tried to put Christine's voice back in my head to fill the void, but it was gone, just as she was. Silence. Only silence and solitude surrounded me. I raised my head and screamed as loud and as long as I could toward the cold stone columns and arches surrounding me. I stumbled and fell to the bottom of my boat, crying into my hands.

I eventually made it back to my feet, disorientated, with the same looming columns and swirling gray mist everywhere I looked. I gazed around, not knowing which way to go. As I turned and turned, the lake began to spin around me, and I staggered again, falling into the water.

The weight of my cloak pulled me down and down, and I lost track of which way was up. I had no strength, and my head started pounding. Then I saw the faint light coming from my boat's lantern, but I couldn't fight against the weight holding me captive. Why was I trying to save my life when I really wanted to die and let it all be over? Just take a deep breath and it will all be over, I remember thinking. Why was I fighting? Why?

Somewhere in the middle of my physical and mental struggles, I had the presence of mind to release my cloak's clasp. Once done, I was free from my anchor, but I still couldn't make any progress to the top. My lungs were beginning to burn when I removed my shoes. Then I saw the lantern's light slowly getting closer.

I could see the bottom of the boat above me, and I pushed off my lungs' desperate desire to expand. Why I didn't give into them and let them have their way, I don't know. Why did I struggle for my life? Why, when I wanted to die? I couldn't answer those questions then, and, to this day, I still can't. None of it made any sense.

I reached for the light from my boat just as my lungs took over and I gasped for air only to receive water into them, lots of it. I came up out of the water and gasped and coughed over and over, trying to stay afloat. I sank again, and again I struggled to reach the light. Once more I came out of the water, and again coughed and choked. Finally, my fingers grasped the edge of my boat.

With hardly any strength left in me, I used my boat to stay afloat until I could make it to the wharf. Somehow I made it, and, after I climbed up, I lay in a pile of wet clothes with my lungs burning. I must have lost consciousness, because I woke shivering uncontrollably. I staggered to my feet, trying to maintain my balance, but I wasn't sober enough for that feat. So, as I reached for a pillar, I fell, one more time, into the lake.

I grabbed the pillar and eventually made it to dry land, completely disorientated. I sat on the wharf until I had my bearing and again began my quest to find out what day it was. I somehow managed to make my way to the street through the back entrance and metal gate. It was a wonder I made it that far, considering I wasn't sober enough to know I was without that one piece of clothing that I was never without—my mask.

Once on the street, lit by street lamps, I leaned back against the side of the building, searching for the right direction to go where I could find a newspaper and the date. I started to cross the street, but I was nearly run over by a carriage, which sent me to the melted snow and slush in the gutter. As my left side slammed into the brick road, I felt the pain in my thigh and hip for the first time. I raised my head out of the freezing slush, trying to focus, when I caught sight of Christine being helped out of a carriage and into the side entrance of the opera house.

"Christine," I whispered. "Christine."

I got on my hands and knees and looked again at the entrance where she'd disappeared, but then, there she was once more, getting out of another carriage and again entering the opera house with yet another man at her arm. As my confusion continued to get in the way of my thoughts, I could feel my anger start to build.

I stood up and leaned in the recess of a doorway, shivering and trying to breathe and gain mastery over my thinking. Then, in the distance, I heard a woman's happy voice call my name, and I jumped. I tried to think, but my mind was being slowed down by the contents of many bottles.

Who knows my name? Certainly no woman in Paris. Again, it called, Erik, and again I jumped. I peeked around the corner just in time to see a blonde woman standing under a street lamp with outstretched arms. Celeste, I wondered, as I wiped my blurry eyes. Celeste? I felt a frown form on my brow when a tall man filled her waiting arms and they embraced.

He was clad in evening attire, with top hat included, and had just stepped out of the side door of the opera house. I wiped my eyes again and strained to see them as they stepped up into a waiting carriage. I slipped back into the darkness and watched as they passed by me, with their gay voices filling the night air around their carriage. It wasn't Celeste. It was another woman, calling her lover who just happened to have my name. Her lover who had my name but not my face and, I'm sure, not my past and not my heart.

I leaned my head back against the door and closed my eyes, thinking. Her lover had nothing more than me, except for a pretty face, a pretty face that wouldn't stay pretty forever. Raoul had a pretty face, but it wouldn't always be that way. Why? Of what use is a pretty face? It doesn't serve any useful purpose except something to look at. Why? Why do women always have to go for the pretty faces? I was sure I had everything else just like him to make a woman happy. Christine, why do you want a pretty face? I have everything else.

I watched as yet another happy couple walked by me. Why? I continued to question. I have all the same parts. Why? Another couple approached, and I stepped out in front of them.

"Why?" I asked.

As the woman shrieked and covered her open mouth with her gloved hand, the man spread his arms out from his sides and moved the lady behind him.

"Why?" I asked, as I also spread my arms out from my sides. "Why not me? I have all the necessary parts to make you happy." I looked beyond him and toward the lady. "I have hands and fingers to caress your flesh and make you tremble."

I stepped forward and the man spread his open hand against my chest, his voice saying something. I didn't even acknowledge his presence and continued to push forward.

"I have arms to embrace you and make you feel warm and safe. I have legs to walk beside you and carry you over the threshold. I have a mind to compose for you great masterpieces and simple love songs. I have lips to speak sweet nothings in your ears and to kiss you tenderly." I turned in a clumsy circle. "Look! I have all the rest of the necessary parts to make you blissful and to give you children."

With that last comment, I felt his fist land against my jaw and lips, sending me to the ground. My world was spinning as they walked away, and then the unmistakable taste of blood filled my mouth. I was shivering badly, and my painful cheek pressed against the cold walkway, while other couples passed by me as if I didn't exist.

I tried to lift myself up, needing several attempts to achieve an otherwise simple task. I managed to reach a lamppost, and then made my way back to the dark doorway. I looked in the direction that the couple had gone in and still questioned why. What is a pretty face? It serves no useful purpose.

Completely forgetting the reason why I was on the street in the first place, I looked in the other direction toward the side entrance to the opera house. Then there she was again, Christine, in her beautiful blue gown and jewels. I took a deep breath, thinking, she must be performing tonight and I won't be there. I must get there. She needs me. But then I felt I couldn't be there and I didn't know why. My confusion was tearing me up, and I buried my face in my hands.

It was only then that I realized I was without my mask. I had a full beard, but no mask. I gasped at my own horror, and, with my hands covering my face, I turned into the corner of the door, crouching in its protection like a deranged patient in a mental ward.

I felt miserable, cold, and frightened. I could smell myself, and I smelled repugnant. I hadn't bathed in I didn't know how long, perhaps a week or more, and I was drunk. I could then add to my list of accomplishments: a drunk, a sloppy, disgusting drunk.

"Christine," I whispered. "What have I done?"

Her perfect face kept swimming around me. I raised my head to the stars in the ebony sky and begged, "Oh, dear God, if you're there, just strike me down and be done with it. If there's any mercy in you at all, you'll end this nightmare right here and now."

I sank the rest of the way down to the step and lowered my head to my knees. I was soaking wet, cold, and shivering. The automatic reaction of years gone by was to reach for my cloak to pull it closer to me. But, since I'd forgotten that it then lay at the bottom of the lake, my attempt for any warmth was unsuccessful.

I heard another happy couple walk past me, without even noticing the dejected man hunched in pain in the doorway. I tried to get to my feet, and then I hung onto the wall as I made my way back to my home through the gate. The gate and trees beyond it swayed and blurred together, and I was so cold.

I stayed, leaning against the gate, with my own words circling around my head. "Why does it have to be pretty?" I spread my outstretched fingers over my face. "Why does it have to be pretty?" I stumbled down the walk, seeking refuge in my shrouded castle, until I finally landed in the bushes where I stayed. "Why does it have to be pretty?" My last thoughts were about the pain in my head and my entire left side.

The morning sun and voices woke me, and I opened my eyes to find several people staring through the wrought iron gate toward me. When I rose up and looked at them, they backed away and gasped. I instinctively reached for the mask on my face, forgetting I was without it. I might as well have been naked.

I heard someone say, "Should we get the police?"

Those words gave me the incentive to get to my feet and limp toward the back entrance, falling several times in the process. I at last reached the wharf and lowered myself into my boat. Then, as quickly as I could under the circumstances, I headed back toward my prison alone. I felt dejected, in pain and sorrow, and in a much worse condition than I had been upon returning from Perros.

I turned up the light and collapsed on the divan, still shivering, and I stayed there in my damp clothes for I don't know how long. I still didn't know what time or what day it was, but I did know something for sure; I was sick and it wasn't just emotional.

I felt that familiar burn in my chest, and I knew my lungs were sick. My first thought was to head for my medicine, but then the second thought was to let the illness take its course until I took my last breath. I vacillated between the two until I became angry at myself for my lack of fortitude. I couldn't even make a simple decision between life and death. I rebuked myself, calling myself a coward. Either do something to end your miserable existence or change it, I told myself after throwing a few of my prized possessions across the room. Fortunately, when I slammed my fists against the ebony boxes on my mantel, they held fast, so, at least, I didn't bring down the opera house that day.

I headed for the bath and my medicine. After taking the proper dose, I stripped my wet and stinking clothes off. In so doing, I realized the odor I'd smelled wasn't coming from my dirty and wet clothes; it was coming from the wound in my leg. I sat on the edge of the tub, staring at my leg in disbelief. I actually had to cover what would have been my nose in an effort to filter out the stench. It was horrible. It smelled like death.

It was the same smell that emanated from a carcass lying in the woods. My leg was rotting off right before my eyes. The entire area where it had broken open in Perros was black and seeping reddish-yellow fluid. I might not have been thinking clearly as of late, but with that sight I knew I was in serious trouble.

I went back to the parlor and managed to find a bottle that had a small amount of brandy still in it. Back in my bath, I poured it over the area, and then, surprisingly, it didn't hurt. Obviously it wouldn't hurt, I finally realized, because I'd killed it. I was managing to kill myself one bit at a time. I felt as if my back was against a wall and all I needed was a blindfold before being shot. Either from my own neglect and hands, or by my lungs or my leg, I was definitely facing death.

Eighteen

It took me looking death right in the face before I knew I didn't want to die, not yet. There were still things I wanted to do with my life, and, as long as I could keep myself from degenerating into self-pity and its accompanying depression, I could still accomplish anything I wanted.

Knowing what I needed to do, I shaved, sank into a warm bath, dressed my wound, got dressed, including a mask, and then I was back in my boat crossing the lake. I caught the first brougham I found and gave the driver the doctor's address. I was finally in control of my senses, so at least I was stable emotionally, but, physically, I was probably at one of my worst times.

I was feverish and nauseated, my head was throbbing, and I was in pain from both my lungs and my entire leg, as well as my right shoulder. I'd never been in so much pain, not when I'd been beaten, not with my worst lung infection in Persia, and not when I was stabbed. My leg literally felt as if it was in a fire and to move it even a little was excruciating. Even when it wasn't bearing weight, the pain was incredible. I honestly didn't know how I'd gotten to the brougham.

On the ride there, I thought about what I'd put myself through, and I really wished there was some way I could stop myself from being so self-destructive. I didn't know why I did it, and it made me quite angry, especially since I knew I was going to pay dearly for my last bout.

By the time we stopped and the driver opened my door, I knew I had as much right to be on this earth as the next man. I'd relived the encounters with Raoul and Christine in Perros, and I had just as much right to fight for her as he did. I couldn't change the past, but I'd been trying to live a relatively sane life, and, more importantly, I could have full control over my future, now that I wanted one.

I rationalized that, since Raoul believed me to be a real man of flesh and blood, so would Christine in time. I had to find a way to win her over before Raoul ruined everything. I had to let her see that I was a man. I realized then, more than ever, that I couldn't win her over the slow way or from behind the mirror. I didn't have enough time with Raoul in the way.

The temptation to get him out of my way permanently was a big one, but, if I wanted Christine to love me, I couldn't expect her to love a murderer, especially the murderer of someone she cared about. In addition, I couldn't live with myself if I became that person again. I had to find a way for her to see the person I was inside. Celeste thought me to be dashing; perhaps Christine would also if she could see me without fear.

While contemplating how to win Christine over, I remembered my father's words; *Give them a chance to see who you are, and they will love you. Give them a chance.*

Somehow, I found myself sitting in the doctor's office, waiting while he finished with another patient. I was kept waiting so long that under different circumstances I would have left. But there was no strength left in me, and, for one of the few times in my life, I was truly concerned for my life.

When the doctor entered the waiting room with a young woman and her daughter, he looked at them with such compassion that it calmed my agitated spirit for his keeping me waiting so long. It was that quality in him that I eventually appreciated, the quality of caring, not about the strict rules of his over protective nurse and secretary, but for his patients. They came first to him, and, at that moment, that quality was what I was counting on.

He looked at me first with a frown, and then one eyebrow went up when he spoke harshly to me. "You promised, Erik. Your one day has turned into ten. Is this how you keep all your promises?"

I took his remark without commenting. At least it told me what day it was and how long I'd left Christine alone with Raoul. I tried to get to my feet, grimacing and faltering as I applied weight on my leg. His angry frown instantly turned into concern, and he quickly helped me support my weight, while barking orders at his nurse. He helped me into a room where I was told to lie down, and then he started his examination of what was left of me.

He first felt my head and wrist, but, when he heard me struggling to breathe, my lungs then got his attention. His face showed the degree of his concentration when he placed his stethoscope on my chest and back. Then he looked sternly at me.

"Why didn't you come back, Erik?"

I couldn't answer, so I closed my eyes and turned my face away, but he promptly turned my face back.

"I have to remove your mask, Erik."

I didn't answer. I felt too bad to care.

His fingers started searching my face, and, when he reached the left side of my jaw, I pulled away in pain. He moved my face back where he wanted it and continued his search. He was frowning the entire time, and, periodically, his eyes glanced at mine.

"You look as though you've been in a horrible fight, Erik."

I closed my eyes without answering, and he turned my head and parted my hair, looking through it like a monkey grooming another monkey in a tree.

"That's a nasty gash you have there. I'll have to stitch that up."

Again, I didn't answer as he continued to probe me. When he began applying pressure to my right shoulder, I once more moaned and pulled away, but that only made him examine it closer. Once he had my shirt laid open and saw the bruising around my shoulder and across my ribs, he looked me in the eyes and shook his head.

"I certainly hope you got at least one good punch in, Erik."

I once more closed my eyes and turned my face away, not wanting to tell him that I'd done it to myself.

He sighed and said, "You have a high fever, and I'm almost afraid to look at your leg."

But he did anyway, and, as my trousers came down, the concern in his eyes increased a hundredfold. When he gently pulled the bandage off, he took a deep breath and actually coughed because of the stench. His nurse had to turn away, and she gladly left the room when he told her to get certain items for him.

"Erik, I can't believe this. What have you done to yourself? Why didn't you come back?"

"It's a very long story, Doctor Leglise, and I don't wish to bother you with it."

"Well, you're going to be here for quite a while, Erik, so you might as well start talking."

I narrowed my eyes and frowned at him. "What do you mean—quite a while?"

"This is very serious and I mean *very* serious," he responded while giving me a sideways glare.

Not certain I wanted to know the answer, I asked almost under my breath, "How serious?"

"Well, to put it in a few words, your leg is rotting off."

Over the last few weeks of working with him on my nose, I knew he had a good sense of humor, but, as I searched his eyes for it, it was nowhere to be found. He was dead serious. The nurse came back in with a tray of medical supplies, but she didn't come too close, and she didn't look at my leg or me.

He began probing around in my wound, and I gripped the table and clamped my teeth together. He took a deep breath, laid the instrument down, and backed against the wall, staring at my leg. He rubbed his jaw and took another deep breath. Then he looked me in the eyes. His nurse, while holding her hand over her nose and mouth, asked if she could be excused, and he granted her that request with a hand gesture.

I became impatient and almost snarled at him. "Well, are you going to stand there holding up the wall or do you intend to help me out here?"

Looking at the wound and rubbing his jaw one more time, he sighed. "Well, Erik, we have two choices. I'll assume you know you have a serious wound here. You may not have a nose but you still have the sense of smell and that alone should tell you the serious situation we're facing.

"I can operate and take out a section of your leg, hoping I can reach all the decay. But, if I do, there's a chance I'll have to go too deep, and there could be nerve damage and you could lose some mobility in that leg. That's if I'm able to get all the dead tissue out, and, if not, it will continue to spread and we'll be back at square one."

I frowned at that prospect, knowing he wasn't joking with me. "Is it really that serious?"

"Yes, Erik. That muscle is actually rotting away, and, if it isn't stopped, you won't last much longer, neither you nor your leg. The infection has obviously started to spread through your body, that's why you have the fever. So, whatever you decide you want me to do, we have to do it quickly."

I thought a moment and then asked, "You said there were two options. What's the other one?"

"It's rather unconventional, but I've had good success with it before. Instead of cutting out the dead tissue, I could implant a colony of live maggots into the wound."

"What!" I couldn't help exclaiming, while trying to rise up.

"I know it sounds repulsive," he started to explain, "but they do a good job. That's their sole purpose in life, to eat rotting tissue, but it's usually that of a dead animal. Although they don't know the difference between the dead tissue in your leg and a dead squirrel lying in the forest. It doesn't make any difference to them.

"And the advantage of using maggots is that they'll usually only eat the rotting tissue and will leave the healthy tissue alone. They can get into spaces and clean out your wound in a way that I can't. Unless there's a nerve that's had its covering infected, they won't eat it and it won't be damaged."

description
headernavigation184	Theodora Bruns

I pictured maggots crawling inside me, and I closed my eyes tightly and shivered.

"What are you thinking, Erik?"

I shook my head slowly. "I'm not usually squeamish about such things. I've had occasions to witness their work during my travels, but the thought of them performing their skills within me I . . . . My stomach has been sick for days, but, right now, that thought I simply can't fathom."

I shivered again, and while he laid a blanket over me, he said, "Let me tell you a true story. There was a miner who got trapped when the mine collapsed. He had a beam across his legs and couldn't move. He was alone with only one water canteen. He was in pain, but he had no idea what was happening to one of his legs as he lay there.

"It was almost two weeks before he was dug out. After being taken to the hospital, the doctors found a large wound on his leg, perhaps like yours, but there was no sign of any infection and it was partially healed. He was badly dehydrated, but he didn't have any sign of infection, which he should have had. When they examined his leg closely, they found, along with the healthy pink tissue, maggots—lots of them.

"I can imagine they were just as repulsed as you are, but, when he walked out of the hospital two days later, they attributed the saving of his leg and his life to those hard-working, repulsive workers." He laid his hand on my shoulder. "If it were my leg, Erik, I'd go with the maggots."

While that story was interesting, I wasn't ready to consent to such a procedure just yet, so I questioned him further. "Are those my only choices?"

He rubbed his jaw again and looked under the blanket at the wound again. Then he looked into my eyes before he gave me an answer.

"Well, we could amputate the entire leg. That's always an option."

"What!" I again exclaimed.

"It's your choice, Erik, but we shouldn't wait too long."

"What's too long?" I sighed, thinking of all I needed to do for Christine.

He looked at his watch and then back at me. "Oh, about two minutes."

I turned my face toward the wall and thought over my options. "How long would the . . . they take?"

"They're pretty fast, but it depends on how much of your leg is diseased. If I were to take a guess, I would say probably no more than three or four days—five days tops."

The thought was absolutely revolting, but it was better than losing the use of my leg. It was at that time, when I thought about the possibility of losing the use or even the partial use of one of them, that I realized how much I depended on them. How would I get up and down all those stairs or ride a horse?

With those thoughts in my mind, I answered, "Very well, what do I need to do?"

He patted my arm. "You don't have to do anything other than stay here and rest. I'll do what's needed. Well, the maggots and I, that is."

I watched him as he started to cross the room. "You expect me to stay here? For how long?"

Then I saw the sense of humor I was used to start to return. "Until they're finished with their meal. It would be impolite to disturb them before that time."

The thought of lying there for up to five days was impossible, so I shook my head slowly, "I can't do that. Why do I have to stay here? Will they refuse to eat unless they're in your company?"

He squeezed my arm and chuckled. "No, Erik, it's not that. You need to be immobile and the wound needs to stay open. In addition, I would need to monitor their progress closely. You can't be wandering around with the little critters crawling in and out of your leg. They might escape or get lost."

His sense of humor might have been up and working, but I wasn't in the mood. The thought of it taking that long was worse news than the seriousness of the wound and the medical procedure combined.

"I can't stay here that long. There has to be another way."

His humor walked out of the door instantly. "Erik! You're in this serious situation because you refused to listen to my advice. You said you didn't have time to take care of yourself properly, and look what happened. Well, you only have one place to go from here. If this isn't taken care of *right now*, your next stop will be a pine box, and I dare say you'll have plenty of time then. Do you want that?

"You need to listen to my recommendations and respect them for what they are. You came to me for some reason, and I can only presume it's because you felt you needed my help. Well, I'm trying to give it to you. You can't expect me to create miracles or work with my hands tied behind my back. You have to listen to me. You need to stay here and let me take care of you."

I took a deep breath and started to get up, causing him to push against my chest with his palm. Not wanting to break the wrist of the man I expected to help me, I gave into him.

"What's so important on the other side of that door that can't wait for three, or even four days?"

I pushed my head back against the pillow and rubbed my fingertips against my forehead. I think I even whined. I looked out of the window at the tree and the pink blossoms falling with the gentlest touch of the breeze. Another season was beginning with new life as its prospect, just as it did every year. The decision I made right then would mean the beginning of a new life for me or the end of it. Could I take a chance of waiting any longer to capture Christine's heart?

I turned my sight back to his waiting eyes. "I respect you, Doctor Leglise, and that's the only reason I came back to you. You're one of the few people in my life that I've allowed to see the reason for my mask. My mask," I repeated with a slight sigh. "You know, I can't remember being without one. As far back as I can remember, a mask was an essential part of my wardrobe. And, believe me, my memory goes way back. I put it on with regularity, just as I would my shirt or any other piece of clothing. Even when I was a small child, I wore the mask."

I took a deep breath and looked again at the pink tree. "I left my home when I was ten. Then I spent the next fifteen years trying to avoid those who either wanted to make a profit off of what was under my mask or wanted to end my life because of it. Then, at the age of twenty-five, something happen to me that I never dreamt would happen. I found a wonderful girl who didn't care what was behind my mask. She looked in my eyes with the same love, whether I had the mask on or off."

I nodded to the gold band on his finger. "You know what it's like to have someone look in your eyes with that special look of love. It's the most wonderful feeling, don't you agree?"

He nodded and I asked, "Do you have children?"

"Yes. Three boys and one girl," he replied softly.

I nodded and went on. "For the first time in my life I had a hope of having children. I don't expect you to understand how that made me feel. You, more than likely, always knew that someday you'd marry and have children, but I never did. I'd reconciled myself to the prospect of never marrying or having children of my own. Then that special girl appeared without warning and changed my world completely.

"But then someone with good intentions talked me into waiting just four days. He said, that's not long, only four days before I could take her for my wife and start a life that I'd never dreamt possible. I respected that man very much and, because of that, I agreed to wait the four days."

With another sigh, I closed my eyes and then looked at the ceiling. "Another man who I dearly respected once told me that you never know what tomorrow will bring, and, in that case, he was so right. Because I never suspected what awaited me at the end of those four days. By then, she was gone from me, she was stolen, I was robbed, and my world was turned upside down. That event changed me into something unimaginable, something I hated.

"That was twenty years ago, and I gave up. No, it wasn't that I gave up because I never gave another thought to ever finding anyone else like her again. For me, the chance of ever finding even one person who could look behind my mask without repulsion was almost impossible, so the chance of ever finding another one would be completely impossible, as far as I was concerned."

I returned my sight to his eyes that were fixed on mine. "Then almost three months ago, there she was. I began to think maybe—just maybe—I might have another chance at love. I've been working with that goal in mind since then. I'm only one step away from finding out if she could be the one. And I've been one step away for several weeks now, while I put that day off for one reason or another.

"I don't know what tomorrow will bring. I could get hit by a runaway brougham, I could fall down a flight of stairs and break my neck, or the next person who wants to end my life could be a better marksman."

I placed my hand over the scar from my knife wound. "I've escaped death more times than I care to remember, and, from what you say, there's a chance I may not outrun it this time." I took another deep breath, closed my eyes, swallowed hard, and then I looked him directly in his eyes again.

"Doctor Leglise, I'm a forty-five year old man who has never been kissed, not even on the cheek by my mother. Never, Doctor, never. I don't even know what it feels like. I don't know where I'll be tomorrow, and I don't know where I'll be in four days. I realize your words are well intended, and so were my friend's twenty years ago, but I can't wait four days. I can't put this off any longer."

His eyes were telling me how much he felt for my plight, so I put the life I wanted with Christine in his hands with my next plea and a smile.

"There has to be a way for me to let your little creatures work, while I continue with my plans to find someone to love me. I'll be nice to them, I promise. I won't hurt them. You have to help me find a way."

He was silently watching me by the time I finished my desperate dissertation. Then he slowly removed his hand from my chest, where it had been lying the entire time, and then sat in the chair next to my bed. After a few seconds of thought, he nodded and told me his ideas.

"You have to agree to stay here at least for the rest of this day. I'll need that time to begin the procedure. I'll see to it that you get home today. But I'll need you to come back every day so I can monitor your progress, or, should I say, *their* progress. Other than that, I only ask that you keep your leg dry and stay off your feet as much possible."

He opened an armoire and took out an ebony walking stick. "Before you leave, I'll show you how to make the best use of this." He paused a moment and looked at the row of medical books on his bookshelf. "I can't treat the area with as strong a medicine as I normally would. It might kill our hungry friends, so you need to take it under your tongue. It's bitter and might sting, but a small amount of wine will take care of that. Will you agree to that?"

I nodded. "Yes, but one other thing." I started, even though I was afraid to. "My lungs—how did they sound to you?"

He came back to me and listened again. "They're tight, but I don't hear any fluid in them. I might have something for them in the other room."

"I already have something for them. I just wanted to know how bad they were."

"Then you've had this problem before?"

Again I nodded. "The first time was when I was five. I nearly died then. I've had recurrences since then—again almost dying."

He shook his head. "It's a wonder you're still alive." I halfway chuckled, and he asked, "Do you do something special when you get a lung infection?"

I told him what I normally did, and he had his secretary go out and buy what I needed, including the hard-to-find shark liver oil, while he began the procedure on my leg. When she returned, she made enough tea to keep me going for a few days. He'd never heard of that particular treatment for lung infections, and he was glad to have the information for future use.

He really did everything he could to help me with my unusual dilemma, not only with the wound but more importantly with my timeline to find someone to love me. He gave me morphine for the pain and instructed me in how to administer it to myself. He wanted me to get proper rest, and the morphine would help in that regard as well as with the pain. I thanked him, without telling him I was an expert in the use of morphine.

I took the drug from him, knowing I would use it in the right way that time, not only to help me sleep, as he suggested, but as insurance against any further harm I could cause others. I would use it to end my life if I felt I was getting out of control and was a threat to anyone else. I would use the morphine instead of a knife across my wrist or a bullet in my brain. Just like my lassos, it would be silent and spill no blood.

As I rode in the brougham back to my home and listened to the comforting clip clop of the horse's hooves on the bricks, I pulled the bottle of morphine from my pocket and held it in my open hand. I gazed at that small bottle, that small bottle of liquid that held a power that I could either control or it could control me.

I believe the amount the doctor had already given me was helping with the pain and making my mind, for the first time in weeks, work properly. So, at that moment, I felt I'd have the strength to use it the way it was intended. The doctor was right, I needed rest if I were to live long enough to see my plans for Christine come to fruition, so I would use it for that and for the pain only.

After that, I would put it where I could get to it if the day came when I would need it for the final time. What I was preparing for was going to be my last try at a normal life, a life I could spend in splendor with Christine. If it didn't work and I botched the job again, then I had to rely on myself to end it. If I couldn't rely on a merciful God to end it for me, then I had to close the curtain on my final scene myself.

I rolled the bottle back and forth across my palm, first in the lamplight and then in the darkness as the light came and went with each passing lamppost. Just like the light, my thoughts came and went, words and pictures, taking their turn wandering through my memories. Papa's words along with Christine's, Celeste's, Oded's, and Raoul's. Pictures of the first house I worked on with my father in Perros and then the palace in Persia; pictures of Christine's face on the other side of the mirror and on the stage. I heard her words of defense for her angel, which had given her courage to work through her pain and fears. I heard Oded's words of encouragement to me right before we left Persia. I heard my father's words to not give up on my goals, along with his words that I couldn't turn back the clock but I could reset it. But would it be possible to undo all that I'd done?

I could do nothing to change the murders I'd committed in Russia, and I could do nothing to change the horrors of Persia, but I could try to control my future. Even though I'd been inebriated to the nth degree the night before, what I'd said to that couple on the street was true. I did have everything it would take to make Christine happy.

In addition to having all the right fingers and limbs, I had something that I didn't think anyone else possessed. Most importantly, I had a heart that was full of incredible love and devotion for only her. A heart I'd never shared with another, and I knew that I would never share with anyone other than her.

But the question remained, could I reset my clock and start again with Christine? I didn't know, but I knew I had to try.

Nineteen

The night passed calmly, with even my night visitors resting peacefully, which was surprising, considering what I'd put myself through and what was crawling around inside my leg. As I lay there in the darkness, I was also surprised that I felt no pain in my leg. Carefully stretching and rolling onto my side, I reached up for my light and then my watch. I was thinking perhaps a night hadn't passed and I was still under the strong influence of the morphine.

Once my watch opened, it told me it was ten o'clock, so I'd either slept fourteen hours or only two. In either case, I was wide-awake, so I threw back the covers and carefully swung my legs off the bed. There was still no pain, and I remember smiling with the prospect of going through my busy day without it. I raised myself up on my feet gingerly, and I was still all right, so I took my first step.

That ended my euphoric thoughts. The pain shot through my thigh and down my leg, as if I'd been sideswiped by a guillotine. I went to the floor on my knees, causing another surge of pain. I then went the rest of the way to the floor, rocking and moaning in agony. What I was experiencing then, and the day before, was much worse than the original gunshot, and I was beginning to think the doctor was going to have his way in the end, and I would end up in his office for the next few days.

With the amount of suffering I was going through right then, I didn't see how I was going to accomplish anything that day, but I had to. By the time the pain subsided enough for me to get up off the floor, I was shivering and recognized the feelings of a fever. Using my walking stick, I made it to the doorway and looked at my tall floor clock, which told me by the length of its chains that it was the next day and a little after seven a.m.

Once in my bathroom, I again sat on the edge of my tub, trying to make a decision while weighing my options. I could go back to the doctor and let him take care of me for a few days until I could function properly, or I could keep myself dosed with morphine enough to accomplish what I desperately needed to do. It only took me a moment of picturing Christine on her toes kissing Raoul to come to the decision of using the morphine.

I couldn't allow any more time to pass before I revealed my true identity to her. So, with the right injection, I was soon dressed and heading for the doctor's office as I'd promised.

He was surprised to see me sitting in his waiting room, and while he jokingly teased me about my ability to keep promises, it wasn't until a week later that he confessed what he was really thinking. He didn't think he'd ever see me again. He thought I would die before he could finish his work.

He first checked the workers in my leg. "I'm pleasantly surprised with the progress they've made. They must be getting paid well or they like the taste of Erik."

I was feeling horrible, so I barely smiled at his remark. While he poked around in the wound, I was close to giving into his wishes and staying there. The thought of someone taking care of my needs was a good one, but I didn't tell him my secret desires. However, I think he sensed them. He had a jar of those creepy things in one hand and tweezers in the other when he began explaining what he was doing.

"I'm going to take the dead ones out and replace them with hardy ones. This you'll need . . ." he stopped mid sentence and looked at me. Then, placing the back of his fingers against my forehead, he asked, "Won't you please stay here? You need more than just this procedure."

I closed my eyes, tightened my jaw, and shook my head.

"Erik, you infuriate me." He paused, but was still intently watching my face. "Will you at least stay here long enough to eat something? You look as if you haven't eaten in weeks."

I opened my eyes and looked at the sincerity in his. "Very well," I replied.

He smiled broadly, as if he'd just won a lot of money in a horse race, quickly set the jar down, and left the room. He was back almost as quickly, telling me his secretary was getting me something to eat. Then he continued with the procedure, while giving me further instructions.

"If you don't stay off your feet, the movement of your muscles could squeeze our friends to death. Then their little dead bodies," he said as he raised the tweezers holding one, "would compete with your needs, because the survivors would use part of their appetites to eat their brothers and sisters instead of you. Do you get the picture, Erik? Can you understand the importance of resting your leg?"

I got the picture all right, and it was gruesome. I would not only have those creepy things eating their way through my flesh but I would also have them dying inside me. I shuddered and nodded, and he smiled and patted my knee. He checked the stitches on my head and then listened to my lungs, asking me how they felt.

"They feel better, thank you. I don't think the problem was an infection as much as the lake water I breathed."

He stopped, raised his head, and looked sternly at me. "Why did you breathe in lake water? Was someone trying to drown you?"

"No," I replied as I relived that frightening moment. "No one but myself. I was careless and fell from my boat. It was a simple accident that almost prevented me from seeking your help."

He smirked. "You know, Erik, unless you change your lifestyle, I believe I could give up my practice and concentrate solely on you. What do you think? Can I come live with you and make your health the source of my primary income?"

We both chuckled, but if he had any idea what my true lifestyle consisted of, *he* would be shuddering and not chuckling.

A few minutes later, his secretary came to the door with a tray containing the food he'd ordered, and a few minutes after that he was finished giving his creatures a new home. He handed me the tray, but I really didn't feel like eating and I think he knew it.

"You'll probably feel better if you eat, Erik. Your body needs nourishment to fight this."

I knew he was right, so I began to eat the soup while he gave me more instructions. I managed to get all the soup down, but I couldn't begin to eat the rice dish, even if it happened to be my favorite one that Oded had always made for me. It made me think of him and what advice he would give me for my new illness. I'm sure he'd have some type of remedy for it, but I had no intention of seeking his help, since it would come with many questions that I didn't want to answer.

Doctor Leglise put the rice dish in a glass jar, telling me to eat it later. Then he put me in a brougham, instructing me to go straight home and rest. I told him I would, but I knew rest was the last thing I'd be doing that day, even if it meant I'd be killing some of my workers.

The first item on my agenda was to find out Christine's whereabouts, because, if she was in another country with my young rival, then the rest of my plans were pointless. But assuming she was still within my reach, I made mental notes of all I had to accomplish, keeping in mind the doctor's words about not walking, especially up and down the stairs.

In addition, I knew I was facing a new challenge, moving around inside the opera house without being seen. For my entire life my biggest asset, other than my intelligence, was my agility and speed. Those attributes had allowed me to live within the opera house all those years without being seen, or, if I was seen, it was only as a shadowy figure that vanished quickly. But, at the present time, I was neither agile nor swift, so I had to use more of my wit. I'd have to use more of my passages instead of the open corridors, which meant a longer walk, but I could take my time.

My first stop was Christine's dressing room. My heart was pounding as I approached it, because I feared she'd be gone for good. Her room was empty, but the lamp on her wall was turned down low, which meant someone had been in there that day. My first thought was to go to the rehearsal studio and see if she was there, but then I decided on a less strenuous solution, her diary.

I entered her room and was instantly caressed with her fragrance. I closed my eyes, smiled, and took a deep breath; she'd been there recently. After making sure her door was locked, I sat down and took out her diary. Again, the sight of her perfect hand made me both ache inside and smile, but I didn't smile for long.

Her words expressed how much distress she was in, much more so than any of her previous writings. She felt she'd done something terribly wrong and that her angel had found her unworthy of any further tutoring. I felt horrible.

Raoul also added to her sadness and frustration. He didn't understand why Christine felt the way she did about her angel's disappearance, and she felt he should have understood and supported her. It seemed his answer for everything that was going wrong in Christine's life was to take her away from the opera house, which wasn't what she wanted. She wanted someone to help her know what to do and how to fight for her rights, not take her away. So, in the end, he only complicated her problems.

While those words were disquieting, they could be rectified just as soon as I could talk with her. But the words that caused me the most apprehension and anger were about her performances.

Carlotta had been slandering Christine and accusing her of trying to sabotage her roles and performances. She'd even sworn to get even with my angel. She was lying to the press about her, telling them that both her appearance and voice were no better than a toad's. She was threatening the new managers in order to get Christine placed back in the chorus, which she'd successfully done.

At that time they were performing *Faust*, and, even though Christine had proved her superior voice and acting skills for the role of Marguerite, she was placed as one of the town's boys. Christine sounded so miserable, and I could feel her tears between her written words. Again, I could help Christine feel better once I could talk with her, but it was going to be more challenging to undo the damage Carlotta had caused her career.

I sat for a while, thinking about what I could do. I didn't have to do anything about Raoul. He was doing it to himself and all by himself. All I had to do was to be there for her and let her know that I did understand how she felt, and that I would take care of Carlotta and our managers so her career could flourish.

What I had in mind for Carlotta would be simple. However, I also had a list of other things I needed to get done during that day, so that added nuisance only increased my hatred for the Opera Populaire's contemptuous prima donna.

I needed to write my new managers a note, but I couldn't use Christine's stationery, and I couldn't go all the way down to my home for mine. Therefore, I opted to find an empty office. The first one I approached belonged to Madame Giry, and, since it was empty, in I went and found some blank stationery that couldn't be traced back to her.

With the anger I was feeling, I wrote my first note to Carlotta.

My Dear Signora Guidicelli,

I'm sorry to say—I'm not pleased with the happenings here at my opera house during my brief hiatus. My, my. I can't leave for a moment without you performers squabbling like a flock of noisy geese. Well, I'm back, so I'd advise you to stop trying to use your wiles on my managers. It won't work. You see, my wiles are much stronger than yours, so it would be an exercise in futility on your part even to try.

If you can remember back that far, I'm sure your first vocal coach told you the dangers of being stressed and getting sick. Why, even the common cold can be devastating to a singer. It could cause irreversible damage. You should value your voice as a gift. If you try to sing with a cold it could be your swan song. We wouldn't want that—now would we?

So, a word to the wise, *my dear Carlotta:* gracefully back out of your part in *Faust* and let the rightful owner of the role of Marguerite take her place. There are much worse things than a cold or a missed performance—much worse than even death. I caution you to take my advice and make the right choice. If not, your voice just might be swallowed up as easily as a fly stuck to a toad's tongue.

The stars aren't aligned properly for you this day, and it would be folly to tempt the hand of fate this particular evening.
The Master of Voice,
OG

While I was sitting at Madame Giry's desk, I discovered *my* Box Five would be occupied that evening by none other than my new managers themselves. If I wasn't angry enough with Carlotta, well, that new bit of information sent me through the roof. I instantly wrote another note to my new managers, mincing no words as to the insanity of their attempt to sit in my box. I was almost too angry even to write, and threatened them grimly if they didn't leave it unoccupied for my use. I was so upset I couldn't even think of a reasonable threat, so I just told them that a catastrophe would happen if they didn't comply with my wishes.

By the time I was finished, I had a tremendous headache and was feeling spent, so, instead of delivering the notes myself, I left a note for Madame Giry and asked her to deliver them for me. I had nothing on me to leave her as a gift, so I told her I would leave her something special in my box that evening. I then left her office and slipped into one of my passages, giving myself a moment to think and rest.

I took out my watch and knew Christine was still in the morning rehearsals, so I headed for my box, thinking I could sit and rest while I watched her. I entered through the column, made sure the door was locked, and then sat down in my chair in the shadows. The house lights were down which helped to ensure I wouldn't be seen while I rested.

I stretched my leg out, laid it over the seat of the chair in front of me, and then I rolled to my right hip, laid my head back against the wall, and took a deep breath. It felt so good to be off my feet, but not nearly as good as the sight of Christine when she appeared on the stage. It was a dress rehearsal and she was in a boy's wig and clothing, but I would know her eyes no matter how much makeup she was in.

My pleasant feelings lasted only until her body language told me the degree of her downcast state. They'd stripped her, torn from her, the confidence that we'd worked on for months. I once more became angry and huffed.

I wanted to go to Christine and comfort her. I wanted to go to my new managers and bang their heads together. I wanted to go to Carlotta and ram my fist down her throat and pull out her vocal chords. I wanted to do a lot of things, but my physical condition was making it necessary to calm down and ration my energy. Therefore, I worked on my main priority, which was to help Christine.

I decided to wait for her behind the mirror and was just inside the marble column when I heard the key in the lock and then voices inside *my box*. I looked through the hole and saw my new managers arguing.

"I saw a head in here, Firmin. I know I did," Armand exclaimed almost angrily.

Firmin, not giving into his partner's anxiety, tried to put it off. "Are you sure it isn't just all this talk about the ghost?"

Still sounding angry, Armand explained, "Don't be an imbecile. I'm not falling for that nonsense, but I do still believe our predecessors are playing a prank on us. I just want to catch them in the act, that's all. Now look around. What could they have used?"

They started searching behind the drapes and in between the chairs, grumbling the entire time. Then they entered a subject that added to the angry state I'd just calmed down from.

"Do you think Madame Giry is behind all of this? She seems to be the only one delivering notes to us. She's also the only one who admits to hearing a ghost," Firmin stated.

Armand, while picking up a chair and looking under it, responded, "I don't think she has the brains to come up with such a scheme. But I definitely think she has something to do with it. I would peg her as a dupe being used by Poligny and Debienne."

"Well, whatever the case, Armand, I'm getting tired of this and we need to put a stop to it. I say we fire her and put someone in her place that will be faithful to us and not our pranksters."

Firmin's words triggered my angry thoughts and started that evening's events in motion, but Armand's response would be the one to make those events disastrous.

"I agree with you completely, and I know just the one to take her place. I have a lady friend who wants a position here at the opera house. She would love this opportunity, and she would definitely be faithful to us. I have a ticket right here in my pocket for tonight's performance that I'd planned to give her this afternoon. It will be the first opera she's attended, and a perfect way to celebrate her new job. I could tell her about the box keeper position when I see her. What do you say?"

Firmin was pleased with the thought, but, needless to say, I wasn't. I wouldn't allow them to discharge my reliable Madame Giry—I wouldn't. I didn't know how I would stop them right then, but I would somehow.

I listened to them congratulate themselves on such a perfect plan and their decision to have dinner after the performance to celebrate. They laughed and talked about sitting right there in my box and then where Madame Giry's replacement would be sitting. They were happy and laughing, but I was the furthest thing from it; I was fuming. So, groaning low and to make a statement, I raised and then lowered the light in the box slowly. They looked around and then into each other's eyes. They shook their head in unison, dismissed my actions as a coincidence, and left my box, but they wouldn't be able to dismiss my actions that night as a coincidence.

By the time they'd left my box, I was dizzy with a splitting headache again and feared trying to move very far, so I entered my box again and took the same position I'd found so comfortable earlier.

I lay back in the chair, telling myself not to be angry but to think of a way around all the events that had transpired during my absence. I listened to more of the rehearsal, closed my eyes and opened them, and then I looked around the auditorium that I'd had a hand in building. I looked at the red velvet stage curtains that held a special place in my theatrical heart. I studied the sculptures, the columns, the paintings on the ceiling, the chandelier, and the seat right under it where the new box keeper would be sitting.

I relaxed and entered a sort of fog with the chandelier as the backdrop for my creative mind. My headache lessened, my anger calmed, my thoughts cleared, and, in those moments, the rest of the day's events were written just as clearly as the score for that night's performance.

The rehearsals ended, and I watched Christine leave the stage, looking so dejected. She wasn't even talking to Meg who was by her side and chattering continually. My heart broke for my angel, so I entered the column and headed for her mirror. Once there, I found her sitting at her dressing table writing in her diary. Her eyes were dry, but her face was drawn and tired. I didn't know what to expect from her after leaving her that way for so long, so I watched carefully for her reaction.

"Christine, I'm here."

She jumped up, sending her quill to the floor. Then her hands went to her chest, her eyes filled with tears, and she sobbed, "My Angel?"

"Yes, Christine, your angel."

"I thought you'd left me for good. I thought I was no longer worthy of you. Why did you leave me alone for so long?"

"I apologize for my absence, Christine, but I was called away on an urgent matter."

"Oh, I see," she said softly.

Then I watched as her countenance changed. Her shoulders sloped and she stepped back and sat in her chair with her head down.

"I . . ." she began to say.

When she didn't finish, I encouraged her. "What is it? Why are you so downhearted?"

She looked at her two drooping roses before she gave an explanation. "I never thought my angel wouldn't be here for me, and it frightened me."

What had her counterfeit angel done this time? How was he going to fix this latest blunder? "Even your angel has his limitations, Christine. But I'm here now, so rise up and don't despair. I can't explain right now, but my delay had nothing to do with your worthiness. You're perfect in every respect, and I'm sorry for your pain. This is not the time for me to explain everything to you, but I will and soon. We'll talk for as long as you wish tonight after the performance, and I'll explain everything to you then. I'll be watching you tonight, my angel, so sing for me."

"I always sing for you, but my role tonight is nothing special, so you needn't bother to attend."

"You're wrong, my child. The role doesn't make the performer special; the performer makes the role special. Do your utmost tonight to make the role you perform special, and I'll be pleased. Then when you come back to your room, *I'll* have something special for you."

We talked for a few more minutes, and then I left the house and caught a brougham. My first stop was a bookstore to find a good book to read to Christine by the fire. I wanted it to take us into a world of fantasy, without touching any tender nerves. A story that would stay clear of anything that would make her think about her father and feel sad. I wanted something that would make her laugh and feel excited.

It took a while, but, after reading several forwards, I found one that sounded like what I wanted. It was titled *Jacob*. The forward described the book as intriguing, funny, mysterious, adventurous, and touching. It was the story of a man who traveled the world in search of adventure, going to places from the North Pole to the South Pacific Islands. His trips included sailing on ships, and rides through jungles on the backs of elephants. The book was hailed as a must read for anyone with an adventurous heart, and I thought it sounded like a safe entertainment for both Christine and me.

In that same shop, I bought her a lavender feather pen and matching stationery, along with a dusty rose diary. Since I knew how much she liked to chronicle her thoughts, I wanted that set in my home for her use when she was there.

Once back in my waiting brougham, I scratched the book off my mental list and went on to the next one; the antique furniture store she'd frequented. There I bought her the dressing table, matching mirror and chair she'd admired. Then I arranged for it to be specially delivered to the props department at the opera house. I had them attach my note to it: "Not to be opened until 1 January, 1900." I figured that would keep the workers away from it until I could get to it.

My next stop was a specialty shop where I outfitted my bedroom to be fit for a queen. Christine's favorite color was lavender and my favorite color on her was blue, so I bought a plush comforter in those colors with a hint of peach. I bought new sheets, pillows, and towels all in the same color scheme, as well as a new painting that coordinated with the room.

Three doors down from there was a woman's fashion shop. I wanted to buy her a complete wardrobe, but I only had enough energy and time to buy her a few things; a powder blue silk nightgown trimmed in cream lace, a matching robe, and a lavender dress for the travel to my home.

Again, I was back in the brougham, surrounded with packages and heading toward the florist. There I bought all the flower arrangements they had and asked them to get as many more as they could before that evening. I arranged for them to be delivered to the back entrance of the opera house at five, thinking there would be so much going on at that time that a few more flowers wouldn't be noticed. Right next door was a candle shop, where I purchased several dozen candles in varying colors, as well as bath crystals and creams for my Christine's pleasure, most of them in lavender scent and color.

One of the things I wanted to do for Christine was to make her fine meals every day, but, in my current condition, I wasn't sure I could pull it off without letting on that I was ill. So for the first night anyway, I purchased only fresh bread, cheese, and some fruit and nuts. I also bought two boxes of English sweets, one for Christine and one for Madame Giry.

Once I was back in my waiting brougham with all my purchases, my next challenge was getting them down into my home. By the time we reached the opera house, I hadn't come up with a solution, so I had no choice. If I wanted to have any strength left in me, I had to have help. So, for the first time during all my years of living there, I had to find someone to help me down to my home—well, to the lake anyway.

I told the driver to take me south toward the poorer neighborhoods. Then, as we rode down a dirt road with muddy potholes, we passed boys playing in the street with a stick and a rock, so I had the driver stop. My only thought was to find willing hands and strong legs to help me, so I hadn't given much thought beyond that.

But my actions became painfully clear to me when I stepped down from the brougham and approached the boys. They stopped playing and stared at me, and their expressions made me realize what I must have looked like. There I was, a tall man with a black mask, hat, cloak, and clothing, and limping with the aid of a black walking stick. And what made it worse, I was about ready to tell them that I would pay them if they took a ride with me and helped me. What was I thinking? Was I crazy?

I looked down at the mud puddle in front of me and sighed, and then I looked at the brougham, full of my packages and shook my head. Then

I looked at the boys and knew I had to make a quick decision, since some of them were scurrying away to their homes. Without further delay, I told them the truth.

"Hello. Can you see all the packages I have in my carriage?" I asked while motioning toward them. "I bought those for a special lady, but I have no way of getting them downstairs to my home because of my injured leg," I said as I stomped my walking stick beside my foot. "I'll pay whoever helps me. With the money I give you, you can buy real toys. It won't take too long. Who of you wants to help me?"

There were eight of them by then, ranging from perhaps six to eleven years of age, but then, one by one, they started backing away and then running away until there were only two left. They looked at each other and then me for some time; during that time, three mothers came out of their homes. With the thought of their fathers being the next to appear, I was ready to give up that idea as a bad one and get back in my brougham. I was in no condition to fight anyone. Then I rebuked myself. Erik, what have you gotten yourself into this time?

Twenty

Finally, one of the boys still standing in the street spoke up.

"Sure, Roland, let's do it. We need a ball."

"Good," I responded quickly before they changed their minds or before an angry parent changed it for them. "Jump on the back of the brougham. As you can see, there isn't enough room inside."

They gladly complied and laughed nearly the entire trip back to my home. However, I was far from laughing. I felt so sick and in so much pain, but, worse than that, I was anxious and expected to see a mounted officer stop us and accuse me of kidnapping, but that never happened. Once we reached the back of the opera house, I loaded my young helpers with flowers and Christine's gifts, while giving them instructions.

"You go first," I said to the largest boy, "and when we get to the doorman, don't say anything unless he asks you a question. He probably won't, but if he does just tell him you were given orders to deliver these gifts to the performers. Then keep walking until you get to the first corridor on your right. Turn there and I'll lead the way from there. Do you understand?"

"Yes! This is exciting! I feel like a spy!" he exclaimed.

I let him lead the way through the iron gate while I took up the rear, holding a large bouquet up in front of my face. As it turned out, the doorman didn't say anything. I didn't think he would, since he's used to seeing flowers delivered on a regular basis.

Once around the first corner, I took the lead. They became quiet as we made our way through one passage after another, and then, once we began descending the stairs toward the lake, their eyes widened, and I could see their fright in them. To keep their minds busy, I started asking them questions. I asked about their brothers or sisters, mothers and fathers, games they liked to play, animals they liked, their friends, anything and everything I could think of until we reached the lake.

Once we were by the lake, they completely changed. They were no longer frightened; they were amazed and awed. They started talking to each other and to me excitedly.

"This is great! I had no idea there was a real lake inside this building," the larger one, Obert, remarked.

"Me neither," Roland added. "I've wanted to go inside the opera house, but my mom always says maybe next year. Wait till I tell her what I saw. She won't believe me."

I smiled. My lake and opera house, that I took for granted by then, was something special for them to see, and they started asking me questions. But I was feeling poorly, so I made them a deal.

"I'll tell you what. As you saw, there are many more packages to bring down here, but I can't make that trip again. So will you go back up and get them? When you're finished unloading the coach, I'll pay you and answer all your questions."

They looked at each other, nodded, and began running back up the stairs. When they were gone, I loaded my boat with the gifts and then unloaded them in my docking room. Then I went back to the wharf and waited for the boys. They made two more trips before they had everything down by the lake, so I paid them enough to make their eyes pop out of their heads. Then we sat on the wharf, and I willingly answered their questions.

"How do you get all this water in here?" Obert asked.

"We don't. It comes from an underground stream. It was an architectural blunder to begin with, but it's now useful in different ways. It's used as part of the hydraulics to lift the sets and scenery up above the stage where they're stored and then lowered during the productions. It's also used to water the horses in the stable."

"Stable?" Roland asked. "You mean there's also a stable inside here along with a lake?"

"Yes, there is." I gestured toward the arches above our heads and continued, "It's two stories above us, and they have beautiful horses there that are used during some of the operas. There's what you might call an entire little city above us. There's a carpenter's shop, a seamstress's shop, something like a clothing store, and so much more. They can make almost anything you want up there, from small feather pens to life-size elephants."

Their eyes and mouths were wide open, and I smiled again. They asked many more questions and I answered them completely, perhaps too completely. In the process, I thought, I should be a tour guide. This is fun, and I'm good at it. I should be good at it, since I'd had a hand in constructing parts of everything that sat around us.

When it was time for the remaining flowers to be delivered, I offered them that job as well. They were happy to comply. Then, while their young and healthy legs trekked back up the stairs, I took the packages I had and crossed the lake. I was suffering in the extreme by then, so I gave myself another injection; then I sat for a bit waiting for it to take effect.

It took my helpers six trips to bring all the flowers down to me, and it took me three trips across the lake to take them to my home.

"I thank you both for your help. I never could have done this by myself. Here's what I owe you for the deliveries and here's a little extra so you can catch a coach back to your home."

They both stared at my outstretched hand holding more money, looked up into my eyes, and then at each other. They thanked me profusely for the extra money to get home. But, from the looks on their faces, I believe they'd already spent it on something they wanted.

As I watched them run toward the stairs and then disappear, Doctor Leglise's warning about losing my leg hit home hard, and I knew I had to take care of it soon. But first, I had to prepare for Christine's visit.

I decided to go to the set department first and find the dressing table I'd bought. It took a while, but I finally spotted a crate under a tarp. Upon examination, I found my note attached to it. It was a welcomed sight, and I immediately began shoving it toward my passage. The job was strenuous, and my weakness truly made itself apparent. It would have been a simple task before I was shot, but, right then, I seriously doubted if I could complete it. Several times, I had to hide and rest while stagehands came and went, and I was exhausted by the time I reached my passage.

Once inside the passage, I put a rope around the crate and let gravity take it from there. I let it slide down each step, while I sat on a step behind it and pulled back on the rope. It wasn't too long before I had it uncrated and in its place in what would be Christine's room. I next hung the matching mirror above it and put the chair in its place. I then stood back and looked at it, remembering Christine sitting at it in the antique shop. I hope she'll be pleased, was my main thought.

After that, I excitedly started cleaning her room from top to bottom. I even had to relocate my eight-legged friends to a beam in my docking room. Then, when I remembered how Napoleon dismantled what he thought were unsightly homes during the restoration period, I felt like him when I dismantled their unsightly but carefully designed homes.

I took all my belongings and put them in the other armoire in my music room and then put everything I'd purchased for her in what was now her room. I hung her gown and robe inside the armoire, but the lavender dress I wanted to take to her dressing room for her to put on before I brought her down to my home.

I put her brush, comb, hand mirror, feather pen, diary, stationery, and box of English sweets on top of the dressing table and then put the two red roses in the slender vase there also. The lavender towels, bath crystals, and creams I put on the marble counter in the bath. All around the bedroom and bath I placed the lavender candles, and, even though they weren't lit, they filled the room with their fragrance. I hung the colorful painting above the bed and laid the comforter over the bed. The room looked like a beautiful picture in a catalog, with only one piece of the picture missing—Christine.

Cleaning. I'd never had so much enjoyment cleaning my home before. Under normal conditions, I kept my home relatively clean, but, with Christine on her way, I wanted it to sparkle. The biggest clutter I had to clean that particular day was the accumulation of liquor bottles and glasses that remained as testimony to my sad state just days before.

Once cleaned, I brought up the assortment of flowers from the docking room and put them around my parlor and dining room; a few of them I put in Christine's room. When finished, I stood back and surveyed my home. It had the effect I wanted. It looked like a bright summer day in a park.

There was only one more important project I needed to do before I brought Christine into my home—put locks on the black boxes on the mantle. I wouldn't want any curious fingers accidentally blowing up my home. Once the locks were in place, I put the keys in a small leather bag and then put the bag on a bookshelf in my music room.

Thanks to my nearly two weeks with the wine, I hadn't gotten that extra bath built. Therefore, for a time anyway, I'd have to use my kitchen for some of my personal needs.

It was a little before six p.m. by the time I finished with my home and headed for my next project—César. With my bosal in hand, I entered the stable. Knowing I didn't have time to wait for laudanum to take effect, I was hoping I wouldn't have more than one groom to contend with, and I didn't. Even in my crippled state, I was able to get behind him, and then, with the right pressure on his neck, he was soon unconscious on a pile of hay.

Since I would be sending César back to the stable alone, I wanted him to be without tack; therefore, my greatest challenge would be to mount him bareback with only one good leg. But, once that was done, we were down the corridor leading up to the dressing rooms.

My plan for that night was to leave him tied at one of the entrances to my passage that led to Christine's dressing room. At the same time, I would lead her through it toward him. Then we would ride together down to the lake, all the while with my arms around her and my voice singing in her ear the romantic piece I'd written in Perros. Then, once at the lake, I would send César back up to the stable by himself.

I'd sent him up alone before and he'd made it just fine, so any concern I had wasn't due to his losing his way. The only unknown factor was the unfamiliar territory I'd be asking him to maneuver in the near darkness. I'd ridden him many times from the stable down to the lake, and through the corridors leading to the loading dock, and through the passage to my secret outside entrance, but I'd never had him in the dressing room section of the opera house before.

Considering the precious cargo I'd be carrying, and the fact that I was without much strength in my left leg, I didn't want anything to go wrong. That's why I wanted to ride him several times over that area to make sure he was familiar with it.

For a stallion, he was gentle as long as he was inside the opera house. I saw a much different side of him when I rode him by the river, but, thankfully, he'd been trained well, and when inside he knew he was working so he behaved.

Once I felt comfortable with his performance, I took him down to the lake for a drink, and then we headed back toward the stable. But we didn't quite make it there. We were almost to the well when a figure stepped right in front of us, catching us both off guard. César reared, and I nearly came off his back, while trying to calm him and examine our intruder at the same time.

Then, with an angered huff, I questioned, "What are you doing here, Oded?"

"I've missed you, Erik. It's been a while since I've seen you," he said while taking a few steps in my direction. "Have you been too busy to visit with your old friend?"

"Yes, much too busy," I responded with my lack of patience showing. "I don't have the time to banter with you, so, if you don't mind, I need to get back to *my* business."

True to form, he stepped in front of us again. "What is it, Erik? What are you so busy with?"

"Just stuff," I grumbled while trying to continue on my way. "It's nothing that would interest a Persian daroga. Now, please, if you don't mind."

"Erik, you're hiding something important from me, and I can't help but wonder why."

"Why? Why are you so unrelenting when it comes to *my business,* Oded? I thought we were past that stage in our relationship. I thought we had a good understanding. I would see you on occasion, beat you in a game of chess often, listen to your chatter continually, and you would leave me alone—always."

"Now I know you're hiding something from me. You're on the defensive and you never get on the defensive unless there's something you want to keep secret. What's going on here?"

He looked at César and then toward the stairs and then toward the lake and my boat. "Why are you always down here, Erik?"

"I could ask you the same question, Oded. I work here, remember? But you have no business here; other than to sit in the audience and enjoy the music. Look around you. Do you see an orchestra? No! So go back upstairs and wait for one."

"Well, actually, Erik, that's what brought me here. You see, I was in the audience enjoying the music the night of the gala, just as you said I should. Everyone was talking about the new singer, Christine Daaé, and her miraculous overnight success. There was much talk about a special and secret teacher. Do I need to tell you where my mind went at that time?

"I remember another young girl who was tutored by a truly special teacher. I heard in Mam'selle Daaé's voice something similar to my own daughter's. That certain great passion that no one knew existed in her until that night. Would you happen to know who that *special teacher* is?"

I slid off César and walked up to him, glaring right in his eyes. Then, in a low tone, I tried to warn him. "You tire me, Oded. You tire me with your continual interference in my private affairs. If you want to know who her voice teacher is, then I suggest you ask her and leave me out of it."

I turned back toward César and started to lead him away, but Oded again stepped in front of us. "Well, I did, as a matter of fact. Her only response was that it was someone her father once knew and had sent to her. But, you see, I know her father has been dead for ten years, so he couldn't have recently sent him. On top of that, it was the way she said it and the look she had in her eyes when she said it. I've seen that look before in my own daughter when she was captivated by her teacher."

I narrowed my eyes. "What are you accusing me of this time, Oded? And what difference does it make who her teacher is? And why are you making this your business? I don't understand your unnatural need to always know everything about everybody."

He walked in a circle around us and then looked back at me. "You know I care about you, Erik. I care for your welfare and your life, and I have from our first meeting. When I hear about strange things happening in your sphere," he said as he circled his hands around the area, "I become concerned.

"As you know, I always find you here, and yet it's strange that no one around here has ever seen you. You're rather distinctive in your appearance, and you really stand out in a crowd, and yet no one remembers seeing anyone who fits your description. I find that rather peculiar—don't you? I know how you feel about music, and yet I never see you at any of the performances—not at the grand opening and not at the gala. You're never seen and you're never heard. I find that difficult to understand."

I snarled. "I really don't get your point. *So* we've missed each other, and *so* no one sees me. You know how I feel about being seen in public. *So* I choose not to be seen in large crowds. I don't think that's really newsworthy, and it's surely a waste of your time to investigate it.

"You know what, Oded? I think you need to take a job with the Paris police department. That's where you need to be so you can do real investigating; such as robberies and murders. You don't need to follow me around trying to understand why I'd rather spend my time down here with César and not up there with the snobbish upper class. That really shouldn't be hard for you to understand. You've known me long enough to know I prefer the company of horses over people."

"Erik, why are you lying to me? What is so secret that you have to lie to me—your supposed friend?"

He'd pushed me far enough, and I lost it, so I turned on him with raised voice and arms. "What is it you expect from me, Oded?"

César spooked and I almost lost him, stumbling over myself trying to calm him. In the process, I also calmed. So, in a softer tone, I asked in all sincerity, "What do you want, Oded? Please stop beating around the bush and just say it outright. What is it you want to know?"

So he did just that; he said it outright. "Are you Christine's teacher? Are you watching the operas, say from Box Five that belongs to the mysterious Opera Ghost? Are you the Opera Ghost? Did you have anything to do with the sudden illness of Carlotta and Mam'selle Daaé's appearance? Did you have anything to do with the unusual demise of Joseph Buquet?"

I stood there with my arms spread. I'd asked him, and he'd replied completely. Now, was I prepared to answer him? Do I answer him honestly?

I turned and faced César, stroking his jaw. "We're friends, right, Oded? You know I visit with César and that he's never been hurt. No one has been hurt by what I've done with him—right?"

"Yes, Erik, and I've kept that little secret of yours."

Continuing to run my hands over César's nose, I went on. "I would never hurt anyone intentionally. Do you believe me when I say that?"

"Yes, I do, Erik."

"If I tell you the truth, will you believe me and keep my secret and stop asking me questions?" He was silent, so I turned back and looked at him. "Will you, my friend?" He nodded. "Then, yes, I'm Christine's teacher and

I mean her no harm. I've only wanted to help her reach her potential the same way I did with Vashti. And, as you can see, it's been working."

"Yes, it surely has. But what about the look I saw in her eyes, Erik. Are the two of you in love?"

I swallowed hard. "Oded, she doesn't even know me, and she's never seen me. She only hears my voice as I instruct her. I've never touched her or done anything to seduce her, so she's safe from harm."

He looked at me strangely. "That's a peculiar type of relationship, even for you, Erik."

Softly, I replied, "Yes, you could say that, but it's working for us both."

There was a moment of silence as I again turned toward César. "And as far as Joseph Buquet goes, that was truly an unfortunate accident." I turned my head and looked at him again. "Do you believe me?"

"Are you telling me the truth, Erik?"

"Yes, Oded. It was an accident."

He nodded and sighed. "And what about this Opera Ghost, do you have anything to do with it?"

I looked back in the direction of the lake. "I've worked on this structure for nearly twenty years, and a big part of the time I wasn't being paid a franc. I did it because I wanted to see it finished and in good repair. I currently still work on sections of it, and I'm still not being paid for my work. I've maneuvered events at times so that certain ones have been assigned the proper place in the casting, which has greatly improved the productions and therefore increased revenue for the Opera Populaire. Again, I'm not compensated for my work. I think requesting a box to sit in is not much to ask for, considering what I've contributed to this place."

I turned my head again and looked back at him. "Is that so much to ask—that I be able to watch something that I've been responsible for making come to life?"

He lowered his head and then looked back at me. "I guess not, not when you put it that way. But why don't you do it openly? You're a talented man in many ways, and they would have to see that. So why don't you do what you do like a normal person and without all this cloak and dagger secrecy?"

"Oh, Oded," I laughed sarcastically. "You know what happens when I try to associate with anyone on a regular basis. It would only be a matter of time before I'd be run out of here, just as I was run out of Persia. It's always the same and it will continue to be the same. I'm not a normal person; I never have been, and I never will be. No, I gave up on that idea a long time ago. You, of all people, should know I'm not allowed to live a normal life, even when I try."

I looked at the lake, then at César, and then back at Oded. "This is the only way I can exist anywhere close to a normal life, here as a shadow where no one gets hurt, not those around me and not me. Is that so wrong?"

He nodded in compliance. "Then you are living here?"

"Oded, you said that if I answered your questions you would stop asking them. Well, I answered all of them, and I really didn't need to. I could have simply left you standing here all alone in the dark with your questions unanswered, but I didn't, because you're my friend and you have been there for me when no one else was. But now your questions are answered, and I don't want to answer any more. Can you allow me to maintain some of my privacy, without continual harassment from my friend?"

"Yes," he replied, with that look in his eyes that told me he wasn't quite finished with me. "I'll leave you alone if that's what you really want. But there's only one more thing, and I won't put it in the form of a question. I can't help but notice that you're favoring your left leg. I hope you're taking proper care of whatever happened to it."

I assured him I was. Then I watched him walk away while thinking about our friendship and hoping he would be at peace with my explanations.

I stood there a minute more, looking at the lake and thinking about the one project left for me to do. It would be the high point in my career as overseer of my opera house. It would also be the statement that would leave no doubt in my manager's minds that I was not one to be toyed with. But it was also the most physically demanding part of my plans, and, since the burn in my leg was increasing, I took César back and went home for another injection.

I was sweaty and out of breath by the time I climbed not only the five flights to the main floor but also several flights more until I reached the ballet studio above the auditorium and chandelier. Then huffing, I climbed another flight to the chandelier's rigging room where its chains and gears were maintained.

Once there, I sat on a crate and stretched my leg out, trying to relax and catch my breath. I laid my head back against a post and looked up at the rigging that was used to raise and lower the chandelier for cleaning. It was then that I started my calculations, calculations that would make my managers stand up and listen to any future demands from their Opera Ghost.

My plan was to let the chandelier fall to within seven feet of the seats below it and then stop. The new box keeper would be sitting right under the chandelier, so my intention was to frighten her and my managers. That act alone should make all of them realize that the one they were dealing with was serious about leaving his box empty for him.

I was also going to write them another note with regard to Madame Giry and her position. I wasn't certain exactly what I would tell them, but, after the near destruction of their chandelier, I didn't think it would take special words to make them reconsider their decision about the box keeper position. That is if after the evening was finished Armand's friend hadn't already packed her bags and left.

My mind was fuzzy, either from the climb or perhaps the morphine, so I gave myself plenty of time to do the calculation properly. Weight times velocity, tensile strength, distance, age and wear, velocity, weight, strength. I went over all the calculations many times. I checked and double-checked my timing while waiting for the overture to begin. I couldn't start working with the lumber and chains until there was enough noise from the orchestra to conceal the noise I would make.

Then I heard it, and my heart began to race. I waited a few moments more, taking several deep breaths before getting to my feet. Before I started, I went to the observation window and looked down over the audience, and what I saw was enough to fuel me on. The unbelieving Richard and Moncharmin were in my box, and I glared at them.

"They'll be wishing I was relaxing in my box during this particular performance of *Faust* instead of doing what I'm about to do," I muttered to myself.

I went to work attaching the extra chains and sheering up the beams and counterbalances to handle the extra weight of the falling 200,000 kilo chandelier. I didn't work fast, not because of my leg and lack of strength, but because I didn't want to make a mistake. I made certain all my connections were secure and the release wheel was ready for its part in my performance.

I'd never done anything so drastic to make a point since the near destruction of the palace in Persia. By the time I was finished with all the double checks, I had to smile. This was going to make a much bigger statement than a note written in red ink or my laughter filling the opera house. This, and my special surprise for Carlotta, would not only disturb the performance but would also bring it to a climatic halt. Nothing like it had ever been seen at an opera, and I was sure it would be talked about for years, if not decades or even centuries, to come.

It was the beginning of the second act and everything was set. The chandelier was poised and waiting for its cue—and so was I.

Twenty-One

I looked toward the stairway and took a deep breath, knowing I had to travel it again. With my walking stick in hand, I went all the way down to my home. Once there, I quickly cleaned up, dressed in my finest, lit all the candles, started a fire, and turned on all the lights. Then I turned off the lake's sensor alarm. With Christine in my home, it needed to be turned off before I left by way of the lake; otherwise, it could frighten her terribly.

After I grabbed the box with Christine's dress in it and the box of English sweets and the silver opera glasses for Madame Giry, I stood at the exterior door. When I looked back into the room, it was exactly the way I'd pictured it: perfect.

I used César to carry me and my packages to the secret passage entrance. After giving him an extra pat, I told him I wouldn't be long. I next put Christine's dress in her armoire and then returned to the passage. After closing the mirror, I looked back into her room and took a deep breath. With a smile in my heart, I pictured her in that dress and willingly placing her hand in mine.

What a beautiful picture that was, but then I also pictured her screaming in fear when she saw me. I shuddered at that thought. I looked down at my hands that were shaky and weak. How can I present a strong figure when I feel so sick? Perhaps I should wait a few more days and get well before I try capturing her heart.

That started another round of internal arguments, the same arguments I'd had before. No! You can't turn back now. Quit using excuses for not moving forward. You're not that sick. Why do I fear her so? Why do I tremble at the thought of facing her rejection? I'd faced a dozen armed men without fear. What power does she hold over me that they didn't? Those men had held the power of life and death over me, but then, so does she.

She holds my heart on her whispered breath. With her *yes*, my heart will soar, and with her *no*, it will plummet to the depths of hell. Oh, Christine, what will it be when you see me? Will you see my devoted heart or my deformed face?

My final decision was that her delicate breath had more power than a thousand mighty men, but if I didn't try to capture her heart and I lost her to her childhood sweetheart, then I was dead anyway. So, I had to try, and I had to try that night. Therefore, within minutes, I was in the column next to my box, waiting for the second act to finish. After the applause subsided, I only had to wait for my managers to leave.

Moncharmin got to his feet first, stretched, and laughingly commented, "It's not a bad house, considering we were to experience a catastrophe this evening."

They both laughed and then Madame Giry came in and they laughed even more. "I thought your ghost always came to claim his box by this time. He's late," Richard joked.

Again they laughed and Madame Giry, undeterred, responded strongly, "I'm going to lodge a complaint against both of you. You had no right to kick me earlier just because I spoke the truth about our Opera Ghost."

I felt a frown form on my brow, wondering why in the world would someone in their station kick anybody, much less a lady. It was such a childish thing to do. I made a mental note to address their uncivilized behavior toward my one supporter at a later time.

Taunting the poor lady even more, Richard jeered, "A complaint? With whom? The Opera Ghost?" They again laughed. "You have no right to file a complaint because this is your last night as box keeper. You've been replaced, so save your breath."

She glared at them, as did I, and then she spoke sternly to them in her impeccable French. "I wouldn't laugh just yet, Messieurs. The night is still young, and the Opera Ghost always has the last laugh. So mind your tongue and my words."

They only laughed more, and she left. Once they left, I slipped in and left her sweets and glasses on the shelf. Then I left with a smile on my lips. She was always faithful to me, but, that night in particular, she had no idea just how true her words were; I would have the last laugh and a big one at that.

Once back in the column, I headed toward my waiting masterpiece far above the auditorium. By the time I reached it, the third act had begun, and I sat down again on the crate and gave myself time to recuperate from the climb. I laid my head back and listened to Carlotta slaughter the role of Marguerite.

I shook my head in disbelief. How could those two fools, who were responsible for the management of the opera house, make such a terrible blunder? Surely they had to have ears and could hear the difference between

Carlotta and Christine. How could they allow themselves to be duped into letting her have that role? What ignorant fools!

I listened to the famous tenor, Carolus Fonta, as he sang the part of Faust and waited for Carlotta's line that would be my cue to get on my feet and start *my* performance.

Then I heard the words from Carlotta's lips. "Oh, how strange! Like a spell does the evening bind me!"

I was on my feet and standing by the observation window when her next lines sung out. "And a deep languid charm . . ."

I took a deep breath and parted my lips waiting for her next line. "I feel without alarm . . ."

Then I sang out strong, letting my voice fall on her throat. "Co—ack!"

I stopped laughing long enough to speak once more in my manager's ears. "She's singing tonight to bring down the chandelier!"

I laughed again as they glanced over their shoulders for the one speaking. I don't know what they did after that, because I was by the gear and released it. I looked up above my head to see the chains start to move, at first almost in slow motion and then swiftly. They sped past my eyes, and I again laughed loud—but not for long.

As cries came up from the auditorium beneath me, I felt the floor under my feet, as well as the walls around me, shake. I looked up, and, at the same time, I heard the unmistakable sound of timber cracking. With that horrible splitting sound, I knew something had seriously gone wrong—terribly wrong.

I shouldn't be hearing that sound, I remember thinking. As I began backing away, I saw the beams and the entire assemblies over my head break away and come crashing past me. As it disappeared through the floor in front of me, my mind flashed faster than lightning, and one phrase repeated in my head.

"I couldn't have made a mistake! I couldn't have made a mistake!"

There were people screaming, glass shattering, chains rattling, and wood splitting. I couldn't have made a mistake. I'd never made a calculation error—never. What had happened?

I felt as if I was in the midst of a slow-moving nightmare. What was happening just couldn't be happening. I stood there staring at the gaping hole in disbelief until the rumble subsided. Then there was no sound, other than the cries from below me. I moved to the edge of the splintered floor and looked down. Why? I don't know.

I watched in stark horror; there were people running, people staggering, people screaming, people crying, and people lying over the seats or in the aisles amidst the twisted and shattered chandelier. I felt my head shake slowly—what had I done?

Above the cries, I thought I heard Christine calling out, "Angel!"

I searched through the mass hysteria in the auditorium below me until I saw her in her little boy's costume, minus the wig. Her hair was tossing from side to side as she searched each aisle, all the while calling for her angel.

I could only watch. I was unable to move or respond to her calls. It wasn't until I saw her start to run back toward the stage that I could move, but not far or fast. I started backing away from the disaster scene, while still telling myself that it wasn't possible for me to make a calculation error of that magnitude.

When I was able to really move, I don't remember feeling any physical pain while running down the stairs toward the main level. All I remember was going over and over the calculation in my mind, trying to understand what had happened.

Then the sight of the bodies lying everywhere woke me up, and I felt truly sick. I then began questioning what was wrong with me. Was I then an intentional murderer without even trying? Had I become so tied in with death that I could cause it even when there was no intent?

By then I was on the main level and running through the corridor behind the boxes with many other people, but I gave no thought to them or being seen by them. I ran down the steps to the auditorium and through the sea of red and gold seats, then past more people and back up the stairs on the other side. Again I ran through the corridor behind the boxes, and then down and around corners, and more corners, and more people, until I was in the hallway leading to the dressing rooms. I kept running into and past people without any regard to who they were or who saw me.

I moved quickly past César, not even halting long enough to give him a pat, and into my dark passageway. By the time I reached the mirror, my mind and heart were a mess. It was only the sight of Christine that gave me what I needed to think. She was pacing frantically across her room, while her fingers tugged and pulled at the belt loops of her trousers, and her whispered voice kept repeating toward the floor.

"Angel . . . oh, my angel where . . . Oh, my angel. If you're not dead . . . oh, please . . . please show yourself to me. Oh, please my angel—answer me."

I closed my eyes for a second and took a breath, trying, unsuccessfully, to control my voice. "Yes, Christine, I'm here."

She leapt and turned in circles. "Are you all right?"

That question only added to my confused state. "Yes, I am."

"Oh, I thought you were . . . I thought you were dead," she whimpered.

"Why would you think your angel was dead?"

Her bewildered voice expressed the confusion in her mind, while she walked aimlessly through her room. "Oh, I was so frightened for you. There were so many who were hurt, and I couldn't find you. I called for you, but you didn't answer. You said you'd be watching me, and I was afraid you were there and hurt. I'm so thankful you weren't hurt, but there were so many who were hurt. Oh, those poor people. There were so many, and they were just . . . oh, those poor people."

I didn't know how to respond to her. My mind was in a shambles and reeling as the vision of the falling rigging swirled around and around in my head. I felt as if I was trying to control a runaway team of horses, heading for a cliff and without any reins in my hands. My so-called superior intellect was as useless as wet paper. There were no quick-witted words to be found anywhere within me. I was in shock, total shock, and her words about my welfare only confused me more.

"I don't understand, Christine. Why would you think an angel would be among those hurt?"

Her hands were covering her face and she was shaking her head. "I don't know. I don't know. I was so afraid. It was so horrible—so horrible."

My eyes were closed as I pictured all the ones lying among the rubble, and I clenched my jaws. Then I responded, almost to myself, "Yes, Christine, it was a horrible accident."

That was one of the times when she turned and looked directly at the mirror, and I knew I wasn't controlling my voice properly, but, at that time, I really didn't care. I was numb and yet in horrible pain at the same time. I didn't know what I was going to do with myself, much less how I was going to help her. She was still moving around the room and speaking to me, but I don't remember what she said from that point on. I just watched her in her fright and I felt so sick in my gut.

My head felt as if it were under water, her words and my thoughts muffled and swirling together, preventing me from hearing either of them clearly. My one thought, that I can remember, was of music. I wanted and needed my music. I think I turned with the intention of going to my piano and my music, but then I must not have, because I was still behind the mirror, motionless and watching Christine sob.

Then, although I don't recollect hearing it, I felt my voice inside me singing. I could feel it inside my throat, but I couldn't hear anything with my ears. I didn't know what the words were or the melody.

Christine stopped crying and raised her head, looking right at the mirror. I watched her eyes and face become as one who was sleepwalking; then she started to approach the mirror. As she got closer, I raised my hand and laid my fingers over the latch, but I don't remember thinking about doing it. The mirror opened and she kept walking and I kept singing. Then I took her by the wrist and directed her inside.

When we were both behind the mirror, it closed. I put my arm around her waist. Then I began walking slowly and guiding her through the nearly black corridor. I don't think I once removed my eyes from her face, and her eyes stayed fixed on my masked face. She walked in her sleep-like state, and I could still feel the music in my throat.

As I led us toward the lone lamp at the far end of the passageway, the passage became lighter. Then, without warning, I watched her eyes wake up and her mouth open, followed by a horrible, retched scream. Within that instant, we were both wide awake, and I automatically wrapped my fingers over her mouth and told her to stop screaming. I repeated her name several times, but her only response was to push against my chest with great force.

But her attempt to be free from me only lasted for a few moments. The next second found her lying limp in my arms and me trying to keep both of us from falling. My masked face so close to hers must have awakened her, and her scream definitely awakened my senses and my body. That scenario cleared my mind quickly, and I registered everything, from the strange situation I'd brought Christine into to the tremendous pain in my left leg and hip.

I slid down the wall with her still in my arms, and then I sat on the floor with her lying across my legs. I ran my fingers over her forehead, repeating her name and telling her to wake up. She was completely unconscious, and I closed my eyes and shook my head. I'd obviously not made a good first impression.

I looked toward the end of the passage, which was a little over six meters away, and tried to make the right decision. Should I try to take her the rest of the way to my home while she was still unconscious or do I stay there until she wakes up?

I laid my head back against the damp stones, closed my eyes, and questioned, what was happening? Nothing was going according to plan. That night was supposed to begin a completely new and different life for Christine and me—but not that different. I could see then that my being shot was only a prelude to the catastrophe that had just occurred with the chandelier.

In addition, there I sat on the cold floor with the woman I loved unconscious because of her fear of me. The woman I was supposed to enchant and sweep off her feet, I'd nearly frightened to death. Nothing was working right, and I couldn't help but wonder what else was going to go wrong.

I looked at the lamp and the way back to my home, and then I looked back at the darkness and her dressing room. I was seriously considering taking her back to her dressing room and laying her on the floor, hoping that when she woke she'd think it was all a bad dream. But then I looked down at the beautiful woman in my arms, and I pulled her closer to me, desperately wanting to bury my face in the creamy skin of her neck. But I didn't. Instead, I ran my fingers along her cheek and knew I couldn't let her go. I had to somehow finish what I'd started and not let another day go by without her knowing exactly who her angel was.

But how was I going to get her out of that dark and dreary place? I thought about sitting there with her until she woke. But I feared what she would do if she woke in my arms and on the floor, if seeing me on my feet was enough the make her faint. I had to get her out of that passage if I could and as soon as I could. With that determination in my mind and heart, I managed to get to my feet and test out my leg.

It took me only one step to wish I had my walking stick. The last time I remembered having it was in the chandelier's rigging room, so I had no idea where it was at that time. But, with or without it, I had to get Christine out of that dark passageway; therefore, I prepared to endure the pain.

I knelt down, took a deep breath, clenched my teeth, lifted her in my arms, got to my feet, and started walking. By the time I reached the end of the passage, I could feel the sweat on my brow, and I can't even describe the pain in my leg. I closed my eyes and laid my head back against the cool wall until I had enough breath and strength to continue.

I hadn't counted on her passing out and having to carry her that far, although it would have been terribly romantic if I could have done it with strength. But even with my carrying her, it wasn't the romantic vision I had as I laid my original plans in order. I shook my head. How did my masterful scheme get to this place? But then I thought about César and was thankful I had him to help me.

At that time, he was truly a necessary part of the equation and not merely a romantic idea. As I opened the door and crept through it, César nickered. Then, leaning against the wall, I looked at him with gratitude and he looked at us with his eyes and ears alert.

While telling him to stand still, I lifted Christine up and laid her over his back, apologizing to her as I did so. Other than dragging her, that was the last way I wanted to transport the woman I loved to my home—throwing her over a horse like a pair of leather saddlebags.

César nickered and started stepping sideways toward the wall, and I instantly reacted. "César, halt! Easy, boy—easy. You're going to squish her. Easy, boy. Good, boy," I said softly.

He halted, and I held her in place by grasping the belt of her little boy trousers. Then I moved around his rear until I was on the other side of him by Christine's head. He'd come close to smashing her head against the wall, and I shuddered at the thought. Then, while rubbing his neck and talking to him, I took a minute to think through exactly how I was going to transport her safely.

I had little choice, and I had to count on his training if we were to make it to the lake without another disaster, so I threw his reins over his neck and prepared to move on. I then spoke to Christine, trying to wake her, but she didn't respond. Therefore, I grasped her belt tightly with one hand and with the other I grasped her upper arm.

I began giving César verbal commands, and he obeyed me perfectly; in fact, he was the only part of my well thought out plans that was working right. That night was supposed to be so romantic. I was the strong and dashing caped man in black who would lift her effortlessly up on the back of his mighty steed. Then, with great ease and grace, I would swing up behind her, and, with my arms around her, we would ride the white stallion down the passageways to my home. All the while I would sing to her a beautiful song composed just for that occasion.

It all sounded so good in my head. So romantic and daring. She would be captivated and overwhelmed by my power and strength and would swoon in my arms. It wasn't to be like this, an injured and deformed man not only unable to whisk her away but unable to stand on his own without wrenching with pain. And she was supposed to swoon, not faint out of fear. You stupid fool, I was beginning to think. Why didn't you wait until a better time?

I stayed by Christine's head, holding her in place on César's back, while we headed for a small bubbling well off the main corridor in the third cellar, hoping I could wake her there. Remarkably, with only my words guiding César, he took us there, and then I slid Christine down into my arms.

After a few agonizing steps, we were by the well and I set her down. Then, pulling my cloak from my shoulders, I laid it down and then laid her over it as gently as if she were a fragile porcelain doll. We were away from the lamps in the passageway, and it was extremely dark again, even for me. I didn't want her to wake to complete darkness, so I lit a lantern that was close by. I'd just pulled my handkerchief from my pocket when I sensed we weren't alone, so I quickly doused the lantern, putting us back in total darkness.

Within a split second, my mind went through several modes. I reached for a lasso, which I couldn't get because it was under Christine in my cloak. Then, wanting to prevent any knives or bullets from harming her, I was on my feet and running toward a pillar. I held my breath, listening. Then, within moments, I heard someone breathing from behind the next pillar. Hoping I was right about the location, I laced my fingers together, making one double fist, and stormed toward the breaths, swinging my fists repeatedly.

With the second swing, I connected but I kept swinging, connecting one more time before I heard his body hit the ground. I lit a match and looked down at our stalker. Oded, you stupid fool, I sighed. Hadn't I told you just hours earlier to leave me alone? I checked him over closely to make sure I hadn't caused him serious harm, and then I grumbled, something else going wrong. Was nothing going to go right that night?

I couldn't allow him to hamper my plans any more than they already had been. I knew then that I had to work fast before he woke up, so I went back to Christine and lit the lantern before I lifted her head to my knee. I wet my handkerchief and ran it across her forehead several times.

At first there was no response, and I gazed at her flawless face in the dim lantern light. I watched her chest rise and fall, and I desperately wanted to raise her up into my arms and hold her close to me. That could be the only chance I'd have to hold her. Once she realized what I'd done, she may never forgive me for taking her away like that, and she could hate me forever for destroying her angel.

I shared my glances between her face and the pillar where Oded lay, while telling her to wake up. César started pestering me, creating an additional challenge by trying to nuzzle her face. But then, maybe that's what she needed, because she started to come around. I wet my handkerchief one more time and again wiped her face, while pushing my mighty steed out of the way at the same time.

She opened her eyes momentarily and then turned her face from me and whispered, "Where's the voice . . . Angel?"

I instantly felt horrible for what I was doing, and an ache flooded through my chest as I sighed.

What was happening was real. No more fantasies of what the evening would be like; no more prince and princess on a white stallion heading for a bright castle on a hill. It was me—a deformed man who'd just kidnapped a beautiful woman who was young enough to be his daughter, and then dragged her to the dark depths of his domain far below the streets of Paris.

This was real, and the princess was about to wake, and I feared she would wake with fright and screaming.

I was about to explode as I waited for her to turn back to me. I wanted to speak to her and tell her not to be frightened, but I seemed to have lost what it took to speak to a beautiful woman without a plate of glass separating us, so I waited silently.

I put my fingers on her cheek and turned her face toward me, and she looked up into my eyes almost as if I wasn't there. I put my hand behind her and lifted her into a sitting position, and then I got to my feet. I offered her my hand, and, surprisingly, she took it, and I lifted her to her feet. When she shivered, I picked up my cloak and wrapped it around her shoulders, clasping it there. Then gently, and with my hand behind her waist, I walked her to César.

She was wobbly, and I feared she was going to pass out again, but she didn't. Clenching my teeth, balancing my weight on my good leg, and trying not to let out any sounds of pain, I lifted her up onto César's back again. Without having to think about it, I knew I hadn't the strength or the agility to jump up behind her, so I needed to find the strength to walk the rest of the way down to the lake.

Christine's eyes were open, but she still didn't present herself as being fully awake, and even began reeling. I was afraid to let go of her; afraid she would topple; therefore, I again had to walk beside her, holding onto her belt to steady her. Once more, César followed my verbal commands as I walked beside Christine. At last, we were at the lake, and, grasping her by the waist, I pulled her down.

The only thing she'd said since her scream was to ask where the voice was. I wanted to reassure her that everything was all right, but I never found the words or the courage to answer her. I steadied her on her feet and then took César's bosal off and sent him back to the stable. I then walked her down to the wharf with my arm still around her waist and directed her down into my boat. I didn't know what to think about her condition. Because of the way she was responding to my unspoken directions, I would have thought she'd been drugged, if I hadn't known better.

I moved across the lake as quickly as I could, since she was still unstable and I feared she would faint again and fall into the water. That night I didn't watch the mist parting before my boat as it had on so many occasions, for my sight was on the beauty before me. Perhaps she was feeling what I was feeling; perhaps that's why she wasn't saying anything.

I felt as if I was dreaming. It was all so unreal, and yet my rational mind told me it was very real. But something, somewhere within me, was afraid it wasn't. I feared, if I made any noise or sudden movements, the bubble would burst and I would wake out of the dream I was in. As I watched her eyes, which were watching me, I wondered if she felt the same.

We reached the end of the labyrinth and I stepped out of my boat, then I held out my hand to her. She looked up at my face and took my hand, but, as she stepped out, she nearly went down again. I instantly wrapped my arm around her waist, and then her knees went out from under her. I lifted her up in my arms, and, with her head on my shoulder, I carried her up the steps to my door, moved the spring, and waited for the door to open.

When it did, we were flooded with bright light, color, and warmth, and both of us turned our faces from it. After stepping inside, I stood her up, holding her shoulders steady against the wall. Then I waited until she was stable before I moved the spring to close the door. I removed my cloak from her shoulders and backed away, watching her closely as she also watched me.

While we studied each other, I tossed my cloak over a chair and then felt extremely awkward, not having anything to do for the first time that day. I felt my arms and hands were strange appendages just hanging from my shoulders, and I needed to do something with them, so I crossed them in front of my chest.

I told myself to speak to her, but for some unknown reason I hadn't a thought in my head, except for the beautiful woman who was finally standing right there in my drawing room. Neither of us spoke for what seemed like an eternity. Then, as I watched her, her breaths started coming closer together, and then, finally, the silence broke with her whisper.

"Where am I? Who are you?"

Her words made my own breaths come quickly. Then, in the room filled with warmth, light, and color, I somehow found my voice.

"My name is Erik."

Twenty-Two

"The voice? You're the voice?" she questioned in an undertone.

She wavered on her feet and reached for the wall; then, with one hand on her forehead, she gazed at the floor. I wanted to go to her and steady her, but she was already frightened, and I feared those actions would only make matters worse, so I refrained and waited for her senses to catch up. Finally, she looked back into my eyes, and her brow wrinkled.

"The voice? My angel?" she questioned again.

I watched her closely as she began gazing around the room and as my heart began beating rapidly. She was so beautiful, even if she wore little boy's clothing and not the lovely dress I'd prepared for that occasion. I watched her eyes as they went from confusion to fear, from anger to betrayal, and then back again in rapid succession. Her breaths came quickly, and she released her hold on the wall and stood up straight. Then her eyes filled with indignation and landed firmly back on me. After taking a step toward me, it began.

"What are you doing? Why am I here?" she questioned with renewed strength.

Thinking, here we go, I unfolded my arms and spoke softly and with control. "Don't be frightened, Christine. I mean you no harm and you're in no danger."

Frowning more, she asked, "If you mean me no harm, then why the secrecy and why the mask?"

I lowered my eyes, and then raised them again to meet hers, speaking softly. "We all wear masks, Christine, you included. The only difference is that mine you see first and not last. Everyone protects their true feelings at first by wearing a mask over their hearts. You're wearing one right now.

"It usually takes time before we let our true selves come to the fore, remove the masks, and bare our souls. But everyone wears a mask to begin with. I'm not wearing a mask on my heart right now, Christine. I've stripped myself of all protection, and I now lay my heart naked and unprotected at your feet. I ask that you please be gentle with it and not trample upon it."

She was still frowning and searching my eyes. Then, in an instant, she stormed up to me and reached for my mask. I grasped both her wrists firmly and looked down at her, shaking my head.

"You can't see what's behind my mask—not yet. A pretty face can distract a woman's eye and prevent her from seeing what's in the heart. I wear the mask so you won't be distracted by my appearance. I want you to come to know what's in my heart before you see what's behind my mask. What lies there doesn't represent the man I am."

I slowly released her wrists and walked past her toward the center of the drawing room and then turned to face her. By then she'd returned to her original place by the invisible door.

"I'm the one you've come to know in your dressing room—the voice that filled the air around you. Remember our conversations and our laughter? That's who I am, Christine, not the face behind the mask. You can see my lips speak words to you now and you can see in my eyes that they speak nothing but truth to you. That's all that's needed at this time. Once your heart can speak to mine with honesty, then, if you wish, you can see my face."

She was obviously confused, and she had every right to be. "But how can you be the same, both the voice and my Angel of Music? And yet be a man who's standing here before me in this place?"

"You can see I'm not an angel, not a ghost, not a phantom, and not only a voice. I'm none of those things." I spread my hands out from my sides and made one complete turn. "I'm just a man, not a composer, not a scientist, not an inventor, not a teacher. I'm only a man right now, a man in love with a beautiful woman—you, Christine."

Her hand went to her throat and she backed up, so I tried to relieve her fears. "Don't be frightened. I mean you no harm. I'll not hurt you in any way. I won't even touch you. I've spared no expense to make your stay here in my home a pleasant one."

"My stay? What do you mean—my stay?" she shrieked, perhaps fearing the worst.

"I love you, Christine, with a love that I don't believe anyone can understand. I would do anything for you. Anything you ask of me, I'll do for you."

"Then let me go," she demanded, as she looked around, obviously for the door. "Let me go!"

"I will. I promise I will. All I ask is that you spend four days here with me."

She backed against the wall again, and panic filled her eyes.

"Don't fear me, Christine. I promise I won't hurt you. You have your own room, and I'll respect your privacy. I won't even enter your room unless invited. You have no need to fear me."

"What do you want from me?" she asked after relaxing a bit.

"I want you to stay here with me for four days. I want you to talk with me and sing with me, that's all. Just like in your dressing room. Nothing more."

She looked around at all the flowers and the fire and then asked, "Why?"

"Because, if in four days you haven't fallen in love with me, I'll let you go."

Her eyes flashed quickly back in my direction. "Fall in love with you? Are you crazy? I don't even know you!"

"Yes, you do," I responded softly. "We've spent much time together, talking in your dressing room. Have you forgotten all those conversations? Have you forgotten how your heart soared when we sang together? Have you forgotten me?"

She shook her head. "But that was with my angel."

Again, I spread my arms out from my sides. "One in the same, my dear."

She looked so confused, frightened, hurt, disappointed, and a host of other negative emotions, and I truly felt bad. I wanted to take her in my arms and comfort her, but I knew that wasn't an option.

"You can't keep me here in bondage," she said with her returning courage.

"You'll be free to leave in four days while I remain here in bondage."

She frowned, "Bondage? I haven't seen any bars or guards. You're not in bondage."

"There are many forms of bondage, my dear. I prefer the bondage of bars and mortal men guarding me; from them I can flee. But my bondage is an invisible one. Just as yours is."

"You're crazy, and you talk crazy."

"Do I? Are you not still held back from freedom of heart by the death of your father and your loneliness?" She only looked at me without a response, so I continued. "We're all held captive in some form. You've made great strides in your music to become free, but you must take the next step now to free yourself completely so your music can continue to grow. You've been held in bondage by lies told by the one person you loved the most—your father."

"My father never lied to me," she replied indignantly.

"No? Then why did you believe so easily that I was your Angel of Music?"

"You deceived me."

"Did I? Did I give myself that label—or did you? I believe it was you, Christine, who believed me to be your angel. I merely used it to teach you. Now, I set you free from that falsehood. I'm only a man who saw a beautiful woman with the potential for greatness, if she could be released from her bonds. I want to continue helping you just as I have been."

I took a step toward her but she backed against the door.

"Don't fear me, Christine. You know me, and you know I've never hurt you. I was the one who encouraged you and taught you all those weeks. If I wanted to hurt you in some way, I've had plenty of opportunities to do so, but I haven't, because I mean you no harm. I only want your happiness and the chance for you to come to know me for who I am.

"Sit down, please," I requested, as I moved aside and motioned toward the divan. She only stared at me without moving until I gestured again, and then she moved slowly toward the divan and cautiously sat down.

"Would you like something to drink or eat? I have a vintage wine, hot tea, or cool water, and I have aged cheese, fresh bread, and apples."

Again, I only got that look of suspicion and a shake of her head. The poor thing was probably thinking I wanted to drug her so I could have my way with her, so I didn't force the issue. Hoping that giving her distance from me might make her feel more comfortable, I stood behind my chair, facing her. Then I tried again to reason with her.

"Christine, how do you feel when you sing now as compared to the way you sang three months ago?"

"There's no comparison," she answered without hesitation. "When I sing now, I feel alive and . . ." She stopped and narrowed her eyes at me. "There aren't words."

"Three months ago," I continued, "would you have expected to feel this way about your voice?" She shook her head, and I went on. "If someone had told you then that you would sing center stage at a special gala in the largest opera house in the world, would you have believed them?"

She shook her head again, and I took a deep breath. "I gave you your voice, Christine, a voice you never thought possible, a voice you wouldn't have if it weren't for me. Give me four days and I'll make your heart soar as your song does and in a way that you can't even imagine right now. Give me four days and I'll give you the world. Give me four days and there won't be words for what you feel inside. Please, just give me four honest days. That's all I ask, and I promise you all this."

She looked around the room. "That's a great deal to promise—the entire world."

"I'm a man of considerable means, although you may not think it, considering what you see around you. I'm forced to live down here not because of a lack of funds on my part but because of a lack of human compassion on the world's part. I beg you, Christine, don't throw yourself in with their lot. Don't become part of an uncaring world and ignore the man I am inside just because of this," I said as I laid my fingers against the side of my mask.

I looked at the floor and rubbed my fingers against the back of my neck, wondering if I should take the conversation in the direction my thoughts were going. When I looked back at her, I decided to take a chance.

"There's nothing your young friend, Raoul, has that I don't, except for a pretty face; in fact, quite to the contrary. Look, Christine," I said as I stepped away from the chair and held out my arms from my sides. "I'm a man in every respect. I have two arms, two legs, all in good working order, but, most of all, I have a heart that I'm giving to you unconditionally."

She also took a deep breath and looked away from me toward the fire. I watched her for a moment, and then, trying not to limp and disprove what I'd just told her, I took another chance. I stepped to within one meter of her and knelt down on one knee, so we could look eye to eye.

"Can't you look beyond this mask, Christine, and look at me?" She took another deep breath and looked in my eyes. Then I spoke softly, "A simple grain of sand in the bottom of your shoe can become quite irritating and you quickly take off your shoe and shake that grain of sand out on the ground. Then you keep walking without another thought about that ordinary piece of earth. But that same grain of sand if put inside an oyster's shell will, in time, produce a beautiful and very valuable pearl.

"Most people, when they first encounter me, consider me nothing more than an irritant that should be thrown away and walked over. But those who give me enough time eventually see how I can produce beauty that has great worth. Give me time, Christine. Just give me time, and I'll give you beauty of greater value than a pretty face."

She glanced down at her hands in her lap and then back into my eyes, so I started again with a tone of voice that showed the depth of my sincerity. "Look in my eyes and see if I'm not telling you the truth. Look deep, Christine, and you'll see my soul. Look beyond this mask and see if I'm whole in every other respect.

"I can offer you the same, if not more, than your young de Chagny. What does he have that I don't, other than a pretty face? His face will change, you know. He'll grow old, or some fate could befall him and he would no longer have his pretty face. Would you feel the same way about him then? What would you do if he lost his pretty face?"

She looked frightened, and I feared my words sounded more like a threat than simple reasoning, so I tried again. "Don't worry. I won't do anything to spoil his pretty face." Although I wanted to add that I was tempted, but I tried changing my direction instead.

"We have something you'll never have with him, and you know that to be true if you listen closely to your heart. You're just too frightened of this mask and all that has happened tonight to let yourself see beyond it. I don't believe you to be so shallow that you would let my mask hamper you from seeing who I am. You can't be."

I felt that ache in my jaw and tears start to form in my eyes, so I glanced at the fire and swallowed hard, trying to maintain control. "You'll never have anyone who'll share your passion for music as I do." I looked back at her and she was also staring at the fire. "Look at me, Christine. Not my mask, but me—look at me."

When she looked back into my eyes, I continued. "I can match or surpass the Vicomte's wealth and his name if you're by my side. I can make my name known on a much grander scale, believe me. I've done it before and I'll do it again—for you. You'll never find anyone who'll love you more than I. Look at me, and see me, not the mask or what's behind it."

She shook her head and frowned. "What are you talking about? Are you seriously asking me to love you and stay forever with you when we've just met? You're mad!"

"Perhaps," I responded with a sigh. "But do you really know anyone who has lived in this insane world who can claim to be entirely sane?"

Her head shook. "I must be dreaming. This can't possibly be happening to me. I don't understand any of this."

She looked around the room again and her rapid breathing was telling me she was about to do something, but I just didn't know what. My leg was hurting severely in my kneeling position, but I was afraid to move, afraid that any movement might increase her fears. Therefore, I stayed put and tried to apologize.

"I'm sorry, Christine. I never wanted you to be so frightened. I had this entire evening planned out so well, but nothing seems to be going the way I'd intended. As we traveled down here, I wanted to be singing to you so you would know who I was and trust me. The last thing I wanted was for you to fear me or my actions. I promise you, I'll do you no harm. I only want you to stay down here with me for four days. That's all I ask."

She was looking in my eyes when I finished, and, at first, I thought everything was all right, but then she recoiled from me and started again.

"What do you mean, down here? Where are we?"

I looked around at all the colorful flowers and burning candles and tried to answer her honestly. "We're in my home, and my home is in the fifth cellar of the opera house. Would you like to see it?"

Clenching my teeth, I managed to get to my feet and hold out my hand to her. She looked at my hand and then up at my face and then back at my hand. I stayed put in that position until she got up and moved past me, without taking my hand and in apparent defiance.

"This room, as you can see, doubles as a library and a drawing room. While you're here, you're welcome to read any of these books you wish. I have a nice selection, so I'm sure you can find something you'd like."

She nodded, and then her eyes scanned the multitude of books on the shelves. She moved closer to them and ran her fingers over a few of the titles, while I stood watching her with my nervous hands holding each other behind my back. That was the first positive response I'd gotten from her since we left her dressing room.

"You have eclectic taste in books," she offered as she glanced over her shoulder at me.

I took a step closer to the bookshelf and also scanned my collection. "Yes, I presume I do. I don't believe there should be any boundaries on knowledge, other than the amount of time we have on earth to take it all in."

I let her stay there until she looked back at me, and then I walked into my music room, turned and waited for her to follow me. Once she entered, I began.

"This is where I keep my most prized possession—my music."

Her eyes came to life and the fear and suspicion left for the first time, causing me to smile. She looked at me, also with a smile, and then she held that position. I then realized that was the first time I'd smiled at her. I felt my smile broaden with her reaction to my music room, or perhaps my smile, or both. She started walking through the room, running her hands over everything. When she came to my violin lying on the top of the piano, her smile softened and she picked it up. She held it a few moments, and then she looked at me.

"This is an expensive instrument. I can tell," she remarked with wonder.

I nodded. "Yes, but with its sound it would be worth any price."

She gently laid it back down on my piano and headed for the door. I started to follow her, but then she stopped and looked back at the violin.

She thought for a moment and then looked up at me. "Perros?"

I nodded, knowing it was going to take her some time to put all the pieces together.

"You were there with me? It was you who played the violin for my father?"

"Yes, Christine. I told you I would, didn't I?"

"Yes, but that was my angel."

"I was playing the part of your angel for you, to help you gain the confidence you needed, the confidence you lacked, the confidence you now have."

She stared at me, and, for only a moment, I don't think she saw the mask.

"My father was right. Your playing is beyond compare. No wonder he thought you to be an angel. You had me fooled."

"I wasn't trying to fool you, Christine. I was only trying to help you."

After a moment more of looking at me, she nodded and started to leave the room once more, but then stopped again and looked back at me.

"The park? You were the man in the park. You were there. I saw you." Her hand went to her mouth and she looked at the floor in thought. "I talked to you—there in Perros and in my dressing room. You were always there. It was you I was always talking to. It was you."

The light had finally come on, and as the thoughts flooded in on her, I thought she was going to faint again. She reached for the piano to steady herself, and I reached for her shoulder, but then I thought again and pulled away.

I motioned toward a chair by the organ and suggested, "You look as if you need to sit for a moment."

She complied, and, after sitting down, she laid her head against its back and looked at me. I stayed by my piano and away from her.

She was gazing at the ceiling as she spoke. "It was always you. All those conversations were with you."

"Yes, Christine. You see, we already know each other. I'm no stranger to you."

She nodded and looked around the room again. "I see you play more than the violin."

"Yes, I have more than an abnormal fondness for music," I replied as I ran my fingers over my piano keys. I waited a moment more and then asked, "Would you like to see the rest of my home?"

She shook her head. "Not right now. I'm tired and I like it in this room. It's comforting. Would you play something for me? Would you sing for me?"

"Absolutely, my dear. It would be my pleasure."

I accompanied myself through one piece, and she kept requesting more, so I complied. Then, at one point, I looked over my shoulder and found her asleep and I smiled. My beautiful Christine was asleep—in my home.

I stood in front of her and spoke her name, but she didn't respond. I knelt down in front of her and touched her hand, squeezing a bit and repeating her name. She opened her eyes sleepily, and I got to my feet, with her hand still in mine.

"Let me show you to your room, Christine. You need rest. It's been a trying day."

She didn't argue with me or pull her hand from mine as I led her to her room. I opened her door and we were instantly caressed with the fragrance of the burning lavender candles. We both took a deep breath at the same time, and I looked down at her and smiled. I stayed in the doorway and gestured with my hand for her to enter. She looked up at me and walked past me so close that I thought I would be the one to faint.

When she looked in, she gasped. "I can tell you put a lot of thought into making me comfortable, and, while I do appreciate it, I'm still angry with you."

I closed my eyes. "I know, and rightfully so."

I was at her mercy and was preparing for the worst scenario: her complete rejection.

She looked around and then looked at me with a strange expression on her face.

"This is my favorite color and scent. Everything is so beautiful. Did you know? Did you know lavender was my favorite color?"

I smiled and nodded. "I wanted you to be pleased with the room. Are you pleased?"

"Oh, yes, thank you," she responded while looking around. "You've gone to so much trouble for me."

"Believe me, Christine, it's been no trouble at all. In the armoire and through that door you should find everything you need to make yourself comfortable."

She nodded. "Thank you, but I'm still angry with you for what you've done to me. You had no right to bring me here this way. I'm not your possession."

"I know, and I do apologize," I replied with lowered head. "I truly do apologize."

She sighed. "I can't imagine the worry those above us must be going through."

I had no answer, for that feature of my plan I'd neglected to consider. I was trying to think my way to a good response when she cocked her head and noticed the dressing table. She frowned as she ran her fingers along its edges, much as she had in the shop.

"I love this piece. I've dreamt of owning it for . . ." She froze and stared at it. Then she looked at me. "Was this merely a coincidence or did you know how much I liked this particular antique?"

"I knew you liked it, and I wanted you to have it."

"But how did you know? I don't remember telling anyone about it, not even Mummy or Meg."

"Your heart knew it, so I knew it," I replied while slipping back into her angel's character.

"No!" she snapped. "No more tricks and lies. You're not an angel. You can't read my heart, so how did you know?"

"Very well, I saw you in that antique shop, and I saw how you looked at it, so in a way I was reading your heart."

She frowned more. "You saw me there? When?"

"Often," was my answer as I shifted my weight and leaned against the door frame, trying to relieve the pain in my leg.

She frowned even more and cocked her head at me that time. "Do you also visit that shop?" She glanced around. "I don't see other antiques in here, only this one. And all the lavender—how did you know that was my favorite color and scent?"

I started to answer, but by then she was putting the pieces together so she asked me outright, "Did you follow me to that shop?"

"I have to admit that I did, but . . ."

Before I could defend myself, she scrunched her face. "You followed me? Like a stalker? That's sick. No, that's demented."

"Demented?" I rebutted strongly, while forgetting who I was talking to. "Really now. Demented?"

Fortunately, I took a breath and a moment to hold my tongue before I did serious harm. She had no idea why certain words cut right through me, so I tried to continue in a softer tone, but, from her reaction, I think my strong feelings showed through anyway.

"Demented? Perhaps some might call it that, but I was acting out of love, and I wanted the woman I loved to have her heart's desire. I also wanted her to be safe, and a woman walking alone on the streets of Paris is not safe. You can call me your unseen escort if you wish but not demented. My *stalking* you, as you called it, was done out of a heart full of love—not a demented mind."

She looked shocked and silently stared at me. Realizing the blunder I'd made, I clenched my teeth and lowered my head.

"I'm sorry, Christine. That was rude of me. There're some subjects that hit . . . I . . . it . . . please forgive my outburst. It won't happen again."

Her face softened, she took a deep breath, and looked around the room again. When her sight came back to the dressing table, she ran her fingers over the items I'd put on top of it, then she picked up the lavender quill and ran it gently across her fingers.

"You certainly captured the essence of my likes," she said softly when glancing at me.

"I tried," was my simple reply.

She looked back down at the items on her table, and then her eyes widened when she looked at the two red roses.

She looked at me again and softly smiled. "It was *you* who gave me two fresh roses every day. It was all you."

I nodded, and she slightly shook her head. She steadied herself with her fingertips on the edge of the table and then sat down in the chair. Her head was down when she shook it again.

"It was always you," she repeated almost under her breath. She raised her head and glanced at her reflection in the mirror. Then she gasped and her fingers covered her open mouth. "The mirror? The flowers talked. The mirror talked. The tree in Perros? It talked. You made them talk? How did you make them talk?" She put her palm against her forehead and seriously frowned. "There's so much I don't understand. I feel so confused. What have you done to me?"

In my most compassionate tone, I tried to reassure her. "I realize there's a lot you don't understand, and I don't expect you to understand it all at once. We'll talk more tomorrow, and I'll answer all your questions then. Try to sleep now, and if you need anything else, just let me know."

She nodded. "I'd like you to play your violin for me. When I was a child and couldn't sleep, my father played his violin for me. It would be comforting to me if you would play yours now."

"It's my pleasure," I responded. Then, as I started to close the door, I added softly, "Sleep well, Christine."

Twenty-Three

As the door clicked closed, I leaned back against it and sighed contentedly. She was here. She was finally here in my home. At that moment, my heart swelled with love and thanksgiving for her.

To fulfill her request, I got my violin and began playing softly. While sitting on the coffee table and glancing at her door often, I played three pieces before I stopped. Then I just sat there, looking at the door and thinking. The day may not have gone exactly the way I'd intended, but it ended with her sleeping under my roof. What more could I ask?

That question triggered the pain of being shot, the sick visions of Buquet hanging in the third cellar, and the horrors of the chandelier falling. Those thoughts took me in an entirely different direction, so I went to Christine's door and knocked softly. There was no answer, and since I needed to be sure she was sleeping before I left her alone, I peeked in. The sight of her asleep, with her golden hair spread out over the lavender pillow, helped to soothe my troubled spirit.

Within minutes after that, my cloak was on, and I was heading up the passage that led from my music room to the main floor. Everyone was gone from the auditorium, except for ten men working around the fallen chandelier. All the restful thoughts I'd had while playing my violin for Christine were completely gone by the time I reached the chandelier's rigging room.

My managers were there with several workers and two uniformed men, so I waited for over an hour for them to leave before I could do my own investigating. What I discovered made my heart ill.

The metal supports for the chandelier's counter balance looked as if they'd been damaged by heat, perhaps a small electrical fire. Earlier that day, I'd opted not to climb any higher and check that one area because of my leg. I reasoned that they were metal and weren't that old so they should have been in perfect condition, but, obviously, they weren't.

I felt so sick, especially since there were many who were injured and there was one death—the new box keeper. I sat on a crate for quite some time, stone-faced and looking at the gaping hole in the floor. I still couldn't believe that I'd made such a gross error. I tried to rationalize that at least there was only one death when there could have been many, but it didn't help. I believe I would have slipped back into a depressed state and used a fatal dose of morphine if it hadn't been for Christine alone in my home. So, with her in mind, I headed back down. On the way, I stumbled across my walking stick, so, using it, I was soon in my lair.

It was almost seven a.m. when I sat down with some hot tea and wrote Christine a note, letting her know where I was and what I was doing. With my physical condition decreasing by the minute, I knew I had to keep my appointment with the doctor if I wanted to keep my promise to Christine about having all my appendages in good working order.

I knocked on her door softly, and, when I didn't hear a reply, I cracked the door open and was instantly caressed with the scent of lavender. I then stepped in enough to lay the note on her dressing table. I was backing out of the room when the beam of light from the drawing room fell across her bed. The temptation was simply too great, so I moved beside her, looking down at her beautiful face and form. I touched my fingertips to her hair, but when she stirred I quickly left.

The sun was shining brightly that morning when I entered Doctor Leglise's office, but, when he saw me, his reception wasn't bright at all. I guess he could tell from my appearance that I hadn't followed his instructions and rested, because he gave me that same look of disapproval without saying anything. He motioned for me to follow him into his examination room and again motioned for me to lie down on the cot.

"Take off your trousers," were his only words, and then he left the room.

When he came back in, he had the tray with his instruments and that jar of creepy maggots. Then he stood beside me, still without a hello or any greeting. He felt my forehead and then proceeded to take the bandage off my leg. He sighed, long and slow, gave me a sideways glance, and then, taking the tweezers in his fingers, he began removing my dead workers.

I finally spoke up, sarcastically. "Well, good morning to you too."

He only gave me that same sideways glance, and then his eyes returned to the work at hand. I folded my fingers behind my neck and closed my eyes, thinking he must have had a fight with his wife or something, and I wasn't up to dealing with it, so I stayed quiet.

Then, after a few minutes of silence, he asked, "Erik, what do you do for a living?"

My eyes sprung open. "What?"

"You heard me. What do you do for a living?"

Naturally, I couldn't tell him the truth, so I asked, "Why, are my workers complaining?"

"No. Actually, they're quite peaceful. *They're all dead.* Now, tell me, what kind of work do you do? Your fingernails aren't dirty and they look recently manicured, so I don't think you do manual labor or work out of doors. I see traces of ink on your fingers. Do you sit at a desk all day? Are you a designer or perhaps a writer?"

Searching his face while trying to understand why he wanted to know, I responded, "You could say that. Why?"

Without looking at me, he asked, "Think of something you worked hard on or created, and then picture someone destroying that design without giving any consideration for the hard work you'd put into it. How would that make you feel, Erik?"

Again, he gave me that sideways glance. Then, without giving me a chance to answer, he went on. "Each time you come here, I can tell you're destroying my work. I've repeatedly told you the importance of getting rest and staying off this leg, but, for some reason, you're refusing to take my advice. I realize the importance of this other person in your life, but if you don't listen to me, you'll not have a life to share with this person. Your leg looks much worse than it did when you first came to me. Sit up, Erik, and look at your leg."

I just looked at him. Then sternly he repeated, "Look at it."

I lifted my head and shoulders and looked down.

"Do you see this?" he said as he pointed to a long red streak going from my wound to my hip. "Now look at the wound itself. It's growing. That streak is getting longer and telling me that the infection is moving through your body and will soon reach your heart or brain. When that happens . . ." He shook his head.

"There's only so much I can do. You have to follow my instructions or you'll be dead within the week, Erik. And I guarantee you—that's no idle threat. You need to stay here and let me take care of you. This leg needs hot compresses with medicated water several times a day, and it needs to be immobile."

I thought about Christine locked in my home with no way out, and said softly, "I can't stay here."

He stopped what he was doing and stared down into the wound, with his hands and instruments poised over my thigh.

"What do you expect me to do, Erik? Create a miracle?" He sighed and closed his eyes. "If you won't stay here, let me come to you. Tell me where you live, and I'll come to you every day and treat you there."

I lay back down and searched for the right words. "That's impossible. It's far away, through a winding territory, and across a lake. Even if I gave you directions, you wouldn't find it. Nobody can."

He went back to his work, but continued with his reasoning. "If your home is that difficult to reach, that's all the more reason for you to stay here."

I shook my head. "I left the one I love there, and she won't be able to find her way out. She could starve."

"She's in your home? Well then, let her take care of you," he replied, thinking he had the solution to his unique problem.

Knowing that was also impossible, I shook my head.

"Erik! Why are you being so difficult?" He huffed, slammed his instruments down on the tray, and walked across the room with his back to me. "Listen to me," he said sternly and then turned to face me. "If she loves you, then she'll be glad to help you. You have to stay off this leg and treat it properly."

Trying to work with him and be as honest as I could, I replied, "Look, Doctor Leglise, I truly appreciate everything you're doing and your advice. I don't want to die and I don't want to lose my leg. I finally have someone in my life, and I want to be the best I can for her. I have to admit that the last few days or weeks have been strenuous on me physically, but the days ahead won't be, and I'll be able to rest."

"Why is it I don't believe you, Erik?" he asked while walking back toward me.

I looked straight in his eyes and my tone was serious. "Perhaps because I haven't been the ideal patient up until now. As I said, I don't want to die; in fact, I want to live now more than at any other time in my life, so work with me on this. Other than a few errands on my way home, I can . . ."

"Oh, Erik!" he shouted as he slammed his fist down on the mattress. "See, you're already doing it. You aren't even out of my office and you're already planning not to listen to me."

"This is the last of it, I promise," I tried to reassure him.

"And you expect me to believe any of your promises, Erik—after your track record?"

I pushed my head back against the pillow. "I know I must sound crazy to you and full of contradictions, but I do promise. I only have three stops on my way home, and then I won't do anything else, except come back here to see you."

He looked in my eyes and then at my leg. Then, with his hands behind his back, he backed away and leaned against the wall. He sighed deeply while focusing intently on my wound. Obviously, he was thinking over something, so I remained quiet and waited for him. After a few more sighs, he covered me with a sheet and left the room.

When he returned, he had two books in his hands. He then sat in a chair and began thumbing through them. Periodically, he made a notation on a piece of paper, and then he continued his reading. I used the time to close my eyes, while telling myself that I had to trust him and his judgment. I didn't want to lose my life, especially now that I had a chance to live it with Christine.

The room was quiet and my thoughts turned to the shattered chandelier and those injured. I spent the next half hour, unsuccessfully, trying to remove those visions. Finally, he laid the books down and left the room again, with the piece of paper in his hand. When he came back in, he pulled the chair up beside me, sat down, and laid his hand on my arm.

"I presume the more we're challenged the better we become, right, Erik? Well, I have to admit you're the biggest challenge of my career, not necessarily your wound but you. I don't want you to come back for at least four days. Especially now that I know how hard it is for you to get here. You're to stay at home and down until then.

"I'm sending you home with all you'll need to take care of your leg. I'll also send instructions for your lady friend on how to take care of you. I'm trying some new procedures on you, although to those in China they're very old. I'll also send a good supply of maggots in their different stages for you or your friend to use, but they'll only be productive for four days, then you have to come back here and let me see how they've done. Anytime during those days, if you feel worse or the wound looks worse, then please, Erik, please come to me right away.

"I'll now finish cleaning out the area, and I want you to sit up so you can see what I'm doing and how to recognize the dead maggots from the live ones. Are you willing to work with me on this or do I throw my hands in the air and forewarn the undertaker?"

"You can count on me to follow your instructions," I honestly replied.

However, I didn't intend to involve Christine in what I was to do, but I couldn't tell him that. It wouldn't bode well to tell him that she didn't love me or that she was my prisoner in what some would call a dungeon. No, that wouldn't do at all. Perhaps Christine was right; perhaps I was demented. What else would explain my keeping a beautiful and precious woman locked in the basement of the opera house?

He sent his secretary out to buy the supplies he needed while he went to work again on my wound. It was almost ten a.m. before he let me leave, but not before he gave me one last piece of advice.

"You have to follow these instructions precisely. Unless you do all that's written here, it'll be tantamount to putting a fresh coat of paint on a barn with one hand and then throwing a lighted match on the hay inside that barn with the other hand. All this," he said emphatically, while shaking his instruction in front of my face, "will be for naught. You'll die, and then what will happen to that woman waiting for you?"

He was right. I had to do it his way for Christine. So I moved quickly to finish some necessary errands and then get back home to her before she woke without me there. After telling the driver that I was in a hurry, he moved us through the streets as quickly as safety would allow.

Once in the dress shop, I picked out three dresses for Christine—a simple blue, a not so simple forest green, and a deep purple, velvet evening gown with a matching cloak. While I rested in a comfortable stuffed chair, the clerk found all the undergarments she would need.

Once finished with that shop, I picked up a fresh bouquet of flowers and then went to my favorite restaurant. I told the proprietor what I wanted, and he happily supplied my needs, especially once he saw the amount of cash I had on me. I took a few items with me, like little shrimps, chicken wings, and bread. Everything else I had him deliver to the back door of the opera house at two p.m. every day for the next week.

One more stop and then I could go home to Christine. I had the driver go to the area where I'd found my young helpers. We had to circle around the area before I found them two blocks away in a field, throwing rocks at tin cans on a fence. They came running when I called them.

"I have another job for you, if you want it."

"Sure," was their eager response.

"A package will be delivered to the back door of the opera house every day at two p.m., and I need it taken down to the lake. Here's a note from the opera management. It will gain you access to the building, and you know where to go from there."

With that finished, my plans were set so I went home.

After I dropped the food off in my dining room, my arms were still loaded down with packages, large and small. I went to Christine's door and tapped three times, and, when I didn't get a response, I opened the door slowly. I was startled when I saw her standing on the other side of the room, but, rather than saying anything about it, I laid all the packages on her bed.

"These are for you. I hope you like them. Once you're dressed, food will be waiting in the dining room."

She didn't respond, so I simply nodded and backed out of her room, trying not to be too distracted by the vision of her in that blue dressing gown. That wasn't the response I was expecting from her; it wasn't nearly as cordial as when I'd said goodnight to her, but I tried not to read too much into it.

While I waited for her, I set the table with my best dishes and glasses and the new bouquet. Then I arranged the prawns and chicken wings on a platter and brought out a bottle of Tokay that I'd brought back from the cellars of Konigsberg. I'd been saving it for a special occasion, and nothing could possibly be more special than that day. I also put the English sweets in a bowl on the table. Once finished with the table, I built a fire, thinking that after we ate we could sit by it and talk.

When she finally came out, she was wearing the simple blue dress, and she took my breath away. Without the ability to think or talk, I could only smile and motion toward the dining room. I held the chair for her and then sat down across from her.

"This all looks so nice," she remarked politely. "You shouldn't have gone to this much trouble. Cheese and bread would have sufficed, but thank you anyway."

I still couldn't find my once eloquent words, so I merely nodded. She began eating, but I wasn't capable of eating anything. I don't think I'd eaten anything in the last two days, but my nerves weren't in the best condition, and the thought of putting anything down my throat was repulsive.

I was feeling bad in every way possible, and it angered me. Here I finally had the chance to be with Christine and eat our first meal together and carry on polite conversation, but all I could see or hear was the chandelier crashing to the floor and people screaming. I tried to erase those visions and focus on the soft beauty before me, but they kept weaving in and out of my thoughts.

While Christine was doing a good job of keeping the conversation light, I knew she had to be thinking about that disaster also. She'd been distraught the night before in her dressing room, so she couldn't have forgotten about it that easily. I feared her bringing up the subject and asking if anyone was killed. I didn't want to tell her that someone had been killed. I wanted the days ahead to be spent with her getting to know who I really was, but then maybe what had happened and any conversation about it was proof of exactly who I was.

Eventually, she began asking me questions, so I was forced to start communicating with her.

"Erik isn't a French name. What's your native country?"

That question caught me off guard, but did help to take my mind off the chandelier.

"I have no country. I picked that name out of a hat, you might say."

"And what type of a last name did you pick?" she asked after she took a sip of her Tokay.

Taking a breath and leaning back in my chair, I had to think seriously about my answer. I hadn't told anyone my last name except for the planning committee, and I really didn't want anyone to know it. It was almost sacred to me, since, to me, it represented my father. But I had to tell her something, so I used my old trick of hiding the answer among a confusion of words.

"I have no need for a last name. A last name establishes genealogy or a legacy, and since I have neither, and quite possibly never will have, there's no need for one. The only other reason for a last name is to distinguish you from others who have the same first name. I don't believe I need that either. Once someone meets this Erik, that one name alone is all they need to distinguish me from any others who might also carry that name. Hence, I need no last name. I'm simply Erik."

While explaining that to her, I'd leaned forward in my chair and laid my hand on top of hers. When I finished my explanation, she discreetly pulled her hand back, and I apologized.

"I'm sorry, Christine. I didn't mean to be so forward. It's just that I've waited so long to have you sit across the table from me that I must have forgotten my manners. I want to stay within the bounds of propriety; however, I presume just bringing you down here has indubitably crossed those boundaries already. I'll try harder not to touch you in any way, but I can't promise that I won't express my love for you on a regular basis, if not by words, then at least through the windows to my heart."

As she patted her lips with her napkin, she gazed at me in silence. I gazed back, so thankful to have her across the table from me at last. Her gaze left me and traveled around my home. From where we were sitting, she could see into every room, so she asked her next question.

"This is all you have—these five rooms?"

I also looked around and nodded, since I couldn't tell her about my mirror chamber, for how could I explain a room filled with mirrors and a lone tree. I couldn't, so my response was simple.

"My needs are few, music, books, and now you. That's all I need."

"You don't need to sleep? I don't see another bed in here. I'm not taking your bed, am I?"

"Oh, no, no, no." I replied while looking down at my hand, tracing a design on the table top with my fork handle. "I have a bed in my music room. That's where I sleep."

"Hmm, I didn't see a bed in there," she mused.

"I keep it covered with a tapestry," I tried to explain with a cleverly woven lie. "That's why you didn't recognize it."

Fortunately, she changed the subject when she looked at my empty plate. "You're not eating. Have you already eaten?"

"As I said, my needs are few. I can eat later. Right now, I'd like to hear more about you—your likes and dislikes."

She looked at me thoughtfully before she responded. "From what you told me last night, you already know all about me and Raoul. So you tell me what my likes and dislikes are."

I leaned back in my chair. "Well, I know you think you love Raoul. I know he makes you angry when he talks badly about other people, and I know you have to stand on your tiptoes to kiss him."

"Kiss him?" She frowned and looked straight into my eyes. "I've only kissed him once and that was in Perros. How could you know that?"

I leaned forward, placed my elbows on the table and my chin on my knuckles before I answered. "I have a way about me, and, when I need to know things, I have ways of finding them out. How else do you think the Opera Ghost got his reputation for seeing and hearing everything—for knowing everything?"

"Opera Ghost?" she questioned with wide eyes. "What are you saying? Do you know the Opera Ghost?" Then she gasped and covered her mouth with her napkin. "Are you the Opera Ghost?"

I smiled and almost chuckled while leaning back in my chair again. Then I raised my arms out from my sides and answered, "One and the same, my dear."

"I don't understand. There are so many things I don't understand."

"Don't be concerned, Christine. It's really not a mystery at all. I had to learn at an early age to see and hear everything that went on around me. It was the only way I could survive with this," I said as I tapped the side of my mask. "Without certain skills, I would have died a long time ago."

"But you are human—aren't you?"

I chuckled, "Yes, I believe so. Although, there are times when I question that myself."

"Then how much can you see and hear?"

"Well, I can't see through walls like a real angel, if that's what you're concerned about. But I do have excellent hearing, so I can hear through them easily."

"Through walls?" she asked rhetorically. "Can you also make your voice go through walls clearly?"

"To a degree, yes," I replied. "You're learning how to control your voice, how to sing softly and yet have it heard in the back of a room. That's the beginning of what I've learned to do. I can make my voice do almost anything. I can make it land anywhere I want it to land. I can make it land so softly that only the ones close enough to it can hear it. I can make it sound like anything I want, whether that's another person or animal. With enough training, anyone can do it. It's nothing supernatural, nothing to fear."

She sat quietly for a few moments, and the expression in her eyes showed she was putting more of the confusing pieces together. Then she started a dialogue that I feared, since I knew it could frighten her.

"There were times when I could hear your voice distinctly, like when it was on the roses. But there were other times when it was all around me, like the air I was breathing. Then there were times when it sounded much different, more human. Those times it came from the mirror. Those times . . . I felt . . ." She almost shuddered and wrapped her arms around herself. "Those times, I sensed I was being watched."

By the time she'd said that, she was gazing at the flowers on the table, and then her gaze came back to my eyes.

"You said you can't see through walls, but could you see me when you were talking to me? I felt you could always see me, but that was when I believed you to be my angel. Could you somehow see me in my dressing room?"

Here we go, I thought. "Yes, but I never watched you if propriety wouldn't allow it. So you always maintained your privacy, if that's what you're frightened about."

She recoiled from me and looked away, still with her arms wrapped around herself. Then she looked toward her room and scrunched her shoulders.

"Can you see into that room?" She looked back at me, almost with defiance. "Are you still watching me?"

"No!" I responded with a strong shake of my head. "In that room you have absolute privacy—I promise."

"Then how could you see me in my dressing room? It didn't have windows, so how did you do it?"

"Your mirror is see-through. When I'm behind it, I can see into your dressing room."

"Behind it?" she rhetorically questioned again. "You were behind it?"

"Yes. That's true, but again you maintained your privacy. I never used that mirror to see anything that I shouldn't have seen. I only used it to get to know you better so I could please you more. I only wanted to help you attain your rightful place on the stage."

She gazed down into her plate and rested her forehead against her fingertips. "Behind the mirror?" She looked again toward her room. "There's a mirror in there. Can you see me through it?"

"No. That mirror is exactly what it looks like—an ordinary mirror."

She looked at me with a slight frown, and then she gasped. "I walked through my dressing room mirror. You called me through the mirror, but how? I thought I was dreaming or dead, but now I know I wasn't. I know I'm human, so how could I walk through the mirror? Explain this to me, please."

"You didn't walk through it. It opens much the same way as a door. I opened it and you walked into the passage behind it with me."

"There's a passage behind it?"

"Yes, it's one the Opera Ghost hides in and travels through."

"I'm so confused. Everything about last night is a blur. I was so frightened after the chandelier fell. I was frightened for those poor people and I was frightened for myself and my angel. I thought I was dead when I entered that passage." She shuddered again. "I don't want to talk about this anymore. It frightens me."

"Then we won't talk about it. Let's do something that will make you feel better. Let's forget about the horror of last night for now and begin your music lessons. We could rehearse for the upcoming production of *Othello*, and when we're finished we can sit by the fire and read a good book together. How does that sound?"

Her eyes lit up. "Yes, I would like that."

We went into my music room, and, while I began playing, Christine sang Desdemona with all the despair the role called for and was so perfect that she almost replaced my horrible visions. Then the lines of Othello approached, and my voice rumbled through the room with all his anger and love, combined with my own, and, with it, the vision of the chandelier returned. I tried harder and focused on the keys. But my fingers, which transferred ruthlessly all the emotion displayed in that scene, kept changing places with the bodies lying under the chandelier. Concentrate! Concentrate, I demanded, while trying to focus on Christine's face.

The very air was charged with such power that I should have anticipated an explosion of great magnitude, but I never did. I never expected the hateful deception of the woman I loved and unquestionably trusted at that moment. I'd just laid my heart open, exposed, and defenseless, and yet she turned on me like Judas, with smiling lips at one moment and a viper's bite the next.

With the sound of our combined voices filling my home and my soul, my heart was ripped from my chest as my mask was torn from my face.

Twenty-Four

With gut wrenching horror, I felt my mask being ripped from my face, ripped by the hand of the woman I loved. I jumped to my feet, with clenching jaws and with my naked and gruesome face exposed prematurely. The sands of time passed in slow motion until Christine's screams instantly woke me to the truth, causing me to storm forward in a rage that easily could have ended the life of that screeching woman.

Quite naturally, she covered her face with her hands, attempting to hide from the monster that unexpectedly appeared before her. She backed away, fell against the wall, and then crumbled to the floor—as if preparing for her death.

In that instant, I felt my life end. Everything I wanted and needed was gone in that one instant. All my hope for a love with Christine vanished along with my mask, and the pain within my chest was so great I could feel it bleeding.

Her eyes cautiously appeared between her fingers, those eyes so familiar to me, those eyes in the street when I was a child, those eyes gawking at me in the cage, those eyes on the streets of Venice, those eyes that haunted my sleep. Those eyes were then sucked into a swirling funnel and combined with my lifetime of emotional anguish and torture. Together, they joined forces and violently exploded—all in that one moment in time.

I screamed and flung slicing words in her direction, words I would never dream of using in the presence of a lady. But, during those horrifying moments, she wasn't a lady to me, so, with a dragon's roar, I began dismantling everything in my path. Time moved strangely, and the happenings of the next span of time blurred and became as difficult to differentiate as ships moving on a vast sea draped in mist.

I rushed back on her again and towered over her, growling insanely. She was crying pitifully, but then she looked up at me with her eyes filled with a different fear, and in them I saw other eyes. I saw the eyes of the men at the campfire massacre in Persia, and together they quickly stopped me. Her eyes were the same as theirs. They saw their deaths coming, and I saw their last thoughts about the monster preparing to end their heartbeats.

I saw the black eyes of those Armenians, and I saw the blue eyes of my Christine; then together they shared the time and space in my darkened memories.

My anger then moved inward, and I turned from her and continued dismantling my music room. The winds of rage tossed everything in the room—sheet music, books, chairs, wall tapestries, paintings, candles—everything in my wake was nothing more than parchment in a hurricane, including my own tortured soul. When there was nothing left to hurl, I slammed my body against a wall. Then I slumped down it to the floor in mournful cries.

Everything was gone. I had nothing left. Christine then knew not only the monster's face but also the monster's heart—everything was lost. She was gone. I'd lost her for good. I had nothing left but my sorry excuse of a body and despicable soul.

Then there was an empty stillness, and I was lying stretched out and face down on the floor, with the hem of Christine's skirt in my hands and pressed against my naked and deplorable face. Gradually, I heard my pathetic crying mixed in with Christine's pitiful sobs, and I felt the hem of her new dress wet with my tears.

"Christine.—Christine," I whispered pathetically.

The room became silent with nothing but our breaths as evidence that life still continued in my dismantled home. Slowly, I curled away from her, turned my back, and got to my feet. A second later, her quivering voice came across the settling air.

"It doesn't matter. Look! It doesn't matter."

I heard her get up and move into the parlor, so, with my hand covering the gaping hole in the center of my face, I glanced over my shoulder. She was hurrying through the parlor with my mask in her hand, and when she was in front of the fireplace she threw it in.

"Look!" she continued to exclaim through her sniffles. "It doesn't matter. Now I know what's behind the mask and it doesn't matter. You don't need to wear it any longer."

I knew her too well, and the act she was performing wasn't a convincing one, which sent me in a more dangerous direction than the calamity we'd somehow managed to live through.

As I headed for my armoire and another mask, I growled low at her. "Oh, really? You're so accustomed to seeing a man without a nose that it doesn't matter to you any longer? Your curiosity, *my little Pandora*, is now sufficiently appeased?"

"No, it really doesn't matter," she tried, unsuccessfully, to convince me.

Her tear-streaked cheeks pressed into an artificial smile, adding more fuel to my fire. Her acting skills were great, but not great enough to pass her teacher's scrutiny. I felt my anger mount with her continued deception, the anger *I* feared the most—my controlled anger. After slipping on another mask, I walked toward her, slowly and deliberately. Her eyes were focused intently on mine, and I heard a small whimper before she tried again to defuse the irate monster approaching her.

"I don't think I told you how beautiful your eyes are, and I love your smile. It makes my heart happy when you smile. Please, smile for me, Erik."

"If a smile is what you wish, then I'll grant you your last wish. Is this better, *my sweet*," I responded with my most sinister smile.

She tried desperately to control her breathing, but a whimper escaped nonetheless. I stopped about two meters away from her and looked at my smoldering mask in the fireplace.

"You really shouldn't have done that—*my dear*. That mask was my favorite one, and it took me a long time to perfect. I wore it for you this day, *Christine*. I've done a lot of things for you, not only this day but for months now. I gave you my heart unconditionally. I gave you my music that made it possible for you to sing center stage." I motioned toward my burnt mask and shook my head. "I gave you so much and this is how you repay me?"

I slowly closed the space between us, and she started to back away but then caught herself and held her ground. When I was directly in front of her, I reached for her hair and smiled wickedly. Her quick and trembling breaths gave away her fright, and I narrowed my eyes with pleasure. Then I grasped the back of her hair tightly, forcing her head to stay in one place. I watched the fear in her eyes mount as I moved my face down until our lips were only a few centimeters apart.

With a tone that would make the devil himself retreat, I hissed, "You deceiving temptress. My face is not bad you say, *my dear*? Well, that's so nice to hear. You see, once a woman sees Erik's face, she's hooked and can never look upon another's the same way again. My face is quite handsome, I agree. A feast for the eyes, I admit. Now, at long last, you know the face of the voice that has comforted you and guided you.

"You're extremely privileged to have seen it. You know, most never have that privilege. But it does come with a price. The Erik with the concealed face only asked you for four days, because after those four days you could have loved him. But now that you know his comely features, you've instantly fallen in love with him, and you're his possession now—*and forever and ever and ever*. Now those four days have turned into four hundred years.

"Oh, what's that you say?—You don't mind, you say?—Oh, you're so brave for such a *young and pretty girl*." I watched my fingertip move across the tears on her cheek. "A pretty girl with a beautiful voice. She could have any young man in Paris if she wanted." I looked back in her eyes. "Would you like this man, Christine?—This man without a nose? Certainly you do, because, I'm a sort of Don Juan, you know. I'm irresistible—wouldn't you say? Yes, I'm Don Juan, because I now have the beautiful young singer to call my own—*forever*.

"What's this I see in your eyes? Disbelief? You say you can't believe the beautiful face of Erik can be real. Perhaps you think the face without a nose is also a mask? Well, do you want to remove it also?" I reached for her hand that was clinging to her skirt and held it in mine. "Well, see for yourself, *my dear*. See that its beauty is real and not merely the figment of your *curious* imagination."

Holding her hand firmly, I made her nails dig into my cheek and then ripped them across it. "Are you quite satisfied now, *my pretty*? Now that you've left a scar on Erik's perfect flesh and made his tears turn to ruby red?"

I looked at her quivering lips and outlined them with my finger. "Have you ever kissed a man without a nose, Christine?" Then, with unadulterated venom and narrowed eyes, I looked back into hers. "I know you haven't. You see, I'm a dying breed—I am." Still with a firm grasp on her hair, I moved my other hand down and wrapped my fingers around her throat.

"They say that, when you lose one part of your anatomy, your body compensates and other parts become more acute, more sensitive. Since you're such a curious little creature, aren't you curious to know what other body parts have compensated for my lack of a nose? Perhaps my fingers," I questioned as I moved them slowly up and down her neck. "Or perhaps my lips, *my dear*. Would you like to find out what my lips would feel like against yours?"

I remained silent for a moment and glared down into her eyes, watching as she struggled to maintain her composure. I could feel her rapid pulse in her throat, and I could feel her quickened breaths as they passed her lips and landed on mine, one after the other.

My voice was not nearly as venomous as I repeated my question, "Well, do you, Christine? Do you want to know what it would be like to kiss the man with the angelic voice, the man with the monster's face, the man without a nose?"

I glanced down at her lips and then back into her eyes. She did the same, and then there was silence again with only our breathing heard. She was so frightened, and it didn't matter that she didn't answer me because her eyes did. But then, slowly, her eyes changed, and my anger began melting under the warmth of her gaze.

The longer we held that position, the more my temper waned and my remorse over what I was doing to her began to slip through my web of revenge. Then my remorse started to gain the superior position, and I softened my grasp on her hair and my vengeful thoughts. Soon my hand was no longer gripping at her hair; it was cradling the back of her head. Then my fingertips woke to the softness of her hair and neck; like the finest spun silk.

I looked again at her rosy lips and was about to back away from her when her eyes changed again and spoke that special language. They spoke the words her voice couldn't convince me of. They weren't frightened any longer; they were telling me to follow through on my threat and to kiss her. I studied their expression until I felt my own breathing start to increase, then I let go of her and backed away.

The tall clock's pendulum was the only marker of time as we fixed our attention on each other's eyes, neither of us knowing how or when to make the next move. After a few tension filled moments, Christine released a slight sigh. I used that one simple movement to back away farther; with my head lowered in shame. Once I reached the door to my music room, I raised my eyes to hers again.

Then, softly, I said, "I apologize . . . . I . . . I don't . . . I'm sorry. My behavior was despicable. I'm so sorry."

I finished backing into my music room and then closed my door. I laid my head back against it and began to cry. What had I done? I'd just ruined everything. My tears came without restraint, and I was soon sitting on the floor with my knees curled to my chest. Oh, what had I done? There was no way she could learn to love me now, not after she'd witnessed the worst of my personality traits. What had I done? What was I to do? How could I go back out there and face her? Again, in anger, I tore my mask off and threw it across the room. What was I to do now?

Two hours passed, during which time I'd cried all the tears I had in me, replaced my mask, and cleaned the shambles I'd made out of my music room. While in that process, I knew I had to take her back to the living above us before I did further harm, a harm that could be irreversible. When I pictured what I'd done to her and what I could have done to her, I shuddered with fear. I could have easily killed her, the woman I loved. What was wrong with me?

Then, pacing, I knew I'd never be able to look in her eyes again, not after what I'd done. But I knew I had to take her back, so I told myself to become a man and go into the next room and face the music. Eventually, I took a deep breath and opened the door. Christine was sitting curled in the corner of the divan, and, as I entered, her eyes rose to meet mine. In shame,

I looked away from her. Then, keeping my eyes on the smoldering fire, I walked to it in silence.

Placing one hand on the mantel, I lowered my head, swallowed with difficulty, and spoke gently. "I'm truly sorry for the way I've treated you, Christine. There's no excuse for my behavior. I hope I didn't hurt you, and I hope that someday you can forgive me."

I could tell she was watching me when she softly replied, "No, you didn't hurt me, and I'm also sorry. I had no right to do what I did, and I don't know why I did it. There are times when I just become so curious about something, and I don't think through my actions or my words. It's a failing I have, I guess, and I'm not sure how to control it. At times, I say or do things that are none of my business. Today was one of those times, and I'm truly sorry for intruding on your privacy that way, and I hope that someday you can forgive me."

By the time she was finished, I was looking over my shoulder at her, thinking about her humility. Then I came to the realization that what she'd done to me, although wrong, was one of the reasons why I loved her so much. Removing my mask was due to her need to know about me, the same need I'd seen in her those days when she questioned everyone she came in contact with. It was a good quality, so how could I be angry with her? I couldn't; in fact, that quality was definitely one of the reasons I loved her so much.

"Christine, I need to take . . ." I couldn't say it. I hurt inside with the thought of taking her back up, so I waited to gather my strength while I gazed at the dying embers. I didn't trust myself, so I knew she had to leave, but I couldn't say it. I didn't want her to leave.

"Yes?" she asked. "You were saying?"

As I clenched my jaws, I gave into my selfish desires. "Never mind. It can wait."

I believe she was just as exhausted as I was, so she didn't pursue it further. Gradually and guardedly, we began talking, first about respecting each other's privacy and about our personal failings. Then we talked for hours about our likes and dislikes that led into a discussion about the different things we could do while she was there, starting with her lessons.

We wanted them to continue each morning as before, and since we'd missed a proper morning exercise, I suggested we practice at that time. She agreed, but as we entered the music room again, I could feel the tension, with even the air around us still remembering those horrible minutes. Therefore, I tried to get us right into the lesson. The sooner we started the better; it was a safe place for both of us to be. But her natural curiosity got in our way.

"May I ask you a question, Erik?"

"Feel free to ask me anything. You've earned that right."

"You said you had a bed in here. Where is it?"

For the life of me, I don't know why I answered her the way I did. I can only blame it on my perverted and sick sense of humor or perhaps I was merely trying to lighten the spirit in the room. I'm not sure, but my answer was ridiculous.

I walked over to my coffin, pulled the tapestry off of it, opened its lid and said, "Right here."

She gasped first with wide eyes, and then she looked up at me and grimaced. "You sleep in a coffin?"

"Why not?" I came back with a snicker and in a matter-of-fact way. "We all end up there someday anyway, so why not get used to it now while we can?" Her eyes were horrified, and it made me respond with a grin. "Feel. It's really quite comfortable. I have it padded and lined with velvet."

She cautiously peeked inside. "I see." Then she quickly backed away.

"I bet you're thinking it would take someone truly demented to think of sleeping in a coffin, or maybe it would take someone truly demented even to have a coffin as a fixture in his home—right? But then, what would you call someone who burrowed a hole in the ground and built a home there like a mole? Demented? Deranged? A lunatic? At the very least—unbalanced?"

The expression on her face was priceless, and I couldn't help but laugh aloud as I closed the coffin and put the tapestry back over it. "No, Christine, I don't sleep in a coffin. I was just playing around. Perhaps someday I'll tell you the story about how the coffin got in here, and then it won't sound quite so insane—well—maybe—maybe not."

She was still staring at it as I headed back to my piano. "To answer your question, you're sleeping in my bed so . . . Oh, I guess that doesn't sound just right, does it?"

She turned and looked at me, and again I felt that irresistible urge in the pit of my stomach to laugh, so I did. Then I tried again.

"I'm allowing you to sleep in my bedroom so . . . No, that won't work either."

Again I laughed and lowered myself down on the piano bench and my eyes on the keys. I tried to maintain myself, but then I looked up at her, and she was smiling and her eyes were beginning to dance, so I lost it again and started laughing uncontrollably. I tried humming as I ran my hands and fingers over my cheeks and lips to stop myself from laughing.

Then, without looking at her, I began apologizing. "I'm sorry, Christine. I don't know why I'm finding this so amusing." I took a quick breath and blurted out rapidly between a broad smile. "While you're here, I'm sleeping on the divan. There, I got it out."

I heard her chuckle, and I made the mistake of looking up at her, and then I lost it again. I got up and began pacing around the room. My eyes were tearing, so, with my back to her, I removed my mask and wiped my eyes, slapped my face a couple of times, replaced my mask, rolled my head and neck around, shook out my arms to my sides, and took a deep breath. Then, when I was in control, I turned back, and, with a staunch demeanor, I went back to my piano.

"Are you ready to start your lesson?"

She didn't answer, which forced me to look up at her again. She was smiling broadly, prompting me to speak up with a large smile of my own.

"Don't smile at me, Christine, unless you want me to lose it again."

"Would that be so bad?" she asked as she walked toward the piano. "I've never seen you laugh. I've seen you smile, and I even remember hearing you chuckle, but I've never seen or heard you really laugh. It was quite enjoyable, to tell you the truth. You should do it more often.

"Don't be such a Frenchman, Erik. Don't hide your feelings. You said you brought me down here so I could come to know you. Well, how do you expect me to know you if you hide who you are? Don't present to me the Erik you want me to know but the Erik you are. I love your laughter. It's just as becoming as your singing and makes me feel comfortable around you. You should really do it more often."

I ran my fingers over a few harmonious chords. "Your presence makes me happy enough to want to let go and laugh. You inspire me in many ways, Christine."

She laid her hands on top of the piano and tapped her fingers on it. "Oh, come now. After what I just witnessed, with only a coffin as a catalyst, I have a feeling there are plenty of times when you find yourself laughing."

Again sending a few chords into the room, I responded, "Well, I have to admit that, at times, my abnormal sense of humor comes to the surface and has even gotten me in serious trouble on occasion, but . . ."

My fingers lay still on the keys, and I looked up at her, unable to finish that sentence, unable to find any words that could express the magnitude of her presence in my life. So I simply sighed and suggested we get started on her lessons.

There wasn't a mirror for her to face, so I had her face the piano while I stayed behind her. As usual, to get her into the right frame of mind to warm up her voice, I had her go to the shores of Perros. Only with our not being separated by the mirror, I was able to feel her closeness.

When I told her to close her eyes and raise her arms from her sides and to feel my wings beneath them, I actually placed my arms under hers and laced my fingers between hers. When I told her to hear my voice in her ear, I placed my lips in her hair and spoke to her, taking in her fragrance at the same time. I could then feel the warmth of her body so close to mine. Fortunately, that segment of her lessons didn't last that long or I don't think I could have maintained a position of propriety.

She was able to concentrate even better than when she was in her dressing room, but it wasn't as easy for me. Her nearness was enough to drive me crazy, and it took all my willpower to resist taking her in my arms and holding her close. The duets we sang together were the most difficult for me, considering they were mostly love songs, and, on the stage, the man and woman would be in each other's arms, right where I wanted to be. Therefore, during most of the duets, I stayed sitting at my piano.

That first lesson didn't last long because, once again, she was putting pieces together and coming to realizations that were both surprising to her and also disturbing. She was singing, and I was at the piano when she stopped and stared at me, and then her fingers pressed against her lips and her eyes began to moisten. Then her soft voice filtered through her fingers.

"If you're my angel, that means there's no Angel of Music."

"Yes, there is, Christine. Didn't you ask for the angel of music that your father spoke of to teach you?" She nodded, and I continued, "Well, I was the man your father spoke of. Remember, I met him in Perros. Just as I told you, he heard me playing my violin and he also played for me. I did give him gifts, just as we spoke of in your room. Now, have I not come to you? Have I not taught you just as you asked? And have you not gained your rightful position center stage, right where you wanted to be?"

Again, she nodded, and again I went on. "Then, just because I don't have wings and fly around doesn't mean I can't be your Angel of Music. I am your angel, just as you are mine. You've saved me from my lonely life. You've given me new meaning and a reason to look forward to the next day. The times I've spent with you in your dressing room were the highlights of my day, and the rest of my day was spent waiting until I could talk with you again.

"I've watched you speak with different ones in the house, like the seamstress or the goldsmith, and the way you treat others is proof that you're an angel in many respects. And now you're here with me in my home, and even if it's only for a few days, you make my breaths worth taking. You are my angel just as I am yours. Nothing has changed."

She sighed and nodded. "I suppose."

We then practiced until she said she was hungry. So I took her to the kitchen and showed her another feature of my home.

"Open that pantry door," I began.

She did and then exclaimed, "It's empty! It doesn't even have shelves."

"Certainly it does, but, like a lot of things around here, they're hidden. Push that button and watch what happens."

She did, and as the sound of a faint motor began, she leaned forward and looked down into the cold, dark hole. Then, as a metal chest rose up to meet her and clicked into place, she chuckled.

"There are the leftovers from our meal," I explained. Then as I took the few items off the shelves and pushed the button to send the chest back down, I explained further. "There's a metal shaft that goes down about ten meters to the level of the lake. Down there, it's cold so it keeps my food fresh longer. It also means I don't have to share my food with the many rodents that inhabit this place."

"That's amazing," she offered. "Ingenious, actually."

I held her chair out for her, and she sat down and began to eat. But, once more, I couldn't, even though I knew I really needed to. I hadn't eaten anything in almost three days, but I was too afraid of becoming terribly ill in front of her, so I waited, telling myself I could eat later when I was alone.

Before I sat down, I put the teapot on the stove to heat water for tea. When I sat down, she stared at me.

"What did you just do?" she asked with her normal curiosity.

I glanced over my shoulder. "I'm heating water for tea."

She frowned. "But where's the flame?"

"Oh, that's a stove I've been experimenting with. It isn't heated by gas flames; it's heated by electric coils under the metal plates. Right now, I have three different plates for three different temperatures, but I'm working on a switch that can be used to change the temperature of each plate."

While she stared at my stove with fascination, I stared at her with fascination.

"I'd be finished with that switch, but I've been a bit distracted lately," I said with a longing glance at her.

She shook her head and looked back at me. "You are an inventor, just like they say."

I nodded, and then we talked while she ate. Once she was finished, she automatically started cleaning up after herself. I wanted to do it for her, but, considering my current physical condition, I let her do it while I enjoyed watching her move around in my home.

Then we retired to the drawing room with a cup of tea, where I made a fire and we talked more. It was then that the inevitable happened. She was still putting pieces of the last weeks together, so that, along with her natural curiosity and caring personality, the conversation began that I should have expected.

"It was your voice I heard on the stage that night with Meg, wasn't it?"

I smiled at her while remembering that pivotal night in my life. "Yes. That was the first time I saw you, and I couldn't believe my eyes. You were so angelic, and I was drawn to you as I'd never been drawn before. I believe I started falling in love with you that very night. Especially when you walked toward me and looked right at me, although I don't believe you knew it at the time."

She lowered her eyes to her lap, almost as if she was embarrassed. "I felt the same, only I couldn't believe my ears. I'd never heard such a voice as yours, and I was also drawn to you."

To hear her say those words sent a flood of warmth through my body, but then she had to spoil it with her next comment. "Meg and others said you were the Phantom, and then there were those who called you the Opera Ghost. Were you . . . are you both those entities in one?"

I sighed. "I've been called by many names by many people, but whatever they choose to call me doesn't change who I am. As you can see, Christine, I'm nothing really that mysterious. I can't walk through walls—well not literally anyway—and I do have feet to walk on. I'm just a man that leads a rather peculiar life—for obvious reasons."

She looked down at her hands again with a serious expression, and then it came out. "The Opera Ghost has been blamed for many bad things that have happened in the opera house, even Joseph Buquet's death. Is there any truth to those accusations? Or are they just more of the superstitions that are rumored?"

The time of true test had just arrived for us both. I wanted a good relationship with that woman I loved, and I could easily lie to her. I felt she would believe me, since she could see so many of the other rumors were false. But I didn't want our relationship to be built on any more lies. I had a way with words and I knew it, so I could easily talk around the subject, allowing her to think I'd answered her question when I hadn't. But did I really want to use that tactic on her? What would she do if she knew the truth? Would that end it all for us before it really began? I struggled a few uncomfortable moments before I could answer her.

"I can assure you, Christine, that some of my accomplishments have been greatly exaggerated. Most are allegations never proved, although, as with all rumors, there's probably a measure of truth in all of them. The challenge comes when we try to sort out the truth from the untruth. If we listen to all rumors spoken by the superstitious, then we could miss the true beauty of the truth that lies beneath the rumor. I'm said to have no feet so therefore I float. Well, it's obvious that I do have feet, and I can't fly around, that I can assure you. However, a long time ago I had to learn how to be agile on my feet, so, I presume, I can give the impression that I'm floating.

"It's said that I can walk through walls. Well, if that's true, then last night you also walked through walls just as I have. I don't walk through walls. I walk through doors just like everyone else does. The only difference is that my doors don't look like doors, but the truth is that they are doors just the same. It's said that my eyes glow like lanterns and that they light my way in the dark. Well, Christine, you're right here with me, so look in my eyes. Are they glowing like a lantern?"

She looked at me intensely and then shook her head. "I can see what you mean, but then . . ."

She stopped right in the middle of the sentence, her eyes widened, her fingers closed over her lips, and I heard a soft gasp.

"Perros! It was you," she whispered through her fingers.

"Yes, but why the shock? I already told you I was there with you."

She lowered her head and wrapped her fingers around her throat. "I know, but you were also with Raoul, weren't you? He talked about glowing eyes. It was you who tried to kill him."

Twenty-Five

I smirked and shook my head. "Again, Christine, an exaggeration. I can assure you that if I'd wanted him dead, he wouldn't have been able to tell you that story."

I bit my tongue when I heard the tone in my voice, a tone that revealed my true feeling about the young fool. I searched her eyes, and I feared she'd also heard it. Trying to think quickly for words that would calm her new fears of me, I first took a sip of my tea.

"Honestly, Christine, I didn't want to cause your young friend harm. Well, that isn't entirely true. I was angry with him and would have liked to slap him around a bit for the way he was treating you. But I knew how much you cared for him, so I couldn't cause him any harm. I couldn't hurt *you* that way. I never even touched him. He simply fainted at my feet."

I smiled, remembering my laughter as he did; however, she wasn't amused. "But you left him there to freeze to death. That's the same thing."

"No, Christine. Believe me, if I'd thought his life was really in danger, I wouldn't have left him there. He's young and strong, and I knew a priest would arrive at some point and find him. He was in no real danger." Then, like an idiot and with a smile I couldn't conceal, I added, "Especially from a big, black bear."

She set her cup in the saucer loud enough to let me know she was irritated. "You may think what you did to him was funny, but I didn't. I was extremely frightened for him."

I nodded and waited a moment to make sure I had the glee out of my voice before I continued, "All's well that ends well, my dear. The two of you spent time together and, I'm sure, had a nice train ride together back to Paris."

She looked at the fire and spoke softly. "No. I came back alone, the same way I went—alone."

"Why?" I asked with sobered thoughts, realizing she'd traveled all that way by herself.

With her eyes still on the fire, she responded, "Because I didn't want to be with him any longer. He made me so angry, and I didn't want to talk with him anymore. I hate to travel alone, but it was better than listening to any more of his accusations, so I left without his knowing."

"Accusations? What accusations?" I questioned, thinking Raoul did it to himself. He'd put himself on her bad side without any help from me whatsoever.

With a solemn expression in her eyes, which were still locked on the flickering fire, she said softly, "He so much as accused me of having an affair with my pure and perfect angel. He accused my angel of having selfish motives and wanting to seduce me. It made me so angry, but then, I presume, there was some truth to his fears, wasn't there?"

The room fell to silence as we looked at each other, and then I shook my head slowly and spoke softly "No, Christine. No. My intention was never to seduce you—never. Perhaps my motives have been partially selfish but not completely. The time I've spent with you, whether it was from behind the mirror or down here, has convinced me that we're meant to be together. There's something between us that can't be put into words.

"Yes, I want you as my wife, but I also want your happiness more than my own. Without doubt, I believe I can make you happy in ways that no one else will ever be able to. I don't know if it's our connection with music, or something else that I'm not aware of at present, but it's there, and I can feel it so strongly. Can't you, Christine? Can't you feel it also?"

Again, there was silence as our eyes spoke, and then she responded in a whisper, "I don't know. I feel something, but I don't know what it is."

Her eyes returned to the fire but mine never moved from her. I watched the firelight dance on her golden curls and bring out the pink in her cheeks. I could have spent the rest of the evening watching her. Then I felt my chest ache when I realized we'd completed one day, and I only had three days left to spend with her. I didn't know how I was going to do it; how I was going to let her go. I loved her so much.

I should have left the conversation on that note; it would have been a good way to end the evening. Our thoughts would have been good ones to take to our beds, but, like an idiot, I didn't. While thinking about the short time I had left with her, my chest began to ache and I'm sure my expression showed it. So, before she looked up and saw my pain, I started talking.

"So, as I said, I can't take credit for all the extraordinary rumors spread about me. While it would come in handy to walk through walls or to fly, I'm only a mortal man with no more unearthly powers than the next man. What you see in front of you is all there is; just a man, no phantom, no ghost, just a man."

She took a sip of her tea and then looked back at me over the top of her cup. "And what about Joseph? It's said you hung him in the third cellar.

Is any of that true? Did he commit suicide like the police said or are you a murderer?"

I leaned forward in my chair and placed my elbows on my knees, then, swallowing again, I began. "It's true I hung him in the third cellar, but he was already dead when I did so. And, as far as it being a suicide, well, in a way it was. He tried to kill me, and in so doing it cost him his life. So, in a way, it was a suicide."

I looked at her eyes, trying to read them, and I didn't like what I saw, so I tried to explain further, "It was self defense, Christine. It was dark, and I couldn't even see him until it was all over. I didn't deliberately kill him. I need you to believe me when I say that. I never intend to hurt anyone."

She glanced at the fire, and I waited to see if that was going to be the end of it, but, sadly, it wasn't, and her need to understand went on. "Perhaps, this isn't any of my business, but I need to know something."

"Christine, I'm asking you to love me, so there's nothing about me that's not your business."

"I need to know . . ." she hesitated and took a deep breath. "I need to know if Joseph Buquet was the only man you've killed. There were rumors that there were many."

I looked at her, thinking, this could be the end of it all, but I had to tell her the truth.

"Because of what's beneath this," I said as I motioned to my mask. "I've been forced on occasion to forfeit another's life to save my own. But, I can assure you, I would always prefer to leave a dangerous situation than to hurt anyone. I don't take death lightly, and it's never my intention to cause it, but there've been more than a few who've felt my life should end."

She curled her legs under her, pulled a blanket over them, and leaned back in the corner of the divan. "Then are you telling me you've never taken a life unless yours was in danger?"

I was afraid she was going to take the natural progression with that question. I closed my eyes and turned to take a drink of my tea, giving myself a chance to think. Do I continue to tell the truth or do I lie? She would never know the difference. But I would—I would. So I took a deep breath and turned back to her.

"Christine, there're parts of my life that I truly regret, and if I could, in any way, do it over, I would change the outcome of certain situations, but, unfortunately, I can't. There was a time in my life when I was a different person than who I am now. It was a long time ago and in a place far from France. I was very young and very hurt and *very* disturbed, and I reacted to the hate-filled world around me in a way that I'm ashamed of. No, being ashamed doesn't come close to how I feel about that time. I did things then that I can't even speak about, and my remorse is beyond words.

"I was once told that we can't turn back the clock, but we can wind it up again; we can try to do better the next time. That's what I've been trying to do. I've tried to stay away from certain situations and, therefore, prevent unnecessary deaths. That's why you find me down here. I live here not only to protect myself but, more importantly, to protect those who wish to do me harm. It never turns out well for those who try to steal my life, and Buquet is proof of that fact."

Her eyes moistened, and I added, "You don't need to look at me that way. I'm not asking for pity. I only want you to know me for who I am *now*. I don't want there to be secrets between us, Christine, and if it means you have to learn about a past that I'm ashamed of, well, so be it. But it's the man I am now that I want you to know. I'm a man who's been given many natural gifts, and I want nothing more than to share what I have, what I've been given, with others. That's one reason why I began tutoring you. I have a need to teach."

I held my eyes on hers as I finished my explanation. "But my greatest need is to share my life and all I have with you, Christine. I love you as I've never loved anyone. I learned at a young age that everything cost something—even love. All my life I was either unwilling to pay the price or others would never consider paying it. I love you not because I was willing to pay the price but because I had no choice. My heart took over my mind's ability to make a decision, and I just love you—plain and simple—I love you."

The room was quiet as we listened to the crackle of the fire, and I believe we were both in deep thought. I was hoping for, even praying for, her understanding and forgiveness, but I couldn't tell what she was thinking. Mostly, she watched her fingers feeling the fringe on the end of the blanket, and occasionally she looked at the fire. When she looked at me, it was truly intense, but she didn't ask any more questions. Eventually, we managed to talk about lighter subjects until she yawned and said she was sleepy.

"Then you should retire. There're nice bath oils and crystals, if you wish to take a bath. If you do, turn the knob that's on the wall at the end of the tub. That will light the gas jets under the tub and make your bath warm and relaxing."

"What a wonderful idea. Your inventions are truly remarkable."

"I've only designed things to make my life easier—better, like my electric lights or my cold pantry. Oh, one word of caution about the jets. Wait until the water is running in the tub before you turn that knob on and remember to turn it off before the water is out of it. If you don't, the tub will become like a huge pot on a stove and get extremely hot. It could cause a nasty accident."

"I will. Thank you for thinking about the bath oils. I noticed they're also lavender."

"You're most welcome. I aim to please. I'll light the jets for you, if you'd like."

"I think I can figure it out. If not, I'll let you know." She got up and started to leave but then stopped and looked down at me. "Thank you, Erik, for being so open with me. It means a lot that you can talk about your past failings like you did."

I looked up at her. "I want you to know exactly who I am. No superstitions—no rumors—only the truth."

She nodded and almost smiled, and then left for her room.

When I heard the water running in the tub, I sighed. She was really here, I mused. After listening to her hum for a few moments, I got up and took our cups to the kitchen. All I wanted was to collapse on the divan and get a good night sleep, which I hadn't had in several days, but I knew I had to fulfill my promise to Doctor Leglise and take care of my wound first.

He'd told me that I needed to treat it three or four times a day, but I knew I'd only be able to do it twice a day, once before Christine woke up and once after she went to sleep. Therefore, I put the pot on the stove to heat the water and then went to my armoire to get the oils he'd given me.

Then I saw, sitting beside the oils, the box with my nose in it. My curiosity triggered a thought and I decided to try it on again, thinking, since Christine knew the reason for the mask, I had nothing to lose. But when I put it on and looked in my small shaving mirror, I instantly took it off. I felt bad with it on. It wasn't me. I felt like a fraud. It just wasn't me. I put my mask back on and then I saw myself. Perhaps I'd worn it too long and relied on it too much. It was by then a part of me just as my eyes and mouth were, and, without it, I didn't feel whole. So I put the nose back in the box in my armoire and left for the kitchen again, thinking it had been a bad idea to begin with.

While the water was heating for the compress, I made a plate of food, since I knew I needed nourishment. Once done, I took everything I needed for the wound along with my food and a glass of brandy to my divan. I then removed my neck scarf, coat and trousers, loosened my collar and lay back against the divan, with my legs on the table in front of me.

Before I tried to eat, I first removed both the dead and live maggots from the dark, stinky hole in my leg, causing me to nearly change my mind about eating. After hiding their jar on the floor beneath my legs and out of my sight, I laid the hot compress over the wound, threw a blanket over my good leg and my body, and then relaxed. I took a sip of my brandy, closed my eyes, and enjoyed the warmth of the compress on my leg and the brandy in my chest. My thoughts quite naturally turned to Christine in the next room, which made me feel warm all over.

I only momentarily gave thought to taking a dose of morphine to stop the pain and help me sleep, but I knew I couldn't do that, not with Christine in my home. I gazed at the ceiling, the wall hangings, the fireplace, and wished I had a window. That was one major drawback to my shrouded castle, no windows. At times like that, I missed watching the trees moving gracefully in a breeze, or the puffy white clouds traveling lazily across a blue sky, or the multitudes of stars on a dark night. Oh, well, I sighed. Be thankful for what you do have, the lovely Christine in the next room.

I must have drifted off because the next thing I remembered was my brandy glass slipping from my fingers. I jumped and grabbed for it, but I was too late.

"Christine!" I blurted out.

She was standing over me with my brandy glass in her hand. "I was afraid you were going to spill it all over yourself. I'm sorry. I didn't mean to startle you."

"What are you doing up?" I stammered while throwing the blanket over my bad leg.

"I heard you scream and feared something was wrong. Do you have night frets?" she asked compassionately. "Sometimes I do."

"You could say that. I'm sorry I woke you. I'm fine. You can return to your bed," I tried to say without showing my embarrassment.

"It's all right. Don't look so shocked. I've dealt with serious injuries before."

She set my glass on the table, stuck her finger in my bowl of water, and picked it up.

"What are you doing?" I asked, still somewhat confused over the new personality I saw emerging from her.

She turned around, heading for the kitchen, and answered over her shoulder, "This is cold. I'll heat it up for you."

"That won't be necessary. Don't bother," I tried to tell her, as I awkwardly moved the blanket to cover myself properly.

"It's no bother," were her last words as she disappeared around the corner.

I looked quickly at my trousers lying beside me and wondered if I had time to slip them on before she came back. My question was answered a moment later when she returned, so the blanket stayed put, and so did I.

Then she acted as if we'd known each other for years and just took over. She tried to pull the blanket off my leg, but I held onto it tightly.

"It's all right, Christine. I'm finished for now anyway."

"I don't think so," she came back with authority. "I saw that red streak on your leg, and you can't have too many hot compresses."

Again pulling the blanket off my leg, she went on. "I've seen this before. Mummy was bitten by a dog once, and this same thing happened to her arm. The red streak went all the way from her wrist to her elbow. I remember being so frightened when the doctor said she could lose her arm, or even her life, if it wasn't taken care of quickly."

She looked at my leg. "This is much worse, so you need all of the hot compresses you can stand, and you really shouldn't be walking on it either."

She started to reach for the cloth lying over the wound when the teakettle whistled and she quickly left. My eyes darted around the room, as I tried to gain back a measure of my dignity. I struggled to think of the right words to dissuade her from continuing with her efforts to help me, without hurting her feelings. Before any reasonable thoughts came to mind, she was back by my side and had set the bowl of hot medicated water on the table at my feet. She reached for the cloth again, and I put my hand over it.

"No, Christine, you don't need to do this. It's not a pretty sight, and I can do it myself."

As she knelt down on the floor by my leg, she answered in a matter-of-fact fashion, "I know you can, but I'm here, so you don't have to. Now quit being such a baby and let me help."

"I'm not being a baby. I just don't want you subjected to this when it's not necessary." She looked at me and shook her head. "Men are such babies."

The next time she reached for the cloth, I didn't prevent her. When it came off, she instantly dropped it, and her hand covered her mouth, so I quickly covered it up again.

"See, I told you it was horrible. Now go back to bed and let me take care of it."

But she didn't go back to bed; instead, she took it off again and started apologizing. "I'm sorry, Erik. It just took me by surprise and . . ."

She rinsed out the cloth and placed it back on the wound, and then she looked up at me and took a deep breath.

"What is it, Christine? You have nothing to fear by what you say at this time. I won't threaten your life again, I promise."

"It's not that, it's . . ." again she stopped and just looked at me.

Through Phantom Eyes   263

"What is it? If you want to change your mind and go back to bed, go ahead. I'll understand."

She sat back on her heels. "No, it's not that either." She stared at my leg and shook her head ever so slightly. Then she massaged her forehead with her fingertips and looked at the door leading to the lake. "I understand now."

"Understand what?" I prompted her.

She looked at my leg again and then in my eyes. She took a breath and then stopped again.

"Christine," I started, "you've seen the worst of me this day, so there's nothing you can say to me right now that would offend me. Please, either go back to bed or speak your mind, because, in case you haven't noticed, patience is not my strongest personality trait."

She lowered her eyes and started feeling the silk ribbon of her gown. That was such a familiar gesture of hers, and it made me relax, but her words brought the tone in the room back to one of a serious nature.

"I was so frightened last night after the chandelier fell. I first thought my angel was dead and then I thought I was dead." She looked back up at me. "When I heard your angelic voice singing, and realized what you were singing, I thought for sure I was among those who'd died. I thought you were calling me home to be with my father."

With true curiosity, I questioned, "Why? What was I singing?"

"You don't remember?"

"I also was in shock, Christine. I don't remember parts of that evening, and what I was singing is one of the missing pieces."

She gazed into my eyes for a moment before she answered, "My angel . . . I mean, you were singing the redeemer's lines. 'Come to me and believe in me. Whosoever comes to me and believes in me shall live. Come to me. Whosoever believes in me shall never die.' I thought I was dead and that my Angel of Music had turned into the redeemer. My room did strange things around me. My mirror wavered, and I followed your voice through it. Then I was behind the mirror, and I knew I had to be dead, because I'd just walked through a wall. It was so dark, and I couldn't see anything, and I thought my eyes were closed in death."

Her sight went to her hands lying on her legs. "Your hand was so cold when it grasped my wrist, and I remember thinking that angels aren't warm blooded as we are, and I wondered how long it would take me to turn cold. At that time, I didn't want to go with the angel. I didn't want to be dead; even if it meant I could be with my father again. But your voice comforted me, and I felt safe with your arm around me, so I willingly followed you.

"But then you turned your head toward a distant light, and I no longer saw a bright white angel as I'd imagined. I only saw a black cloak and mask, and I instantly thought the ghost of the commune had me, and I was going to die again or be imprisoned in his cellars."

She paused, and I uttered my heartfelt thoughts. "I'm so sorry Christine. I never meant for any of that to frighten you. It was supposed to be beautiful and take your breath way, but not like that."

She nodded and went on. "I remember screaming, and when you put your hand over my mouth, I . . . I . . . I smelt death. This smell, Erik," she said as she pointed to my wound. "Then I thought you were the angel of death. I thought you were going to take my soul away. The next thing I remember was the smell of death again—all around me. When I opened my eyes and saw your mask again, I wanted to scream, but then I saw a white horse, and I thought I was in heaven. I was so confused. My mind was so tired, and I no longer wanted to think or fight what was happening to me."

I looked at her with tenderness. "I'm so sorry. I'm so sorry."

She nodded slightly and went on. "I remember telling myself not to fight, to let go and I would soon be with my father in heaven. I just wanted to sleep, and I felt as if I'd had too much to drink. All I could think about was to lie down. Then I kept changing places between being in your arms and in hell with the smell of death around me, and then on the white horse and in heaven.

"At one point, I even felt as if I was floating on a cloud. I felt weightless, and I could see its white mist moving around me. Then it was dark and I again smelled death and you were carrying me to hell once more. Then there was a bright light and many colors and I thought I'd arrived in paradise. I was so confused.

"Then, when I saw you standing there among the bright flowers and candles, I couldn't breathe; my mind was reeling. You looked so human, so tall and strong, and yet the way you moved wasn't human. You were so . . . I don't know how to describe it. So fluid . . . weightless . . . graceful . . . almost like a beautiful angel in black, and I again thought you were an angel and that I was in heaven a . . . a bright colorful heaven, not at all what I'd pictured all my life."

She rinsed the cloth and laid it over my leg again. "Well, you know the rest of the story. When we began talking, I came to understand who you were and why I was here. So you see, it wasn't the sight of your wound that caused me to gasp, it was the smell of it that brought back all those fearful feelings.

"Now I understand why I smelled what I did. You were injured, and you had to have been in such pain. At the time, I wondered why you put me though such an ordeal, but now I'm wondering why you put yourself through the pain that you must have been experiencing."

I couldn't answer her right away, because I was so taken by her rendition of what had happened that I could only stare at her. She rose up on her knees and again rinsed the cloth in the hot bowl and once more gently laid it over my leg. Then she sat back on her heels and looked up at me.

I shook my head. "I love you so much, Christine, and I don't think I'll ever be able to express to you the amount of love I have for you. I would walk through fire for you, so a nasty hole in my leg wasn't going to stop me last night. I'd watched you for months, and I so often wanted to tell you exactly who I was and how much I loved you, but I was so afraid."

Her eyes widened. "You were afraid? I don't see you being afraid of anything."

"My worst fear, Christine, is never having you return my love. But I'm prepared to face that fear if that's your decision. You've probably seen me at my best and my worst; everything in between is just filler." I knew I shouldn't ask what I was thinking, but I had to. "Do you think the day will ever come when you can see me for who I am, and love me just a little?"

She sighed and warmed the cloth again. "I don't know, Erik. I honestly don't know."

I closed my eyes and laid my head back. "Well, I imagine an indecisive answer is better than a negative one, right?" I opened my eyes and looked at her, and she smiled. "You need to go back to bed. I can finish dressing the wound."

"I want to finish the job. What's next?" she insisted.

"This next step is really—really repulsive. It's much worse than the wound. You don't need to be involved in it."

She again insisted on helping, so, thinking she'd seen my face and my decaying flesh so what was there to lose by allowing her to decide for herself if she wanted to continue or not. Therefore, I reached down and grabbed the jar of maggots, and when they came into her view, she scrunched her face and halfway turned away.

"What's that?" she grimaced.

"I told you it's repulsive. They're maggots."

"Maggots! What do you do with them?" she asked, as if she really didn't want to know the answer.

When I explained the procedure to her, she drew back, but I couldn't blame her.

"Go to bed, Christine, I can do this myself," I encouraged her softly.

"I know you can, but you don't need to," she replied while cautiously reaching for the jar.

She then took the tweezers from my hand and cautiously began. After the first two, you'd think that working with maggots was her vocation. She even continued our conversation just as if she were making me a pot of tea or something else of a *normal* nature.

As she was taping the clean bandage over my leg, she looked up at me and asked, "I'm curious . . ."

"When aren't you?" I interrupted.

She just smiled. "How did this happen?"

"My leg happened to get in the way of a projectile, and, in my own stupidity, I tried to remove it myself."

"A projectile? What kind of a projectile?"

I looked at her and it was then that I realized how hard it was going to be to always be honest with her. I saw in her, right then, what I'd seen all those weeks when I followed her around and watched her talking to everyone. What she was doing with me was just who she was. She had such concern for others and a true desire to be a part of their lives. It was that aspect of her that I loved the most.

"As I told you before, there have always been those who want to end my life. Therefore, I sometimes have an injury to contend with. This one happened to be a bullet. You could call it, a bullet wound gone bad, although, I suppose, there aren't any bullet wounds that are good, now are there?"

"A bullet? Someone really tried to kill you? Why?"

"As I said, I'm not always certain why. I just have that effect on certain people, but I've learned to accept it."

She sat back on her heels again and shook her head. "You shouldn't have to accept such a fate. That's a terrible way to live. Who was it anyway? Anyone I know?"

I took a deep breath and laid my head back on the divan. "Our former chief scene-shifter."

"Joseph?" she gasped.

I nodded. Then she stared at me with concern. After a moment, she looked down at the bandage on my leg and commented in an undertone, "Then it was self defense?"

My head came up quickly, and I frowned at her while my voice came across too close to the edge of anger.

Twenty-Six

"Did I not tell you it was? Did you think I was lying? None of it was a lie—none of it! I've told you nothing but the truth, Christine. I've told you things that I haven't even told my best friend. I've not lied to you once and I never will."

Her eyes were wide again, and I saw in them a moment of fear. I'm sure she was preparing for my full rage once more. She nodded and began speaking softly, trying to defuse the situation.

"I know you were telling me the truth, Erik. I'm sorry. This last day has just been so much for me to absorb. I feel as if I'm living in the middle of a novel and that none of this is real. I expect to have the book close and then to find myself back as a chorus girl and living with Mummy where nothing has changed. I'm sorry. Please be patient with me."

Then I felt terrible again. "No, I'm sorry. I have a quick temper that can be nasty at times. I'm really trying to improve, so I ask *you* to be patient with *me*. You've been more than kind to me. When I think about it, if someone had done to me what I've done to you, I think I would have . . . I don't know what I would have done, but I do know it wouldn't have been pretty."

She gazed at me in thought. "Joseph died weeks ago. That means you traveled all the way to Perros with this. I could tell by the feel of your leg that you have a fever. You're really sick, and probably have been for some time. And to think you carried me down here with this leg. Why? Your pain had to be unbelievable. Why did you do it?"

"As I told you, I would go through anything for you. I'd waited much too long to tell you who I really was. The closest I came was the night before the gala when we were on the roof. At that time, you asked me never to leave you. Do you remember that?"

She nodded. "I'll never forget it."

"I almost revealed myself to you right then, but I feared it might cause an upset before you could show Paris the true Christine Daaé, and I couldn't do that to you. I also came close to letting you know who I was while in the inn in Perros. Actually, I was the one who knocked on your door after you came back from the cemetery, but, by the time you opened your door, it was Madame Mifroid you saw."

"What? Really? You were in the inn?"

"Yes, and when I heard you crying, I couldn't stay away. I wanted to comfort you, so, if it hadn't been for Madame Mifroid's sudden appearance, you would have known who I was that night."

She slowly shook her head. "I can't believe this. So much was going on around me and I suspected nothing." Her eyes widened. "You heard me crying? Then you must have been close. Where were you?"

"In the room next to yours."

"What? I feel like such a . . . such a blind and ignorant fool! I had no idea!"

"Don't feel that way. I'm a master at deceptions—illusions. No one would have known I was there unless I let them, so you weren't a fool. You were in pain of heart—not a fool."

She looked at me and again shook her head. "You were right next door?"

"Yes, but at times I was even closer to you than that. Remember when you were in the inn's restaurant and Raoul was making you angry, and a man bumped into him and knocked him to the floor?" She nodded. "That rude man was me."

"What?"

"Yes. I was so angry for the way he was talking to you, and . . . well . . . I guess it was a prelude to what happened in my music room earlier. My temper took control, but it was only a hint of what he deserved."

Her eyes were wide and her open mouth was covered with her fingers, but then her eyes began to smile, and she whispered through her fingers, "You were protecting me?"

"Yes. You shouldn't be talked to that way. He deserved a lot more than what I gave him, and under different circumstances he would have gotten it."

"Raoul's words weren't nearly as cutting as yours were earlier, Erik," she said softly.

Oh, with those words she stabbed me in the heart. I closed my eyes and laid my head back. "Please, don't remind me. My actions were despicable, and someone should beat me royally for them." I looked back at her. "I wish I could turn back time. I feel you'll never forget or forgive my actions."

"I didn't mean that as a reminder. I don't believe in that. I was only trying to help you understand that Raoul means well, even if he says improper things to me. He's not a bad person, and I don't believe you're a bad person either."

"Christine, I don't think it's in you to believe someone is a bad person. That's not who you are. That good trait can make you vulnerable, though, and put you in dangerous positions. That's one reason why I wanted to accompany you on your trip to Perros. That's one reason why I watched you the entire way—to protect you."

Again she exclaimed, "What? You were on the train with me? Where were you? I don't remember seeing you."

"I was in the back and in the corner, on the other side of the train from you. But as I just said, I'm a master when it comes to being concealed. When you couple that with your trusting and caring quality, then quite naturally you wouldn't see me."

"Just who are you, Erik? You're such a contradiction. You can be so . . ." she stopped and looked toward my music room, I'm sure remembering her harrowing moments. Then she looked at my leg. "From what you've told me, you put yourself through agony just to be my guardian angel—just to make me happy.

"You shouldn't be living down here like this. You should see the sunlight and share your smile. You're a brilliant musician and you should share that gift. You shouldn't live your life like this," she said as she circled her hand around the room and then let it rest on my knee.

With the feel of her hand on my leg, I took a quick breath and felt sensations travel through my body, premature feelings that I couldn't let begin—not yet. Therefore, after bundling the blanket on my lap to hide any outward signs of my true feelings, I forced myself to think about her welfare and not my pleasure. I looked into her sincere and innocent eyes, eyes that were completely unaware of what her touch was doing to me. With another quick breath and slight shake of my head, I tried to explain my living situation as best I could.

"It sounds so simple, doesn't it? Just live my life like *a normal* person. I explained before why I've locked myself down here. I can't bear . . . I can't witness . . ." I laid my hand on top of hers and tried again. "You're very young, Christine. I know you've seen a lot of suffering in your short life, but you can't begin to imagine the suffering I've seen or . . ." I was about to tell her about the suffering I'd caused, but I couldn't right then. Perhaps another time, I thought.

"I know I've expressed how much I love you during this day. I've also told you that I could leave this place if I had you by my side. While I was trying to tell you the truth, I don't want you to view it as pressure. Whatever decision you make has to be made because it's something you want. It can't be out of pity for me. You must take what I'm saying to heart. I truly want your happiness much more than my own; however, I do believe that you'll never be truly happy with anyone other than me.

"You might be happy, but not truly happy. There's a difference, and since I met you I've known that difference. To settle for *only* love, I now know, would be hollow. We might be able to love many, but what I'm feeling for you, and what I believe you'll feel for me, is a love without words. It's not a love you learn or expect just because someone loves you or because you've known someone for a long time; it's a love that captures your heart and takes control of your life—a love that you willingly surrender to. That's what I feel for you and what I believe you'll feel for me soon."

I removed my hand from hers and leaned back. "Don't do this for me. I've learned to lose loved ones. I'll survive with or without you, but I don't want to survive without you. If you decide to leave here and never see me again, I'll leave this place. I won't be able to stay here with memories of you surrounding me. But if I'm able to leave this place with you on my arm, I'll be the happiest man alive, and I'll conquer the world for you. I'll share the gifts I've been given with the world—for you.

"But, again, no pressure. You make your decision for you—not for me. And, by the way," I added with an eyebrow raised, "don't make it for Raoul either. Don't let him persuade you into making a decision you're not 100 percent in agreement with. That's all I ask."

I was really feeling terrible physically by then, so I laid my head back on the divan and closed my eyes while waiting for a response from her. The room became quiet. Then she gently squeezed my knee before covering my leg with the blanket. When she got to her feet, I opened my eyes and watched her.

"No response?" I questioned.

"Not now. You've given me a lot to think about. So much has happened, and I need to process it all before I can respond. You're a fascinating man, and there's much more I want to know about you. But we can talk tomorrow. You need your rest."

She then picked up all my medical supplies and started for the kitchen.

"I can clean this up, Christine. You really should go to bed now. I thank you for your understanding and all your help."

She looked over her shoulder at me. "Certainly you can, and you're welcome," but she kept going.

I was glad she didn't listen to me. I really didn't know what would happen if I tried to stand up at that moment. She might have fainted in my arms, but I certainly would hate to faint in hers. Spending so much emotional energy that day had left me without any strength to spare. In addition, I was sick to my stomach and my head was throbbing.

Once she was back, she stood at my feet and looked down at me.

"That's the worst wound I've ever seen. It's much worse than Mummy's dog bite. I don't understand how you're still alive. You're a seriously ill man, Erik, and you need lots of rest and proper care. I hope you'll put away your pride for a few days and let me help you while I'm here."

"Very well. I surrender," I responded with a smile while holding my hands up.

"Good. Now tell me where you keep your bedding."

"You don't . . ."

"Erik! Please don't be stubborn and make this harder on me."

That was my last attempt to take care of myself. I gave in to her and soon she had a comfortable bed made for me on the divan, and I was lying in it. She set a glass of water on the table beside me and gave me instructions on the importance of drinking a lot of water. Then she tilted her head and looked at me in thought. I started to tell her again to go back to bed when she asked me a question that no one had asked me before.

"Is what happened to your nose another attempt on your life?"

With that question, I took a deep breath, closed my eyes, and nestled my head in the pillow. "No. I was born without certain wayward cells that would have been my nose. They're probably still wandering around somewhere. Too bad it wasn't wayward ear cells. A missing ear would be much easier to hide."

"You have an unusual sense of humor. Do you mind my asking you these questions?"

"Not at all, Christine." I spread my arms out wide. "I'm an open book. Ask away."

"Not now. You really do need to sleep. I can ask them tomorrow. I hope you can sleep well. I feel bad about your sleeping out here though. You should be in your bed."

I turned my head and looked up at her. "Don't be silly. I'm used to sleeping almost anywhere. I'll be fine. Now, go to bed."

I finally convinced her to retire, and then I lay there, thinking about our conversation and smiling with the warmest feeling inside me. While it was a strange conversation, it was an informative and honest one for both of us. As it turned out, during the next few days, the times when she took care of my leg were the times when we had the most interesting conversations and learned a lot about each other.

I sighed in the silence, thinking that one day was gone and I had only three more left to spend with my Christine.

Even though I was on the divan, I had a good night's sleep, but I woke abruptly when I heard a loud whistle. I barely cracked my eyes opened in time to see Christine streak through the parlor and into the kitchen. The whistle stopped, and then I saw her slowly peek around the kitchen door. She was so cute and childlike at times, and she made me smile often.

"Oh, Erik, I'm so sorry for waking you," she began while coming back into the parlor. "I wanted to have some tea and your compress ready for you when you woke up, but I really didn't want you to wake until you were ready. I'm sorry. I got distracted by your library."

I chuckled, stretched, and rubbed my two-day old beard with my fingers. "It's all right. I don't want to sleep away my time with you. What time is it anyway?"

"A little past noon," she replied while looking at the tall clock.

I groaned. "It's past time for me to get up," I said as I tried to maneuver into a sitting position.

"No, you stay put. I'll bring the tea and your compress water and what little food we have left." She hesitated and added, "If I promise to return, will you let me go shopping for some food? We're going to get really hungry soon."

"No need," I said with a twinkle. "My elves will be delivering it soon. Then we'll have plenty to eat."

"Elves?"

"Yes. You know what elves are, don't you? Those busy little creatures?"

"Certainly, but they're not real."

"Oh, you with little faith," I teased. "Yes, they are. I talked to them in my dreams and gave them our food order. It sounds scrumptious."

"You're teasing me, Erik."

"Am I? Watch! They'll bring it to our door in less than two hours."

She looked around. "What door?"

"My door."

"Where?"

"Right there," I replied as I pointed behind her.

"I don't see a door."

"You're not supposed to."

"Why not?"

"Because, you might escape, my curious Christine."

"Erik, please stop teasing me. Be serious. We need food," she insisted, while placing her hands on her hips.

I chuckled. "Seriously then. All my doors are invisible. All 56 of them, and I'm the only one who can open them. That's the only way I can survive. And, seriously, our food will be delivered to my wharf in two hours. I arranged for our needs before this began. Any other questions?"

"No. That answers them. But why couldn't you just say that to begin with?"

"Because it wouldn't have been nearly as much fun."

"For you, maybe," she said with her hands still on her hips.

"I'm sorry, Christine. It seems I do have a weird sense of humor. I'm sorry."

She only nodded and turned to get our tea and sparse food. I think she was irritated with me, so when I asked for permission to use her bath for a minute, her only response was a wave of her hand.

While she treated my wound, she eventually talked to me again, so our food wasn't eaten in silence. Before long, everything had been cleaned up and she went to my bookshelf.

"There's a book here I'd like to look at. I have a few ideas, so do you mind if I take it to my room and look through it? I'll bring it back."

"That's why they're there, so be my guest."

She left and I sat in the quiet for a moment, thinking about my lack of privacy. Then I decided to use the time while she was reading to clean up and give myself a shave. So, after I built a fire, I gathered everything I needed from my armoire and went to the kitchen. I had my trousers on but not my shirt as I bathed my upper body.

I put my shaving mirror on the edge of an open cupboard, took my mask off, and had the lathered brush in one hand and the razor in the other. Then I heard a loud pop from the fireplace. Not wanting a hole burnt in my rug, I turned and started for the parlor. But I'd only taken one step when I saw Christine standing in the dining room, watching me. I was embarrassed and began stumbling over my words and fumbling with my mask and shirt to get them on quickly.

"I'm sorry, Christine. I thought you'd take longer than that."

"No, wait," she said while rushing toward me.

After placing the book on the counter, she took my shirt and mask from my hands and then stood there, staring at my chest and shoulders. Then her eyes traveled to my face.

"You didn't get enough of my beauty yesterday? You want a repeat? You certainly are a curious little glutton, now aren't you?" I said sarcastically, but then I tried to cover my naked face with my fingers and nearly begged, "Please, Christine."

While gently pulling my hand down, she explained, "You're asking me to stay with you forever. You're asking me to marry you. Will I never be able to see the face and body of my husband? You want me to know you—to understand you." She gestured to my chest. "I can't help but think that this is partly what has shaped the man you are." She raised her hand to touch my face, but asked first. "Do you mind if I touch you? Do the scars hurt?"

"They happened a long time ago. They don't hurt. In fact, I hardly notice them anymore."

"Not even inside?" she asked with compassion.

"I can't live in the past," I replied, while placing my knuckle under her chin. "My future is what really counts, especially now that you might be in it."

That's what I told her, but the truth was that they did hurt inside, and my nightmares were proof that each strike could still feel new. And even though it was emotionally painful, I acquiesced to her wishes, so she ran her finger over the scars on my cheek and forehead that were normally hidden by my mask. Then she touched the scratches that her nails had caused.

"I'm sorry, Erik, to have caused you more hurt."

"Don't be. It was my fault," I faintly responded with closed eyes.

Then she ran her hands over my exposed ribs.

"I know." I tried to explain. "I look like a skeleton, but I don't normally. If I don't eat properly, I lose weight quickly, but I also put it on quickly. I'm sorry you had to see me like this."

"I'm not looking at your lack of weight, Erik."

She then ran her fingers over a few of the scars on my chest and neck. Under different circumstances, her touch would have excited me, but, at that time, I was too embarrassed, too anxious. I wasn't prepared for what she was doing, so I was nearly frozen in fear while waiting for her response to the scared and deformed man she was examining.

She looked up into my eyes, and the sorrow and compassion I saw in hers touched my heart and eased my fears. She then moved around to my back and did the same. Her fingers hesitated a moment longer over the scar from the bullet wound on my right side. When she came around the other side, she touched the deep gash from the dagger in my left side and again looked up in my eyes.

"Who whipped you like this, Erik? What kind of a man could do this to another man? Who could be this heartless?"

"He didn't do it to a man; he did it to a child," I responded, with my emotional scars surfacing in my tone.

She shook her head. "A child? How old were you?"

"10—11."

She looked deep into my eyes. "Was it your father?"

"No, not my father," I answered adamantly. "He would never . . ."

"He may not have caused this but he didn't prevent it either."

I took a breath and tried to bury more of those emotional scars before replying to her harsh appraisal of my father. "He had no control over it. He was dead. I was kidnapped and then sold to the owner of a traveling circus where I was kept in a cage like the rest of his animals."

"That's horrible!" she gasped. "A child?" she looked deep into my eyes while tears formed in hers. "How could they do that to you—a child?" Her brow furrowed and her fingers gently brushed the lash mark on my neck. "Oh, Erik, how could you survive such an ordeal at such a young age?"

"Stubborn determination, I suppose. I don't like to be forced to do anything by any man."

Once more, she ran her fingers across the scars on my chest and shoulder. "If I wasn't looking right at them, I don't know if I could believe you. It's all so hard to understand. How could he do this to a child?"

"Believe me—it happened, and as I told you before, many don't consider me human. They see me as an animal and often treat me as one. In this particular case, I wouldn't submit to him treating me like one of his animals or one of his oddities, so he tried to force me into submission. But I don't want your pity. It was a long time ago, and I lived through it."

"Perhaps, but not completely." Her head shook again when she looked back up at me. "Even if you were an animal, how could they do this? I couldn't do this to an animal."

"You're cut from a different cloth than most, Christine. That's one reason why I love you so much."

"I still don't understand how anyone could do this."

She looked up into my eyes again and I looked down into hers with so much love swelling in my heart. I was somewhere in deep thought about her purity when she interrupted my thoughts.

"Erik?"

"Oh! Yes! I apologize. You mesmerize me."

"I would say quite to the contrary. Now that I can really see your eyes—without the mask—I can understand something else I heard about the Opera Ghost. I've heard that he . . . that you have the power to hypnotize people. So with your voice and these eyes, I now understand how. They are . . ." She intently focused on them. "They're . . . I've never seen eyes like yours. They're captivating and I guess hypnotic. They're beautiful. I wish you wouldn't wear that mask. I can't see your eyes that well with it on. I love your eyes—especially when you smile."

At first, I didn't know how to respond to her, so I just stared down into her deep blue pools until the perfect and honest response came to me.

"I could say the same about yours. They're what captivated me that first night on the stage." I brushed the back of my fingers across her temple and into her hair. "I know you're probably so tired of hearing me say this, but I love you so much, and I love you more each time I learn something new about you. What you've just done makes my heart swell." Then fearing what she was going to ask next, I added. "But I can't go without my mask. Not yet anyway."

"I'm not asking you to—not yet anyway," she said with a teasing smile. "Back to this power you have with your eyes. Is this how you got free from the cage? Did you hypnotize that cruel man?"

Another moment of truth was upon us, so I closed my eyes and lowered my head. I didn't want to tell her the truth, but when I looked back into her concerned eyes, I knew I had to.

"No, unfortunately. That would have been nice, but it wasn't that easy. I tried to escape many times, but, each time, I was caught and thrown back in the cage. Then, one day, something happened that made me go mad." I looked toward my music room. "Mad like I did when you removed my mask. Only . . . ." I had to breathe a moment before I could finish. "I managed not to kill you yesterday, but my captor wasn't as fortunate." I lowered my head again and closed my eyes. "I'm sorry to say, he was my first victim. My freedom cost him his life."

"I now understand a lot. I know this had to be hard for you to discuss, but, again, I thank you for being honest with me." I nodded, and she smiled while turning toward the door. "I'll leave you alone to finish what you were doing. Oh," she added while turning halfway back toward me. "You don't have to shave on my account. I like what I see."

She spoke with such unabashed flirtation that it left me dumbfounded, and I couldn't respond to her. I almost followed her to question her; however, I was so emotionally drained by her examination that I had to lean on the counter to support myself before I did anything. But, after thinking more about her last comment, I didn't bother to shave.

As I was buttoning my shirt, I heard her humming, and, at first, I smiled, but then I recognized the melody and took off at a full run toward my music room. When I saw her, she was standing with her back to me and facing my organ. She had my score of *Don Juan Triumphant* in her hands and was humming softly. Without saying anything, I reached around her and took it from her hands. Her eyes showed surprise along with a bit of shock.

"It's not finished, Christine, you must be patient."

"You wrote that? Then another rumor is true. You're also a composer."

I nodded while putting the score in a folder. "Yes, but it's not ready for anyone to see or hear just yet. It's not ready for you, Christine, and you're not ready for it."

"You thought I was ready enough for the gala," she responded while leaning back against the wall. "Are you saying your work is better than Gounod's, that I couldn't sing it?"

I looked at her for a moment, trying to find the right words that would be honest and yet not send her screaming from the room again. "No, I'm not saying that at all. But just as you needed special tutoring to sing Marguerite's and Juliette's roles, you'll also need special training to perform the part of my heroine in this opera."

"Will you also tutor me for that part when you're finished?" she asked with a slight smile.

Oh, what a loaded question she asked, and if she knew exactly what she was asking me, I don't believe she would have asked it.

So while turning my back to her and placing my score on a shelf, I answered her honestly, "That's just what I look forward to doing in the near future, my dear."

With innocence, she asked, "When do you think it'll be ready?"

"Well, that's hard to say," I began as I turned around to face her. "I still have much work to do on it, and, at the rate I am going, by the time it's full grown, I'll probably be ready to crawl into my coffin," I snickered, while looking at my tapestry-covered casket.

"If that's the case, then I never want you to finish it, Erik."

I looked at her, wondering if she took me seriously, or if she was serious, or if we were just playing word games with each other. Then she moved away from the wall and toward the bust of Molly, stroking its nose as if it was a real horse.

Then she asked, "I've never spoken to a composer before. How long does it take to write an opera? How long have you been working on yours?"

I joined her at Molly's bust and also ran my hands over its mane. "A very long time. Its conception was just after I met your father, and its birth was after I had enough of my home completed to have a place to work on it. So it's been, probably, close to fifteen years.

"But then it wasn't a continual work. Sometimes I'd go for long periods without inspiration, so I wouldn't work on it at all. Then there were other times when I couldn't stop working on it, and I'd go for weeks at a time doing nothing but composing. There have been times when I didn't even eat for days at a time, or sleep for that matter. It all depends on my inspiration."

"What is it that inspires you to work on it?"

I looked down into her innocent eyes and placed one finger under her chin, raising her head up until our eyes met.

Then I spoke softly, "You do, Christine. You inspire me. You make me want to work only on it so I can start on your tutoring. Perhaps with your nearness, I'll be done soon."

She sighed and playfully turned from me, heading for the drawing room. "Good! Because from the little I just read, it sounds . . . what would I call it?" She stopped, looked back at me, and coyly smiled. "Intriguing. Yes—that's a good word—intriguing."

Then her eyes danced as she looked at me for only a moment longer before she headed for the dining room. I knew the game I was playing with her, but I wondered, was she also playing a game with me? At that moment, I wasn't sure if she was as innocent to my desires as I thought she was. I wondered how much of the score she'd read.

I followed her into the dining room. But before she entered the kitchen, she hesitated a moment and smiled temptingly over her shoulder.

"Please, hurry won't you, Erik? I can't wait to have you tutor me for the part of your heroine."

I felt my eyes narrow as I watched her complete her journey into the kitchen, and I felt warm inside, but not necessarily in a good way. Relax, Erik. She's nowhere close to where she needs to be for you to make that type of a move yet. But then, as she came back into the dining room and smiled that same smile at me again, I asked myself—or is she?

Twenty-Seven

I leaned against the wall and watched Christine come back into the parlor and replace the book in its spot on the bookshelf. She was talking to me the entire time, but I wasn't hearing what she was saying with her lips; I was trying to read her eyes. I couldn't help but wonder how much of the score she'd read or just how much I should read into her words about my tutoring her.

She was staring at me, and then my name came across loud and clear. "Erik!"

"What?" I replied, as I came off the wall and out of my daze at the same time.

Cocking her head at me, she asked, "You didn't hear a word I said, did you?"

"I'm sorry, Christine. My thoughts were elsewhere, but they were about you, if that's any consolation."

She smiled. "I was asking you if it was time for our supper to arrive."

I quickly glanced at the tall clock. "Yes, it certainly is. If you'd like, you can set the table while I step out and get our supper."

"Step out? To where?"

"To where I can get our supper, silly," I replied while grabbing my cloak out of my music room, turning off the lake's motion sensor, and releasing the latch for the door.

"I thought your elves brought it."

I smiled broadly. "*Touché*. You got me there."

She started to ask another question about where I was going, but I stopped her and motioned toward the cupboard in the kitchen where the plates were. When she turned in that direction, I pulled the door open. When she turned back and saw me standing there with part of the wall open, she gasped and hurried toward me.

"What's this? What have you done?"

Teasing her, I replied, "It's a door. Certainly you've seen a door before."

She looked up and down and out into the dark passage. "Yes, but not like this one. So this is your secret door. I don't see a knob. How did you open it?"

While stepping out into the passage and lighting my lantern, I replied, "All in good time, my sweet. If after the four days you want to stay with me, then I'll show you my secrets, but not until then. My hidden doors are my protection. Without them, I could no longer stay here. I'd be overrun by curiosity seekers or by those wanting my unique head to mount over their fireplace. I won't be long, only a few minutes."

"But, Erik . . ."

"Hold your thoughts. I won't be long."

I then heard her huff as I closed the door.

When I approached the dock, I could hear and see rats around the packages, and I feared our supper was ruined, but they hadn't broken into it yet. Instantly, I made a mental note to get there before the rats the next day. When I returned and opened the door, the first thing I saw was Christine staring right at me. Then she examined the door and the passage I'd just come from.

"Where does that passage go?"

I smiled. "You're so cute. All in good time, Christine. All in good time. Now here, take these," I said as I handed her two packages, and then I picked up the other four. She watched me closely as I came inside and leaned back against the door until it clicked. Her inquisitive expression was so adorable, and I again smiled at her. "Let's eat. I'm hungry. Aren't you?"

"Yes," was her reply, but her eyes and thoughts were still on that door.

Soon, the table was set with an abundance of food, a linen tablecloth, fine china, crystal wine glasses, burning candles, and a new arrangement of fresh flowers.

"Before we sit down to eat," she said, "let me get these roses in water." She left the room but continued her thought along the way. "You really don't need to feel obligated to get me new ones every day. A rose lasts longer than one day."

"I don't feel obligated by any means. It's something I want to do," I responded as she came back in the room. "Don't forget what they represent. I always want your present and your future to be as fresh and new as the first roses of a new day. That way, each day will be what you deserve, a day filled with life and beauty."

"Well, thank you, but I have an idea. Instead of throwing so many of these roses away, I think I'll hang them up to dry, and then I can put the petals in a bowl to keep the room smelling sweet."

"Sounds like a good plan to me," I replied, while hoping she would be there long enough for those roses to dry.

I pulled out her chair for her and then sat down across from her. She smiled and the conversation went on about the nice meal we were eating. Then she suggested something that turned out to be a fun adventure for me.

"Why don't we make out a shopping list for *your elves* and then I can cook for you?"

I stopped eating and just looked at her. I should have guessed she would want to cook for me. That's who she was, my special Christine. So we did just that, made out a shopping list that I could give to Roland and Obert.

We ate and cleaned up, and then she made me surrender to her care of my leg, which was already looking better under her attentive nursing. Then, with a nice warm cup of tea, we sat and talked about the different places I'd seen and the places she'd been with her father. I watched her as she talked about him, with many smiles on her lips and some tears in her eyes.

I was kneeling on the hearth after lighting a fire, rolling the match between my fingers, when a conversation started that I hadn't anticipated.

"He loved his music so much, Erik, and I loved to listen to him play his violin. He had such passion."

"Yes, he did, I could feel the depth of his love when he played my violin."

She nodded. "He spoke about that day often, and I listened with rapt attention every time he told me that story. He tried many times to recreate the piece you were playing that drew him to you that day, but he could never get it right. He was excellent when it came to replicating a piece of music. But he said you put something into that piece that he couldn't match. I think that was part of the reason why he thought you were an angel, because he just couldn't get it right."

I looked over at her, knowing what it was that he couldn't get. My pain. My heart and soul were in that piece, along with tears and incredible pain. I got up and sat in my chair, and, as I crossed my ankle over my knee, I watched her looking down at her fingers running over the brocade pillow on her lap. Then she continued.

"He finally gave up trying to recreate it, and when I asked him why, he told me that when a composer is inspired to write something, the inspiration goes into the piece. He said the only one who can truly play it properly is the composer, because it's he alone who can feel what is written between the notes. He told me he could tell that piece was written with pain and love combined, and that he simply couldn't do it justice, so he stopped trying."

She became quiet, and I could tell she was in deep thought, so I sat without speaking and let her have her time alone with her father. I also used the quiet to think about my father and relived the circumstances under which I'd written that music. Eventually, she looked at me and asked something of me that made me lose my breath.

"Do you remember what it was that you played that day? Do you remember it? If you do, would you play it for me?" I believe I just stared at her for a moment without answering until she spoke again. "I realize it was a long time ago, so you probably don't even remember what it was."

"No, Christine, I remember well what it was."

"Then will you play it for me. It would mean so much to me. It would make me feel closer to my father. If you could, I'd really appreciate it."

How in the world could I possibly refuse her? I didn't know how I could play "Papa's Song" with anyone else around though. I'd only played it twice before, and both times it took everything out of me, and both times my mask was soaked with my tears before I finished. So how could I pull it off with her in the room? But when I looked at her pleading eyes, I had no choice.

"Certainly, Christine. It would be an honor."

While I tuned my violin, I told myself that I could pull it off if I concentrated and tried not to remember the tragic situation under which I'd composed it or the meaning behind it. But I soon forgot about that remedy because it was the emotion I'd put into it that made it special, and it was that special quality that her father was unable to duplicate. So I had to play it the way it was written—with my bleeding heart leading the way.

I stood by my piano and she was curled in the chair as I laid the bow to the strings and let the first note of "Papa's Song" emerge. I had to keep my eyes closed, hoping she wouldn't notice my mask soaking up my memories. I soon stopped thinking about what she was thinking and let myself feel all the emotion that piece was meant to express. My body swayed with the melody until my bow lay still on the strings, and then there was silence. I turned and began putting my violin in its case, without saying anything and neither did she. I used that time to make sure my eyes were free from tears before I turned toward her.

"Thank you so much, Erik. It was breathtaking. I now understand why my father couldn't recreate it. I can hear him playing it, and I can see what he meant about what was missing. I can also understand why he tried so hard to play it properly; it's . . . . it's haunting . . . it's tragically haunting."

"Thank you," I barely replied, as I sat down on the piano bench.

We both sat quietly for a while, and it was then that I realized how much she'd also been crying. I gave a momentary thought to reciting the lyrics for her so she could experience the full meaning, but I couldn't. Perhaps at another time, I told myself.

The conversation moved on, as did the day, but as night fell a related subject started. She'd gotten up and left for her room and then had come back out with her hair brush in her hand. I'd taken a book off the shelf and was thumbing through it when she expressed her view about our stroll with our fathers.

"You know, Erik, one of the things I've always admired about certain people is when they're able to express emotion without fear of what society says about them. I love Mummy with my whole heart, but that's one of her flaws. She may say she loves me, but when it comes to really showing it physically, she shies away.

"I think that's probably one of the reasons why I like the hard workers here in the opera house so much. They're just people without a hard exterior, and they're not afraid to express themselves. That's one of the things that makes me uncomfortable around the rich, even Raoul—their unwillingness to let me see who they really are."

By then I was sitting in my chair and she was standing in front of the fireplace and brushing her hair.

"I know how much that piece of music means to you, Erik, and I could feel every bit of it in every note you played. I'm certain if it weren't for your mask, I would have seen tears streaming down your cheeks as they were mine. I know you've been trying these last two days to let me come to know who you are. What I saw this day probably told me more about you than all the rest of the time I've been here. Don't hide anything from me, Erik. I want to know more; I need to know more."

I just looked up at her and was without words to respond. I loved her so much, and every time she spoke or did anything at all it made me love her more. She smiled, and I think I smiled back. Then she walked past me toward her room. As she passed my chair, she laid her hand on my shoulder for a moment before she squeezed it.

"Goodnight, Erik."

I closed my eyes and took a breath with her touch. "Goodnight, Christine."

Then she left me alone with my thoughts about her and her words, which filled me with an indescribable feeling deep inside my chest. I laid my book in my lap and my head back against the chair and gazed into the fire. The next day marked the third day, and as she closed her door, I hurt at the thought of her leaving me. I didn't want to let her go, but I'd promised her that on the fourth day she would be free. I didn't know what I was going to do without her around.

With a heavy sigh, I picked up the book again, hoping I could read until my eyes wouldn't stay open any longer. But with so many thoughts about her in my head, I couldn't do either, sleep or read. So I'd read a sentence, gaze into the fire, read a sentence, gaze into the fire.

That was my condition for about an hour. Then, abruptly, my motion sensor for the lake started going off in my music room. I nearly jumped out of my skin, while thoughts circled in my head about the possible trespasser. I turned it off and then went to Christine's door and quietly opened it. She was still asleep; thankfully it hadn't awakened her.

In all the years I'd lived there, it had rarely sounded the warning, and it could mean only one thing; someone was on my lake and near my home. I left instantly and headed for my docking room where I climbed the steps and looked out the observation window. I stared into the darkness and listened carefully, but I saw and heard nothing. After an uncomfortable few minutes, I realized I had to venture out on the lake and find out who was there before they got too close.

While running back down the stairs, I took off my coat and started looking for the long reeds I'd hid for just such a time. After finding them on a ledge, covered in dust and cobwebs, I placed one between my teeth and took off my shoes and mask. Then I slipped into the water by my boat and went to the end of it. Once there, I went under the water and through the small hole at the bottom of the invisible docking door. After coming up out of the water on the other side, I remained still and listened and watched for any sign of life.

When all remained quiet and dark, I swam quietly and slowly until I saw it, a faint light through the labyrinth of columns and mist. I kept swimming until I could see a boat, probably my old boat that I hadn't seen in years. I'd tucked it away out of sight, or so I thought. I swam to a column and hid behind it, waiting until the boat got closer so I could see who was stupid enough to venture into my territory. I feared it might be the police, searching for Christine.

I had to strain my eyes to see through the mist, but, eventually, I could see one man in the boat, and, thankfully, no more. My thought then was that the intruder was Raoul. Who else would be dumb enough to attempt finding me? He'd shown his stupidity in Perros, so it was probably him, the idiot. With my heart rate up a notch, I put the reed in my mouth and lowered myself completely under the water, humming and breathing through the reed.

That was a trick I'd learned from Tonkin pirates during my younger years. I'd used it to hide under water when someone was pursuing me. That trick had saved my life and my pursuers' lives more than once. The humming disorientated the one chasing me, which always gave me the position I needed, the superior position.

I came up long enough to get my bearings and take a few good breaths, and then I went down again and swam under the water, occasionally humming through the reed. I watched the light from the lantern in the boat get closer until I was right next to it. Then I saw the shape of a head appear over the edge of the boat. You young idiot, I thought. He's falling for it. Like so many others before him, he wants to know what the strange and haunting sound is and where it's coming from.

Then, like a fish jumping out of water, I came up quickly, grabbed him by his head, and pulled him under the water with me. Along with him, the lantern fell into the water and sank down with us, extinguishing it and leaving us in total darkness. I took him down with my arm around his neck, turning him in circles to confuse him even more.

He was fighting me and struggling hard, but I kept command of the situation. Once I heard him start to let his breath out, I knew I had to return him to the surface. Once there, I grabbed the back of his collar, looked up and around, trying to locate the air vent and light in the ceiling. When I spotted it, I knew what direction the wharf was in and began swimming toward it, with him gagging and coughing the entire way. My leg, which had been feeling good that day, was beginning to hurt and that angered me even more.

I reached the wharf and shoved the fool's head hard up against a pillar. Then I turned quickly and started swimming back toward my home, thinking that should teach him to try to enter my domain. I was maybe six strokes away from the wharf when I heard my name called out by a familiar voice. Then I stopped and turned around.

"Oded?"

I swam back and found him still clinging to the pillar, so I lifted myself up on the wharf and helped him up. After getting to my feet, I lit a lantern and stood over him.

"Oded, you fool. What do you think you're doing? I could have killed you. Are you sure you aren't Irish? With the number of times I've almost done you in, you surely must be carrying their luck."

"I could also ask you what you thought you were doing. Do you often try to kill those who get too close to your lair, Erik?"

Moving my dripping hair from my face, I rebuked him, "I wasn't trying to kill you, you fool. If I had been, you'd be at the bottom of the lake by now, along with the lantern. That cold bath was only a warning, but then you don't know how to take warnings, do you? You're such an imbecile! I thought our last conversation was clear. I just want to be left alone. This desire of mine isn't hurting anyone. Why did you do this, Oded? Why can't you just respect my privacy?"

He got to his feet and then answered me. "Because there's a young lady who's missing, Erik, and you're the first person who came to mind."

"Oh, thank you, *my friend*," I responded with a contemptuous tone. "Do you automatically think it must be Erik's doing every time something goes wrong?" He couldn't answer. "Go away from here, Oded, and leave me in peace while you still can."

I started to turn to dive into the lake again when he grabbed my arm. "There are those who are frightened for Mademoiselle Daaé. The Vicomte Raoul de Chagny for one, and he has the police looking for her. Wouldn't you rather have me find you down here than them?"

"I'd rather be left alone. But no matter. They'll never find me, Oded; not unless you're heading up the search. Is that what you're doing now? Are you the advance party? Will you go back now and tell them what direction to look in?"

He started rubbing his arms and shivered. "No, Erik. I only want to make sure she's safe. I know you won't harm her, but, if you don't have her, please tell me, so we can stop looking within these walls and start looking elsewhere."

After a moment of gazing out over the water, I answered him. "Yes, she's with me, but she'll be returning soon. I only asked her to stay for four days—that's all."

He moved in front of me and looked into my eyes. "Why four days, Erik?"

"I wanted her to come to know me without being frightened of me, and that would take time. I couldn't simply walk up to her and ask her to accompany me to dinner like any other man in Paris, now could I? She has to come to know me so she can make an educated decision."

"Decision? About what, Erik?"

"About whether or not she wants to stay with me."

He frowned. "Stay with you?"

I turned on him with contempt. "Yes, is that so absurd to think that a woman like Christine would want to stay with a man like me? Someone else wanted to, remember?" There was silence before I asked, "Will you go away peacefully and let me have this one chance?"

"I know you, Erik, and I know the power you can have over people, especially women. Are you certain you want her to have an educated decision or a seduced one?"

I ground my teeth, first turning away from him in anger and then turning back toward him with clenched fists.

"How dare you! Remember, Oded, she's not your daughter, and I'm no longer under your jurisdiction with a leash wrapped tightly around my neck. I know what I'm doing, and I don't want what you're suggesting. How dare you, you ignorant, meddling nuisance! How dare you! I should thoroughly thrash you and send you back into the blackness of my lake for what you're suggesting."

He didn't respond, and he didn't move. I growled and turned away from him, wrapping my fingers behind my neck before I followed through on my threat.

I looked over my shoulder at him and snarled in frustration. "Just for your information, and not that I care what you think about me but I do care what you think about Christine, I still haven't received my first kiss. And, furthermore, I have no intention of ever receiving it unless she initiates it from her heart. I won't receive one until then. Years ago, perhaps, but not now.

"My first kiss is almost sacred to me now, since I've waited so long for it. And I don't intend for it to be anything other than what it should be, something exquisitely special. I don't intend to steal a kiss from her, Oded, or to steal anything else from her for that matter. If I were to seduce her, and I'm sure I could if I really tried, then I would be stealing it from her, and I don't want that. I won't accept a kiss from her until I know it's for real."

"How will you know the difference, Erik? How will you know if she's under your spell or if she's giving her heart to you?"

I turned to face him with a softer tone. "Because a special young girl, who I met a lifetime ago in a far away land, taught me the difference. She taught me how to read the language of the eyes, and the eyes don't lie, Oded. The tongue quite often does, but not the eyes—at least not to me. I won't accept that first kiss until I see in Christine's eyes that language that tells me she loves me and wants to spend her life with me.

"Over these last two days I could have taken that kiss; she would have been willing, but I haven't and I won't. Not until it's right. You don't need to fear for her, but you do need to trust me, and leave me alone. I'm not *asking* you to stay away from here, Oded, I'm *telling* you. Don't come down here again. Next time, the luck of the Irish may not accompany you."

I turned once more, preparing to dive in the water, and once more he grabbed my arm. With a sigh of frustration and a look of annoyance, I turned back. "What now?"

"One more thing, do you know anything about the chandelier tragedy?"

Raising my hands in the air, I huffed. "Why do you automatically think I know something about everything that goes wrong around here?"

"Remember, Erik, don't get on the defensive or you only increase my curiosity."

"Is that a threat, *Oded*?"

"No, just the truth, *Erik*."

"Well, *you* need to remember, my friend, you're the only man who has ever come so close to me, and the skills I'm not proud of, and on so many occasions and still lived to talk about them."

"Is that a threat, *Erik*?"

"No, just the truth, *Oded*."

"By that comment, I figure you do know something about it then?" he insinuated while running his fingers across his beard in thought.

Sighing deeply, I answered as truthfully as I was going to. "It was a tragic accident. I also wanted to know how it happened, so I did my own investigating. The result: I found the metal supports for the counterbalance had been damaged by what looked like heat. Perhaps it was a small electrical fire that burnt itself out before being detected. Perhaps it happened during the war; that's the best scenario. It's really a wonder and a blessing that more weren't hurt or killed."

He looked at me with narrowed eyes, trying to read mine, and then responded, "Yes, it surely was. No one likes to see anyone get hurt, right, Erik? Oh, by the way, because César has been missing so often, the entire stable has been fired, with the exception of Lachenel, the stud groom. I hope the men who were fired didn't have families to support."

He got his message across easily. I was causing others harm when I was certain I wouldn't.

"Point noted, Oded. Now go home."

Before he had a chance to say or do anything else, I dove in and swam home. On the way there, I told myself that I had to find that old boat and sink it before another fool made the mistake of trespassing into my domain.

By the time I got back and put on dry clothes, I was quite agitated. That meddling fool was getting too close. It began with him appearing on the main floors of the opera house much too often, and then he started searching the cellars, but now he was actually on my lake. He was too close. I reasoned, the next thing I know he'll be knocking on my door.

His actions had me too tense to sleep, but I knew I should try. So I poured myself a small glass of brandy, turned out all the lights, and stretched out on the divan. After a few swallows, I put my hands behind my neck and gazed at the remainder of the coals in the fireplace changing colors.

I was still thinking about Oded and how I could prevent him from getting any closer, without doing him harm that is, when I heard Christine's door open. I looked up at her as she entered the parlor and thought; she's exactly what I need to soothe my spirit. But then she threw herself back against the doorframe, covered her face with her hands, and shrieked.

Twenty-Eight

"What is it, Christine?" I questioned quickly while jumping to my feet. "Did you see a rat?"

I glanced around, looking for a rat while closing the space between us, while she shook her head and cowered in the doorway.

"Then what's wrong? Is it a spider? Show me where it is and I'll relocate it." By then I was next to her and could see her trembling. I took her shoulders in my hands to comfort her, but it seemed to make matters worse. "What's wrong, Christine? Did you see someone?"

Then I thought about Oded, and my own heart skipped a beat. I turned quickly and ran to all my doors, checked them, and searched each room, even the trap door in the ceiling above her bed. Then, with panic filling my gut, I ran to the wall to the mirror chamber and leaned against it, listening closely. That lasted only a few seconds before I realized I was being ridiculous. She'd evidently seen something that frightened her and she couldn't see into the mirror chamber. So I went back to her.

"Christine, please tell me what frightened you."

"Erik . . . Erik . . ."

"Oh, Christine, please, for the love of God, please, talk to me."

Her face was still down, so I placed my fingers under her chin and tried to lift her face, but she turned away.

Then she barely whispered, "Please, turn the lights on."

"Certainly," I immediately answered and began moving around my home until they were all on.

"I'm sorry," she finally offered. "I shouldn't have screamed. I'm sorry."

"Can you tell me now what's wrong? Did you have a nightmare?"

"No, it wasn't that."

"Then, please, tell me what it was. What did you see?"

She slowly looked up into my eyes. "Raoul was right."

"What?" I questioned out of confusion. "How did he get in this conversation?"

Her head shook. "The lighting made . . . ." Her head shook more. "Don't be mad at me."

"I'm not going to be mad at you, Christine, but please tell me what happened."

"Your eyes . . . your eyes glowed like a flame."

"What?" I gasped and backed away from her. "What?" I questioned again. "Are you sure?"

She nodded. "Please don't be mad at me for telling you. You obviously didn't know."

I shook my head and lowered myself down on the coffee table. "No, I didn't know. All these . . . all the rumors . . . the rumors were true? No one ever told me. Not even my best friend. Although . . . ."

My thoughts took me back to the story my father told our good doctor, about my eyes frightening my poor mother. I was only a few days old when she said they were glowing like a demon's. I put my elbows on my knees and buried my face in my hands.

"Was she right? Am I? Could it be true? Am I?"

Christine stood beside me and laid her hand on my shoulder. "I'm sorry, Erik. I should have controlled my reaction more. I was just . . . it surprised me, that's all. I'm sorry. Please, forgive me."

I released one hand and laid it on top of hers, all without raising my head. "It's not your fault. There's nothing to forgive. I am what I am. I . . . I just didn't want it to be true."

"Do you want to talk about it?"

"No, not now. Go back to bed or whatever you were about to do."

"I was hungry and wanted a piece of cheese."

I patted her hand and spoke softly. "Then go."

She left for the kitchen and on her way back to her room she again asked, "Are you sure you don't want to talk about it?"

"I'm sure."

When her door closed, I nearly collapsed. This couldn't be happening to me. I looked at my brandy, got up, and drank it down. Then I headed for my piano, knowing I really needed my music. I played for over an hour without much help. My mother's reaction to my demon eyes, all the talk about the Opera Ghost and his burning eyes, and Christine's reaction mixed together and kept repeating in my head.

Then I thought about Oded, *my supposed friend.* Why didn't he ever tell me? And my father. Why didn't he tell me? Both of those men I'd spent a lot of time with, so they had to have seen what Christine just saw. Why didn't they tell me? Why did they keep it a secret? I felt like a fool. I felt duped. Since I couldn't be angry with my father, all my anger turned toward Oded, and I was compelled to tell him how hurt I felt. So I quickly wrote Christine a note, telling her where I was going just in case she got up again before I returned. Then I left and showed up on Oded's doorstep after three a.m., banging on his door.

It was a sleepy Darius who opened the door. "Erik!"

I burst in and harshly insisted, "Get Oded."

He didn't say anything as he left the room, and then Oded appeared, also sleepy.

Ruthlessly, I demanded. "Oded, *my friend*, why didn't you ever tell me about my eyes?"

"What?" he questioned while checking the clock on his mantel.

"You heard me. Why did you keep it a secret?"

"Erik, what are you talking about, and why are you so angry? I'm not at your home this time—you're at mine, so that can't be the reason. Sit down."

"I don't want to sit down. I want answers."

"Well, I'm tired, so I'm going to sit. Now, will you start at the beginning and explain what you're talking about?"

"Why haven't you been truthful with me? After all the conversations we've had, I thought you would never fear to tell me anything. If I'd known the truth, I could have prepared Christine."

"What?" he replied, and woke up quickly. "What about Christine? Has something happened to her?"

"Other than being frightened to death—no. Why didn't you tell me?"

"Listen, Erik, you have to explain what you're talking about instead of accusing me of something I have no knowledge of."

"Are you trying to tell me you never saw my eyes glowing?"

He frowned but looked relieved. "Oh, that."

"Then you did know. Why . . . oh why didn't you ever tell me? Why did the woman I love have to find out without being prepared? I'm 45 and no one has ever had the courage to inform me."

"Erik, think about it. I never gave a thought to *telling* you. I thought you already knew. I never thought I had to tell you that your eyes are nearly black. I figured you already knew that. Are you mad at me because I never told you that? There are a lot of things that are different about you, but I never brought them to your attention, as if you had no brain or memory and had to be reminded about them.

"Like the time when you collapsed at the Shah's residence. That was the first time I saw your need for the mask and all the lash marks on your face and body. I didn't feel a need to tell you that your nose was missing or about the scars. I figured you had to already know about them."

"But this is something different, Oded. The lash marks I received from someone else, while my eyes glowing yellow is a part of me. You should have told me."

"Erik, you're not being rational. I'm sorry you had to find out this way—after all these years. But I'm not to blame."

There was silence and my angered breaths could be heard as I stared down at him. Then I walked to the window and tried to think. He waited a few moments and then tried to be rational with the irrational man in his parlor.

"I've always known how different you are, from our first meeting on that road to Mazenderan. Watching you move was like watching slow moving water falling over rocks. You were liquid—so smooth that it was nearly hypnotic just watching you do ordinary things. And when you intended to capture my attention, it was even more so, like when you were teasing me with that watch chain. But did I tell you then that your hands were graceful? No, it would have been out of place.

"With each encounter after that, I learned more about your abilities, but did I bring them to your attention? No. Not until I saw your skill with the lasso did I mention anything about your speed or graceful movements, and that was because I could see how that skill could save lives.

"Then, once you started going on those rides with us, I really began to appreciate your unique abilities. When I saw how you could hear and see in the dark even faster and better than our horses, I was amazed. But, again, did I ever discuss it with you? Absolutely not. I believed you already knew about your ability to see and hear so well, so it would be ridiculous to think I had to inform you about such a thing.

"And, as far as your eyes glowing, well, it was the same thing. The first time I noticed it, it fascinated me. After really watching you and thinking about it, I came to realize it was all in the makeup of your eyes themselves. If you could see in the dark like an animal, then, structurally, there was something similar inside of them that was like an animals. But just like your good eyesight, I never gave consideration to telling you about it. I didn't know that you didn't already know."

"Oh, but Oded, you could have brought it up as just another part of a conversation. You always managed to ask me every other question under the sun."

I heard him sigh. "I knew you were a private man, Erik. I knew there were certain subjects that were too painful for you to talk about, your need for a mask, for one. You may not have thought it at the time, but I held my tongue often when it came to your physical appearance. It was only when

I needed to know something or needed to explain to you something that I let it be a part of a conversation."

"And what about your men? Did they also see *my glowing eyes*?"

"Some did. But your eyes didn't always glow. The circumstances had to be just right, and the glow only lasted for a few seconds at best. I only noticed it when you were around fire. Actually, I believe it wasn't your eyes glowing as much as it was your eyes reflecting a fire or light if the rest of the area was otherwise dark. It's truly a strange phenomenon, but I don't see how it could frighten anyone. It only lasts a few seconds. If it was continual, then I could see how it could get intense."

He got up and joined me at the window. "Does that help? Does that answer your questions?"

"Perhaps. It does explain a lot, but it doesn't make me feel any better about it. To know I'm feared for yet another reason bothers me." I shook my head. "I don't know how I'm going to return to Christine. I don't know how I can face her. I don't know what to do."

He was silent, and, I'm sure, picking his words carefully. "How was she when you left?"

"She said she was fine and went back to bed. She was very kind about it—once she got over her shock. But then that's who Christine is. She's kind to everyone. Even me, after . . .'"

Thankfully, I stopped myself from making that huge mistake and letting him know how I kidnapped her and that she originally wasn't a willing participant in my endeavors. Not to mention that I'd gone into a tyrannical rage in front of her.

"Thank you, Oded, and I'm sorry I jumped on you. I guess I needed someone to blame. I am sorry."

We talked for a few more minutes and then I started to leave. I was out on the landing when he just had to have the final word.

"I'm glad to see you're not favoring your left leg as much."

"Now, see, Oded. That's what I was talking about. If you want your curiosity appeased, you always manage to make me a part of a conversation."

"Yes, but it's only when I have a need to know. I was concerned about your leg, so that's why it became a part of a conversation. And someday, when you're not so guarded, I hope you'll tell me what happened to it."

I shook my head and started down the stairs. "Goodnight, Oded."

On the way home, I decided to make Christine my favorite breakfast, the one Geanne had always made when I visited them. She deserved to be pampered more than normal after what I'd put her through.

The eastern sky was beginning to lighten once I got home, and when I didn't hear Christine moving around in her room, I went in the kitchen and began preparing breakfast. The eggs were scrambled and seasoned, the potatoes were cleaned and boiling, the cheese was finely sliced and waiting, the bread was buttered and ready to be grilled, the leaks were cleaned and diced, and the bacon was frying when I heard Christine's door open.

I'd decided to start that day off well and explain my unusual eyes over breakfast and with a lighthearted attitude. So, with a pleasant feeling inside me and a smile on my face, I grabbed the dishtowel and was drying my hands as I walked to the kitchen door. But once I reached it, I froze in place, with the dishtowel hanging limp from my hands. She'd just entered the dining room, and, when she saw me, I think she told me good morning, but I'm not certain.

She was wearing the dark green dress, and I was stunned. She was so beautiful. Her cheeks were rosy and her hair was curling softly over her shoulders. I'd previously thought that blue was my favorite color on her, but, as she moved across the dining room toward me, I had to reconsider. I don't believe I'd seen her look more beautiful, not even for the gala.

She had to say 'excuse me' several times before I could move out of her way and let her enter the kitchen. But, even when she was in the kitchen, I still stood in the doorway, mindlessly watching her.

She was talking to me and I think asking me questions, because periodically I uttered a noise of some sort. But it was only after she walked up to me and waved her hand directly in front of my eyes that I responded like an intelligent human.

"Oh, I'm sorry, Christine. You look stunning in that dress."

"Why, thank you, Erik—for the compliment and the dress. This is my favorite one."

She started helping me with breakfast, and, eventually, I was able to gather my thoughts enough to apologize for my childish behavior the previous night. Then I explained what Oded had told me about my eyes.

"Since he believes the dim firelight causes the problem, we can leave all the lights on from now on—if that will keep you from being frightened."

"That won't be necessary, Erik. I didn't expect to see what I saw, that's why it frightened me. Now that I know what can happen, it won't frighten me anymore."

We sat down to eat, and the conversation continued in a wonderful way, just like any normal couple exchanging thoughts over a meal. Once finished, we took care of my leg, which was looking much better, and then we had her lessons. After that, she asked if I would read to her.

"I can't get enough of your voice," she began. "I could listen to you talk all day."

I chuckled, "Oh, I think you would eventually get bored."

"I don't think so, and I want to get as much of it as I can before I leave here." Then she added softly, "If I leave here."

I wasn't sure how she meant that statement, and I was almost afraid to ask, but I did. "Do you think I won't let you go?"

"No, I know you'll honor your word. It's just that . . ." She stopped and looked at me in thought. "When you first brought me down here and explained everything to me, I was counting the minutes until I could leave, but now . . ."

Again she stopped, and I held my breath. Could she possibly be thinking what I hoped she was thinking?

"I'll miss being able to ask you a question just to hear your voice. I'll miss it. I'll miss you. So, if you don't mind, I'd like you to read to me."

I sighed. "I'll miss you also, Christine." Then, when the moment became too intense, I asked, "Do you like Shakespeare's sonnets?"

"Yes, I do. Is there anyone who doesn't?"

"To some they are mindless, indiscernible babble, but I find them thought provoking. I think the hundred and sixteenth is appropriate.

> *Let me not to the marriage of true minds*
> *Admit impediments. Love is not love*
> *Which alters when it alterations finds,*
> *Or bends with the remover to remove:*
> *O, no! it is an ever-fixed mark,*
> *That looks on tempest, and is never shaken;*
> *It is the star to every wandering bark,*
> *Whose worth's unknown, although his height be taken.*
> *Love's not Time's fool, though rosy lips and cheeks*
> *Within his bending sickle's compass come;*
> *Love alters not with his brief hours and weeks,*
> *But bears it out even to the edge of doom.*
> *If this be error, and upon me prov'd,*
> *I never writ, not no man ever lov'd."*

We sat quietly gazing into each other's eyes, attempting, I believe, to understand each other's thoughts.

"That was beautifully spoken, Erik. You do his sonnets justice."

I thanked her and then read more until it was time for me to meet my elves again. Then we decided what we wanted to eat for supper, and she said she'd get it started while I was gone. After I clicked the door closed, I smiled the biggest smile. I absolutely loved surprising Christine with gifts. But to get this one was going to take me farther than the wharf; I would have to go up to her dressing room.

I was a bit surprised and then concerned when I neared her mirror and saw light coming from it, but I didn't need to be. It was Meg and Madame Giry, discussing where Christine could be. It had been over two days since she'd been seen, and they feared she'd been hurt when the chandelier fell. They'd gone to Madame Valerius' home to see if she was there, and they didn't know where to look next. I was waiting for an opportunity to calm their fears when Sorelli came to the door.

"Madame Giry, the Vicomte de Chagny would like to speak with you as soon as you can."

Immediately, Madame Giry and Meg got up from the lounge and headed for the door. Then right before Madame Giry left, I spoke to her.

"My friend, don't worry about Mam'selle Daaé. She's in good hands and will return to you soon. Please let the concerned ones know that she's safe, but not who has care of her."

As expected, she nodded and closed the door. I waited a moment and then entered and locked the door. Once I had Christine's lavender dress in arms, I started home, smiling the entire way. I came in the door to my home quietly and listened for Christine. When I heard her in the kitchen, I quickly went to her room and laid the dress on her bed. Then, with an even larger smile, I left.

While trying to control the degree of my exuberance, so she wouldn't suspect anything, I entered the kitchen, but, when I saw her, my mood automatically changed. She was standing on a chair in front of the pantry, holding my jeweled dagger. I started toward her, and when she noticed me she started with her questions.

"Erik, this is beautiful. It looks like a family heirloom—is it?

"I believe so," I replied while taking the dagger from her hands and placing it on the table. Then I reached for her hand. "Come down from there before you break your neck. What were you doing up there anyway?"

"I was looking for more spices and saw something shiny. I just wanted to know what it was."

"I should have guessed. You're letting your curiosity get you into trouble again, my dear."

I replaced the chair at the table and then started to put the dagger back on the top shelf of the pantry.

"Wait, Erik! May I look at it for a moment? It's the most beautiful dagger I've ever seen."

I sighed and handed it to her. "Be careful. It's extremely sharp. It would be a shame if you sliced off your curiosity," I said sarcastically and with a bit of my irritability showing.

"Is it your heirloom, Erik? Did it belong to your father or mother?"

"No," was my curt answer.

"Please tell me about it. Was it a gift?"

"No."

"Did you buy it?"

"No."

"Are you teasing me again, Erik?"

"Do I look as if I'm teasing?"

"What's wrong? Why are you angry? I only want to know who gave it to you. Or did you find it somewhere?"

I looked at her inquisitive eyes and sighed, trying to release my unwarranted irritation. "Very well, if you must always have your curiosity appeased, I found it—right here," I said as I held my hand on my left side. "Remember this ugly scar? That *beautiful* dagger nearly took my life."

"Oh!" she gasped and scrunched her face. Then she looked at the dagger and set it down on the table.

"Does that change your view of it, my dear?"

She nodded. "I'm sorry. I shouldn't have been so nosy."

"It's all right. It also captured my attention."

"Why do you keep it around?"

"At first, I was going to throw it into the lake, but then, like you, I was mesmerized by its beauty. So I decided to remove the blade and keep the jewels and gold handle as a paper weight, but I never did," I said as I ran my fingers over the handle.

"I'm sorry," she said in a somber tone. "Sorry for the pain it caused you. But, at least . . . ."

"At least, what?" I asked when she didn't finish her thought. She shook her head. "Come on, Christine. You can't start a sentence like that and not finish it. But, at least—what?"

She took a deep breath. "At least it wasn't a weapon you used to kill someone."

At first I was hurt by that reminder, but I couldn't let anything spoil our day, so I tried to be honest with her. "You've got that right. I've never used a blade or a gun as a weapon. I have an aversion to blood. I would never use such a ghastly instrument." She was quiet and stared at me for far too long. "What now? What are you thinking of asking me this time?"

She shook her head again. "It doesn't matter. It's none of my business anyway."

I replaced the dagger on the shelf and sat down across from her, laying my hand on top of hers. Then I said softly, "Remember, Christine, my life is your business. I don't want to keep secrets from you, even if it's a subject I don't like talking about. If there's something you want to know, I'd rather you ask me. If you don't, then my imagination conjures up the worst, and I get unnerved. So, if there's something more that's bothering you, something about me, then I want to answer your questions so they won't be blown out of proportion by some false rumor."

She nodded and lowered her sight to our hands on the table. "You've admitted that there have been ones you've had to kill or be killed yourself. Was the one who stabbed you one of them?"

"Unfortunately, yes," I replied after a deep breath. "He thought it would make him someone important if he captured the Opera Ghost. Foolish man. That was his last attempt at trying such an unwise endeavor."

She thought for a moment and then asked another question. "If you don't use a gun or knife, then how did they die?"

I ground my teeth, released her hand and sat back. I looked at my hands lying on the table, and I truly hurt inside. I never expected her to ask such a pointed question, and I didn't know if I could answer her. I removed my hands from the table and almost sat on them. They were disgusting to me when I viewed them in that light. Christine knew I was troubled and tried to correct the situation.

"See, I told you I should mind my own business. I'm sorry. Forget I said anything."

"Forget? If it were only that easy. Something else you'll discover about me is that I never forget anything. I can remember every word in every conversation I've ever had, every word in every book I've ever read, the details of every place I've ever visited, every piece of music I've played and every note in it, along with every fight I've ever fought. Forget? If it were only that easy."

"You don't have to answer that question, Erik. I don't want to cause you more hurt."

I looked at her. "Will you be able to forget the question if I don't answer it?" She quietly gazed at me. "That's what I thought. If I don't answer it, you'll always wonder, won't you? I'd rather you know the truth than to wonder and perhaps envision something worse than the truth—if there is anything worse than the truth." I added as an afterthought.

She gasped and exclaimed, "The Punjab lasso! Is there truth to the rumors I've heard about it? Is that your weapon?"

"Yes, but it isn't the type of weapon that's rumored. It's more like a violin string than a traditional lasso."

"Really? A violin string? How did you discover such a thing? Or did you invent it?"

I took a deep breath and laid my face in my palms, closing my eyes and rubbing my temples with my fingertips.

"Oh, Erik. Again, I'm sorry. You don't have to answer. I can tell it's hurting you."

"I want you to know the truth. I don't want there to be unanswered questions swimming around in your inquisitive head and bumping into each other. It's just hard to talk about it. I hate that time in my life, but you need . . . you deserve to know." I raised my head and looked at her. "It was when I was very young and full of hate for everyone. If anyone crossed me, they only did it once. I was feared, and people steered away from me, which is what I wanted—to be left alone.

"Then one day something happened, and I woke up to the horror of my existence, causing all my hatred to move inward. I hated myself and wanted to die. Then, when others recognized my vulnerability, I became the target of extreme abuse, but I didn't fight back. I felt I should be punished for my crimes, so I let the abuse continue until one night when I thought I was going to die.

"At that time, I became a victim of the Punjab lasso. But the one using it didn't want to kill me, he only wanted to rob me without my fighting back, and it worked. When he had what he wanted, he took the lasso off my neck and ran away. I instantly realized the potential the lasso had, so I ran after him and made him tell me about that strange weapon.

"After that, I spent over three months learning how to use it in such a way that it wouldn't cause any harm. From then on, I was never abused, and I never inadvertently killed anyone in the process of trying to save my life, with a few exceptions like Buquet. Since I was shot, I couldn't get to him in time to release the lasso, and, regardless of what others might think, I do regret his death.

"The lasso has saved many lives. I know there are those around here who fear it, but, as long as everyone leaves me alone, they have nothing to fear. In fact, while I was in Persia, I was even called upon to use my skills with the lasso to help track and capture criminals. When I did, no blood was spilled and no lives were lost. It's saved many lives over the years. And, in a way, it's caused others to fear me enough to leave me alone."

I brought my hands back up on top of the table, opened them, and looked at my palms. "I've been gifted, as you know. Between my hands and my mind, I can do almost anything. While I've done ugly things with my hands, I've also created beauty with them. I have to remind myself about that beauty often, or I'll go crazy over the ugliness they've caused."

The fright and disgust left her eyes and her compassion returned. Then she laid her hands on top of mine and looked in my eyes.

"Thank you, again, Erik. I can tell it's hard for you to answer my questions. Thank you."

I nodded and then watched her face. I knew there was another question forming behind her eyes, but I didn't know if I wanted to ask her what it was, but I had to.

"Go ahead, Christine. I know there's another question on the horizon."

She shook her head slowly. "No, not a question. A realization. I now understand why you left me alone for so long on the day of the gala, and why you sounded the way you did. You'd just been shot and could have died. You were so hurt, and I was so angry with you and spoke so rudely to you—so harsh and even cruel. You must have been in such pain and yet you were there for me.

"You were always there for me. You've walked all over the opera house with your poor leg. You shopped and purchased all you gave me, all the time with that wound." I tried to get a word in, but she kept going once the pieces started falling into place. "And then Perros. You were there in Perros with that leg—all the way to Perros. Oh! And then the cemetery and playing for my father, and then you were with Raoul. Oh! Erik, why did you put yourself through that?"

Without giving me a chance to answer she went on. "And the park. You were there with your poor, poor leg. You were walking all over Perros with it. Oh, Erik, why did you do that? Why did you put yourself at such a risk?"

"I told you I would walk through fire for you, Christine. A walk through Perros was nothing. I had to be there with you."

"Oh, Erik, I'm so sorry. I was so selfish. If I'd only known . . ." She stopped and shook her head again. Then, as silence settled in, she searched my eyes and spoke softly. "If I'd only known a lot of things."

Twenty-Nine

As we made our meal, Christine continued to talk about her new understanding of her Angel of Music. She also teased me about my unusual approach to cooking.

"Perhaps my many years of being a bachelor have made me lazy. That's my only excuse for my lack of culinary skills. But I'm willing to learn. Would you like to switch places and be my tutor?"

"Certainly," she eagerly began. "This is how you prepare asparagus."

We laughed and we talked and, eventually, the table was set and we were eating stuffed chicken with garlic potatoes, asparagus with hollandaise sauce, and chocolate cake. As we ate, my thoughts started turning serious. We had only one more supper to share together and then she'd be gone, and I fought my natural tendency to become depressed.

So, instead of thinking, I watched her and soaked up her essence. I watched her eyes as she spoke, and I watched her hands as she moved them from her fork to her wine glass. She was mesmerizing—every bit of her.

Once we were finished with our meal, I wanted to encourage her to go to her room so she could see her new dress, but the paintings I had scattered on my dining room wall caught her attention. Some of them depicted places I'd been, and I explained that to her. While she studied them, I studied her. When she was satisfied, she glanced around the parlor and then looked up at me.

"Are these all the rooms to your home?"

Surprised by that question, I also looked around. "Why do you ask? Is my castle not large enough for you?"

"No, it's not that at all. It's perfect for an ordinary bachelor, but you're not an ordinary bachelor. You've traveled far and, I'm sure, have seen wonderful sights, so you seem out of place here. Now, if there was more to your home that would allow you to expand your mind and . . . and do or . . . ." She sighed, "I'm not sure how to explain what I'm feeling. I sense there has to be more to this place than meets the eye. So I was wondering if there are other rooms that I haven't seen; ones with hidden doors perhaps—ones I can't see."

I took a deep breath and looked down at her. "I have a wine cellar that's below us, and there's one other room that's a security room of sorts. I've never used it or had a need to use it—thankfully."

She cocked her head and frowned. "I'm confused. What do you mean—a security room? You mean it's filled with weapons—weapons that you say you don't use?"

"No, not at all like that. It is, I suppose, a weapon in itself." She looked even more confused, so I tried again. "Remember, Christine, there are always those who want to do me harm. Well, that extra room is a precaution in the event that someone should discover I live down here. It's a guarantee that no one will ever do me harm in my own home. No more scars while I'm in here.

"I guess you could say it's like having locks on your doors. They would have to get through that room before they could get in here, and it's nearly impossible to get out of that room without my help. Thankfully, though, no one has ever made it this far down to find me. No one except you, Christine. So I trust that, when you leave here, you'll keep my secrets."

"Yes, I will. Besides, from what I've learned about you, if I were to send anyone down here I would be sending them to their death."

I closed my eyes and turned, taking a few steps away from her. "It makes me feel sick that you know these things about me. I hate the things I've done or have had to do. I don't want a life like this any longer, a life where I'm always on guard, always looking over my shoulder, a life where I have to hide behind a moat, trap doors, mazes, and a secret chamber. This isn't what I want. This isn't who I am."

I turned back to face her. "That's why I need you so badly. With you by my side I would have the strength to leave this place and to walk in the sunlight and build another home with windows and many more rooms, and none of them would be a weapon."

There was moisture forming in her eyes when she spoke. "I believe you really mean that." I nodded and she shook her head. "That was much more information than what I expected. I really wasn't trying to pry into your security. I only felt that a man like you might have a laboratory or work room where you experimented with things or built things, like your cold pantry or electric lights and stove."

I rubbed my chin and thought, my guilty conscience is getting in the way of ordinary conversation. I suddenly felt a need to be more guarded. I looked at her and knew she was being honest with me right then, but what about in the future? I needed to be more careful. But I could explain that concern of hers easily.

"Since I do live here alone and have never had visitors until you, it doesn't matter where I experiment or build. It doesn't matter if I make a mess out of my drawing room with an experiment or two. And, as far as building, well nearly everything you see was built right where it sits." I glanced around at all my furniture. "Yes, it all sits right where I built it." Then in a more teasing tone, I added, "It saved my back that way—no need for moving furniture around."

"You mean you built all your furniture?" I nodded. "Even the divan and chair?" I again nodded and she looked completely surprised. "What about the dining furniture?"

"Yes," I said as I swept my arm around the dining room and parlor. "All but the paintings, tapestries, books, and a few trinkets, I've made."

She looked around again. "What about that tall clock? You surely couldn't have made that."

"Au, contraire, my sweet. I once built 24 tall clocks that were much larger and much more complicated than that simple one. Those other ones . . ."

I stopped myself from telling her that those other ones were also weapons, but I think she was so astounded with her new understanding of the man in her midst that she didn't catch my near blunder. Instead, she rushed toward the music room.

"What about your piano and organ?" Again I nodded, with an increasing smile at her excitement. Then she scrunched her nose. "And that casket? You also made it?"

"Yes, Christine." I stood behind her and also looked into my music room. "Well, there are a few things in here that I didn't make, like my violin, and that horse bust, and the paper, and uhh my clothes in the armoire, the feather pen, and . . ."

"All right. All right. I get the picture. But that's still remarkable, Erik. I could understand you building your home, but . . ." She stopped, turned, and looked up at me. "Then the rumors are true about you also building this opera house?"

"Well, parts of it," I admitted. "I didn't build the entire structure myself, but I studied the plans and built enough of it to know it very well. It's all up here," I said as I tapped the side of my head. "I know it well enough to build another one exactly like it in another land—if I was asked to do so, and the same goes for the Palace in Persia."

"You built a palace?" she asked as her eyes widened even more.

"Yes, I designed and built it for the shah, but I had 1,000 men working alongside me, so it wasn't as if I hammered every nail."

"You're much too modest, Erik. Now I know you don't belong down here like this. What a waste. Just think what you could do if you lived outside these walls."

"Modest?" I chuckled. "I've never been accused of being modest before. I've been called many other things, but never modest." Then, in sincerity, I reminded her. "Again, Christine, I've tried to live outside these walls, but it never ends well. You've seen my body—you've seen the results of my close contact with others, and I've told you my past and what can happen to others when they get too close to me and try to do me harm.

"At times, I feel like a volcano. After a violent eruption, a volcano produces new land mass that, in time, can turn a barren sea into a beautiful island. And even during their eruptions, especially at night, their powerful explosions are beautiful to watch and even captivating. But, if anyone dares to ignore warnings and get too close, they can lose their lives or at least be seriously harmed.

"That's what I feel like. I have the potential to create beauty, but something always seems to go wrong and someone gets hurt—even me. I often hurt myself," I said as I ran my fingers over the self administered scratches on my cheek and then patted my leg.

She took a few steps toward me. "And yet you feel you could succeed if I left here with you? How would that be any different?"

"Because I would have the right incentive beside me all the time," I replied as I took her hand in mine. "I would have more reason to control my actions and responses when others tried to do me harm. And, with you, I could build a castle on a hilltop and not have to come in contact with others that often. With you, I could do anything."

The compassion in her eyes and the softness of her hand in mine was moving me in a direction that I knew I couldn't handle right then, so I tried to change the subject.

"On a lighter note, my dear, there's something in your room that I didn't make. Our own little elves left it for you today. You should take a look."

She looked up at me with a smile and shake of her head, and I held out my arm, motioning toward her door. She headed in that direction while glancing over her shoulder at me, and I followed her, opening the door for her. When she spotted the dress, she took a deep breath and moved quickly to it. Then, grabbing it up in her arms, she turned quickly and almost ran to me. She looked as if she were going to give me a hug, and I was about ready to let her, but she stopped just short of it.

"Erik, this is so beautiful. I love it. Thank you . . . I mean, thank your elves for me."

I was smiling broadly the entire time, but when she continued my word game, it made me chuckle.

"That dress was meant to be what you wore on your trip down here. I'd put it in your armoire for you, but . . ."

"Oh, you mean your elves also know how to get into my locked dressing room?" she questioned, while holding the dress against her and turning in circles.

"Apparently."

She looked down at it again and added, "Seriously, Erik, you don't need to keep giving me things. It's terribly sweet of you to do this, but you've already given me so much." Then after looking back up at me, she questioned. "You're not, by any chance, trying to buy my affections, are you?"

I shook my head adamantly. "Absolutely not! That tactic would never work on you. You're not shallow like so many other women. I would never try *any* tactic on you. You deserve to know the truth about me, so that's all I'm doing—being honest. I love giving you gifts, so to not give you gifts would be tantamount to being dishonest. You don't want that do you?"

She smiled at me and then hung the dress up in her armoire while thanking me again.

Oh, how I wanted to grab her and hold her close to me. Every moment I was with her was making it extremely hard on me to resist her. It was only the vision of her giving me my first kiss of her own free will that kept me in line, so I had to maintain strict control over my actions. Therefore, once more, to change the dangerous direction my thoughts were taking me, I offered to read to her.

"There's something else I bought for you; well, since I haven't read it yet, I actually bought it for both of us. It's a book named *Jacob*. You haven't read it, have you?"

"No, I haven't, but it wouldn't matter. I'd want you to read it to me anyway."

So I started a fire while she put on the kettle for some tea and hot water for my compresses. I got comfortable on the divan with the book in hand, and she started with my treatment. The story began well, although it had an unexpected feature that wasn't described in the forward, and it made me uncomfortable at first.

I wanted a book that wouldn't remind either of us about any painful memories from our pasts, especially anything about a close father and child relationship. But, within the first few pages, we discovered Jacob had a ten-year-old son named Matthew, and a wife who had just died. To console himself with his grief, he left with Matthew and started their adventures.

I glanced at Christine a few times during those pages, considering that was what had happened to her. The only difference was that she was a six-year-old girl when her mother died and she and her father started traveling. But, according to her expression, it wasn't bothering her, so I continued on, even though it did bother me, considering it was about a father and son.

The story kept both of us intrigued and in anticipation of what was going to happen next in the pair's exploits. Their adventures covered territories from the North Pole to the South Pacific Islands. They traveled on dog sleds across frozen tundra, on horseback over Arabian sands, on sailing ships during turbulent storms, on a raft down the Amazon River, and on a train across Africa, to name a few.

The writer kept our attention as we waited to learn how they managed to escape being tracked by a hungry polar bear. Then we laughed along with a village of Eskimos when the father and son team built their first igloo and forgot about making a door. Next we were on the edge of our seats again when they hid in a cave on an island inhabited by headhunters. From there we laughed wholeheartedly as they bathed in a clear lake in South America where their clothes, and all they owned, were taken by a troop of monkeys.

Because of our laughter, I actually had to stop reading when, in their efforts to retrieve the only clothes they had, they entered a village that was swarming with Catholic missionary nuns. The writer painted a clear picture of their plight, which was funny to us, but I'm sure it wouldn't have been funny had it really happened.

Along with the story, the author gave us interesting history and geography lessons along the way. One such time was about a historic lighthouse on the rocky coast of Maine in the United States. Jacob and Matthew fell in love with the peaceful area, its history, and the majestic waves crashing on the rocks. Consequently, Jacob purchased the lighthouse and they moved in and prepared to end their journeys.

All went well for the first week, but then a terrible storm hit that nearly sent them to the bottom of that dark sea. They soon realized why that quaint lighthouse had been put there to begin with. It was to warn sailors about the dangerous waters and not to invite them to the warm sunny beaches. As a result, Jacob took the first offer to sell the lighthouse, and they continued their journeys toward calmer waters.

I would look at Christine periodically over the top of the book to make sure she wasn't getting bored, and, although I found her in different positions, she never looked bored. Sometimes she was curled in the corner of the divan, or lying on her stomach with her hands under her chin, or sitting on the divan with her knees against her chest, or lying on her back with her head resting on a turquoise pillow. She was distracting to watch. I wanted so badly to be sitting beside her and holding her in my arms as I read to her.

There were times when she would get up, and, after telling me to not stop reading, she would walk past me and lightly brush her hand across my shoulder. Then she would continue on her way to the kitchen to fill up our teacups. We took breaks to eat a snack and discuss what we'd already read, but, other than that, we read for the rest of the day and evening.

The book did keep us both intrigued and amused from beginning to end. There were times, though, when I had to stop and pretend I needed a drink to clear my throat. Those times, my thoughts turned to my father and me and the times we spent together, and, as I looked at Christine, I believe she also was having the same feelings about her father.

We were nearing the end of the well-written book, and I think both Christine and I were having good feelings about our day of reading. But then, when we were down to the last three chapters, the scenario became uncomfortably familiar, and I looked at Christine often to see if she also saw it.

Matthew was forty-three by then and Jacob was sixty-seven. They disembarked from a ship that landed in Port Elizabeth, South Africa. They both fell in love with the beautiful terrain and the people, but Matthew also fell in love with a blonde girl named Mary who was twenty-three years younger than he was. There was stiff opposition from her family, since Matthew was not from the rich upper classes as she was. Plus, he was considered a drifter and much too old for her.

Then Matthew had to make a serious decision. Jacob wanted to leave on another sailing ship and head for India, and, although Matthew loved his father more than life itself, he was also in love with a beautiful girl for the first time in his life. They had such a connection. She was also adventurous and wanted to sail the world with him and his father. Mary's parents finally agreed to let her marry Matthew, and Jacob agreed to stay in Port Elizabeth until after the large and expensive wedding being planned by Mary's mother.

To show Mary's parents that he wasn't completely without refinement, he wanted to get Mary a strand of Tahitian pearls for her to wear on their wedding day. He'd first seen them when he was a boy and traveling with his father through the South Pacific, and, like most people, he found the pearls to be extraordinary in their size and hue. But he was having difficulty locating them anywhere close by.

He was told that, because of their rare beauty and size, poachers had all but destroyed the oyster beds around Tahiti and their oysters were nearly extinct. If the French government hadn't stepped in to protect them and build new beds, it was certain they would have gone out of existence. So after months of searching, Matthew was able to find only one pearl. He had it made into a necklace just in time for the wedding.

After the wedding, everything looked as if it was going to work out well for all involved. However, while in the process of making their plans for their next adventure, Mary became with child. So the decision was made to wait until the child was one year old before they started their voyage.

Life was good for the adventurous threesome as they waited for the big day. In the meantime, they made small trips in South Africa. Finally, they were only one week away from the biggest adventure for them all, the birth of the baby.

I was down to the last six pages of the book when the story took a turn that I hadn't seen coming, but, at that stage of the reading, I was committed to finishing it. Jacob fell ill with malaria and lay dying with Matthew at his side. The writing was excellent and captured my heart, causing it to lay bare on my sleeve.

I struggled to finish the last few pages without my voice breaking, but my throat tightened, and my words were more than difficult to get out, and, at times, it was even impossible to enunciate properly. I stopped often, cleared my throat, and squeezed my eyes closed tightly, removing my tears so I could read the print on the page. I don't believe Christine even tried to conceal her sniffling, but I hid like a coward behind the cover of the book, unwilling to let the woman I loved think I was weak for crying over a fictional story.

The child was born during the early morning hours, and, while Matthew held the new baby boy in his arms, he sat on the edge of his dying father's bed. Jacob smiled at his first grandchild who was to become an adventurer just like his grandfather and father before him. Jacob kissed the baby boy on the top of his head, looked at Matthew, smiled, and squeezed his hand for the last time. Then, with the tender coos of the baby in Matthew's arms, Jacob slipped away.

Somehow, I managed to finish the last words on the last page. "As one adventurous soul traveled his last road and left this world, another entered and began anew."

By then, the inside of my mask was soaked. I didn't look at Christine—I couldn't. I lowered my eyes and laid the book on the small table next to me. Quickly getting to my feet, I picked up a log and laid it on the fire, buying myself time before trying to say anything to her.

It was finally Christine who spoke first. "Thank you for sharing that story with me, Erik. It was beautiful."

I nodded and added, "Yes, it was adventurous, wasn't it?"

I quickly glanced over my shoulder and saw her smiling warmly at me. She knew I'd been crying but was kind enough not to damage my masculine pride by bringing it to my attention. However, when the room became too quiet, I struggled to find a safe topic. The first thing was about the book.

"I think my favorite part was their trip on horseback through Arabia. Their horses reminded me about some of mine. There's nothing like a horse, and I think that's what I miss most about living down here. I can't have my horses around me all the time."

"Horses! Then that's another true rumor? It was you who kept stealing César," she exclaimed.

"No!" I came back quickly. "That's a gross lie, and anyone with half a brain would see right through it."

"If it wasn't you who took him, then do you know who did?"

"Oh, I took him sure enough and often, but I always returned him. So it wasn't a theft—it was a loan," I explained with a grin.

At first she smiled at me, but then she looked serious and her brow wrinkled as she whispered, "César. It was César that was with us as we came down here—right?"

I nodded. "Yes, he was supposed to be the prince's white stallion taking his princess to his shiny castle in the sky. Silly—right?"

"Not really. I wish I could remember more about it. It sounds romantic. I wish it had worked out the way you'd planned it."

"Me too, but it ended well. You're here with me now, and I'm enjoying myself very much."

"Yes," she said softly while gazing at the fire.

We were quiet for a while. I don't know what she was thinking, but I was thinking it was the end of the third day, and I had only one more day to spend with her. I told myself not to think about it because it made me sad, and I didn't want to be sad while she was there, but I couldn't help it. I didn't know what I was going to do once she was gone.

Fortunately, she broke the silence and my sad thoughts by informing me it was time to treat my leg again. So, as she took care of me, we talked more about the book and how much fun it would be to travel the world. We even got my atlas down and let our fingers travel the same path that Jacob and Matthew had traveled. Then we made a path of our own with all the places we'd like to travel to.

It had been a wonderful evening, but, all too soon, it was time for her to retire, and she once more stood in front of the fire, brushing her hair. Then, as she had the previous evening, she walked passed my chair and laid her hand on my shoulder.

"Thank you for reading to me and doing so with such passion. I could tell you were feeling what the characters were feeling, and I could feel your pain along with theirs. I don't expect you to tell me your entire life story during these few short days, but I beg you not to hide who you are when you have a chance to let me see you in a true light."

I reached up and placed my hand on hers—slightly nodding. The tone of her voice touched my heart, and I couldn't stop myself from expressing my love on a different level. I grasped her hand gently and turned my head, resting my lips on the back of her tender hand. I held that position, and she didn't pull away, so I didn't hide the next tears that formed in my eyes. Then, releasing her hand, I looked up at her.

"Thank you, Christine, for being the person you are, and for being here with me. Regardless of what tomorrow brings, I'll always cherish the time we've had together. Thank you."

"You're welcome, Erik, and so will I."

With that, she ran her fingers across my prickly cheek and left, while I closed my eyes and let them fill with more tears. I loved her so much, and I hurt inside in both a good and bad way. I laid my head back and gazed into the fire while twisting the gold band on my finger. With a sigh, I looked down at it and watched it sparkle in the firelight, just as I'd done so many times when it was on my father's finger.

Then, the more I twisted it and the more I watched it sparkle, thoughts, wonderful and daring thoughts, began forming in my mind. With them, I felt fear and contentment at the same time. I glanced over my shoulder at Christine's door and thought, do I try? Would I dare try?

Thirty

Thoughts and ideas about our last evening together built on each other and worked themselves into a cohesive plan. I felt excitement and fear at the same time. It would be wonderful if she accepted my offer, but I feared she wouldn't. After all, it was a rather strange request.

Once my thoughts quieted down enough, I prepared to sleep. I hadn't slept the night before, so I figured it shouldn't be difficult to sleep that night. To make certain I wouldn't frighten Christine again with my *fire* eyes, I lay in the opposite direction on the divan, so I couldn't see the fire. I closed my eyes, and, with a soft smile on my lips, I drifted into sweet sleep. Then, abruptly, I was jolted off the divan with Christine's scream.

I expected to see her standing in her doorway again, but her door was closed. Without even thinking about knocking, I burst into her room.

"Christine! What's wrong?"

She was sitting on her bed in the dark with her face in her hands and crying hysterically.

I immediately turned on the light and knelt beside her. "Christine, you're trembling. What's wrong?" Her only response was more tears. "Did you have a nightmare?" She managed to nod but didn't stop crying. "Oh, Christine, Christine. It's over. I'm here," I said softly while stroking her arm.

I took one of my handkerchiefs from the drawer of my bedside table and put it in her hand. She took it, but she still couldn't stop crying. After a few moments, I couldn't refrain from automatically taking the next step to comfort her. I rose up and sat on the edge of her bed, facing her, and then I gently took her shoulders in my hands and pulled her into my chest, wrapping my arms completely around her.

"Shh, my angel. It's over. You're safe. Shh."

She melted into my chest, and I stroked her back while whispering encouragingly to her. We stayed in that position until she started to calm down. Then I realized what a dangerous position I'd brought us to, so I gently released her and started to get up.

But she grasped my shirt strongly and pleaded, "No, please don't leave me."

A plethora of thoughts and feeling surged through me, from me begging my father not to leave me when I had a nightmare to my silent pleas on the roof that night when she begged her angel not to leave her. She said it. She asked *me* not to leave her, and I closed my eyes, wrapped my arms back around her, and soaked in the precious moments.

My logical side knew she was searching for comfort, and it didn't matter who was sitting in front of her; she would have asked the same thing regardless. But I didn't want to be logical. I wanted the feel of her against my chest, a feeling I'd only imagined before. So I laid my cheek on her head and listened to her breathing until it slowed. Then, sadly, the moment came when she was composed and moved away from me. Those precious moments were only a memory then.

"Are you feeling better?" I asked.

Her head was still down, but she nodded. Then she laid her palm on my chest and said with a sniffle, "I'm sorry. I got your shirt wet."

"No matter, my sweet. They won't hurt it, but they hurt me. I hate to see you cry."

I lifted her hand and kissed her fingers, which was the catalyst she needed to realize I was sitting on her bed with her. She lifted her head and looked at me, with fear rising in her eyes. I instantly released her hand and sat on the floor beside the bed before I said or did anything else.

"Do you have these often?" I asked quickly, trying to relieve the tension in her eyes.

"Often enough. I hate them."

"I know. Would you like to talk about it?"

I expected her to refuse, since I never wanted to talk about mine, but she nodded and began explaining.

"They're always the same. I'm dancing, but then I have a horrible pain in my chest, and, when I look down, all I see is a black hole. There's no skin, no heart, or anything—just a black empty cavity. Then there's laughing and girls in strange costumes all around me—laughing at me. They tell me to go away and that I don't belong there. They say I'm fat and ugly and that I can't dance or sing, and they dance around me, laughing. Meg's face laughing at me is what wakes me. I feel horrible when I wake—hollow, and like I need to wash and hide."

I knew what she was feeling, and I felt I had to do something to make her feel better. I started to lay my hand on her arm again but then held back.

"Would you like me to run a bath for you? Would that make you feel better?"

She looked at me. "Thank you for being here and being so kind, but what I want most is to listen to your music. Will you play for me?"

"Certainly," I replied. "I never have to be asked twice to play my music. What would you like to hear?"

"It doesn't matter. You decide."

I got to my feet and went to my piano. I was about to begin when she walked in with a blanket over her arm.

"I don't want to be in there alone. May I stay in here with you?"

"You don't ever need to ask that."

I got up and took the blanket from her and then waited until she was curled in the stuffed chair. I then covered her and tucked the blanket around her feet. I started to turn and go back to my piano, but she grabbed my hand and squeezed it.

"Erik?"

"Yes? Is there something else I can get you?"

She shook her head. "I just wanted to thank you for not taking advantage of me in there. I appreciate that."

"There's no need to thank me. You deserve respect, and I always want to give that to you. I do apologize though if I crossed any boundaries. I knew you needed comfort and that's the only way I know how to give it. At a time like that, words can fail."

"You didn't cross any boundaries, and I understand."

I then began playing soft melodies and periodically glanced over my shoulder. She'd respond to my glance with a smile. During the third piece when I glanced at her, her eyes were closed. I finished that piece and then waited in the silence to see if she was asleep or only resting her eyes. When she appeared to be sleeping, I smiled, knowing she was at peace.

I got up carefully and knelt beside her, watching her sleep. She was so beautiful, but what was continuing to grow within me wasn't connected to her beauty; it was something unexplained, something much more encompassing.

Her hand was lying limp over the arm of the chair, so I raised it and laid it on the arm. When I did, I let my fingers hold her wrist for a moment, and then I laid my forehead on the back of her hand. I stayed there, feeling her blood pulse through the veins in her wrist, and, at the same time, feeling my own pulse in my fingertips.

I raised my head and looked over every bit of her flawless face, wanting to kiss her lips tenderly. But that forbidden desire would have to wait for an invitation. As a substitute, I moved her curls from her cheek and placed my palm there, feeling her breath on the inside of my wrist—so soft and sweet.

I thought about everything we'd done in the last three days, the three most precious days of my life. With each day that had passed, my love for her had increased immeasurably. Have your feelings for me increased at all, Christine? I wondered. She started to stir, so I got up and moved over to my organ.

"Oh, I'm sorry, Erik. I must have fallen asleep."

I smiled. "There's nothing to apologize for, my dear. I thank you for the privilege of watching you sleep. Are you feeling better? Do you feel well enough to return to your bed or do you want to spend the night here?"

"I'm feeling much better, thank you. I'll go back to bed now so you can get some sleep. Thank you for your music. It really helps to calm my nerves."

I offered her my hand and helped her up. "If you'd like, I'll keep playing until you get back to sleep."

"That would be nice, but don't tire yourself too much. You still need to be careful about your leg."

"Don't worry about me. My music is also good for me."

I followed her to her door, we said goodnight, and I went back to my piano. After four pieces, I checked on her, and, when I saw she was sleeping peacefully, I went back and lay down on the divan, thinking about what had happened in her room. I'd just gotten a taste of what it would be like to be her constant companion and protector, and so had she. I liked the experience, and I hoped she did also.

I took a deep breath, closed my eyes, raised my arm and laid it across my forehead. I relaxed and could still feel her breath on my wrist and her blood pulsing through her veins. I took another deep breath and was moved instantly with inspirational thoughts. So, bounding off the divan, again, I headed for my piano—again.

The notes and words forming in my imagination came one after another, and one after another I wrote them down. They were coming so quickly that it was hard to keep up—a note here, a word there. As at so many other times in my life, I was unaware of time passing until I felt a hand on my shoulder, and I turned with a start.

"I'm so sorry for waking you. Was I playing too loud?"

"No, it was perfect. There's nothing better to be awakened by than your music. That melody is beautiful, but I don't recognize it."

I smiled and looked at my watch, realizing I'd been composing for over nine hours; then I responded, "Yesterday I wouldn't have recognized it either." Then my smile softened and I looked in her eyes. "You inspire me in many ways, my dear."

"You mean you've been up all night composing?"

"Well, let's say it's a work in progress," was my attempt at modesty.

She looked at the scribbles on the pages in front of me and softly read its title, "'One Beat.' Play it for me and sing it for me, please."

"It's not finished yet," I tried explaining. "Wait until it's finished."

"Please, Erik."

Then I realized she could be gone forever by the time I had the finishing touches on it, and I may never have another chance to show her how much of an inspiration she was to me. So I laid my fingers on the keys and began playing and singing for her.

"Don't leave me here all alone; stay close to my heart.
Keep your soul near to mine, don't rip them apart.

Two lives—one devoted breath.
Two hearts—one unswerving beat.

Our lives entwine and move as one, sharing breath and beat.
One true touch, forever paired, together they're complete.

Two lives one breath, together they'll stay.
Two hearts one beat, their love will find a way.

Their love will find a way with their heart's one beat,
With their heart's one beat,
With their heart's one beat.

Hair turns to silver, a breath still speaks of love.
Bones thin and tremble, a heart still beats for love.

Two lives—one joined breath. Two hearts—one strong beat.

My melody without your voice is like a bird without a wing.
My life without your heart is like a world without a spring.
A wingless bird, a darkened day, is what time will bring.
Without your breath, without your heart,
to make our one beat sing.

Please keep your breath inside my song.
Please keep your heart within my life.
Then through ages, our one true love,
Will stand the test of time.

Sharing life, sharing love,
With our heart's one beat.
With our heart's one beat.
With our heart's one beat."

While the last note was fading, I was watching her closely and silently pleading for her to love me and not leave me alone. Slowly, one tear escaped the corner of her eye and she stepped closer to me. She gently moved one finger, as well as her eyes, across the scratches her nails had made on my cheek. Then they both moved across my forehead, moving my hair from it. Next her eyes moved to meet mine, and we stayed locked in that space of hushed time with only our eyes communicating our innermost thoughts. I didn't move, afraid to fracture the precious moment, afraid I would wake to find she was gone and that it was all only my pleading heart's dream.

Time has a way of appearing different at different times. It can move so quickly that one feels he can't keep up with it, and then other times it stands still. That moment with Christine's finger moving across my forehead was one of the times when it stood still. I studied her eyes and I believe she knew exactly what I was wishing for, but she was unable or unwilling to give into my desires at that time; however, she was kind nonetheless.

She smiled while studying my eyes. "It's breathtaking—both the melody and the lyrics. You're a gifted man in every respect, Erik. It's rumored that the Opera Ghost is a genius. Well, the rumors don't come close to the facts, that I now know. The rumors speak about your brilliant mind, but the facts speak about your magnificent heart.

"Regardless of what this day brings, I want you to know how much you mean to me. If time should separate us, I'll never feel this way about another man. What I feel for you is without description, and that's why I can't give you the answers you're asking for. I honestly don't know what they are—at least not right now.

"Be patient with me, Erik. I don't want to say the words you want to hear and then find out that what I've been feeling is only your magic and mysterious ways captivating me. I can't say yes now and then no later. I know what that would do to your giving heart, and I can't do that to you. I care too much for you to hurt you that way.

"You told me that I deserve respect. Well, so do you, and I wouldn't be giving you that respect if I said yes too quickly. Can you understand what I'm trying to say?"

I took her hand and kissed her wrist. "Yes, unfortunately, I do understand. You've only been here three days, so what can I expect? As long as you're not saying no, then I can be patient. I've waited for you my entire life, so what are a few more days, or weeks, or months? I can be patient."

She gently pulled her hand from mine and then watched her fingernails run across my temples and into my hair. Then, with a sigh, she said, "I'll go put on the water for tea. Then would you mind showing me how you made that omelet the other day? I'd like to make it for Mummy."

"It would be my pleasure," I answered while getting to my feet.

She started to leave but then stopped and looked at my scribbled notes for "One Beat" on top of the piano. Then she turned and looked up at me.

"Erik, I'm curious."

"Now, where have I heard that before?" I said teasingly.

"Seriously, you say you never forget anything—that you can remember every note and every word. If that's true, then why do you have to write your music on paper?"

"I don't write it down to remember it; I write it down to organize it. When I have inspirational thoughts, they come at me so fast that they blur together, and I can hardly recognize them. They swim around in my head and won't stay still long enough for me to categorize them."

She frowned, so I tried a different approach. "Like the omelet we're going to make. If I put all the different ingredients in different bowls and set them on the counter, you could easily tell what they were, right?" She nodded. "Then when I put all the ingredients in one bowl and mix them up, it becomes more difficult to tell what each of them is, right?" Again she nodded. "Now imagine if I threw that bowl of ingredients at your face . . ."

"That would be really messy. I sure wouldn't want to clean it up," she said with a wrinkled nose.

"Exactly my point. Now imagine you have not only one bowl thrown at you but many—all at the same time. Would you be able to identify every ingredient as it came at you?"

"No, not at all."

"Well, that's how my thoughts are when I become creative. They are extremely messy and drive me crazy until I commit them to paper. Just like you wouldn't be able to stay very long with that omelet mixture on your face and in your hair; you'd have to clean it off as soon as possible. So that's what I have to do in a figurative sense.

"Once they're on paper, I can organize them and they become a melody or lyrics or even a house or a palace. It doesn't matter what the inspiration is; I have to treat them all the same. Depending on the size of the inspiration, it can sometimes take me a long time to complete the process. That's why I told you there are times when I'll stay at my piano or organ for days or weeks at a time. I become a slave to those inspirations.

But once I have everything down on paper, they no longer own me—I own them. Does that make any sense?"

"Yes, completely. You're a good teacher."

"Why, thank you, my lady."

From there we went into the kitchen and I showed her how I make my omelet. We ate, had her lessons, and then treated my leg, which was looking good. The last of the maggots had been used up the day before, but they did their job before they died. The black and dead tissue was gone and so was the red streak; however, there was still a deep and wide hole in my leg. I gave thought to stitching it up myself, but then, remembering what happened the last time I tried doing it myself, I chose not to.

I was planning to go back to the doctor the next day when Christine was gone, but then she insisted that I really shouldn't wait any longer. Under the circumstance, I decided to let her think that going to the doctor was her idea, when actually it fit nicely into my thoughts of the previous evening.

Therefore, I cleaned up, including a shave, and dressed in my three-piece dark brown suit, complete with cream ruffled shirt, dark brown silk neck scarf, and my tan mask. Christine was on the divan reading a book when I walked out of my music room. She glanced up at me, back at her book, and then back at me quickly. Her jaw literally dropped, and she laid the book down.

"Erik, you look so . . . so handsome!" she exclaimed.

I never had taken compliments about my appearance well, so I responded simply. "Thank you. Are you sure you don't mind staying here alone? I could wait and go tomorrow."

"No, you need to go now. The doctor should look at it and decide if he wants to stitch it up. I'll be fine. I'll probably still be right here with this book when you get back."

"Well, if you're certain. Depending on how long I have to wait for him, I shouldn't be longer than two hours."

After positioning my hat, I turned off my motion sensor so it wouldn't frighten her when it went off, and then headed for the doctor's office. I didn't have to wait long before Doctor Leglise came into the waiting room, and he had almost the same reaction as Christine, although for a much different reason.

Once we got in his office, he explained, "I'm so glad to see you. Honestly, Erik, I didn't think I'd ever see you again. I felt certain you wouldn't make it through that infection, but you seem to be looking good. How are you feeling and how is your leg?"

By then I had my trousers off and was sitting on the bed. "I'm feeling much better. I think the fever is gone and I'm able to eat again. Your new treatment seems to have done the job nicely. As for the wound—you tell me how it is. That's why I'm here."

He examined the wound, and stood over me shaking his head. "Well, whoever this lady friend of yours is, I would keep her around if I were you. She's obviously good for you. I've never seen you look so well."

With a sincere smile, I replied, "Keeping her around is exactly what I have in mind."

He studied the wound carefully and then gave me instructions that took the wind out of my sails. I was thinking it really looked good, and I had nothing more to worry about, but according to him, that wasn't the case.

"I think I should stitch it up to encourage it to heal quicker, but you still need to be careful. Basically, you're now where you should have been a month ago. You need to keep it dry, keep using the hot compresses, stay off of it as much as you can, and get lots of rest. I want you to come back here in a week, unless you see signs of another infection setting in. If you do everything right this time, we shouldn't have a repeat of the infection. Can you do that for me, Erik?"

I just stared at him, and I think he knew what I was feeling.

"Oh, don't look at me that way, Erik. I'm not sentencing you to life in prison."

"Then why does it feel like it?" I rebutted.

He patted my shoulder. "I think you'll live. Do it right and it won't take long."

He left to get his instruments to stitch my wound, and I tried to talk myself back into the good mood I was in when I entered his office. It didn't take me too long once I thought about my plans for the evening ahead.

Within the hour, I'd left his office and was at a jeweler's shop. After looking over his premium selection, I picked out a strand of the purist Tahitian pearls and had him wrap the box in deep purple paper with a white ribbon. With a smile, I slid the gift into my inside coat pocket, picturing Christine's face when I gave it to her.

After that, I went to the market and purchased everything I needed for the evening, still with a smile on my lips. Then, once back at the lake, I waited for ten minutes for Roland and Obert to arrive. I was prepared to tell them I wouldn't need their help any longer, but they looked so disappointed that I made them a different offer.

"If you want, I'll pay you to check in with me every day in case I need anything."

"That's great!" they both said as they jumped up and started running back toward the stairs. "See you tomorrow, Erik."

I snickered and thought that was probably the best decision anyway, considering Doctor Leglise wanted me to stay off my leg as much as possible. I knew I had to be more careful this time around. I certainly didn't want a repeat of that last episode.

I was smiling broadly as I walked in and saw Christine still on the divan with her book.

"My! That's a big smile. Did you have a good trip?"

"Yes, my dear. The doctor said my leg looked great and that you were good for me and that I should keep you around. See, even he thinks you should stay with me."

I left to put the packages in the cold pantry, but her words followed me.

"You're teasing me again, Erik. What did he really say?"

Coming back into the dining room, I responded, "Seriously, that's exactly what he said. I'll take you with me next time and you can hear it from his own lips."

She cocked her head and squinted at me. "I never know if you're teasing me or not."

"Honestly," I said while holding my hands up in the air. "That's just what he said. So, you told me that I needed to obey him—does that go for you also? Do you need to obey his advice and stay here with me?"

"Now I know you're teasing me."

"Am I?" I asked, as I entered my music room and shut the door.

Before long, my clothes were changed, and I was explaining to her that we needed to have an early supper because I had something special planned for the evening. Quite naturally, she was curious, but I managed to put her off. Shortly after that, we were making chicken cordon bleu, seasoned rice, cucumber salad, and hot rolls. By the time we sat down to eat, I had her convinced I was telling the truth and that she was good for me.

"You're good for me also, Erik. I haven't felt this carefree in I don't know how long. Thank you for being such a good host."

"You're welcome. It's been my pleasure." I took a sip of my wine and looked at her in serious thought. "So these last four days haven't been as bad as you thought they were going to be? Do you view me differently now than you did four days ago?"

She stopped eating and looked at me, also in seriousness. "You were right—there's no comparison."

Thirty-One

Her words warmed my heart and gave me hope. Perhaps after she experiences all my special surprises, she might decide to stay with me. I could always hope.

While we ate, we talked about light-hearted subjects for a short time and then there was a long silence, which was strange. Nearly the entire time she'd been there, my home was flooded with sound, either music, with our voices in song, or talking, or reading, or even laughing. What was I going to do when she was gone?

I was beginning to think the entire idea of bringing her down to my home was a bad one. My loneliness had moved in on me horribly from time to time in the past, and that was when I didn't know what it was like to actually live with someone special around all the time. But right then, I knew what it was like, and I cherished it. I didn't know how I could go back to the way it was. Yes, those four days were spent in heaven, but would the following days be spent in hell?

Perhaps I wouldn't be able to spend much time in my home ever again. I wouldn't be able to handle the silence. I would just have to spend my days following her around again, was my only answer to the problem. I was moving my food around on my plate, and silently bemoaning my coming state, when she broke the silence.

"Erik, you're not eating. Don't you like what we prepared?"

I smiled at her. "No, Christine, the dinner is delicious. I guess I don't have much of an appetite today."

It was then that I slapped myself around. There was my last chance to have a nice meal with her and I was ruining it. I reached across the table and ran my fingers over hers. I didn't have to say I love you; she knew by then what my look meant. Our eyes stayed on each other's for a few thought-filled moments before I smiled, took a deep breath, started cutting up my chicken, and began a conversation. However, the subject to come wasn't going to be pleasant for either of us.

I sat up straight and, while trying to hide my emotions, spoke nonchalantly. "I'll be taking you home this evening, so things will be changing. I'll continue your lessons every morning at eight if you like. You would be advised to carry through with them if you want to continue to progress, but if you choose to find another instructor, I'll understand.

"You're welcome back down here anytime you wish. We could dine, or sing, or I could read to you if you like, that would be up to you. If you choose to never see me again, then I ask you to please tell me now, so I can prepare for my future accordingly."

I took a drink of wine and held my breath while waiting for her response. Her eyes were fixed on mine, and she also took a sip of wine. She patted her lips with her napkin and then sat back. There she remained, peering into my eyes so deeply you would think she was trying to read my mind.

Finally, she took a deep breath and responded, "My voice has received the kiss of my Angel of Music. There's not another who can possibly follow his lead. I would like you to continue with my instruction for as long as you're willing."

I allowed myself to breathe once more. She accepted my offer. Now, would she accept the ones that were yet to come so I could continue to breathe?

"Your angel will always be willing to help you in any way, Christine. While I'm flattered and pleased with your decision, the price of such a valuable instruction comes at a cost to you and one you may not be willing to pay."

Her eyes filled with questions along with a hint of fear.

I smiled at her. "Don't worry, Christine. I won't ask you to betray your chastity, but I do require a high price." I took another sip of wine and watched her face, waiting in anxious anticipation. "I ask that you don't see any young men, and especially Raoul, within the walls of my domain—this opera house. You know I love you. I've not kept that a secret. I cherish being able to watch you here, but to see you with someone else is a price I'm not willing to pay just for that privilege; therefore, I would have to insist on your obedience to my one demand."

She thought for only a moment before responding, "That's not too high a price to pay."

Breathing again I went one step further. "Your mind has made a wise decision in continuing under your angel's wing, but what about your heart, Christine? What is your heart telling you about the man you see before you?"

She closed her eyes, lowered her head, and whispered, "I don't know, Erik. I just don't know."

I reached across the table and lifted her chin until our eyes met, and then I spoke softly. "I can be a very patient man while in the pursuit of something I desire." I glanced around my home and then back into her eyes. "What you see around you is the fulfillment of a dream that took me nearly thirty years to achieve. Oh, I realize to most it doesn't look like much, but for me it was the culmination of a long awaited dream.

"What surrounds me day and night is wood and stone with my musical notes in between." I ran my finger across her forehead and down her cheek. "Of what greater worth is the heart of this exquisite creature who has entered my life and taken control of my heart. I dare say a million times a million more. As long as I continue to see a flicker of hope somewhere in these eyes, I'll wait with the patience of Job."

She took my hand and pressed her cheek into my palm. I closed my eyes and took a breath, savoring her touch. Not wanting to, but knowing I needed to in order to keep my composure, I slowly pulled my hand away and changed the subject.

"I'd like to take you on a carriage ride around the city before I take you home. Would you like that?"

She looked at me, almost expressionless. "That would be wonderful, and it's very thoughtful of you, Erik."

I wanted to ask her how she felt about gaining her freedom back, but then I decided I may not want to know the answer, so I didn't ask.

While we were cleaning up from supper, she questioned me about the doctor's instructions. When I told her I was basically back at square one, she insisted that she treat it again. I didn't resist her, since it was probably the last time she'd be doing it. So, soon the teakettle was whistling and we were back in our usual spots.

She was exceptionally gentle, saying she didn't want to disturb the stitches. I would have enjoyed her final touch more if I weren't watching the clock and nervously anticipating the coming hours. By the time five p.m. rolled around, we were finished with my treatment and sitting by the fire talking.

"Christine," I began, "I'd like you to pamper yourself for an hour. Take a bubble bath or whatever will make you feel good—feel relaxed. Then I'll have a surprise waiting for you when you're finished. But, remember, don't come out here until the hour is up. Understand?"

Then she gave me that face that drove me crazy. I wanted to grab her and kiss her face all over every time she did it. She cocked her head, looked at me, and wrinkled her nose.

"What are you up to, Erik? Why can't I be out here? Are you also going to pamper yourself?"

"Sure. Whatever you want to think, my sweet. Just don't come out until then. Oh, and if you don't mind, I'd like you to wear the deep purple velvet dress tonight."

"Won't you give me a hint, please, Erik? How can I relax in a bubble bath while not knowing what you're doing out here?"

I walked up to her, held her chin in my hand, and looked down at her. "Let me put it this way, my curious little temptress. The sooner you get out of here and leave me alone, the sooner you'll know what I'm doing. Is that fair?"

"No," she pouted, as she turned around and headed for her room. But when she reached her door she stopped, tuned, and smiled. "Not even one little hint?"

"Get out of here, or do I have to put you in the tub myself?"

I started toward her and she quickly darted behind the door and closed it. I chuckled and thought, too bad. That would have been fun to do."

With her gone, I headed for the kitchen where I started our dessert, made of fresh strawberries, melted chocolate, and sweet cream. I then spread a new linen cloth over the coffee table and set up candles all around the room. When everything looked the way I wanted it, I took care of myself.

I washed up and dressed in one of my finest black tails, white ruffled shirts, small white silk neck scarf, and black brocade vest, along with the proper number of rings. I put the box of pearls in my pocket and patted it with a smile.

Then I went back and finished the dessert, turned out all the lights, and lit all the candles. I set the dessert on the coffee table and left to get a good port wine and glasses. I was walking through the dining room with the bottle in one hand and the glasses in the other, when I heard her door open.

When she appeared, I stopped in my tracks. I knew she was beautiful, and I knew that dress was beautiful when I bought it, but I wasn't prepared for the way the candle light flickered on the rich purple and the way she filled out every curve in that dress. Together, they defied description. I couldn't move. I couldn't take my eyes off her. She was more than beautiful; she was gorgeous. I don't know how long we stood there gazing at each other before she broke the silence.

"Erik, what's this all about?"

"Spending the last evening of a momentous adventure with the woman I love." I moved to the coffee table without taking my eyes off her. "You look gorgeous tonight, Christine."

"I could say the same about you, Erik, but I'm not sure I'd use the word—gorgeous."

"Well, thank you, my dear. Won't you please sit down," I said as I took her hand and guided her to her usual spot on the divan.

I prepared a plate for her, poured her a glass of wine and one for myself, and then I sat on the other end of the divan, instead of my chair. I started up a light conversation about how well her lessons had been going since she'd been here and wondering what the weather was like. Then with a nervous smile, I handed her the gift box.

Her eyes widened. "Erik, you've given me so much these last few days. You really didn't have to give me anything more."

"I know I didn't, but I wanted to," I responded as I turned sideways on the divan and spread my arm out over its back. "Now, open it."

When she took the top off, she stared down into the box. Then she looked up at me. "Are they real?"

I actually laughed aloud. "Certainly, Christine. I would never think of giving you anything other than the genuine product."

She was stammering over her words as she tried to thank me, while I got to my feet and moved behind the divan and behind her. I took the pearls, which by then were lying over her fingers, and placed them around her neck. I ran my fingers slowly against her neck and under her hair, pulling it out and over the pearls, and allowing my fingers to enjoy their journey in the process.

She was rolling the pearls between her fingers as I sat back down. "They're so beautiful, Erik. I've never seen such pearls. I've looked at pearls in the jeweler's window before, but I've never seen such large ones, and the color is exceptional. They're exquisite."

"Now we can both appreciate that section in the book *Jacob*."

"Really? These are Tahitian pearls? But I thought they were hard to find."

"They were, but that was a hundred years ago. They've repopulated, but they're still considered precious and are protected by the French government."

She was looking down at them and shaking her head. "I don't know what to say."

"You've already said enough. Now let's eat so we can go for a nice ride."

We finished and put on our cloaks, Christine in her deep purple and me in my black. I made sure my hat was pulled down, Christine's hood was up, and both our heads were down when we approached the side door.

It was dark and one of the busiest times at that door, so we slipped through the people and outside without much notice. I hailed a brougham and gave him a list of all the places I wanted him to go, with Madame Valerius' as the last stop, and then we were on our way.

We traveled slowly to the different sites. All of them I'd seen while riding alone; such as the Cathedral of Notre Dame, the Champs Elysées, the Luxembourg Palace, the Longchamp race course, and we just had to ride along the Seine River. It was a beautiful evening, with a slight breeze, and I was cherishing every minute of it.

I watched Christine as the shadows moved across her face, and I listened to her sweet voice while she talked about how much she'd enjoyed all we'd done and how much she loved her new dresses and pearls. She made a comment about not being able to bring all I'd given her with her and that perhaps she could visit me and get the rest at another time. I naturally agreed.

I had to keep taking deep breaths, while trying to calm my stomach. I was both excited and anxious over what I was about to do.

We rode around for almost two hours and talked about many things, and I believe we were both comfortable in doing so. She looked so relaxed and that also helped me to relax my nervous stomach. It was so easy to talk with Christine, and while I'd tried to be honest with her during the last four days, right then it was especially easy to let my guard down and talk freely, even more than I could with Oded.

I knew I was running out of time and would miss my opportunity if I didn't speak up soon, but I couldn't get those first few words out. I watched one scenic location after another pass by, and I started several times to begin my strange request, but then I backed out. Finally, there was a lull in the conversation, so I took a deep breath and began. I leaned forward, placed my elbows on my knees, took another deep breath, reached for and held her hands in mine, and began.

"I realize, Christine, that this is all very strange for you, but I only ask that you listen with your pure heart and hear what mine is speaking to you. I love you, and I have since the first time I saw you on that stage with Meg. I know it's no secret to you by now, but I want you to be certain of my motives. It's because of my love for you that I speak to you at this time.

"I'm laying my heart at your feet and telling you what I want out of my life—and yours. Raoul was right on many occasions when he spoke about me, but he was also terribly wrong. I am just a man and I do want something from you for selfish reasons. But I won't take anything from you that you don't want to give me.

"I didn't take you down to my home to take advantage of you or hurt you in any way, and I believe you know that now. I love you, Christine, above all else I love you, and I could never hurt you. I want you to love me, and I want you to agree to marry me, but only if and when you're ready to and not a second sooner.

"Oh, I know you're probably thinking it's impossible, since it hasn't even been a week since you came to know my true nature, and in another time and place I might agree with you. But I've seen many things during my life come to pass that I at one time thought impossible."

I lowered my sight to our hands together and ran my fingers over hers, and then in a reflective tone I continued, "I had a wife once, well, almost a wife. She loved me and was willing to marry me, but she died before that could happen. So now I only have the memory of a dead wife, and she can't ever be a living wife for me." I looked back up at her. "But you can, Christine. You can be a living wife for me.

"Perhaps I'm crazy for telling you all of this so soon. Perhaps I should have waited until you came to love me, if that day ever comes, but I wanted you to know everything up front. I never want there to be any question in your mind about my intentions.

"I want you to marry me. That's my intention, and if you agree I'll lay the world at your feet. You've already seen that I've withheld nothing from you, whether it was in the form of something monetary like your jewelry, or emotional comfort such as at your father's gravesite, or something inspirational like your voice.

"I want to give you everything and take care of you. I want to take you anywhere you want to go. I wouldn't expect you to live down in my home with me. But, in time, if you agree to marry me, it will no longer be my home, unless you want it to be. We'll live wherever you wish, anywhere in the world."

I looked down at my hands and twisted the gold band on my finger. "This ring means more to me than anyone can imagine. I haven't been without it for thirty-five years, and it carries a piece of my heart and always will."

I slid it off my finger and turned it in the passing lamplight. "I never thought I could be without this ring. It actually means more to me than the finger I wear it on, if that gives you any idea of the value I put on it. But I'm now asking you to wear it. Not for real, but just pretend.

"When I lost my almost wife, I had nothing of her in the way of a wife to remember her by. But now that you have spent these days with me, I can see and feel what it would be like to have a wife to share my life with. I only want to pretend that I have a wife for however long it takes you to decide if you can become my real wife. So I ask that you wear this ring for me, just until you make your choice."

I made sure I was looking her directly in her eyes and she was looking into mine when I made my next comment. "I'm not asking you to betray your chastity. I'm not asking you to invite me into your bed or anything of that nature. I only want to pretend for as long as I can. Just pretend. It would only be a pretend marriage.

"While you're deciding, and if you want, you can visit me just as often as you'd like. We can sing and eat together, or read and talk. I only want to pretend that you're my living wife. That way, if you choose to leave me forever, I'll at least have that memory."

I held out my hand toward hers and waited for her response. She studied my eyes intensely, and I remained silent and still while I waited for her to answer my most unusual, and a bit pathetic, request. Then slowly she did it. She raised her left hand out of her lap and held it close to mine.

I took a breath of relief and reached for her hand. Then, through the moisture in my eyes, I watched our hands together, and as the lamplight came and went, and as the rhythmic sounds of the horses' hooves on the cobblestones kept time with my beating heart, I slid my gold band on her finger. Then I closed her precious hand in mine for a moment before I kissed the back of it.

"I thank you immensely, Christine. You have no idea what this means to me. I'll now have memories of a woman with my band of gold on her finger and the memory of me putting it there. If nothing more, I'll always have that special cherished memory. Thank you, my angel."

I again raised her hand and kissed its back along with the ring.

She smiled warmly while looking into my eyes and then said softly, "Erik, you're a very unusual man. You have so many skills and such deep passion. I've never met anyone like you; in fact, I never dreamt anyone like you existed. I know you want me to be honest with you, and that's what I'm trying to be. Although I'm not sure just what honesty is at the moment. I'm not sure what my heart is telling me right now.

"These last few days have been a whirlwind of everything I love, singing, reading, stories, cooking, and simply sitting and talking. While they may not have started out that way, they've been some of the best days of my life. You make me feel safe and at ease. Being with you is like having a warm blanket around me on a cold winter's night. You make me feel secure, without having to make decisions about anything. The most I've had to decide is what to prepare for our dinners. It's been like a glorious vacation."

She stopped talking and looked out of the window, and I didn't know what to say or do since the tone in her voice left the conversation up in the air; therefore, I waited. I let go of her hand, sat back up, leaned against the seat, and watched her. I glanced down at her hands in her lap, feeling the ring on her finger. She appeared to be captivated by the trees passing our windows, but I knew she was in deep thought.

There wasn't another word spoken between us. I wasn't sure why she was quiet, but I was quiet because I didn't want to say or do anything that would spoil the precious moments of watching the woman who'd just agreed to be my living wife. I also glanced out of the window and recognized the street we were on. After that, I kept my sights on the marvelous woman in front of me, knowing that she would soon be stepping out of the carriage, and we would both be stepping into the unknown.

When the carriage came to a halt, I waited for the driver to open the door. Then my heart tore apart when I stepped down, knowing I would be returning to my home alone. I gave Christine my hand, and she graciously accepted it. All was quiet, and even the air was still as she stepped down and looked up at me. I searched for the courage to tell her goodbye, but she laid her hand on my arm before I found it.

"Wait here a minute, Erik. I have something I want you to have. I won't be long."

Then she turned and walked up the steps and in the front door. I didn't know what she had in mind, but I was glad I was rescued from having to tell her goodbye just yet. The minutes passed as I waited. Nervously, I leaned against the carriage, I paced on the walkway, I leaned against a lamp post, I climbed the steps and paced more, I thumped my fingers rhythmically on the carriage door, and I looked at my watch several times.

It had been over fifteen minutes since she left, and I couldn't help but be concerned about her delay. Is this it? Is this how it ends? Is she not going to grant me one last and final goodbye? My imagination sprung open and out of it walked Raoul. He had to be inside and preventing Christine from leaving. Why else would she take so long? I went back up the steps and tried to see in the windows. The lights were on but I saw no one. I listened carefully for his voice, but I heard no one.

I went back to the carriage and watched the windows, waiting for a sign that she was coming back. I headed back toward the steps with the intention of knocking on the door, but then, through the lace curtains, I saw her coming down the hall. I was pacing beside the carriage when she finally appeared in the doorway. I rushed up the steps and took her arm as she came down them. I waited breathlessly for her to explain her actions.

"I'm sorry to keep you waiting so long, Erik. I thought Mummy would be asleep but she wasn't, and she had many questions. However, she wasn't concerned about my disappearance; in fact, she even told the police that I was probably with my Angel of Music and that they had no need to fear for my safety. I'm sorry she told them that. I hope it doesn't cause you more trouble."

"No need to apologize. I'll be fine."

"I have something I want you to have. This was my dear father's. It was part of his performance attire when he was with the symphony. Here, open it," she said as she handed me the long, slender black box.

"Why, thank you, Christine. What a nice thought and surprise. I'll cherish it."

When I opened it, I saw a white silk neck scarf with a treble clef embroidered on it in black. Attached to it, was a gold pin in the shape of a violin.

"Oh, Christine! Are you sure you want to part with this?"

"Yes, and I believe my father would approve. He was proud of this and often mentioned that he wouldn't have them if it weren't for his Angel of Music." She looked up into my eyes. "You were his angel, whether you were heavenly or not. You and your words rescued him at a time when he was nearly lost. You gave him hope. You gave him courage. So you deserve to have these."

"But are you su . . .""

She placed a finger against my lips. "Hear me out. I've been fortunate to have had several angels in my life. First my parents; they were heaven-sent and gave me a life filled with love and music. Then, when I lost them, Mummy became my rescuer, my angel, and saved me from a life in an orphanage and who knows what else. She's my dear sweet Mummy, and I love her very much.

"And whether you're heavenly or not, you also rescued me and saved me from a lonely life of despair and doubts. Your angelic voice caressed my soul and made me look forward to each morning. You gave me courage and hope, just as you did my father. I honestly don't know how much longer I could have remained in the state I was in." She placed her palm on my cheek. "You've truly been my Angel of Music, even if you are a man of flesh and blood."

"And you . . ." I tried to say, but again she placed one finger against my lips.

"Wait! There's something Mummy said to me just now, and you need to know what it was."

Then she looked down at my gold band on her finger and twisted it, and my heart pleaded, No! Don't take it off! Don't give it back to me—not yet! Then she looked back into my eyes.

"When she saw this, she made me tell her what it meant. I tried explaining it to her simply. I told her my Angel of Music wanted me to wear it for a while because I was his student. She smiled and said, 'That is natural and proper.' I was surprised by her comment until she explained her thoughts. She called me privileged. She said I was singled out by an angel who wanted to look after me, and, as long as I wore his ring, I was under his wing and would be safe.

"I knew she meant those words in a heavenly way, but, when I thought about what she said and realized the truth of the matter, I could also understand her words in earthly terms. These last four days, well, the last two days anyway, I've felt safe in a way that I haven't since my father's death.

"When I close my eyes at night and know you're in the next room, I'm comforted; I feel safe. Then when you play your violin while I'm going to sleep, I'm filled with warmth, and I believe I even drift off with a contented smile on my lips. And when I wake, it's the same thing. I know you're in the next room and I feel safe—contented.

"You said you wanted me to get to know you. Well, four days isn't nearly enough time to get to know a prospective husband, especially a prospective husband as complicated as you. I need more time. I want more time to get to know you.

"I'm still not certain how I feel with regards to you and Raoul or what my future holds, but there's one thing I know for sure. When I fall asleep tonight I want it to be with sounds of your sweet music filling my room, and, when I wake and eat breakfast, it's your eyes I want to see across the table from me.

"So, my Angel of Music," she said as she held her hand up for me to take, "if you still want me, I'd like to return with you to your unique home. But only as a pretend wife and not a real one."

I thought for certain my knees were going to give out under me. I instantly felt that ache in my jaw and the tears swell in my eyes. I felt like crumbling at her feet and kissing her feet in sobs of great joy. I wanted to grab her up in my arms and dance in circles. I wanted to sing out—I love this woman, this Christine Daaé. But I couldn't do any of those things. All I could do was gaze at her and silently say 'thank you' a million times to the heavens above.

In order to get me to respond, she finally had to say in a teasing fashion, "That is, unless you're tired of sleeping on the divan."

I shook my head adamantly. "I would sleep in my boat if that's what it took to keep you with me."

"That won't be necessary, Erik. I like having you sleep in the next room. It makes me feel safe."

When I took her hand to help her back into the carriage, she hesitated. Then she looked up at the driver. "Please, monsieur—take us back to the Opera Populaire."

Thirty-Two

On the ride back to the opera house, the air was filled with something electric. Neither of us talked much, but I believe I was smiling the entire way. Several times I glanced at my ring on her finger while feeling my naked one. We shared smiles and an occasional touch. The same was true as we made our way back down the steps toward the fifth cellar and then across the lake. My eyes stayed on hers and hers were on mine as we made our way through the mist.

I knew what I was thinking, but I wasn't sure what she was thinking, and I was afraid to ask, afraid it would somehow change the direction my life was going in, so I remained silent.

I helped her out of the boat and then up the steps to my door. Once inside, I took off my cloak and laid it over my chair, much the same way I had on that first night. She also was standing in almost the same position, and I walked up to her with gladness in my heart.

"Four nights ago we were in this same position, remember?"

"I don't know about you, Erik, but I was in a much different position than I am now. I was frightened and angry. I'm no longer angry with you and you no longer frighten me."

I replied while releasing her cloak from her shoulders, "I'm so glad to hear that." I started for her door and continued, "If nothing else, I never want you to fear me." I opened her door and waited for her to enter. "I'll never hurt you, Christine, you can take my word on that."

I was standing in the doorway, holding the door and her cloak when she walked in front of me and then stopped and looked up at me.

"I . . . I . . ."

I cocked my head when she couldn't find her words. "I thought you said you weren't afraid of me; then you shouldn't be afraid to speak your mind to me."

"I guess that's my problem. I'm not sure I know my mind right now."

She may not have known her mind, but I did mine, and she needed to get away from me quickly before I gave her something new to fear me for.

But, instead, she made it even worse. She placed her palm on my jaw and searched my eyes. Then she looked at my lips and back in my eyes, and there it was again. Not the look of love I'd been waiting for, but the look of temptation. She was asking me to kiss her, and right then that desire almost took control of me.

My body was screaming to take her in my arms and kiss her passionately, but a part of me, my heart, was still holding out for that look of love. Besides, if I kissed her, I didn't know if I could stop. And if I kissed her and then in the days ahead she left me, I think I would go mad for sure. So, instead of kissing her lips, I closed my eyes and kissed the soft inside of her wrist, savoring the sensation of her skin on my lips.

"Perhaps you might think with a clearer mind in the morning, Christine, and then we can talk. For now, I'll play my violin for you."

She nodded. I handed her cloak to her and started to move away, but she reached for my arm.

"Thank you for everything, Erik, the ride, the pearls, and," she added while rotating the band on her finger, "the ring. I'll take good care of it."

"I know you will, my dear, or I never would have entrusted you with it." Then I picked up her hand and pressed my lips over the ring on her sweet-scented fingers. "Sleep well my cherished, living wife."

I closed the door and looked at it with contentment. I was glad I'd told her I would play my violin for her. It would help soothe my feelings as well as hers. If she keeps tempting me this way, I thought, I'll be playing my violin more than usual.

During that first piece, every time my hand came into my view it felt strange to see my finger without Papa's ring on it. I'd worn it for 30 years, and it was a part of me. It felt so strange that I had to put another ring on that finger so it wouldn't look and feel so naked.

I felt at peace when I lay down on the divan. That was the first time since she'd been there that I wasn't making plans for the next day, the first time I wasn't thinking beyond the moment, and it was a good feeling. Therefore, I floated on it and drifted into sleep quickly.

I woke early, cleaned up, and dressed for the day, although I had no idea what the day was going to bring. I was at the dining table, working on a new mask, when I heard her moving around in her room, and then I heard her run the water for her bath. I closed my eyes with a warm smile. Mmm. My wife is bathing, I allowed myself to think, but only for a few moments before I snapped myself out of my wayward thoughts.

When she came out of her room, I was on my feet to greet her. "Good morning, Christine. I trust you slept well."

"Yes, I really did. That's the best night's sleep I've had in a long time. How did you sleep?"

"Like the proverbial baby. See, we're good for each other."

She shook her head, smiled, and then noticed the beginnings of my new mask.

"You make your own masks?"

"Yes. I always have. This one is to replace the one that got caught between two fearful hearts," I teased.

"Oh, Erik, I'm sorry about that; I really am. I don't know what I was thinking."

"Not to worry, my dear. You were probably thinking about staying alive. I was the one who pushed you to that point, so I'm to blame, not you."

She sighed and picked up the piece of leather. "I would imagine the props department could make your masks for you."

"Probably," I replied. "But, from what I've heard, they don't like working for or with ghosts, and I must keep that persona—for a while longer anyway. In addition, I'm rather particular when it comes to my masks. How they fit and look is important to me. The wrong fit could make it harder for me to see and therefore easier for someone to catch me off guard."

"I understand," she said as she placed it back on the table. "But I still feel bad." Then abruptly she pulled a lavender envelope addressed to our managers from her pocket, handed it to me, and exclaimed, "Oh! Here! I almost forgot! Would you deliver this for me, please?"

"Surely, but is there a reason why you don't want to deliver it yourself?"

"I think it would be best if you delivered it. I don't want to be seen just yet. Besides, according to another rumor, you're an expert in that field," she commented with a teasing smile. I nodded sheepishly, and she went on. "Don't you want to know what it says?"

"It's your business, Christine. If you want me to know, then I'll know." I tried to answer without my curiosity showing.

"Go ahead and read it. I want your opinion."

She headed for the kitchen, and I followed her while reading her note.

My Dear Messieurs Moncharmin and Richard,

I trust my note finds you both well and in good spirits.

At this time, I request permission to take a holiday for an undetermined period. I hope it won't cause you too much of an inconvenience, and I want you to know that I wouldn't be taking this liberty if I were in an important role that would be difficult to fill on such short notice.

Please accept my apologies.
Respectfully,
Mademoiselle Christine Daaé

As I placed the note in my shirt pocket, I smiled. "So, an undetermined period? That's good to hear."

She was pouring herself tea and looked up at me with a nod. "Any other thoughts about the note—since you're the expert?"

"I'd say it's well written. I couldn't have worded it better myself, and I'm proud of you for taking that stand. Our managers need to learn their place, and this note just might help them find it. They're idiots for placing you in such a menial role to begin with. They have no right being in this business if they don't have an ear for excellence. Furthermore . . ."

"All right, Erik! All right! I didn't mean to get you in such a state. Calm down."

"I'm sorry. It's just that ignorance in those trying to put on airs of superiority angers me."

"Obviously," she replied.

She wanted to make me breakfast, so we ate sweet cakes, sausage, and hot chocolate that she confessed was her favorite breakfast.

"I thought so. That's what you ordered while in Perros, right?"

She shook her head. "Is there anything you don't see?"

"Not much," I teased.

We were still eating, and I was again stirring my chocolate and somewhere in thought when she questioned what I was thinking about.

"Hot chocolate will always remind me of a kind man who came into my life when I was desperate. I honestly believe if it weren't for him I wouldn't be alive. I was starving to death when I found him—or when he found me."

"It appears to me that you've led a life of many twists and turns."

I looked back up at her. "Yes, and if I don't get back to my job of running this opera house, we're both going to be twisted and turned right out of our jobs."

She chuckled. "These last four days have been nice, being away from all the turmoil of the outside world, but I presume we can't stay here forever. There are things I also need to attend to. Last night, I arranged for a neighbor of Mummy's, Madame Boulanger, to stay with her. I think I should talk to both of them about the possibility of her staying with her for an extended period. I could check in on her daily and shop for her needs and visit, but I'd really like to spend most of my time here."

I stared at her in deep thought, and then she asked, "Why that look? Don't you approve?"

"Oh, no, no, no, not at all. That sounds like a perfect idea. I was just thinking about the wonderful woman you are, and how proud your parents would be if they could see you now. They've missed seeing the woman you've become."

She looked down into her hot chocolate as if she was going to cry, so I jumped in quickly. "I'm so sorry. I should have thought before saying such a thing. I'm sorry."

"No, it's all right. I'm glad you see me that way. Your opinions are important to me." She gained her composure back and asked, "So, what kind of trouble are you going to get yourself in while I'm gone?"

"I believe my first order of the day should be to whip our managers back into shape. I'm sure they've become lax in their jobs and perhaps have forgotten how to do my bidding."

"Very well put, but be careful. Don't catch anymore projectiles, and mind what the doctor said about staying off that leg. I know you can't do it completely, but be careful."

I smiled and reached across the table, taking her hand in mine. Then, running my fingers over our ring, I offered another opinion. "Spoken like a true wife. I get the distinct feeling that, by the time you've finished being my living wife, you'll slip right into the next role perfectly."

She put her other hand on top of mine. "I hope that's the way it works out, Erik. I really do."

"You make me feel like dancing, Christine. You make me so happy."

"My actions aren't entirely selfless. You also make me happy, Erik."

Before I envisioned what it would be like to have a real wife and get all flustered again, I suggested we start our day. So, before long, we'd cleaned up, had my leg treated, and were finishing her lesson. Then a sobering thought hit me, and I had to enter a sobering conversation.

"I think it's important for you to have certain instructions before either of us goes anywhere. You jokingly told me earlier not to catch any projectiles while you were gone. Well, as you know, that's always a possibility, no matter how careful I am, so you need to know how to get in and out of my home without my help. I'd hate to think of you trapped down here. So, are you up to an adventure?" Her eyes got wide and she nodded, so I continued. "Go change into that little boy costume. It will make this easier for you."

She went off to change, and I went into the kitchen to get a stool and lantern. I was back in my music room and removing the large tapestry from the north wall when she came in.

"Considering you've had a daily dose of my wound, and you've seen my many scars, it should be apparent that you need to keep what I'm going to show you a secret. Without this secret, I probably wouldn't be alive. So, never reveal this to anyone, not even to Madame Valerius, and especially not to Raoul."

She looked at me seriously for a moment and then responded with thoughts that both comforted me and yet made me feel horrible to think she felt that way about me.

"I would never tell anyone about your home or how to get here, Erik, not even if I hated you and wanted to see you locked up, which I can't see happening. Not even if I hated the other person and wanted to see them dead, because that's how it would turn out, right? Someone would die? I would never do that to you, Erik. I would never want to be the one to put you in that position. I believe what you've told me about your remorseful torment. You can trust me."

"I thank you in advance for your discretion" is what I told her, but I had to tell myself to let go of the horrible feeling her words gave me. Fortunately, she began asking me questions about taking the boat, so I had to concentrate on her.

"No, absolutely not! Don't ever try to take the boat under any circumstances. It's much too dangerous. It's dark so you have to take a lantern, and then the lantern light reflects off the mist and makes it almost impossible to see where you're going. I can't tell you how many unnecessary and extremely cold baths I've taken in that lake because of the mist and a pillar looming up in front of me; and I'm skilled at it, so you wouldn't have a chance. On top of that, the clothing you wear would weigh you down and you would drown for sure. No, never take the boat—never!"

"All right! I have the picture. Never take the boat."

While we were discussing the lake, I told her about the motion sensor and how to turn it off, just in case I forgot to do it before I left. She was again amazed, and I went on to caution her about other dangerous areas in my home.

"I think it goes without saying, never try to find your way out through my security room. That again could end in a disaster. I have another trap door above your bed, but that one isn't a good idea either. It's difficult to get into and the first 20 meters or so have to be traveled on your stomach. You can't even crawl in it. It's mostly there as a failsafe in case something happens to the others.

"While this one I'm going to show you is the easiest for you, it will still be hard. It's narrow and steep. That's why I wanted you in that costume. This passage wasn't designed with a woman in mind, so I don't know how you'd make it in a dress.

"As you've already experienced with the door to the lake, most of my latches are hidden and much too high for you to reach, thus, the need for the footstool. The latches leading away from my home will be easy enough for you to reach without the stool, but the ones coming back are high and a puzzle. You'll be able to get out without getting lost. It's a single passage that will take you to the main level. Getting back down here is a different story, but I'll explain that as we go. So, are you ready?"

"I think so," she replied without much conviction.

"Don't be frightened. You can do it. I'll show you everything you need to know, and it might answer a lot of questions for you."

She shook her head and looked around the room and then at me. "It shouldn't be like this. You shouldn't be living like this, buried down here, with all this precaution around you. It shouldn't be like this."

"My sweet, Christine," I said as I placed my palm against her cheek. "Perhaps, in the near future I won't be living like this." I looked in her compassionate eyes for a few moments before I asked, "Are you all right? Do you want to do this now or wait?"

"I'm all right. As you said, I need to know this, so let's go."

"Very well. Stand right here," I said as I positioned her in front of another invisible door. "Since I'm left-handed, all the latches will be on your left. So raise your left hand to about the top of your head and feel for a slight indentation."

She did as I asked, and when she felt it she looked at me and smiled. "Is this it?"

"Well, I don't know," I teased. "Push it and see what happens."

When the door moved on its pivots, she, at first, gasped and then looked up at me and smiled even more broadly.

"Here, you take the lantern and go first so you'll be familiar with the area. I know it's not the gentlemanly thing to do, but, under the circumstances, I think it's more important to be behind you to catch you if you fall than to follow proper decorum."

"Yes, you and your proper decorum." She looked down at me. "We always have to follow that, don't we?"

There, she did it again. that teasing little flirt. She'd just given me an open invitation to forget propriety. I shook my head.

"Pay attention, Christine. Don't distract me. Now, once you're through the door, wait a moment until the door closes and clicks. It should do it on its own, but if it doesn't, shove it open and wait again. That should do it. You never want to leave it until it clicks. If you do, then you're leaving it open for uninvited guests. Listen," I said as I let go of the door and let it close. When it clicked, I asked, "Did you hear that?"

"Yes, and I'll remember."

"One other thing. Never leave a lit lantern alone in one of these passages. A rat could come along and knock it over and start a fire. We wouldn't want that now, would we?"

"I understand. My father actually told me similar things about lanterns."

She started up the stairs, and I tried to keep my eyes on the steps in front of her, but it was terribly hard with her adorable derrière in those little boy trousers swaying back and forth right in front of my eyes. Keep your eyes on the steps, I kept telling myself, and, to help me in that pursuit, I began explaining things to her.

"My home is above the lake and on the same level as the fourth cellar, so when we get to the top of this passage, we'll actually be in the third cellar. Oh, and by the way, don't be startled if a rat or two runs in front of you. Unlike most rumors about them, they won't harm you. But they are some of the unwanted guests that I don't want in my home."

She let out a little gasp. "Really?"

I smiled when her steps became more cautious. Good, I thought, that will give her something to think about other than teasing me. Now if I could find something for my mind to think about other than her derrière. Fortunately, we were soon at the end of that passage.

"It's a dead end, Erik. Now what do I do?"

"The same thing you did in the music room."

She did and we walked through the door and waited for it to click.

"Turn around and look at me, Christine." She did and I went on. "If you turn to the right like I just did, you can feel for another latch. That passage leads to the set department. At the end of it there'll be another door with another latch just like this one. But if you turn this way to your left and go through another door, you would be in big trouble. That passage leads to my security room, and there you would be trapped with no way out, like a rat in a trap. Do you understand? This is extremely important. Never take the passage to your left."

"Yes, Erik. I understand."

"Good. Now, keep going. The next time you hit a dead end, we'll be on the second level. This time if you go to your left you'll be in a passage that leads to another door not too far from the workings under the stage. But if you take the passage to your right, you'll enter a passage that is long and eventually leads to the outside. But there won't be an easy latch there, because I don't want anyone to know I have a secret outside door. Did you get all that?"

"Yes" was all she said.

We were soon through the next door without any instruction from me. Then, as we were traveling up the last flight of stairs, I gave her the final directions.

"Once you reach the end, you can make several decisions and they will all be safe ones. If you go through the door straight ahead of you, you'll enter a secluded corridor behind the ballet studio. If you go to the right, you'll enter another passage that goes behind different offices. If you go left, that passage takes you to your dressing room."

She turned immediately with her eyes wide. "I want to take that one."

"Are you certain, Christine? That one doesn't go straight; it takes several turns. You'll have to pay close attention or you could get lost and frightened."

"Yes, I'm sure," she replied with excitement. "I want to know how to get there. And what better way is there for me to get out of a passage without being seen?"

"I believe you're right, so, when we get to the end, open the door to your left and let's begin."

"Oh, Erik, this is exciting. I feel as giddy as a child."

"You are a child."

"No, I'm not."

"Yes, you are."

"Erik, stop teasing me."

"Then pay attention. We're almost there. This won't be as easy as what we just came through. You'll turn several corners, but you won't have any choice in the matter since that's the only way the passage goes. But then you'll start to see passages, without doors this time, on both sides of this passage. Take the second one on your right." I waited until she did it and then told her "Take the first one on your left." Again I waited. "Now go straight, but hold the lantern behind you so you can watch for any light up ahead of you."

"We're at a dead end, Erik. I didn't see any light. Was I supposed to?"

"Not necessarily. Now, hold the lantern up and see the difference in the walls. You'll find one is smoother. That's the backside of your mirror."

She almost squealed, and I had to caution her. "Shh, Christine. Some of the bricks in this section are hollowed out and can be heard through."

"All right," she whispered. "But I can't see anything."

"That's because it's dark in your dressing room. Now feel the edge of the mirror, this time with your right hand until you feel the latch."

"I feel it. Should I push it?"

"If you want to go into your dressing room, yes."

"Oh, I'm frightened. Maybe I shouldn't go in," she again whispered.

"That's up to you, but what are you afraid of?" She was quiet, so I asked again, "Christine, what are you afraid of?" Finally, I had to lift her face toward me and ask a third time, "What are you frightened of? No one is in there."

I could barely hear her when she answered, "What if Raoul is in there in the dark?"

"I highly doubt that's the case, but there's nothing to fear. If he's in there and you want to talk to him, that's up to you. If you don't, then I'll take care of it." She looked really frightened. "I mean, I'll show him the door, so you won't have to talk to him. I won't hurt your friend, Christine. You can trust me."

There was silence until her answer came by her releasing the latch. There was a slight rumble as it turned on its pivot, and, as the light from the lantern shone into her room, she took a deep breath and stepped in. I stayed in the passage and took the lantern from her.

"Make sure your door is locked, and then go to the center of the room." She did and I continued. "I'm going to let the mirror close and watch what happens."

I let the mirror close, and she spread her arms out and shook her head. "I can see you. I'm confused."

"That's because the lantern is on. Now watch when I turn it off."

I turned it off, and she instantly started talking to me. "This is spooky, Erik. I know you're there, but I can't see a thing. Erik, are you still there?"

I smiled and opened the mirror. "I'm always here, remember? Now turn your wall lamp on."

She did and then asked, "May I come back in with you now? I feel strange in here."

I opened my arms wide. "Always."

When she was inside the passage again with me, I let the mirror close and click into place.

With wide eyes and parted lips she turned and looked up at me. "Erik, this is what you saw?"

I gazed down at her with a pleasant smile and nodded. "Yes, this is how I watched and sang to my angel all those weeks."

She looked back into the room, and then she took a quick breath, and her hand covered her mouth. "Erik! You saw everything I did in there?"

"Well, almost everything. I can assure you I was gentleman enough not to watch as you undressed. Although, I have to admit, I sometimes was tempted," I finished with a smile of a different sort.

She was still looking into her room when her head nodded. "I believe you." Then she looked up at me. "You've been nothing but a gentleman, Erik."

At that moment, in the semidarkness, and with the back of her shoulder lying against my chest, and her perfect face gazing up into mine, I thought I wasn't going to be a gentleman much longer.

Then she turned to face me and asked softly, "Erik, will you hold me, please?"

"My dear, you'll never have to ask that question twice."

She melted into my chest, and I wrapped my arms around her, savoring her touch.

"This seems strange, Erik. When I look in that room, all that happened in there seems like a lifetime ago, almost as if it happened to someone else and not me."

"Yes," I whispered. "I understand what you mean."

"Erik, I was wondering. When I first arrived here and was so discouraged, Meg told me there was a time when she was ready to quit performing. She was working so hard. Her toes were always bleeding and she even broke two of them, and she was never promoted to the front row. Then the Opera Ghost talked to her mother and told her not to fret because she would be in the front row soon and later in life she would marry wealthy. Now that I know the Opera Ghost is you, are you the one who got her to the front row?"

"I confess—that was me."

"Just like the way you got me noticed?" I nodded. "She also told me that her brother was gravely ill and needed an operation but they hadn't the money. She said the Opera Ghost gave them the money for the operation. Was that you?"

"Again, I confess."

"Oh, my! She also said the first time she saw the Opera Ghost was in the ballet studio. She said he walked through the mirror. Was that also you?"

"Yes, that was me. I was careless. That was a lesson I learned the hard way."

She pulled away from me and looked into my eyes. "Then you're a philanthropist. More people need to know this. Can I tell Meg that my angel and that philanthropist are the same? Then she wouldn't be so concerned about me."

"I'm not sure about that, my dear. Let me think on that. It could have far-reaching effects on my life here. Let me think about it."

She nodded, and laid her cheek against my chest again, and I laid my cheek on top of her head, and then we silently gazed into her empty room, remembering, I'm sure, both blissful and frightful moments. It was at that precise moment that I seriously began to question my desire to have her give me that look I was waiting for, that look Vashti gave me.

I loved Vashti, but not like she loved me. I never gave her the look she gave me or the look I'm sure I was continually giving Christine. Perhaps Christine would never be able to give me that look. Perhaps the look and desire I'd seen often in her eyes were all I could reasonably hope for.

I was going to marry Vashti without having that love because Oded helped me to believe that in time I would grow to love her. Is that what it was going to take with Christine? Or perhaps, she needed that desire filled before her love could grow any further. Perhaps I needed to give in to her wants and forget about my strange one.

If I waited for that special look before I kissed her the way she was asking me to, then everything could be for naught. It may never happen that way. I suddenly felt defeated. Maybe what she was waiting for was that first kiss. Maybe that's what I needed with Vashti—that first kiss.

I took a deep breath, closed my eyes, and kissed the top of her head. I loved her so much. What was I waiting for? Just lift her chin and kiss her, you fool.

Thirty-Three

During those silent moments while I waited for the battle between the two halves of my heart to end, we heard a key turn in the lock of Christine's door. She gasped, and I put my hand on her cheek and pressed her head against my chest.

"Shh," I whispered.

The door opened, and we heard an excited voice cry out, "She's here!" Then we saw Meg charge into the room. "Christine! Christine!" she cried. She went behind the sheers to the dressing area. "Christine?" Then Madame Giry entered. "She's not here, Mama, but she must have been! Her light is on! I'll go to the rehearsal studio! Maybe she's there!"

"No, Meg, wait!" her mother told her. Then she moved to the center of the room and slowly looked around. "Yes, she was here, and he was with her. They were both in here. But I don't believe you'll find her in the house. He still has her."

Meg quickly moved beside her mother and grasped her arm. "Really? How do you know?"

Almost expressionless, Madame Giry gazed around the room again and even at us behind the mirror. "Because I smell the mist from the lake. Can't you smell it? I smell it often when he speaks to me."

Meg took a deep breath. "Yes, I do. Should we wait here until they come back?"

"No need, Meg. When he's ready, she'll return. She's in no danger. We can stop worrying."

Madame Giry turned the lamp off and motioned for Meg to leave, and then they both left and closed the door, leaving us in total darkness.

"That was close," Christine whispered. "My . . ."

"Shh, wait," I cautioned her. After a comfortable amount of time, I asked her, "You were saying?"

"I was saying—my stomach is all in knots. That was frightening and exciting all at once."

"I know. It can be. Do you want to continue with your instruction, or would you rather do it at another time?"

"No, let's finish while we're here."

"Very well," I said while lighting the lantern again. "But keep your voice down."

She opened the mirror without my instruction and we stepped back into her dressing room and checked the lock on her door.

"First thing, Christine, if you don't intend to stay in here long or you don't want to be seen in here, then you need to prop the mirror open so you can leave quickly if you hear a key in the lock. Here," I said as I placed the stool behind the mirror. "This will work. I learned this the hard way and almost got caught in here."

"Really? Who almost caught you?"

"Actually, it was you."

"Me? When?"

"The first night we met. You and Meg were going to supper, and I wanted to follow you, so I was about ready to open your door when you put your key in the lock. Because the mirror was almost closed, I knew I couldn't make it back in there, so I hid over there behind your curtains. Then I held my breath, just like we just did, while you came in and got your necklace."

She gasped and covered her open mouth with her hand while gazing at the curtains. "I never suspected." Then she looked up at me. "You're very good at this hiding thing. Are you sure you never, uhh, watched?"

"I'm certain, my sweet," I replied softly while looking directly in her eyes.

I almost told her the real reason why I never watched, but that conversation would have been too deep to go into right then, so I didn't.

"Therefore, always block the mirror open with enough room for you to get in the passage before you let it close."

She nodded and then looked at the door. "They were really concerned. Perhaps I should go find them and calm their fears."

"That's your call, Christine."

"No, I think I'll wait. I want to see Mummy first, and then I'll find Meg."

"Do you think you'll be able to find your way here on your own?"

She sighed, almost with frustration. "Certainly I can. It wasn't nearly as difficult as you made it out to be. Don't forget, I'm a dancer, so my legs are strong, and my mind is not weak, *monsieur*."

I chuckled. "I wasn't suggesting it was. I just wanted to make sure. I would hate for you to go missing without me knowing it." She gave me that sideways glance of disapproval, so I changed the subject. "Is there anything in here you want before we leave?"

She looked around and opened her armoire. Then, slowly, she lifted the skirt of a dress.

"This is what I wore to the theatre the night of the disaster." Then she looked at me. "Have you heard anything? Was anyone seriously injured?"

The moment of truth had come, and I took a deep breath in preparation. "Yes, I'm sorry to say. One woman was killed, and I'm not certain about the injured."

She closed her eyes and lowered her head. "Do you know who it was?"

"Not really. I didn't catch her name."

She nodded and looked back into her armoire, barely whispering, "May her soul rest in peace."

I didn't respond. I didn't know what to say. I felt so guilty and needed to get out of that room quickly.

She turned and looked at me. "Are you all right? You look distraught."

"Death has a way of making me feel sick, but I'm fine. Don't worry your pretty little head."

She closed her armoire and looked back at me. "You told me that night when the chandelier fell that you would explain later why you left me alone for so long."

How could I tell her that I was on a two week bout with depression and a drinking binge? Although I'd promised myself that I would be completely honest with the woman I loved, I just couldn't confess that to her, not yet. So I did the next best thing; I told her the part of the truth that I could speak about and the part that she could handle.

"I was very ill, Christine, very ill. You have to understand that it would take something of a serious nature for me to abandon you the way I did. I feel just awful that you had to endure everything on your own—just awful."

She was frowning by the time I finished, and then she asked, "What was it?"

I only patted my leg, indicating the reason for my absence.

"Oh, Erik, I'm so sorry. It was entirely my fault. You went to Perros to help me and made yourself sick. I'm so sorry for being that selfish."

I shook my head, "No, Christine."

"Yes, Erik. You got sick and could have died all because of me."

"It wasn't your fault, Christine," I groaned as I placed my forehead against the corner of her armoire. "I did it myself after I got back to Paris. It was my neglect. You had nothing to do with it."

"You said you would be honest with me, Erik. Are you telling me that if you didn't go to Perros that you would still have gotten sick?"

"Oh," I groaned again. Telling the truth was so much harder than I ever anticipated. "No. If I hadn't gone to Perros I probably wouldn't have gotten sick, but honestly, Christine, it had nothing to do with you, it was all me."

She put her hands on her hips and demanded, "Then why are you acting this way? Why are you acting as if someone is threatening to pull your fingernails off?"

"Oh, Christine," I murmured, as I turned from her and laced my fingers on the back of my neck. "I told you that there were things in my past that I was ashamed of. Well, I saw someone while in Perros who I knew as a child. She was kind to me and her kindness made me feel so disgraced. She was so pure and I was so vile, so once I got back to Paris I felt unworthy to be in your presence, and I knew you would be better off without me around. So I stayed away from you, and I neglected my wound, and I got sick."

I lowered my arms, turned, and looked at her. "So, see, it had nothing to do with you. In fact, it was you who saved me. It was the vision of your face and my love for you that gave me the strength to care about getting help. You've saved my life in many ways, my dear sweet Christine. Please, don't blame yourself for my stupidity."

She walked up to me and placed her palm on my cheek. "Very well. I'm sorry to have made you explain that. I know it was hard on . . ."

"Shh," I interrupted. Then we heard, what sounded like a group of chorus girls passing in the corridor. "We need to get out of here soon. Come, let me show you the latch."

I put the stool under the latch, the mirror closed, and I asked her to step up on the stool. She did, but she was still too short.

"Hmm, I'll have to make a stool just for you, but for now let me lift you. Now remember, use your left hand. It will make it much easier."

I lifted her up by her small waist while telling her to feel for the indent in the center of a rose on the wallpaper. She found it with glee and pushed it. We heard the low rumble, and the mirror opened.

"Here, Christine. Take the lantern and lead the way again."

She did and I was pleased with the ease with which she chose the right door and passage; however, I had to lift her at every one. I could have released the latch for her, since she knew approximately where they were, but I wanted her to be familiar with the feel of each one. Besides, I didn't mind holding her one bit.

When we neared the last door, she thanked me, and then explained, "I now understand why you wanted me in this costume. It was much easier with these trousers on, and I think I know what I'll do when I go back up. I'll always take that same route to my dressing room, and then I can change into that dress before seeing anyone."

"Good idea," I replied as the last door opened.

As soon as she walked in, she plopped herself down in the stuffed chair and sighed. "That was quite a trip."

I replaced the tapestry and smiled at her. "Yes, one of many."

"Just how many of those passages do you have?"

I sat down on the organ bench facing her and looked at the walls surrounding us. "It's hard to say. I would have to actually count them. Let me just say that this entire structure is honeycombed with my passages. That's why so many think I can walk through walls. So be careful, Christine, or you'll soon have that same reputation," I added jokingly.

"I don't think I'll try going through any doors where there are people around. I'll just use my dressing room. I think that would be safer."

"I agree."

"Tell me something, Erik, how long did it take you to build so many passages?"

I shook my head. "Let me think. I started in 1865, so about 16 years, and I'm still constructing them. It's an ongoing project, you could say. But, like my music, I don't work on them all the time, just when I have a thought and the time and the opportunity all at the same time."

That conversation went on for an hour or so. She had many questions and was always fascinated with my answers. We eventually decided we both needed to start on our tasks for the day if they were going to get done. So, while she made us a snack, I got some scrap lumber from the docking room to make longer legs for the stool. When I was finished, we both started back up the stairs. Once at the top, I nervously sent her off toward her dressing room while I headed for our managers' office.

I was waiting for half an hour for them to leave their office, and while at any other time I would have kept on waiting, with Christine in my passages my patience was wearing thin. Therefore, I took a bold move and, when the corridor was clear, I entered it and headed quickly for the office of their secretary, Monsieur Remy. Without a word, and with my head held down, I opened the door and quickly laid the envelope on his desk and then left. I didn't see anyone in the office, but then I didn't take the time to look either. I went back to the passage behind the managers' office and waited another five minutes before Remy came in holding the envelope.

Richard opened it, read it, discussed it with his partner, and then put it away. I turned to leave and was part way down the passage when I heard the words, Box Five. So I went back and listened to them laugh.

"They must have given up on their jokes," Richard said scornfully.

Also chuckling, Moncharmin added his thoughts. "And if we had crumbled under their threats, think about the money we would have lost. That box has been sold almost every night."

"Let that be a lesson for us," Richard replied.

I grumbled while thinking, lessons—your day is coming for your lessons to begin in earnest. But, right then, my only thoughts were about Christine and not about teaching them their proper place in *my* opera house.

I once more turned and was on my way home when I heard an angry voice, and one I easily recognized, Raoul's. Needless to say, I was back at the small hole and listening within moments. Raoul was irate, and while our managers tried to calm him with their recent information about Christine's holiday, he accused them of being deceitful and that he was going to see the magistrate. That wasn't a calming thought.

By the time I reached the last passage down to my home, I realized what time it was and that I might miss Roland and Obert if I took that passage. So I circled around and took the stairs down to the cellars. It was a good thing I did, because I met them on the stairs in the third cellar, and I was actually shocked when I saw Obert carrying two red roses.

"There you are, Erik. We thought we wouldn't see you today," Roland said.

"I've decided you'll probably be seeing me every day. But what is this?" I questioned while gesturing to the flowers.

"You always had them on your list so we thought you would want them today as well. I hope that's all right with you," Obert questioned.

"It's more than all right—it's perfect, and I'll want them every day until I tell you otherwise." I handed them an envelope and explained, "Here's a list and some money for the items. You can keep the change as your pay. Can you read it? Do you understand it?"

The list I'd given them not only had our food for the next day but also another dress and an everyday black cloak for my love. I'd written the store's name and location along with a complete description of the dress and cloak, if they were available. If not, then I was leaving it up to the proprietor to find something similar. They said they understood and I sent them on their way.

From there, I went to and entered the trap door in the third cellar and then down into my home. I cleaned up the mess I'd made from the stool and was preparing to have some food ready when Christine got home, but my stomach was in knots. I was so worried about her getting lost in my passages, so I went back up again and waited in the passage behind her mirror. I sat on the floor that time, since my leg was complaining loudly by then.

I turned out my lantern and laid my head back and tried to relax, but that wasn't going to happen. The more time that passed the more anxious I became, so by the time I heard that familiar sound of a key in the lock, I was a mess. It had been almost two hours, two hours of torture. This was going to be harder than I thought.

As soon as the door opened I heard Meg's chatter, and I was terribly disappointed. But then I also saw and heard Christine. They both came in with Meg questioning Christine like an investigative reporter.

"But are you sure you're all right? What did he do with you all this time? Are you sure he didn't hurt you?"

"Meg, please stop. He's a perfect gentleman. Other than that, I've told you everything I can. I'll tell you more tomorrow or the next day. Right now I really don't feel well, and I need to lie down for a while. Can I answer your questions later?"

"But what about Raoul? What should I tell him?"

"Don't tell him anything. You didn't see me, remember. I'm on holiday. Now, will you please leave me alone?"

Meg finally agreed to wait and Christine almost shoved her out of the door and locked it. Then she hurriedly grabbed the costume out of her armoire and darted behind the curtain. I smiled; she didn't trust that I wasn't watching, was my first thought. She came back out in just as much of a hurry and quickly hung her dress up and then started to climb on the stool. At that time, I released the lever and the mirror began opening.

She jumped down, and just as soon as the opening was large enough, she squeezed in and wrapped her arms around me tightly.

"Oh, thank you for being here. Hold me, Erik."

I did that easily enough, but then I began questioning her. "What's wrong? Why are you in such a shambles?"

She looked up at me. "Oh, Erik, please just take me home. I want to go home. I'll explain when we get there." Then she laid her head back against my chest.

"Certainly, Christine. Certainly. Whatever you want," I replied and laid my head on top of hers.

She called my home her home, causing my heart to beat calmly with a new type of warmth flowing through it.

The mirror had closed, so, pulling away from her, I opened it again and grabbed the stool. Then with the lantern in one hand and the stool in the other I moved us quickly through the passages and doors. I looked back at her often, and each time she was right with me. Then, once we were in the music room, she barely gave me time to sit the stool and lantern down before she grabbed me, again asking me to hold her.

"What's wrong, Christine? What's happened to you?"

"It was horrible. Just horrible."

"What was? Did our managers do something to you?" she shook her head. "Was it Meg's pestering you?" She shook her head again. "Raoul?" She nodded. I grabbed her by the shoulders and pushed her away from me, looking directly in her eyes. "What did he do to you?"

She was tearing up by then. "He didn't do anything to me. He didn't even see me. He was yelling and cursing at a stagehand and then at Madame Giry. He was accusing them of keeping him away from me, and he just kept yelling and cursing in a horrible way. I was trying to get back to my dressing room, but then Meg saw me and started squealing and talking loudly to me. I was so afraid Raoul was going to see me.

"I couldn't see him right then. Not with him in such a fit. He was treating everyone like they were . . ." she shook her head and clung tighter to me. "He was treating them so badly, and I knew how he would treat me if he saw me. I wasn't prepared to defend myself. Maybe when I'm more prepared I can, but not now.

"I had to put my hand over Meg's mouth to keep her quiet and then hid around a corner until he left. Oh, how I wished I knew where one of your passages were right then. I was wishing I could slip into one of them like you do." She looked up at me. "Can you please show me more of your doors so I can hide if I don't want to be seen?"

"I'm sorry, my dear, but that wouldn't be possible. Remember where all my latches that lead down here are? They're all too high for you, and you can't continually carry that stool around. The object of the doors and passages is to maneuver them quickly and you simply couldn't do it quickly if you had to climb on a stool first. Do you understand? It's not that I don't want to show them to you, it just wouldn't be practical or wise to do so."

She nodded. "I'm sorry, Erik. He just really unnerved me. I'll be all right."

"Let me get you some tea. Maybe that will help your nerves."

"You've already helped them, but tea would be nice also."

We went into the kitchen where she saw her new roses and we talked about her visit with Madame Valerius. We got the leftovers out from the day before and ate them while we continued to talk. We discussed Raoul's actions and what she might do about them, and I told her about our managers' reaction to her note, but I somehow neglected to tell her about my seeing Raoul and about him going to the magistrate.

Then while she was pouring herself more tea she realized that we were way overdue for the treatment of my leg, so that was our next job. When she removed the bandage she frowned and laid her palm over the stitches.

"It's hot, Erik, and it's getting red again."

I looked at it carefully. "Doctor Leglise said if this should happen that we were to use the oil full strength on the stitches."

"I'll get it. Which one is it?"

"The one in the green bottle," I called to her.

She came back and dropped a few drops of the oil on the area. At first I didn't feel anything, but after a few seconds, it felt like someone had driven a hot poker into my leg. I gasped, grabbed my leg, squeezed the wound, threw my head back against the divan, clamped my teeth closed, and closed my eyes tightly, groaning.

"Oh, Erik. That must really hurt."

I couldn't respond and she didn't ask again, but she did rub my knee softly. Gradually, the sting subsided, so I opened my eyes and began breathing normally.

"Wow!" I finally exclaimed. "That was unexpected. Next time I'll prepare beforehand—like drink a full bottle of brandy first."

"Are you ready for the compress now?" she asked guardedly.

I nodded and she began with the first hot cloth, which actually felt good.

"You used it too much today," she scolded like an aristocratic governess.

"I agree, but I won't have to in the days ahead. We accomplished much today. Now you know how to get in and out of here on your own, so you can come and go whenever you like."

"Not really. Not if I might run into Raoul." Then she looked like a light turned on inside her head. "Erik! you said you had an outside entrance that you use. Can I use that one? Then I wouldn't have to chance running into Raoul or Meg."

"No, I'm sorry. And again it's not that I don't want you to use it, it just wouldn't be possible. You see, I only use it when it's dark outside and when I'm totally in black. That's what keeps me from being seen. If I used it at any other time of day, I could be seen. And again, the latch coming back this way is too high for you. You couldn't be out there in the dark that way alone. It wouldn't be safe."

"Well, I won't worry about that right now. I won't have to go out tomorrow. Mummy and Madame Boulanger are going on an outing for most of the day, so perhaps by the next day I'll have more courage to face Raoul."

"You do what you think is right for you, Christine. You shouldn't be pressured by his domineering ways."

"Oh, you're a fine one to talk. You're the one who kidnapped me and held me in bondage for four days."

"Christine, are you serious or are you joking?"

She looked up at me. "I'm sorry," she said softly. "I guess I'm still upset with Raoul."

"Am I domineering?"

"You were, but you're not now."

"I'm sorry. Perhaps I should have tried a different approach, something other than kidnapping you.—No! What am I saying? I wasn't kidnapping you. It wasn't supposed to be that way. You were supposed to see and know who I was and then go willingly with me. So, in my mind, I wasn't kidnapping you. I was offering you a chance to come to know me for who I really was."

She said she understood and the conversation became lighthearted and we even laughed. The hours ticked by until she yawned.

"I guess I'm sleepy. It's been a long day. I think I'll retire. Thank you for helping me and encouraging me. I feel much better now."

She hesitated for a moment when she neared my chair, and I looked up at her and told her she was welcome. She was looking at my hair and moved a few strands from my forehead, and then she let her fingertips run across my temples. By her forthcoming question, she must have been looking at the gray streaks at my temples.

"How old are you, Erik?"

"Of what relevance is an instructor's age to his pupil's age?" I asked nonchalantly.

"None. It's just that . . ."

"Yes, it's just what, Christine?"

"Meg said the ghost, or what she now knows is my angel, is old enough to be my father."

"Then Meg is right. I am. Does that bother you?"

"No, not really," she replied.

"Did Meg say something else that *did* bother you?"

"She said it isn't right for a man of your age to be in love with a girl my age."

"How does she know I'm in love with you?"

"I guess I sort of told her," she replied as she lowered her head, looking like a little girl who'd just been caught using her mother's perfume.

Then I asked guardedly while studying her eyes, "Does *that* bother you? That I'm older and in love with you?"

She shrugged her shoulders slowly before replying, "Not if I don't think about it for too long."

Then, abruptly, that conversation that could have led somewhere important, changed with the changing of her womanly attitude into one of a perky schoolgirl.

"Well, I'm off to bed." She then darted behind my chair and headed toward her room. "Goodnight, Erik."

I turned halfway in my chair and watched her leave. "Goodnight, Christine."

Her door closed and I shook my head. She so often perplexed me. I was turning to sit back when her door opened again, so I looked over my shoulder at her door just when her head peeked around the doorframe. Then the face I saw and the voice I heard had once again changed, that time into the soft seductive voice of a woman that can melt a man instantly.

"And, Erik, I choose not to think about it."

She smiled for a second and then once more disappeared and her door closed again. I didn't move that time. I stared at her closed door wondering, what was she telling me? Did she mean the thought was too disturbing to think about or that she disagreed with Meg and our age difference didn't matter to her? Was she saying she was developing feelings for me regardless of our age difference?

Perplexed didn't come close to describing my feelings right then. When she ran to me and asked me to hold her, she clung to me like a child would cling to a father. Was that what I was becoming to her? Was I merely taking the place of her absent father? If that was so, then how could I explain that look she'd given me several times, that look that sent sensations through my body, that look that positively said, "kiss me?"

I groaned and looked into the fire. That woman was driving me crazy. Am I to be her father or her lover?

Thirty-Four

Sleep didn't come easily for me that night; most of it was spent trying to understand Christine's quick change in moods. But I did manage to fall asleep for a while, and, by the time Christine was awake, I'd finished my morning routine and was at my piano playing softly. Even though she was frustrating me completely, I couldn't help but smile when she entered the room, still in her nightclothes and wrapped in a blanket.

"Good morning, my sweet. Did you sleep well?"

"Yes, but I'm freezing. My room is cold, so I thought I'd leave the door open until it gets warm enough in there to take a bath."

"Cold? It shouldn't be cold," I replied while getting to my feet and heading for the heat vent in her room. When I found it closed, I asked, "This shouldn't be closed. Did you close it?"

"Yes, but that was days ago. There was cold air coming from it so I closed it. Was I not supposed to?"

I opened the small vent, and asked her, "Was that the day you got up before me?"

"Maybe. I don't remember."

I put my hand over the vent and then asked her to do the same.

"It's warm," she said with surprise.

Then I explained, "There's one of these vents in every room. They're connected to a main tube that runs against the sheet metal in the fireplace. When the fire is lit, it heats the air in the tube and carries it to every room. It usually keeps my home comfortable, but since you got up before me that day, I hadn't started a fire yet. I apologize for not explaining this to you sooner. Did you close the one in your bath also?"

She nodded and headed for her bath. "There, that one is open now. Until it warms up in here, would you finish playing the piece you were just playing? I've never heard it before. I like the rhythm."

"Certainly, I like the rhythm also," I replied, as I headed back to my piano. "It was inspired by a horse. That's the rhythm you hear."

By then I was sitting at my piano and starting to play, and she was asking me questions. "Was it César?"

"No, not César," I answered with a smile. "This particular horse I named Molly, and she came into my life when I was about five and then left it when I was 24. She was my only companion for many years, and we had a special bond. She liked to steal handkerchiefs from my pocket and wait for me to chase her. She made me laugh often."

"I can hear that in the music," she offered.

"That bust of the horse beside you is the likeness of Molly."

"Really?" she responded, while reaching over and running her fingers over Molly's nose. "How did you find one just like her?"

"I actually didn't. Someone made it for me."

"Someone made it? Whoever it was is extremely talented."

"I agree. He was and still is talented. His entire family is exceptional. I consider it an honor to know them." I stopped playing and gazed at Christine. "They're the type of people you would find so fascinating. Would you like to meet them? We could go for another ride this evening and stop by to see them. I know you'll fall in love with them and them with you."

"I'd like that, Erik. Let me take my bath, and then you can tell me all about them over breakfast."

She took off for her bath and I headed for the kitchen to get breakfast started. By the time she came out of her room, the table was set, the water was hot for the tea, and I was just finishing the sweet cakes. We sat down and began eating and she began questioning me.

"So tell me, how long have you known this family?"

"Well, Dominick, the oldest boy, began working with me when I first started working on this opera house. That was in 1862, and I met his family almost a year later. They impressed me so much. Dominick had 8 siblings, and all 11 of them lived in a small, one-bedroom home in a poverty stricken area on the south side of Paris. The father had been paralyzed in an accident, and his only means of supporting his family was to carve likenesses of animals and sell them. The mother took in washing, ironing, and mending to help."

I shook my head. "They were such an inspiration to me. They helped me to be content with what I had."

"I can't wait to meet them."

I smiled with excitement at the thought.

We finished eating, took care of my leg, and then began her lessons.

"I believe they're planning to do *Faust* again soon, so we'd better add those pieces to your lessons to keep you well prepared to sing Marguerite."

"But they have Carlotta slated for that role."

"No, I'm certain you'll be in the lead this time. It appears Carlotta has refused to sing ever again. I suppose losing her voice like that really crushed her confidence. What happened to her is a singer's worst nightmare, as you're probably aware, and it's such a shame that she didn't heed any warning signs and rest her voice when she had the chance.

"Let that be a warning to you, Christine. Your voice is a valuable instrument, and you must take extreme care of it and never take it for granted. Not all are privileged to have what you possess."

I thumbed through my sheet music while her fingers traced the lines in Molly's mane. Then she added another comment to the subject.

"It was the strangest thing. Did you hear it?"

While trying not to smile too broadly, I responded, "Yes."

She frowned ever so slightly. "I've never heard a soprano release such a deep sound from her throat before. It was most unreal."

Hiding my smile, I turned from her and pretended to be looking through more sheet music. "As I said, let that be a warning to us all. The vocal chords can do strange things when not protected. They can embarrass a rich baritone with the squeaky sounds of mice, or the sweet sound of a soprano with the hoarse sound of a toad."

There was a moment of silence before she started again. "It's interesting that you should use that description, 'toad.' A short while ago, Carlotta used the same word to describe my voice. She told the press that my voice was like a toad's croaking."

"Is that right?" I asked as I sat down on the bench. "Well, perhaps karma has caught up with our *diva*. Perhaps, if she's superstitious enough, that episode might teach her a lesson—she needs to watch her viper's tongue."

"It really hurt and made me afraid to sing. I knew Carlotta had been in the business for a long time and must have known what she was talking about. She had me convinced that my angel had heard me with the ears of a heavenly creature, while those here on earth could hear the truth—I was worse than nothing.

"I actually felt relieved when I was cast as part of the chorus during that production of *Faust*. I felt safe there. Especially when I couldn't find you, I thought for sure I'd lost everything. I felt like such a failure and disappointment to my father and such a failure to you. I'd lost all confidence in myself; even though I knew you wanted me to have that confidence, it was all gone."

The look in her eyes and the sound of true sorrow in her voice only increased what I was feeling toward the Opera Populaire's lead soprano, and my next words expressed just how I felt.

"Carlotta is an arrogant fool. She's grown too old and too comfortable with her past laurels. She's neglected to remember the beautiful tale of the princess and the frog. Everything isn't always what it seems, Christine, remember that. What's beauty in one's eyes is ugliness in another's.

"Carlotta sees through eyes of jealousy. She sees how you've improved, and she fears you'll take what she thinks is her place center stage. Well, in her arrogance, and by her own mouth, she's cast a spell on herself, and now you'll sing Marguerite in place of her—mark my words."

I believe my tone had sparked a hint of suspicion, so I tried to give her something else to think about, something other than my possible involvement in Carlotta's downfall.

"If you want to be a great singer, you must develop a tougher skin, Christine. It was once said that, the closer you are to the fire, the more you'll feel the heat. Well, the same goes for the stage. The closer you are to center stage, the more you'll feel others' jealousy and hear their bitter words. But that's all they are, my dear, just words. They can't hurt you if you don't let them. You'll be twice the star that Carlotta has ever been, and you'll shine twice as brightly, I guarantee it. Now, you must stop your doubting."

"I know you're right, and I'll try. Thank you. You always manage to make me feel better."

We began her lesson, and I watched her expression and movements closely for any signs of insecurity, but I didn't see any. I was grateful for that, and I knew, as long as she was with me, I could keep her feeling confident, but I was still concerned about what would happen the first time she had a confrontation with Carlotta. I would just have to watch her closely and intercede if necessary.

We talked until it was time for me to meet the boys at the dock, and then I left. When I returned, I left her boxes in the docking room until I could get them inside without her seeing me. So, when I entered the parlor, I was carrying only our bags of food. I smiled when I saw her walking toward the fire, but the smile quickly left my lips when I saw what was in her hand. I gasped, dropped the bags on the floor, and rushed toward her, causing her to jump and drop the small bag on the floor, the small bag containing the keys to the black boxes.

"Oh! Erik! You startled me."

"Likewise, my dear," I said as I picked up the bag. My teeth were clamped tightly, and I glared at her while shaking my head. "Christine, you must control your curiosity or it might be the end of us all. Didn't I tell you not to touch this bag?"

"I don't think so. You took it away from me, but that's all I remember."

I glanced at the innocent looking bag in my hand and then at her. "What were you planning to do with this?"

"I was curious and . . ."

"Oh," I growled. "You and your curiosity. Christine! Please, don't ever experiment with anything in my home. You have no idea what could happen. If you're curious, ask me about anything you want, but restrain yourself from trying to figure things out on your own. These . . ." I stammered as I tried to explain the keys. "These aren't . . ."

"What is it, Erik? I know they're keys. They look like they could go to those black boxes. Do they?"

I tossed the bag in one hand a few times, still shaking my head. "Very well, you want to see what these unlock?"

I took her by the shoulders and moved her close enough to the fireplace to see into the boxes but far enough away so she couldn't touch them. Then I held her hands behind her back.

"Here, hold your hands. Don't move them, and don't try to touch what's in the boxes. Do you understand?" she nodded. "Do you agree not to touch them?"

"Yes, but why are you being so cautious? Whatever's in those boxes can't be that dangerous."

I chuckled and unlocked the boxes. "A scorpion can kill, and it could also fit in that box?"

"But it couldn't stay alive in there," she rebutted with a slight frown.

"Perhaps, but remember what I told you earlier about things not always being what they seem. So just don't try to touch it."

"You're acting so strange, Erik. You're almost frightening me."

"Good," I replied as I moved behind her, preparing to grab her arms if she moved them. "In this situation, being frightened is a good thing" Then I reached around her and opened the boxes. "Now you can see what's in my black boxes, but be careful. They both hold great power."

She turned her head and looked up at me. "Maybe I no longer want to see."

"Will your curiosity be appeased if you don't? Will you no longer want to know what's in those curious little black boxes?" She didn't answer. "That's what I thought. You started this, Christine, now I'm going to finish it, once and for all. Just look inside. As long as you don't touch them, they can't hurt you." I nudged her gently and she leaned forward.

"Oh! They're delightful, Erik."

I felt her arms start to move forward and I grabbed them. "No, Christine, don't touch."

"I don't understand. They're nothing more than metal replicas. They're not alive so how can they hurt anyone?" She looked up at me again. "You're teasing me again, aren't you? There was never anything dangerous in there, was there?"

I took a deep breath, moved her to the divan and sat her down. Then I started to lock the boxes.

"Erik, are you going to answer me?"

I turned and looked at her. "Christine, you know only a small part of what my life has been like. And this . . . . Perhaps you don't want to know about it. Perhaps you don't need to know or perhaps you do need to know, since it involves who I am or at least who I was or could be."

"You're not making any sense, Erik."

I put the bag of keys in my pocket, with the intention of hiding it somewhere that she couldn't go. She was much too curious for the good of either of us. Then I sat in my chair and began my strange story.

"During the war with Prussia, I was living right here. It was a dark time for Paris and for me. This opera house was used by the military, and death was a daily occurrence. Death not caused by me, by the way. I was sick of the death, and I was sick of the men who were causing it.

"But when the communes took over this house, it was even worse. They brought in hundreds of barrels of gunpowder and it angered me terribly. I pictured them, or the next power to be, blowing up my home that I'd worked on for years, and possibly killing me in the process. If they did succeed in destroying the opera house, they would also be destroying my childhood dream.

"I wasn't going to let that happen, so I took those barrels and hid them all around the foundation of this place. Therefore, I would be in control, and if I discovered they were going to take this place down, I would do it first.

"Those innocent looking replicas hold great power. One is connected to that gunpowder, and, if turned, it'll take this place down and everyone in it. So you see, my curious Christine, that's why they're under lock and key. And these keys," I said as I patted my pocket, "were kept far from the boxes as a safety precaution. But now I see I have to find a better hiding place."

"You can trust me now, Erik. I won't touch them. But, if I may ask, that was during a war so I can understand your thinking—in a way. However, it's been many years since that war, so why don't you disconnect the gunpowder so there won't be a threat?"

"Good question, my dear," I replied as I looked at the boxes. "Good question indeed, and I don't know if I can answer it. I believe I was nearly mad when I designed that scheme, and perhaps I still am for not dismantling it. But I've learned over the years that my life can have unexpected and instant twists and turns. You even commented on that aspect of my life.

"As an example—you heading for those boxes with those keys in your hand. If I'd taken just one more minute to get home, I may not have had a home any longer or a living wife. Get my point?" Her eyes were wide and she nodded slowly. "I still might need that mad scheme at some point, but I hope not. We never know what tomorrow will bring. I can assure you though, if I ever leave this place, I'll disconnect their power and take those replicas with me."

Her curiosity was finally appeased and we started on supper. Time passed and I still hadn't had the opportunity to sneak her surprises in, so I made up an excuse about checking something in my boat before we left. Therefore, I was shortly in my docking room and hiding that bag of keys and getting her presents. When I walked in the door she was on the divan with a book and her chocolates. I stood in the doorway with my arms loaded down with the large boxes until she looked up at me. She frowned as she got up and began walking toward me.

"What have you done this time, Erik?"

I set the boxes on the coffee table and replied, "Open them. They're for you."

As she started to take the lid off the top box, she shook her head. "You must stop this, Erik. You're spoiling me."

"Then I'm doing my job properly. That's exactly what I want to do, spoil my love."

"Oh, Erik! It's beautiful! Thank you!" she exclaimed as she picked up the dress made from a teal, lavender, and rose print fabric, the one I was hoping they still had.

I loved buying things for her, and I cherished the expression on her face each time she opened a package.

"And this one will help you in many ways," I said as I gestured toward the second box. When she picked up the black satin cloak and matching gloves, I explained. "These will go with any of your dresses, and they can double as a hiding place. With them on, you'll be harder to spot if you stay in the shadows. Then you won't have to talk to Meg or Raoul unless you want to."

She looked at me, nodded, and smiled. "Spoken by the Phantom?"

I sheepishly grinned. "Perhaps."

We talked about what she should say to Meg or Raoul when she met them again, and then we prepared for another carriage ride. I changed into a nice suit and she put on the new dress I'd just given her.

"Once again, my sweet, you look stunning."

She twirled. "This one is so gorgeous. I wish we could go out to a nice restaurant. I'd like to show it off—and you," she responded while placing her palm on my chest.

"That's one of my fantasies, my dear. I dream of taking you shopping and letting you buy whatever your heart desires, and then spending an evening at a fine restaurant and listening to soft violin music." I took her hand in mine. "That's what I hope for in the not too distant future."

I could tell she was struggling to find words, so I abruptly turned around, shut off the alarm, opened the door, and held out my arm for her. "Shall we go, my lady?"

I'd decided to do something different that evening, so I had the driver of our coach take us to the livery. Once there, I had Christine wait in the brougham out of sight while I rented a covered carriage for the evening, thinking it would be more private. But I had to prepare the horse and carriage myself since the owner was busy with the veterinarian and a sick horse.

No problem, I thought. I've done this a thousand times. I hurried through the process and then headed back to the brougham and Christine. But before I got out of the stable, I was caught off guard by a figure who'd stepped out of the shadows right in front of me, and I gasped.

"Christine, you startled me!"

"Good," she replied. "Your black cloak idea works. You didn't see me."

"Oh, my sweet Christine. I don't know why you're always so surprised when something I tell you is true."

"Because sometimes I like to experience things for myself, that's why."

"In other words—you were curious." I shook my head at her. "There was a reason for you staying in the coach. I didn't want you to be seen."

"Well, you didn't see me, so I doubt anyone else did."

"*Touché*, my dear."

Soon we were on a back street and heading south.

"Erik, I was surprised to see you hitch the horse so easily. You really can do everything."

"I don't know why that surprises you."

She was quiet for a bit before she offered an explanation. "I guess I'm always comparing you to Raoul. He can't do nearly the things you can. I know he can't hitch a buggy or cook, and he certainly doesn't know how to build anything."

I shook my head before I spoke my mind. "I can't believe what I'm going to say, but I have to. In his defense, you can't fault him for his lack of skills. He's still young, and he's been trained by aristocrats to have everything done for him, so why should he learn how to do anything? I was forced to learn. I was alone for most of my life, so if I was hungry or needed to travel, I had to learn how to cook or work with horses. If I didn't do it, no one would do it for me."

"Yes, I guess you're right. Oh! I keep forgetting to ask if I can take the book *Jacob* to Mummy for her to read. I think she'd really enjoy it."

I told her certainly, and then we talked about the beauty of the moon and stars and other safe subjects until we pulled up in front of Lapierre's home. Then, nervously, and with Christine on my arm, I knocked on their door.

Geanne answered the knock. "Erik! What a nice surprise. Come in, please. Lapierre, look who's here."

Lapierre was at the table carving and immediately dropped what he was doing and rolled toward us.

"I wanted you both to meet Christine. She's a promising student. Christine, this is Lapierre and Geanne—the most remarkable parents you'll ever meet."

They greeted each other cordially, and Geanne headed for the kitchen to get us tea.

"Erik told me you made a horse bust for him. You're extremely talented, and that was such a nice gesture to do for him. When he looks at it, I can tell how much it means to him."

"Well, making that for him was a drop in the ocean compared to what he made for us. It was the least I could do." I tried to change the subject, but he wouldn't let me. "Oh, by the looks on your faces, I suspect you didn't tell her about why I made that statue for you, did you, Erik?"

"That's not important. Now tell . . ."

"Not important!" he exclaimed, cutting me off.

About then, Geanne came back into the room. "Lapierre, where are your manners? Erik, Christine, won't you please have a seat?"

As she was pouring the tea, Lapierre told her, "Erik doesn't think what he did for us is important."

"My husband, don't embarrass Erik."

"I'm not embarrassed, it's just that . . . let me put it this way," I tried to explain. "I brought Christine here to meet all of you, not to talk about me. So tell me, do you think we could get everyone to come here?"

"I'm sure we could," Geanne replied, and then she went to the back door and called Alphonse. "He still takes care of the chickens for me," she offered as she came back to the table.

Shortly, he came in with a happy smile, and I introduced him to my student. Geanne told him what we wanted and he left right away. While we were waiting, I tried to keep the conversation directed away from me. Lapierre was right. Talking about me was embarrassing, and surely not needed. Christine already knew about me, and I wanted her to know about them. It wasn't too difficult to do once the children started to arrive with their spouses and their children. Brie even brought a freshly baked chocolate cake.

"Oh, Christine, look! Chocolate—your favorite," I teased.

We all laughed and had a great time either telling stories, or listening to them. Christine learned that night and understood why I felt they were so exceptional.

She was by the shelf where Lapierre kept his work and running her fingers over a sleek black leopard in a crouching position. I could tell she wanted it, so I picked it up and put it in her hands.

"Here, it's yours," I said softly.

"I would love to get this for Mummy. How much do you think he wants for it?"

"It doesn't matter. I'll take care of it."

"No, Erik. I have my own money. I just don't have much with me."

"But I want to buy it for you and Madame Valerius. Tell her it's a small token of your angel's appreciation for taking such good care of you all these years."

She smiled and agreed, and I took out what I thought Lapierre would want for it plus a bit more. When we returned to the table, I slid it in his shirt pocket and told him about Christine wanting it. He immediately took the money out of his pocket.

"No, Erik, I won't take your money. You take this back."

At first I argued with him, but then I let him win. After all, I knew I could slip it on their bookshelf before we left. I might have been able to work out that problem easily enough, but it quickly triggered the conversation that I'd managed to avoid all evening.

It was Lapierre who started it again when he asked, "Dominick, can you believe that Erik thinks what he did for us was nothing?"

"Certainly, I believe that, but it's not true, and we all know it."

From there, anything I tried to say to maintain control of the conversation was for naught. There were about 20 of us in that room and they all agreed with Lapierre. One after the other they began telling stories about the things I'd done. From the very beginning when I was teaching Dominick at the opera house to the renovation of the neighborhood. Everything I'd done or inspired was brought to the surface, and, while Christine looked at me and smiled a lot, I lowered my head and shook it in defeat.

Eventually, when everyone had had their say, I was able to slip in a question to move the conversation in another direction.

"Speaking of renovations, how are they coming? Are all the homes now finished?"

"Nearly," Dominick offered. "We have only one more home that we'll be starting in a few weeks, and then we're finished with the building part of the renovations. The next project in place is a program to save the money to have the streets paved. We even have the contractor lined up to help us. We were hoping to get it finished before winter set in again, but it looks like it might take us another year or maybe two before we can do it. It will be nice to be rid of those muddy potholes."

"That's quite a large project, but I'm sure you'll do it. After all, look what you've accomplished so far," I replied encouragingly.

By then, the hour was getting late, and many had already left to get their little ones in bed, so I whispered to Christine, "Do you want to leave or do you want to stay longer?"

"We should probably leave. I don't want to overstay my welcome," she whispered back.

I got up. "We should also be leaving, and thank you for welcoming us into your home."

"Yes," Christine added. "Now I understand why Erik spoke so highly of you. Thank you, Lapierre, for the statue. My guardian is going to cherish it. And thank you, Brie, for the chocolate cake. Erik was correct in saying it was my favorite. You could even say I have an addiction to chocolate."

"As do I," Brie replied.

While they were talking and the attention was on Christine, I stepped closer to the bookshelves and left the money for the statue there. Then I put my cloak on and placed Christine's over her shoulders.

"Won't you please come back soon?" Geanne asked. "It's been such a nice visit."

"We'll try. I'm not certain about Christine's future plans, but I'll try."

I opened the door and let Christine leave first, then, while I was positioning my hat, Lapierre rolled up to me.

"Erik, she's lovely, but I get the distinct feeling she's more than just your student."

I looked at Christine who'd turned back to look at me. "Yes, she is, but only time will tell how much more."

Thirty-Five

As soon as we pulled away from their home, Christine turned toward me. "I now understand why you said they were special people. They made me feel at home. Thank you for taking me there." She paused a moment and I looked at her. "I'm proud to be in your company, Erik, and now whenever I look at Molly I'll be reminded about how special you are also."

"I'm not special, my dear, but thank you anyway. Remember, I was given gifts—I didn't have to work for them, so what I did for Dominick and his family was nothing special."

"I beg to differ. Everything you did had to cost a lot of money and time. Are you going to tell me that those are also gifts?"

"No, I won't say that exactly. I did have to work for every franc I have, but the work came easily for me because of my gifts, so, in a way, it was also a gift. And, as far as time goes, I enjoyed myself immensely while I was working there. It was a wonderful experience for me. So, again, it was nothing special."

"Erik, you're impossible. Why don't you take credit for what you do?"

I didn't answer that question, but I did ask one of my own. "I'd like to make just one more stop while we're here. Do you mind? It won't take long."

"That's fine with me, but you didn't answer my question."

"I'll give you an answer just as soon as I find one," I replied with a smile and a wink.

I pulled up in front of Joubert's place, tied the traces, and set the break. "Christine, I need to talk with this man in private, so, when we get in there, please don't be offended when I take him into the kitchen alone."

"Secrets, Erik?"

"Not really."

"Then what do you call it if it's not a secret?"

"Christine, there are just some things that . . ."

"Yes. Some things that what, Erik?"

"Some things that are hard for me to . . ."

I closed my eyes, lowered my head, and ground my teeth, while she waited patiently for me to complete my sentence. I didn't want her to know what I was about to do, so it was a secret, but we'd agreed there wouldn't be any. How was I going to get around this one? Finally, she sighed deeply and deliberately.

"Very well. No secrets," I said as I got out and helped her down.

While walking up to the door, she looked up and saw what type of building it was, causing her to stop short, press her hand against her chest, and look up at me.

"Erik, this is a church! What are you doing?"

"No, no, no, my dear. We're not here for that, although I have to admit I wish we were. I only want to talk to this man—that's all. He's a man of God who answered some of my long-time questions about why there's so much suffering in the world. I know him to be kind and honest, and that's why I chose him for this project."

Joubert greeted us just as warmly as Geanne had. I introduced him to Christine, and he asked what brought us to that neighborhood.

"I have a request, and I need you to keep this a secret for me. Dominick just explained to me the town's desire to have their road paved and their hope to have it completed in a year or two. Well, I'd like to help so they won't have to wait that long, but I don't what anyone to know. If you could find out how much they need, I'll come back and give you the money and you can give it to them. Just tell them it was from an anonymous traveler passing through their quaint community."

"I'd be glad to help you, but they're going to know who that *anonymous traveler* is anyway."

"Hmm, you're probably right, but it's worth a shot. I'll be back in two days. Will that give you enough time to find out how much they need?"

He agreed and we left. I expected more questions from Christine, but she was unusually quiet the entire ride back. She even stood silently in the shadows as I unhitched the horse. Without being reminded, she stayed in the shadows while I called out for a brougham, and then she remained quiet on the ride back to the opera house. It wasn't until we were standing in my parlor that she spoke.

"Thank you for this evening, Erik. I enjoyed it and learned so much."

"You're welcome, my lady," I said as I took her cloak.

She then stepped closer to me and laid her left hand on my chest, gazing at it in total silence. I believe she was looking at my ring on her finger. Then she closed her eyes and moved closer, and with her next move she took my breath away. She wrapped both her arms around me and laid her cheek on my chest. I took a deep breath, closed my eyes, and returned her embrace.

"They're so wrong," she whispered, with a slight shake of her head. "They have no idea about what they speak. All the rumors are so wrong. They talk about a frightening monster who wantonly murders. They gossip about a ghost's extortion and his lurking in the cellars. The only rumor they have right is that the Phantom is a genius in every respect, but they still have no idea about who lives down here. But now I do.

"Lapierre and his family know who you really are. They weren't talking about something rumored. They've seen you work and have been the recipients of your generosity. They've seen your real personality. They know you and now so do I. I'll never look at that bust of Molly the same way again. That statue speaks volumes about your character.

"I feel I now know what a true gentleman should be. I don't mean the ones who open doors for me or give me their hand as I step down from a carriage. I mean a real gentleman who truly cares what I think and what my needs are, a man who's willing to forgo his own desires just to show respect for mine. That's what you are, Erik.

"All the time I've been down here, I've watched you, and I've been in awe, but there was always a doubt that it might not be the real you—that it might be an act. But now I know. Tonight I saw the truth. Tonight has given me much food for thought."

She pulled away from me and looked down at the ring on her finger, twisting it. Then she looked up into my eyes. "I feel privileged that you've singled me out and have let me come to know the real Erik. I thank you for that privilege."

"You leave me speechless, Christine. I don't know how to respond."

She laid her palm on my cheek and spoke ever so softly. "No need to, my Erik. No need to."

I took her hand and kissed the inside of her wrist tenderly. "I love you so much, Christine, and I want you as my real wife as never before. With each passing moment, that desire grows stronger."

She barely whispered, "I know." Then she turned and looked at the tall clock. "I realize it's late, but we shouldn't neglect your treatment. I'll get the water boiling."

I knew I should have told her that I could do it and that she should go to bed, but I didn't want her to leave me, so I let her continue into the kitchen. Then I backed into my music room and changed into my dressing robe, all the while thinking about my special angel. Soon I had a fire started and was in my usual spot on the divan with my injured leg on the table in front of me.

Christine smiled softly when she returned but didn't say anything, and neither did I. She knelt beside me, removed the bandage, and when she laid her palm across the stitches, I almost lost complete control. Her touch only increased my desires, causing me to hold the pillow on my lap, lay my head back on the divan, and close my eyes.

"Erik? What's wrong?"

I cracked my eyes open and looked at her, trying to find a good lie, since I obviously couldn't tell her how badly I wanted to take her as my real wife.

I shook my head. "How is it looking? Do you think I need to use the oil again?"

She scrunched her face. "I'm sorry, but, yes, I'm afraid so. It's looking better, but just to be safe I think we should do it again."

"I figured as much, so I'm preparing for the pain. Go ahead."

I closed my eyes and waited. It hurt but not nearly as bad as before, and not bad enough to stop my desires. Then to make matters worse, she laid her hand on my knee and massaged it as she applied each new compress. By the time the treatment was finished, I thought for sure I was going to explode. It was probably the longest 20 minutes of my life.

She cleaned up and then stood behind my chair and looked at me on the divan. "Is there anything I can get you before I retire?"

Oh, if she only knew what I wanted to ask for she wouldn't call me a gentleman again, but I continued to play the part she wanted and needed. "No, thank you. You've done enough. I hope you sleep well."

"Thank you again, Erik, for the splendid evening."

"It was my pleasure."

Then she was gone, and I could bang my head against a wall or do something to get my feelings under control. The majority of my life I'd been able to control those desires, but I was totally unprepared for true love to be thrown into the equation. In the past, it was always only lust I had to control, and I did. But, with love at the core, my lustful feelings were quadrupled, and I feared they would overtake me if I didn't find a way to control them.

I got up and began pacing through my parlor, trying to cool my body and change my thoughts. I walked into my music room, at first, thinking my music might help, but, with a second thought, I knew even it wasn't powerful enough. I put my hands behind my neck and stared at the ceiling, wishing I had Molly or any of my horses to ride and ride until I could gain mastery over my torturous thoughts and desires. I would have gone to César, but, with additional police on the lookout for Christine and me, I knew that was impossible.

Then, abruptly, I opened the door and charged up the passage to the third cellar and back down again. I repeated that process a few times until my wound was beginning to burn and I stopped, but my lustful desires hadn't. I growled with frustration and turned in circles with my palms pressed against the sides of my head. When I stopped, my sight landed on the switch to the motion alarm on the lake, and I felt for sure I had the answer to my problem.

I quickly turned it off, stripped off all my clothes, including my mask, grabbed a towel, and ran for my docking room. After opening the viewing window and turning on the light, I dove into the water beside my boat and swam down through the small hole; then I swam and swam without letup. I kept swimming until both my limbs and lungs were burning, and then I stopped and floated on my back until I caught my breath.

I was extremely cold, but that was better than what I'd been feeling. This will have to do until she's my wife, I told myself. I then swam slowly in circles, looking for the light from my docking room. Shortly, I spotted a faint light, and I headed for it. It was either the light from my home or the light that streamed down from the air vent on the other side of the wharf, so I wasn't certain where I'd end up.

I was freezing by the time I recognized it as the light from my docking room, and my teeth were chattering by the time I was climbing the stairs to my door. I was still drying off as I cautiously cracked the door open and looked for any signs of Christine. Without seeing any, I walked into the warmth of my parlor.

I quickly entered my music room and shut the door; then I put a dry bandage on my leg and warm clothes on my body. After I got a glass of brandy to warm my insides, I wrapped in a blanket and sat close to the fire. While gazing at the flames flickering, I felt in control again, and knew then how I could survive my new challenge until Christine made her decision.

I couldn't let her dress my wound again. That was too close and too dangerous. My emotions were becoming harder for me to maintain, and I couldn't be less than the gentleman she expected and deserved. I'd have to take care of my wound before she got up and after she retired for the night. Then if I waited for her to leave in the afternoon, I could treat it myself at that time. All my problems were solved, or so I thought.

The next morning went fine. I was finished with my wound and had breakfast ready by the time she was up. Then while eating, she expressed her disappointment.

"I apologize for sleeping so late and making you care for your wound by yourself." I shrugged it off, but then she announced, "I don't want to go to see Mummy today."

I swallowed hard, thinking this could be a problem. "Why not?"

"I don't know. I just want to stay here with you. I noticed you have a chess board. Would you teach me how to play? I'd like to learn."

"Certainly," I replied eagerly. "How about after your lessons?"

She agreed, and I was relieved. Teaching her would be a good distraction for both of us. Hopefully, she might get so wrapped up in it that she'd forget about my wound, and I might get so caught up in it that I could forget about her. It was a perfect solution, and it worked out perfectly. She was just as good a student in chess as she was in music, and before either of us knew it, it was time to meet the boys with our food. Then over supper she made another good suggestion.

"Do you think we could go for another carriage ride tonight?"

I set my wine glass down and smiled at her. "I would like that." I laid my hand on top of hers. "Perhaps, soon, we can take a carriage to a restaurant where I can show off my wife to something other than these cellar walls."

She nodded. "I hope so."

"However," I told her, "if we're going to make a habit of these rides, we need to change our routine. I've found it's easier to stay ahead of those looking for me if I don't have a regular pattern to my activities. So, tonight, I'll take you out my private entrance in the back."

Her eyes widened, like a child expecting something special, and I smiled. Sometimes she was simply too cute, and it was hard to keep my hands off her.

That night, the carriage ride was similar to our first one, and so were the ones to follow, but I changed the order of the places we visited. We rode around the city and out into the countryside. We talked about the moon and the stars, and I showed her some constellations that she didn't know about. We'd even burst out in lyrics when one of us said something that reminded us of a line in an opera, and then we'd laugh.

Part of the time we sat quietly, with both of us in thought about memories unearthed by something we'd said, or we were simply silent and enjoying what we were looking at, especially me, considering I was watching Christine.

During those rides, I felt my life was near perfect, and the only thing left for me to ask for would be to take her out in the light of day and eat and shop in public. Well, I could ask for more, but that was all I could ask for as long as we were only playing at being married.

While I really wanted her as a real wife, the part we were living right then was very important to me. To be close to her and to share my thoughts and feelings with her and then to watch her as she shared hers with me was precious.

Then there were times when I was so comforted by the sound of her voice, along with the comforting sound of the horses, that I drifted into a hazy tranquility. It was during one of those times that I envisioned another special evening for us, and I knew exactly what I wanted to buy her for that occasion, a red evening dress, a ruby necklace, and gold hair combs adorned with rubies. I would have a special dinner prepared for us so we wouldn't have to cook, and I would play my violin. I smiled at her across from me and could picture the evening perfectly.

That first night, I kept us out extra late, hoping she would be so tired she wouldn't want to treat my leg, but it didn't work. She was talkative all the way home, even bubbly. When we entered the door, she turned in circles with her arms out, making it difficult to release her cloak from her shoulders.

"What a wonderful night for a ride," she sighed with a large smile. After taking a few pieces of chocolate from the bowl, she headed for the divan and picked up the book she'd been reading. "I only have two chapters left in this book, and I'd like to finish it before I retire. Do you mind?"

"Not at all. I also have something I'd like to finish," I replied while walking into my music room.

Good, I thought. I'll play something soft and relaxing, encouraging her to get sleepy, and then maybe she'll forget about my leg. But it didn't work out that way. After about an hour, she appeared in the doorway.

"That was a good book, but not as good as *Jacob*. I'll get the water hot, and when you're finished we can take care of your leg."

She started to leave, but I stopped her. "No! Wait! I don't know how much longer I'll be, so you should go to bed. I can take care of my leg myself."

I returned my sight to the keys, but she stayed in the doorway until I finally said, "Good night. Sweet dreams."

She still didn't leave, and then she started that dreaded conversation—or should I say argument.

"What is it, Erik? You're not acting right."

"Am I? I'm sorry," I said, hopefully convincingly. I waited and then glanced up at her for only a second and then quickly lowered my eyes again.

"You're hiding something, Erik. What is it?"

"Who? Me? No, I'm not. I'm just concentrating on this piece. I'm sorry if I gave you the wrong impression."

I looked back down at the keys and she stayed where she was. Then she blocked my beautifully executed plan.

"Very well, I'll find another book and be reading until you're ready for your treatment."

"No, Christine," I said with a bit too much emphasis. "I can do it myself. You need to go to bed."

"Now I know there's something wrong. I can tell when you're not being honest with me. Why aren't you letting me help you tonight?"

"It simply isn't necessary any longer. It's nearly healed, and in two more days I'll be going back to the doctor and he'll take the stitches out. I've appreciated your help, but your sleep is more important tonight. It's very late."

She almost started to leave but then stopped. "Did I do something wrong? Is that why you don't want me to help you?"

"No, you didn't do anything wrong. It's just not necessary. I don't need to burden you any longer."

"But I enjoy taking care of you, and isn't that what a wife is supposed to do?"

"Well, yes. But then a wife is supposed to do a lot of things that you can't do."

I bit my tongue and knew that was a stupid thing to add to the conversation, and she knew it also. I struggled nervously for a simple way out, but I couldn't find one. Apparently, my lack of quick thinking also added to her concern.

"Erik, what's wrong? What is it that you're hiding?" All I could do was stare at her blankly. "Well, I know I've done something wrong, and you just don't want to hurt my feelings and tell me. So, I'll leave you alone."

She turned and left the room with such a hurt expression replacing her earlier happy one that I had to follow her.

"No, Christine, listen to me," I blurted out. She turned and looked at me, and I shook my head. "You've done nothing wrong; in fact, you've done everything right—that's the problem."

"Then there is a problem."

"No . . . Yes . . . The problem is in me, my sweet, not you." I groaned, turned, and leaned my forehead against the doorframe. "Oh, Christine."

"What is it, Erik?"

I looked at her. "It's no secret how much I love you. And you know I want you for a real wife." She nodded slightly. "Well, the longer you're down here with me the stronger those desires are becoming. I'm trying to be a complete gentleman, but . . ."

"And you have been, Erik, amazingly so."

"And I want to keep it that way. But there are times . . ."

"Yes?"

"There are times when you drive me crazy."

She frowned. "Why? What do I do wrong?"

"As I said, you do nothing wrong, that's the problem. You do everything right, and my responses to your actions are perfectly normal. But they're premature. I shouldn't have . . . I shouldn't allow these feelings I have for you to be so strong. But I can't seem to help it. There are times when you touch me . . . especially when our skin touches . . . especially when you touch me here," I said while laying my hand on my wound. "I nearly go mad with desire, Christine."

"Oh!" she gasped as her hand covered her open mouth. "Oh! I'm sorry, Erik. "Oh!" she said again while turning away from me. "I see." She turned back and looked at me and then nodded. "I understand. I thought it was . . ."

She just stared at me until I encouraged her. "You thought it was what?"

"Never mind."

She turned and started for her bedroom, but I stepped quickly toward her and grabbed her arm, turning her around. "Wait a minute, my dear. You won't let me get away without finishing my sentences. Now you have to finish yours."

She looked down at her fingers twisting my ring. "I thought I was the only one who was having that problem. I didn't know I was causing you . . . I'm sorry, Erik. I never want to cause you more harm. I won't pressure you again about your leg." She looked up at me. "Please forgive me."

The moments that followed were silent as we both looked at each other in a new light, a very dangerous light. I let go of her arm and moved back, uncertain what I should do or say next, and I believe she also was uncertain. Ultimately, she was the one who gained her wits enough to break the silence first.

"Good night, Erik. I hope you sleep well."

I believe I only nodded, and she stepped into her room and shut the door, while I stared at it. When I finally managed to move, I did so slowly. The realization that she felt about me the way I felt about her was actually frightening for me. How was I going to cope with this new information? I thought about Oded and all his advice to me when I was courting Vashti, and I felt a desperate need for him and his advice. I felt I needed him to stay in my home with us until she made her decision. I didn't trust myself, and from the expression on Christine's face, neither did she.

We'd just stripped off a layer of that mask I'd told her about the first night she was there with me, and I wasn't certain if it was a bad thing or a good thing. Removing our masks from our hearts was necessary if we were ever to reach that point I wanted us to reach, but I never imagined it would be so frightening. I looked at her door and wondered if she was also frightened.

The night was long and slow. I only gave a momentary thought to sleeping, but I knew it wasn't in the cards for me—not that night. By the time Christine came out of her room in the morning, I had our breakfast waiting to be cooked, and I was in my chair by the fire with a cup of tea in my hands and many thoughts in my head.

Our morning routine was a subdued one; neither one of us ventured into a conversation about what had happened the previous night. I presume we were both cowards. By the time she was prepared to leave for Madame Valerius', I was working on my mask at the dining table. I looked up at her when she came out of her room, wearing the boy's costume with her new black cloak over her arm.

"I think I'm ready for my visit, but I don't know if I'm ready for Meg or Raoul. That's why I thought I'd wear this cloak. Maybe I can hide from them if I see them," she explained.

"It's worked for me nearly my entire life," I replied. "However, you might be anticipating more of a problem than you need to. I saw how you handled Raoul in Perros, so I'm sure you'll be fine if you have to do it again. But the final decision is yours, Christine. I don't want to push you into anything."

"Perhaps you're right. But it was stressful for me to *handle* him in Perros, and I'd rather not, if I don't have to."

"I could follow you to make certain he doesn't cause you problems, if you'd like."

"Oh, no thank you! I'd like to keep the two of you as far apart as possible."

"Christine, listen to me. You don't have to fear me doing him harm. I would never hurt him, unless . . ."

She looked at me, waiting. Then she asked, "Unless what?"

I shook my head. "Unless he was harming you in a physical way. That I couldn't stand by and watch without stopping him. But, even then, I wouldn't do him lasting harm. You can trust me. So, do you want me to go with you?"

She sighed. "No. I have to learn to stand up to these people myself. You may not always be watching me or protecting me. No, Raoul and Carlotta I have to face myself, but thank you." She looked down at me and ran her fingers along my jaw. "You're so sweet to offer."

She then turned and headed for my music room, and, at first, I watched her walk away, but then I had to force myself to look away. She was so adorable in that costume, and I wanted so badly to grab her, but instead, I got up and followed her. When she bent over to pick up the stool and lantern, I again had to look away, so much so that I sat on my piano bench and began dusting off the keys with my fingers. Then I counted my breaths, waiting for her to leave.

I'd managed all morning to keep my thoughts decent, but the sight of her in those trousers was making it difficult to continue doing so. Therefore, I didn't get up and help her with the door as I should have; I kept on dusting and concentrating on good thoughts.

But then, she walked up behind me, placed her hands on my shoulders, and whispered something in my ear. I didn't hear one word she said; I only felt her breath on my ear, which sent shivers up and down my spine, and I automatically closed my eyes and took a deep breath. What was she doing?

I got up quickly, but by then she'd turned and was at the door. Against all my good judgment, I followed her and opened the door for her. She looked up at me and thanked me—I think. She started up the stairs, and I watched her, with my heart pounding and my thoughts twisting. Once again, I was out of control, and I shook my head hard.

"No! No! No!" I grumbled. "You're an adult, so act like one."

I'd planned to follow her to make sure she was safe, but at that moment she was safer without me around, so I went back to my piano. I tried playing, but the damage had been done. I was, again, locked in lustful thoughts, but I wasn't going to be tormented by them the way I'd been before.

I knew what I had to do, so, within a few minutes, I'd stripped all my clothing off and was swimming. Once cooled enough, I headed back to my home. My teeth were again chattering as I ran up the stairs, trying to dry off at the same time.

I was thinking about dressing and finding Christine to protect her when I opened the door and charged in to the sound of two gasps—one from me and one from Christine.

Thirty-Six

She quickly turned around and I, just as quickly, covered my body with the towel and my face with my hand, while we both questioned simultaneously, "Christine! What are you doing here?" "Erik! What were you doing?"

Again simultaneously, we both started stammering and apologizing. "I'm so sorry, Christine, I didn't know you'd returned." "I'm sorry, Erik, I needed you."

Still stammering, I suggested. "Uh, hold that thought. Mm, let me get some clothes on."

I started for the music room, but she stopped me. "No! Wait! Answer my question first. What were you doing out there without your clothes?"

"Uh," my eyes darted around the room, while I tried to think of a reasonable lie. "Uh, exercising? Yes, that's it. I enjoy swimming, especially if I can't run or ride a horse. It relaxes me. And, uh, I used to get lots of exercise by running all over this place, but that was before you came and before this injury. Now that you're here, I sit most of the time, and, uh, I'm going to get fat and lazy. We can't have that," I tried to say jokingly.

"And you used a freezing lake to get it? And what about your clothes? Do you have to swim without them? I somehow don't believe that, Erik. You're so cold your lips are blue."

At least she was looking at my lips, was my first thought, and then I decided to use her own words to escape her curiosity.

"Since you're so concerned about me freezing, may I please get dressed?"

I started for my music room again, but again she demanded, "No! I'm not going to give you a chance to think of a better lie. I know you're not telling me the truth. Your words are only hesitant when you're not being forthcoming. Tell me the truth. What were you doing out there?"

"Please, Christine, I am freezing. Let me dress and then we can talk."

"No! I know what you were doing, and it makes me feel sick inside to know my being here has pushed you to this."

Oh, great, I thought. She knows. Now what do I say?

"Admit it, Erik. You're taking your baths in that dirty and freezing lake, aren't you?"

I think my mouth dropped open before I thought, perfect. She gave me an excellent excuse. Now if I can keep from stumbling over my words, I'll be fine. So, "Touché," was all I said.

"I knew it! And I won't hear of it."

"It's really all right, Christine. I'm used to it. For a big part of my life that's all I had to bathe in, the closest body of water. Sometimes it was only a small stream and other times it was a large lake where there was snow on the ground. So, I'm really all right with this arrangement."

"Well, *I'm* not all right with it. You have a nice tub in here with lots of warm water, and you should be using it."

"But I wanted you to have your privacy, Christine. I wanted those rooms to be yours."

I couldn't see her face, but from her folded arms and her shaking head, I knew what her face looked like—determined.

"I won't let you take a bath out there again—I won't. So, unless you promise to stop this ridiculous behavior, I'll leave. I'll return to Mummy so you can have your warm tub. I won't be the cause of your getting pneumonia."

"Very well, I concede," I replied, hopefully with the sound of defeat. "I won't take another bath in the lake. May I dress now?"

She nodded, and I again started to leave, but once more she stopped me. "Erik?"

"What now?" I asked, fearing her reply.

"It's good to see you have more weight covering your bones."

"I told you I could put it on quickly" was all I could think of as an answer, since I was terribly embarrassed about the entire episode and wanted to get out of there.

I continued toward the music room without her interference that time. Then I put some oil on my wound, redressed it, and dressed myself. I was still shivering, and I wanted to sit by the fire, but I didn't know how to face her. I didn't know how much of my body she'd seen, and I feared the worst. I paced for a few minutes, trying to gain my composure back so I could put on a good enough act for her. If I stammered again, she might not continue to believe the bath story. When I felt I had command of my actions, I opened the door and headed for the fire.

I didn't see her anywhere, but I did hear her in the kitchen. By the time I did see her, I'd just sat in my chair, holding my hands out to the fire. At first, I couldn't look up into her eyes, but when she handed me a glass of brandy with a huff, I had to.

"I can't believe you've done this to yourself," she criticized while tucking a blanket in around me. Then she felt my ears. "Your ears are like ice." She huffed again and shook her head. After she put another log on the fire and stoked it, she held her hands close to the fire and rebuked me again. "I can't believe you could be this careless with your health. After all you've gone through lately, how could you do this?"

I was trying to choose my words carefully, so I wouldn't stammer again, when she walked behind my chair and placed her warm hands over my cold ears.

"Your bathing out there makes me feel just awful," she reiterated with a sigh.

"Please, Christine, don't. You're not responsible for anything I do. Don't berate yourself for my stupidity."

I closed my eyes, allowing myself to enjoy her touch and relax in the silence, but I couldn't relax completely. I sensed a tension building in the room, and I feared what she was thinking. I was thinking about the possibility that she'd seen too much of me when I entered the room, and I couldn't help but think she was also visualizing that moment.

Her seeing me naked, or even near naked, and our not talking about it, was like having an African lion pacing in the room and neither of us saying a word about it. I knew we needed to talk about it to clear the air, but I certainly wasn't going to bring it up. No way. I'd much rather have that lion pacing in my parlor.

Then my way out of that uncomfortable situation dawned on me, so I asked, "Why did you come back, Christine? You seemed so determined and confident when you left. Why did you say you needed me?"

She sat on the divan, shrugging her shoulders. "I don't know what happened. I did feel confident while on my way to my dressing room, but by the time I reached it I'd lost it all. I just don't want to hear any critical talk or answer probing questions. I do want to visit Mummy though and give her that book. She understands our relationship, so I don't mind talking to her. When I realized that's what I wanted to do, I decided to ask for your help. That's why I came back so soon."

"I'll be glad to help. What is it you want from me?"

"I think it would work better if I went to see her during our carriage rides. It would be dark, and there is less chance of anyone around here seeing me. What do you think?"

"I think that's a wise choice, and I think I need to make an equally wise choice. I usually try to change my routines around from time to time. There's less chance that way of someone following me and discovering my home. So, if we're going to take more evening rides, I think we need to use my secret exit. If we're careful, no one will see us leaving the opera house, no one such as Meg or Raoul.

"But you do realize, don't you, that eventually we'll both have to face the music and face Raoul? That is, unless you intend to spend the rest of your life down here with me, which I wouldn't mind at all."

"I know, but I'm not ready to face that time just yet."

"Well, I'll never push you into a rash decision. We'll take each step at your pace."

"Thank you. I knew you'd understand. Oh," she added as an afterthought. "When I couldn't find you here, I wanted to go to your docking room to see if your boat was gone, but, as you know, I don't know how to open that door. I tried to find the latch, but I never could. Can you show me where it is, just in case I should ever need to go out there?"

"I'm sorry, Christine. I can't show you that one. Like I told you the other day, that boat is dangerous and so is the area where it sits. Also, I know your curiosity and your adventurous spirit. I can think of several scenarios in which you might try taking that boat out on the lake." I stopped and shook my head. "I shudder to think about you out there alone."

She nodded. "I understand."

"And while we're talking about it, that safety room is the same. Please don't ever try to find the door to it. I have two motion sensors. One is on the lake to warn me if someone is near, and the other one is in that safety room. The one on the lake triggers a bell, which is not dangerous in itself, but the one in the safety room triggers gas jets, which are very dangerous.

"Please don't be curious about either of those locations. If anything happened to you because of those areas, I would never forgive myself—no, I would end my life for a certainty."

She looked at me with serious concern. "I won't, Erik. I promise. I won't do anything to hurt you."

"Good," I sighed, as I laid my head back against my chair.

We talked about the people and events in our lives, but we never did acknowledge that lion by talking about what had happened when we innocently appeared in my parlor unprepared. Even when he walked right between us and roared, we refused to acknowledge him. So he remained a feature of my home, and, from the look in Christine's eyes now and then, he was sitting right beside us.

Christine was once again like an excited schoolgirl when I led her through the long passage to my secret outside door. She marveled at my ingenuity while I hailed a brougham, and then we entered it stealthily.

Our using that door proved to be good timing, because as the driver neared the corner, I saw Raoul. He was leaning against a lamp post just outside the side entrance, waiting for us or at least Christine. Christine was happy and talkative, so I didn't tell her what I'd seen. I didn't want to spoil her positive mood.

When we pulled up in front of Madame Valerius' home, I asked, "How long do you want to visit?"

"Perhaps an hour," she replied.

I pulled out my watch and checked the time. "I have errands to run, so I'll be back at 9:30. Enjoy your visit."

Actually, I only had one errand to run, so I told the driver to take me back to the opera house. Once there, I waited up the street and watched Raoul, pacing in front of that side entrance. Periodically, he'd stop someone coming out and talk to them, asking, I'm sure, about Christine. I almost felt bad for him, until I realized it was probably more his defeated pride than his love for Christine that was driving him.

I was back and waiting for Christine when she came out of the house. Then we continued our evening ride. Much the same as before, we talked, laughed, and even sang short verses. The same was true the following night, with an added small celebration because the stitches were finally removed and my wound was healed completely. But then the inevitable happened, and, as with all my dreams, I was forced to wake up when it turned into a nightmare.

On a clear evening during the middle of May, my perfect little play marriage came crashing down around me, all because of one changed expression on Christine's beautiful face. We were traveling down the Bois, and I was watching her talk while she watched the people we were passing. She was smiling as she told me a story a seamstress had told her, and then she stopped mid-sentence. She lost her smile, and her eyes fixed on something outside her window.

I also looked out that window to see what had captured her attention, and, within a few seconds, a group of men, nicely dressed and laughing, came into my view. Her eyes searched them as we passed and so did mine. Two of the men locked their sights on our brougham and followed it with their eyes. I was searching them, looking for young de Chagny, and I knew she was also searching for him. Thankfully, he wasn't there.

Once they were out of our view, Christine's small frown and blank gaze told me her thoughts were important to her and also private. I sat quietly, waiting for her to pick up her story, or to tell me what she was thinking, but she never did. In fact, I was the one who started the conversation again, just to end the silence.

By the time we got back to my home, she was talking again, but I could tell her thoughts were still back on the Bois, and, I'm sure, on Raoul as well. I wanted to draw her out, but I couldn't bring myself to do or say anything that would actually end my perfect little paradise. She retired to bed while I sat and gazed into a dead hearth, occasionally twirling the brandy in my glass. I had to find the strength to face what was to come, good or bad, so I spent the night making plans to uncover what was in her heart.

The next day, I was back from meeting the boys, and we were eating our supper when I reminded her about the annual masquerade ball. "I thought it would be fun to attend. That's the only event held here that I can participate in openly. Since everyone will be wearing a mask, I don't believe I'll even be noticed. What do you think? Would you like to go?"

"Yes, that would be fun," she replied without her normal enthusiasm.

The ball was always filled with merrymaking; however, my real reason for going was to put her back in her old environment and see what she would do with her freedom. I knew it was a necessary move on my part, but I truly feared the outcome.

As I sipped my wine, I watched her closely. She was in deep thought, but I wasn't going to encourage her to talk about it. I didn't want to interfere with what was to come. Since I'd first seen her, I'd maneuvered events to meet my wishes, and, at the end of it all, I was still uncertain about her feelings for me. So I had to let her take the lead and pursue what was in her heart, no matter what it was or how painful it might be.

I felt sad. The atmosphere in my home was solemn, devoid of our usual chatter or banter. Then she asked me a question that I knew was only the prelude to the rest of her story.

"I think I'd like to go as a black domino. Do you think you could find me that costume?"

"Certainly, my sweet. I know exactly where it is."

"What do you think you'll be wearing?" she asked, almost cautiously.

"I'm not certain, but I do know it'll be something spectacular, something that will be remembered by all."

The evening moved on as usual, but I don't think either of us were feeling the same as before. It had been thirteen days since I'd brought her down, and I believed we'd grown close. But something had happened to her heart when she'd seen those men—something had changed.

I was ready to stay in for the evening instead of going out for another carriage ride, especially after what had happened the prior night. But if I was going to allow her to make all the decisions, I wasn't free to use my persuasive skills against it when she asked if we were going again.

When we pulled away from the opera house, I felt so sad. Those rides were special to me, filled with our happy voices and the sight of her across from me. But that night it was quiet, and to watch her was actually painful.

She was no longer my bubbly Christine or my seductive Christine—she was a different Christine.

Once we were on the Place de l'Opera, she kept glancing out of her window. Then she'd quickly look back at me, all the while painting a smile on her face. I'd smile back and make some comment about the trees or weather. I eventually stopped watching her directly and only watched her out of the corner of my eye, while pretending to be gazing out my window.

Then I saw her do something that made my heart tear apart. Secretly, she dropped something out of the window, and I unintentionally frowned at her when I recognized it as her lavender stationary, the stationary I'd bought for her. My thoughts were painful the rest of the ride, fearing I'd lost so easily all that I'd gained.

We were on the return part of our trip, and once again traveling down the Bois, when she became extremely nervous. Again, she was glancing at me and then out of her window. Then, at one point, she held her breath, and the look on her face signaled me that something significant was about to happen. I was watching her face and out of the window at the same time, and then we both heard it, Raoul calling her name. Within a moment, he came into my view, running after our brougham.

He'd obviously seen her and she'd seen him, so there wasn't a logical explanation for my next actions. I reached over and pulled the shade down on her window while explaining my abrupt move.

"It's chilly tonight, Christine. You shouldn't be breathing this night air. Remember what happened to Carlotta?"

All in that same moment, she gasped, flinched, and backed away from me, and I frowned at her, with my heart fracturing into a million pieces.

"You act as if I'm going to strike you. You break my heart, Christine. I've never hit you, not even while in an uncontrolled rage. What makes you think I'll strike you now? You break my heart."

"I . . . I was just startled. That's all. I'm sorry."

She was lying, and that made my hurt worse, so I clenched my teeth and turned away. I couldn't look at her, not then and not again for the rest of the ride, which passed in complete silence. There was hardly a cordial good night from either of us as she went to her room and closed the door.

I sat in my chair, watching the dead coals and waiting for her to fall asleep. Then I went to the costume department where I found her black domino costume. I also found the red death costume I'd decided to wear. I thought it was appropriate, considering my past and my current hateful thoughts.

The red death costume was made out of scarlet velvet with a huge hat adorned with feathers. It came with an immense velvet cloak that trailed on the floor. Written on the back of the cloak in gold script were the words, 'Touch me not. I am red death stalking abroad.' It also had a full skeleton skull as a mask.

I next went to Christine's dressing room and put her costume in her armoire. As I was leaving, my sight fell on her dressing table. There I saw her dead flowers, and I sighed. I stared at them with a somber heart, fearing their condition was a glimpse into the future of our short-lived relationship.

Once back in my home, I hung the red death costume in my armoire, and then I lay on the divan with my hands behind my head and stared at the ceiling for the rest of the night. I was sitting in my chair with a cup of tea when she came out of her room. She was in better spirits, and we even talked cordially over breakfast and as we went through her lessons. But I was reading between every letter in every word that she spoke the entire time. However, she honestly sounded excited when I told her what to expect.

"I've put your costume in the armoire in your dressing room, and I'd like you to go up before me. I don't want it to be obvious that we came together, just in case. If we don't meet up at the ball, then I'll meet you back in your dressing room when you're ready to leave. That way, you won't have to struggle with the latches. Any questions?"

"No. It sounds like you have everything planned out perfectly. This is going to be an interesting night," she finished, with a tone that I didn't quite understand.

When the time came, I opened the door for her and watched her ascend the steps before I closed the door. Five minutes later, I was dressed and not far behind her when she reached the main floor. Since everyone was in costume, I had no problem following her through the throng of paper faces. I tracked her for three hours while she laughed and talked to everyone. I was beginning to think I'd made a mistake in thinking she was going to secretly meet Raoul.

But then she started looking around nervously. Shortly, she started making her way through the crowd as if she had an agenda. It was almost midnight when she entered the big crush room and meandered through it.

I glanced around the room and easily spotted Raoul, leaning against a doorframe next to the rotunda. His face was covered with a lace-trimmed mask, but I recognized his fair hair and mustache, not to mention his costume—a white domino costume. I glared at him, knowing then why she'd wanted me to get her a black domino costume. Together they made a pair and could recognize each other easily.

I then watched Christine as she approached him but then kept on walking, with Raoul following her. My eyes were still on her as she headed straight toward me, with an occasional turn from time to time to make sure he was following her. They walked right in front of me, and my eyes burned hatred as I glared down at them both.

Then Raoul looked up in my eyes and held his sight there, even though he was still walking. Our eyes stayed locked on each other's until, in anger, I turned from him and moved through the throng of merrymakers. I glanced over my shoulder in time to see Raoul turn and start to follow me, causing me to defiantly turn back toward him.

But then Christine turned and looked at me, and instantly I knew they both realized who was wearing the red death costume. I started walking toward Raoul, that arrogant and stupid fool, but Christine grabbed his arm and quickly pulled him away. I laughed aloud and wickedly as they disappeared among the colorful costumes.

I climbed a few steps and could easily see the two spotted costumes. When I saw what direction they were going, I circled around in another direction until we were two flights up where there were fewer party makers. As I was descending a few steps, I saw them both slip into a private box, his brother's box, so I entered the box next to them with my personal key. I stood in the front of the box and pressed back against the wall so I could listen carefully. I had to maintain my temper as I listened to Raoul's accusations.

"I know you're not being honest with me. Why are you scheming with this man? Why did you pull me away from him? That was my chance to unmask him and hand him over to the police, ending his charade once and for all. Just get out of my way, Christine, and let me confront him."

Then she used words that gave me my first fearful sign of her true thinking. "Not in the name of our love will you pass me."

"What do you mean, in the name of our love, when you love him and are trying to protect him? I despise you, Christine. You're driving me crazy," he said through sobs.

Then I heard in Christine's voice the tone that always tore at my heart, and I knew she was crying. "I'm not trying to protect him—he doesn't need protection from anyone. Someday, Raoul, you'll understand what I'm doing, and then you'll be sorry for your harsh words."

"Understand? What's there to understand? I'm not a fool, Christine. You go away with a man for weeks without a word to me, and you expect me to believe nothing happened? Oh, how my friends are making fun of me. You know the kind of fool they're calling me? They're right. I have been a fool to think I was willing to give my reputable name to an opera wench—a lying opera tart."

"Raoul! How can you speak to me this way? I've never once lied to you, and I've never asked you to give me your name. How can you treat me this way? I came here to explain everything to you, and you treat me this way?"

My eyes were closed, my jaws were clamped shut, and my fingers were gripping the drapery beside me. I didn't know how much more I could listen to without interfering, and then it got worse. His words were so slicing that it took more than I thought I had to stay focused on letting Christine make her own decisions, for all of our sakes.

"That's right. Leave me again. Are you going to go to your lover and reside in his paradise for another two weeks? Well, go ahead and go, Christine, and perhaps I'll come and listen to you sing from time to time. And, if you're very, very good, I might even shout *brava*."

Christine answered softly, "No, Raoul, I'll never sing again—never again."

"Oh," he sarcastically ridiculed her. "Is he going to take you away somewhere? Is he so rich that you'll never have to work again? Well, how nice for you, Christine—how nice. I applaud you. Very well done. You played us both. I imagine he must have a larger estate than the de Chagny family. Well, maybe I'll see you again on the Bois before you leave."

Christine came back quickly. "No, Raoul! You'll never see me again, never. It was useless for me to try to explain anything to you. It was foolishness on my part to think you would give me a listening ear and understand."

I heard the doorknob turn and then Raoul's words again, only softer. "Wait! Christine. I only want to know the truth. Can you tell me the truth? Where have you been for two weeks? I don't see any chains on you, so you must not be in any sort of prison. What kind of a hold does this freak have on you?"

"You wouldn't understand now, Raoul, even if I could explain it. You've lost faith in me, and it's just too late. It's finished, Raoul. It's finished."

The door opened, and I heard Christine's steps move away and then Raoul sigh. I waited until I heard him leave, and then I started following him, because, by then, I was more interested in what he was thinking than in Christine's thoughts.

It looked as if he was heading for the dressing rooms, and, while I followed him, I was thinking over their conversation. Even though it was painful to hear Christine's hurt, I was pleased with what I heard her say to Raoul. But I couldn't help but feel her words were more because of his attack than her true feelings. I wondered what she would have said to him if he hadn't been so accusing.

Once I was certain he was heading for her dressing room, I slipped into a passage and headed for the mirror. I was there only a few minutes before I heard the dressing room door open and saw Raoul walk in.

He shut the door, and we were both in the semi-darkness of her low-lit wall lamp. Then he started looking around her room. He kept up his search until he abruptly stopped and looked at the door, and then he quickly ran behind the curtain to her dressing area. Within a moment, the door opened again and Christine walked in. She sat down on her dressing chair, tearing off her mask and throwing it on her table.

She laid her face in her hands, and I heard her whimper, "Poor Erik. Oh, poor Erik."

I wanted to reach out to her, but I waited for Raoul to make his move. When he didn't, I knew what he was doing. He was spying on her and waiting to see if I was going to appear. The stupid fool. He had much to learn about Christine's angel. But then I guess it was only fair. I'd just listened in on their secret conversation, so why shouldn't he be allowed to listen in on ours?

So you want to see what happens between Christine and her angel? You want to know what power I have over her? You want to see her invisible chains? Then watch!

I removed the death's head and laid my voice tenderly on her shoulder, singing softly Romeo's part of the wedding night song. Her face lit up, and she smiled while getting to her feet and turning toward the mirror. Then I heard honest relief and caring in her voice as she spread her arms out and answered me.

"I'm here, Erik. I'm ready to leave now."

I first watched her beautiful face for a couple of bars, and then I looked beyond her to the curtain and let my voice settle right where it belonged—in my throat. "Fate links thee to me forever and a day."

Then I did it, and with my entire body prepared for what might happen next, I released the latch to the mirror. With a slight vibration, it moved on its rotating pins. I kept singing as I reached my black gloved hand out to her, and she placed her delicate white gloved hand in mine. Then I guided her inside the passage with me.

I kept singing softly to her, and, as the door closed behind her, I looked back through the mirror in time to see Raoul on his way toward it. Then he stopped and just stood there staring at the mirror with his mouth open.

Defeated, he sat in her chair, dropped his face in his hands, and began crying.

I watched his pathetic form, causing me to smile through the notes leaving my lips. Regardless of his wealth, regardless of his youth and handsome face, regardless of his long-established relationship with her, he would never have or understand the connection we had—never in a thousand lifetimes.

I felt victorious, and my heart swelled as I looked down at the beauty who'd made the decision to take my hand. She'd gone to him, but she'd come back to me, her tutor—her angel.

Thirty-Seven

Christine watched my face intently during our trip down to my home. By the time we reached my boat, I'd finished Romeo's lines, and from there we were both quiet. There was much I wanted to say to her, but there was one huge distinction between what I wanted to say and what I could say without letting her know I'd been listening in on her conversation with Raoul. So I remained quiet.

We changed out of our costumes, and I was in the kitchen getting a glass of water when she came in. The serious expression on her face told me she had a heavy weight on her mind, and I could completely understand, considering their heated argument.

Then she said it. "Erik, I need to talk to you about something important."

Fearing the worst, I motioned toward the parlor. "Certainly. Shall we sit?"

All my fears were quickly washed away once she explained. "Someone at the ball told me Mummy has taken ill. I'd like to spend a few days with her. Would you wake me at six in the morning so I can be with her first thing?"

"Absolutely. Did this person describe the illness?"

"No, he didn't say. But I know she wasn't feeling her best when I left her last. I'm worried about her."

"Would this other person happen to be Raoul?"

She broke eye contact with me and looked down at her hands. "Yes." Then she looked back at me. "Thank you for not causing a scene and for not following us. When I saw Raoul on the Bois, I realized I wasn't being fair to him, and he was probably worried about me. I felt really bad about being childish and avoiding him for so long. I knew I needed to talk to him and let him know I was all right and what I was doing, and I needed to do that without anyone around, especially you. I didn't want there to be a confrontation between the two of you. I'm sorry I didn't talk to you about it first. I was just frightened and confused."

"I understand. And you certainly don't have to discuss everything with me, although I cherish it when you do. Was your conversation productive?"

She looked down at the blanket beside her and felt its fringe, thinking, and I waited for her to sort out her thoughts. When she looked back at me, I think she was holding back tears.

"Yes and no. It didn't go as I wanted it to, but it did give me insight into his thinking."

"Would you like to talk about it?"

"No, it tires me just to think about it, and I don't want to go over it again."

I nodded and changed the subject. "Since you're worried about Madame Valerius, do you want me to take you there now?"

"No, it's late, and I'm sure everyone is in bed. In the morning will be fine."

"Very well. Then I'll take you there in the morning."

"No, I need to go alone. By the time I get upstairs, Meg should be getting ready for rehearsals, and I want to talk to her. She asked me some questions at the ball. I couldn't answer her then, but I can now after talking to Raoul. If I go before rehearsals, there's less chance I'll run into Carlotta, and Meg won't have the time to corner me. I can answer her questions without having to go into too much detail."

My disapproval must have been written on my face, because she came back quickly.

"Don't look at me like that. I'll be fine. Talking to Raoul has given me courage. If I could confront him and everything he said, then I can confront Meg or Carlotta with confidence."

"Well, if you change your mind, you know where to find me," I said with a light-hearted flair. Then I added, "You'd better get to sleep. Morning will come soon."

"Thank you, Erik." Then she walked past me, again running her hand across my shoulder as she did so. "Thank you also for always being there for me. It's comforting to know I have someone close I can talk to without arguments."

"*Always* is the prime word, my dear. I'll *always* be there for you."

Her door closed, and I wondered if she was talking to her father's replacement or the man who loved her. There were still so many unanswered questions in my mind. After hearing that conversation between Raoul and Christine, I didn't know where I stood in her heart. I also remembered how fickle she'd been in Perros, one moment being terribly angry with him and the next minute kissing him.

It appeared my idea about the ball didn't work out well. I still didn't know her true feelings for me, but I did know more about my hatred for Raoul. If I never heard his name or never saw him again for the rest of my life, I would be blissfully happy. But I knew that wasn't going to happen any time soon.

I couldn't sleep, so I spent the night working on my mask and cleaning my music room. I'd neglected the proper maintenance of my instruments since Christine had come down, and that night was a good time to get it done.

When morning came, I went into her room to wake her, but, as I stood over her, I hesitated and seized the opportunity to watch her in silence. I went down on one knee and watched her breathe, she was so beautiful and I loved her so much. I glanced at the pillow on the other side of the bed and closed my eyes, picturing myself lying there holding her in my arms as she slept.

Oh, would that door ever be open to me? Would I ever be granted that privilege? I opened my eyes and gazed at her hand lying limp over the pillow, her left hand with my gold band on her finger. Would she ever be mine to keep?

Taking a much needed deep breath, I got to my feet, and ran my fingers across her cheek. "Christine—Christine, it's six a.m.—Christine."

She moaned, stirred, stretched, and I ached. "Time to get up, my sleepy angel."

Her eyes fluttered open and then closed again. "Thank you."

Then I made my exit before I lost control and was forced to take another cold bath. I had some tea and toast ready when she came into the kitchen, and we ate quickly before I took her across the lake. We were standing at the foot of the stairs, and I was stalling, since I didn't want her to go alone.

"I hope her illness is nothing serious. Also, remember I have a good working knowledge of natural oil remedies, and I know someone else who has a better one, so, if you think she might benefit from them, let me know. Be careful on the stairs. Sometimes they can be slippery. And if you see Carlotta, hold your head up. Remember, you'll shine twice as brightly. And don't let Meg dominate the conversation. Tell her what you're ready to tell her and nothing more. Also . . ."

"I know, Erik, I know," she interrupted with a smile. Then she laid her hand on my chest. "Thank you for your concern."

"Are you sure you don't want me to go up with you?"

"I'm sure. Today I have a good excuse for not talking to anyone, so I'll be fine. Besides, you're the one who said we can't be seen together."

I nodded and took her hand from my chest, kissing her fingers and the ring. Shortly, she was gone, and I felt truly uneasy. I waited until I couldn't hear her footfalls, and then I knew I couldn't let her go alone. So I quickly started following her, while listening carefully for any sound that might signal her distress.

I hadn't gone far when I heard steps coming down toward me. At first I smiled, thinking Christine was coming back, but then I realized they were too heavy for her steps, they were a man's steps. So I charged back down until I was at lake level and behind a column. I looked at the lit lantern in my boat, but I knew I didn't have enough time to extinguish it, so I remained hidden until I heard him leave the stairs.

My next thought was that it was Oded again, but I didn't recognize the strides as belonging to my friend either. When he was beyond the column I was hiding behind, I peeked around it and saw a man approaching the wharf—Raoul!

I moved back out of sight and pressed my head against the column, closing my eyes tightly. My thoughts went to Christine's words about not wanting to send anyone to their death by sending them to my home. I felt certain she wouldn't have betrayed me that quickly, so the only explanation was that he was waiting for her to unwittingly betray my location. In either case, I was angered to the point that I was getting a headache, and the fact that I had to make a quick decision wasn't helping either.

Do I remain quiet until he tires and leaves? Do I wait and give him a chance to try to find my lair—perhaps drowning in the process? Do I confront him once and for all and try to end his meddling?

He was on the wharf and looking down at my boat when I made my decision, so I moved from column to column until I was closer to him. Then I stepped out from behind the column and spoke to him.

"It can be dangerous to lose your way in a strange territory, *my boy*."

He jumped, gasped, and turned with my cold threat, and I smiled—but only inside. My exterior posture was absolutely serious, and I began walking parallel to his position, slowly. I kept my eyes on him across my shoulder and continued my taunt.

"Straying a bit far from your comfortable and *safe* home, aren't you, *young de Chagny*?"

When he finally gathered his wits, he asked, "You know my name?"

"Oh, yes," I replied confidently. Then I turned and started in a casual and yet deliberate pace toward him, all without breaking eye contact. "I know many things about you. I know your name as well as where you live. I know what you do with your extra time. I know who your friends are—and who your enemies are. I know where you go for holiday, and I know why you came down here to this unlikely habitat for the wealthy." By that time, he'd left the wharf and I was a meter away from him, glaring down into his eyes with my narrowed ones. "I know what it is you're looking for down here, and I know it isn't a bear."

Again I was smiling inside as I watched his breathing increase, and I could smell his fear.

"It's you! Erik, right? Your name is Erik. You're the deceiver."

"Deceiver?" I questioned, while taking a few backward steps with my hands spread out from my sides. "I deceive no one. I may be hard to find at times, but to anyone who really wants to know me, I am what I am, and I hide nothing. Now, if there are those who choose to believe outlandish stories instead of looking for the truth—well, what can I say? There will always be a measure of ignorant fools in the world."

He squinted at me. "You talk in riddles and make no sense."

I cocked my head. "As I said, there will always be a measure of ignorant fools in the world."

He took a step toward me, studying me. "You're old."

I laughed aloud, and, as if our bodies were chess pieces making one move at a time, I took a step toward him.

"I prefer to say I'm wise, since wisdom comes with age and is lost on the young, which you're proving by being down here where demons and ghosts are said to lurk."

"You can't hide your old age behind clever words."

"You seem to have a problem with the French language, don't you?" Without giving him a chance to respond, I continued. "Listen, my *young* de Chagny, age is relative. To Methuselah I'm young, very young, whereas to a newborn baby you're old, very old. Everything is relative, including wisdom. I would never give up the wisdom I've gained with my age for the foolish meandering of a young man. Meandering that, in his lack of wisdom, has led him to a place he should not be."

He took a step sideways, and I slipped my fingers through a coil when I heard the anger in his next words. "Leave her alone. You have nothing to offer her. You're nothing more than a tired old man."

"There you go again, using that relative label." I started walking circles around him while he turned to keep facing me. Speaking slowly, deliberately, and low, I rebutted, "An old man, *young* de Chagny? Have you not heard that there are certain things that are better with age? Cheese—wines—experience—*making love!*

"I can offer her more than you could ever imagine. And what do you have to offer her besides a pretty face, youth, and money? You know—youth and money are both greatly overrated. I've had both, so I speak from experience. One day your youth will be gone and with it your pretty face.

"As for your wealth, well, it doesn't take much, a fire, a war, or simply a disagreement with your aristocratic family, and everything you depend on could be gone. What then? What will you have left to give, my *young* de Chagny?" As I finished, I was right at his shoulder so I spoke softly in his ear. "What would you have to give her if something unexpected happened to your pretty face?"

He quickly moved away from me, glaring up at me. "You can't frighten me away, not that easily. I have so much more to offer her than you'll ever have. I can offer her my love and a respectable name. And you, you can offer her what?—A life of running from the police and living in darkness? Yes, I know all about your cold-blooded murders and how you're continually pursued."

Running my fingers over the coil, I resisted my urge to silence his arrogance permanently. I kept my eyes on him as I continued to walk back and forth in front of him. My voice was still controlled and low as I tried to warn him.

"If you want to listen to drunken men and silly girls, then you'll be underestimating the simplicity of the truth. But I strongly suggest that you never underestimate my ability to hold onto what is mine just because of my *old age*. This old man doesn't take lightly to being tested." Then I added with a sarcastic smile and tone, "Especially when it's past my nap time and I'm tired and cranky."

The foolish boy continued to taunt me with his haughty words and his overconfident body language. Then he dared to hold out one fist in front of him and waved it at me.

"If they're wrong and what you say is true, then why is it that you live behind a mask and lurk in the shadows?"

With his remark about my mask, a measure of my restraint slipped from me, causing my body to stiffen and my jaws to clench. Then, when I took one quick and long stride toward him, a measure of his confidence left him and he retreated to stay out of my reach.

With a deep breath I growled at him, "I've been forced to wear this mask and to lurk in the shadows, as you call it, because of *ignorant fools* like you! Now, I'm warning you, leave me alone. Leave my shadows so I can return to my lurking. I tire of this trivial conversation with your ignorant arrogance. Leave now while you still can. I won't warn you again."

There was an uncomfortable period of silence while we glared at each other. Then he nodded, turned his back on me, almost as if he was heading for the stairs. But when he turned back toward me, he had a smile on his face and a pistol in his hand.

I looked quickly at his weapon, enough to know it wasn't cocked, and then at his face, in a sickly and premature smile of conquest.

I shook my head at him and gave him a smile of my own. "Now, what do you expect to do with that, *you fool?*"

"Take you to the police and end your deception with Christine," he responded with a smirk on his face that was pushing me closer to the edge of my tolerance.

I snickered. "Your confidence in your manhood and your ability to hold onto Christine is surely lacking if you feel the need to have me behind bars before you can do so."

He started moving toward me with his voice raised in his half-grown victory. "Now, what was that you were warning me about? Warning me that you were going to kill . . ."

Before he could finish his sentence, the last of my patience was spent and my lasso sliced through the air and was around his neck. Then with one simple move, I was behind him, holding the lasso tight, but not tight enough to deprive him of air.

"Kill you, you ask?" I hissed.

I heard his pistol hit the ground as his hands clawed at his throat. My voice was low and cold, as I seethed my hatred for him directly into his ear.

"No! I'm not going to kill you, at least not right now. But can you see how easy it would be for me? You stupid fool, do you see how I hold your *young* life in my *old* hands? A few seconds longer, or tighter, and your life will be snuffed out, just as easily as I blow out one of my candles. But, I let you live this day, not because I care about your puny life, but because I care about Christine, and for some unknown reason she wouldn't want your life to end."

I loosened the noose just enough for him to breathe easier, while I again whispered in his ear, "Do you see now how easy it would be for me? I haven't kept track of all the times I've had you in my sights, *young man*, and I haven't the patience or the inclination to explain all of them to you.

"I can only suggest that you take my advice and not come down here again. I can't guarantee the next trip will go as well as this one, with you still on your feet and breathing. So I advise you not to tempt me further. This *old man* may not always be as benevolent as he was that night in Perros or this day. If you value your life at all, don't enter my domain again."

I jerked on the coil for emphasis. "Are you smart enough to believe what I say?" Still holding his throat securely, I pulled him backwards a few meters toward the well and warned him again. "Or do I have to drag you to the same place I buried another man who thought he could capture me like a hunter's trophy?"

At that threat, he held both of his palms out from his sides and whispered, "All right—All right."

I let him go completely and shoved him away from me, kicking his pistol into the lake at the same time. He coughed a few times while rubbing his neck, and then he just stared at me. As silence fell over the lake, I coiled my lasso, just in case he was a bigger fool than I thought. We held our sights on each other, and I contemplated remaining quiet or speaking further to him. Then, once again, my concern for Christine moved in and became the stronger of my desires.

"My advanced age, which you've so thoughtfully reminded me of, has given me well-developed knowledge when it comes to human nature. So I advise you to use what I'm going to tell you with wisdom. Christine is an adult and a highly intelligent and compassionate woman who has a mind of her own. I respect her for that, and so should you."

I motioned toward the stairs. "Did you see her when she left here? Did you talk to her? Did you see her face? Did she look as if I had her in chains? She is free to come and go from here just as often as she wishes. I hold no physical bonds on her. What holds her to me is something you would never understand, and I in no way intend to explain it to you."

I shook my head. "To try to explain it to you would be akin to explaining to an ant the functions of the sun and moon. Just take my word for it. There's something between us that you can't possibly comprehend."

I scowled at him. "I shouldn't be giving you this advice, *you arrogant fool*. I should let you have all the rope you want until you strangle yourself with it. And if I were only thinking about our animosity toward each other, then I would keep quiet and watch you kill what affection she has for you. But what I say is about something larger than the two of us put together. It's for Christine."

He was still staring at me, and for the first time I glanced at the lake in a moment of thought before I looked back at him and continued. "Don't press Christine too hard to make a decision between the two of us. It will only backfire on you, or you could do the woman I love irreversible harm.

"You can't force the petals of a rose to open too quickly or the rose will be ruined and no one will be able to enjoy its beauty. Don't push Christine, Raoul. Let her make her own decision, and then it will be obvious who the better man is in *her* eyes, not yours and not mine."

I walked up close to him and looked directly and strongly into his eyes. "Don't do anything further to hurt Christine. I don't like it when she's distressed. It angers me, and to see her shed tears . . . well, let me just say that it doesn't put me in a very good mood.

"The sting you're experiencing on your neck right now is the result of only a tip of my temper being released. You don't want to be around or know what happens when I'm really angered." I backed away from him and crossed my arms across my chest. "Now, leave here and never come back."

As I waited for him to respond, he looked at the lake, he looked at me, he looked toward the stairs, he looked back at me, and then with a deep breath, he turned and headed for the stairs. I held my position until he was out of sight and for a few more minutes for safety.

I was in a terrible mood by the time I returned home. My encounter with that fool kept replaying in my mind and joined with memories of Christine's argument with him. I was so angry with him and his arrogance that I could hardly think. However, I was somewhat pleased with my own actions. I might have allowed him to anger me, but he was still alive. That was a great accomplishment, considering how much I hated everything he represented.

I began playing my music to calm my nerves, but I soon realized I needed to get out of my home and do something to get my mind off Raoul. So I headed for César, but that thought was thwarted instantly. There were four grooms and two officers guarding him, making my head hurt even more.

I was so angry by the time I got home again that I nearly lost my temper completely. My furnishings were only rescued because I refused to let those men control me. They weren't going to make me a prisoner in my own home, so I changed into my riding clothes, grabbed all my water canteens, all the cash I had on hand, and a hand full of jewels from my old chest and cloak. Then I moved fast but not hastily toward the passage leading to my outside door.

I didn't like using that door during daylight hours, but I managed to leave without being seen. Soon I was in a brougham and heading for the livery, and shortly after that I was on a horse and leaving the city. When I could do so without attracting undue attention, I ran the sorrel I was riding and finally felt relief. I hadn't had a good run with a horse in a long time, not since that last newspaper article about César's disappearance.

When I knew I'd run him long enough, I dismounted and walked him out. I kept walking with him until we were both cooled down, and then I found a brook and a nice tree with tender new grass growing under it. After putting a lead around the sorrel's neck, I removed his bridle so he could enjoy the grass without that piece of metal in his mouth. Then, while he grazed, I sat beside him and enjoyed his sounds and smell and the peaceful countryside.

I'd nearly forgotten how much I missed my hoofed friends and the great outdoors. Regardless of what Christine's decision was, I knew then that I had to leave the opera house. I wanted horses back in my life, but then I remembered the reason I was living where I was, and I began to feel trapped again. Fortunately, I told myself, no, I won't think about that right now. My time with the sorrel was too peaceful to complicate it with my torturous thoughts.

While I was sitting there, I smoothed out my plans for that special night with Christine, and I used the rest of the day to prepare for it. I eventually mounted again and headed for Obert and Roland to let them know I wouldn't need them for a few days. Then I went back to the city where I shopped for that night.

I found the red evening dress I wanted for her, and I also found a jeweler who could make the hair combs and necklace I had in mind out of the rubies I'd brought with me. While I was there, I looked over his selection of ladies watches and decided to get one for her. The jewelry would take a couple of days to finish, but the engraving I wanted on the inside of the watchband he did while I waited. Then I went to my favorite restaurant and ordered our special dinner. From there, I went to see Joubert.

"Have you found out how much Dominick needs for the paving of the street?" I asked as I walked into his kitchen.

"Yes, and he didn't look suspicious when I asked him. But I don't think that will be the case when I give him the money."

"Just do the best you can. If the truth comes out, I'll deal with it at that time."

I gave him the money, and he made us hot chocolate, and then we talked. He willingly answered more of my Bible questions and even gave me scriptures to look up when I returned home. He was such an easy man to talk to, and I would have stayed longer but I wanted to visit with Lapierre and Geanne before I left the area.

They were pleased that I'd returned so soon, but they weren't pleased that I hadn't brought Christine with me. Geanne insisted that I have a piece of cherry pie and tea while we talked about their new grandchild. As usual, their company made me feel warm inside and helped to erase my vengeful feelings towards Raoul.

I stayed there until an hour before sundown, and then I headed home. It was dark by the time I'd returned the sorrel and made it to the opera house. I was thinking it would be easy to slip in through my secret door, it usually was after dark, but it wasn't that night.

I'm not sure what had happened, but there were police patrolling the walkways circling the opera house. I couldn't help but wonder if Raoul had had anything to do with it. I stayed a block away, leaning against a corner, and watched the patrols. Again, the actions of the police department were absolutely absurd. They made it so easy to evade them.

After a half an hour, I had their patrol pattern down and moved in closer, waiting for my chance to sneak behind their lines and into my secret door. Their presence made it more of a challenge for me, but it didn't stop me by any means.

Since I smelled like sweat and horses, I decided to take a bath in the tub as Christine had ordered, and, at first, it was relaxing. But since I was surrounded by all her things, it made me miss her, so my bath wasn't a long one. While I dressed, I realized the next few days were going to be extremely long and lonesome. To overcome that problem, I decided to spend them working on Don Juan, and, so I wouldn't lose myself in my music and forget to eat, I made a plate of food and a pot of tea and took them to my music room.

Before I got started, I took Christine's watch out of my cloak pocket and put it in my armoire. While I was there, my sight fell on the green, velvet bag with my mother's locket, so I opened it and looked at it. Memories of my conversation with Celeste visited me, and I felt even more alone.

I was in that thought process when I heard something behind me, and I instantly dropped the locket and turned. There was someone on the other side of my secret door, and I automatically reached into my pants pocket for a lasso, but it was empty. I grabbed the one from my other pants, the one I'd used on Raoul, and another one in my cloak. Then I faced the door, and, with a coil in each hand, I waited.

By then the door was opening slowly, and the tapestry over it was swaying. Triggered by the happenings of the day, with Raoul and so many police on the premises, many scenarios flashed through my mind. Had Raoul found his way down? Had the police found my passage? Had Christine betrayed me?

Thirty-Eight

With the coils steady in my hands and my heart beating steady in my chest, I was prepared for whatever awaited me behind the tapestry. It moved, and I heard Christine's concerned voice.

"Erik, are you there?"

Without moving, and preparing to see or hear Raoul, I answered guardedly, "Yes."

"Then could you please help me?" she asked, with frustration growing in her voice.

I moved toward the tapestry and cautiously pulled it back; what I saw made me laugh softly. She was flattened between the heavy tapestry and the wall with her hair all a muss and in her face. While chuckling, I slid my lassos into my pockets and released the hanging from the wall.

"Perhaps I should leave this down, yes?"

I laid it over my coffin with the other one. When I turned back toward her, she was still by the invisible door with her hands on her hips and her hair in her face.

"I still need your help, Erik," she said, as she gestured toward the floor on her right side.

Then I saw the cause of her frustration. The hem of her dress was closed in the door, and, from the position she was in, she couldn't reach the latch to open the door again. I went to her rescue, trying not to laugh as I removed a few gold tendrils from her face and opened the door.

"Thank you," she huffed.

"You know, Christine, I warned you about trying to maneuver those steps in a dress."

"You men," she snapped, taking me aback. "You think we can't do anything on our own. Don't forget, I'm a dancer, and my legs are as strong and as steady as a cedar tree. In addition, women can maneuver quite easily in a dress, we've been walking in them from our first steps, so it's natural and not difficult by any means. Now, you men, on the other hand, I'm sure you would be completely helpless in a dress. That would be an interesting experiment, don't you think? I'd like to see you in my dress and then try to climb those stairs. I bet you wouldn't be your powerful and agile figure for long, and you wouldn't be laughing either."

"It's all right, Christine. I'm sorry. Calm down. I have to agree, you're probably right, but, even though I'm fond of experimenting, I think I'll pass on this one."

Still not satisfied, she continued her angry defense. "Besides, it wasn't the stairs or my dress, it was that ridiculous tapestry. Why do you have it hanging there anyway?"

"I like it. I think it's a restful scene, don't you?"

She shook her head and snapped again. "Perhaps, but that's a preposterous place to hang something that large. For a man who's supposed to be intelligent, you didn't show it when you chose that wall for it to hang on. Why don't you put it somewhere else—out of the way?"

"Christine! Calm down. What's wrong? This isn't like you. I have a feeling this isn't about the tapestry or the steps or your dress or men. What's happened?"

She sighed and sat down on the piano bench, looking quite dejected. "I don't know. I think I need to visit Mummy more often. I suppose she's just getting old. She looked so frail in her bed, and it reminded me too much of my . . . of my father before he died. I hate the thought of losing her. Oh, I'm only being a baby," she said softly, while looking at the ribbon on her dress sliding between her fingers. "I should have stayed with her longer, but I needed to come home to you and your encouragement."

I gazed at her with a heart full of love. Once more she used those words. She considered my home her home and she said she needed me, which was almost as important as saying she loved me, or maybe it was more important.

"Christine," I said as I picked up my plate of food and the teapot. "Why don't I get you a cup of tea and we can sit by the fire? Then you tell me more about your visit?"

Once we got settled, the real reason why she was so troubled was revealed.

"I enjoy looking after her, that never bothers me. I think what really disturbed me was Raoul showing up. He was so accusatory."

My heart quickened, and I prepared for my defense. I felt for sure he must have told her about our encounter by the lake and probably accused me of trying to kill him again. But if he had, she didn't mention it, and it goes without saying that I didn't question her about it either.

She gazed into the fire while twisting my ring on her finger, and her voice expressed the degree of her hurt and anger.

"When he saw this, he became so angry. Then, when I wouldn't explain what it meant and that it was none of his business, he said such hurtful things. He accused me of horrible deeds—and you too. I don't know how he could think such awful things. They were even worse than what he accused us of at the ball." She took a deep breath and shook her head. "All I could think about was coming back here. He can't find me here. I'm afraid to go back there, but I know I need to for Mummy's sake."

By then, I was also gazing into the fire and trying to put out the flames in my thoughts. I wanted to find him and give him a stronger lesson. But the only stronger lesson would involve death, so that wasn't an option. I was also tempted to use her anger with him and bring out more of his bad qualities, but, knowing Christine the way I did, I knew she would only come to his defense, so, for a while, I remained quiet on that subject.

"Christine, I want you to know that my natural inclination is to find him and give him a lesson in proper decorum. But . . ."

"Oh, no, Erik. Please don't," she begged. "I shouldn't have said anything to you."

"Christine, listen to me," I said softly. "What I was going to say was that I couldn't go to him because I know you don't want me to. You have nothing to fear on my part. Besides, I highly doubt he would listen to anything I'd say anyway. Please, don't hold back from talking to me on that account. I want to be here for you."

She nodded. "Thank you. Now I just need to decide what to do."

"Would you like my advice?"

"Yes, that's why I came back."

"Then tell me—if Raoul weren't in the picture, what would you be doing right now?"

"I'd be taking care of Mummy."

"Then, if that's what your heart is telling you to do, you need to do it." She laid her forehead in her hand and shook her head. "Christine, let me tell you something I've learned during my life. Money has a strange power over most people. The rich think they're better than those without money, and the poor think they're worthless because they don't have it, when, in reality, they're no different. If you stripped the clothes from both sets of people and gave them a bath and a haircut, you couldn't tell one from the other—they're all the same. It's only their money or lack of it that sets them apart.

"Now, you may not want to hear what I'm going to say, but hear me out. Raoul, through no fault of his own, was born to parents who had money, so he was brought up believing he was better than those without it. Along with that belief comes a domineering spirit. I'm certain he was taught from an early age how to order servants around. His word became law, so when anyone opposes that law he doesn't know how to conduct himself.

"You've shown Raoul that you have a mind of your own and don't necessarily want to live by that law, and his only way to express his frustration is to get angry with you. I'm not saying he's right in doing so, but that's *why* he's doing it. If you stick by what you believe in your heart and don't back down from him, he'll do one of two things. He'll either learn to respect you for having your own will or he'll despise you because of it. You need to be ready for either outcome.

"Don't let Raoul stop you from going to Madame Valerius and caring for her. You have a right to do that, and he shouldn't be a reason for not doing it. Don't back down from him, Christine. Remember, without clothes we're all the same, so don't let him make you cower just because he shows a superior attitude. Show him your strength. Show him he's no better than you are.

"Don't let him hurt you by the things he says. I know that may not be easy, especially for someone like you who holds your heart on your sleeve, but it's the only way to deal with someone like Raoul. If you don't want to talk to him, then tell him so and show him the door—or don't let him in to begin with. If he doesn't show respect for you, he doesn't deserve to be in your company.

"And, one more thing. Watch out for a repeating scenario. If he hurts you and then comes back on bended knee, that's a good sign. But if it's repeated over and over again, it's a bad sign, and it will never change. If that happens, you have to decide if you're willing to put up with the hurt or leave it.

"In the end, all the choices are yours to make. Don't let him or anyone else make them for you. Not even me, Christine. It's your life, and you only have one to live, so don't live it in fear or in hurt."

She agreed and thanked me, and then I heated up our tea and gave her chocolates to her. We talked for hours after that, and she decided to go back to Madame Valerius' home in the morning. Eventually, she started yawning, and we decided to call it a night. She headed for the music room to get her cloak, and I took our plates and cups into the kitchen. When I came out of the kitchen, she was walking toward me, looking down at her hands.

"Erik, I found this on the floor," she said as she looked up at me. "I'm not being curious—honest. I just didn't think you would want this on the floor."

By then we'd met in the dining room, and she handed me my mother's locket.

"You're right. I must have dropped it. Thank you," I replied while heading for my armoire to replace it, but then I glanced over my shoulder when I got to the door. She was still standing in the dining room and watching me, and I knew she was curious, regardless of what she said, so I asked, "Do you want to know about this locket?"

She nodded and started walking toward me. "This is a locket I gave my mother when I was just a boy. When you and I made that trip to Perros, the friend I told you about gave it to me. Does that appease your curiosity?"

"Yes, thank you."

When I put the locket back in its velvet bag, I saw and remembered Christine's gift. "Here," I said as I handed it to her, "this one is for you."

Her eyes widened, but then she shook her head. "You really need to stop buying me things, Erik."

"You give me one good reason why I shouldn't buy you trinkets, and then I'll consider it."

"Because you've already given me too much, that's why."

"No, I said a good reason. That's not a good reason."

She smiled and opened the box. "Oh! Erik! This is gorgeous. I've never seen such a beautiful watch. This had to cost you a fortune."

I was smiling from ear to ear while she examined it. It was stunning, and that's why I wanted it for her. Its face was delicate and was surrounded by two rows of diamonds that sparkled and made the white gold also sparkle. The band was nearly solid, with only one section that expanded to fit over the hand. The inside of the band is where I had the jeweler put the inscription.

"I'm glad you like it. Now you won't have to ask me what time it is so often. Look at the inscription."

She turned it toward the light and read it. "Until the last hour of forever~~my heart is yours." She looked up at me and barely shook her head. "Oh, Erik, what can I say? I love it. It's perfect."

"Just like you, my dear," I replied softly while running the back of my fingers down her cheek.

Then she started bubbling over like the excitable schoolgirl she became from time to time. "Oh, I can wait to show Mummy—Oh, and Meg. I can't wait."

When she finally calmed down, we retired to our respective beds, and then, during breakfast the next morning, she told me her decisions.

"I thought a lot about all you said last night, and you're right. I don't like confrontations—they hurt, but if that's what it's going to take to make Raoul understand my position, then that's what I'll have to do. These weeks I've spent with you have been like a fairytale, and I've felt like the princess in it, but it's time to close the book and come back to reality.

"I'd like you to take me across the lake again so I can wear this dress. It's one of my favorites, and I also think it's dignified, and I want to look dignified when I talk to our new managers. I'm going to tell them I want lead roles or I'll be leaving." She scrunched her face and shoulders, and asked, "Do you think that's too strong? Would you suggest a better approach?"

I smiled at her. "No, my dear. That approach is perfect, and the dress is also perfect for the occasion. I'm proud of you. It's time you stood up for yourself, and I'm pleased you now realize it."

"Good. Then that's what I'm going to do. If they accept my demands, I'll be starting back in rehearsals soon, but I want to continue my lessons with you, if that's all right."

"You know it is and always will be." Then, taking a chance, I asked her, "Have you thought any more about Raoul?"

"Yes. I'm going to give him one more chance. I'm going to tell him exactly what I want out of my life. I'm going to tell him I want to stay at the opera house and perform. I'm going to tell him about you and how I feel about you, and that I'll be visiting you just as often as I want. If he doesn't like it, then he doesn't have to see me anymore. I'm also going to let him know that I'm not his property, so he has no right to accuse me of any wrongdoing. I simply won't put up with it any longer."

Nodding in thought, I replied to her decisions, "I see. I hope he doesn't give you more problems. And while we're talking about your life and decisions, there's another special evening I've planned, but, if it interferes with your new schedule, I can change the night."

"I'll know more after I talk to the managers and Gabriel. When I do, I'll be able to schedule my time with Mummy and you. Can I let you know then?"

"Certainly. Well, my dear, it sounds as if you have it all worked out. I'm proud of you."

She thanked me for the encouragement, and we began her lessons. After that, I took her across the lake and part way up the stairs. Then I kissed her fingers and the ring and told her I hoped her day went as planned. She turned and started up the stairs, and I turned and started down, but I was much too curious and concerned to continue. So I slipped into one of my passages and went to our managers' office and waited for Christine's appearance.

I was once again pleased with her actions. She talked to them with respect and almost like a true diva, minus the arrogance. She had no problem getting what she wanted, especially since Carlotta had refused to come back to the stage since her visit with the toad. She even was trying to get out of her contract, and I had to place my fingers over my smiling lips, feeling quite accomplished.

From there she went to the rehearsal studio and waited until Gabriel was free to talk to her. She told him what was happening, and he was also pleased. It appeared he'd been having problems with Carlotta's understudy and was beside himself with frustration. He suggested she start rehearsals the next day, and she could start in the productions when they both felt she was ready.

While she was in the studio, she also talked to Meg. They were too far away for me to hear them, but it looked as if Christine was telling her about the gifts I'd given her. She held her skirt out and turned in a circle, and then showed her the new watch. They talked for a few minutes, hugged, and then Christine left. I followed her until she was in a brougham and drove away.

Excellent, was my thinking. It looked as if the day was going to go her way, and it made me smile on my way home. I hadn't gone far when I realized I had no reason to go home, but I did have a reason to stay on the main levels. I'd been so busy with Christine since the gala that I hadn't taken the time to get to know my new managers, and I knew the importance of knowing my opponents before doing battle with them.

Therefore, I stayed in that area and listened in on every conversation I could. I listened to workers, ballerinas, Madame Giry, and my managers. When they left to have lunch, I snuck into their office and went through their files. After several hours of reading and listening, I'd found out all I needed to know about them and what they were currently doing.

Armand Moncharmin knew nothing about music and was more of a silent partner while Firmin Richard was a distinguished composer in his own right. He'd published a number of successful pieces. But he also had a nasty temper, so he was the one I needed to focus most of my attention on.

They'd been selling my box on a regular basis, and my wages were overdue, causing me to think, how quickly they forgot about the chandelier disaster. But then perhaps it was partially my fault for neglecting my note writing, which would have kept my wishes in the forefront of their thoughts. I knew I had to start whipping them into shape, but the timing was wrong. I was still too focused on Christine and her success on the stage, and in her personal life, so I needed to wait until I could talk to her again before starting anything with our managers.

I was home for about two hours when I heard Christine enter the music room, and, in an instant, I was on my feet and joined her there. Then

I chose my words carefully, since I couldn't let on that I already knew how part of her day went.

"Well, Christine, you look much better today than you did yesterday."

"And I feel much better also. The managers agreed to my demands easily, and I felt such relief."

"That's wonderful, Christine. I knew you could do it. And how did it go at Madame Valerius'?"

"It went well there also. Mummy is so sweet. I explained I would be spending more time here rehearsing and performing, and she understood without complaint. When I told her I would be in lead roles, she was even more pleased. She gave all the credit to my angel, and she was right in doing so. I wouldn't be where I am if it weren't for you."

By then, she'd walked up to me and placed her hand on my chest. That familiar action of hers made my heart smile, and I laid my hand over hers and gently squeezed it.

"And you wouldn't be where you are if it weren't for you. It's your voice. All I did was direct it."

"No, it's more than my voice. You gave me confidence. Without that confidence, I couldn't sing, and I think you know that."

I nodded. "And what about Raoul? Did you see him today?"

She removed her hand and sighed deeply. "No, he didn't show, and Mummy didn't say he'd been there."

"Now, about your schedule, do I keep my plans for a special evening tomorrow night or do I cancel it?"

"Tomorrow night will be fine. I probably won't be performing for a few days."

We went in by the fire and talked more until she left for bed, while I sat there for a long time, thinking and making the final arrangements for our special evening. The next morning when she headed for rehearsals and then a visit with Madame Valerius, I headed out to do my errands. When I got back, I put her packages on her bed, three black boxes tied with red silk ribbons. After I got everything ready for our meal, I spent the rest of the day composing something inspired by Christine's new zeal for life. That's where I was when I heard her coming down the steps toward my music room.

She smiled when she saw me sitting at my piano, and I smiled when I saw her in that little boy costume.

"Working on something new?" she asked.

"As a matter of fact, yes I am. Again, you inspired me," I replied while getting to my feet and taking a tapestry satchel from her hands. "And what is this?"

"Just some things I needed, and my green dress is in there also. I didn't want to leave it in my dressing room."

"You seem in better spirits tonight," I commented while following her into the parlor. "Did things go better today? Did you have that talk with Raoul?"

"I'm not sure if they went better or not. I did have a nice time with Mummy. I gave her that leopard statue and she was so thrilled, and she's really enjoying the book. But I didn't have that talk with Raoul; however, I did see him, and I'm sure he saw me."

She stopped and turned toward me with her hands on her hips. "Can you believe it? He sat in his coach up the block from Mummy's home for over two hours, I'm sure just waiting for me to do something wrong. He doesn't trust me, and he must think I'm an idiot not to recognize his team and coach. I think that angers me more than his out and out accusations. He was spying on me as if I were his chattel."

She huffed and shook her head while I stammered, knowing I'd done exactly the same thing. "Hmm, that's interesting. Perhaps, it's not so much that he doesn't trust you as much as he doesn't trust me."

She shook her head adamantly and spoke just as strongly. "No, no. It's the same thing. If he trusted me, he wouldn't have to worry about you. No, he doesn't trust me to make the right decisions and to handle myself if necessary, and that angers me."

Since I was feeling quite guilty, I tried to change the subject. "Well," I said as I walked up to her and took her hands from her hips and held them between us. "No more anger tonight. I want you to relax. You're starting off on a new and exciting career, and we're going to celebrate in a fine fashion." I ran my fingers across her forehead and then shook them. "I want you to wipe all thought of Raoul out of your mind and enjoy the evening. Can you do that?"

"Yes, I can," she replied with determination and then headed for her room.

I followed her since I wanted to see her reaction to her presents. She opened the door, and, shortly after she turned on her light, she gasped.

"Erik! You must stop this!" she exclaimed. Then she turned and looked at me. "But I know you won't, right?"

"I can't stop. Every time I see something beautiful I think about you, and I just have to get it. Please, don't make me stop."

"Very well," she said softly while placing her palm on my cheek.

When she opened the large box and saw the red evening gown, she actually got tears in her eyes.

"It's the most beautiful gown I've ever seen. Thank you so much."

Then she rushed toward me and gave me a big hug before s
up against her chest and turned in circles. When she'd examined
to her satisfaction, she sat in her chair and opened the other boxes. Unlike
the dress, when she saw the ruby necklace and hair combs, she was almost
speechless and sat quietly running one finger over them.

"They're so gorgeous. I don't know what to say or how to thank you."

"The expression on your face is all the thanks I need. Now, you take
all the time you want to relax and get ready, but, again, give me at least an
hour to get prepared. Understand?"

She gave me another hug and then looked up at me, but only for a few
seconds. I couldn't take more than that without having to take another
cold bath, so I left and prepared for the evening. After I got myself ready in
my best evening attire, I set the table with a white linen cloth and candles.
At the turn of the hour, the place was lit by only candles and the fire, and
the food had been warmed and was on the table along with one of my best
wines.

Then I leaned against the doorframe to my music room and waited.
After about ten minutes, her door opened and she stepped out. At that
time, my heart stopped, my lungs stopped, and I believe all brain activity
also stopped. She was radiant. No, she defied description, and all I could do
was stare at her. She moved across the room toward me like a goddess, and
I could swear there were clouds encircling her.

"Do you like it?" she asked, while holding her arms out from her sides
and turning slowly.

I stepped toward her and shook my head. "I love every bit of it—every
bit of you." I took her hands in mine and kissed them repeatedly, since I
didn't dare think about kissing her ruby lips. "You make all the goddesses
in the universe envious tonight, my angel. I've never seen a more lovely
vision—and neither have they."

Then she turned from me and looked over her shoulder, batting her
eyelashes. "Why, *monsieur*, you surely make me blush."

In that instant I knew I was in serious trouble. I'd like to say I had a
wonderful evening, but I didn't. I was miserable from beginning to end.
She was breathtaking. She'd swept her hair up on top of her head and held
it in place with the gold and ruby combs, completely revealing her soft and
sensuous neck. A few tendrils hung loose on her neck and around her face,
and I would normally sweep them back, but I didn't dare come that close
to her right then.

Once she was sitting, the small lace sleeves fell from her shoulders,
revealing the creamy skin of her bare neckline and décolletage. It was there
that the ruby teardrop hung from a delicate gold chain, much too close to

those smooth curves. Like a child sneaking a cookie, when she looked away, I snuck repeated glances at her feminine beauty and wanted to caress her so badly.

Therefore, I spent the entire time fighting my desires, so much so that I don't even remember what we talked about. While I watched her talking, with the candlelight flickering on her perfect complexion and her golden hair, I made the decision never to buy her another dress or prepare a special evening like that one.

Somehow, it bought out the seductive side of her—or maybe it was the red dress coupled with my growing weakness, I'm not sure, but I couldn't put myself through another evening of torture like that again. It was too dangerous. I was nearly going mad with passion, and my thoughts were far from gentlemanly.

She smiled across the table and acted so flirtatious and alluring, as if she actually knew what she was doing to me, but I'm sure she didn't. My thoughts almost embarrassed me, so, if she had any idea what was going through my mind, I'm certain her face would turn just as red as her dress.

I'd fought many battles in my life, but none was as hard as the one I fought that night. I wanted her so badly, and in every way possible. And, what made it worse, I knew if I maneuvered the situation properly, I could seduce her and end up in her bed before the night was out, and that's where I battled the hardest. I knew I had powers, and if I locked my sights on something I wanted I could always attain it, and that night my sights were locked on her.

Since I first met her, I'd gone through advancing stages of love, and I believe I'd managed to conquer each of them successfully, but what I felt that night was new, and it frightened me terribly. I'd had to take cold baths to overcome my lustful desires fueled by love, but right then a cold bath would be as impotent as death.

I can only explain it as being akin to my anger. My violent anger was fearsome to anyone watching me, but my controlled anger was much more dangerous and death-dealing. Oded had questioned if I was seducing her, and I could honestly say I wasn't, at least not intentionally. But that evening the stakes had changed, and I was on a deliberate path of seduction before I realized it. Then, once I realized it, my full power was in play, and I knew she was no more than clay in a sculptor's hands—my hands. For the first time, I saw myself lying on that pillow beside her—not as a wish but as a reality.

It's strange how the most unlikely thoughts or memories can surface at the most inopportune times. While taking her hand from across the table and kissing it tenderly, I thought about my father and his conversation with our doctor about my birth. He said it was his lack of discipline that led to it, which led to my mother's guilt and fear, which in turn partially led to my lonely life.

In addition, I also thought about the role I'd coached her in so often, the role of Marguerite. If I took her to her bed and she became pregnant and then something happened to me, I would be leaving her as a living Marguerite. My insides trembled at that thought. So, with my lips pressed against her tender hand, I knew I couldn't do that to the woman I loved.

In the end, it was my love for Christine that saved us both from what could have been a terrible mistake. That one act could have destroyed any respect she had for me. I loved her too much to treat her the way Raoul believed I would or already had. I didn't want to lie beside her for only one night—I wanted to lie beside her for the rest of our lives.

Thirty-Nine

For almost a month, we continued in our new routine. She'd have a small breakfast and a short lesson with me to warm up her voice, go to rehearsal, spend a few hours in the afternoon with Madame Valerius or Raoul, who was temporarily keeping his thoughts to himself, be back at the opera house to perform, and then come back to me for a simple late supper by the fire before retiring.

She wanted to spend the house's dark days with me, and that pleased my heart. Since she needed to rest her voice those days, she only had her lesson if there was a problem she was trying to work out, but even then it was a short one. We would spend the day playing chess, reading a new book, cooking, and usually going on a carriage ride in the evening.

I stayed away from my home as much as possible when Christine was gone, it was simply too quiet. So I'd take long rides in the countryside on the back of a horse or conjure up ways to whip my new managers into shape. My wages remained overdue and my box was still being sold on a regular basis, and I wasn't going to allow them to continue in their neglect. So I did what the Opera Ghost was famous for—I wrote them a note.

My Dear Managers,

I believe you've had sufficient time to settle into your new positions; therefore, I'm now reminding you about a matter you must have overlooked. I trust your intelligence would prevent you from trying to test my power, especially after the costly repair of our magnificent chandelier.

If you'll recall, your predecessors showed you clause sixty-three, the additional clause to the building's lease. Now just because it's an addition doesn't make it any less important than the rest of the contract. That clause is just as significant as the section regarding the lighting, the props and sets, the security, and the use of certain sections of the building, such as the foyer of the ballet that was used the night of the gala. If certain aspects of the lease are neglected, then use of those props or premises could be rescinded, which would make producing an opera extremely difficult.

You might consider my demands to have Box Five reserved for my use as being of little concern to you, but, I can assure you, it's of no little concern to me. It's quite disturbing to arrive at the opera and have nowhere to sit comfortably. I really dislike having to wander around and miss out on a line here and there. It's most distracting.

In addition, for any true lover of opera, which I'm certain most of your patrons are, it's rather unsettling to be disturbed during a performance. It almost makes you wish you hadn't bothered to attend at all and perhaps even reconsider ever attending again. Therefore, to make sure my wanderings don't distract someone else, I recommend you make certain I have somewhere to sit—namely Box Five.

And, by the way, I now have a lady friend who'd like to attend the opera with me, so if you would be so kind as to provide her with a small stool for her feet, we would both appreciate that kind gesture. And while you're supplying me with the stool you might as well supply me with my wages for the month also, considering they're late. Just leave it in the usual place on the shelf in my Box Five.

I look forward to an uneventful and successful performance this evening. I so hate a scandal and the effort it takes to create one. I much prefer to live in peace and harmony—don't you?
Respectfully yours,
O.G.
P.S. Enclosed is your misplaced watch. I hope when you look at it you'll be reminded about the importance of always taking the time to consider my needs.

I delivered the note and then waited for them to enter and read it. It took a while, but it was worth the wait in order to understand their thinking. After reading my note, they called in Madame Giry and questioned her about the history of Box Five.

"The former managers," she began, "learned the hard way that the Opera Ghost always gets what he wants, so they stopped trying to prevent him from having his Box Five to sit in during the performances. Over the years, I've learned to understand him well, and I know he's unhappy about the way you're behaving, namely selling his private box to someone else. When he's pleased, he leaves me a token of his appreciation, so, since I haven't heard from him in a long time, I know he's displeased with the way his opera house is being managed."

If she had left it at that, I think they might have given consideration to her advice, but she continued in a direction that put them on the defensive.

"I don't understand how two men of your station can be so stupid and stubborn when the Opera Ghost isn't asking for that much. Everything here at the opera house would run smoothly if you'd stop trying to fight against his wishes."

"Stupid?" Firmin shouted.

"Stubborn?" Armand chimed in.

"Listen, lady, we're not stupid," Firmin angrily shouted. "We know you're in league with the former managers. We've heard about their sense of humor, and we don't think anything they're doing is funny. We know they're the ones who want Box Five left open for them, and you can call us stubborn if you like, but we have no intention of falling for their pranks again."

Pranks, I thought. Is that what they think this is all about? Well, perhaps I needed to give them a reminder along with more proof of my existence.

Christine was performing the lead in *Faust* that night, and, while I hated to cause a disturbance in anything related to her career, I couldn't let my managers continue to think I was nonexistent. Therefore, I dressed for the evening and arrived in the column at the beginning of the second act. Much to my surprise, the box was empty. I entered, and after making sure the door was locked, I sat down and prepared to watch Christine for the first time from my box.

I was there about fifteen minutes when I heard a key in the lock. Instantly, I was on my feet, had grabbed my cloak, and was through the column just as the door opened. To say I was irritated wouldn't cover what I was feeling when a young couple came in, preparing to enjoy the rest of the opera. I don't think so, was my first thought, so, before they had a chance to sit down, I began.

"This box is already taken."

They looked at each other and then around. The woman shrugged her shoulders, and the young man took her wrap and stood at the back of her chair until she sat down.

Shaking my head, I tried again. "Did you not hear me? This box is already taken."

Again they looked at each other, and then the man went to the door and looked outside. When he didn't see anything, he came back in and sat down.

I took a deep breath and silently apologized to Christine for disturbing her role as Marguerite, and then I started laughing loudly. The couple looked at each other, and I kept laughing until an usher came in and asked them to please be quiet. They tried to tell him that it wasn't them laughing. The usher left, and within a minute I started laughing again. Once more the usher came in and asked them to please be quiet, and again they tried to explain that they weren't the ones who were laughing. One more time, the same scenario occurred, and that time when the usher came in he told the couple they had to leave.

The young man became irate and refused to leave, which meant they were then creating their own disturbance by their arguing, and I smiled. The usher left, the man sat back down, and I started laughing again. The next time the door opened it was an inspector who literally dragged them away. Again I smiled, and there were no more disturbances to Christine's performance. I felt it was too risky to stay in the box, so I left and watched the rest of the performance from the catwalks.

After the last curtain call, I went home, wrote a note, waited until all were gone, and then I went to the managers' office. The note was simple, but, to anyone with half a brain, it was worth a million words.

> *I didn't realize Faust was a comedy.*
> O.G.

The next night my box was empty the entire evening and there was a footstool for my lady friend. In addition, there was an envelope with my wages on the ledge along with my program. That didn't take too much work, I remember thinking. During the third act, I went home and wrote a note of appreciation to Madame Giry. Then I took the note along with a box of sweets and left them on the ledge in my box for her.

After my successful performance the previous night, I think I was smiling the entire way home, and I believe I was still smiling as I sat by the fire with a glass of brandy in my hands. I still felt a smile on my lips when I heard the door in my music room open. When Christine entered the parlor, I got to my feet, still smiling, but she wasn't. She looked extremely upset. While the disturbance to the opera had worked out well for me, it came at a cost to Christine, and that made me feel really bad.

"Why the frown, my sweet?" I asked while taking her satchel from her hand.

"Were you at the performance tonight, Erik?"

"Yes, and you were magnificent. I don't believe there was a dry eye in the house."

I put her satchel in her room and returned to her just when she rebutted, "Well, there was at least one. How could someone laugh during such a dramatic scene? Was I that bad? I thought I was expressing the right emotion, but he evidently didn't. His laughter really shook my confidence. What did I do wrong, Erik?"

"Oh! No, no, no, Christine. It wasn't you. Your performance was perfect. I have to apologize. It was my fault, but I don't believe it will ever happen again."

She scrunched her face. "You? How could you do that to me?"

"I didn't. Here," I said while motioning toward the divan. "Have a seat and let me explain." She sat, with confusion written all over her face. "I don't believe we've discussed this yet. Somehow this subject managed to get overlooked during those days when you were questioning all the supposed rumors about me. You see, I have a fondness for Box Five, and when someone else is sitting in it I get . . ."

"Oh!" she gasped and covered her mouth with her fingers.

"You're remembering the rumors now?" She nodded slowly. "Well, they weren't rumors. You see, for personal reasons, I literally built that box along with many other things around here. I alone worked on this place during the war when everyone else was off playing their silly war games. I even believe I alone prevented it from being destroyed during that time. I wasn't being paid to be Garnier's watchman—it was something I wanted to do.

"I believe I was born with music in my blood, and my childhood desire was to live where I could listen to music and watch operas whenever I wanted. So, as the Opera Ghost's persona grew, I saw that box as a way of fulfilling my dream. In my mind and heart I've felt I deserved to have that box for my personal use, and that's what I've demanded from the management. My old managers conceded to my wishes long ago, but with the new managers in the house, I had to make it clear to them that they weren't to sell that box."

She was frowning at me by then, so I tried to explain my thinking in another way.

"You've seen the packed house. You've experienced my tutoring and seen the results. The reviews written about you and the performances bring in revenue. I'm partially responsible for those good reviews, so shouldn't I be paid for my efforts? Is requiring one box too much to ask for? I'd like your honest opinion, since I know mine is twisted at times."

She stared at me for a moment and then gradually lowered her fingers from her lips and nodded. "I agree with you. You deserve your own box, but I don't see how you laughing during my performance would help you attain it."

Once I explained exactly what happened, she understood. However, I didn't go into my demands for my wages. I figured one explanation at a time was enough.

Our routine remained status quo until the first week in June, and then something happened that started a series of events in motion—a series of *serious* events. I can only compare that event to the onset of childbirth. Once it starts, there's no stopping it.

The moment I first saw Christine on that stage, my love for her was conceived, and in the months that followed, it, along with our entire strange relationship, grew and brought with it tremendous pressure to have her all to myself. Most of the time, what I felt was beyond our little game of only playing the part of having her as my living wife—I needed her as a real one.

My efforts at staying busy were honest and valiant, and, for the most part, I'd managed to keep my thoughts and emotions under control. But, during that fateful day in June, there was no stopping what finally broke through my stern resolve and fine-tuned self-control. The full expression of my love and passion for her was imminent, with only one question remaining, would it be born alive and well or impotent in death?

The morning that opened that climatic chapter of my life started much like many others. It was a dark day for the house, so we had a leisurely breakfast with light conversation about the way I sang Romeo's lines to her after the masked ball. She asked about a certain transition I'd made and expressed her desire to use the same transition during a part of Juliette's lines. Even though she wasn't supposed to sing that day, we agreed a short experiment wouldn't hurt.

We went to my piano and I sang the part she was referring to, and then to get the complete feel for that piece, we went through the entire scene together. I was accompanying us on the piano, and she was standing beside the piano when our voices began harmonizing. Then it began.

We were in the middle of the scene when we somehow merged. We were no longer only Erik and Christine—we were also Romeo and Juliette, with all their passion and love seeping from every note. All four hearts had fused and began beating as one. Soon my piano sat silent and only our voices could be heard. Then I was on my feet and facing my Juliette, which I'd already learned never to do.

I took her hand from off the piano and held it in mine, while moving closer to her. My other hand found its way around her waist, and I slowly pulled her close to me. As I gazed into her captivating eyes, I no longer questioned if it was an act or if her true feelings were showing through. I simply drifted in the incredible moments filled with music and our feelings for each other.

Our voices eventually faded into silence, but the performance continued on. Our clasped hands at our breasts were the only barriers preventing our bodies from closing the gap and embracing. I stood motionless, and for the first time I wasn't thinking about whether I should move away or continue with the emotions that had taken me over so completely. I was merely following a course designed millennia in the past by an irresistible force much more powerful than myself.

My fingers felt the soft skin on the back of her hand, and my other hand pressed on the small of her back, registering her increased breathing. My eyes traveled the contours of her beautiful face and sensual lips, and then I gazed deeply into her eyes that were uttering that unspoken language, and my questions commenced.

Neither one of us was seducing the other, yet we were both being seduced by that invisible power. Were we merely music's captives or had we finally reached that point in our relationship that we'd been progressively traveling toward? I couldn't answer that question, and, furthermore, I didn't want to answer it. I wanted to experience it. I wanted to travel that path to its end.

Therefore, I only half-heartedly called upon my learned self-control to prevent what I feared would be a catastrophe. But, the more seconds that passed, the larger the crack in my control became and the more of it helplessly slipped through that crack and beyond my reach. The result—I tilted my head and lowered my lips to hers, and she responded as if being directed. She tilted her head, lifted her chin, and prepared for our lips to meet.

Our lips were only a few centimeters apart when we received the encouragement we needed to prevent that catastrophe from happening. The tall clock in the parlor announced the tenth hour by chiming abruptly, and we both jumped out of shock. I quickly squeezed her hand and then released it just as quickly. Within the next few moments, I was back on the piano bench and running my fingers nervously over the ivory and black keys, while praising her for her excellent skills.

She didn't respond at first, but then, while placing a hand gently on my shoulder, she asked, "Do you really think so, Erik?" I closed my eyes and took a deep breath. Then she asked, "You would tell me if I'd done something wrong, wouldn't you? I never want you to hold back and not tell me if my performance wasn't what you wanted."

With my eyes still closed and turned away from her, I questioned if she was speaking about her singing or our close encounter. Then I answered,

"No, Christine. I couldn't have asked for a more perfect performance. You were excellent." Then in an undertone meant only for my ears, I added, "You're exactly what I want."

"What?"

I took another deep breath and turned toward her. "You're exactly what the public wants. Now it's time to rest your voice. You don't want to overexert it."

"It feels fine, Erik. I'd like to continue."

"We can't chance it, Christine. We can't task your voice any more this day."

Then I added silently, and we don't dare task my will power any more this day.

I left quickly for the kitchen and a much-needed glass of water, but, while it cooled my lips, it did little to cool my thoughts. Each encounter we had brought us closer to what I feared was a great disaster. I knew myself well, and the pressure mounting within me was giving me a clear signal. There was definitely danger on the horizon if she didn't make her decision soon, but I'd promised her I wouldn't force her to make that decision prematurely.

I felt trapped and was actually thankful that most of the days she was rarely in my home. If I could make it through that day, then maybe the pressure would subside, and I could gain my control back.

I set the glass in the sink at the same time that Christine asked, "Erik, what is this?"

She was standing in the doorway to the kitchen, holding two small boxes, wrapped in red paper and tied with black ribbons. They were the gifts I'd bought for her the day before. I'd placed them on one of the shelves in my music room, intending to give them to her at breakfast, but I'd completely forgotten about them.

Trying to lighten my mood, I teased her while walking toward her. "Oh, my Christine, you're so inquisitive. One of these days you're going to let your curiosity get the better of you, and you just might find yourself somewhere you didn't intend to be." I took the boxes from her hand and put them behind my back. "These were supposed to be a surprise. So call upon that excellent acting skill I just saw and be surprised, all right?"

She smiled and nodded, and I handed them to her. Without moving from the doorway, she quickly opened them. Inside the one box were two matching gold hair combs in the shape of a base clef. They were inlayed with onyx stones and adorned with diamonds. She squealed with delight, and her eyes danced with glee as she started to run to her room, but I stopped her.

"Wait! Open the other one first."

With the largest smile, she opened the second one and found a companion piece made with the same gold, onyx, and diamonds, only it was in the shape of a treble clef and hung from a gold chain.

"Oh, Erik. You somehow always manage to outdo yourself. These are breathtaking. Where did you find them? They're so perfect, with the music clefs and all."

"They were hiding somewhere in my imagination, waiting to be released. Again, my dear, you're a great inspiration."

She stared down at them, shaking her head. "I say thank you so much that it hardly seems to mean anything anymore. What more can I say?"

"You've already said it. Now, go try them on."

She nodded and nearly ran to her room, while I walked there slowly, still uneasy after our close encounter. I reached her room and leaned in the doorway, watching her sitting at her dressing table and trying to put the necklace on.

Huffing, she asked, "I can't seem to work this clasp. Can you help me, please?"

Against my better judgment, I stood behind her with the necklace across my fingers while she lifted her hair off her neck. Trying to concentrate on the job at hand and not the nearness of the neck I desperately wanted to kiss, I hooked the clasp and stepped back away from her. She looked at it in the mirror, fondling it with her fingers, and then she looked at my reflection in the mirror and thanked me again.

I nodded, and she began brushing her hair in preparation for the combs, while I watched on just like another member of her captive audiences. The entire time, she was chattering about something, but I didn't hear what. I was too engrossed in watching her adorable expressions change as she talked and her fingers moving gracefully through her hair. I was mesmerized as I watched her hair repeatedly fall softly over her shoulder.

Then, without thinking of the consequences, I reached over and replaced a few strands of hair that she'd been missing, and, in so doing, I let my fingers linger on her bare neck for a few moments. After I realized what I was doing, I quickly removed my fingers and looked at her eyes just in time to see her open them wide and look up at my refection. Then my heart began to race while she continued talking. She gracefully, and, seemingly without forethought, pulled back the sides of her golden locks and slid the combs into place.

"Erik! Erik!" she had to repeat to get my attention. "Are they straight?" she asked while trying to adjust them properly.

"Yes," I replied breathlessly. "They look perfect."

I remained standing behind her, watching her reflection in her mirror, and she was looking at my reflection and speaking relentlessly. How I wanted to silence those chattering lips with mine, and when I looked beyond her reflection to her bed, I ached to take her there.

But I could only watch and admire from a distance, barely coming close enough to reach out and gently touch the outline of those soft curls. Any amount of strength I'd gained since we sang, which wasn't much, was gone, and I suddenly became painfully aware of my idle hands that appeared to be too large and conspicuous, like some foreign and strange appendages that had no purpose or assigned place on my anatomy. It was as if they'd stuck themselves to my body without permission.

I knew what I wanted to do with them, but I didn't know what I should do with them. However, I did know I had to put them somewhere out of harm's way, and I started fidgeting with them. I ran them through my hair, I laced my fingers on top of my head, and then put them in my pockets where they remained until they became much too warm; in fact, my entire body became too warm. So I pulled my sweaty hands from my pockets and put them behind my neck, trying to find someplace to put those unwanted attachments.

Holding them behind my neck only intensified my uneasy posture, so, lowering them, I placed them behind my back and clasped them together, hoping they would stay there and not embarrass me further. But then they began to tremble along with my knees, and I felt weak all over, as if I was suffocating. I had to place my feet farther apart to steady my balance, which made my entire body feel conspicuous.

I felt sweat begin to roll down my neck, so I lowered my head and placed my hands on my neck to conceal the visible evidence of my sad state, but my hands were more sweaty than my neck, making me even more uncomfortable. While in that position, I could see the ruffles on my shirt pulsate with each beat of my pounding heart, and I feared she would notice, so I put my arms across my chest and grasped my upper arms tightly. Then I stood there like a full-sized portrait of a staunch totalitarian in a museum.

I knew I had to leave while I still had any self control left, so I started backing up until the back of my leg touched the end of her bed. Then my picture came to life when Christine repeated my name once again, but I don't think I answered with anything coherent. I only stuttered and stammered and struggled to find a way out of the very dangerous situation we'd somehow again entered into.

I glanced around the room, like a trapped rabbit with nowhere to hide. Then the urge to run surged through me, and I felt as if I was going to explode or go mad or melt or do something bizarre.

Finally, I managed to produce something resembling human speech. "Christine, please excuse me. I need a drink of water."

Without waiting for a response, I tried to conceal the outward appearance of my passion and left for the kitchen. After taking several large swallows of water, I removed my mask and splashed water on my face, trying to gain a semblance of sanity. I spread my arms out on the countertop and lowered my head, trying to relax so I could return to her. Once I was back to a presentable state, I left the kitchen, knowing what I had to do. She was standing in front of the bookshelves by then, so I walked to the hearth and gazed down into the fire, preparing my apology.

"Christine, I'm sorry, but I feel a desperate urge to compose, and I'd like to be alone so I can work. Would you mind spending the rest of the day with Madame Valerius?"

I felt her watching me for a moment, and then she reached over and placed her hand on my arm. "Is everything all right? You don't look well."

"I'm fine. I just need to work."

"Are you sure? Have I done something to offend you? Did I not show enough gratitude for your gifts?"

I turned my head and looked at her for the first time since my ridiculous actions. "Oh, no, Christine. You've done nothing wrong. I've told you that I sometimes have a compelling need to compose. That's all it is. Don't worry your pretty little head about it."

"Then let me pack a few things," she replied, while heading toward her room.

I took her across the lake and up the steps mostly in silence. Then when we reached the spot where we normally said goodbye, I kissed her fingers and the ring.

"I love you, my angel. I hope you have a nice afternoon with Madame Valerius."

She smiled and I started to turn, but she laid her hand on my arm. "Erik?"

I looked back at her. "Yes."

She studied my eyes and placed her palm on my cheek as she so often did. Then she started to say something but stopped.

"What is it, Christine?"

"You have a good afternoon also, Erik. I hope you can accomplish what you want."

I smiled faintly, nodded, and again turned and left. When I reached the dock, I stood for a few minutes, looking toward the stairs. I had more hope for our future than I ever had before, but there was something in her heart that her mind was preventing her lips from expressing, and her eyes had just told me so.

I closed my eyes and sighed as I thought about the power that was continuing to grow between us. It was a power that frightened me, and a power I wasn't able to describe, and I feared I wouldn't be able to outmaneuver it much longer. I felt something of gigantic proportions was building, and I was torn between running away from it and embracing it.

Unfortunately, the ability to see into the future wasn't one of the gifts I'd been given at birth. If it had been, I would have raced after her at that moment, and I wouldn't have let her out of my sight until she told me what was in her heart. But, since I didn't have that ability, I was forced to let the sun rise and set until that power revealed itself to me in full. At that time, my earnest prayer was to understand that power and learn to control it before it destroyed us both.

Forty

I spent a few more moments in thought, and then I turned and left for my empty home. Less than an hour later, I realized I was in more trouble than I'd originally thought. No matter what I tried to do, Christine's vision brought fourth that ache in my chest, that need to hold her close to me and to hear her return my words of love.

As I drank my tea, there was her face across the table from me. When I tried to read by the fire, there she was on the divan smiling at me. While I played my piano, there was her angelic voice caressing my soul. When I reached for my portfolio of Don Juan, there were her inquisitive eyes, waiting for an explanation from me. It was hopeless. I was hopeless. Everything around me reminded me of my angel.

I went to the kitchen and, without thinking, reached for a bottle of brandy. I was ready to pour a glassful of comfort when I realized what I was doing. I was preparing to bury my problems in liquor, and I knew I was completely lost if I thought I could hide from my pain in that fashion ever again. So I put it back in the cupboard where it needed to stay.

Shortly, I was standing halfway between the door to the lake and my music room door, looking at both of them. When the deathlike silence pressed in on me, I knew I had to get out of my home. I had to get away from her memories and the nearness of the wine cellar before I did something crazy, something I might regret.

Therefore, I headed up the stairs toward the floors above me. Once there, I figured I could keep busy walking through my domain and listening in on others' conversations as I'd once done. But, again, every sight and every conversation made me think of Christine. She'd taken over everything, and I didn't feel safe anywhere.

I was in the third cellar by the sets and had just decided to head home when I heard Christine's voice. It was so clear, and I knew for sure I was going crazy, but then I realized she was actually near. She was talking with Meg about Raoul, so I stopped and listened.

"You mean you left him like that, Christine?"

"Yes," was Christine's reflective and soft reply.

"Oh, Christine, why did you do that? I thought you loved Raoul. You could be a countess someday. Don't you want that?"

"I don't know what I want, Meg."

"Well, don't you love him?"

"Yes, I do love him, and I think I would go away with him and marry him if he were to ask me in earnest, but then . . ."

"But then—what, Christine?"

"I don't know, Meg. I just don't know. I have fun when I'm with him, but something doesn't feel right, something is missing, and I get confused. I just don't know."

Her words hurt and made me feel conflicted. I had to get away from her and any thoughts of her, but how? For starters, I knew I had to get out of the opera house, so, after looking at my watch and knowing it was after sunset, I headed for my outside door.

Once outside, I lowered my hat and head, raised my collar, and started walking toward the Seine. I stood for a few minutes, watching it slowly move past me, but it wasn't any help, it only reminded me of our carriage rides. I growled and started running along its banks. At that point, I didn't care if I was seen or heard, I just had to run. I only stopped when I could no longer breathe and all my muscles burned.

I spent the rest of that evening and then the entire night walking or sitting and trying to gain control of my mind. After hearing Christine's last words, I knew she was truly being tormented by her own indecision, so I couldn't blame her for not giving me an answer. But that knowledge didn't help my thoughts or feelings to quiet down. I couldn't gain back my patience, and, without it, I knew I was a walking fuse just waiting for the right explosive to ignite.

My strongest urge was to run, and it had to be more than a foot race along the Seine. I needed to be on the back of a horse and running where there were no buildings or people or carriages or streets and no sounds of wagon wheels or voices. I needed to get away from the city and everything in it. Perhaps then my mind would clear and I could gain mastery over it once again. Once I came to that realization, I knew what I had to do, and I began preparing for it.

As I made my way back to the opera house, I prepared what I needed to tell Christine. The light was still on in my music room as I entered it and clicked the door closed, but the rest of my home was dark. So I walked softly toward the kitchen and washed quietly, trying not to wake Christine.

I was walking toward the fireplace, preparing to light a fire, when her door opened. She walked out in the lavender negligee and robe I gave her, and instantly that same passionate feeling surged through me, leading me down that path of no control.

"Erik!" she exclaimed, while starting to rush toward me. "You're home! I was so worried. Are you all right? Where have you been all night?"

Knowing she was probably going to hug me, I barely looked at her and continued on my way toward the fireplace. "I apologize if I worried you. That wasn't my intent. I've been walking and thinking."

"All night?"

"Yes. Sometimes I have to walk in order to think."

She sighed, "Oh, I see. Do you want to talk about it?"

I shook my head, took a deep breath, and prepared to tell her my first real and deliberate lie.

"What's wrong, Erik? I thought you were acting strangely yesterday. What is it?"

Motioning toward the divan, I began. "Nothing that serious. Please, sit down." After we both sat in our respective places, I continued, "I need to leave Paris for a while, so I won't be able to continue with your lessons for a few days."

Placing her hand on her chest, she sighed, "Oh, is that all? The expression in your eyes had me frightened. I thought I'd done something seriously wrong."

I managed to smile as I lowered my head. "No, my dear, you did nothing wrong. It's just something I need to take care of, and it requires me to leave Paris."

"How long will you be gone?"

Keeping my sight on my hands, I tried to explain. "That depends. I'm not sure how long it will take to correct the situation. I hope it will only take three or four days." I looked her sternly in the eyes. "I need you to know that if this weren't important I wouldn't abandon your lessons."

"I understand. I'm not having any problems right now with the score, so it'll be fine."

"I'm glad to hear that." I sat back in my chair and tried to sound nonchalant. "While I'm gone, you're welcome to stay here if you like. I want you to feel like this place is also your home, whether I'm here or not."

"Since you won't be here, I might stay with Mummy. This will give me a chance to reassure her of my love and care."

We talked for an hour or so, during which time I almost changed my mind. The conversation was relaxed and without any pressure from either of us. She didn't tease me, and I was free from those passionate feelings. But I knew I still had to get away, and, since the curtain was up on that scene, I had to finish what I started.

While she packed her things in her tapestry bag, I packed what provisions I felt I needed in my canvas bag. Once we were ready, I took her across the lake. We were at that same place on the stairs when we said goodbye.

I held her shoulders in my hands, laid a kiss on top of her head, and whispered, "I love you, Christine Daaé. Never forget that."

She pulled away from me and looked into my eyes, with hers filling with fright. "Erik! What's wrong? Something is wrong, I can feel it. Tell me what's wrong."

I looked away, swallowed hard, and then looked back at her. "The only thing wrong is the depth of my love for you, the depth of my need for you, that's all. Don't worry about it. But, if you would while I'm gone, please search your heart for your true feelings. I know I told you I'd be as patient as you needed me to be, and I'm truly trying to be just that. But, just like so many people who've underestimated my power, I fear I've also underestimated the power of my love for you. I just need some time alone, some time to think."

She touched my cheek, I took her hand and kissed the ring on her finger, and we said goodbye. Here nearness in the semi-darkness didn't help my tortured emotions, so I hurried my steps toward what I'd hoped would rescue us both from what was to come.

Shortly, I was on the back of a horse and heading for a store where I could purchase what I needed to stay out of doors for a few days. I never made it to that store though; there were too many other shops along the way. All those shops reminded me of that special woman—the florist, the dress shop, the restaurant, the book store, the grocer, and even all the broughams with their matched teams of horses. I felt pressure on my chest and that uncontrolled urge to run again, so that's just what I did—I ran.

Once out of Paris, I slowed my dapple-gray mare to a walk and tried to enjoy the scenery, but just as my journey down the Seine, I couldn't get Christine out of my mind. I headed for the area where I'd spent those days during the war, knowing it was a good location with ample water and perhaps food, but it didn't have enough influence over my emotions. I wasn't any better off there than I was in Paris; in fact, I believe I was even worse.

Not only could I not stop thinking about her but I was also burdened with an overwhelming sense of loss. I missed her terribly. When I closed my eyes, I could feel her fingers brush over my shoulder or through my hair. I could see her adorable face when she scrunched it and wrinkled her nose. I could see her wide eyes and hear her excited squeal every time I gave her a gift.

I could picture the way she changed in an instant from an excited schoolgirl to a seductive woman, and it made my heart race. I pictured the way she fidgeted with her fingers or a ribbon when she was anxious about something, and it tore at my heartstrings. I pictured the way she looked in that little boy costume, and that made my heart feel warm. I pictured the way she held her hands on her hips when she was angry with me, and that made my heart laugh. But then the way she placed her palm on my chest when she was going to say something important or my cheek when she was feeling compassion made my heart ache and brought tears to my eyes. I missed her so much.

Then, after two days of that torture, that other emotion that I hadn't learned how to control became so strong that I thought I would destroy something, anything. It was jealousy. Having never been in love before, I was completely unfamiliar and unprepared for the strong passion of love and jealousy combined.

The passion of lust I'd had in my past couldn't compare to the passion of true love. It overpowered me completely, and all the intellect I had couldn't fight against it. Then that helpless feeling added fuel to my fire and made me angry.

I'd always come off the conqueror in any battles I'd fought in my past, whether it was against someone simple like Oded or someone powerful like the Shah of Persia. Those were battles I knew how to fight and win, but, with this new one, I was floundering like a wingless bird.

When I thought about my feelings for Raoul and how close I'd come to taking his life, and his attempt to take mine, I pictured us only a little higher than unreasoning animals. Two stags come together in a forest to fight for a doe, one fights off or kills the other and the winner gets the doe, so simple an arrangement.

But we weren't unreasoning animals, or at least we weren't supposed to be. We were civilized, although I'm sure if anyone had been watching us at the lake that day they might disagree with that statement. But since we were trying to be civilized, we had to leave the decision up to Christine, and I then realized it was going to be one of the hardest battles of my life. And as with many other lessons I'd learned, I was learning that one the hard way.

As each day went by, I kept waiting for the surroundings or the constant companionship of the faithful horse with me to help me feel better, but none of it did. I'd only brought a small amount of food with me, but I wasn't eating it. While the days were getting warmer, the nights were still cold, and, without proper cover, I was spending my nights awake and shivering, although I don't think a tent would have helped.

If I slept, I either had passionate dreams about making love to Christine or horrible nightmares about killing Raoul, and if I was awake it was pretty much the same. I was so miserable in all ways.

By the fourth morning, my decision to leave Paris started hitting me hard, and I became angry with myself. I was going crazy knowing Christine was free to do with her life as she wished, and the more time I spent on that hill the more jealousy took over my thoughts. I was beginning to think I was a fool to leave her there alone with Raoul. He had an open door to influence her without my counter balance.

By late afternoon everything came to a head, and I knew I had to go back, even though my time there hadn't done the work it was supposed to do. I was weak from lack of food, and my sleep was rare at best. I felt simply horrible emotionally and physically. My throat was beginning to burn and my lungs felt suspicious.

I was lying on my back watching the sun move in its orderly fashion across a clear but cold sky, and I was still watching as a cloud formation began concealing it from my sight. Then I felt the first drop of rain, and I knew I had to leave right then.

I was halfway back to Paris before the clouds let go and it began pouring. By the time I reached the knoll over the city, I was soaked and chilled to the bone, but my physical condition paled in comparison to my emotional state. My feelings for Raoul stayed steady, while my feelings for Christine fluctuated. At one moment I had myself convinced she'd made her decision and I would never see her again, and then in the next I felt terrible for leaving her alone and frightening her the way I did.

It was during one of those remorseful times that I made the decision to buy her another gift, a gift of apology. I'd wanted to get her a jewelry box from the first day I'd seen it in the jeweler's shop. It was made from carved polished mahogany with a red velvet lining and a mirror inlay on the lid. When the top was opened, a man and woman in evening attire popped up and began twirling to a Strauss waltz. With the inscription I had in mind for the mirror, it was just perfect.

Trying to keep that remorseful feeling in my heart, instead of the possessed one, after I returned my faithful mount, I caught a brougham and headed for the jeweler's shop. It was dark inside, and my heart sank. I really wanted to get that box for her before going home. Sadly, I prepared to give the driver new instructions, but then I saw a faint light move in the back of the store, so I jumped out quickly and began banging on the door.

"I'm closed," the man shouted.

While pointing to the box in the window, I shouted back, "I'll pay you double for that box."

That did the trick, and before long I was crossing the lake with the music box. The opera had ended, and I was hoping to find Christine in my home so I could be freed from my self-torture. But when I opened the door to complete darkness, I knew she wasn't there.

I turned the lights on and searched my home, not for Christine but for some sign that she'd been there. When I found nothing that indicated she'd spent part of her time there, my fears increased tenfold. Quickly, I placed her wrapped jewelry box on her dressing table, dropped my wet cloak and saddlebags on the floor in the music room, had a dry cloak on, and was up the passage from my music room and heading for her dressing room.

I found it just as dark as my home, and again my fears grew. Her dark room meant she wasn't in the house at all, but, just in case, I walked through the shops she frequented. Then, with a heavy heart, I finally gave up looking there. Next I thought about Madame Valerius, so, with my stomach turning with anxious anticipation, I was back in a brougham and heading there.

To keep from being detected, I had the driver stop two blocks away, and I ran the rest of the way to her home. Then, like a thief in the night, I crept around the exterior of the house, looking for the back door. Once I found it, I let myself in through the locked back door. I sneaked through the upstairs and where I thought Christine's room was, but, other than the two ladies in the parlor and a maid in the kitchen, the house was empty.

I can't explain the amount of dread that swelled in my heart as I left and headed back to the brougham, with only one explanation left—Raoul. Refusing to believe the worst, I told the driver to take me past the nicest restaurants. After an hour of searching for his carriage and matching stallions with no results, great apprehension surged through my gut. With my jaws clenching, I told the driver Raoul's address, and then I had him drop me off two blocks away from the de Chagny estate.

I didn't run to Raoul's residence, I walked slowly, and by the time I neared it, I was convinced he was going to take her away from me. I just knew it. I also knew if he hadn't taken her to his bed yet, that I couldn't allow him to make her his own that night. But then what in the world did I expect to do once I got there? What if she was there? Was I going to drag her out by her hair? What if he'd already taken her to his bed? Was I going to strangle him in his sleep with her watching on? What in the name of everything sane was I doing?

Trying to keep my steadily growing cough under control, I made my way around his home, looking for a lit window. When I found none, I went to a back door, and, for the first time in my life, I found a lock I couldn't unlock, which made me feel defeated before I really began.

I started searching for a way inside and shortly had my sights set on a pair of French doors off a balcony. Without stopping to think of what I was going to do next, I put a lasso between my teeth and started climbing a lattice until I reached the balcony. As I climbed, a faint little voice, somewhere in the deep chasm of my twisted mind, was telling me I was acting like a madman and to leave and go home. But I didn't listen; instead, I stepped over the railing and took a few steps toward the doors.

It was then that the words I needed stopped me. They were my own words to Raoul, and they shouted painfully loud. *Don't force the rose open or the flower will be ruined.* That was my advice to him, and yet what I was about to do could damage Christine beyond repair. That one thought forced some part of my insanity to respond to my sanity, so I turned and retreated.

I was one step away from the railing when it happened, a familiar piercing burn in my back along with the explosion of a pistol and the shattering of glass. I was thrown against the railing, forcing the lasso from my teeth, went down on my knees, and then within the smallest fraction of a second, I searched my options. I could turn on my attacker and chance another bullet in my chest, I could jump over the railing and run and chance another bullet in the back, or I could go up on the roof and hide. My decision was instantaneous and so were my actions. I was up on the railing and on the roof within a heartbeat.

After a quick moment of rolling in pain, I lay perfectly still, not even breathing. Then I listened to the door open, glass crunching under steps, and Raoul's voice booming in his true dictatorial tongue.

"Quick! Get the police!"

I continued to lie still and listened to him moving around on the balcony and discussing with someone what he shot at.

"It was him—I know it. I saw his yellow eyes," Raoul insisted.

The other person was more logical. "A man with yellow eyes? I think you're over stressed. It was probably a cat. Look! Its blood is on the railing. And look here! There's more blood up on the drain pipe. Only a cat could get up there that quickly without help."

"No! I'm sure it was him. That freak came to strangle me in my sleep. Quick! Get me something to climb on. Do we have a ladder?"

"I believe so. But, Raoul, I think we should wait for the police!"

"No, Philippe! He's injured. Now's my chance to put a stop to his influence over Christine. I'm going after him to finish this."

"Raoul, don't be a fool! Don't climb on that!"

That was all I needed to hear to stir my anger more and give me the strength I needed, so I held my breath and rolled over. I took a slow breath and held it again as I got to my feet and started for the peak of the roof. I searched the other side of the roof, looking for another balcony to escape to, but I didn't find one. Then I heard voices again coming from the balcony where I was shot, and I stood still and listened.

It was Raoul and Philippe again, discussing my fate, and that discussion, along with the growing pain in my shoulder, altered my mental status. I was no longer the one being pursued but the one doing the pursuing. I was no longer just angry—I was in my controlled anger state.

I headed back toward that balcony, with my hatred for Raoul taking on new and frightening proportions. When I reached a chimney, I stood on its dark side, with my blood dripping from the fingers of my right hand and a lasso in my left hand, preparing for that stupid and arrogant fool. He thinks this is his chance—he has no idea what awaits him if he dares to follow me.

While I stood there waiting for him to approach, the words of my little trainer began to surface. At first they were faint, and I struggled to silence them. But the louder they became the harder it was to hold onto my anger, the anger he said would blur my vision and lead me down the wrong path. It would be so easy to end his life within the next few minutes, but as I contemplated it, another force entered. In the end, it wasn't the words from my trainer that saved Raoul's life that night. It was, once again, the vision of Christine's eyes filled with tears when she heard about his death.

Her sad blue eyes encouraged me to find the lowest part of the roofline, and Raoul's conversation about catching me for the police encouraged me to lower myself from the roof with only the aid of my left arm. The thought of dropping two stories was most unpleasant, but it was a picnic in comparison to the vision of sitting in a jail cell.

The fall took the breath out of me, and the pain in my shoulder and back was fierce, but I managed to get back on my feet, knowing if I didn't there was a good chance I might pass out. Cradling my right arm with my left hand, I started running away from the house until I reached a wrought iron fence.

I was feeling faint by then, but I made it over the fence and then started running once more. I ran for three blocks before I stopped and took note of where I was. I was close to the river, so I walked to it. Once there, I sat and tried to decide what I was going to do. Do I go back to my home and take care of my wound, yet another time, or go to the doctor, yet another time?

While I tried to decide, I examined my wound, or should I say wounds. I had two of them in the muscle between my neck and right shoulder; one in the back where the bullet entered and a larger one in the front where it exited.

The more I thought about everything that had just happened, the angrier I became. I was angry enough to know I didn't want to die before I had a chance to play out a final act with Raoul, and that anger gave me direction. Also, I didn't want a repeat of the last time I tried to doctor myself, so I hailed a brougham and headed for Doctor Leglise's office.

When I stepped down from the coach, I was definitely suffering from the effects of blood loss, and by the time I climbed the stairs to his office, I was barely crawling. I sat on the landing, leaned against his door, and took out my watch. I had another hour to wait before he'd arrive, and I honestly didn't know if he'd find me alive or dead.

The next thing I knew, there was sunlight coming through sheer white panels covering the window in the same room I'd been in so many times before. I remember groaning and closing my eyes, and, when I opened them again, there was Doctor Leglise standing over me. I blinked a few times and tried to get up, but he quickly pushed me back down, without a word. He laid his hand on my forehead and then pulled up a chair and sat down.

"I'm glad you're awake, Erik."

I nodded. "I need you to stitch me up again."

"I already have," he responded with a touch of frustration in his normally jovial voice.

I reached for my shoulder and found the entire area between my shoulder and my neck, front and back, bandaged. I also realized I was without any clothing, not even my mask.

"Thank you," I whispered with my eyes closed. "I need to go. Where are my things?"

"You're not going anywhere, Erik. You've lost too much blood, you have a fever, and you have fluid in your lungs."

He wasn't wearing a smile or his normal sense of humor that morning and neither was I.

"I have to leave now, so please, where are my clothes and my mask?"

He stood up and stared down at me. "Erik, what happens to you? Why do you keep getting shot? Are you a jewel thief or something of that nature?"

"As I've told you, Doctor Leglise, I don't lead a normal life. I thank you for your help, but I can't stay here, I need to go."

"We've been through this many times before, Erik. You need to stay here. Your clothes are wet and soaked with blood. They should be washed and dried before you wear them."

I looked at him sternly. "I believe you've taken liberties that aren't yours to take, Doctor. Their condition doesn't concern me, so hand them over."

He took a deep breath and let it out slowly. "Well, since you can't very well leave without them, if I refuse to give them to you, do you think you have the strength to fight me for them?"

I closed my eyes. "No, I don't, but I'll walk out of here with only this blanket if I have to."

Testing me, he backed away, shook his head, and motioned toward the door. "You know where the door is."

He was a fool to test me, so I tightened my jaw and managed to get to my feet, while he watched on. Then I wrapped the blanket around myself and staggered toward the door, but he grabbed the blanket and easily pulled it away from me. I groaned in pain and fell against the door, while he wisely moved to the other side of the room. I glared at him and shook my head.

"Don't play this game with me, Leglise. It's not wise."

He held the blanket out from his side. "I don't believe you're in any condition to fight me for this, so just lie back down and let me care for you."

While trying to steady myself, I shook my head again. "You really want to play this game?" Confidently, he just smiled at me, and I nodded. "Then let's play."

When I started to turn the door handle, he cautioned me. "There are people out there, Erik."

"They're your patients, Leglise. I don't care if they're traumatized—do you?"

Forty-One

I had no intention of walking out there. The most I had on me was the bandage over my shoulder, so I was counting on him giving in before I had to. I slowly opened the door about 6 centimeters, and then he rushed over and slammed his body against it.

"All right! You win! You're just crazy enough to do it. Stay here while I get your clothes."

When he left, I clutched the blanket, collapsed on the bed, and leaned against the wall. I was in so much pain, and all I wanted to do was take a healthy dose of morphine and never wake up. It seemed that all my battles of late I'd lost, and I was so tired in every way possible. I really wanted to cry.

As he came back in the door, he asked, "Are you sure you want these back?"

When he opened my brown shirt that was half red with my blood, I replied softly, "Yes, they'll help me find my way in the days ahead."

He looked at me as if I'd truly gone mad, but he didn't question me since he already knew I was a bit off center when it came to sanity. He only frowned at me, helped me sit up and put my clothes on. He made a sling for my arm and gave me familiar instructions. There was one new one though. I couldn't rest in one position for too long. Since there was fluid in my lungs, I needed to move around so it wouldn't settle in one spot and cause additional problems. I took everything he said without argument; I was simply too weak and tired to argue.

Eventually, he wrapped my cloak around my shoulders and helped me to my feet. That movement made me start coughing, and I felt as if my neck and shoulder were tearing apart, so, while he steadied me on my feet, I told myself not to do that again. He then helped me down the stairs and into a brougham.

He closed the door and then slapped it as he said, "I would give you advice, Erik, but you've heard it all before, and I know you'll do just what you want to do anyway. So all I can say is, take care of yourself." He nodded. "Until next time, Erik."

On the way back to the opera house, I leaned my head back and closed my eyes, trying to relax and listen to the rhythmic sounds of the horses. I tried to clear my mind and think of what I'd done and the stupidity of it all. I was angry with myself for losing control, angry with Raoul for a number of reasons, angry with Christine for what I felt was her betrayal, and just plain angry with the world in general. My mind was twisting in a crazy fashion, and I knew I had to do something about the situation the three of us were in before it was too late and someone died.

Nearly my entire life I'd felt as if I was walking a tightrope without a net and ready to topple off to my death at any moment. While I had a long pole in my hands to keep me balanced, what sat on its ends either helped me or hindered me. It was only my awareness of what balanced on its ends that prevented my death.

What sat on my left side was that happy and inquisitive child who looked at his passion for music and the beauty in the world with fascination. That child loved to laugh, to experiment, and to play tag with his horse. Along with that child sat my father and our loving relationship. I'd feel warm inside when I remembered his eyes and his instruction about life and especially about construction. To this day, when I think about him and all his guidance, I have to smile.

But on any balance beam there has to be a counter balance. So on the right end of that pole sat my temper and anger for the world, along with my unique mind, which was capable of conjuring up anything it desired, good or bad. However, I believe even with those negative attributes, if I'd had a normal face that was accepted by the world, I could have made a success of my life.

While I had my issues with my mother, it was that attack by Franco and Pete Jr. that gave the most weight to that right side. That was the true turning point in my life, and it increased my hatred and anger to a place that I'd never been able to come back from. Then, with my attack against those boys, I gained abnormal confidence in my ability to use my mind to control others, along with the beginning of the skills I used to defend myself throughout my life.

I meditated on all that had happened in my life and how that balance beam had tipped to one side or the other, with good times or horrible times as a result. That was especially so once I met Christine. She sat like a shining star on my left and gave me hope, but when Raoul entered and sat on my right, my world darkened and my real battle to keep that pole balanced began.

I'd almost let my hatred and anger tip me completely off that tightrope the night before, and, considering that Raoul had managed to put one bullet through me, I honestly felt, if it hadn't been for Christine's counter balance, both Raoul and I would have been dead before sunrise. That would have tortured Christine and ended her indecision in the process.

As I watched the trees passing my window, I could see clearly just how dangerous our situation was. And as strange as it sounded, out of the three of us, I was the only one sane enough to know we couldn't continue the way we were. So I had to make the change. I had to make the decisions that could put all of our lives back into balance.

While I honestly believed that what I'd told Raoul about not forcing a rose to open was true, I knew that was exactly what I had to do. I questioned my motives as I replayed both Raoul's and Oded's words in my head. Was I being deceitful? Was I seducing her unwittingly? Was I really being honest with her and myself? Did we really have the connection I believed we did or was it just my imagination fueled by years of unsatisfied needs?

I thought about Christine's words to Meg. How could I know for sure what she was thinking or feeling when she didn't? But then, I couldn't just sit around and wait for her to completely betray me without having my heart prepared. If I wasn't prepared and in a balanced condition before that decision was made, I didn't want to think about how far off that tightrope I might fall or how many people I might take down with me. My thoughts were torturous, and, with a heavy heart, I came to only one conclusion.

Both Christine and I had to know the answers to those questions, and as long as we were in each other's company I didn't see how we could be sure of our true feelings. I was too blinded by my love for her and she was also being blinded, perhaps by just who I was or whatever it was that Oded said I possessed. I didn't know, but before I went completely off on the right side of that tightrope and committed a deliberate murder, I had to know the truth about what we were feeling.

Therefore, I knew I had to do something that I wouldn't have imagined I could do. I was going to tell her I needed to be alone to work on Don Juan for two weeks. So she could come to know me, she'd stayed with me for two weeks willingly. Now I had to give that two weeks back to her without my influence in her life and see what she did with it. If what she was feeling for me was real, then I had nothing to fear and at the end of the two weeks she would still be mine. And, if not, I had to set her free before the unimaginable happened. As at so many other times in my life, what I was going to do wasn't necessarily what I wanted to do, but it was what I knew I had to do. I had to be prepared to let her go.

When the carriage stopped behind the opera house, I nearly stumbled out of it and barely made it to the lake, only to remember that my boat was on the other side of it. Therefore, I was forced to go back up two flights and take the passage down into my music room. Once inside my home, I leaned against the wall, closed my eyes, and began coughing, causing me to drop helplessly to my knees in pain. Then Christine's tender and worried voice reached my conflicted senses.

"Erik! What's happened?"

I tried to focus on the wavering room and saw her coming toward me; then my thoughts also began to waver. I pictured her with Raoul the night before and anger swelled inside me, while, at the same time, her concerned face and compassionate voice became music to my soul.

"Oh, Erik, you look horrible."

Without answering, I got to my feet and headed for the drawing room, steadying myself on pieces of furniture along the way. I stopped in the doorway and leaned against its frame, while Christine followed me, repeating her question. She walked past me and stood in front of me, still asking me that same question. I wanted to fall into her arms and sob, but my thoughts of what might have happened the night before caused me only to glare down at her.

"Erik, please, answer me. What happened to you? Where were you last night?"

Coldly, I responded, "I would like to ask you that same question, *my dear.*"

Her brow wrinkled, and, with a tone of confusion, she replied, "I was here waiting for you."

"Oh, really?" I questioned with sarcasm while lifting myself from the frame and heading for her room. I opened the door, looked inside, and then looked at her coldly. "Your room looks undisturbed. Are you sure you want to stick to that story?"

She frowned seriously and stepped back from me. "Erik, what's wrong with you? Why are you questioning me this way? You sound like Raoul, and I don't like it, and I won't allow it."

"Raoul? Don't compare me with that scoundrel. I was here last night and you weren't here, Christine, and now your bedroom is confirming that fact."

She frowned even more and shook her head slightly. "I didn't sleep in my bed. I sat up in your chair, waiting for you to return. Since there was little food in here, I decided I'd go across the street and buy us dinner after the performance. When I got here and found your wet cloak and soaked saddlebags just lying on the floor, I got so worried. It wasn't like you to do such a thing. I was so troubled that I couldn't go to bed, so I sat up and waited for you."

Still not convinced, I again accused her. "You say you bought food. Then where is it? I didn't see any food. Do you want to stick to that story also?"

"What do you mean, stick to that story? That's what happened, so there's no story to it. You told me you'd be back in four days, and yesterday was the fourth day. I was hoping you'd be here after the performance, and I wanted to surprise you with a nice dinner. But when you didn't show up, I put the food in the pantry. Why the interrogation, Erik? What are you trying to insinuate?"

"You weren't with Raoul last night? You haven't spent these last four nights in *his* bed?"

She took a step back from me, and her frown turned to a scowl. "Erik! How dare you accuse me of such a thing? What makes you think I'd give away my love prematurely? Do you think that little of me? Furthermore, how do I know you weren't sleeping in someone else's bed?"

Ignoring that ridiculous question, I kept asking, "Are you expecting me to believe that, with me out of the picture, Raoul didn't seize the opportunity to have you all to himself? Are you telling me that you haven't been with him this entire time?"

"Well, yes, I've spent time with him, but not during the nights and certainly not last night. We had supper together two nights ago, but last night I was here waiting for you."

I closed my eyes and leaned against her bedroom doorframe. Could I be wrong?

"Your restrictions were that I didn't see him inside your opera house, Erik, and I haven't. Are you now suggesting that I did something wrong by having supper with him away from here?"

I sighed and looked at her for a moment, and then I started for the divan before I fell over. Keeping my cloak wrapped around me, I lay down and started coughing again.

"Erik, what's wrong with you? Why are you so suspicious? Talk to me?" she insisted.

I closed my eyes and took as deep a breath as I could. I didn't know what to say to her. I was so angry, but, at that moment, I wasn't really sure who I was the angriest at—her, Raoul, or me.

She knelt down next to me. "Erik, please talk to me. You're frightening me."

I looked at her and searched her eyes for the truth and my heart for proper words, and then she laid her hand on my right shoulder and squeezed. I groaned and tried to move away. My eyes were tightly closed when she gasped, and I opened them to see her with my cloak laid open.

"Oh, Erik! What's happened to you? You're bleeding badly!" She jumped to her feet. "We have to get you to a doctor right away."

I closed my eyes again and responded softly, "I just came from there."

With the true caring voice of my Christine, she questioned, "Oh, my poor Erik. I'm so sorry. What happened?" I scowled at her, and she backed away with a frown. "Erik, what's wrong? Why are you angry with me? What did I do?"

With the full degree of self-pity and self-loathing, I responded, "I'm sorry. I suppose you didn't do anything wrong. This blood was caused by another person who wants me dead, nothing more. Just the same thing over and over and over again."

She ran her hand over my forehead, and I wanted to give into her care, but I was so confused and still partly angry and still very jealous.

"Oh, Erik. Oh, my poor Erik. What can I get you? Oh, my poor Erik."

"Will you stop saying that!" I ordered harshly. Then I glared at her. "I've been in worse shape—much worse. You need to leave and go home."

Almost stomping her feet, she insisted, "I am home, Erik, remember? I'm not leaving you, so don't even try to tell me to go because I won't. In addition, from the looks of you, you're in no position to make me. Now, please, tell me what happened, and let me help you. What did the doctor say? What do I need to do?"

Closing my eyes again, I said softly, "I need to sleep. So leave me alone and let me sleep."

"Very well, but do you have medicine you need to take before you sleep? Or how about a clean shirt? Can I get you a clean shirt?" she asked as she started for my armoire.

"No, Christine!" I snapped. "Let me sleep!"

She continued on anyway and then came back with a pillow that she placed gently under my head and a blanket that she put over me. She took off my wet shoes and socks, and then looked down at me.

"Your trousers are damp and so is your cloak. You should really change them before you go to sleep. Sleeping in damp clothes won't help your cough any."

"Please, just leave me alone," I replied softly.

She did as I asked, but only after she placed a clean pair of socks on my feet and another blanket over me. Then she went around the room and turned all the lights off except for the one in her room. I don't remember anything else for I don't know how long, and, when I opened my eyes again, I saw a lit fire with Christine curled in my chair and watching me. As soon as she saw me open my eyes, she was by my side again.

"Can I get you anything, Erik? How about some tea?"

I sighed and looked at her beautiful, compassionate eyes, and then I surrendered to her care. I told her how to make the tea for my lungs, and asked for a clean shirt and the medicine for my lungs that was in my armoire. When she came back, she also had a clean pair of trousers and two more blankets.

"These," she said while removing the blankets off me, "are damp from your clothing. I'll put them by the fire to dry."

When she held out her hand to me, I placed my left hand in hers and let her help me sit up. She gently took my cloak and coat off me, and then, kneeling in front of me, she started unbuttoning my bloody shirt. As I looked at her caring face, I felt my wildest fantasies coming true, which I felt could never be fulfilled, so I grabbed her wrist.

"I can dress myself, but, if you could, please get me some warm water to wash with, and give me a few minutes to change my clothes."

Reluctantly, she did as I'd asked and left me to fend for myself. Somehow, I managed to get my shirt off and my trousers changed, and then I lay back against the divan with the blanket over my bare chest and legs. Shortly she came back with the warm water, a rag, and a pot of tea. I sat up, and she started washing the remainder of the dried blood from my arm and hands. My emotions started moving toward passion, so I took the rag from her and did the job myself. But when I couldn't reach my back, she once more took over.

She sat beside me, and I leaned forward. When she took the rag from my hand and began running the cloth over my back, I heard her sniffle. I tried to glance over my shoulder, but I could barely move my neck without additional pain. So, when she moved forward to wash out the rag, I saw her face wet with tears, and her brow was furrowed, as if she was in personal pain.

She ran the rag over my back again and whispered, "I'm so sorry, Erik. This is so wrong. I just don't understand. Why would anyone want to hurt you like this?"

My anger over Raoul's attack returned, and the inflection in my voice registered its degree. "More of the same, Christine. Just someone who didn't want me in the way any longer. You've had the tour of my life by way of my scars. Treat this one the same, and then put it behind you, because that's what I'll have to do."

She was silent for a moment, and then she asked in a tone that told me she really didn't want to know the answer. "And this attacker—is he dead?"

I shook my lowered head slightly and answered softly, "No. This latest threat to my life has been kissed by a special angel and seems to carry with him a secret potion that makes him immune to my curse."

She sighed, in relief, I'm sure, and then asked, "Will you tell me what happened?"

I shook my head slightly again, closed my eyes, and willingly let her clean my back, relaxing and enjoying her loving touch. I thought about all the scars she was looking at and cursed myself for being so careless and letting someone add another one. I felt so stupid for turning my back toward my enemy. It was the strong passion of jealousy that had caused my latest scar, and, as Christine's gentle touch caressed my back, I wondered how many more scars I would receive before a fatal blow hit.

I think I might have been able to keep my emotions in check if I'd kept my eyes closed, but, once she dried by back and started to help me on with my shirt, I opened my eyes and watched her face. The anger I'd been feeling for her drifted away and only the love remained.

When she knelt down beside me again and started buttoning my shirt, she looked up into my eyes and then at her hands on my shirt and then back into my eyes. Oh, how I loved that woman. She had to love me. She just had to.

By the time she finished the last button, I was once more thankful I was sufficiently hidden behind the blanket, or I wouldn't have been able to conceal my feelings for her.

She straightened my collar and then ran her palm across my cheek, smiling softly. "You're fuzzy, Erik. I like it."

The innocent way she made that gesture and the childlike tone in her voice made me chuckle and helped me keep my thoughts clean. But, from the effort to chuckle, I started coughing, increasing the pain in my shoulder, and, I'm sure, the grimace on my face.

Her smile quickly turned to a frown as she laid her fingers across my forehead, and, in her true caring fashion, she asked, "Where have you been, Erik? You're very sick."

Trying to relieve some of her concern, I partially explained, "I'm not that sick, so you don't need to worry. This is a problem I've carried from my childhood, another scar you might say, although invisible. I can assure you, I've been much worse off and survived. So don't worry, my dear. Enough of this tea and medicine and I'll be fine."

She came back quickly. "Maybe enough tea along with good food. You don't look as if you've eaten much lately. There's the dinner I got last night. Would you like some of it?"

"Not right now. I don't have much of an appetite."

"That's not a good enough reason, Erik. You should eat, but I won't force the issue right now."

She picked up my dirty clothes, took a strong look at my bloody shirt, and, as she started leaving the room, said, "I'll put these in to soak and wash them in the morning."

"No, Christine. You need to leave. You can stay here tonight, but tomorrow I want you to leave, and I want you to stay away from me for two weeks."

She stopped instantly and looked back at me. "What?"

I swallowed hard and went on before I lost my determination. "At the end of the two weeks, your performance as my living wife will end, one way or the other."

"Erik, what are you talking about? What have I done wrong?"

After a long slow breath, I continued, "You've only been you, which is nothing bad or wrong, but you do act as a catalyst between Raoul and me, which is bad. Not only can none of us be happy as long as we remain in this triangle but it's becoming increasingly dangerous for us to do so. I fear a calamity of gigantic proportions is on the horizon. Therefore, I need you to leave for two weeks, which is how long you originally stayed with me and away from Raoul. I'll stay down here and work on Don Juan for the two weeks and allow you time to spend with him or Madame Valerius or whomever you wish."

Then, with lying lips, I planted the seeds that would enable me to keep close watch on her thoughts. "I do want to caution you though. While the sky looks peaceful, it's dangerous this time of year. The air is full of pollen that will play havoc with your vocal cords if you allow it to. So I strongly advise you to stay either inside Madame Valerius' home or inside the opera house as much as possible. No walks in the park or carriage rides for sure.

"Since I'll be absorbed in Don Juan, it doesn't matter if Raoul spends time with you here; in fact, it's preferable to your being outside. Do you understand, Christine? This is an extremely important role for you to perform. It can either make or break your career."

She nodded and naturally thought I was speaking about her theatrical role and career; however, I was really referring to the test I was putting her through. I feared what the test results would reveal, but I had to know for sure. I'd already given my heart to her on numerous occasions, but, before I lost it—and what was left of my mind—completely, I had to know her true heart's condition.

I took a deep breath and went on with my scripted deception. "You have no further need of tutoring for the role of Marguerite, but you'll always need to make sure you exercise and warm up your voice properly every single day. Since I want to spend all my time on my opera, I won't be present at any of the performances. But, at the end of the two weeks, I'll be in the audience listening, probably for the last time, so I ask you to sing for me that night."

She responded softly, "I always sing for you, Erik."

I thoughtfully acknowledged her kind reply and continued, "After you change out of your costume, I'll be waiting right here for you. I ask that you come back down here and give me one of two things—either your heart or my ring—since our little make-believe opera will be over and your performance will end at that time.

"Then all of us will be able to breathe safely, and you'll be free to become a real wife to either Raoul or me or no one. The choice will be entirely yours, Christine. I'll not beg or cry or badger you in any way. I'll be a gentleman about it, I promise. My only request is that you make sure you come back and give me either my ring, which you know holds dear memories for me, or your heart, which I value more than my own."

She walked listlessly to my chair and sat down with my dirty clothes piled on her lap. Then she looked at me with a somber, deeply thoughtful face.

"What happened, Erik? Why this sudden change?"

I laid my head back on the pillow and looked at the ceiling, searching for the proper words. "I know I told you that I wouldn't pressure you, and I don't want to give you an ultimatum, but things have changed and a decision is necessary. I've grown to love you more than I thought humanly possible, Christine, but, as with all things, that love comes at a great cost to all concerned." I looked back over at her. "I never expected my love for you to be this powerful, but since it is, I have to change our original agreement."

I motioned to the walls. "This has been my home for over fifteen years, but now it's my prison. I can no longer look at it the same way when you're not here. I can make it through the next two weeks down here if I know there'll be an end at that time—whatever it is.

"If you decide to stay with me, we can leave together and start a new life somewhere else. Wherever you want to go I'll go: Spain, Italy, Austria, England, America, it won't matter to me. But if you choose Raoul, then I'll leave here alone and travel. Perhaps I'll become like Jacob and go to the North Pole or the South Pacific Islands, I don't know. Maybe I could even go to Port Elizabeth and find someone who could love me, the way Mathew did. I don't know where I'll go, but I'll most assuredly leave here—that I know for sure."

I looked back at her as she gazed into the fire for a few moments before she looked at me. "I don't understand why you feel I have to make a decision between you and Raoul. It wouldn't matter if I chose him, he could never marry me, his brother would never permit it."

"Is that the only reason why you couldn't choose him? Do you not love him enough?"

Her eyes went back to the fire, and she responded softly, "Yes, I love him, and he says he loves me, but I believe it's all just a fanciful game we play. He knows he can't marry me, so we just play games like we did as children. We have dinner together and we talk about how it used to be and we laugh. It's all just a fun game."

"As Raoul once told you, Christine, you're no longer children, and you have to face an adult life and the adult decisions that come with it. The game you play is becoming much too dangerous for you to look at it in the same way."

She looked at me quickly. "Why do you keep using that term, dangerous? How can any of this be dangerous?"

Turning my head and closing my eyes, I sighed, "Oh, Christine, you're such a naive and terribly innocent child. I'm trying to tell you that, if you don't make a decision, then one is going to be made for you, and you'll have no say in the matter. In two weeks, I'll be gone. Either I'll be dead or I'll be out of France altogether. Preferably, I'll be out of France."

When I looked back at her she was frowning seriously. "Dead? What are you suggesting?"

Quickly, I answered, "I'm not only suggesting but I'm telling you that if Raoul and I stay in the same city much longer, one of us could easily turn up dead."

"You wouldn't," she exclaimed as she sat forward. "You wouldn't kill him! You promised!"

I again sighed as I closed my eyes and pressed my fingers across my forehead. "Not intentionally, my dear. But you've heard my track record and you know what happens when someone tries to take my life from me." Sarcastically, I added, "I don't appreciate it very much, and I can get a tad angry."

"Raoul would never do that, Erik. He's a gentleman. He talks about finding you, but I can't bring myself to believe that he'd hurt you—much less kill you."

With that ridiculous statement, I laughed aloud, causing me to wrench in pain, cough a few times, and then I let her have the truth. "Gentleman? You call this a gentlemanly act?" I laid my hand on my shoulder and my voice rose. "Does this really look like the results of a gentleman's hand to you? Should I take the bandage off and show you the results of that *gentleman's* efforts to get me out of his way?

"Should I show you where the bullet entered and where it exited? It entered in my back, Christine. He shot me in the back, and what makes it worse is that he thought he was doing the world a favor in doing so. Therefore, if you're still going to call him a gentleman, then you have to at least call him a cowardly gentleman."

I looked sternly at her sitting in my chair with her mouth dropped open and shaking her head. "I don't believe you," she whispered.

"Oh, Christine, you need to wake up," I rebuked harshly. "Right now we're moving around in the eye of a hurricane and at any moment its walls could move in on us, and its gale winds would take complete control of our actions and our very lives, ripping them apart. If the three of us stay here together, then we'll be allowing that to happen, and we're all doomed to failure.

"I'm trying to prevent a disaster from happening, with or without your cooperation. Therefore, in two weeks, I'm leaving France. If you go with me, then you'll make my dreams come true and make me the happiest man alive. If not, then I'll leave alone just as I have so often in the past."

She was still sitting there with disbelief flowing from her eyes. So, shaking my head at her, I tried one more time in a soft and loving tone. "Christine, I love you with a love that's worth more to me than my own life. Everything that I'm telling you is based on that love. The fact that I'm lying here like this, with yet another hole in my body, should prove to you that what I'm saying is the truth. Something horrible is going to happen if we don't act on what I say. I would rather set you free, Christine, than to see you hurt any more than you have been."

She stared down at the rug at her feet. "I'm sorry. It's my fault. This is entirely my fault. You're fighting over me. My indecision has caused this. I can't let this happen. I'll go away—far away from both of you." She shook her head. "If one of you dies because of me . . . ." She shook her head again. "I never saw this coming. At times I was afraid you might kill him but never the other way around."

"Oh, I see! In your eyes, he's too much of a *gentleman* while I'm the *murderer*, right? So, your fair-haired boy would never do this? Ha," I laughed.

"No, Erik, it's not that. Raoul also has a bad temper; plus he's spoiled and always wants his way. He's told me he wants you dead, and I could tell in his eyes how he felt about you. I could see him trying to find you and fighting with you. I've even had to stop him from doing so. But I never thought he would catch you in a vulnerable position and be able to kill you.

"But I know your strengths, and I know what you could do in self defense. I never thought or imagined that you would ever kill him without being provoked. Oh," she gasped. "Joseph." She looked at my shoulder. "If Raoul shot you, what happened to him? Is he hurt?"

"No, he's not hurt. He's still just as aristocratic as ever. The last I heard from him, he was giving orders to his servants. No, he's not hurt—yet."

"No, Erik, this has to stop." She got up and started pacing. "This has to stop. This is my fault."

"No, this isn't your fault, Christine. I went mad with jealousy. It's not your fault that I'm crazy, and it's not your fault that Raoul has such low regard for my life. It's not your fault. We're grown men and are responsible for our own actions—not you."

She stopped and looked at me. "Had you done anything to deserve getting shot in the back?"

Forty-Two

I huffed and shook my head in disgust. "Well, let me see. Why, yes, I believe I did do something to deserve a bullet in the back. Yes, I did—I turned my back on him, that's what I did. I learned a long time ago never to turn my back on an enemy, so it was my error. Sorry, I presume I did deserve it—right?"

She looked dumbfounded. "I can't believe this is happening."

"Well, believe it, my dear, because it's real. You might look at your fair-haired, childhood sweetheart in a different light now. He's not so fair, is he? He's not the innocent young man you thought him to be, my benevolent Christine, he's one of them. One of the long list of people who've wanted me dead, and the only reason why his life hasn't ended like the rest of the many who've tried to take my life is because of you and my love for you."

She was staring down at her hands when she responded softly, "I'm having such a hard time visualizing Raoul actually pulling the trigger and shooting you in the back. I can't believe it really happened."

"Well, it did happen, and, furthermore, let me tell you that if he were a better marksman I would be dead and it would have been by his bullet."

"Could you possibly be mistaken?" she almost pleaded.

"I don't think so, Christine. It's hard to mistake the pain of a bullet tearing through your flesh. It's something you remember and you unquestionably mark the person who was responsible."

"No!" she exclaimed. "I don't believe you. You're just telling me this to influence my mind."

"Oh, really? Is that what you truly think? Do you honestly believe I did this to myself? Many have thought me to be crazy, but can you visualize me doing this to my own body just to influence you against Raoul?"

Her hand went over her mouth and she shook her head. "No, I didn't mean it that way, I only meant that you're blaming Raoul for something someone else did to you, just as he blamed you for trying to kill him."

Every syllable I spoke next came laced with venom. "No, Christine. I've had many opportunities to end his miserable life and without anyone suspecting me. I could have killed him right in your own dressing room or that night in Perros. And then there was the time down by the lake when we argued. He pulled a gun on me then also, so it would have been self defense.

"I could have ended all of this then and had you for myself. And then last night, I could have killed him easily, but no, because of my love for you, I didn't. Instead, I turned my back on him and he shot me as if I was an open target in a practice field. No, my dear, this wound has his name on it for sure.

"Actually, I have two scars from him, and they both have his name written across them. Each of my scars has a name, and every time I see one of them, the memory of what happened flashes before me. So, with his name on two of them, my thoughts of him will be twice as frequent and twice as hate-filled."

I took a much-needed breath and tried to calm my spirit before I went on. "This game is getting much too dangerous and you must stop it, Christine. I know you believe that Raoul can't marry you, perhaps that's adding to your indecision, but my many years have taught me that time has a way of changing our lives. I can think of several different scenarios where he could change his situation and marry you. Therefore, you must make up your mind and heart, either Raoul or me. If not, then one of us is going to end up dead, and you'll have to bury one and live a life with that memory of your indecision. Two weeks, Christine—Raoul or me."

She laid her face in her hands. "No, I can't listen to any more of this. I can't listen to any more."

I was beginning to feel bad for my harsh tone, so, with all the caring I could give her at that time, I spoke to her. "Then go to your room and try to rest. Tomorrow you can pack what you want and leave me, and then I'll see you in two weeks."

She got up slowly, laid my dirty clothes in my chair, and left for her room, all without looking at me or responding in any way. I sighed, closed my eyes and melted into the divan. I felt horrible. I felt as if I was in another living nightmare, and I couldn't even imagine how Christine must have felt.

I was lying there thinking for a few minutes when I heard her door open. I looked toward her and watched her cross the room toward me. Then she sat on the coffee table close to me.

"I'm sorry, Erik. I wish I could freely tell you what you want to hear, but . . ." She stopped and stared at the floor. "I care for you deeply, and the thought of never seeing you or not having you in my life is very painful for me, but . . ."

She stopped again and looked at me. "I'll do what you ask, because I trust your wisdom more than my own, so I'll stay away for two weeks, but not right now. I can't leave you in this condition. I just can't, and you can't ask me to. I need to stay with you until you're better and in a safe condition, and then I'll do what you ask. Will you at least agree to that much?"

My heart was melting. "Oh, Christine," I reached over and touched her hand. "I love you so much. You're truly my angel. You may stay and help me. Please, don't fret. Everything will work out for the best in the end. Believe me, it always does."

She tried to smile and then she took my clothes into the kitchen, telling me she was going to put them in to soak.

"Seriously, Christine, don't bother. The jacket and shirt have holes in them, and I don't want them as another reminder."

She nodded, but kept on walking. She was gone for some time, and when she came back, she had a plate with some cut up fish, some spiced rice, and two celery stalks.

As she poured me some tea she said, "You need to eat something and you need to start drinking your tea."

She held out her hand for me to take, and I did, letting her help me up. She sat with me as I ate, but we didn't say much, at least not verbally anyway. In the dim light from the dying fire, our eyes did most of the talking. She did, however, thank me for the jewelry box and said the inscription made her cry.

I finished eating, she took the dish to the kitchen, and, when she came back, she pulled something from her pocket, two lassos.

"I almost forgot," she said as she walked toward me. "I found these violin strings in your coat pockets. Where would you like me to put them?"

"Those are my lassos, Christine," I replied grimly.

"Oh!" she gasped.

I gestured toward the coffee table. "You can leave them right there."

After taking a guarded glance at them, she laid them on the coffee table as if they were diseased.

We said goodnight, and she left, closing her door and taking the remainder of the light from the room. I lay there watching the last of the red embers turn to black, while I tried to sort out what I needed to do in order to keep myself on a straight path. Having her stay with me any longer was going to be hard, but I told myself that it could be the last I saw of her, so I needed to enjoy it while I could.

I'd told her I was going to stay down in my music room and work on Don Juan, but that was far from the truth. I needed to watch her with Raoul. I wanted to see how she reacted to him. He'd made her angry during the masked ball and also in Perros; therefore, I didn't believe she was able to tell him what she was really feeling. I needed to give her the opportunity to be with him and let him bring out his true colors to her, and for her to bring out her true feelings for him, which would help me to know what her true feelings were for me.

The next day, and each day after that, she was gone from me only during rehearsals, performances, or when shopping for food. She made three full meals each day, not just tea and toast, and she kept me filled up with my tea and herbal medicine along with lots of fruit.

I slept as often as I felt the need, and, while she tried continually to get me to sleep in my bed and let her take the divan, I refused. To me, that bed was hers, and I couldn't bring myself to sleep in it unless she was there with me. Therefore, I slept on the divan and woke many times to find her curled in my chair with a book or just watching me. When that was the case, she would instantly ask if she could get me anything. I soaked up everything she did for me and cherished every movement she made.

The pain I was in was severe most of the time, and I wanted to give into the soothing effects of morphine, but, as tempting as it was, I couldn't do that with Christine in the house. I didn't trust myself while under its influence, and, since my last encounter with it in Perros, I feared depending on it for any reason other than physical pain. Especially was that true right then, with the very real possibility that Christine could be gone from me forever.

The first two days passed like a dream, and we were playing house again just as before, but, toward the end of that second day, the air once more became charged with our conflicting feelings. Without my asking, she prepared to change the bandages on my shoulder.

"I don't want another bottle of maggots around here, and I'm sure you don't either, so we'd better take care of your shoulder properly."

"You've got that right," I replied.

She sat on the divan next to me and helped me off with my shirt, and then, as she removed the bandage, I clenched my teeth, causing her to apologize. When she became quiet, I glanced at her frowning brow.

"Oh, Erik, your poor shoulder. I didn't realize a bullet could do this much damage," she said, as she ran her finger gently across my shoulder.

"Come now, Christine, this is nothing compared to the last time you dressed my wound."

"I know, but that was more than a bullet wound. I didn't expect this to be so bad. It almost took off the top of your shoulder."

Her words made me think about Raoul, and I'm afraid my voice showed my continued irritation with him. "That's because it not only entered but also grabbed hold of my muscle before tearing through the front and taking a portion of my flesh with it."

She closed her eyes and took a breath. "I'm so sorry."

I should have kept my mouth shut and stayed on her compassionate side, but I let my bitter thoughts take hold and come out mockingly. "Oh, are you seeing Raoul in a different light, my dear? Can you see he's not the sweet, debonair young man you think him to be?"

"Please don't, Erik. Don't start again."

"I'm sorry, Christine. I just know your nature and how you always see the very best in people to the point that you see no wrong. You've worked so hard to get where you are right now, and you deserve only the best. I don't want to see you reduced once more to a common chorus girl in the arms of a common mortal, a mortal who doesn't care enough about you to know what you're about, who doesn't know what you want most in life.

"While you're gone from here, try to remember that you deserve someone who truly cares about what you want—your music. That's the only way you'll be truly happy, and that's what I want, for you to be happy. Please don't forget that."

While running the medicated water over my wounds, she said softly, "I'll remember."

I was watching her face as I made an even bigger mistake. "Keep your guard up, Christine. Don't let that handsome, young fellow make you his Marguerite. He may only be after one thing."

She turned on me in a fury. "How dare you, Erik! Raoul is not like that, and he would never treat me that way. He's a gentleman and a nobleman and he would never treat me with such low regard. He wouldn't treat any woman that way."

She was furious by the time she'd finished her childhood sweetheart's defense, and she was not that gentle as she dried my shoulder.

Then she glared at me and hissed, "If anyone would play the role of Faust, *my good monsieur*, it would be you—not Raoul."

As soon as she finished rebuking me, she sank back on the divan. I don't know if it was actually hearing her words out loud or seeing the expression in my eyes, but she sank back. I turned my face away from her, but I couldn't be mad at her; she was right. If either of us had a reason to make a pact with the devil in order to win a beautiful woman, it would be me.

She sat back up and placed the clean bandage over my shoulder, while I tried to soothe my hurt feelings. I told myself that it was my fault, and I never should have pitted myself against him. It was a stupid and careless move. I obviously still had a great deal to learn about proper decorum in a relationship, especially one that was three sided, and especially when I felt the way I did about my competition.

She helped me put my shirt back on, and then, once again, was on her knees and buttoning my shirt.

"I'm truly sorry, Christine. I never should have said that. Please forgive me."

She looked up at me and nodded. "I'm also sorry, Erik. What I said was uncalled for."

I watched her face as she finished the last button and then straightened my collar. Our eyes met and we stayed there for a few special moments before she again ran her palm against my unshaven cheek. Then she smiled. That silent and precious moment was repeated many times in the days ahead, and nearly every time I was thankful for the blanket that was folded over my lap.

It was nearly three weeks before she felt I was well enough for her to leave. I was no longer coughing and the fever was gone. Even though it still hurt to do so, I could button my own shirt, bathe, and shave myself. With her tender and vigilant care, I was actually feeling good physically. I'd been to the doctor and he removed the stitches, telling me again that the care I was receiving was good for me and to keep my special lady friend around. Oh, how I wished I could, was my unspoken reply.

The day came when it was decided the two weeks needed to start and the morning passed by us with our silent tongues and talkative eyes. She went into her room and picked up her cloak and satchel from her chair, and I groaned inside with anxious anticipation for what the days ahead might bring. With her cloak over her arm, she walked back into the drawing room and then looked toward my music room.

"May I hear one more piece of your music before you take me back?"

"Certainly, Christine. What would you like to hear?"

"Anything, I don't care," she said softly.

I followed her into my music room where she sat in the stuffed chair she liked the most. I sat at my piano and began playing the first thing that came to my mind, "One Beat," but my heart wasn't in it. I feared it would be the last piece I'd ever play for her, and my fingers lacked their inspiration.

She listened for a few moments and then walked over to me, and, with an ever so faint frown on her perfect brow, she placed her hand on mine, releasing them from an impossible task. I looked up at her, and, as her eyes began to moisten, she looked into mine.

"I'm sorry, Christine, my heart isn't in it."

"I can tell, and I'm sorry. I wish I could tell you what you want to hear now, but I can't, not and be honest to us both. I'm really trying to do what you ask of me. I know you want me to be 100 percent sure of my feelings. And, as yet, I'm not."

I closed my eyes, nodded, got to my feet, and took her cloak from her hands. Then, placing it around her shoulders, I paused with my hands on her shoulders for as long as I dared before releasing her. I had the door to the lake opened and waiting for her by the time she came out of the music room and joined me.

It was extremely quiet on the ride to the dock, with only the sound of the pole in the water as we went. When we reached the spot on the stairs leading to the main floor where I usually left her, I paused and waited for any further word from her. As the clock ticked away, she only looked at me with eyes that were speaking volumes, but they weren't speaking that one word I was waiting to hear.

"The two weeks will end on the eighth of July," I reminded her. "I'll be in the audience, watching and listening. Then I'll be in my home, waiting for your heart or my ring." Again there was silence, and when I was at the end of my composure, I placed my fingers under her chin and whispered, "I'll miss you, Christine." I laid a kiss on top of her head and whispered again in her hair, "I love you."

I stood there with my lips in her hair, feeling her softness, smelling her fragrance, sensing her essence, listening to her breaths. She didn't pull away; in fact, she put her arms around my back and laid her cheek against my chest. Then we stood there together in the silence. I knew that could be the last time I would hold her, and, from the way she was holding me, I sensed she felt the same. The precious moments ticked by, and, when I felt my eyes begin to fill with tears, I pulled away.

Then, after kissing her fingers, I turned to leave, and she said, "Please take good care of yourself, Erik."

I looked back up at her, nodded, and answered, "I'll do that for you, My Angel."

I then headed toward the dock and stayed there for a while. I looked out over the water and then back at the stairs, wondering what would return to me, her heart or my ring? I was sad and yet calm. If she gave me back my ring, it would break my heart in such a way that I knew it would never heal. My flesh had always healed from its wounds, but I knew my heart could never heal from her loss.

On the positive side, I also knew I was prepared for whatever happened, and I felt I could go on without her if that was what she wanted. I loved her that much, and that love gave me the strength I knew I would need. She'd been honest with me from the beginning, and I drew strength from that knowledge. She could have tried to play me, but she never had. Her deep compassion was her strongest attribute, and I was counting on that quality to continue through to the end.

Eventually, I entered my boat and started for home. I fought my tears and tried to fill the void she'd left me in with anger, but I was without it or anything else that was going to help. I stepped out of my boat and stood for a moment gazing out over the dark lake. Taking a deep breath, I thought, this is it, either the beginning of a wonderful dream with Christine as my wife or a closing curtain. Which will it be?

If the curtain closed on me that time, then it would take from me all I'd come to love and cherish—My Angel—my Christine. As I watched the ripples in the water calm and the lake become still, I hoped I could survive with dignity the wave her presence in my life had started.

I went inside and headed for my fireplace where I placed one outstretched hand on the mantle. I lowered my head and closed my eyes, listening to the silence inside my home and inside my heart.

Silence. The biggest part of my life I'd spent in silence, with only sounds of nature around me or my own voice or music. I'd learned to accept that and live a life that could be content with only those sounds, but Christine had entered my life and it would never be the same again.

Right then, the sound of nothing around me was like a heavy weight that pressed down on my chest. I imagined it having a will of its own and that it was testing my endurance. I knew if I thought about the silence and what it represented, Christine's absence, I could do something foolish. So I forced myself to think that I still had a chance to win her heart.

I also knew I needed to keep myself busy; therefore, I concentrated on what the two weeks were for, to help Christine and me understand what was in her heart. My conscience had pricked me every time I read her diary in her dressing room, but, right then, that was the only way I could hear her thoughts.

Over the years, I'd found that any private thoughts that flowed from the heart and off the end of a pen were truthful, whereas, public words that flowed from the heart and off the tongue were somehow distorted and twisted to please the ears. So reading her diary was a necessary tool to help me understand her private thoughts.

I hadn't read her diary since I'd brought her down to my home; in fact, I wasn't sure she'd been writing in the one I bought her. Relief was the emotion I felt when I opened it and saw her immaculate writing. I took it to my chair in the drawing room, and, with a glass of brandy in my hand and uncertainty in my heart, I began reading.

She'd started writing the first day she came down to me, and, with only a few exceptions, she wrote every day. She started by describing her fear after seeing my face and witnessing my insane anger. She actually thought she was going to die right then, and I felt horrible. I had to lay the diary down and gaze at the tapestry on the wall for a moment; then I also relived those harrowing moments. That fear surfaced off and on throughout the rest of her writings. She feared my temper more than anything else.

She said her feelings for me were growing, but she couldn't describe what those feelings were. She knew she loved Raoul, but how she felt for me was much different, so she didn't think that feeling was love. What she felt for me was powerful, and she never wanted to leave my side. She described how she felt for her father and how similar her feelings for me were, that safe feeling.

As the time passed, her feelings for me changed. She still had that safe feeling while in my company, and yet she had another fear that was growing. At times, she felt helpless in my company and only wanted to do my bidding. At other times, she was embarrassed about how she felt, such as when I gave her the onyx combs. She wanted me to make love to her, and she felt guilty because of those feelings.

My jaw dropped, and I had to read that passage again to make sure I'd read it correctly. I even read it a third time. I couldn't believe it. She was feeling exactly the same as I was feeling. I laid her diary on my lap and stared into the fire, frowning. She wasn't teasing me, she wanted me, and my heart began racing.

"If I'd only known," I whispered.

Then I relived those moments and realized it was best that I hadn't known. It was hard enough to resist her without knowing she was feeling the same way. No telling what would have happened if we had shared our thoughts at that time. However, I couldn't help but wonder, if I'd kissed her, where would we be? Maybe that would have solved everything.

Knowing it was too late to do anything about it, I went back to reading. Then, what I read next brought out in me what Christine feared the most, my temper. It appeared that after I made her leave that day and left her on the stairs, she realized who she wanted to spend the rest of her life with—me. She said for the first time that she was 100 percent sure. She was on her way back down to tell me her decision when she met, who she called, the Persian on the stairs.

I frowned and began grinding my teeth when she described how he warned her about me and my powers of seduction and persuasion—even hypnotism. He asked her enough probing questions to make her start to question her own feelings for me again. Therefore, she didn't come back to me.

At that time, I didn't lay her diary down, I threw it across the room and charged to my feet. I stormed around my parlor, cursing Oded and his meddling. I threw my brandy glass, with the small amount of liquor left in it, into the fire, creating a minor explosion. How could he do that to me? If he were standing in front of me right then, I swear I would have strangled him. That meddling fool!

I even started up the stairs, with his flat as my destination, but, thankfully, I came to my senses before I got very far. The damage had been done, and giving him a thrashing wouldn't change anything. It would only make both of us unhappy. Eventually, I was back in my chair with Christine's diary in my hands.

The remaining part of her diary covered the time when I was shot and the days of my recuperation. Her fear for my life was great, as well as her fear of what she was feeling for me. But with the way I was talking about death and Raoul, her fear of something happening to him grew, along with her fear of my temper.

She believed what I said about someone dying and she was tormented severely. She wrote about leaving Paris and disappearing so that there wouldn't be any further confrontations between the two men in her life. But then she realized that if she disappeared, each of us would blame the other one, and there would still be the possibility of someone being killed.

She felt trapped, with no way out and nowhere to turn. She couldn't talk to either of us about it, since we both got angry quickly. It made me feel terrible to know she felt that way. I'd always wanted to be there for her to talk to, and yet, during such a traumatic time in her life, I wasn't there for her. I wanted to go to her and comfort her, but, again, it was too late.

There were a few times when she was trying to explain how she felt about me, but she couldn't, so she scribbled out the writing and only wrote that it was a wonderful and powerful feeling.

Once I was finished reading, I put her private thoughts back in her drawer and sat in my chair, digesting its contents. The strongest recurring theme through her writing was that of fear for all three players in that strange and unexpected tale of our encounter.

It was easy for me to see then that she was telling both of us a version of the truth, but neither of us the entire truth about the way she really felt. Or perhaps she was just trying too hard to keep both of us happy, while being completely untrue to herself. I then wished I'd read her diary sooner and maybe I could have helped her through her thoughts.

I felt sorry for her during that time of personal struggle, for hadn't I done the same thing in my past when I tried to hide what I was feeling in order to protect my father from the truth? It's hard enough to tell yourself the truth when it's a subject you don't want to think about, much less be truthful with another person when their heart is lying open and unprotected in your hands.

I didn't sleep at all that night. I only stared at the ceiling wondering what Christine was thinking about. It was almost morning when I realized that, during the time she'd been there with me, I nearly always slept well, and my nightmares were few and relatively mild. Doctor Leglise was right. She was good for me in so many ways.

Forty-Three

I began my day early, knowing I'd be returning to my old ways of watching Christine's every move, or, should I say, listening to her every thought. I was up the street from Madame Valerius' home in a brougham, watching the sunrise. I felt both gladness and sadness when I saw another brougham pull up and Christine come out of the house and enter it. She went straight to the opera house and then straight to her room. I was behind the mirror and watching as she entered and leaned back against the door, looking at the mirror.

"Are you here, Erik?" she asked softly.

It was difficult, but I didn't respond. Then she lowered her eyes, lowered her head, and covered her face with her hands. She remained there for a few moments, and when she raised her head again, there were tears streaking down her cheeks.

I pressed my teeth together to prevent my heart from speaking to her and telling her not to cry. I wanted to tell her I was always there for her, but I had to see this through. She had to understand what she was feeling, and, as painful as it was going to be for both of us, it was necessary.

She wiped the tears from her cheeks as she walked to her dressing table and sat down. Then she took out her diary. She wrote a few pages, and, after replacing her diary in the drawer, got up and started unbuttoning the bodice of her dress. I was about to turn and leave, giving her privacy, when she suddenly stopped, turned, and looked at the mirror. She squinted in thought, and then picked up her rehearsal clothing and went behind the curtain.

I smiled. Even though I hadn't answered her, and I'd told her I would stay down in my home for that two weeks, she wasn't certain I wasn't there. For some strange reason, that made me feel good, causing me to shake my head and smile even broader. She would never again undress in front of a mirror.

She went to rehearsals, came back and changed, and then sat at her dressing table, straightening her drawers for some time. Once she had them the way she wanted them, she started rearranging the top of the table.

She picked up the vase containing the dead roses and started across the room to throw them in a basket, but then she stopped and went back to her table. She took a handkerchief out of her drawer and spread it out on top of the table. She then cut the long stems off and laid the roses on the handkerchief.

She ran her fingers over them for a few moments before she folded the edges of the handkerchief over them, and then she placed them in the back of her diary. She closed it and held it to her chest, gazing at the mirror, I believe thinking about their history. Once more, I saw tears appear in her eyes, and my vision also started to blur.

That poetically sad yet beautiful moment ended when someone bounded into the room—Raoul. She smiled at him and then gently put her diary back into her drawer. By then Raoul was on one knee in front of her.

"Oh, Christine, I was so glad to get your note, and I'm so glad to see you. I was worried about you. Where have you been?"

Raising her hand and running it across his boyish cheek, she replied, "I'm glad to see you also, Raoul."

He placed his hand over hers and then turned his head and kissed her fingers, whereupon he felt the ring. "You still wear this? Why, Christine?" he demanded.

"Raoul, please don't speak of this, not now. I only want to spend time with you. I need to spend time with you."

He sighed and ran his fingers and eyes over the back of her hand. "How can you expect me to simply ignore this visible token of love?"

"Because this is not what it seems. I wear this as a favor to the one who gave me my courage and my voice. I owe him so much, so this is the least I can do to repay him."

"Is that all, Christine? Are you sure you don't love this man?"

She was quiet as her eyes fell to their entwined fingers; then she looked at the mirror. "Let's go for a walk."

They got up and left, with me following them. Thankfully, she took him to the huge prop room, which was packed with large and small items. If she planned to speak to him in private, that room, other than her dressing room, was the best location for me to listen in. It was crowded with lots of places I could hide while being close enough to them to listen in on their conversation.

"Christine, why are we here in this place?"

"Because this is a private and safe place for us to talk."

"Safe?" he questioned while looking around. "Are you afraid of him?"

"For me, no. But . . ." She stopped and also looked around before finishing her thought. "I don't want to hurt him, and it would hurt him if he saw me with you. So this is a good place to talk."

"Why do you care if he's hurt? Do you love him?"

"I care deeply for him, Raoul, and maybe I love him, but it's different than the way I feel about you."

"I knew it!" he exclaimed, while putting his hands behind his neck and turning in a circle. "I knew you loved him. What happened while you were with him, Christine? Did he . . ."

"Raoul, please don't do this again. He never touched me in that way. He was a perfect gentleman." She took one of his hands that was still behind his neck and held it in hers. "We can love many people and all in different ways. You loved your father and now your brother and your aunts—right?" After a moment, he nodded. "Well just because you have love for an aunt doesn't mean you don't love your brother. I love many people, but what I feel for you is special in one way, and how I feel about Erik is also special in another way. You don't need to be jealous. It's not a becoming quality."

"But can you answer this one question, Christine? The love you feel for this other man, is it a romantic love?"

"I don't know how to explain what I feel for him, Raoul. He's a very complicated man and my feelings for him are just as complicated. But, please, I don't want to talk about Erik. I want to talk about us. In less than a month you'll leave again on expedition, and I want to enjoy the time we have left. So can we not think about anything serious and just have fun?"

Raoul nodded, and they were quiet as they walked hand in hand through the props for *Juive*.

After a bit, Raoul asked, "Christine, will you still be a free woman when I get back, that is, if I get back? This expedition isn't going to be easy, and I may never return. I could die out there."

There was quiet again, so I moved and looked between two pillars and saw Christine with her head down. Then she spoke so softly that I could barely hear her.

"I could also die."

I don't believe Raoul heard her, because he lifted her head with his fingers under her chin and asked, "Christine, will you wait for me? Will you not marry this Erik before I return? If you wait for me, then we could be married."

She shook her head, turned from him, and started walking again. "Raoul, you know we could never marry. You're brother would never permit it."

Then, as if a bright light of inspirational thoughts flooded through her, she quickly turned back toward him and clapped her hands in front of her chest.

"Oh! Raoul! I know what! We could have a pretend engagement, a secret pretend engagement and no one would have to know but us. People have secret marriages, so why can't we have a secret engagement? It would be fun to pretend—don't you think? We could be engaged for a month until you leave. This would make us happy without hurting anyone else. It's perfect!"

Raoul stood there, shaking his head and smiling at her. Then he went down on one knee and spread his arms out from his sides.

"Very well then, my lady. Will you marry me, Christine Daaé?"

She laughed, handed him her hand, and responded; "Why, yes, my good *Monsieur*."

He jumped to his feet and grabbed her, and then they began twirling in circles and dancing around the props. Their hearts were happy, but mine was beginning to bleed. I was only into the sixth hour of the first day and my heart was bleeding. I questioned if I could withstand two weeks of that kind of torture.

For an entire week they did just as they said they were going to do, they pretended they were engaged. Whether they were somewhere in the opera house or at a restaurant, they pretended. They talked about wedding plans, who they'd invite, what they'd have to eat, where they'd go on their honeymoon, and where they'd live after the wedding. They even talked about how many children they would have.

Raoul was at every performance and sent large bouquets of flowers to her room every day, and every day he would take her in his arms and kiss her, and every day she would kiss him back, and every day my heart broke, and every day I cried, and every day I questioned my sanity and my strength to see through to the finish what I'd originally thought was a necessary scheme. The only good thing that happened every day was that Christine would return to Madame Valerius' and sleep in her own bed.

The first day of the second week brought with it an unexpected bit of news, not just for me but more so for Christine. As usual, Raoul showed up after rehearsals with a basket of biscuits and wine. They spread out a blanket on her dressing room floor and pretended they were in a park with birds singing and white clouds passing overhead. Christine was laughing at something she herself had said when Raoul reached for her hand.

"Christine, I have something important to tell you."

"And what would that be, my sweetheart?" she asked with a large smile and a giggle. "Are you going to add a cruise to our honeymoon, or are you going to buy me that fur coat I saw as a wedding gift?"

"No, something better."

She grabbed his other hand. "What, pray tell, could possibly be better than an adventurous cruise?"

"Seriously, Christine, I've decided not to go to the North Pole on expedition."

She instantly dropped his hands and lost her smile. Then, just like a turtle retreats into the safety of its shell when threatened, she retreated into herself. Her face lost all color, and I couldn't even tell if she was breathing. She stared at Raoul, whose expression was also changing. He looked confused.

"Why this strange reaction, Christine? I thought you'd be happy to hear this good news."

She got to her feet, looked around, and landed her sight on the mirror and me. She was breathing hard by then, and her fingers were at her waist and twisting the ribbon of her bodice. I recognized that gesture all too well, and the terrified expression on her face.

I had to clench my teeth to keep my compassionate reaction to her silent cry for help from escaping my lips. The fright in her eyes was truly great, and I believe she was finally realizing the truthfulness of my words about playing such a dangerous game. She looked up toward the latch for the mirror, and I believe she was considering escaping through it right then and there.

I was holding my breath by then, not sure just how to play out the scene, in which I was only supposed to be a spectator and not a participant. Raoul rescued me when he stood behind her, taking her shaking shoulders in his hands.

"What's wrong, Christine?"

She was holding one arm at her waist and her other hand was at her throat when she answered breathlessly, "I don't feel well. Perhaps I had too much wine. I think I need to go home."

Raoul took her by the arm and gently sat her in her chair. Then he gathered everything up, put it in the basket, and took her by the arm again, leading her out of her room, as if she was an elderly convalescing patient. From there he took her home, went inside for a few minutes, and then left.

I was down and across the street from the lady's home when I told the driver I wanted him to wait until I gave him new instructions. We were there for over two hours when a carriage pulled up in front of the house, and Christine came out and got in. She'd changed her clothes and looked in a hurry.

They headed back toward the opera house, and once she got there she was nearly running as she entered and started through the passageways. She was moving so fast that I almost lost her a few times. Once I knew she was heading for her room, I took a shortcut and headed for the mirror. I was barely behind it when she came rushing in. Within a second, I knew what she was doing. She placed her chair by the mirror, and I quickly turned and ran down the passage, knowing she would soon be in the passage with me.

Naturally, my longer legs and arms gave me the advantage, so I was in my music room, had a moment to catch my breath, spread out my score of Don Juan on top of my organ, and was playing it before I heard the door move on its pivots. I stopped playing and turned to watch as she entered, completely out of breath.

"Christine," I said, with wide-eyed innocence. "What are you doing here? It hasn't been two weeks already, has it?"

I rose to face her as the door closed behind her. Her fingers began twisting the lace on her skirt and she whimpered, "Erik, I . . ."

I frowned at her. "What is it, Christine?"

She walked slowly toward me, stopped right in front of me, looked up into my face, and then the tears began filling her eyes.

I placed my hands on her trembling shoulders and spoke words that were only partly an act. "My dear, what's wrong?"

She lowered her forehead against my chest and sobbed. "Erik, please hold me."

I needed no further invitation. My arms went around her, I closed my eyes, my face went into her hair, and my entire body melted against hers.

"Oh, my Christine," I whispered. "What happened?"

She shook her head slowly and said softly, "Just hold me."

We stood there holding each other, and I felt so bad for her and the stress I'd put her under. She'd always been so soft, but right then I could feel bones that I'd never felt before. She'd lost weight, so her health was being compromised, and I questioned if I should put a stop to the entire affair. Was what I was doing that important?

Before I could answer that question, she said, "I'm sorry, Erik. I know I wasn't supposed to come back for another week, but I had to. I was so frightened."

"Of what?"

She looked at me intently but only shook her head. "I don't want to talk about it. I only want to stay for a while. Please let me stay."

Although her request in no way fit into my plans, I couldn't refuse her, so she stayed the rest of the day and night. She had me deliver a note to the managers giving her apologies for missing the performance along with assurance that she would return the next night. We talked only a little and then she asked me to read to her, which I did until she fell asleep. The next morning I had tea and toast ready for her when she woke.

When she sat down across from me at the table, she again apologized. "I'm sorry for ruining your plans, but I didn't know what else to do."

"Plans can always be altered, my sweet. They weren't written in stone. It's obvious you're in serious distress, and I can imagine it's about the decision that's facing you. Am I right?"

She lowered her eyes and nodded.

"Christine, I've discovered that you can't please everyone. You have to pick your battles. You're a wonderful and caring woman, and, as I've watched you these last months, I can see you're always trying to make everyone around you happy, perhaps to your own detriment.

"While that's an admirable quality for anyone to have, it comes with a cost, and, from the looks of you, that cost could be your health. I suspect you're trying to please too many people at once. You need to step back and ask yourself what it is you want and not what those around you want.

"While others may be pleased with your efforts to make them happy, you can't keep it up forever. Something will break, and I fear that something will be you. If you aren't happy, my dear, then those who love you won't be happy either, so all your efforts will be for naught."

She looked at me soberly for a moment and then asked, "But what if any decision I make will hurt someone I love, Erik? How can I think about what I want when what I want will hurt someone I love?"

I knew she was talking about either Raoul or me, and I had to remove myself from the equation before I could answer her with truth.

"Will the decision make you happy, Christine?"

"It would if it didn't hurt someone I loved," she replied with a slight shake of her head.

I sighed. "Does that person you love also love you?"

She looked me directly in the eyes for a moment before she answered, "Yes."

"Then tell that person the truth, and that person, because of his love for you, will understand. Nothing lasts forever, Christine. Time moves on, and, with its movement, it soothes our pain. Nothing lasts forever. Whatever decision you make won't stop the sun from rising, and it won't stop life from moving on. Don't take so much on your delicate shoulders. You can't please everyone."

Her eyes filled with tears again, and she placed her hands over her face and began to sob.

"Oh, Christine. My poor, Christine," I whispered. "Pease don't cry."

I reached across the table and took both of her hands and held them between mine. Then I told her what I would tell myself.

"Pour yourself into your music right now. Take your disquieting thoughts and set them aside for a few days, and place your heart between the notes on a score. Perhaps things will look differently once you've given your heart time to rest."

We talked softly for a while longer, and then our conversation moved on to the current production and questions she had about parts of it and how she could improve them. I gave her all the direction and encouragement I could, without actually making the decisions for her.

When she was in better spirits, I reminded her, "The eighth of July will be here soon, and I'll be in the audience to see how you handle that segment. Will you still sing for me that night?"

She blinked slowly and responded as before, "I sing for you every night, Erik. No one else—only you."

I squeezed her hand briefly before she left for rehearsals, and I continued with my observation of her encounters with Raoul. I believe my suggestion about pouring everything out in music must have helped, because she did wonderfully during both the rehearsals and the performance that night. I was watching from my box, and I couldn't have been more proud of her, especially considering I knew the emotional trauma she was going through as she sang. The audience went crazy with their applause. She was truly superb.

The main downside to the evening was that Raoul was also present and just across from me, and after the performance he ran to her dressing room. I was also there behind the mirror as he came in and took her in his arms, congratulating her on her wonderful voice, and then kissing her. She didn't turn away from his kiss, but the air around them was different, and Raoul knew it. His voice wasn't totally sincere when he said she'd sung the best ever.

She smiled softly, turned toward the mirror, with one hand at her throat, and replied almost under her breath, "Yes, I felt it."

I watched Raoul closely as he watched her. He scowled at the mirror and at her. I could tell he understood her tone and her expression. He knew she was silently talking to me, and it then became obvious to him how deep her feelings were for me. He was jealous, and that pleased me.

His next words were slicing as he took her left hand in his. "You still wear his ring—this common band from a commoner."

"Not much longer, Raoul, and it'll be finished," she replied softly and yet with conviction.

"What do you mean, finished, Christine? What will be finished?"

She took her hand from his while shaking her head. "You must go now. I'll see you tomorrow."

He argued a bit more about not wanting to leave, but she held her ground and he left. The expression they both had when he left told me that the make-believe was over, and he knew it. There was a different and unexplainable air around her when she sat at her dressing table, taking off her jewelry and gazing right at me. I was curious. Had she finally made her decision?

"Erik, are you here?" she asked softly.

Even though I was curious, I didn't answer. She had to believe I was never watching her or she might not be true to herself, or Raoul, or me.

She got up and headed for her curtain, then stopped and looked over her shoulder. "Erik?"

When I didn't answer, she continued on. Once she was dressed, I followed her back to Madame Valerius' home.

For the next three days, everything went much the same as it had before Raoul announced that he wouldn't be leaving, with the exception that the make-believe was gone. Christine was real, and, while she still continued to drag him all over my opera house with constant chatter, she wasn't playing. She showed him everything in my domain, with the exception of the cellars.

On many occasions she'd stop talking and gaze at something, becoming very still. She acted as if she was listening for something, and I knew that something was me. Raoul would ask her what was wrong; then she would start up again and they'd be off in another direction.

On the fourth day, which was seven July, she was different. Her mood was low, so much so that I feared something bad had happened to Madame Valerius. But once Raoul showed up and she didn't disclose it to him, I knew her changed attitude was because she had only one more day before she had to make her final decision—if she hadn't already. I felt badly for her, leaving her with that weighty responsibility, but she was the only one who could make it.

As the day moved on, she became more and more withdrawn, and Raoul asked her about it often. She'd shrug it off and continue on with what they were doing. That continued until she had to prepare for the performance, but then continued on after it was over. The tension was thick enough around them that even I was finding it hard to breathe, and I think it was making Raoul angry, because he then took a stronger hand.

He started with his domineering ways when they were sitting on the stage by an open trap door and among the sets for the opening scene of the next performance.

"Christine, I can't stand this. I demand to know what's wrong. You answer my questions by changing the subject and dragging me off to show me a new location. Also, I've noticed you never show me what's in the lower stories. Why is that, Christine?"

I believe he already knew the answer, considering he'd met me by the lake, so that question had to be his way of testing her truthfulness. That tactic worked and he got what he wanted when she finally answered his question outright.

"That's because those cellars belong to him, and you can never go down there."

He raised his head and his chest went out, like a bloodhound when catching a scent. "Does he also live down there?"

"He lives far away, Raoul, so don't question it."

She remained faithful to me with that response, but by then his superior attitude was getting on my nerves, so I gave him something else to think about. I closed the trap door. They both gasped and stared at it for a few moments, and then Christine quickly took Raoul's hand and dragged him away.

He was walking away with her but he was looking back at the closed trap door when he asked, "It was him that shut the door, wasn't it Christine?"

"No, it couldn't have been him, Raoul. He's working on something important, and when he works he's much too involved to do anything else, especially something as trivial as closing trap doors. The managers pay men to do that, and that's all they do all day long, close this door, close that door, all day long. I'm sure it was one of them—not Erik."

Raoul stopped and frowned. "Christine, your hands are like ice, and you're shaking. What's wrong? Are you afraid of him?"

"No, certainly not, Raoul," she replied, but not convincingly.

"Christine, you're lying to me. Has he hurt you?"

"Raoul, no! He would never hurt me," she insisted, while dragging him up one level to another.

"Christine, if he's hurt you or you're frightened of him, then why stay here? Why not leave? Come with me, and I'll take you so far away from here that he'll never find you."

She stopped and looked at him, as if she was contemplating his words. "No, Raoul, I could never marry you, you know that."

She continued with her upward climb, and he continued with his plea. "That's not necessarily the case, Christine. But, even if it was, I could still take you somewhere where this monster won't find you."

Again she stopped and looked at him. "Why do you speak that way, Raoul? He's not a monster as so many claim. He can be very kind and gentle and caring, and even wise."

"Kind and gentle? He killed Joseph Buquet. Do you call that caring?" he demanded.

Still defending me, she rebuked him. "You don't know that for sure. It's just a rumor."

"How do you know that, Christine? Did you ask him?"

Without halting her upward climb, she answered, "As a matter of fact, yes, I did."

"And what did he say?" he asked, while trying to keep up with her pace.

She stopped momentarily and looked back at him. "That it was an accident caused by Joseph."

With spread hands he asked, "And you believed him?"

She turned and kept moving. "You don't understand, Raoul. He was telling me the truth, and I even saw the proof."

"Proof? What possible proof could he show you?"

She turned and looked at him again as if she was going to answer, but then started running up another flight of stairs, with his steps and words following her.

"What proof?"

"Just forget about it, Raoul. Forget I said anything."

"How can I, when you're obviously frightened to death by him?"

"It's not that," she yelled over her shoulder, without missing a step.

He managed to grab her arm and stop her, and, while trying to catch his breath, he questioned, "Where are you going? Stop running."

"Let's go to the roof. He won't be there, so we can talk."

He complied and said no more until they were on the roof, and so was I. It was a beautiful summer night, with bright stars and a few wispy clouds. But we were all much too concerned with the direction the conversation was going in to enjoy what surrounded us. They were both out of breath and moved to a bench where they sat down.

My own heart was pounding, more from anticipation of what was to come than from exertion. I moved slowly and quietly through the shadows until I was as close to them as I could get without being seen. A large bronze statue of Apollo served as my shield where I could listen and watch them through the strings of his huge lyre.

As far as I was concerned, a foreboding air encircled the top of the opera house that night, and I feared the stage was already set and just waiting for the players to begin their final lines. I believe we would have had more success in changing the course of a river than to change the course of the events that were beginning to unfold that fateful night.

Forty-Four

Christine glanced in all directions, as if she was a frightened fawn hiding in a thicket, and I could hear her quick breaths from where I stood.

"Tell me, Christine," Raoul started again. "What has he done to you to make you so frightened of him?"

"Nothing, Raoul. I'm not necessarily afraid of him—not like that—not for me."

He kept moving her face toward him as he spoke. "Well, something has happened. Why do you continually go to him and then act the way you are now? What is he holding over you—love or fear? I've seen love in your eyes when you speak about him, a strange love that's driven by passion. Why do you deny it?"

"Oh, Raoul," she sighed and lowered her head again. "You can't possibly understand, because I don't."

There was silence while he gently ran his hand across her back, and then, much to my heart-stopping fear, she began from the beginning and started telling him everything about us. She told him things that were to be our secrets. She divulged everything, and I felt so betrayed. She even told him about the secret passage and how she came and went from my home.

How could she? How could she tell him those things when she knew how important my secrecy was to me and my existence? My emotions began to flip flop rapidly, from pain to anger and back again. But, in the end, it was the pain that remained, and my eyes began to burn and my chest began to ache.

The first thread snapped, and a rip began to appear across my heart, and with each of Christine's words that followed, another thread broke, and through each broken thread my heart seeped my life sustaining blood. I believe that, during those moments, if I'd looked down at my chest it would have been crimson. She'd shot me in the heart just as her lover had shot me in the back.

Once she was finished with the first of her betrayals, Raoul spoke softly to her. "Please, Christine, this is breaking my heart. Let me take you away from here where he can't find you."

"I can't leave, Raoul. It would kill him if I left and he didn't know where I was."

"Christine, from what I've heard, if we stay here, he could kill both of us." She stared at him, and then lowered her shaking head. "Then let me take you away someplace safe," he continued, "and I'll come back and deal with him."

Her head sprung up. "No, Raoul, never! You must never meet him. It wouldn't be good for you, and something terrible could happen. Please, tell me you'll never try to find him. Oh, I shouldn't have told you about the passage. Please, Raoul, promise me you'll never try to find him."

He didn't divulge that he'd already met me, but he did expose more of his stupidity. "I'm not afraid of him, Christine. He's nothing more than a diabolical old man."

"Raoul, don't be a fool. He has . . . I know you wouldn't survive if there was a confrontation between the two of you."

"Oh! I hate him, Christine. I hate him for what he's doing to us. You think this Erik is stronger and more powerful than I am, don't you?"

With her hand over her mouth, she stared at him. "You can't possibly understand him and what he can do, Raoul. He has an incredible mind, and I . . . I . . . he uses powers and . . . he's unbelievable. You wouldn't survive, Raoul. You wouldn't survive. He would . . . He would kill you. I know it."

Raoul sat quietly, perhaps thinking about the two times we'd already encountered each other. In a moment he said, "Then I'll take the police with me. I'll take lots of them. He can't fight us all."

"Oh, no, Raoul, you mustn't. Promise me you won't do that. I don't want him hurt. You can't let anyone hurt him. So many have already . . ."

He took her hands in his and ran his fingers over my ring. She was still looking down until he spoke her name, and then she looked up into his eyes.

"Do you love this monstrous man, Christine? Please tell me the truth. I need to know the truth, so I can be put out of this misery I'm in."

She took her hand from his and began rolling my ring around her finger. "I wish I could answer that question, not only for you but also for me, but I don't know, Raoul. I honestly don't know or understand what I feel for him. His music and his voice make me feel as I've never felt before. It's like being in a dream. But then there are times when he makes me so very angry, and we argue." Then she looked directly into his eyes. "You know when he makes me the angriest? It's when he's talking badly about you, Raoul, just like you're talking badly about him. You make me angry when you speak about him this way."

Raoul looked away from her. "Christine, you're confusing me. How can you pity him, be angry with him, and fear him all in the same breath?"

She lowered her head into her hands. "Oh, Raoul, I don't know what I'm saying. I feel as if I'm going crazy. I just know that I need to . . . I want to be honest with you just as I've tried to be honest with Erik. But, most of all, I need to be honest with myself. Sometimes I get so confused that I just want to go away from both of you so I can think. You both make me angry, and yet what I feel for you both is so strong."

She looked back up at Raoul. "I know I love you, Raoul, and I think I want to go away with you and try to forget all of this. But then there's Erik, and I don't know if I can live without him. I can't leave him, and I can't hurt him. He's done so much for me and my career, and I know it would make him cry if I tell him I'm leaving, and I don't want to see him cry anymore."

While Christine continued to twist and twist my ring on her finger, Raoul came up with what he thought was a simple answer.

"Then don't go back down there anymore, and you won't see him cry. Let me take you away from him and his influence over you."

She sighed, "It's not that simple. If I don't go back down there, he'll be hurt and come looking for me, and he'll call me with his voice, and I won't be able to resist him. And if he suspects that you had anything to do with it, he could lose his temper, and no telling what he'll do. He has a very bad temper, Raoul, and when he loses it, it's most frightening."

"Then that does it, Christine, you can't go back to him. I won't let you go back to him."

"Oh, Raoul, you can't say that. I have to make this decision, and he isn't always a frightening demon like you think. Most of the time, he's so gentle that he can cry out of tenderness. He reminds me so much of my father at those times, and I feel safe when I'm with him. He's such a contradiction, and that's what makes me so confused, that and how I feel about you."

Before she twisted her finger off, Raoul took her hand. "If you fear him at all, why do you go back?"

"I'm not sure. I'm drawn to him for some reason, and, once I get down there, I don't want to leave. There have been many times when I'm down there and it's Erik who tells me it's time for me to go, not me. He makes me leave, telling me he has to work on his opera. But I would stay there if he let me, and sometimes I think I want to stay there with him forever."

Raoul's voice was definitely irritated. "Christine, you frighten me when you speak like this. I think you might love him more than you're willing to admit. I sense you're not being honest with me."

"Raoul, I brought you here so I could speak to you without hindrance. I want to be honest with you and myself, but I just don't know for sure what honesty is right now."

She turned her face away from him, and he spoke softly. "Do you love me, Christine?"

"Yes, Raoul. I do love you, that I know for sure. I know what love is, and I love you. I love Meg, and I love Mummy. I know what love is, and what I feel for Erik is not like that, and yet I'm compelled to go to him. When I'm with him, I feel safe in a way that no one else can make me feel. What I feel for him is so powerful and almost supernatural."

There was silence before Raoul spoke again. "I think you're being hypnotized, Christine, and that frightens me even more. He could make you do things without your permission." She looked at him sternly for a few moments, prompting him to question her. "Why do you look at me that way?"

Hesitantly and slowly she responded, "You're the second person to tell me that."

"Who else told you that? Certainly not this man," he said with scorn.

"No, it was the Persian. He once warned me about Erik's power to control minds."

Oded, I growled under my breath. His interference would surely cost him dearly if he were within my reach right then. My anger instantly flared, giving me a few brief seconds of relief from the stabs to my chest before I once again focused on their conversation.

"Then that's what it is, Christine. You're being tricked into going down there, tricked into doing his bidding. You must not go there ever again."

She looked at him again, and I watched her eyes fill with tears, and she once again twisted my ring around her finger.

"What's wrong, Christine? Why do you cry over this monster?"

She turned her head and didn't answer, but I almost did. Between Christine's betrayal and Raoul's arrogance, my strength to bridle my actions was being tested to the fullest. I clutched the back of Apollo with my fingers, wishing it was Raoul's neck. Often, I had to close my eyes and press my forehead against the cold metal in order to push aside emotions that were wearing away at what little restraint I had left.

"Christine, please don't lie to me. I can take the truth even if it hurts, but please don't lie to me."

"I don't want to lie to anyone, and especially not to myself. I'm trying so hard to be honest with everyone, but it's driving me crazy."

"Oh, Christine," he said as he pulled her into his chest, "don't cry."

Her words were muffled and spoken through tears. "I don't want to hurt Erik . . . poor Erik. He loves me, Raoul, and I feel something for him that frightens me, and I don't want to hurt him."

He took her shoulders in his hands and looked right into her eyes. "Christine, listen to me. This man is a monster, and he's only going to hurt you if you keep going back down there."

"Oh, Raoul," she sobbed and melted into his arms. "I don't know what to do. Poor Erik. I don't think he would hurt me, although there was a time when I thought he was going to kill me, all because I saw his face, his horrible face. Oh, poor Erik. But then he turned as meek as a lamb and cried like a baby and begged me to forgive him.

"Think of him at my feet, Raoul, cursing himself, begging for my forgiveness, and confessing his immense love for me. He crawled on the floor before me and begged me. I told him if he loved me that much, he would let me go. From then on, he showed me nothing but respect and explained to me when he would let me go, and he did. He kept his word, and he let me go. A monster wouldn't do all that."

"Christine, you mustn't go back down there. This man is mad."

"I know, Raoul, I know. If I go back down there with him, I fear I'll never see you again. I won't have the strength to leave him again if he cries."

"Christine, listen to me. I don't care what my family says. I don't care about my inheritance or my name, I only want you. These last two weeks have made that clear to me. I only want you. Go away with me now, right now. We can move up north away from all of this, and our secret engagement can become a real one. Marry me, Christine, for real, and you'll no longer live in fear. Come with me, right now," he said as he got to his feet and took her hands, lifting her up.

"No, I can't Raoul, not now. He expects me to sing for him tomorrow night, and if I'm not there his heart will surely break. He tells me that often, and I can't be responsible for his heart breaking, I just can't."

Raoul huffed. "Why do you care about this man? He has caused both of us so much heartache, not to mention the deaths he's caused. He's nothing more than a diabolical, cold-blooded murderer."

"No, Raoul, you don't understand. He's not like that, I know."

"Oh, Christine, you've just been duped by this man, can't you see it? Come away with me, and, in time, you'll see it was all a sham of his to lure you into staying and living a life such as his. Please, Christine, let me take you away."

She turned away from him, sat back down, and looked out over the city and then at the sky. Her hands were limp in her lap, and she spoke as if in a dream.

"Will you take me far away where the clouds are going?"

Raoul sat back next to her. "Yes, Christine, I'll take you far away."

She turned back toward him and took his hands in hers. "He'll be watching me during the performance tomorrow night, and then he'll be waiting for me to return to him with my answer. Meet me in my dressing room, and then we can leave before he knows I've left. See if there's a train leaving for the north so we can leave before he finds out. Can you do that, Raoul?

"If I'm faint and fear to go with you, make me go, Raoul. Don't let me change my mind. I can't go back to him and look into his pitiful eyes, I just can't. I can't watch them fill with tears again. I can't listen to him tell me he loves me and plead with me to love him. If I see him and hear his voice, I won't have the strength to refuse him, I know I won't."

My fingers pressed hard against my face in a pitiful effort to silence my cries that were demanding their say. I can't find a word that can come close to describing what those words of my lovely Christine did to me. I felt as if the last weak thread holding the fragile remaining portion of my soul had been ruthlessly ripped from my chest, leaving my defenseless and trusting heart to plummet to the cold stone beneath my feet.

I stared at her in disbelief. I'd been trying to prepare myself for what I thought would be the worst case scenario, but I was completely unprepared by her traitorous actions. My eyes blurred as I watched on, feeling I no longer had any control over my life, while they heartlessly moved on with theirs.

He took her in his arms, and she sobbed and pleaded with him to help her. He raised her chin and kissed her, and I felt my heart at my feet struggling to beat just one more time when it no longer had the will to do so. With her hand in his, they left the rooftop, and the stars, and the wispy clouds, and the beautiful summer night, and her downed angel with his bleeding heart.

The air on the rooftop became silent, with only my muffled sobs left as evidence of the sad scene. Christine had the soft shoulder of Raoul to fall against, while I was left with the cold bronze of Apollo as comfort.

"Oh, Christine, how could you?" I whispered into his back. "How could you?"

My fingers wrapped around the metal strings of Apollo's lyre, and I cried tears of such agony. How could she? I began to question, I gave her everything I had. How could she do this to me? How could she leave me without even a goodbye? Did I not tell her I was prepared for a refusal, and all I asked of her was to be honest with me and give me back my ring? Was that so much to ask—just to be honest?

I didn't even ask for my first kiss, not even a goodbye kiss from the woman I cherished, the woman I'd given everything to. I could have. I could have taken one anytime I pleased, but I didn't. I'd been nothing but a gentleman to her, and she turned into a Delilah to me.

I started moving across the rooftop still questioning, Oh, Christine, how could you do this to me? I sat on the same bench where they'd just been, and I cried. I removed my mask, and laid my naked face in my hands, and I cried. I doubled over and rocked in pain, and I cried.

I only had enough strength to whisper, "Christine—Christine, why?"

My sobs subsided, my tears began to dry, and I focused on my feet, now left to walk their path alone once more. Where will you take me, my feet? How far can you walk without your heart? Italy? Spain? America? Or perhaps, the North Pole or the South Pacific Islands? How far can you walk without your heart?

I was using all my brain power to work out what I had to do next, but it's hard for a brain to work without a heart. I did know though that I had to interrupt their plans just a bit. I couldn't let her leave with my ring. I had to get it back. She could keep her heart, I finally decided. I didn't want anything that treacherous lying around anyway.

Also, I had to let both of them know that I was still in control, and that I, and I alone, would be directing the last scene of our near love affair. I couldn't let either of them leave without knowing that they hadn't outsmarted me. So, after a few minutes, I had the final scene of the final act of our little drama written to my satisfaction.

They would be meeting in her dressing room after the performance, thinking they'd sneak away without my knowing. Well, I'd have a surprise waiting for them. I'd be there, dressed in my finest evening attire. I'd be staunch and in control when I reminded them that I always see and hear all that goes on in my domain, and that they're both fools to think they could slink away without my knowing about it.

I'll criticize Raoul by telling him that he didn't get a very good deal on those tickets he bought. I'll tell him he should have consulted me first, and I could have gotten him a much better deal. I'll take the gowns and jewels I'd bought Christine to her dressing room and give them to them as her dowry. Perhaps, I'll even buy something new and expensive for them both, perhaps a silver platter engraved with something special for the newlyweds, just to pour salt in their wounds.

If it weren't for the stern air I planned to use, our meeting would be cordial, but my sarcasm would definitely get my point across. I'll be anything but the wimpy, tearful fool she thought I would be. If any tears are shed, they'll belong to my traitor. I even had the staging set. I'll be sitting in her chair with my feet propped up on her dressing table and perhaps thumbing through her diary when she enters.

My planning was doing its trick, and it helped soften my pain. Now, I thought, if I can only keep up this attitude until the following night, we might all make it through this long and ridiculous ordeal in one piece.

I was leaning back on the bench and looking at the same wispy clouds that Christine was looking at when she made her final decision to leave without giving me my ring and without a goodbye. I'll be much more of a gentleman than she was a lady, I thought. I was always more of a gentleman than she was a lady.

I should have known from the beginning that I couldn't trust her. My first clue should have been when she ripped off my mask. If I couldn't trust her with my face, what made me think I could trust her with my heart? She couldn't be trusted. She says one thing and then does another, the lying wench.

I started to get up when something caught the moon's light and sparkled under the bench. My automatic reaction was to look toward it, and then, once more, in disbelief my emotions took off in another direction without me. I reached for it. I reached for my ring. Rolling it between my fingers, I shook my head. She knew what that ring meant to me, and yet she treated it as no more than a child's toy. I only asked that she give it back to me if she didn't want it. That was all I asked.

I slid it back on my little finger where it belonged and where it should have remained, and then I walked to the edge of the roof, twisting my ring as I went. My jaws were tightening as I replaced my mask and glared down on the street below and the people carrying on their lives, with no regard for this fallen angel's despair.

I'd turned my suffering into a cold resolve with my plans to rewrite the last scene, but with this new evidence of her betrayal, that cold resolve moved easily into uncontrolled anger. I cursed God for my pitiful plight, and I beat on the cold stone that surrounded me. Then I cursed myself for being so brainless as to allow another human to have that much control over me. But then my worst fear moved in and started a steady path toward the surface—my controlled anger.

It was that anger that had allowed me to plot against Franco and then to carry out my desire to kill him, and I would have succeeded at that young age of ten if it hadn't been for the loving care of a father. My mind and heart could plan such a murder because of my controlled anger.

It was that anger I'd carried with me during that year and a half when so many lost their lives because of it. It was that controlled anger that nearly got Christine killed once before, and with what I was feeling for her right then, I feared where my thoughts were going. But as it began to take over my mind and heart, I once more became a spectator, merely watching myself from another sphere somewhere.

I was no longer cursing, my voice was silent, and the air on the rooftop became tranquil once more. My heart slowed to a steady beat as I looked out over the rooftops and into the distant hills. I looked to the north and wondered if Raoul had bought their tickets yet. I pictured both of them smiling, thinking they had it all worked out so nicely.

I huffed. She's broken her last heart. She's trifled with both of our hearts, Raoul's and mine, long enough, and she won't be permitted to do it any longer. No longer will I be the gentleman she's known. I'll take from her what I've wanted, what she's refusing me. I'll take that first kiss and much more. I only asked her to be my living wife in name only. Well, her little game of betrayal is going to come thundering back on her.

I felt my eyes narrow as I began envisioning my plans to make her completely my own. My lifelong dream of living within the walls of an opera house had been ruined, and I was then being forced to leave my piano and almost everything else I cared for. Everything was ruined because of that tramp, so she'd be made to pay for her folly.

She'll either marry me for real or she won't live long enough to marry anyone. She thinks she can play a game with the master of games and win. Well, I don't think so. This master always wins—always.

As I walked slowly and deliberately down from the roof, I worked out the details that would put an end to the game we'd been playing. This will be the end of my lonely and tormented life one way or the other. I'd only asked her for my ring or her heart, and she thought that was too hard a decision to make. Well, she'll soon come to realize what a simple decision that was—simple in comparison to my next demand.

She'll either lie with me in *my* bed as my real wife or we'll both be dead and buried within two days, one day to maneuver my plans, and one day for her to make her decision—my wife or death.

With my heart no longer in pain, I walked slowly through the empty corridors, probably for the last time. I went to the stable, rendered the grooms unconscious, and took César for a ride along the Seine for one last time. I didn't care who saw me, and those who did received my icy glare as a warning. I took him to the lake, kissed him goodbye, and left for my home, all the while knowing exactly what I was doing, and I was doing it grimly.

When I knew the city was awake, I left my home and set out for the dress shop, and there I purchased the last dress for my deceitful wife, a bridal gown. It was a beautiful dress and such a shame it couldn't be worn on a more festive occasion. Its white satin was overlaid with delicate

Venetian lace, and small pearls were scattered throughout the bodice, truly a piece of art.

The shopkeeper smiled warmly at me. "It appears the other dresses you've purchased for your lady friend must have paid off."

Coldly, I responded, "Perhaps," and nothing more.

I next went to the pharmacist and bought a bottle of chloroform. Once home, I checked the connections to the two boxes on my mantle, both the grasshopper and the scorpion. Then I went down to my wine cellar and checked the connections to the gunpowder. Finally, I checked the connections on the barrels of gunpowder around the foundation of the opera house. I had no intention of doing the job halfway—I never did anything halfway.

Once that was completed, I poured myself a glass of brandy and sat calmly in my chair by the fire, while I wrote what I imagined would be my last words in my journal. After that, I played all my instruments: organ, violin, cello, Spanish guitar, and French horn, thinking it could be the last time I'd hear their special voices. Once finished, I played my piano for a long time, fearing it would be my last musical experience.

I played Chopin and Mozart peacefully and then all my own compositions, which almost started to break through my cold anger and make me start to question what I was doing. Therefore, I went back to my organ and moved into the more angry pieces of Don Juan, and, considering what was to take place shortly, they were most appropriate.

Then I dressed properly for the opera, and, once the second act of *Faust* started, I entered Box Five through the marble column. Casually, I took my cloak off, laid it over the back of a chair, and sat down. Then I proceeded to glare at Raoul and his brother across the auditorium from me. Christine appeared on stage and sang Marguerite beautifully, and I could tell she was pouring her soul out, and I knew it was my swan song.

Once more her voice almost broke through my determined hatred, so I moved my sight back to Raoul and pictured the train tickets in his pocket. That's all it took to revive my anger, so, along with my glare, I silently told him to tell her goodbye, because that was his last chance to do so.

The time for the prison scene approached, so I was up, replaced my cloak, and entered the column again, heading down to the lighting organ and the two men in charge of raising and lowering the lighting for the stage. With a chloroform soaked cloth in each hand, I stood in the shadows, waiting for the prison scene to start, but, before it did, a man came out of a door beside me. So I quickly grabbed his head with the cloths, dragged him back into that room, and left him there unconscious. Then I again waited in the shadows until just before Christine was due to be the closest to the trap door in the stage floor.

Then I was around the corner, with those same cloths in each hand. I put one hand over each of the two men's faces, and pressed their heads against my body until they went limp. Then I listened to the music and waited for my cue, while I pictured the players moving around the stage. Then, just as Marguerite began invoking an angel for guidance, I threw the switches and darted up the stairs toward the dark stage.

There were a few screams and a rumble of voices by the time I reached Christine. Then my hand, still with the chloroform cloth in it, went over her face, and within moments she went limp in my arms. Instantly, I tossed her over my shoulder, and we were both down through the trap door, and it was shut before the lights came back up. I carried her through the maze of beams and gears until I reached my passageway. From there it was only a matter of minutes before we were in my home.

I took her to her bed, or, should I say, my bed, and laid her down with cold indifference. Any other time in our relationship those moves would have been a dream come true, but that night I wasn't even tempted to stroke her cheek. I didn't allow myself to be moved by her beauty or my love for her, and I didn't even cover her. I was too angry for those niceties.

While trying to rub the pain out of my injured right shoulder, I glared down at that temptress, that liar, that cheat. Knowing she would be out for several more minutes, I headed for my kitchen, and, when I returned, I was swirling brandy in a glass. Setting the glass on her dressing table, I locked her door and dropped the key in my vest pocket. Then I took the wedding dress from its box and spread it out over the bed beside her. Smirking, I thought, how foolish for anyone to try to outsmart me, especially a flirtatious and insensitive woman such as she.

Next, I went to the trash where I found the last two roses I'd given her, which were by then dead and dry. Hoping she'd remember what her roses stood for, her future, I crumbled them over the dress, making the silent statement that her future was dead.

After pulling out her chair, I turned it toward the end of the bed, sat down, and then, with disdain, I propped my crossed ankles on the bed's railing. I slid my ring off my finger and put it in my vest pocket so it could wait for its cue to take its place in that night's drama.

Taking my glass of brandy in my hands, I took a sip and prepared to wait. I relaxed as I placed my elbow on the arm of the chair, my chin on my knuckles, and my eyes on my soon-to-be wife. Then I watched her and waited for her to wake and for the first scene of the real last act to begin for us both.

While I waited, my eyes wandered around the room and landed on her music box, the last gift I'd given her. I set my brandy glass down and picked up the box, reading the inscription: *Music has joined one angel to another forever.* My eyes narrowed, and I squeezed the box as hard as I could. I visualized it disappearing into dust under my grip, but it didn't.

Then I read the inscription again and thought, no, don't destroy it, this is perfect. She is joined to me forever, and there's nothing she can do about it. I smiled and replaced the box on her table. Then, with repeated sips of my brandy, I continued waiting.

It took her nearly ten minutes to wake, during which time her beauty and my love for her almost took control of my hate-filled plans. To force their control away, I replayed the rooftop scene over and over in my mind until my anger pushed my love for her away.

When she started to stir, I watched her with narrowed eyes and a silent tongue. Another few moments and her eyes fluttered open and she looked around. Once it registered where she was, she jolted up and gasped.

I looked at her and snidely smiled. "Well, *my dear*, here we are again. Welcome home."

Forty-Five

"Erik? What am I doing here? What happened?"

"Oh, my dear, you look confused. Don't you remember?"

Her hand went to cover her open lips. "You? You did this? Why?"

"I did what, my sweet? Rescued you? Why, yes I did. You see you fainted right in the middle of your aria. You were praying for angelic help, so, being the upright angel that I am, I couldn't leave such a lovely Marguerite sprawled out over the stage that way, now could I?"

"No—you . . ."

"I what?"

"I felt your hand on the back of my neck and a cloth over my face."

"My hand? Oh, I don't think so. It must have been a pigeon's wing. You know how they like to roost on the rafters."

She looked down at the floor and began shaking her head. "No, it was you I felt."

"It couldn't have been me. Perhaps it was the Opera Ghost. Oh, no, wait a minute. It couldn't have been him, because he and I are one, right? So I would have known it."

She swung her feet off the bed and sat on its edge, waiting, I'm sure, for her equilibrium to return. "Erik, I demand you stop playing with me. This isn't funny."

"You demand?" I parroted with raised brows. "Oh, is this the part where I'm supposed to crumble at your feet and cry and dry my tears with your hem? I don't think so, my dear. You see, while I've been tutoring you, I've also been learning. I learn constantly—did you know that? I soak up information like the dry desert soaks up moisture. I've learned much from you.

"I've learned not to let my heart be moved by a traitor's tears or smooth tongue. There's nothing you can say or do that will influence my decisions. My plans are in motion and so solidly set that they might as well have been played out already. Nothing can change them, so save your breath."

She huffed and headed toward the door, scowling at me. "Plans? You're talking in riddles again, Erik, and I'm not in the mood." She was halfway across the room when she stopped and put her hand on her forehead. "What did you do to me? I can still smell what you put over my face, and it's giving me a headache. Oh," she grumbled, "I'm so tired of you men treating me as if I were a rag doll between two dogs. I'm fed up with it! I'm fed up with both of you!"

"If you feel that bad, then you shouldn't be wasting your strength walking around, my sweet," I said snidely, as I held the key to her door out toward her and twisted it between my fingers. Stubbornly, she jerked on the door handle several times anyway.

"Erik, let me out of here! They might be holding the act for me."

"Oh, I don't think they can wait that long. I'm sure your understudy has finished the act for you by now. But, sad to say, you don't have an understudy for your current role, do you?"

She rubbed her forehead again, frowned at the floor, and looked at me angrily. "Erik, please stop playing this game with me. You know Jolene is my understudy. Will you just let me out of here?"

"Why? So you can catch a train with your lover and leave me with nothing but a void? Tell me—why should I do that? Why should I make it easy for you? That's what I've done since day one, and how do you repay me? By leaving without a goodbye or an explanation? No, I don't think so. You were about to run out on our contract, and . . ."

"Contract?" She cut my words short with defiance. "I have no contract with you, so quit talking this way and let me out of here."

"Oh, but you do have a contract. Have you forgotten so quickly? Remember—in your more appreciative days—when you pleaded for me to stay by your side, and you asked how you could repay me for what I'd given you?"

"I spoke those words to my angel," she rebutted.

"Yes, but that angel and I are one—you know that. *I* was the one who gave you your talent, so the contract is with me and still binding. Nonetheless," I continued, nonchalantly, as I flicked a speck of dust from my knee, "remember what I told you to do? I only asked you to stay true to the course I'd started you on. At that time, you willingly agreed—you signed a verbal contract with your promise."

Her eyes narrowed, she shook her head slowly, and I continued, "You know that in some cultures, if you renege on a contract, you could lose your head. Should I take your pretty head as payment for your betrayal? Yes, perhaps I could have it mounted on the wall above my mantel like a trophy. Perhaps that would fill the void after you're gone."

That last statement removed some of her confidence, and she took a step back and a deep breath. "That's a sick thought, Erik. Have you gone mad?"

I laughed wickedly. "Yes, I presume I have. But this isn't the face or the posture of a madman. I've kept my insanity from you. You might have seen a glimpse of it the first time you were down here and tried to take something that belonged to me, but that was only a glimpse. If you'd seen it completely, it would have been the last thing you saw."

I shook my head. "Believe me, I've kept that monster hidden deep inside here," I said as I thumped my chest with my fist. "No, what you see right now is not insanity, but," I continued as I rose slowly to my feet, "if you try to take something else that belongs to me, namely you, then I fear you might see the full extent of my insanity."

As if testing her senses, she tried the door again. Then, when she looked up at me, I could see the fear in her eyes being to grow.

"What do you want from me, Erik? Are you threatening again to keep me locked down here to sing for you forever?"

"No, my sweet. The stakes have changed, thanks to your deception." I motioned to the wedding dress lying on the bed. "I want you to put that on."

She looked at it and moved closer to it. Then, as her fingers covered her open mouth, she exclaimed, "That's a wedding dress!"

I laughed again. "Why, yes, so it is. Now that you've proven your fine knowledge of women's fashions—put it on," I slowly growled.

Her head barely shook. "Erik, I don't understand why you're doing this. You keep talking about deception. How have I deceived you? I don't understand, and you're frightening me with all this crazy talk."

"Yes, you have a right to fear me now, my dear. You never had a reason to fear me in the past, but you changed the script, and now you have every reason to fear me." I motioned toward the bed. "Please, sit down and conserve your strength. You're going to need it."

"Erik, please, what are you doing?"

"Just playing out the scene as you wrote it."

"What are you talking about? What did I write?"

"I believe we've had a similar conversation, don't you remember? Although, at that time, I promised I wouldn't hurt you and that I'd be a gentleman, didn't I? Well, I can't guarantee the script is written exactly the same way this time around."

She frowned, and her hand went to her throat. "I don't understand."

"Oh, come now, *my sweet*, don't try to play the innocent with me. Don't you know by now that this is my domain, and I know all that goes on within it? I know when there's a casting change. I know when new sets arrive or when old horses leave." Then slowly and deliberately, I added, "And I know when the trap doors are opened and closed. I know all, Christine."

With my last words, she started putting the pieces together. With my next words, she lost all her color.

"I have eyes and ears all over my realm. They're in the props, they're in the curtains, they're in the catwalks, they're in the stable. I know everything, from my home in the fifth cellar to the highest pinnacle on the roof. I even know when train tickets are purchased and what time the train leaves the station. I'm very well informed. Oh, speaking of trains, I believe you're going to miss yours tonight, since you have a most important wedding to attend."

She hadn't taken her eyes off me the entire time, so I gestured toward the wedding dress again. "You didn't tell me how you like your wedding dress. Do you like what I picked out for you? I know it's not conventional for the groom to pick out the wedding dress for the bride, but then I think you probably realize by now that I'm rather unconventional in most of the things I do."

Without a word, she stared at the dress, and I went on. "Do you like the accents of scarlet roses? I do apologize for their condition though, I would much rather give you live roses. But then, perhaps their condition is perfect, considering they're supposed to represent your future."

Her eyes took on more fright and she shook her head. "Erik, what are you saying?"

I sighed slowly. "Don't you know by now, *my dear*, that everyone has to die sometime? And didn't you tell your young lover that you feared I would kill you? Didn't you tell him that, if you came back down here, you wouldn't be able to leave? Well, what can I say, *my sweet*, you set your own future in motion with your ill spoken and treacherous words, and they've been indelibly entered into the script."

She shook her head. "Erik?"

The look she gave me almost broke through to me. So I rushed toward her, towering over her.

"How could you, Christine? Why? I told you to tell me what you wanted—Raoul or me. I was prepared for you to reject me. I was ready for that, Christine. But, no, you were going to sneak away from me, without giving me so much as a 'thank you, Erik, for my voice and my career, but I don't want to marry you, and I'm going away with my childhood sweetheart and leaving the stage and all your hard work behind.' No, you couldn't give me the decency of being honest. You were going away without even a goodbye, Christine. How could you? How could you?"

I charged toward the opposite side of the room and nearly slammed my fist through the wall, and then I turned back toward her with my voice raised even more and out of control. "I gave you everything I had. I gave you my heart. I gave you your voice. I gave you my music. Why couldn't you give me just a simple goodbye? You liar—you cheat—you traitorous, deceitful wench."

She shook her head. "That's not true, Erik. What's wrong with you? You have to have gone mad."

"Mad? You ask a second time if I'm mad. You must really think I am, but I don't believe so. You see, I was born this way. Everything else you see, the voice, the music, the intellect are just a façade, much like my opera house. She's made from bricks and steel, but the fancies in Paris wouldn't consider sitting on dirt surrounded by unsightly iron and rock. They must have the niceties of arches and angles and gold and plush red velvet to enjoy music. It's not necessary, you know. They don't have to have the colorful costumes gliding across the stage like a gigantic kaleidoscope to enjoy her music. It's just what they prefer.

"I'm much like her—my opera house. At the heart of me, I'm unpleasant to look at, and I'm not talking about my missing nose. I'm talking about my heart and mind. Without the smooth and carefully chosen words, my heart is as cold and frigid as her bricks and my mind is as unyielding as her iron. So, mad? No, I don't believe so. What you see now is who I am."

"Erik, stop this. I know this isn't you. For some reason you're putting on an act for me."

"Putting on an act? You honestly think this is an act, a simple illusion? While I am a gifted illusionist, what you see right now isn't an illusion. What I've allowed you to see up to this point has been an artfully crafted illusion, but the illusion has vanished, the curtain has closed on that act. Now you have to come back to the real world. This is real, Christine—deathly real."

"Erik, stop this. You're frightening me."

"Oh, am I now? Well then, *my sweet Delilah*, you should have considered the consequences of betrayal *before* you betrayed me. If you had, I never would have stripped my appealing façade and revealed my true structure to you. You would have remained innocent, and I would have remembered you as an innocent—not as the Judas you turned out to be."

"What are you talking about? I didn't betray you. Why are you accusing me of such a thing?"

I laughed loudly. "Now you're teasing me, right? I heard it from your own lips, so don't lie to me. Lies make me quite irritable, and I sometimes do things of an unpleasant nature."

"What are you talking about?"

I shook my head. "Remember my last words to you? Remember all I asked for?"

She frowned. "Yes, to give you your ring or my heart. And that's what I was going to do."

"If I didn't know you better, I'd almost believe you were telling me the truth. But, as I said, I heard it from your own lips, spoken under the stars and the wispy clouds. You were going to fly away on those clouds and leave me without a goodbye, without giving me my ring."

"No, you're wrong. I wasn't, Erik. I wasn't leaving with Raoul. I was coming back to you."

I leaped toward her and growled. "I warned you! Don't lie to me!"

"I'm not lying, Erik. You don't understand. I wasn't going away with him."

"That's not what I heard."

"You were obviously listening to our conversation on the roof. Well, what you heard was my confusion and fear. Yes, I told Raoul I would go away with him, but I knew I needed more time to think. I couldn't think with him being so demanding. He was pushing me, and you'd pushed me into a corner, and I didn't know what to do. I was out of time, and I was frightened of making the wrong decision.

"With the way you looked and what the Persian said, I was so confused, and felt I didn't even know my own mind or heart. I was about ready to leave without either of you knowing about it and disappear completely. I was going mad. So I went home to think about everything. I didn't even sleep, and my final decision was to find you after tonight's performance and talk with you. I knew for sure I had to talk to you before I did anything."

"Nice try, my sweet, but it's too late to throw the blame on Raoul or me, much too late. You've been fickle from the start, and you've driven both of us, Raoul and me, crazy. Well, no more."

"But, I was coming back, Erik. You can even ask Raoul. We had a huge argument this afternoon about it. He said he refused to let me come back down here, but I told him he had no choice in the matter, and that I couldn't do anything unless I talked to you first."

I nodded slowly and moved toward the door; then I spoke softly and deliberately. "So, are you sure you want me to ask him? Well, let's see." I started going through my pockets and watched her face in the process. Then I took out a lasso and said, "There it is." I held it up between us. "Do you still want me to ask him?" She just stared at the lasso. "Well, what will it be—yes or no?"

She slowly shook her head.

"That's what I thought. Your time is up, Christine, and the hour is late." I looked at my watch. "It's now 10:10, and if you don't make the right choice by 11:00 tomorrow night there won't be any more choices for any of us."

"What are you talking about? What choices? What are you planning?"

"Plans. Let's see. You know, my first plan was to find Raoul and end his pathetic life before this scene we're now playing even started. But then I thought, no. If he isn't destroyed when the Opera Populaire comes down, then he'll have to spend the rest of his life with the knowledge that I had the last laugh.

"My word is law around here, and he'll have to concede to it. He'll know he was powerless against my forces and couldn't protect his love from the fate I'd given her. For him to lose to me will be a fate worse than death."

"Bring the house down? What do you mean? Oh!" she exclaimed when the pieces fell into place. "The gunpowder—the black boxes. Erik, you wouldn't!"

"Remember, I told you I left them connected just in case there was another twist or turn in my life when I might need them. Well, here we are, and I need them. I never expected you to make the decision you did, so you created this twist and my need for those boxes. This will be my final act—and yours."

"Erik, you can't do this. Think about all the people above us. All the innocent people."

"Innocent people! None of them is innocent! They all scorn me! They're all the same!"

She shook her head and faced me. "But, Erik, I was doing just what you wanted me to do. I was coming back to talk to you. I was even considering going away with you, not Raoul."

"Well, well. I'm a much better teacher than what I've given myself credit for. That was excellent, my dear. You've learned how to think on your feet and present a convincing lie. But it won't work on me. Not anymore."

Seriously frowning, she shook her head strongly. "This is all wrong. You're not being logical. There has to be an explanation for your actions. What has happened to change you? Have you been drinking?"

Laughing again, I replied, "I have no need of alcohol to fuel my sanity, or insanity if you wish."

Once I stopped laughing, I became very serious and almost lost my composure. My hands pressed into fists and my jaws clenched. I even slammed one of them into the doorframe before I calmed myself and took a deep breath.

Her lips were parted, and her eyes were wide as they stared at me, silently. I walked back to her, lifted her left hand, and stroked the back of it gently, while moving my glance between her eyes and her hand. My voice was tender and charming as I started my next taunt.

"You have such lovely hands, my sweet, very smooth and slender. But they look so terribly naked now. I liked them much better when this one was adorned with my ring. By the way, where is the gold band I gave you? You know, the one I asked you to be careful with, the one that holds sentimental value to me alone? You remember, don't you, Christine? The one you wore for several months as my living wife? Where is it now? Don't tell me you've misplaced it? Or did that young man of yours remove it for you?"

I squeezed her hand to the point of pain, and I'm sure my voice was just as agonizing. "You could have had the decency to return it to me. Was that too much to ask? How could you treat it with such apathy? But then, why should I think you would be careful with a ring when you weren't careful with a living, beating heart?"

I gave her hand a stronger squeeze until she moaned. "You're hurting me, Erik."

"Oh, really? Is your heart bleeding yet? No, you say. Well, until your heart bleeds, don't talk to me about hurt. You know nothing about hurt." I gestured to my chest. "Can you see my heart bleeding? I know you can't, because it's bled itself to death. It's now dead and feels nothing, no more joy, no more hurt, no more empathy for the desires of a diva.

"Did you know its death was slow and painful? Well, it was, so be thankful you weren't looking on as it died. It was most unpleasant. Your compassionate heart wouldn't have been able to withstand its torture. Oh! But, wait a minute, there was no compassion in your heart while mine was dying. Yours had only one agenda, to fall into the arms of your lover and let him kiss away your compassion. Am I right?"

I let go of her hand with a shove, and walked back to the chair and sat down. "My ring," I said softly. "Do you know where my ring is, Christine? Perhaps I can remember seeing it somewhere if I try hard enough." I started going through my pockets as if I was confused. "Now, where is it? Where did I put it? Oh, getting old is such a bother. I can't seem to remember anything these days. Don't get old, my sweet, it can be most unpleasant. Oh! Here it is."

I pulled the ring from my pocket and held it up between us. I held it to my open lips and huffed on it, and then I took a handkerchief from my pocket and polished it. "There, good as new. It sure is a good thing I'm a magician. If I wasn't, my precious ring might have been lost forever. Oh,

I can tell by your expression that you're wondering how I found my ring. Well, I just told you. I can make things appear and disappear—like this."

I held my ring up in the air between two fingers, and then I closed my fist and turned it in a circle. When I opened it, my ring was gone. I did the same thing in reverse and then my ring was back.

"Fascinating, isn't it? People have always loved watching my hands and fingers as I've made things appear and disappear. But, you know what I love? I love to watch their faces and eyes while they watch me. It makes me laugh inside. They're so dimwitted. They can't figure out such a simple trick with a ring or a note. And then when I do something really big—oh, my, you should see their faces then.

"I have to admit that some illusions are a bit more difficult, like the appearance of a toad in a diva's throat or the disappearance of a white stallion from a stable or how about a diva disappearing from center stage right in front of thousands of people? I wasn't around to see or hear the reaction to that accomplishment. That would have been fun to see.

"However, even that one didn't require too much thought. But there are those that require a great deal of expertise, such as taking down a section of a palace with my hands tied behind my back. Now that was quite a feat, and you should have seen the Shah's face. It was worth a thousand laughs. But large or small, it doesn't matter to me. I can handle whatever challenge is put before me."

I sighed loudly. "But, sad to say, I don't think there'll be any laughing going on in the hours ahead. Too bad. Too bad."

Christine was silent and almost seemed to be in shock, while I casually studied my ring and put it on my finger. Then I sighed again and started walking around the room slowly, looking at and touching different objects as I went. I began twisting the ring on my finger and glancing at her as I traveled through the room that once held the calming fragrance of lavender and so much promise.

"Oh, Erik, I'm sorry. I tried to look for it. I . . ."

"Never mind the ring, my dear," I growled low. "It's now back where it belongs."

"Erik, please let me explain."

I huffed and growled loudly at her. "Save your breath, *my dear*. You're going to need it."

By then, I was close to her again, and I once more raised her hand, but, that time, I kissed the back of it and whispered, "So sad. So sad. Such a lovely hand, and to think it will die naked."

Her eyes began to fill with tears. "Erik, please don't talk like this. Let me explain."

"Talk? Is that what you think this is about?—Just talk? Oh, my dear, how could you possibly think you could get away with being so traitorous?"

"Traitorous?" she questioned, as I started my tour of the room again. "You're not making any sense, Erik. How was I . . ."

"You don't understand? Well, then, let me explain. I see all, Christine, and you never should have forgotten that or underestimated my scope of knowledge. So, because of your lack of foresight, you'll now pay for your traitorous deceit. All traitors are executed you know. No one has ever crossed your—*poor Erik*—and escaped being eaten up with worms—no one. Well, no one except your young lover, and the only reason he's still breathing is because of my love for you. But that is all in the past now. No more love and no more deceit and no more sparing lives for you."

By then, tears were streaming down her cheeks, meaning she was acting very well or her acting skills were slipping away from her. In either case, I kept up my taunts.

"Do I execute you, my dear? Is that what I should do to my traitor? No, I don't think so—not just yet anyway. I get everything I want, my dear sweet Christine." I spread my arms out around the room. "I wanted this home down here, and do I have it? Yes, I do. I wanted to become your Angel of Music, and did I become your Angel of Music? Why, yes, I did. I wanted you to sing center stage, and have you sung center stage? One more time, the answer is a resounding yes.

"I wanted you to come down here and stay with me for a few days, and did you come down here? My, my, yes, you did. And I wanted you to come back of your own accord, and did you? Again, yes, my dear. Are you getting the picture? I get everything I want." Then I said coldly and deliberately, "Once I go after it."

I walked slowly back to her and placed my knuckles under her chin. "Now follow me, if you can, you foolish woman. I asked you to play my living wife, and did you? Yes, you did. What's left, *my dear?*"

I moved to the other side of the bed and ran my hand over the dress. "Oh, you can't say it out loud, now, can you? I want you to marry me for real and be my real wife; my real living wife. Do you doubt that I can also accomplish that feat? Oh, I see in your eyes that you're now following me, aren't you? Can you see where this is going? You've often told me I should sleep in my own bed, remember those times? Well, depending on the outcome of certain decisions, I will be sleeping in my bed shortly—but I won't be sleeping there alone. Are you still following me?"

"Erik, please don't do this," she pleaded. "I can explain everything if you'll just give me a chance."

"A chance?" I yelled. "Is that what you gave me? A chance? A chance to say goodbye?"

I went back to the chair, leaned back in it, and propped my foot up on the end of the bed again. "I wouldn't be doing this, my dear. I would have let you go if you had been honest with me and given me a chance. It would have torn my heart apart to see you go, but if that's what you wanted and that's what would make you happy, then I wanted you to be happy, more than I wanted happiness myself, and I would have let you go.

"I would have cried, yes, but I would have let you go. But then you said you couldn't bear to see me cry. Well, let me tell you something. It would have been much easier to see me cry than to watch what I'm about to do, much easier than what you'll have to bear in the hours ahead."

She tried her plea again. "Erik, this isn't you. Please, don't do this."

My tone was harsh as I responded, "Don't do this?—It isn't me?—In case you've forgotten, you senseless creature, it was you who broke our agreement. It was you, remember? I promised I'd never hurt you, but you broke our agreement, not me. So I'm no longer under any restrictions to comply with what I said I would or would not do. I don't need to let you go now because you tried to deceive me. So now I can do whatever I like with you. I'm free to do whatever I want."

I lowered my foot and leaned in toward her, speaking softly. "Do you know what I want, Christine? I want you as my wife. Therefore, you must dress for your wedding day, my dear. The chapel waits, as does the pastor. And we mustn't keep our guests waiting, so you must dress quickly."

I got up and moved next to her, holding out my hand for her to take, but she looked away from me and refused her hand. "Oh, come now, my dear. We're not going back to that place, are we? We've been through too much together for you to refuse to give me your hand."

Her breaths were coming quickly when she glared up into my eyes, so I shook my head. "Then have it your way, *my sweet*." I grabbed her arm and brought her to her feet. "Our guests await the bride and groom, *my dear sweet betrothed*, and your groom waits for you. So dress quickly." I put my fingers under her shaking chin and lifted her face to mine. Then I lowered my face to hers and whispered slowly, "Your groom awaits, Christine."

I started backing out of the room, watching her. There was true fear in her eyes, but she didn't move, so I walked back to her.

"Now, come, my dear, you're not moving very fast. Do you need my help? I'll be more than happy to help you dress, if that's what you wish. I've never played the part of a wardrobe assistant before, but I'm always willing to learn new roles, so this should be fun—don't you think?"

I reached for and released the tie on the bodice of her dress, but she grabbed it out of my hand and backed away from me.

I smiled, and said softly, "Remember, Christine, I always get what I want. You'll be in that dress. Whether you dress yourself or I dress you, the end will be the same. You'll be in that dress and you'll be my bride. So make up your mind. Do you dress yourself, or do I?"

Her jaws tightened. "You can't force me to do this."

I smiled, sighed, and took another step toward her. "Oh, I could force you easily enough and enjoy it as well. But I won't force you. You'll put it on willingly."

She looked at the dress again and then at me. "No, I won't."

"Perfect, Christine, you're playing right into my hand, just the way I've scripted it. I knew you would refuse; in fact, I was counting on your refusal. I've pictured this moment—you refusing." I took another step toward her and then reached out and placed my fingers gently under her chin. Then I said, barely above a whisper, "I would prefer to undress you myself."

Indignantly, she shoved my hand away and stepped back, which put her back against her armoire. "You wouldn't dare."

"I wouldn't? You accused me of being mad. Don't you think a madman would enjoy undressing his bride? I think he would." I turned and stepped away from her, and then I looked at her coldly over my shoulder. "I know I will."

Her chest rose rapidly several times, and then she darted for the door again. Fruitlessly, she shook the door and whimpered, while I took out my watch and looked at the time.

"Time is wasting, my sweet. We don't want to be late for our nuptials."

As she turned and looked at me, the amount of fear in her eyes began to penetrate my hardened heart, and I again questioned what I was doing. I couldn't hurt my Christine—not my Christine. Buying time to think, I slipped my watch back in my pocket and then looked at the gown on her bed.

My thoughts fluctuated between my choices, and then I looked back at her. But when I saw a tear slowly roll down her cheek my heart broke completely, and the only choice I could make became clear. I stepped closer to her and removed that tear with the back of my fingers, ready to apologize and beg for forgiveness. Then, out of nowhere, she slapped me across my face. It stung, but not nearly as much as her words.

"Don't touch me! You're evil—all the way through! I hate you, Erik! I hate you! Raoul was right! You're evil. He'll come for me. He'll find the passage I use and come for me. Then he'll kill you for what you're doing to me."

That was all I needed to erase my benevolent thoughts, and I came back at her with cold indifference. "You think you can stop me or hurt me with your *little* slap? You have no idea what others have done to get me to bend to their wishes. Remember all my scars, Christine? Remember what happened to all the ones who gave me those scars?

"Your slap means nothing to me. Your attempt is nothing more than an irritating mosquito bite. It can't begin to compare to the others. And I hope your lover does come for you. But if you think your precious *Raoul* can stop me from attaining what I want, you've been reading the wrong script.

"I've taken down those who were much more numerous and mightier than he will ever think of being. I took them down without ever laying a finger on them, and I'll take that *simple aristocrat* down without laying a single finger on him. Trust me. It will not turn out well for him when he arrives. I'll have a *very, very* warm welcome waiting for him. I stand here today as living proof that no one, no matter who they are, can outmaneuver or outsmart me. I always get what I want, Christine, and I want you."

I looked down into her fearful eyes with pure venom in mine. Then I gently began to unbutton the top button of her bodice. Once more, she raised her hand, preparing for another slap, but I grasped her wrist quickly.

"I don't want to play rough, my dear. Please, don't make me."

With her wrist still in my hand, I prepared to unbutton her bodice again with my other hand. But she raised her other hand, forcing me to grasp it. So there we stood, with both of my hands holding her wrists back against the door. I shook my head and smirked.

Then I lowered my face, placed my cheek against hers, and whispered in her ear, "Have it your way, *my sweet.*"

Instantly, I let go of both her wrists and ripped the front of her bodice open in one quick move.

"All right! All right! I'll put it on!" she shrieked, while grasping her bodice closed.

I stepped back from her and bowed low. "I know you will, my dear. Didn't I predict you would?" Then I spread my hand out toward her wedding gown, and, after she walked toward it, I went to the door. I opened it and looked back at her, giving her some final instructions.

"I know you're an expert at changing costumes quickly, so don't try to play me the fool again. Your bridegroom will be waiting, impatiently, for his bride."

She silently glared at me, and I smiled and bowed low again.

Then, after rising, I said, "Yes, you'll make a most beautiful bride—and wife." I took my watch out of its pocket and looked at the time. "I'll be back through this door in five minutes sharp, my dear, so either be ready for me or—well—let's just hope you're ready."

I started to close the door when she whimpered, "Erik, please don't do this."

I cocked my head. "Erik? Who is Erik? I remember you calling me a madman. From now on you can call me *Monsieur Folle* if you like, but no longer call me Erik." Then I closed the door and turned the key in the lock, ending the first scene of our final act.

Forty-Six

I stood in the middle of my drawing room and literally watched the pendulum in my floor clock sway as its hands ticked away the five minutes. Just as soon as they were up, I opened her door without knocking, carrying my superior strength and confidence in my stride. But I was completely unprepared for what awaited me.

Christine was standing across the room with her back to me, trying to fasten the laces on the back of the dress. As the door opened, she turned and looked at me, and I lost my breath completely. Everything in me, all my plans and schemes, began to crumble at my feet like so much rubbish. She was the picture of everything beautiful, everything feminine, everything wonderful, like a fragile snowflake on pure driven snow. My only desire was to hold her gently in my arms and never let her go.

I swallowed hard, clenched my teeth, and took a deep breath; then I closed the space between us, determined I wouldn't lose my protective covering—my controlled anger. I wrapped my fingers around her arms and slowly pulled her close to me. She was drawing on her acting skills, but they weren't strong enough to cover the expression in her frightened eyes.

"Erik, please don't do this. I know this isn't you."

"Don't do what, my dear? I only want to lace the back of your dress. You can let your betrothed do that much for you—can't you?"

I reached around her back, feeling for the laces and hooks. Then methodically I wove the laces around the hooks, pulled them tight, and tied them in a bow. Taking another hold on her arms, I moved her back, so I could look in her eyes that were speaking of her pain and fear.

Her chin was quivering when she spoke again. "Erik, please. Think about what you're doing. Don't do this to me."

"Don't do what? Can't you speak the words? Can't you speak honestly in front of your husband?"

I began backing her toward the bed and she whimpered, "Erik, please."

Once the back of her legs touched the bed, I let one of her arms go and ran my fingers along her cheek and down her soft neck. The fright in her eyes was immense, and while I could have told her not to worry, and that

I had no intention of taking my first kiss much less taking her against her will, I didn't. I wanted her to suffer as she'd made me suffer.

But with the feel of her so close to me and dressed the way she was, I was the one who was suffering. Like a willow in the wind, my anger began to sway, allowing fresh breaths of my love for her to tug at the pieces of my broken heart. Without any forethought or script, my heart began to speak softly, while my fingertips caressed her tender neck.

"My heart was waiting just for you its entire life, My Angel. It recognized you from the first moment you appeared on my stage, and it will beat only for you until I take my last breath. You alone were allowed to unlock my guarded heart, you alone, Christine. But now that it's opened, and you're no longer inside it, I'm lost. If I let you go now, my heart will be left open for the world to enter and trample upon. If that happens, there'll be no reason for me to live any longer."

Her eyes pleaded, and her lips again whispered, "Oh, please, Erik. Please, let's sit and talk."

Once more my resolve began to crack under the pressure of my immense love for her, and I could feel myself crumbling at her feet if I didn't return to the security of my anger, so I quickly led her out of that room of temptation. I locked the door and put the key in my vest pocket, making sure she saw my actions. I then motioned around the drawing room and began directing the second scene.

"You might notice, my dear, that all the doors are shut and locked, so there's nowhere for you to go. I've also securely locked the passage in the music room, just in case you have any ideas about escaping through it. This room, where we've spent so much time together, will be where we share our last moments. Well, perhaps not, that will be your choice."

She looked as if she was about to faint, so I took her by the arm and sat her on the divan, right where she always sat. I took the bag of keys from my pocket and tossed it from one hand to the other as I began instructing her.

"Perhaps you should stay seated, my dear, while I read through the script for you. Remember this little bag of strange keys that opened those black boxes? Well, now they'll do more than what they did in that first scene. You'll see the complete act . . . Well, again, that depends on you."

I dumped them out on the mantle, picked out the key to the scorpion's box, unlocked it, and removed it from the brass figure.

"Look at the intricate workmanship on this piece of art. You can see it much better now that it's released from its prison. Remember when I told you I had to keep my little friend in here because he's so dangerous? And do you remember why he's dangerous?"

She barely mouthed, "Gunpowder."

"Hmm. Perhaps—perhaps not. I'm not sure now. They've been in there so long. Perhaps I'm remembering wrong. Perhaps the scorpion isn't the dangerous one. Hmm. Well, a scorpion is dangerous if you're stung by one. Have you ever been stung by a scorpion, Christine? No, there's no way you could have been stung by one.

"You've led a life of protection, haven't you? First your father, and then Madame Valerius, and then me, and we can't forget about your young de Chagny, now, can we? Protected? Yes. I'm quite sure you've never had to outwit a scorpion."

My questions kept flying at her, but she barely responded to any of them; in fact, I wasn't certain she was hearing me most of the time. She was nearly as white as her dress, and she looked as if she was going to topple over at any moment. I might have felt compassion for her, but my anger was much too great to feel anything, so I kept up with my taunts.

"Well, let me tell you that its sting is most unpleasant, most unpleasant indeed. It can even kill you, so it's very dangerous, and you must always stay on your guard. When I think about how dangerous it is, I think perhaps it's the scorpion that's connected to the gunpowder." I shook my head. "If I could only remember.

"Anyway, let's think about this one," I said as I unlocked the other box. "If you can remember, this box holds a rather unthreatening creature—a grasshopper. Aha, but a grasshopper can jump very high, now can't it? Very high indeed. But, it doesn't sting, it only jumps, so why the box and key?

"I wonder what I was thinking. Was I protecting the grasshopper from the scorpion or was I protecting the scorpion from the grasshopper? Perhaps the grasshopper could jump away and lead the scorpion to its death in the fire below. Is that it? Do you think that's it, Christine?"

She stared at me, blankly, while I replaced the keys in the bag and laid it on the mantle; then I continued, "My, my, decisions, decisions. I know decisions aren't your forte, my dear, but you need to make one soon. I gave you two weeks to make your last decision, but this time you'll only have 24 hours."

I motioned to the floor clock in the corner and rephrased my statement. "Actually, you have less than 24 hours. I'll give you until 11 tomorrow night to make your final decision. Oh, I almost forgot to tell you what your choices are—how forgetful of me. Well, let's see now. On the one hand, you'll become Erik's wife for real, and we'll live happily ever after. Won't that be nice?" I sneered through a sinister smile. Then I lost the smile, looked directly into her eyes, and nearly growled. "But, on the other hand, if you won't become his wife, then you'll become no one's."

With that threat, I got a reaction out of her. She took a deep breath, shook her head, and I smiled at her.

"Oh, rather harsh, you say? Perhaps, but then life can be harsh, my dear, or haven't you heard that yet? Don't fear though, I've tried to make this decision much easier for you, *my sweet Christine*. The last choice you had to make put you through such turmoil, and it was only between two men. Well, this one should be easier for you, my dear precious Christine. I've made sure of that."

I sat on the coffee table in front of her and reached for her hand, only to have her pull her entire body away from me. I sighed and took her hand anyway.

"What? No thank you, Erik? Are you not going to thank me for my consideration of your feelings? Well, never mind. I'm most used to being unappreciated, but I'll explain my efforts anyway."

I got up and sat in my chair, crossing my ankle over my knee. "By 11 tomorrow night, you'll either be my wife, willingly, I might add, or you'll die. Does that make it easier for you? Well, if not, then let me up the ante a bit. If you die, so will thousands of others. Oh, that got your attention now, didn't it?

"Yes, Christine, were you not the least bit curious to know why I gave you until 11 tomorrow night? Think, my dear, when is the opera house filled with the most people? Oh, the light is getting brighter now, isn't it?"

I got up and started walking slowly around the room, listening to the beginning of her soft sobs. I ran my fingers over the walls and a few fixtures as I went.

"This place has served me well in my life, and I'm sure it'll also serve me well in my death."

I turned and looked at her soberly. Her face was streaked with tears, and the fright in her eyes increased with each word of explanation I gave her. I went back to the fireplace before I continued my derision.

"But, then, let's not jump ahead of the script. Perhaps you'll choose this *poor Erik* over death, the death of thousands." I walked over to her again and took her hand. "Such a small hand to hold the fate of so many people. Such a small and delicate hand."

I turned and started toward my music room, and then I turned quickly back toward her. "Oh, I almost forgot. There's one other small detail I should mention. There's a slight chance—well, I guess I should say a 50-50 chance, if you decide not to marry this fine dashing man before you, that you'll not die, and neither will the thousands above us. But, then again, that's going to mean you have to make yet another decision."

I went back to the mantle and put a hand on each of the brass figures. "Our little friends here will be the final judges to decide what will happen to us if you refuse me." I tried to move the scorpion with my finger for effect. "You see they're firmly placed here so they'll not fall off and so they can't be moved easily, but they can be moved or turned, I assure you.

"When they're turned, they know it's their cue to start their part in this little drama we're involved in. The grasshopper might jump far away from the scorpion and be free or the scorpion might sting the grasshopper and it will die or the grasshopper might lead the scorpion to both of their deaths in the fire below. The choice to have them jump or sting is yours. You can direct the players at will. You can turn the grasshopper or the scorpion and then watch what happens, the choice is yours.

"But, keep in mind, this is a serious decision, much more serious than the last one you were trying to make. One of these small innocent creatures will set us all free to move on through our lives the way we wish, and the other will bring our last act to a conclusion in a thunderous instant. We'll die and be buried all in the same move. Which will it be, my dear—the grasshopper or the scorpion?"

I turned and headed back to my music room, sighing deeply. "I feel a need to compose, my sweet. I'm nearly finished with *Don Juan Triumphant*, and I want it finished before you make your final decision."

I put my hand on the knob, and she stopped me with her wavering voice. "Erik, please don't do this."

I didn't feel a need to compose. I felt a need to leave her sad eyes, to leave the sound of her pleading voice that easily made its way to my guarded heart. I squeezed my eyes tightly and slowly looked back at her.

"It doesn't have to be this way, Christine," I said softly. "All you have to do is tear up this script right now. Tell me you love me. Take me by the hand and lead me to your room. I'll unlock the door for you if your intention is to give me my first kiss. Give me my first kiss and agree to marry me, and I'll put my little creatures back in their ebony boxes. Then we can leave this place of death and live on in peace. No one will die with that ending, Christine."

I gave her a moment to answer, and, when she lowered her head without an answer, I continued, "Very well, my dear. The sands of time are sifting through your delicate fingers. I'll leave you alone to contemplate our fate. But, if you make your decision soon, there'll be no need to put either of us through the torture of waiting out the full amount of time. Come to me if you wish. Come to me if you make your decision."

I waited another moment for her to respond and then left the room. I closed my music room door and lowered myself into the stuffed chair, the one spot Christine enjoyed the most. She said it was comforting to her, and she was right. It was a comforting place, but not right then.

My feelings were swaying like the pendulum in my floor clock, and, just like those pendulums in the clock tower in Persia, they ticked away toward either destruction or peace. And, just like that time in Persia, I was the only one who knew exactly what lay ahead and had the power to control the outcome. But, one more time, it was the decision of someone else that would determine the lives of many.

I laid my head back and gazed around my music room, while fighting to maintain my vexation for that woman I loved and for the entire world. For so long in my life, I carried the hope of living in an opera house with music surrounding me continually. But right then I wanted nothing to do with it, because, along with an opera and music, would be thoughts of Christine.

So I no longer wanted to sit in Box Five and watch the action on the stage. I didn't want to see the colorful garments of the many ladies escorted by their aristocratic suitors. I wanted nothing to do with them. They served only one purpose—a continual reminder about what I'd lost—Christine.

I sighed, closed my eyes, and pressed my fingertips against my forehead. Why, oh why did I allow someone into my heart? Why? How stupid could I be? I glared at the wall separating us. Christine, you Delilah. You stripped me of my power. How could you leave me alone like this? How could you do this to me, you heartless tramp?

With sufficient anger replacing my moments of weakness, I went back to the drawing room, preparing to taunt her further. But my tormenting thoughts were interrupted when I walked in on an unexpected scene. She was sitting on the hearth by the fireplace, slumped over, sobbing, and holding her face in her hands.

"Oh, you sob so well and so easily, my dear," I sneered while walking toward her. "Perhaps I trained you too well. There are other emotions to express, you know, such as the glee of a maiden on her wedding day. Should I instruct you personally in how to convey that passion?"

When I reached her, I leaned down and lifted her face up to me. I was ready to tell her she was a beautiful bride when the blood on her forehead silenced my tongue. I was stunned and had to take a moment to understand what had happened.

The right side of her forehead was badly scraped, swelling, and bleeding. I could tell it wasn't a fall that had caused it. So when I spotted some blood on the stones on the fireplace at the same level as her head, I knew she'd done it to herself. She would rather kill herself than to give me my first kiss.

That didn't give me much hope for the hours ahead. However, I'd had little hope to begin with.

I went down on one knee and touched the blood traveling down her forehead and across her tear-streaked cheeks. She lowered her head again, and I closed my eyes tightly, questioning what I was doing.

"Christine, forgive me. Please look at me." She didn't look up, so I continued, "I know there's something between us. I know it. I can sense it, and I know you feel it also. I've seen it in your eyes. Please look past this face. Please see me for who I am—a man in love. Just a man, Christine. I'm not a monster, not a genius, not an angel, just a man. Look at me, Christine, and please see me. I'll do anything you ask of me. I'll go anywhere you ask. Just see me and love me."

She looked at me, and I searched her eyes, trying to understand her continual emotional changes. Then it became clear to me. She also was being torn between contradicting feelings, just as I'd been. What she saw with her eyes was telling her mind one thing, that the man before her was some sort of monster, but what she was feeling with her heart was telling her another, that the man in front of her was someone she cared for. Those two emotions were so foreign to each other that they confused her.

She turned her face from me, and I frowned, once more being torn between pity and hatred. Unfortunately, it was my hatred that won that battle, and I easily began taunting her again.

"My dear, what has happened? Have you injured yourself? And on our wedding day? What a shame—what a shame. Oh! Look at your pure white dress now damaged with your blood."

I lifted her to her feet, walked away from her, and then turned back. "My poor sweet bride. Were you not listening to me earlier when I told you I always get what I want? Do you think you can end your life by such a trick as this—and in my own home? In case you didn't know, I don't like the spilling of blood. Maybe I never spoke to you about that one aspect of my peculiar personality. I detest the spilling of blood. There are much better ways of ending your life, ways that don't spill blood. Did you know that?"

I pulled a coil from my pocket and opened it to its full length, holding an end in each hand.

"Now, if you really wanted to end your life, you should have asked me to help you. Some call me an expert on the subject of death, and I never cause blood to flow—well, almost never. This small innocent looking piece of catgut is a very useful tool and can perform your task for you. Do you want my help, my dear?"

I walked toward her with my hands still spread out, and she backed away from me until she hit the fireplace. I slid the lasso under her chin and raised her bloodstained face up toward me. "This would have ended it all for you and without any blood being poured out. In fact, it wouldn't have even chafed your delicate skin. It's not rough and hard like most hangmen's nooses. No, it's very smooth. Feel it, Christine."

I moved the lasso back and forth across her neck. "See how easily it moves. It wouldn't have hurt a bit, and it never would have caused your blood to flow from your pretty face. But you didn't think to consult the expert—what folly. You didn't bother to ask me for help, now did you, just as you didn't bother to say goodbye to me?"

I lowered the lasso and ran my finger down her bodice where her blood had dropped. "You've tainted our perfect day with blood, and that angers me. You're responsible for ruining my dress that I picked out especially for you and especially for this day, our wedding day. And to think you ruined it with the crimson of blood that I detest. You would have been better off if you'd cut it up with a knife than to spill blood on it. I don't like blood, Christine, and now look what you've done. What a shame, my sweet," I said softly as I moved her hair from her bloody forehead. "What a shame."

I sighed and she whimpered, "Oh, Erik, please let me go."

I studied her pleading eyes for a few moments, and then I turned from her, fighting the compassion moving into my frigid heart. Then I looked back over my shoulder.

"You must have a headache and probably don't feel like celebrating a wedding right now, but we're not going to put this off. I've waited a very long time for this day, and a little blood or headache isn't going to stop me."

I ran my fingers across her bloody forehead again and spoke softly. "I'll be gentle, Christine. I'll be most gentle." Then I lowered my hand and backed away. "I have only a small matter to attend to, and then I'll be back. Just in case you decide to do something else that will anger me even more, I'll help you restrain yourself from further harm."

I got a chair from the dining room and set it right in the middle of the drawing room. "Sit down, my dear," I hissed as I motioned to the chair. When she didn't move, I grabbed her upper arm, dragged her there, and sat her down. "Now you'll see how versatile my lassos can be."

I pulled her arms behind her and wrapped a lasso around one wrist and one slat in the back of the chair. After I wove the loose end of the lasso around itself, it was firmly in place. Then I did the same with the other lasso and her other wrist.

"Now the catgut is smooth and won't chafe your wrist, but if you struggle against it, it will quite likely tear into your flesh. We don't want any more blood, now do we, my dear?"

I stood beside her and listened to her sobs, and then, with my fingers around her neck, I forced her to look up at me one more time.

"Oh, what sobs. If it weren't for the sobs of my own heart, tearing apart while it listened to you and your lover make plans to rip it out of my chest, I might be inclined to hear your sobs more clearly. But my own pain is blocking the path to my heart. What a shame.—What a shame."

"Erik, please. This isn't the man I've come to care for. Don't do this."

My jaws were clenching, and I felt like screaming. I needed to run. I couldn't go through any more of this twisting and turning. One second I could ruthlessly strap her wrists to a chair, and the next second I wanted to fall at her feet and slit my own throat if she asked it of me. Right then, the pain in my chest was so great that I would have welcomed death. Consequently, I knelt down in front of her and made her look at me.

"My heart would have listened to your wants and needs forever, Christine. I never would have made you cry—never. I would have given you everything. Why did you turn betrayer and spoil all my wonderful plans for us?"

"Erik, please listen to me. Hear me. I didn't betray you. I was coming back. Honestly, I was coming back. You must believe me."

The expression in her tear-filled eyes almost made its way through to me, but then I recalled so many of her words, the ones revealing my secrets to her lover, so I rose to my feet, backed away from her, and took out my watch.

"You're running out of time, my dear. You have less than 22 hours to make your decisions. The grasshopper or the scorpion?"

I started to leave but then turned back toward her. "You'll be my first. Did you know that, Christine? If you make the wrong decision, you'll be my first. Yes, all those who've crossed me in my past and ended up being worm food have been men, so you'll be the first woman to have that distinction."

I opened my music room door and looked back at her again. "Oh, no, wait a minute. There was one other woman just recently, but that wasn't deliberate. Her death was an unfortunate accident. She happened to be sitting in the wrong place at the wrong time. But it might interest you to know that her death was a direct result of her getting in the way of something I wanted. And, since I caused the accident, I guess you could say she was the first woman I killed.

"And to think, she was going to hurt someone I only cared about, not someone I loved as I do you, Christine. Do you have any idea the mountains I would have moved just to give you everything you wanted? I would have stopped at nothing to make you happy. But, now, look at you. I'm the cause of your tear-streaked face. I'm the cause of your blood being spilled. Such a shame—such a waste."

I looked at my watch again. "Running out of time, my dear. Make your choice soon before it's made for you. And, don't forget, if you make the wrong choice, you'll cause many more women to take their last breath along with you."

I bowed low and closed the door.

I headed straight for my organ, where I played the worst of my music from Don Juan and the other dark periods of my life. I played ruthlessly, trying to prevent any human emotion from surfacing again. But I couldn't prevent Christine's bruised and sad face from passing repeatedly before me.

I played for over two hours before I made the decision to plead with her gently one more time. Each time I did, a small piece of my resolve must have somehow been buried, because I had to fight to maintain my staunch demeanor. This time when I saw her, her tears were dry.

"I've finished *Don Juan Triumphant*, my dear," I said as I walked in front of her. "Do you remember what I told you would happen when I finished it?" She barely shook her head. "Then I'll help you remember. I told you that once it was finished, I would take it in my coffin with me and die. Remember now? Therefore, if you won't marry me, the only task left for me to do is to crawl away and sleep forever."

After a silent moment of watching her, I went on one knee before her. I searched her eyes, looking for that one expression I'd been waiting for, but then I presume that was the wrong time to look for it. When I thought about what I was doing, I knew there was no way she could love me, but that didn't stop me from trying again to persuade her.

"I'd like to compose one more piece before the day is finished, and I'd like you to pick the theme. Should I compose a wedding mass or a requiem mass? Which would you prefer?"

She shook her head slowly. "Please, Erik, in the name of God, let me go. You know you don't want to do this. You say you love me, but if you love me you couldn't be doing this."

"Yes, I do love you, Christine, more than life itself. That's why I beg you to let me compose a wedding mass for you. It'll be magnificent, and I promise I'll be the best husband a woman could ask for. I'd appreciate you more than any other man could even comprehend. We could live a life of music and sunlight. I no longer want to live like a rodent underground. I want a wife who will walk beside me through a park and let me ride with her in a carriage in the light of day.

"I spared no expense or effort when I brought you down here to stay with me, and I would do the same if you'd only agree to marry me. I told you I'd give you the world, and I will, if you'll only give me a chance. Love me for the man you've come to know."

Tears started forming once more, and I lowered my head and closed my eyes tightly. "Please, don't cry, Christine. It pains me so when I see you cry." I looked back at her face, and once more saw tears streaming down her cheeks. "Oh, Christine," I moaned.

In the silence, with both of our eyes pleading, my resolve was ready to break completely, but then the motion sensor on the lake went off, and I jolted to my feet in an instant. I turned quickly and left to turn it off. My heart was pounding as I contemplated who it could be. Oded was my first thought, or Raoul, probably with a police escort. My anger was instantly rekindled and was burning through me stronger than ever as I went back to Christine.

"Have you made your choice yet, my dear? Why are you putting it off? You're only tormenting yourself—and me, I might add. Just make your decision and get it over with. Or perhaps I should make it for you."

I moved quickly toward the mantel and placed one hand on each figurine. "The grasshopper or the scorpion? Which one will it be, *my deceitful Delilah*?"

Forty-Seven

With my hands still on the figurines, I glared at her. "You can end it all right now, my sweet, or I can leave and escort the first of our guests into my home to join us in our merry-making. Which will it be?"

She turned her face away from me, and I closed my eyes tightly, hung my head, and felt each figure under my palms. If I moved one, it would bring instant death to many, end my life of perpetual torment, and end Christine's need to make a decision. If I turned the other, our lives would go on, my torment would go on, and Christine and Raoul would leave and marry. Oh, how my heart ached, as it waged a war with my mind.

"Which do I turn, my dear?"

She lowered her head and began sobbing again, so, growling, I stormed toward the door to the lake and away from her and the two figurines vying for our attention.

"Then I must leave you alone and escort them in." I opened the door and turned while laughing at her. "You won't go away now—will you?"

My boat wasn't on my side of the lake for me to use, which was just as well. So I found a reed, took off my coat and shoes, slipped into the water, and began swimming through the labyrinth toward the wharf. I kept watching and listening, but there was nothing for about five minutes. Then I saw a faint light that I thought was coming from my lantern in my boat.

Oded, I thought, he's doing it again. No need to hum through the reed, he would never fall for that trick a second time. Therefore, I kept swimming slowly until I could see my boat, but I couldn't see a man's form in it. So I continued on, preparing to dip below the water just as soon as I saw someone.

The closer I got, the more cautious I became, feeling I could be swimming into a snare. Slowly, I swam closer and closer. When I was right up against it, I went to its bow and placed my palms on the hull. When I didn't feel movement inside, I knocked on it, put my palms on it again, waiting to see if I felt anything. I repeated that movement two more times, and when I still didn't get a response, I cautiously lifted myself up and looked inside. Then, with only a moment of confusion, I found just one item in the boat, a long white silk scarf like the one Raoul wore.

Since I still felt I might be sitting in the middle of an ambush, I hung onto the side of the boat, watching and listening. I was there for some time before I felt safe enough to turn the lantern off and start pulling my boat toward my docking room.

After throwing the scarf around my neck, I entered the drawing room where Christine was still tied to the chair. She looked up at me, and I instantly felt something was amiss. She appeared to be in shock, as if she didn't expect me to return. I walked in front of her, dripping wet, and holding the scarf out in front of her face.

"Does this look familiar to you? I believe one of our guests decided to leave it as a wedding present. And look at this beautiful crest. It's engraved with a large C, perhaps for Christine, so this one must be for you. Perhaps mine will show up before the day is out."

She looked at the crest, and her eyes became wide, so I pushed her further. "Oh, it does look familiar to you. I thought it might."

"What have you done?" she accused.

Like a caged animal, I paced slowly in front of her, and mocked. "Oh, my dear, dear Christine, why does everyone expect the worst from me? Why do you think I did something wrong just because someone left us a gift, our first wedding gift?"

I tied it in a fashionable knot at my neck and turned in a circle. "Well, my dear, how does your groom look? Quite dashing, you say? Now I'm just as prepared for our wedding as you are, except my attire isn't splattered with blood." I spread my arms out from my sides. "I've even taken a bath for my bride. I know I promised I wouldn't take another cold bath in that lake, but I had to be presentable for our nuptial chamber."

I wasn't getting the response I thought I would, so I studied her eyes for a moment. Something had changed. She now looked more nervous than frightened, and it wasn't an act. I looked at the door to the lake and wondered, had I unwittingly led someone to my home? Was the empty boat and scarf only a ploy after all? Had someone managed to outsmart me?

I stood perfectly still and listened for any sound on the other side of the door, but all I heard were Christine's nervous breaths. She was definitely anxious, but why now? She had every right to be nervous when I was threatening to take her to her bed, but not now. Something had unquestionably changed.

"Remember, Christine, when we promised we wouldn't keep secrets from each other? I believe you're keeping a secret from your betrothed now. Are you going to go to our wedding with that secret? Or perhaps you'll go

to your grave with that secret. I see it in your eyes, so don't try to deny it."
She looked down, and I placed my fingers under her chin and lifted her
face. "Look in my eyes, my love, and tell me your secret," I said softly.

She squirmed, but she didn't turn away. Then she looked me directly
in the eyes and presented her case. "There's no secret, Erik. What you see is
my pain. My wrists hurt badly. Please, Erik, untie me."

"Untie you? Do you really think I'm that much of a fool? You want me
to untie you so you can stab me in the back? You and Raoul make a great
pair. Neither of you has the courage to face me while trying to rip out my
heart. Well, let me tell you something. Not since I was a child have I ever
walked into a trap—never, and I'm not about to walk into one now."

"Just look at my wrist and you'll see I'm not lying or laying a trap for
you."

I stepped behind her and knelt down, and then my heart sank. Her
wrists were welted and bleeding, and I hung my head in sorrow. In that
instant, I felt my staunch demeanor slipping beyond my control, and I
refused to let that happen. Therefore, after a deep breath, I calmly stood in
front of her and continued my mocking.

"Shame, shame, shame," I hissed. "I warned you. I told you my lassos
wouldn't hurt you if you didn't struggle. From the looks of your wrists, you
really must have been struggling. Do you want to get away from me that
badly?" I wagged my head. "When will you learn? Do things my way and
no one gets hurt."

She looked directly into my eyes again and then slightly shook her head.
"Erik, think about what you're saying. Think about what you're doing. Do
you honestly expect me to just sit here and wait for you to kill me? I'm not a
lamb you can simply lead to the slaughter. I will fight you in any way I can.
I've tried telling you the truth. I've tried reasoning with you, but you don't
want to believe the truth or be reasonable, so I'm going to fight you until
you either let me go or kill me. I won't simply lie down and die.

"I know you're larger and stronger than me, and I know you could
snap my neck in an instant if you really wanted to. So, since I'm still alive, I
know you don't really want to kill me. You tied me to this chair so I couldn't
try to kill myself again, so I know you don't want me dead. Please, Erik.
Your lassos are truly hurting my wrists. Untie me—please."

I stood up straight and looked down at her. Something had changed
while I was gone, and she had newfound emotional strength because of it.
I glanced around the parlor and wondered what it was. Perhaps someone
was in the mirror chamber. After a few moments, I knew the only way
I could know was to leave her alone again and see what happened. So I
untied her and then stood back in front of her.

"I apologize for your poor wrists, Christine. I hurt you, and I never intended to hurt you. I love you, and I only want you to love me. I never wanted to hurt the woman I love. Perhaps I am crazy as you suggested. Perhaps I deserve nothing more than death. Perhaps I should sing my own requiem and crawl into my casket." Then softly, I added, "Forgive me."

Without another word from either of us, I turned and walked into my music room and shut the door. While I changed into dry clothes, I thought over what had just happened. My apology to her began as an act but ended with my heart sensing pain. I heard my words to her and began to believe they were right. I deserved nothing more than death. But since I didn't want to feel pain, I pushed it off and began demanding my organ to cover over my torture with music. The shelves on the walls vibrated with the thunder of sound when I sang out my own requiem.

Once finished, I sat there until the objects in the room came back into clear focus. In the silence, I massaged my aching neck and shoulder and knew I had no choice. I was insane. What I'd done to her proved it, and I had to let her go before I did something that couldn't be undone.

I lowered my head and sighed, "I have to let my Christine go."

When I entered the parlor, she was standing behind my chair, but I didn't even glance at her. Instead, I headed for the bag of keys on the mantle, intending to lock the ebony boxes and bring the curtain down prematurely on my demented opera. But, when I got there, the bag was gone, and it didn't take a genius to know where it went.

Scowling, I turned instantly toward Christine, who was by then standing in the center of the room with one hand hidden in the folds of her skirt. Her deceit was written clearly across her porcelain face, and I shook my head in utter disbelief that she would turn on me again so quickly. However, she did warn me that she wasn't going to simply lie down and die.

"What have you done with my bag, Christine? You aren't hiding it in your skirt, are you?" She just stared at me. "Give me my bag!" She still didn't respond. "Don't make me wrestle you for it, I don't believe you'll win." She still stood still. "Very well then," I said as I started slowly toward her, smiling. "I've never wrestled with a woman before, but how hard could it be? I imagine it might even be fun."

She turned and darted toward the dining room, and I laughed. "Where do you think you're going? There's nowhere to go, but around in circles like a child's merry-go-round." By then she was at the end of the table by the kitchen, and I was at the other end by the parlor. I laughed more. "Silly child. I'm not in the mood for your childish game. Give me my bag."

I stood motionless and watched her eyes, intently, waiting for her slight distraction. She couldn't handle my stare for long, so, when she glanced behind me, I jumped up on the table, and she darted for the parlor. Then I jumped down right in front of her, wrapping my arms completely around her. She squirmed and moaned, and I laughed and lowered my face to hers.

"That was much easier than I thought it would be, even with my painful and damaged shoulder. You make lousy prey, my dear. No challenge at all." I ran one hand down her arm until I had her empty hand and pressed it against her back, which pressed her entire body against mine. Within the next few seconds, I had her other hand in mine and then wrenched the bag from it, causing her to cry out. The entire process took less than thirty seconds, but I held her in that position for a bit longer.

"You know, my dear, under different circumstances, I'd have cherished having you this close to me, but there's this nagging little voice somewhere inside my head that's distracting me from enjoying this moment. What could it be?" I cocked my head and narrowed my eyes. "Oh, yes, I believe it's called anger, my anger over your continuing deceit.

"You know something else? I was on my way out here to release you. Oh, you look surprised. Well, I was. I felt bad about my conduct, so I was going to cage our friends over there and set you free from your cage. But, once again, your traitorous actions have nullified all my benevolent and *mistaken* feelings. Too bad. Too bad."

Then I hissed, "You fool. Do you still doubt that I get what I want? How much more is it going to take for you to become a believer in what I say? What more do I have to do to you, you foolish, foolish woman?"

"No, Erik, let me explain. I only wanted to lock the boxes back up. I know you don't want to do this. I know you, and I know you're going to be so sorry when this is over. I know you're not going to go through with what you say, and I just wanted to help you get to that point. I swear. I was just going to lock them back up."

Her lips spoke to me such nice words, but her eyes were telling me she was holding something back. There was something she wasn't telling me, so I jerked her closer to me, causing her to moan.

"Erik, you're hurting me."

"And what do you call what you've done to me?—Something pleasurable?—Perhaps a Sunday stroll through the park?"

She doubled up her fist and began beating on my left shoulder, but I only laughed at her. "You're not using your head, my sweet. If you really want to hurt me, you should try beating on my right shoulder. Have you forgotten its condition? Have you forgotten how your lover shot me in the back?"

She groaned and tried to reach over to my right shoulder, but I had her wrist in my hand and pinned it to her back along with the other one. I laughed again and jerked her closer to me.

"Erik, you're really hurting me. Let me go!"

At the end of her words, I heard a sound behind me, like a groan, and I turned both of us quickly. Then I remembered how she'd given away my secret passage. I looked down at her, and, within a second, the expression in her eyes as well as the scene we'd just played spelled everything out to me.

"My dear, did you hear that? I think we have more guests."

"No, Erik. That was just the rats. Remember the rats in the walls?"

"Is that why you're trembling? Are you that frightened of rats? I don't think so, my dear. Shall we take a look and see if it's truly rats or more guests?"

"No, Erik. It doesn't matter. I don't want to see rats."

I laughed at her. "Christine, Christine, Christine. Don't try to deceive the master deceiver. I know you gave away that secret passage to your young de Chagny. Why do you think I locked that door? Just a coincidence? Think again."

"No, Erik," she begged. "I didn't give it away. I never told him where it was or how to work it. I wouldn't do that to you."

I shook my head, released her, and walked into the parlor. "You know what the chances are that someone could find my lair without help?"

"It wasn't me, Erik! Honestly!"

"Such words, and so easily spoken," I taunted, while slipping the bag in my pocket and walking to the wall separating the parlor and the mirror chamber. "Look here, Christine. Have you ever taken a good look at this painting? It's a truly peaceful painting, don't you think? Beautiful trees—a clear sky—a babbling brook. Here, let me take it down so you can see it closer. Oh! What do we have here? Another painting? Now who in their right mind would put one painting over another one?"

I looked at her and cocked my head. "Someone surely had to be senseless to do such a thing. But wait! This one isn't very pretty. It must be of a dark night—there's nothing to see. Who would paint such a thing? No talent at all, this painter has."

I pretended to try to take it down, and when it wouldn't move, I growled, "I can't get this one down. Perhaps it's not a painting after all. I seem to remember someone saying that things aren't always what they appear to be. Perhaps it's a window and not a painting. Let's look through it and see if it's a window."

"No, Erik, it doesn't matter."

"Doesn't matter? I can't believe you actually said that. You're always curious and want to know who and how and to touch and to feel. Are you quite all right?" I asked, while stepping toward her and feeling her forehead. "Hmm, no fever. Oh, well, if you're not curious then I am. I want to see if it's a window, and, if it is, I want to know why it was concealed."

"Please, Erik, go play your piano for me. I want to hear the wedding mass."

"Nice try," I laughed. Then I became staunch, stood close to her, lowered my head, and glared into her eyes. "Wouldn't you rather see your lover, especially after he made the long trip down here just for our wedding?"

Pathetically, she tried again. "You're wrong. You're just teasing me. There isn't anyone or anything there. Please, Erik. Play your piano for me. Play "One Beat" for me."

"How dare you," I growled. "That piece represented my heart pouring out to you during a beautiful moment between us, and you ask me to play it now?—Just to save your lover? How dare you! How dare you, you despicable traitor!"

She was stammering, trying to find words to calm what she feared was coming, my violent anger. I clamped my teeth together and gave her a defiant stare. Then I moved to the corner of the room where I pressed two hidden springs; one turned a light on in the mirror chamber, and the other one opened a small door and allowed steps to fold down under the window. As she watched them click into place, her eyes widened and she began twisting the fabric of her dress. I then took her by the arm and led her around the room as I turned off all the lights. Then, with only the dim light coming from the chamber, I took her to the steps and looked coldly at her.

"Step up, my dear, and watch the picture turn into the man you were going to run away with and marry."

"I don't want to marry anyone, Erik."

"Don't play me the fool, Christine," I demanded harshly. Then I put my lips next to her ear, and whispered, "With the lights just right, you'll be able to see him clearly. Won't that be nice?"

"Please, Erik, don't do this. You're frightening me."

"What? Are you saying you're afraid of the dark? You shouldn't be afraid of the dark while in the arms of your husband. I'm very strong, Christine. I'll protect you." I grabbed her in my arms and held her tightly, while she struggled against me and moaned, so I released her. "Will you make up your mind, you fickle woman. Do you want me to protect you or not?"

She looked up at the window and then back at me, and I knew she was desperately searching for the right words or actions to alter my course.

When she didn't respond, I took a firm hold on her arm and shoved her up one step, and then we both heard movement on the other side of the wall.

"See, my dear. I told you we had guests in there. Now step up further and see who it is. Also, let me know how many are there so I can set more places at the banquet table."

"Please, Erik. If you love me you won't make me do this."

I gently pulled her down from the step and let go of her arm.

"Very well, my dear. I'll go up and see who's come to celebrate with us," I said as I took one step up.

"No!" she quickly exclaimed while grabbing my arm. "I'll go!"

"Why, thank you, my sweet. You're so thoughtful to save me the effort of such a climb at my advanced age. Now, tell me, who's come to call?"

She looked inside and nearly fell from the steps. Then, with trembling lips, she continued with her lies. "No one is in there, Erik. It must have been the rats we heard."

"If there's no one in there, my dear, then describe what you see. Do you like what you see?"

"Oh, yes," her shaking voice tried to convince me. "It's filled with the most beautiful trees. How did you create such a lovely painting?"

"It was nothing really, just something to occupy my solitary hours spent alone in my home. But with your abnormal curiosity, aren't you the least bit interested to know *why* I created such a masterpiece and then hid it behind a wall?"

"No, not really," she tried to say bravely. "You do many things that are unusual, and I've learned to see them as just your way, without asking questions." As she started to climb down from the steps, she made another attempt to deceive me. "I'm finished looking at your painting, Erik. You can turn the light out now."

I moved close to another painting and began running my finger along its frame. To anyone who might have been watching, I might have appeared almost normal right then, but I'm sure my tone had to be sending chills up her spine.

"I'll make you a deal, Christine. I'll turn that light out—if you agree to marry me for real. I won't even ask you to say you love me anymore. I can be patient for that. We could be married before you love me. There are many places in the world where people marry before they love each other; sometimes they don't even know each other when they marry. But, as time goes by, they learn to love each other with a love that's precious and true.

"Just as that grain of sand can become a beautiful pearl in an oyster, two unpolished people can produce a beautiful marriage, if they try. Try with me, Christine. Try with me. Take me to your bed, and I'll turn the light out in my mirror chamber."

She was just ready to answer me when a voice, Raoul's voice, came from the other side of the wall. "Christine! No! Don't do it!"

She nearly jumped out of her skin, and, looking me straight in the eyes, she began shaking her head. The expression on her face told me she felt the next step was going to be Raoul's death. But I wasn't ready for his death just yet. I wanted to continue with my power game a little longer, so I narrowed my eyes, smiled, and backed to the middle of the room, facing the mirror chamber. Then, with my hands on my hips and my head wagging, I taunted her.

"My, my. I had no idea the rats in this building were so intelligent—or was it rats? Perhaps it was Erik's voice we heard inside the room. Just as I have eyes and ears everywhere in this opera house, my voice is also everywhere. Were you aware of that, my dear? Watch and listen as another skill of your betrothed is unveiled."

I tossed my voice toward the scorpion. "Turn me and watch me sting." Toward the grasshopper. "Turn me and watch me hop high." Toward the bag of keys as I tossed them in the air. "Let us out so we can work our magic." To myself in the mirror chamber. "Erik wants out! Let me out! It's getting hot in here!"

Her hand went to her mouth, and she looked at the lighted window, and I smiled. "You've heard me before, I'm sure. Did you not hear the toad in Carlotta's throat?—Co—ack—good imitation, don't you think? And how about the laughter in Box Five, did you not hear that? And then there were your roses who spoke of tender love and hope."

I began sending my laughter all around the room in rapid succession, until, with her hands over her ears, she began begging, "Stop! Erik, please, stop!"

I sneered. "Stop? I thought you could listen to my voice all day long, but now you want me to stop? Why is that, my sweet?"

"Because" was all she could say.

"Aha, it's because of the hurricane, isn't it? You feel its approach, don't you?" I paced beside her, goading her. "Well, tell me, my dear, how do you like being tossed by the gales of a hurricane? Not very pleasant, is it? I told you we were in the eye of the hurricane—now didn't I?

"If you'll remember correctly, I tried to warn you about the dangerous game you played, trying to work both ends. I tried to tell you to make your decision before it was too late and the churning walls came down on us. But you didn't listen to me." I stopped pacing, grabbed her by the shoulder, and glared down into her eyes. "Well, perhaps you'll listen now that you can see all my predictions are coming true."

She was breathing hard and kept glancing over my shoulder toward the window and then back into my eyes.

"Why do you tremble, Christine? If there's nothing but pretty trees on the other side of that window, then why do you tremble so?"

"Because you frightened me, making me think someone was being tortured in there."

I released her shoulder, took a step back, and cocked my head. "Tortured? I've never said anything to you about torturing anyone. Why would you think I would be torturing someone?"

She tried to fabricate more lies while twisting her fingers. "I don't know. I'm just frightened, I guess. I don't know."

I watched her face as she looked at the window again, and it told me much. Raoul was in there sure enough, but who else? The police? Why did she use that term, torture? My suspicions were strong that there was only one person who would use that term with regard to my mirror chamber, so I probed Christine further.

"Don't try to hide it, my dear. I know your young lover is in there, but I don't believe he has the intelligence to find my special room by himself. So, since you say it wasn't you who showed him the way, then I suspect someone else is also in there with him. Say, perhaps, my so-called friend, the one the chorus girls call the Persian?

"Now, it's not that I think my friend has any more intellect than your friend, but he has had many more years to study my work, and he is a *very tenacious* fellow. He once told me he always finds the man he goes looking for. Well, *Mon Ami*," I said as I turned toward the mirror chamber and gave it a knock. "Do you think you've found me? Can you see me? No, so you haven't found me yet. You've only found my trap. How does it feel to be on that side of Erik's invention? Isn't it wonderful?

"Oh! Let me give you a few words of caution. Don't bother to look for a way out. Since you last saw them, my creations have advanced along with my imagination. They're held back only by this weary and broken body I drag around. But still, what I can imagine I can create, and I imagined a better way of supplying you with a desert heat. So don't bother trying to find a lantern to turn off and stop the heat. I use electric coils now. They heat much more efficiently and are well out of your reach. Are you enjoying their comfort yet?

"And the most important caution for you to remember—it won't work to use your shoe or pistol butt or your strong shoulder to break those mirrors. It will only cost you valuable energy. And, no matter how bad it gets in there, I strongly advise that you don't use a bullet from that handgun strapped to your ankle to shatter my mirrors. If you do, it just might be tantamount to committing suicide.

"Oh, that reminds me. You might caution that *young fool* who's in there with you to keep his pistol in his pocket. I know he's fond of pulling it out at any opportunity and shooting blindly, but now is truly a bad time. Let me explain why. You see, those aren't ordinary mirrors you're looking at. They're special—like me. They're deceptive—like me. They'll deceive you and come back to kick you in the rear—like me.

"How is that, you ask? Well, those panels aren't what they appear to be. They're made from thick, polished steel. Oh, what's that you say? You like my new mirrors? You think they're pretty? I did a good job? You thought they were real mirrors? I know. Aren't I ingenious? But you do remember, don't you, that they're only reflecting the iron tree and its branches, and, if you look closely, you'll find one of my lassos under that tree, just in case you should need it before the night is over.

"Anyway, back to the mirrors. It took a long time to get every one of them just right. Not only did they have to have hours and hours of polishing but they also had to be meticulously painted with lacquer to fill in any minute flaws. But, I guarantee, they're all equally dangerous.

"If you should shoot at them, the bullet would only ricochet around in there until it loses velocity or embeds itself in something soft—say, human flesh—say, the back of one of you. So take my warning seriously. I know Raoul is good at shooting others in the back, and, if he doesn't maintain his self control while in there, he just might perform a difficult task—shooting himself in the back. Wouldn't that be funny—in a strange way? At any rate, be careful. One of you could end up dead before your appointed time.

"Do you get the picture, Oded? Good. I thought you would. I would hate to have to clean up large amounts of blood again—especially if it belonged to the one who used to be my friend. You do remember how terribly ghastly it was to remove all that blood, and I'm sure you still remember how I feel about that stuff, don't you, *Mon Ami*? So please be kind. Don't spill any of it if you take your own lives. Use my lasso. It's most clean and silent."

"What, you say? Is this an idle threat? How often have you heard me give anyone an idle threat? That's what I thought. Never! The last time I saw you, I warned you not to get too close, now didn't I? I told you the luck of the Irish may not be with you the next time you invaded my territory. Now you can see for yourself that I wasn't giving you an *idle threat.*"

For the most part, I'd been carrying on a one-sided conversation, and I was tired of hearing my own voice, so I looked at Christine, who was leaning with one hand on the back of the divan. Then I spread my arms out, shrugged my shoulders, and shook my head.

"Oh, sigh, sigh. It appears no one wants to talk to Erik. Poor Erik.—Poor me.—Poor Erik."

There were a few moments of complete silence, and then a familiar voice entered the conversation from the other side of the wall.

"Erik! Remember, I saved your life."

Forty-Eight

"My, my, if it isn't my old and foolish friend Oded. I knew it had to be you in there. You were always the best tracker. Well, almost. You never were able to track me successfully, now, were you?

"At any rate, it's so good you could make it to our wedding celebration. How thoughtful of you. But don't you think it would be proper etiquette to congratulate your old friend on his upcoming nuptials rather than bringing up such a tired and worn-out subject? And, if I'm remembering correctly, which I'm certain I am, I've more than paid you back for that ill-advised error in judgment, so it's too late to claim anything for that one act of mercy toward me. I've lost track of all the times I held back from killing you, *Mon Ami*, so we're even.

"However, I can't help but feel you must be regretting that decision about now. If you hadn't helped me falsify my death—you wouldn't be facing yours. But don't fret too much about it. We all make bad decisions from time to time." I chuckled. "Though, under the circumstances, that decision was a truly stupid mistake. But never mind that now."

"Yes, Erik, never mind that now. That was a long time ago, and it has nothing to do with what's happening now. I don't regret saving your life in Persia, and I don't regret what I'm doing now. I would do it all over again if it would prevent *you* from making a terrible mistake."

"Prevent me? What makes you think *you* can prevent me from doing anything I want when no one else has ever been able to? Have you forgotten our time together in Persia? You couldn't have forgotten how I nearly destroyed the palace I'd just built in order to get my way. Were the Shah and all his armed men able to *prevent me* from achieving my goal? Did I get what I wanted? I believe you know the answers to those questions. And do you remember what happened to those men because of their error in misjudging me? One was left as a baked good in my mirror chamber and the other to live out his life in emotional torment.

"And another case in point, what about the dozen or so mighty fighting generals, men in charge of other fighting men, men who'd won so many battles that the medals on their chests weighed them down? Think about them. Were they able to finalize their plans to hurt those I cared about? No! With the wine still in their mouths, they dropped where *I wanted* them to drop. None of them could stop me from what I set out to accomplish.

"So, now I'm a bit confused. If those two powerful nations couldn't *prevent* me from getting what I wanted, why do you think you and that silly naval officer in there with you can do it alone? Ha! I laugh at your feeble efforts. I take it you must have seen me enter my trap door in the third cellar, right. But now, think for a moment, *Mon Ami*. Did you honestly believe I would leave a straight path to my dining area? Ha! I laugh again at your stupidity.

"No, I take that back. You're not stupid, so there has to be another explanation for this bad decision. Perhaps age is catching up with you. Either that or your stubbornness has gone to new heights. I can understand your bad decisions when it came to our chess games; after all, they were only games. But, even with them, can you ever remember winning one of them? Were you ever able to lay my king down? Yes, I thought you would agree with me there.

"Well, how about real life? Can you ever think of a time when anyone was able to beat me, to force my king to lay down? No, I didn't think so. While still a child, I started learning how to win, with a cold-hearted mother as my tutor. Did she beat me down? A resounding no! I learned from her and got better and stronger at what I did.

"When I was only nine, did the boy who was much bigger and stronger than me beat me down? No! He might have beat me up, but not down, and, when the dust settled, it was he who was struggling for breath and fearing for his life. And if it hadn't been for a kind-hearted man, his life would have ended that day.

"Did a full grown man, with a cage and whip at his service, beat me down? Again, he might have beat me up, but not down, and he paid with his life for that error in misjudging me. We'll forget about the dozens of other men who thought I was a weak target and who never lived to know the truth. They mean nothing to me, nothing more than the dust under my feet.

"No, my friend. After each conquest, I learn and get better. So your frail attempt to outsmart me, to have me surrender my king, is a mere practice in futility.

"No one, and I repeat, no one will ever take me down. Now, I, on the other hand, have full control over my destiny. Well, almost. If this seductive temptress here with me chooses that ignorant fool beside you instead of me, well, then that will be the end of us all. I'll end this game I've played my entire life and lay down my king willingly.

"But, since my life is so much more valuable than all of yours, it will come at a very high price. I dare say, hmmm," I said as I looked at the ceiling and pictured the ones that would be filling the auditorium, "hundreds? Thousands? Yes, I believe thousands will go down with me.

"So you see, since there's no way you can win this battle you've entered into, I believe it's in your best interest to keep your mouth shut. If you don't, I just might get a tad angry, and you know what can happen when I get angry. You know what happened to those men at the campfire site in Persia when they angered me. It wasn't a pretty sight—was it? They didn't fare nearly as well as those generals fared. At least the generals' bodies were intact when they were buried."

"Erik, I came here to help Christine, not to do battle with you. You should know by now that I don't fear you. All those times when you say you could have killed me, you didn't, and I don't believe you will now."

"Well, you see, *Mon Ami*, that's where you and I differ. With each flirtation with death, I learn and become better at what I do. But you, you crazy fool, each time you encounter me, you dig your grave deeper. And I believe this time it's much too deep for anyone to raise you up out of it."

"Erik, listen to him," Christine tried again. "This isn't you. I know that. I know this is one of those times in your life that you'll regret later. This isn't what you really want to do. I know that. Please, stop this insanity before someone gets hurt."

"Oh, how sweetly you plead. How sincere you sound. How comely you appear. But you're forgetting who taught you this skill you're trying to use on me. Like Oded, you test me and my limits. Oh, yes, if I wanted, I could stop this. I could simply turn around and walk out of my invisible door and leave all of you here to try to figure out my brilliance and free yourselves on your own.

"I could go to the stable and pick my favorite horse, and I could leave this stinking structure and this disgusting city. I could leave it all, and I could start all over again, with a new script, and a new cast, and a new venue. I could do it all over again—*if* I wanted to, but I don't want to. I'm bored with the same old and tattered script that always ends the same, with me surviving and leaving turmoil in my wake.

"You're all fools! Fools I tell you! The whole world is nothing more than a stage cast with a company of ignorant fools. I tire of you all. I want to try something different. I want to see if I can outsmart—outmaneuver—the angel of death. I want to take him on and see who wins. Doesn't that sound absolutely thrilling?"

Undeterred, Christine demanded, "Erik, please! Look at me! Look in my eyes and see if I'm not telling you the truth. Look at me!"

"Oh, we're demanding now? How terribly brave of you to demand anything from this monster."

"Look at me, Erik!"

"Very well, *my dear*," I said coldly.

I slowly moved next to her, narrowed my eyes, and glared down at her. Considering the circumstances, she was showing an abnormal amount of courage when she tried again to reason with the unreasonable madman before her.

"We all know what you're capable of, both the good and the bad. You have nothing to prove, at least not to me. I've always told you the truth."

"What!" I screamed and grabbed her shoulders. "You little deceiver! You're now lying about lying?"

Without fear, she continued, "I know I was wrong to tell Raoul I would leave with him, regardless of the circumstances. That was my weakness—my failure. I was scared and so confused. But that's not an excuse, and I was wrong. You deserve so much more than that from me. I've watched you these last months, and I've come to know you and appreciate you for the man you are. I believe I even lo . . ."

"Don't say it, Christine!" I bellowed. "Words are cheap!" I shoved her away from me and turned from her. "Don't insult my intelligence with mere words twisted into lies, lies spoken with the intent of saving your lover. Oh!" I growled and turned back, facing her. "You infuriate me!"

Softly, she responded, "I'm not lying, Erik. I'm really not. I've been confused since you first came into my life. My life has changed so much. I still feel I'll wake from a nightmare in my bed and all this will disappear."

"Well, now," I sneered, as I spread my arms out and began walking backwards away from her. "Wouldn't that be nice for us all, my pretty little thing?"

She looked at the window. "Erik, this is between you and me, not between them and us. Let them go, and I promise I'll stay with you again, and we'll work through this nightmare together."

"Are you saying you agree to marry me?" She looked down at her hands and sighed. "Just what I thought. It's your agreement to marry me that will rescue them and the thousands of others, but we're running out of time," I said as I motioned to the floor clock. "Decide quickly."

"Erik, please listen to me. Remember the day I took your mask off, and remember what you did? You were out of control, violently out of control. You could have killed me easily that day, but you didn't. Why?"

I sarcastically laughed at her. "You were fortunate that day. Your stars weren't aligned for your burial."

"Erik, don't use word games. This is serious. You didn't hurt me because it wasn't in you to hurt me. There was something, and not the stars, something deep in you that was protecting me. That same quality is still in you, and I don't believe you'll hurt any of us. It's not who you really are or who you want to be. You're in pain, and I'm so sorry for that. I never wanted to add to your scars, never. You're going to let us all go eventually, because you can't murder, not anymore. So just let them go now, and I'll stay with you longer, I promise."

Her reasoning almost reached me, so I again moved close to her and said softly and honestly, "I've been so patient, but I don't think I can be patient any longer. You don't understand how hard it's been for me to have you so close and not be able to take you as my wife. It's taken everything I have to prevent that from happening, but I don't think I can do it any longer. I love you too much, Christine."

She ran her finger down my cheek. "You once told me that any decision I made had to be made for me and not for you or Raoul. Do you remember that?" I nodded. "Well, you also said I had to be 100 percent sure of my decision before I made it and not to let Raoul pressure me into a decision before I was that sure. After I left him on the roof, those words of yours about being that sure made me realize I couldn't leave you.

"Well, I'm still not 100 percent sure about my decision. I can't make it with this much pressure on me. You have to know and appreciate that. I could tell you, yes, I'll marry you, just so you'll let them go, but that would be a lie. That's what I did with Raoul on the roof, and you know how that turned out. It didn't come from my heart then, and it wouldn't be coming from my heart now. I can't do that to you. You would eventually know the truth, and I fear what that would do to your already scarred heart."

I spread my arms around the room. "And this doesn't frighten you?"

"No, not like that would," she said softly.

As a hush fell over the room, I searched her eyes, and, with only the sound of the clock's pendulum swaying, I moved her hair away from her bruised forehead. I loved her so much, and, when I took a silent moment to realize just how much, that all too familiar ache surged through my chest.

I ran my fingers down her soft cheek and under her chin, and then I followed the contours of her lips with my eyes. With the sight of them, I saw Raoul's lips on hers, and I heard her betrayal again just as I had on the roof, so I turned abruptly and took a stride away from her. When the stabs to my heart returned and I feared crumbling again, I headed for my music room, unwilling to let her see me fall apart.

"I need to be alone," I grumbled as I shut the door.

That time, I didn't want the loud chords of my organ to cover over my pain. I wanted and needed the soft refrains of my violin to soothe it. So I closed my eyes and let the melodies take me to the shores of Perros with the sea mist bathing my naked face, to the green hills in Mazenderan, to the feelings of my first opera, to my games of tag with Molly, to the tranquility of that little lake in northern Italy, to the conversations with my father among the smell of fresh cut timber, to the slow lope on the back of Déchainé under the blue sky, to those precious carriage rides and laughter with Christine.

Once thoroughly soothed, I sat with my violin lying across my legs and with my eyes still closed. I thought over Christine's words and I knew she was right. I didn't want to kill anyone. My remorse was already great, but it would be worse if I didn't release them now before they did themselves harm.

By the time I'd put my violin in its case, I had the plans for my future already made. I would leave everything behind and head for Southern France where I could build a home with lots of windows in a remote area close to the sea. There I could live out the remainder of my days with only music and horses as my friends.

With my hand on the doorknob, I knew I had to rewrite the last act. I had to release my captives in the mirror chamber, and I had to set the love of my life free, regardless of the emotional cost to me. I'd started that deadly game we were all a part of on that night when I first saw Christine's eyes, so I had to end it so her eyes could smile once more.

However, when I stepped into the parlor and saw Christine leaning up against the wall with her ear to it, I knew my new ending wouldn't have a chance to be played out, since she was right then writing an additional and unrehearsed scene with her own deceiving lips.

"Hold on just a little bit longer. Oh, Raoul, I love you too. Both of you need to be quiet. Don't say anything. It makes him worse when he hears either of you, even if it's only a sigh. Please, be quiet and let me handle Erik. I've learned how to handle him."

My jaws clenched, my fists tightened, my breath turned hot, and I finally saw everything clearly. Christine was part of them and so was Oded, part of the world that hated me. The fact that the three of them were strategizing to outsmart me proved that in a most painful way. To have the two people I cared the most about treat me that way made my anger take me to that place I feared. I felt I no longer had a heart. So, with another protective barrier built securely around me, I stormed upon her and growled.

"Handle me?"

I grabbed her shoulder and flung her around. She hit the wall and looked up at me in total shock. Then I pressed her shoulders against the wall.

"Handle me? You mean like an animal in a circus cage? You know how to handle me? You . . ."

I shook my head slowly and breathed pure fire. She started to open her mouth, and I shoved her across the room, causing her to trip and fall.

"Handle me?"

I picked her up from the floor with one hand and shoved her down in my chair.

"Handle me?"

"I didn't mean it like that, Erik."

"Shush! No more of your lies. No more of your deceit. Your innocent play is over. The game is back on. You almost had me, you seductive, lying little . . . Only 13 hours until the truth be told, grasshopper or scorpion, my dear? The final test. Which will it be?"

"But, Er . . ."

"Shush, I said.—Oded!" I shouted across the room. "Will you please describe to this creature what happens when I'm angered beyond control! Describe to her the fate of those men at the campfire! Tell her how inhumane their deaths were! Tell this lying temptress to stop angering me! She needs to comply with my wishes while she still can."

My chest was heaving as I glared down at her, but she was unnaturally composed, and I was trying to understand why when she again tried to reason with me.

"Would you want me to agree to marry you even if I wasn't 100 percent certain that I wanted to?"

"Oh, my sweet," I sneered, "we're way past that point in this script. I'll take you any way I can get you. Since you've used up all my tolerance, your wishes are no longer a consideration. We'll be together one way or the other—alive or dead—you'll be by my side. However, I would prefer you alive. I would imagine it's rather difficult to enjoy the marriage bed when it's also your death bed."

My harsh words still didn't ruffle her, and she spoke ever so softly. "You once told me you would do anything for me. Well, I'm calling you on that now. I'm asking, no, I'm begging you to let them go. You don't have to let me go, but please let them go."

It was so silent that you would imagine all the players in that drama were holding their breaths. Christine held her sight on my eyes and mine was on hers. A part of me wanted to believe her, but her words about handling me seemed to fill the room with so much clutter that it was hard to reason with her pleas. Abruptly, I stormed across the room with my hands behind my neck and my voice growling loudly.

"Erik! Listen to her," came Oded's voice from the mirror chamber.

"You stay out of this, you meddling fool! You have nothing to do with this. But then, yes, you do! This is entirely your fault! Just as in Persia, you had to stick your nose into my affairs, and look what's happened. The first woman who loved me is gone, along with the woman who loved you—all because you had to have things your way. And, here in Paris, if you had minded your own business, none of this would be happening, and many lives wouldn't be in peril.

"Remember the day when you cautioned Christine about me, as if you couldn't fathom the thought that there was a woman who could actually love me—without being hypnotized first, that is. You idiot! Well, it's because of your interfering that day that we're standing here now—on the brink of a catastrophe.

"Did you know she was on her way to tell me she wanted to be my wife? My wife, Oded! I'd given her a choice, her heart or my ring. It was that clean and simple. No mirror chamber, no threats of imminent death, no tears. No one would have gotten hurt. Well, not entirely. If she'd given me my ring and not her heart, I would have been hurt, but no one else would have been. If you had stayed out of my business, we would all be living out our lives the way we wanted it and not the way *I* want it. But no, you pious fool. You knew best, right? Well now, look where we are.

"You'll be responsible for the deaths of so many tonight, even that young man in there beside you. He never would have come this close to finding my lair. You had to be leading him the entire way. Well, aren't you proud of yourself? You thought you were leading him to my door but you've only led him to death's door. Congratulate yourself!

"When will you learn? You have no control over any of this, so keep your mouth shut. I'm the only one with a queen and she's heading straight for your king without any protection left for you. The only hope any of us have is that Christine will make the right choice. She's the only player strong enough to help.

"Tell me something, Oded. What did you hope to accomplish by coming down here anyway? Did you think you could simply walk into my home, uninvited, and tell me you were here to take my bride away from me—and on my wedding day, no less? Did you think that would checkmate me? Did you expect me to say, here she is, take her away with you? What were you thinking, you fool? You've seen enough of my work. You had to know you couldn't get past my perimeter of protection. What were you thinking? Now, stay out of this or there's no hope for any of us."

"Please, Erik, let her go!" Raoul interjected.

"Erik? Now you call me Erik? Now you say please? What happened to your demands? What happened to the designation—old man or demented monster? Your tune has changed now that the demented monster has control over your destiny, now that you can't settle this with another bullet in my back, hasn't it? Well, maybe you'll think twice from now on before judging a book by its cover. Oh, no, wait a minute. You won't have another chance to judge anything, unless your sweet Christine makes the right choice and marries me."

I heard him let out a sob and another feeble plea that only angered me more. "You simpleminded unbeliever, you have no say in this either, so you also need to keep your mouth shut. This is between Christine and me. Besides, this isn't only Oded's fault. You have to accept your part in this drama. If you had let Christine come to me and talk as we agreed, I would have let her go if that's what she truly wanted. But being the arrogant know-it-all that you are, you wanted to decide her fate for her.

"Well, look what's happened. Now she has an even larger weight on her delicate shoulders. Are you proud of yourself? Your strategy surely didn't work out well, now did it? Oh, by the way, do you still have those train tickets in your pocket? Weren't they to be the way to end Christine's problems? They aren't doing any of you much good right now, are they? Perhaps they could be used as a fan to keep you cool, but that's about all they're good for. I believe it's getting rather hot in there about now. The desert sun can certainly be a bother, can't it?"

Christine whimpered, and I looked at her. "Oh, I'm sorry, my dear. I've left you out of the conversation. I'm so sorry. That's truly rude of me. Is there something you'd like to say to your young lover?"

She just stared at me and shook her head. "What? No questions from this sweet curious creature? How strange. No more questions? That's hard to believe. Those days you spent with me were filled with questions. Did you run out of them? That's really hard to believe."

She looked truly exhausted when she softly asked, "Erik, why are you doing this? You have a brilliant mind. There's so much you could do in a positive way. Why use your intelligence to create ugliness?"

"Why? Why?" I laughed. "Because this is all I've been allowed to create. This ugliness, as you call it. Oh, I've made an effort to use my intelligence for positive creations, as you called them, but no one ever wanted them if they had to take this along with it," I said as I tapped the side of my mask. "Why even this structure we're in right now, as magnificent as all claim it to be, is nothing compared with my design."

Her forehead slightly furrowed. "Oh, you didn't know I also designed an opera house for Paris? Well, I did, but did they accept it? Another whopping no! And why? Again, because of this," I said as I again tapped the side of my mask.

"My opera house," I mused, while I looked up, spread my arms out, and turned in a circle. Then my tone almost lost its venom. "My opera house wouldn't have moss-covered corridors or cold and drafty rooms. My opera house would have ventilation that would keep it cozy warm in the winter and refreshingly cool in the summer. My opera house wouldn't have smelly and dirty gas lighting, it would have clean and bright electrical lights, just like my home down here does.

"It wouldn't have a lake in its cellars. Its arches and architectural design would enhance the skyline of Paris and bring beauty to the eyes. My opera house would have an opera company that would never be matched. I would tutor each one of them as well as the orchestra. There would never be an out-of-tune instrument or a lazy musician. And my opera house wouldn't be run by those who know more about shoveling horse manure than creating breathtaking music. No, my opera house would astound the world.

"Yes, people come to see the famed Opera Populaire, but most do so because they were coming to Paris anyway. But my opera house would draw people to it simply because of its beauty. I could build my opera house in the middle of a desert, and people would still come."

I stopped and took a breath. Then there was quiet, complete quiet, until Christine tried again.

"You could still do that, Erik. You could still build and teach. I know that's what you really want to do."

I laughed loudly and stormed toward the chamber wall. Banging on it, I shouted, "Are you still alive in there? Are you listening to dear Christine's try at saving your miserable lives?

Sure you are. Your trials have only just begun. It's a shame you didn't listen to me, Oded. Now my friend has thrown his lot in with my enemy and your fates are the same. You can't be separated now. One in the same. No separation. One in the same.

"And as for you, my sweet pretty thing," I said as I turned back toward Christine, "I don't want your questions or comments to go unanswered. You see, I have tried. I'm 45 and I've tried. Repeatedly, I might add. But if a son can't have a mother's love then what hope is there for him to receive acceptance from anyone else? Absolutely no chance. That's why you found me here, trying to live out the remainder of my life without interference. But was I even allowed that modest request?"

I turned my head toward the mirror chamber and shouted, "No! I'm hunted even here and even by those claiming to be my friends," I said as I glared at Christine. "Well, no more. No more. The world has never won a game played against me, never. I always win, don't I, Oded?

"Oh, it's managed to check me at times and block my way, but I always find a way around those efforts. And, when I find that way, I only get better at what I do. Like that mirror chamber. The original had many flaws, but I learned. I'm always learning, and I never forget anything. Like this opera house. If I'd been in charge all these years, I can't begin to describe all the advancements I could have made to it. I can't even begin to explain them all.

"And you, Christine. Your voice is unmatched right now, but, with my further training there would be no limits. Can you imagine what an entire opera company would sound like under my tutelage? I'm only bound by human limitations. This broken body is all that prevents me from even grander inventions—unimaginable inventions. You've seen only the beginning of them, Christine."

I closed my eyes, lowered my head, and spoke softly. "But, no matter—no matter. It's over now. Unless," I said as I looked back at Christine. "Unless you agree to marry me, then all of this—this drama—this opera house—this thing called life will be over."

Forty-Nine

My rant over, the parlor became silent. Christine was standing behind my chair, and I was standing in the middle of the room, listening to my own labored breathing. Then, when I suddenly had difficulty focusing both my mind and my vision, I walked to a dining chair and leaned with one hand on its back. I closed my eyes and tried to relax my stiff neck and aching shoulder, but it didn't help. Then I became seriously hot and sweaty, and instantly I felt sick to my stomach.

When I realized what was happening to me, I glanced at Christine, knowing I was about ready to fall into unconsciousness. Unable to fathom what would happen to us all if I did, I instantly went to the kitchen and locked myself in.

I couldn't remember when I'd slept or eaten last—probably several days—and the last I'd had anything to drink was at least fourteen hours earlier. Therefore, I instantly began drinking all the water I could take in while grabbing cheese and bread out of the pantry. I stripped my mask and shirt off and sat on a stool, shoveling all I could into my mouth and washing it down with wine. At the same time, I fanned my body, trying to cool it down.

I stayed in that position, sitting on the stool with one elbow on my knee and my head in one hand, while, with the other hand, I kept feeding myself and drinking wine. Eventually, I began to feel better, physically, that is. Emotionally, I was somewhat numb, and I wasn't sure why I was forcing everyone to bend to my will.

Once I felt good enough to get to my feet, I replaced my shirt and mask and put the cheese and bread on a plate and poured another glass of wine. Then, with two glasses of wine and the plate of food, I returned to the parlor and found Christine standing by the steps in the wall and whispering to the muffled voices on the other side of it. I didn't even try to understand what they were saying. I knew they were again plotting against me, and then I remembered why I was forcing my will.

Nevertheless, I set everything on the small table by the couch and calmly told her, "You need to eat and drink this. It's been awhile. You need nourishment."

She ran her hand over her forehead, and, in a faint voice, asked, "Erik, it's much too warm in here. Can you make it cooler?"

"Aha! The wall you're beside is warm because of the African forest on the other side of it. That's what you saw when you looked in. It can be quite beautiful, but it can also be quite deadly. Oh, the climate," I sighed dramatically while walking toward her. "Sometimes we're at the mercy of the weather changes without warning—are we not?

"But then sometimes," I added, while projecting my voice toward the chamber, "we have ample warning and can protect ourselves from it quite nicely. Ah, but if we choose to ignore the danger signs and proceed without caution, can we blame anyone else for our error?"

I looked down at Christine and snarled, "Those fools, who now find themselves in my ingeniously constructed African forest, must pay the price for refusing to heed my warnings about staying away from my lair."

She was breathing with difficulty and lowered her head and eyes, so I lifted her face with my fingers under her chin, forcing her to look into my eyes. I began laughing at her and the other ignorant fools who thought they could outsmart me. I continued to laugh until I heard banging and yelling on the other side of the wall.

It sounded like Raoul, and I looked at Christine just as she went limp and collapsed on the floor. I picked her up by the shoulders and dragged her the few meters to the divan where I laid her down. Without feeling any emotion for her, I stormed across the room and into my music room, slamming the door behind me. I released my anger one more time on the keys of my organ until I was spent, then I sat with my eyes closed, listening to the silence.

When I returned to the drawing room, Christine was still on the divan. The only light in the room was coming from my music room and the window to the mirror chamber. Since I wanted to get a closer look at Christine, I replaced the picture over the window and turned on a light. Then I sat on the table near her and laid my fingers along the side of her neck, feeling for a pulse. I sighed when I found a strong one.

It was very quiet, both in the drawing room and on the other side of the wall, so I sat and watched her. With her there before me like that, without the fear and treachery in her eyes, my love for her began to flow again, and one more time I began to question what I was doing. Perhaps I should let her go and then end my life and all the suffering it brought to others.

"Oh, my dear God, what am I doing?" I whispered. "Oh, Christine, what am I doing to you?"

I removed my mask and laid my face in my palms, listening to my father's words. *Don't let others determine who you are, Erik.* I'd heard his voice often during my life, but never before was so much at stake. Was I allowing Christine's and Raoul's words and actions to control who I was right then? I don't believe I'd ever plotted to murder anyone before just for my own will. Could I go through with my plans and kill so many people? If I didn't, could I live with the thought of Christine in Raoul's arms forever? Could I do either?

Don't let others determine who you are, Erik. I heard his voice again. But who was I, and why was I there? Why was I even born?

I was in that mode of thinking and seriously considering letting everyone go when I heard pounding on the wall and loud voices coming from the mirror chamber. So I got up and moved close to it.

"Oh, how foolish some of us are, now aren't we, you tenacious daroga? Just like my sweet bride here. Her decisions aren't coming easily, and soon she'll pass her decision-making over to me. But you've already made your decision, and now you'll pay for it, you and my wife's lover.

"Bad decisions—bad decisions. How often we might make them, but you'll not have long to suffer the consequences of this one. We don't have much longer before the opera house will be full of arrogant ones, so unsuspecting of the fate that will befall them. Not much longer and we'll all sing our swan song together—all together Oded. Then it will be over—finally, all over."

"Erik, please," was his only response, to which I paid no attention.

"You sound as if you're getting tired, *Mon Ami*. Would you like to rest now?"

There was still no answer, so I pressed the spring that turned the bright light out in the chamber and another one that made a thousand twinkling stars appear above their heads. Then I spoke in a hushed voice.

"Night has fallen in the jungle, so, if you rest, rest cautiously. The night creatures are on the prowl, especially the black panther who is so silent—so deadly."

I waited a few minutes, and then I began to growl low, mimicking our four-footed predators. I heard their voices and movement, and then after a few minutes I did it again. I repeated it one more time, and then, while smiling, I went to my chair and sat down, watching Christine once more.

I wasn't there more than a minute and was looking at the clock, calculating how much time she had left before I would make the decision for her, when I heard a gunshot. It took me so much by surprise that I jumped to my feet with my heart pounding. My first thought was of blood, and that perhaps one of them had shot himself. But when I listened to their conversation, I knew the hallucinations had completely taken them over, and that someone, most likely Raoul, had shot at an imaginary predator.

Oded was fighting desperately to keep his senses by talking almost nonstop to Raoul. Courageously, he tried to explain to him that everything was only due to my tricks. He was trying to find the spring that would open the door but kept losing his place because of having to take care of Raoul. At one point, Raoul must have put the pistol to his head, and I'm sure, if it weren't for Oded, he would have finished himself off right then.

I was surprised they were still alive. I don't know how long they were in there before I found out about them, but it had been over fourteen hours since I first discovered them. I'm sure it was because Oded knew what he was fighting that gave him what he needed to survive. Again I thought about the importance of always knowing your opponent. He knew me too well.

I went back to sitting in my chair and listening to the silence, with the exception of occasional voices from the other side of the wall. Christine was beginning to stir when I heard a gasp from the mirror chamber, so I moved to the wall to listen more closely.

"Raoul!" Oded exclaimed. "Come toward my voice." There were a few more silent moments until I heard another gasp. "Can you feel that cool air coming from this crack? I believe we've found one of Erik's trap doors. This could be our way out."

I knew then that somehow Oded had found the trap door leading down into my wine cellar. I sighed and went back to my chair, preparing for my next move. They might have thought they were saved, but they'd only moved their pawns to a different space. They in no way had me checkmated.

Only a few moments of angry thought, and I was back at the wall, turning off the heat and chanting, "Barrels—barrels—any barrels to sell?"

I chanted that same phrase a few more times, and then went to the fireplace and looked at my two bronze figurines. I stretched out both my arms on the mantle and tried to think. I hadn't figured on that change in events, so I had to think clearly. With them in the wine cellar, with the barrels of gunpowder, if they disturbed them in any way or lit a match for a lantern, we could all be blown up prematurely. But the gunpowder was my power right then, and if I flooded the cellar then I would lose that power. I felt I had no choice except to silence an explosion before it could occur. I had my hand on the scorpion and prepared to turn it when Christine shrieked.

"Erik! No!"

I was standing with my hand on the scorpion, and over my shoulder I glared at her sitting on the divan. "You've used up your time while you slept, my dear. I must make your decision for you."

"No, Erik, please wait. I'll tell you yes if you let me in the other room."

I laughed at her, knowing the wine cellar, and eventually the mirror chamber, would be flooded with water, so there was nothing for her to worry about, but she pleaded anyway.

"Please, Erik, let me go into the next room and I'll stay with you forever."

"Forever? Are you certain? And what about a wedding? Will there be a wedding?"

"Yes, I'll marry you without delay, just let me in there."

"You lying wench. You told me you would marry me if I turned off the light. Well the light is out, so where is my yes?"

She was quiet, with an open mouth and wide eyes, while I waited for her response. I could hear my breathing increase along with my temper.

"I tire of this game, my dear. I tire of this game called my life. I want a normal life, Christine, with a wife and walks in the park. But all you care about is your lover in the next room. Your lips may tell me yes, but your heart will always tell me no, isn't that right? So what difference will it make? None whatsoever." I scowled at her. "Then you do it. You turn the scorpion, and it will all be over. Do it—turn the scorpion!"

We stood staring at each other with only our labored breathing being heard. Then I growled and turned back to the mantle and again she screamed while getting to her feet.

"No, Erik, don't! How do I know you're telling me the truth and the scorpion is the one I should turn?"

My anger was rising quickly, as I stepped toward her and grasped her shoulder. "You're accusing me of lying to you? No—I don't lie. Unlike you, who promised you'd return and tell me goodbye, I'm not lying. But then, am I lying about not lying. Lies, lies, lies. You know, sometimes I tell so many lies to cover lies that I forget where I was going or where I came from. Lies, lies, lies. If you tell enough of them they can twist into knots and choke you. Now where was I? Was I trying to tell you the truth or was I lying. I can't remember.

"No matter, I guess. You won't know the truth until you find the courage to turn one of the figures. I tell you turn the scorpion, and you'll save the lives of many Parisians above us this evening, but that will mean you're saying yes to me. If you turn the grasshopper, then I'll only have a moment to suffer the pain of knowing that your final answer is no."

She couldn't respond with anything other than a blank stare and a whimper, so I interceded. "Where's your curiosity, Christine? Don't you want to see what will happen?" She still didn't move, so I ground my teeth. "Turn one of them quickly. You're running out of time, and I'm running out of patience with you and your fickle indecision."

I pulled her close to me and glared into her eyes. "I'll leave you now for the last time, my sweet. When I return, if you haven't made it, I'll make it for you. Do you understand?"

She barely nodded, and I released her shoulder with a shove. Then I stormed back into my music room and slammed the door. I charged back and forth and came very close to dismantling the room again. I paced and fumed, paced and fumed, until I swung the door open again.

"Have you made up your mind?" I demanded, as I started across the room toward her, but then I heard another voice, Oded's.

"Erik, listen to me. It's not too late to do the right thing."

"Be quiet, you foolish, persistent daroga," I demanded coldly. "I don't want to hear your voice again. If I do, then it's over. This is none of your affair. It's Christine's decision to make. Stay out of it."

I glared at Christine for only a moment and then at the figurines. I shook my head at her and then started quickly toward the mantle. She turned instantly and grabbed for the scorpion.

"Look! Erik! I turned it! I turned the scorpion!" she screamed and began crying again.

We stood in complete silence. Christine was looking at the floor, and I was looking at her.

It was done—finished. We'd completed the second scene, and we were exhausted.

She looked as if she was going to faint again, so I took her gently by the arm and sat her on the divan; then I placed the glass of wine in her hands. I stood back, watching her, and began to feel the slicing claws of remorse tearing my flesh. She'd turned the one I wanted her to turn, so, in my power play, I'd won. But, at the heart of it all, I'd lost miserably. I still didn't know exactly how she felt about me, although, at that moment, I didn't see how she could feel anything but loathing for me.

That should have been the end of the second scene, as far as I'd written the script, but the intruders in the mirror chamber had complicated the plot, and I was forced to do some instant rewrites. As I watched Christine, and my temper began to wane, I started to feel weariness and the beginning of one of those mental positions where I no longer wanted to think. I wanted to be with Molly, riding across a green plateau. I really wanted to be anywhere other than where I was.

My exhaustion from no sleep and constant emotional drain was taking its toll on me, and my thinking ability was severely hindered. I needed to say something to Christine, but the only thing I could think of was to tell her how sorry I was and to send her on her way. I was ready to speak her name when Raoul's voice came through the wall.

"Christine, are you still in there?"

She looked at me quickly, with wide eyes, and I narrowed my eyes and shook my head at her. She began breathing deeply and my own thoughts were charging back and forth within me. I wanted to release her, but the sound of his voice filled me once more with hatred. Again, there was a cry from behind the wall and, as she started to answer, I said her name and softly told her to be silent.

Quietly, I told her, "His pleas are pathetic, don't you think? But don't worry about him, he'll not die alone. He has good company in there, and they'll be able to help each other during the ordeal of their last breaths."

Her body stiffened and she verbally charged on me. "You lied to me. You said it would be safe to turn the scorpion, and I turned it, so now they should be safe. What is this talk of death? What have you done?"

I jumped to my feet and growled, "There you go again, blaming me for everything that goes wrong. I've kept my end of the bargain. I gave you a choice of the scorpion with a yes and life, or the grasshopper with a no and the death of thousands. You chose the scorpion, and with it came forth water to render lifeless the power to destroy so many. That has been done. I kept my word. The thousands are saved.

"Is it my fault there are foolish ones in the world who trespass where they don't belong? Is it my fault they were in the way of the water? Can I be charged with their ignorance and lack of forethought? Can you blame the lion tamer if he warns people to stay back and they don't and the lion eats them? No, I don't think so. Can I be blamed for the deaths of the two fools in my home when they were both warned to stay clear of my lair? No, I don't think so."

I could see her chest rise rapidly and her eyes widen as she looked back over her shoulder toward the chamber. Then the sounds coming from the chamber spoke loud and clear that both Oded and Raoul feared they were soon to drown, and the panic set into her eyes again.

"Oh, Erik, please, please, don't let them die. This isn't the Erik I knew. This isn't the Erik who took my hand so gently. This isn't My Angel who instructed me with soft words and patience. This isn't you, Erik." She looked frantically at the chamber. "Erik, please."

"You beg me for their lives? How often have I been on my knees before you begging for my life, Christine?" Mockingly, I went down on one knee before her with spread arms. "Perhaps when you've been in this position as many times as I have, I'll listen to you."

There were sounds of splashing water and groans on the other side of the wall and her eyes were so frightened, more so than during all the previous hours. I felt my jaws ache, and that sting in the back of my eyes increased. I lowered my head and tried to bring back the rage, but, all of a sudden, I didn't know what it was all for.

I struggled to think about what I was doing and why, but I was feeling just as confused as I imagined the men in that chamber were. What was I trying to accomplish by forcing the woman I loved to tell me she loved me? What good would it do if it were forced? I couldn't think. Again, my exhaustion was fogging my mind, and I struggled for clear and quick thinking ability, but it was hard to come by.

"Please, Erik," she begged again.

I looked up into her eyes as they filled with tears, and I began to ache all over. I wanted to double up and groan in agony. What was I doing? I felt my heart cracking in two as I watched Christine in such anguish before me. She looked deep into my eyes and began pleading away the remainder of my hardened shell.

"Where is the Erik I've come to cherish? Oh, Erik, please."

I lowered my head and laid my forehead on her knee, and then I felt her hand on the back of my head. I sighed deeply as my eyes swelled with tears, and I allowed my pain to sink deep into my chest.

"Christine, please love me," I sobbed.

I felt her fingers moving through my hair, and I heard her sniffles and her soft voice caress my senses.

"What happened to that man who shed tears over a piece of music? What happened to the man who cried because of the death of Jacob, a fictional person in a novel? Are the flesh and blood men here with us who are fighting for their very lives not worth more than a fictional man written on the pages of a book? Where's my Erik? Where's that man who kissed César's nose with the tender care of a gentle mother? Where is he, Erik?"

She ran her fingers along the side of my jaws and asked, "Where's the Erik I knew, whose eyes moistened every time we sang the death scene from *Romeo et Juliette*? Oh, Erik, where is he? What happened to that man who captured my heart as none other? Where's the Erik I sang and laughed with? Where's the man who marveled at the beauty of a tree? Where is he, Erik?"

Then I felt her hand under my chin, and she raised my face up to her. She ran her fingers across my forehead, moving my hair aside.

"Please, Erik."

I watched her eyes closely, and I finally realized if she stayed with me it would only be to save her lover and not to stay with the one man in the world who loved her the most. She cradled my face in her hands and her eyes once more filled with tears.

Her head slightly shook, and she whispered, "This can't be happening. Oh, Erik, please tell me this is nothing more than a terrible nightmare. Please let me wake up to your music the way I did once. Oh, Erik," she whimpered, and then my lifelong dream began to unfold.

She closed her eyes, and her soft lips pressed against my forehead, and they remained there for a long kiss while my heart ruptured and seeped tears of ruby red. I received my first kiss, and I couldn't hold back my tears—even if I'd tried.

My long awaited kiss had finally arrived. After 45 years of wishing for the touch of a woman's lips on my skin, I finally felt it, and I wanted it to last forever. But, along with my first kiss, I also felt the pain of her tears as they mingled with her kiss on my face. My heart was pounding as never before, and I struggled for breath as her lips parted from me. Her lips were only a breath away when I felt her next words on my forehead.

"Where's that man? Oh, Erik, where is he? I miss my Erik, my poor Erik. Please bring him back to me."

She pulled back, and, when I opened my eyes, she was again looking into mine. Her tears were streaming down her cheeks and my heart swelled and my breaths increased with the feel of my first kiss. We stayed locked in that precious moment until she lowered her face to mine and kissed my forehead once more. Her lips remained there longer that time, and when she backed away, I opened my eyes and searched desperately for that expression in her eyes that I'd been seeking.

Her palms were still holding my face, and her pleading eyes and voice beseeched me, "Erik, please."

Then it happened, something much more important than my first kiss. Her eyes changed right before mine, and I saw it. There it was. There it finally was, that look I'd been waiting for, for so long. That look of love that only the eyes can speak. She loved me, and I could see it, I could finally see it. She loved me.

I broke. My face fell upon her knees, and I sobbed like a baby.

"Erik, please let them out," she whispered to me.

Other than my sobs, the room fell to silence while she continued to run her fingers through my hair. Gradually, enough of my awareness returned, and I realized it was much too late. I moved back on my heels, releasing my face from her hands, and then I actually chuckled, causing her to look strangely at me. I was laughing and crying all at the same time, and all I could think about was, why now? Why now when all was lost? Why now?

I laughed softly, and Christine frowned. "Why are you laughing?"

With my arms spread and my palms and cries directed toward the heavens, I begged our maker. "Why now? Why the look of love and love's first kiss from the woman I love, now? Why now?" I looked back at her and wagged my head. "If I were a jester in a court of appeals, perhaps a chance to love, perhaps a chance to live, perhaps a chance to appeal. I'm but a jester on life's stage, and there's no court of appeals. It's too late. The judges are back, the stone faces with the verdict of death."

"Erik! what are you talking about?" she asked, with concern in her crystal pools.

"Who would have thought—death by love's first kiss? I'm but the jester who laughs as a madman at injustice. Life—thoughts, desires, and twisted riddles in a hurricane—nothing more. Now that love's first kiss has awakened the madman's heart, the verdict is in. Love's first kiss surrenders my soul in place of my accuser's. This jester is ready and laughingly waits at death's door, prepared for a madman's sentencing. The supreme judge is seated and casts his sight on me. A thumb down is his only response. I could perhaps have a chance if I were a jester in a court of appeals."

"Erik! You're frightening me."

"If I but a jester be, I could change the tides, I could alter the course of a river. With the slight movement of my fingers or the quick variation in thought, I could transform the course of events. But I not a jester be. I not a jester be. No change in tides, no alteration in rivers, no transformation in events. I not a jester be in a court of appeals. I be mortal, frail, broken. I not a jester be, Christine. Not a jester be."

Her eyes filled with panic, and she shook her head and then seriously frowned.

Without breaking our eye contact, I rose to my feet, and asked, "Why now?" I shook my head and spread my hands, again asking, "Why now?" I stepped back until I was against the fireplace, and once more asked, "Why now?"

I reached for the scorpion and turned it one more click, causing Christine to jump up and scream, "No!"

Then with total fear on her face, and I don't know what on mine, we felt the floor rumble slightly as the pump in my wine cellar reversed gears and started pumping the water out of the mirror chamber. I was watching Christine's face closely when I realized it was too quiet. There was no more splashing water or struggling voices, and then it was no longer only Christine who was filled with panic. I also feared the worst. I feared it was too late for the latest victims of my brilliance. Her eyes were desperately searching mine for an answer to her plea.

She came up to me, and breathlessly pleaded, "Please hurry and open the door."

I looked at her and felt so much pressure inside my chest, as if my heart was exploding. How could I tell her I was helpless? How could I tell her I couldn't open the door for probably another ten minutes? I moved over to the door to the mirror chamber and leaned my chest against it, with my arms outstretched and groaned.

She was right beside me when she asked again, "Erik, please open the door."

I looked down into her fearful blue eyes and her bruised and tear-streaked face and asked myself, how can I tell her they were trapped in there until the water receded? How can I tell her the chances of them surviving their ordeal were almost nil? How can I tell her I'd killed her childhood sweetheart? How can I tell her?

Fifty

"Erik! What are you waiting for? Please, open the door!"

I lowered my head between my arms and whispered, "I can't."

"What do you mean, you can't? You can't or you won't?"

I laid my forearms against the wall and my forehead against my doubled fists, and then I whispered again, "I'm only mortal. I'm not a god. I'm only mortal. I can change nothing. The script is written and being played. It's too late for a rewrite."

"You're not making any sense. Talk straight to me." Then while shaking my arm, she pleaded, "Help them."

My head shook. "I'm not a god. I'm only mortal."

"Erik, look at me." She took my chin and turned my head, saying again, "Help them!"

I couldn't look her in the eyes, so I again shook my head and repeated, "I'm not a god. I'm only mortal."

Softly, she said, "Erik—hold me."

She got my attention with that out-of-place request. How could she want me to touch her—much less hold her? But she repeated it again and then moved in close to me, wrapping her arms around my back. Slowly, my arms found their way around her back, and then I broke completely. In sobs, my gruesome face fell on her shoulder, and I stayed there, sobbing.

In retrospect, I now realize how close I was to losing my mind completely that day, and, to this day, I shudder to think about what would have happened if I had. But my precious, precious Christine somehow brought me back to a semi-sane state. When I calmed, I backed away and then turned my face away from her pleading eyes.

"Erik, help them," she again tried.

Again, I shook my head. "There's no way. My brilliance has outsmarted us all—even me." I huffed and almost laughed. "Oh, how my own brilliance has outsmarted me. If there were only a way around it, a way to unwind it, a way to turn back time, I would dance on my own grave."

"Erik, please don't talk in riddles. Not now."

I shook my head one more time. "Riddles? My life is a riddle, a twisted, lying riddle!"

"Oh, Erik, please. We need you. Please help us. No more lies and no more riddles."

I couldn't bear to look at her, so I looked at the floor and tried to explain in straight-forward words. "No more lies. What I say is truth—the horrible truth. My safety room is meant to protect me. It has protected me from those men in there who meant to harm me, and now it's protecting me from anyone on this side of the wall harming me. It's protecting me even from the woman I love and from me."

"What are you saying?" she asked while looking intently at the wall. "You built it. You have to know how to get in there."

With more sorrow than I can express, I replied, "It's because *I* built it that I know there's no way of getting in."

She whimpered, "No! No!" Then, with courage, she gathered herself together and told me, "You always have a way of solving problems, Erik. Find a solution. Explain to me how that room works and maybe you can hear in your own words the solution."

I was still shaking my head, but I agreed, mostly because it would help pass the time until we could enter that room.

"Oded found my passage in the third cellar and led Raoul into it, thinking it would lead them into my home. But, true to my design, they entered the passage that I told you never to go down, instead of the one leading to my music room. When they reached its end, there was only one way for them to go and that was down through a trap door into the mirror chamber.

"Once in there, they couldn't go back up through the trap door, because I deliberately placed it too high to reach, not even if they stood on each other's shoulders. So they were trapped in there with no way out, except through this hidden door right here," I said as I knocked on the wall in front of me.

"It probably didn't take Oded long to realize where they were, even if it was completely dark in there. He's been in one of my mirror chambers before, but as my helper and not as my enemy. As soon as the motion sensor in that room was triggered, it clicked on the heating mechanism. Then, when I suspected someone was in there, I switched on a bright light. The light and heat, along with an iron tree that was reflected a hundred times by the mirrors, were designed to disorientate my enemy and allow me time to decide what to do with them.

"The original idea was to let whoever was in there become so exhausted by the heat and dehydration that they would pass out. I would be able to keep track of what was happening to them through that window up there. When they were unconscious, I could then go in and get them and take them across the lake without a struggle and without them seeing me or knowing what had happened to them. Once on the other side of the lake, where it's cool and damp, they'd eventually regain consciousness and be able to drink from the canteen I'd leave for them.

"Well, that's how it was supposed to work, but Oded, that tenacious fool, knows how I work. I imagine he was looking for the spring that would open this door but instead found the spring that opened the trap door leading down into my wine cellar. With his actions, everything changed.

"You see, the gunpowder is in my wine cellar, and I feared they might set it off accidentally, so I had to intervene to prevent an explosion. That's where the scorpion came into play. It's connected to the water pump that's also in my wine cellar. I put it there just in case the lake water started to seep through the retaining walls or just in case the water level rose high enough to threaten my home. With it, I could keep the water pumped out and my home would be safe.

"But with my meddling friend interfering with my plans, I had to pump water into my wine cellar and saturate the gunpowder. Again, these are all safety precautions to protect my home and me. When I heard the water reaching the mirror chamber, I could have turned it off, but, I was so angry and perhaps even out of my mind, I didn't. That's when another safety feature came into play.

"Just in case the gears jam and I can't reverse the water pump, when enough pressure is put on the other side of this door, six steel locks slip into place to prevent the door from opening and the water flooding my home. This door and the trap door in the ceiling of the chamber are water tight, again, to protect my home.

"I've reversed the water pump, and it's now pumping the water out of the chamber. That's where we are right now. There's too much water in there, so I can't open the door until it goes down enough. There's nothing I can do until then—nothing."

She'd been watching me intently during my entire explanation, and once I was finished, she looked at the door and began shaking her head. Her eyes started to tear up again, and she looked back at me.

"What about the trap door in the ceiling? Can you get in there that way and help them?"

I closed my eyes and lowered my shaking head again. "No, again, there's another safety feature. When this door locks," I said as I again knocked on the wall. "The same type of locks seal that trap door. No one can get in or out of that chamber, no matter how hard they try. It's that secure. It's made of thick steel, and even if I, or anyone else, set off explosives at the room's weakest point, it wouldn't affect it. It would take my home down and the floor above us, but it wouldn't damage that room."

I again shook my head. "That's why I said my brilliance outsmarted even me. How sad a scenario is this? It was all designed not only to protect me from outsiders but also to protect me from my own weaknesses and opening the door prematurely, thus ending my life along with theirs. There's nothing I can do. I'm so sorry. I would gladly trade places with those men in there if I could. I truly would.—I'm so sorry."

She moaned and slapped her hand on the wall several times. "Raoul! Raoul! Answer me!" She was near hysteria but then calmed and looked at me. "Erik, I know you. I've watched you and been a part of you doing things that are unbelievable. There has to be a way to get in there and help them. Think, Erik, think."

"Oh, my sweet, Christine. You don't understand. My thinking is what's brought us to this place. I thought this entire scheme out completely, and there are no flaws in my design. I wish there were. I honestly wish there were."

She shook her head and almost lost her control again, but then asked, "Are you lying to me now, Erik? Is this just another one of your tricks so you won't have to save Raoul?"

"Oh, if only I were, this would all end right now. No, my sweet, unfortunately, this is not one of my tricks. My brilliance has truly done its job well in protecting me. That room is impossible to escape from, and, unfortunately, it's also impossible to break into."

She was quiet for a moment or two, but she wasn't about to give up on her sweetheart. "How can I know for sure you're not lying?"

I took a long, slow breath and tried to think of how I could help her cope with the awful truth, the awful truth about how far my genius had gone.

"Come near to the door, and, when you hear the lock release, you'll know I was telling the truth, and you'll know it's safe to enter and help them."

She joined me at the wall and began beating on it. "Raoul, can you hear me? Raoul!"

I wanted to scream. I couldn't bear to watch her in such a pathetic state. I was tearing apart inside, but, then, I deserved to be torn in two.

"Christine, you need to be quiet if you want to hear the locks release," I said calmly.

She nodded and pressed her poor, bruised forehead against the wall, and I tried to apologize.

"I swear, Christine, I'll spend my last breath trying to help them. Saying I'm sorry for what I've done in no way comes close to how I feel. If I live to be a hundred, I'll never find a word to express how I feel. If you weren't here with me, I know I'd take my last breath and end all the brilliant tricks once and for all."

Without opening her eyes or removing her head from the wall, she whispered, "Don't talk of death anymore. I'm tired of thoughts of death."

I began backing away and only glanced at her pitiful sight once more. When in my music room, I closed the door, with her vision embedded in my mind. I looked around the room as if I was in a dream, or, should I say, a nightmare? What had I done? I felt so helpless. I tried to grasp onto some form of helpful thoughts for Christine, but my thinking slipped away from me, repeatedly, like a distant tree in the fog that vaguely appears and then disappears before you can reach it.

I knew it would take at least ten minutes before there would be enough water out of the chamber for the door to be opened, and by then they could be dead, if they weren't already. What had I done? I couldn't even begin to curse my horrible existence enough for what I'd done, not only to Oded and Raoul but also, and most importantly, to the woman I loved. I was a monster. I deserved the worst kind of death possible.

I lowered my head and closed my eyes, again asking myself, why now? I'd just destroyed that special woman and killed her childhood sweetheart as well as my only friend. Why did she love me now when it was too late? My head began to shake harder and harder until I opened my eyes and growled in full fury, why now?

I began to tear the room apart as my mind tore itself apart in search of an answer to the hardest and most serious decision in my life—the taking of my own life. Nothing was sacred in my music room as I released my anger on it. I stormed through it, wiping the top of my piano clean in one motion. I ripped everything in my reach to shreds.

"Why now?" I screamed loudly.

Nothing escaped my wrath; wall hangings, sculptures, pictures, cloths, pillows, even my scores didn't escape my anguish. Also, Molly's bust received a smashing blow, sending it off its pedestal and across the room. Why now, after I'd destroyed everything around me? Why did she show me love now?

When I had nothing more to destroy, I threw myself against the wall, cursing my demented existence and tearing at my hair. I'm truly a monster in every way possible. I deserve nothing more than death. No, even death is too good for me. I should be thrown to wild dogs and be eaten alive. My death—the only answer and end to a tragic but true opera—my life.

I cursed myself and my inhuman existence. I'd been playing the role of an angel, but I was far from it; I was a demon in every respect. I had to end the hellish nightmare called my life. The only thing that stopped me right then was the wonderful and brave woman I loved. She was shouting my name and shaking my arm.

"Erik! The lock released! We need you! Please, help us! Please, open the door!"

I looked at her poor face, bruised and streaked with tears mixed with stage paint and blood, along with a red nose, evidencing her many hours of crying. Her golden curls were matted together around her face with more dried blood. I looked into her pleading eyes for only a moment and then had to look away.

Knowing I was the cause of all her grief, the little bit of my heart that remained in my cold chest shattered into small pieces. I couldn't speak, and I couldn't look into her beautiful eyes, knowing what awaited her in the hours ahead. I felt a sickness inside me that rivaled what I'd felt the days when I became aware of the campfire slaughter. I desperately needed to get her out of my home so I could finish it all.

I took her by the arm and told her, "I'll take you to Madame Valerius now."

But she pulled away. "No, Erik! You have to let them out first!"

I swallowed hard, not knowing how I could tell her it was too late. I looked at the floor clock that told me it was past midnight, which meant the two of them had been in the chamber for perhaps twenty-four hours. I felt the chance of their surviving the heat and then the flood of water was nearly impossible, but how was I going to tell my poor and pitiful Christine that the monster before her had killed her childhood friend and love?

I swallowed hard again, and she pleaded again, "Please, Erik, let them out now—please!"

Without looking at her, I went to the door to my dungeon of horrors. When it opened for me, a small amount of water trickled into the parlor. I turned on the light, and although I was hoping to find them on their feet and fighting mad, I was not to be favored with that sight. Therefore, it was no surprise to see them both lying lifeless in glistening pools of water.

Christine rushed past me, and, with several gasps and cries, she fell at Raoul's side. I wanted to stop her, but I knew she wouldn't believe me unless she saw his death for herself. How could I help her through this? What had I done? I wanted to slam my head through the wall. What was I going to do? I couldn't stand her sad sight, so I turned and pressed my face against a mirror.

Then, within an instant, I knew for sure I was truly crazy. All the people in my past were right. I'd been crazy all along. I'd talked myself into believing that no one understood me, but all of them were right. I was mad. Only a madman would have conceived or even considered what I'd just done.

Oh, dear God, what am I? I almost killed Christine, the woman I loved more than my own life. What had I done? And Oded, the man I loved as a brother. What had I done? I thought about all the people above me who were almost killed and the children who would be left without a mother or father. What had I done? I should have been locked up as a child in Perros, and so many lives would have been spared. All of them were right. I should have been locked up behind bars. I should die for all I'd done and could yet do in the future.

I cried unimaginable anguish within myself and slumped against the mirrored wall, with myself and my hideous crimes reflected a thousand times around me. I finally had Christine's kiss upon my skin. Now all I deserved was death's kiss upon my dark soul.

"Erik!—Erik!"

Christine's pitiful cries weaved their way through my exhausted and foggy mind. I turned and saw her still on her knees by Raoul and looking up at me.

"Erik, please help!"

I managed to make my feet move toward her; then, taking her shoulders in my hands, I tried to lift her up, but she pulled away from me.

"Erik, help them!"

I knelt beside her and took a deep breath, preparing to tell her the truth of the matter.

"Christine . . ."

Then I heard it. I could hear water gurgling in his throat with each feeble attempt at a breath. Every sense in me came alive in that moment, and I quickly felt for a pulse. It was weak, but he had one. With renewed hope, I looked at Oded and charged toward him. He was in the same condition.

When I went back by Raoul, I laid him flat on his stomach with his head to one side, and placed his arms above his head. Kneeling with one knee on either side of his head, I began applying pressure to his back and ribs and then pulling his arms and shoulders toward me. I continued using all my weight on his back, pulling on his arms in repetitive motions, and with each movement a small gush of water escaped his throat and passed his blue lips.

I could hear Christine crying softly beside me, and I knew I needed to get her out of the chamber if I couldn't revive him, so I gave her a job to do. With emotional control, I gave her my bag of keys.

"Christine, put a kettle of water on the stove for tea."

She didn't move and I almost had to yell at her to get her to obey me. But she finally left me alone, with what I feared were my most recent victims. All too soon she was back and knelt beside her sweetheart.

Time seemed to move on forever as I watched and listened to both Raoul and my old friend all alone across my horrible room. I knew the longer I worked on Raoul, the less chance Oded had of surviving, but what was I to do? I couldn't leave Raoul there in that condition. I had to keep trying.

I was ready to give Christine another job to do, not wanting her to be present if her love took his last weak breath, but then there was a larger gasp, gagging, coughing, and more water began rushing out of his open mouth.

"Oh, Raoul!" Christine cried while throwing herself down next to his blue face.

He was barely breathing and Christine was losing more control, becoming almost hysterical. So, once more, I sent her out of the room.

"Christine, listen to me. Go get all the blankets you can find and take them into the parlor, and then check the teapot."

She left, and I continued to work with his meager breathing, trying to encourage his lungs to work on their own. I was at the same time watching my friend at death's door, trying not to become so emotional that I lost my focus. I knew I had to remain in control and separate from emotional feelings if I was to accomplish the impossible and save both the lives I'd just endangered.

Christine came back in the chamber and again fell on her knees beside Raoul. She was running her hand across his cheek and speaking to him softly, telling him how she loved him. At any other time that would have been a very dangerous action for her to take, but, at that moment, I knew it was all over. I'd resigned myself to that fact. So, while her words were like swords through my heart, I had no thoughts of letting her young man die. Once the color started to come back into his lips, I moved on to Oded and sent Christine away again.

"He's breathing on his own, but now he needs your help. You need to make a large amount of tea, the same you made for me when I was sick. Do you remember how?" She nodded quickly. "This is important. He'll need it to protect his lungs from infection."

She again nodded and left the chamber.

I didn't get as good a response from Oded as I had from Raoul, and I feared I was too late. At that point, the tears began fogging my eyes, unchecked by any effort on my part to conceal them.

I was close to losing my emotional control and began talking to him.

"You're not going to die on me, you stubborn daroga. Where's you fight? Where's your tenacious spirit?"

Each time Christine came back, I gave her more instructions just to keep her mind busy and her body out of the mirror chamber. I had her build a fire to warm the parlor, get two sets of dry clothes from my armoire, and put some brandy in the tea to warm their bodies.

Oded still wasn't responding, and I had to turn my face away from him, but I kept on working on him and talking to him, even though I feared the worst.

Raoul's coughing echoed through the barren chamber, mingling with Christine's whispers. I looked toward them just as she tried to help him to his feet, only to have him fall and take her down with him. I charged toward them, lifting him up over my shoulder and then carrying him to the divan.

"Cover him, Christine, and force just as much of that tea as you can on him."

I worked a long time on Oded, waiting for him to have the same response that Raoul had had. I waited for that gasp and flush of water from his lungs, waited for some color to return to his blue lips. Time became nonexistent as I worked, only faintly aware of Christine moving around and speaking my name.

I no longer felt the need to keep her mind occupied, as my own need to help my friend became all-encompassing. On occasion, I felt the pressure of her hand on my shoulder and heard her soft words, without ever registering their meaning.

I don't know how long I was there while my mind traveled through the forest of Persia with Oded by my side. I saw his face on the other side of the campfire as we talked. I saw my own face smile at him each time he stormed away from me in frustration. I saw his frown and the concern in his jade eyes during those days he nursed me back to health. I saw his tears and heard his sobs the days after the loss of his family.

At one point, I was ruthlessly beating on his back with my fist and cursing him. "Don't you dare die on me now, you cursed daroga! Don't you dare leave me! Don't you die on me!"

Then I heard a strong gasp, and the flush of water I'd been waiting for escaped from his lips. Overcome with emotion, I collapsed on his back and sobbed like a child. It was Christine's hand on my shoulder that brought me back to the need to continue to help him recover. So I returned to pushing on his back or beating on it, much the same as he'd done to me while I was on my own death bed in Kord Kay, Persia.

By that time, some of his color was returning, and I was in control again. I carried him to Christine's bed and took off his wet clothes; then I wrapped him in blankets. I gave him some of my herbal medicine and made him drink some tea before I let him lie down and rest.

Then I sat at his feet and began massaging them in the same areas the doctor had shown my father when I was a boy. Once done, I knelt on the floor beside him and watched his breathing and checked his pulse. He was very weak, but at least he was alive.

I was still on my knees, holding his hand, when the tears started again. I lowered my forehead to the back of his hand and released my tears in sobs, knowing I'd nearly ended the life of my best friend. The pain from that realization was beyond words. I was still in that position when I heard Christine approach. I turned and looked at her standing in the doorway, not even trying to conceal my tears. She'd seen me in almost every possible situation that a woman could see a man, so what were a few tears?

"Raoul is starting to wake, Erik."

I nodded, released Oded's hand and placed it under the blanket.

When I checked on Raoul he was stirring, so I gave him a healthy dose of my herbal remedy, to which I added rum, laudanum, and an oil to help him sleep. I needed to keep him under control until I was ready to deal with him.

I was calm, and, much to my surprise, so was he. I told him what I was doing and the importance of the tea. After sending Christine into the kitchen, I stripped his wet clothes off him and helped him put the dry ones on. Then after wrapping him in more dry blankets, I laid him down and worked on his feet for about fifteen minutes.

During that time, I heard Oded coughing, so I looked toward Christine's room. Oded was raised up on one elbow and watching me. We stared at each other for a few moments, but no words were spoken. When he lay back down, I said a silent thank you that he was well enough to move on his own.

Once I was finished with Raoul's feet, I turned out the light in the mirror chamber and locked the door, and then, as I was throwing another log on the fire, I realized I hadn't seen Christine in a while. I'd all but forgotten about her, and as I looked around, I saw her standing in the kitchen doorway, watching me, without much of an expression on her tear-stained face.

"You should take this time to get out of that wedding dress. It won't be needed ever again."

"I will," she responded softly.

"I need to get more firewood, but I won't be gone long," I assured her.

She nodded, and I headed for the door to the lake. Once I reached it, I turned briefly and saw my beautiful Christine holding Raoul's hand and talking softly to him. I lowered my eyes and head and left them alone and in love—just the way it should have been all along.

Fifty-One

Christine had changed into her blue dress and was back by Raoul's side when I returned, so, without saying anything, I put more wood on the fire. Resting one foot on the hearth, I stared down into the flames. The warmth penetrated my legs, but my heart was not to be warmed that night.

I then sat in my chair, and, with my chin resting on my knuckles, I was almost hypnotized by the flickering flames. For all outward appearances, I might have looked like a normal man enjoying the warmth of an evening fire, but, inside, I was nothing even remotely close to that man.

I thought about Oded in the next room sleeping, also appearing as a man at peace and not a man who had barely escaped death. I looked at the fair young de Chagny, also sleeping, and then at Christine, sitting on the floor at his side and running her fingers across his brow.

The two men and the woman I'd almost killed would live to see another day, but my life, as I knew it, was over forever. Content in my shrouded castle I could no longer be. For how could I walk through my domain without knowing I was on my way to meet her? How could I play my piano without seeing her face beside it? How could I raise my voice in an aria without hearing her voice join mine in harmony? How could I sit in my box, overlooking the audience, without seeing all the deaths I'd almost caused? How? I could not. Each time would be like a knife entering my heart anew.

What had I done? My thoughts went to my life of taking lives, and I closed my eyes and shivered. I once excused each and every one of the lives I took as being necessary for my own survival, that is, with the exception of a few. My months of insanity as a teen and then the massacre at the campfire in Persia I couldn't excuse as self-defense.

And then there were the times when I came close to taking the life of my best friend, Oded. It took an assassin's bullet to prevent me from succeeding the first time, the flicker of a struck match the second time, Darius' strong voice the third time, and the pleading eyes of an angelic woman the last time.

What kind of a monster had I become? While sitting in my chair before the fire, I felt I was sane, but I knew I wasn't. Only an insane, a monstrously insane, mind could ever do what I'd just tried to do. I studied Christine, still beside her young love, and realized how close I'd come to causing her death, along with the death of who knows how many thousands above us.

I glanced up to the mantle and the figurines. What kind of a monster would place them there in the first place? This hideous nightmare had to stop, but how? I'd felt that burying myself in the depths of the opera house would protect others from me, but somehow it hadn't. Where could I go or what could I do that would prevent a recurrence of some disaster at my hands?

I was mad for sure, with only moments of seemingly sane episodes in between. It was just as Doctor Faure once said when describing my actions: *The division between an insane mind and a genius mind can often be fragile.* Apparently, I'd managed to dissolve that fragile division, and it no longer existed. I had to do something to prevent any further danger to others, but my insanely genius mind was refusing to be of any assistance. What was I to do?

My sights were fixed on Christine, but it appeared she didn't even know I was in the room, since her attention stayed on Raoul. Without removing my sight from her, I laid my head back against the chair and took a deep breath and then let it out slowly. When I did, she turned her head and looked at me, with the stain from her tears and stage paint still visible on her cheeks. She sighed and then spoke to me.

"Thank you, Erik. Thank you for saving his life."

I stared at her, without any physical or verbal response. She could have slashed me with her tongue and cursed me to hell. She could have beat me with the fire poker or embedded my jeweled dagger into my heart, but she didn't. She thanked me, and those words tore through me worse than anything else she could have done to me. She thanked me for saving the life of a man I almost killed. How ludicrous was that?

Without expression, I looked back at the fire, and she turned back to the young man sleeping at her side. What was I to do with myself? What was I to do?

On the train ride to Paris with Oded, I remember thinking my presence couldn't possibly cause more harm than the slaughter of his family or the campfire massacre, but I was so wrong. The crime I'd almost perpetrated was a hundred times worse. What was wrong with me? I had to end the deaths. If no one else could end my reign of terror, then I had to. I couldn't continue moving from one tragedy to a worse one anymore.

I looked back at Christine and Raoul again, and I knew in that instant what needed to be done. Since burying myself in my home in the cellars of the opera house hadn't worked out so well, I had to literally bury myself under layers and layers of dirt in its cellars. That would have to work.

Christine shivered, and as if that was my cue to begin the closing scene, I got up and went to the kitchen where I prepared a fresh plate of cheese, apples, and bread. Then I made her tea with a small amount of brandy to warm her. I took it back into the parlor and placed it on the table by my empty chair. I grabbed another dry blanket, and, after wrapping it around her shoulders, I tried to help her up.

"Come, Christine, you're chilled. You need to get warm, and you need to eat." She, at first, resisted, so I encouraged her. "He's going to sleep for a few hours. I'll watch over him. You need to rest and get warm."

She let me lead her to my chair and sat down. I then tucked the blanket in around her body and handed her the cup of tea, telling her to drink it. She looked at me, then at Raoul, and then back at me.

"I don't want to sleep. I want to be awake when he wakes."

"You should be. The tea won't make you sleep, it will only warm you."

She nodded, and then, with trust which I didn't deserve, she began drinking it. I could have been poisoning her or drugging her to take her away while she slept, but still in her sweet innocence, even after all I'd done, she trusted me and drank.

I knelt in front of her with two cold, wet rags and wrapped them around her poor welted wrists. Then I gently rubbed another one across the blood on her forehead. Once that was done, I stayed on my knees before her, watching her for a moment while she gazed into the fire. Before I lost my determination, I sat on the coffee table facing her and watched her as she sipped her tea. After only a moment's hesitation, I began the most important act of my career.

"Christine, to give you an apology after all I've done to you is such a hollow gesture. There are no words to describe how terribly sorry I am for all my actions, starting with the first time I saw you behind your mirror right up to and including this moment. I've put you through unspeakable grief, all in the name of my love."

She stared at me blankly, and I clenched my teeth before continuing. "The only truth to any of this is my deep, and, I presume my abnormal, love for you. But that in no way is an excuse for all the atrocities I've committed over these last months. I can't and I won't even ask for your forgiveness, since it would be preposterous to do so, and because I don't deserve to be forgiven.

"When I asked you to marry me and go away with me and live a long life somewhere, it was all a fabricated delusion formed in my demented mind, a desperate mind searching for some facsimile of what was normal, but it was all a lie. I told that lie to you and myself so often that I even believed it could happen.

"But I'm trying to be truthful with myself and, more importantly, you, right now. Even if I was capable of reaching into the heavens and grasping a star and then placing it in your hands, I would never be able to live the life I believed I could with you."

I had to look away from her eyes for a moment, since I was yet again telling her a lie. "The beauty in your heart is pure and powerful, Christine, and perhaps if I'd moved these latest events in a different order, your splendid qualities would have allowed you to marry me. But it would have only been a sham, because I wouldn't live long enough to see it through."

She looked at me over the top of her cup and then prepared to speak, but I silenced her, needing to finish my last untruth before I lost my courage.

"I'm so sorry for everything, Christine, everything. I don't deserve anything from you, but I have one last request."

She slowly nodded, although I couldn't understand why.

"What I'm going to tell you is in no way meant as an excuse for what I've done to you and everyone else, but I do want you to know the reason why I went completely mad." I lowered my head again and took a deep breath. "I've never made a secret of just how much I love you."

I looked back at her. "Perhaps the type and depth of love I have for you is wrong, since it enabled me to commit this ghastly deed. Or maybe it's just me, along with my insanity, but, in either case, I lost what mind I had with the thought of you going away without a goodbye and never seeing you again. I was so wrong, and there aren't words to express just how much remorse I feel for what I've put you through."

She started to respond, but I held up my hand and cut her off.

"I don't want you to feel you have to say anything to me in reply. I only want to explain. Remember that night when I came home after Raoul shot me and you were confused about the degree of my anger?"

I gave her a chance to nod, knowing I needed her to follow my thinking if my lies were going to help her through the coming events.

"One of the reasons I was so angry was because I felt that fate had once again moved me into a place that was so unfair. My entire life I'd been waiting for you, and I believed we were on the way to something very special that even my wildest dreams couldn't conjure. I knew we had something between us, and in time it could turn into a love that would never be matched—all we needed was time. But, that night, the doctor told me I didn't have time, and that I would be dead within a matter of weeks."

She instantly sat forward, her eyes opened wide, and she covered her mouth with her fingers. "No, this can't be. Tell me it isn't so. Tell me this is one of your tricks—one of your lies."

I lowered my face from hers and shook my head. "I'm sorry, Christine. I'm so sorry. I wish I could tell you it was a lie, but I can't."

"Erik, no, no. This can't be happening. You always find a way. What about one of your herbs or oils? Won't one of them help? One of them has to work."

I looked back into her frightened eyes and shook my head slowly. Then, before I could continue, she tried again.

"What did the doctor say was wrong? Is it your lungs?"

Again, I shook my head. "No, it's my heart this time."

"Your heart? What happened?"

Preparing to tell probably the most contrived lie I'd ever told, I lowered my eyes to my hands again. "My heart has been dying since I was five. That's when I had my first lung infection. I nearly died then, but our doctor's expertise saved me; however, the infection took its toll on my heart, damaging it beyond repair.

"I had many repeated lung infections after that, and every one of them weakened my heart more. The last crushing blow came with the infection in my leg that I fought for so long. That infection invaded my heart muscle, damaging it even more. The doctor told me then that I wouldn't live long, but I'd just found you and I convinced myself to believe that if I took good care of myself, if I ate well and slept well, I would be fine.

"I'm so sorry, Christine. I was being selfish. I should have ended my charade before I brought you down here, and you never would have been involved with any of this. I'm so sorry."

"I can't believe this is happening. I watched you take care of Raoul and Oded. You were so strong. You worked for over two hours on them, and then you carried both of them out of that room. You were so strong. How could you do that with a dying heart?"

She was making this lie most hard to make believable, and I had to really concentrate on what I was saying. If I stammered at all over my words, she would know I was lying, and I had to make her believe I was telling the truth. It was the only way I could set her truly free. So, while rubbing my fingers together, I looked right in her eyes and answered her question.

"During my life, I've learned some extraordinary things about our bodies. They have a wonderful power to heal themselves, and when they're called upon to perform heroic feats, they come to the call. I once saw an elderly man lift his heavy wagon that had overturned on his dog. He only lifted it about a meter, but he lifted it, while it took three grown men to lift it up after him. When called upon, our bodies can perform impossible acts. I was called upon in there, and my body came to the call. That's all. Nothing more."

There was silence, and I lowered my eyes again, but my angel wasn't about to give up just yet.

"We have to find a doctor who can help you. Oh," she whimpered. "This can't be happening."

"I know. I felt the same way when I came to the realization of my mortality, but, please—I need to finish my explanation."

I looked up at her, and, with her chin quivering, she nodded.

"All I have left is a short time, perhaps only a few days, so when I heard that Raoul was going to steal those last few days from me, I truly went mad. I only wanted to pretend I was married for a few more days. That's why I told you I would be leaving at the end of the two weeks. I felt certain, if there was a deadline on a decision from you, you would have to choose Raoul over me. I knew you loved him and not me, at least not yet. And that's why I told you to spend time with Raoul, to help cement your relationship for when I was gone. That's also why I told you I needed you to come to me and give me back my ring, so I could be buried with it and tell you goodbye."

"Oh, Erik, this can't be happening. I'm so sorry . . ."

With anger, I rebuked her. "Don't you dare, Christine Daaé! Don't you dare try to apologize, not after what I've done to you. Don't you dare!"

There was silence for a moment before I gathered myself and continued, "Based on that knowledge, I'm going to ask you for one last thing. You're in no way obligated to grant me my final request, but, if you could find it in your pure and honest heart to do so, it will help all concerned, especially you, to put all of this behind us."

I waited for a nod before I began rolling the gold band around my finger and then went on. "Can you find it in your heart to pretend you're married to me for a few days more? That's all I ask. Just keep the ring for a few more days and pretend."

Her eyes widened, and I could see the fear returning in them, and I realized she must have thought the entire episode was going to repeat itself, so I tried to calm her fears.

"Don't worry, Christine. I won't ask for a marital due. I won't even ask you to say you love me ever again. I won't ask you to stay down here with me either. Just say you'll keep my ring and stay mine until my life is over, which won't be much longer. If you could refrain from marrying Raoul until then, I can go to my grave in peace.

"You can give my ring back to me and bury me, along with this impossible script called my life. This will free you to marry Raoul and become the wife you were destined to be. I'm comforted, knowing you have someone like Raoul to care for you. He loves you very much, and I know you love him, and the two of you can live a good and long life together."

I sighed as I looked at the fire, but I didn't give her time to respond before I continued, "I thank you for my first kiss, Christine. You have no idea what it meant to me for you to give of yourself in that fashion. I've reconciled myself to the fact that it's the closest I'll come to the intimacies of a wife, and I thank you for that touch."

"Oh, Erik," she whimpered as the tears continued to form in her most beautiful blue eyes.

But, once more, I stopped her. "Please, Christine, don't feel sorry for me. I don't deserve it, and I don't deserve your consideration in this matter. But if you agree, it will make my last days bearable."

She nodded and whispered, "Certainly, Erik."

I again looked into the fire and gathered more courage before I went on. "But please give me my ring back. As I've said before, it has sentimental value to me, and I'd like to be buried with it on my finger. However, put it on my left hand and not my right. I want to take my make-believe of being a husband into the grave with me. Can you do that for me, Christine?"

Her eyes were filled with more tears by then, and she nodded.

"Please, don't cry, my sweet. This can be a happy day. It can be the beginning of a new life for you and Raoul, a life without my insanity tormenting either of you."

"I'll do whatever you ask of me," she replied softly.

I knelt before her, and, for the last time, I slid the ring off my finger and onto hers. I held her hand as I kissed the ring along with her fingers. I kept my eyes closed until I could contain my own tears, knowing that was, more than likely, the last time I would feel her touch.

She raised my head and looked into my eyes, and what I saw surprised me. To this day, I'm at a loss to describe it. There was sadness, yes, I expected that, but there was something else as we stared into each other's eyes. It was only the chiming of the clock that broke our gaze.

"I'll stay with you and take care of you for as long as you need me," she offered sincerely.

Considering how my death would be played out, it wouldn't do to have her around to witness it. So I managed to convince her that it would only make it harder on both of us if she did; therefore, she agreed to stay with Madame Valerius.

She looked past me at Raoul, still asleep on the divan, and then back at me and asked, "Would you do me one last favor, Erik?"

"Anything you want, my sweet."

"Play your music for me and sing for me."

"Absolutely," I replied as I got to my feet. "What would you like to hear?"

She listed a few of her favorites, one of them being "One Beat." I honestly didn't know if I could play that piece again, but I couldn't refuse her. When I reached the door to my music room, I turned back toward her.

"I also have one last request to ask you. Don't lose your courage, Christine. I may not have been a real angel, but the advice and instruction I gave you was true and pure. You are a great artist, and you must never listen to the harsh criticism of those who will only be jealous of your talent. Never lose your love for music, and, once in a while, think of me when you sing." I tried to smile as I said one last thought. "Who knows, perhaps I'll still be able to hear you sing, and as a real angel this time."

Those were the wrong words to use, and she broke down. She jumped to her feet and ran to me, throwing her arms around me and sobbing against my chest.

"This can't be happening. Everyone I love leaves me. You can't leave me."

I wrapped my arms around the woman I loved and the woman who'd just acknowledged her love for me. I held her close, and bittersweet tears filled my eyes. Forty-five years I'd waited for a woman to both love me and kiss me, and to think I received and lost her all in one day.

I closed my eyes, lowered my face down into her hair, and whispered, "Oh, Christine, I'm so sorry for all of this. I never meant for you to be hurt by my presence in your life. I only wanted to help you and love you. I'm so sorry—so very sorry."

She continued to cry against my chest, and I continued to hold her tightly and cried into my mask, never wanting to let her go. We stayed in that position until she stopped crying and pulled back from me, and then I looked down at her face and wiped her tears away with my finger.

Some of my resolve began to slip away from me as I studied her eyes. I saw in them what she really felt for me—love. In a moment of weakness, I questioned if maybe we could still make it all work, but it was only a moment. In the end, I knew what I was doing was the best thing for her. Living with me would be like playing Russian roulette on a daily basis. She'd never know when the fatal hammer would strike, but it was sure to strike.

She wanted to sit in what she considered her chair in my music room as I played, but I knew I wouldn't be able to concentrate on my last pieces for her if I was in a position to look over at her, especially during "One Beat." So I convinced her to stay in the parlor so she could let me know when Raoul or Oded woke up. She finally agreed and went back to my chair by the fire.

I first went to my armoire to close the doors that had been left open, but before I could close them, I saw the small box containing my supply of morphine. Then I felt a peace pass through me, a peace that was so long in coming. A peace much like the effect a large dose of that drug could bring, a calming and serene peace. Soon, I thought, there'll be complete peace.

I closed the doors and then went to my piano and sat on the bench. But I didn't play right away; instead, I spread my fingers out over the keys and looked at them, remembering my long history with music. I felt calm and at rest as never before. I knew what I had to do, and I was in harmony with my decision. I loved Christine enough to set her free in the only way she could ever be truly released from me.

I played all the pieces she'd asked for, including the emotional "One Beat." I continued to play more soft music, trying to remove the horrors of the night from my home. After about an hour, I felt someone's presence, and I looked up and saw Raoul standing in the doorway, wearing my oversized black clothes. I got to my feet, not knowing what to expect from him.

After an uncomfortable few moments, he turned without saying a word and left. I followed him back into the parlor where he sat down on the divan. Christine was asleep in my chair, which was better than I'd hoped for. She needed rest, and I needed to speak with Raoul in private.

"More tea?" I questioned as I filled his cup back up. "It's best if you drink just as much as you can stomach. It'll help you recover from the effect of your near drowning."

"Yes, the drowning caused by you," he responded, with a tone showing his return to the angered living.

I looked at the locked door to the mirror chamber and replied, "It's most unfortunate you stumbled upon that room, but you should count yourself blessed to have survived it."

He sighed and managed to talk to me in a civilized tone. "That's what I don't understand. I can understand why you tried to kill us, but I don't understand why you rescued us."

I stood behind my chair and looked down at our sleeping Christine. "It's all about her, Raoul. It's always about her and her welfare. I've wanted only what's best for her. Sometimes I might have gotten a bit off track, but it was always for her or about her."

He also was looking at her and started to curse me, while I held my tongue and took his abuse.

When he was finished, I continued. "I can definitely understand your anger and hatred for me, and that's fine and probably just as it should be, but I ask you to trust what I'm about to say."

"Trust you? You expect me to trust you after what you've done?"

"Yes, I do. I easily could have let you die in my mirror chamber; in fact, I was looking forward to it, but I didn't, and that was for one reason—Christine. She saved us all. I strongly suspect that you and Oded went down into my wine cellar and saw what I had stored down there—am I correct?"

"Yes. A madman's wine cellar filled with gunpowder."

"Well, I do have some very good wines down there also, but, yes, the gunpowder is what I was referring to. With the turning of a simple switch, all of us would have been gone, along with thousands above us. You're a military man. You know the power of just one of these barrels. Can you imagine the explosion that would have occurred if I'd set all of them off at once? In addition, I have 10 times that many strategically placed around this building, and they would have gone off one after the other until this building was leveled."

He shook his head. "That's demented."

"Perhaps. It's all a matter of perspective, though. To me, your chosen profession is what's demented. You put a uniform on your back, a sword at your hip, a gun over your shoulder, and you kill other men just because their uniform is a different color. Then, when you send enough men to their graves, you let other men pin ribbons on your chest and call you brave; now, in my book, that's demented. At least I don't expect to be congratulated or patted on the back or given ribbons for what I nearly did.

"And another thing, what I was preparing to do had its start in love, perhaps a crazy love, but love nonetheless. Whereas your profession is based on hate, hate for anyone of a different nation. Again, I call that demented, so I believe it's *your* thinking that's a bit twisted."

By then I was pacing through my parlor and prepared for him to blast me with his haughtiness, but he didn't. Instead, he sat quietly and appeared to be in deep thought, so I used that grace period to continue with my original thought.

"At any rate, you know the power I had at my disposal—actually, it's the power I still have, but I no longer want it. I want you and Christine to leave here and live a happy life with lots of children. But, to make that happen, I need your help. Are you willing to set aside our animosity long enough to help Christine through what's ahead of her? You can blame me for everything if you wish, it no longer matters. But I ask you to please help me help Christine."

With his usual arrogance, his words cut at me. "What are you talking about? You don't need to do anything. I can take care of Christine without your help."

I stopped pacing, put a dining chair in the center of the parlor, and straddled it facing him. I knew I needed to keep my voice calmed and unruffled if I were to get my logic through to him, but at times it wasn't easy.

"Under different circumstances," I started again, "I'd agree with you completely, but we're living in the midst of a bizarre love triangle. You criticized my age, but you need to use my age and the wisdom that comes along with it to help this wonderful woman who's caught between us. She's what matters, not you and not me. Once she wakes, you're free to take her away with you, with a promise from me that I'll no longer interfere with what you want for her. I only ask that you treat her well. She's quite precious you know."

He scowled at me. "You monster. You think you have the right to say when and where I do what and with whom? You're wrong. I'll take Christine away from this place of death, but not because you give me your permission, but because it's my right."

I took a deep breath, trying not to lash out at him or strangle him, but he was making it extremely hard. I knew what I needed to do, so I tried not to let his words distract me; however, I just had to give him a reminder about his close encounter with the Grim Reaper.

"Absolutely, you're right. But, in the process, don't forget where you are and who holds the only keys to the exits from this place. It would also be good to remember who your host is. It's the wisest gentleman that shows respect for the host who invited him in, and that goes double for this particular host."

"Respect for you? Why?" he came back in his true form.

"Let me put it this way, I might have saved your life this night, but try to keep a clear picture of what you went through before I did. Then remember, with the snap of a finger, the diabolical mind that put you in harm's way to begin with could do it again and again and again, perhaps in the next minute or perhaps in the next year.

"For how do you know that, before you reach your carriage tonight, you won't fall into another one of my torture chambers? How do you know that it won't be worse than the last one? How do you know that, before you get home, all the wheels won't fall off your carriage and you'll have a terrible accident, perhaps bad enough to send you to your grave?"

With indignation, he accused me. "You're lying just to frighten me, but it won't work, because I don't fear you."

"Lying? A question can't be a lie. A statement can be true or false, but a question can be neither. Didn't you know that?"

"You're mad and only know how to talk in riddles."

"You might be right about that, but then I'm also right about something. I get what I want, Raoul, and the fact that you spent last night in my chamber of horrors and that you're sitting in my parlor right now should prove that. I get what I want. So take the advice of this elderly madman—don't test me."

Fifty-Two

He didn't respond verbally, but his eyes told me I'd gotten my warning across, which was a good thing, since I was in no mood to waste any more of my energy contending with that young and arrogant fool. I took a deep breath and thought about my next words before I spoke them. Then I lowered my eyes to my hands and rubbed my naked little finger, causing him to gasp. When I looked back at him, he was studying Christine's hands.

"You're doing it again. You . . ."

"Raoul, please! Regardless of what you think of me, try to think of what's best for the woman we both love. I'll be out of your life forever in a very short time, so please stay focused on Christine and what's best for her. Can you be man enough to do that?"

He glared at me but didn't answer, so I went on. "I have a request of you, and remember, it's not for me but for Christine that I ask this. Within a few days, I'll no longer be a living ghost but a dead one, and, while I'm capable of many things, there's one thing I can't do for myself. I'll need someone to bury me.

"Christine has agreed to come back to me at that time and give me my ring. I don't want her to be here alone, so I ask you to accompany her here and help her with that final scene in this twisted drama. While you're here, I'd like you to bury me."

His eyes showed his confusion, and he frowned at me. "If this is another one of your tricks, I'll not be a party to it."

"I no longer need tricks," I replied sincerely, and then spread my hands out from my sides. "My hands are wide open. This is all very real, Vicomte. This is no act, unless you want to call it my swan song. You can join in and dance on my grave if that will make it worth your while."

I took a deep breath and looked at Christine. "Everything I'm asking you to do, Raoul, is for Christine's happiness. You and Christine will leave here soon, and I'll be leaving this earth not long after that. Shortly, you'll read in the obituaries the announcement that Erik is dead. When you see it, I'm asking you to bring Christine back here and watch you bury me."

"What? That's ridiculous! That's mad! You just want to go out in a grand manner. If you really care about Christine, you'll simply let her go without making such a big show of it."

"That might sound true at first thought, but think deeper. She knows . . . you both know me to be a master deceiver. I'm someone who can appear and disappear in the blink of an eye. Unless both of you see me dead, unless you can feel my cold skin, unless you see the dirt being shoveled over me, would you ever truly believe I was dead? Wouldn't you always wonder if it was all another game—another trick on the eyes?

"If you ever saw a black-caped man slipping around a corner, would you wonder if it was me? Would you suspect me of being the culprit of every strange occurrence in your lives? If you heard a creaky floor in the middle of the night, would you wonder?

"Raoul, I know how much Christine loves you, and I think if you're honest with yourself that you have to know how much I mean to her. If I just disappear, without her having the chance to say a final goodbye, there might always be a portion of her that will wonder—what if? And with that portion she might always question where I am or if I'm really dead or alive. That same portion could be a wedge between you and her and her happiness.

"I don't want Christine to be left with any doubts, nor you. You'll never be able to live a happy life if you're always second guessing my death and looking around every corner and listening to every strange noise. Wouldn't you rather know for sure that I was dead and not preparing some new diabolical calamity for you? Do you understand what I'm trying to explain to you?"

"Yes," he said softly. "I see what you mean."

"I know it won't be the easiest job, watching Christine mourn over my dead body, but it'll be momentary, and then you can move on and have the rest of your lives together—in peace."

We sat quietly for a minute or so, watching Christine, and then I presented my next request.

"In addition, I ask that you not take her for your own until then. I know my request sounds absurd, but right now Christine is my living wife. And since I'm certain you wouldn't want to make her an adulteress, I ask that she be allowed to wear my gold band until she returns it to me and I'm buried.

"Perhaps this is ridiculous, my being concerned about a wife who really isn't mine, but I ask you to allow me this one last fantasy in my life, to have a living wife. I only want her as a wife for a few more days, and then she'll be yours for the rest of your days."

He was still looking somewhat shocked and confused, so I tried to clarify any doubts in his mind.

"Christine is a good girl and always has been in my presence. She's still chaste and virtuous, so you have no need to be concerned about how much of a wife she's been to me these last months or what I'll expect from her in the days ahead. She'll remain in your company and care. I only want to pretend she's my wife with my ring on her finger, that's all. I only want to pretend much the same way an actor pretends he's married on the stage. I only want to pretend for a few more days. Please allow this insane man his one last idiosyncrasy."

His eyes softened when he realized our precious Christine hadn't been spoiled by my insane love for her and that she was still a virgin. It also made me feel better to know he wouldn't accuse her or cause her any hurt because of his uncertainties. I looked at our sleeping beauty for a moment, and then I looked back at him and continued softly.

"I want Christine to be happy more than anything else in the world. I can only hope you also want the same thing. Do you love her that much, Raoul? Do you love her enough to put aside our rivalry and your pride and think about her? Do you love her more than you hate me?"

He just stared at me with the strangest expression. He then looked at Christine for a few moments and took a deep breath. When he looked back at me, it was without a verbal response, but he did nod.

"Good. Then watch for an advertisement in the *Epoque* announcing Erik's death. That will be your cue to return to my home and bury me."

"Erik? I still suspect you're not telling the whole truth. You're much too calm for a man who's about to die. It's not natural."

I chuckled softly. "Can you name me one thing I've done or said that seems natural?"

"I suppose not, but it still seems strange."

I looked around the room and then back at him. "Because of this," I said as I tapped the side of my mask, "I felt I would die young. I never expected to live to the age I am now. I've managed to live many decades past my expected death. I've accomplished much, seen much, learned much, and I've received a kiss of love from a beautiful woman whom I love dearly. I'm ready for this, so it isn't at all strange for me."

He nodded, and I got to my feet, explaining, "I need to leave for a while to take Oded home. I trust you'll stay here with Christine while I'm gone. I won't be long."

He nodded again, and then, without further words between us, I left to check on Oded. I sat at the foot of the bed and watched him breathing more easily than before. I stayed there in the silence and said a thank you to our Creator for any help he might have rendered us that night. I was thankful that lives were saved, the life of my old friend, my enemy's life, Christine's life, and the lives of a multitude of others.

I wanted and needed to get Oded out of my home while he was still under the strong influence of the drugs I'd given him. Even though I would be leaving my home for good, I still didn't want him to know how to maneuver the passages and reach my lair. Also, I didn't want to explain my plans to him right then.

Shortly, I pulled Oded into a sitting position while telling him I was taking him home. He mumbled a few jumbled words that told me he was incoherent enough, which was good. I wrapped his arm around my neck and lifted him to his feet. He could hold at least part of his own weight, so I didn't have to carry it all, but he still walked like a drunken sailor.

As we crossed the parlor, he looked at Raoul, and mumbled, "What's he doing here?"

"He's being enlightened—nothing more, *Mon Ami.*"

When we entered my music room, I locked the door behind us, and unlocked the door to the passage. Then, after several falls and stumbles, we were on the street and I was hailing a brougham. I didn't try to conceal us, since we looked like two men who'd been too long with the wine. Once I had him at his flat, I sat him on the step, propped him up against the wall, and rang the bell. I left quickly before Darius had a chance to open the door. Knowing he was safe, I could then concentrate on Raoul and Christine.

Christine was awake when I returned, and they were both sitting on the divan and looked surprised when they saw me.

"What? You didn't expect me to return? You didn't expect me to keep my word?" Neither of them responded, so I did. "Gather what you want, Christine, and I'll take you both across the lake now."

In the silence that ensued, she left for her room and Raoul followed her. I left for the kitchen and a much needed drink of water and a much needed talk with myself. I glanced around the room, and, when too many wonderful memories began to surface, I repeated several times—I want Christine to be happy—I want Christine to be happy. Over and over again I told myself that same phrase, since I didn't want to forget the importance of what I was doing.

All too soon, I heard Christine's melodious voice. "Erik, we're ready whenever you are."

I turned and looked at my precious Christine standing in the doorway. I swallowed hard, set the glass in the sink, and nodded. When we were all back in the parlor, I pulled out a paper from my coat pocket and stood next to Raoul.

"This is a map of the lake and the labyrinth." While pointing out the different features, I explained, "This is my docking room and this is the wharf. The Xs are pillars. The Xs with a circle around them are the ones you want to follow to get to my docking room or back to the wharf. Each of them has a special mark on it that you can feel with your fingers. They'll help keep you from getting lost. I'll show them to you when we pass them. The X with a square around it is the pillar that has the spring you need to push to open and close the docking room door. It also has special markings on it.

"Raoul, I know you wouldn't consider us friends, but there's one more thing. All I've asked of you thus far is for Christine and her happiness, but what I ask of you now is of a personal nature. When you leave my home with Christine for the last time, I ask that you close that door and listen for it to lock into place. Christine knows what it sounds like.

"I know I won't be around to see it, but I don't want all my things scavenged by curiosity seekers. I may not have much, but what I do have I made with my own hands, well, most of it anyway. All this came at a high price to me, on a much different level than monetary. It would be a gross insult to me to let it fall into uncaring hands. It goes without saying, though, that if there's anything in here you or Christine want, you may have it. Will you agree to this?"

Raoul nodded and Christine replied through her tears, "We'll gladly do everything you ask."

"Before the end comes, I'll securely seal all the passages that lead down here. I wouldn't want anyone to accidentally fall into one of them and be trapped forever. Now follow me," I said as I unlocked the music room and walked in. "Feel here," I said as I ran my fingers over the spring to the parlor door. He did and I continued, "Those small springs you feel control the door to the lake and the motion sensor on the lake. Press the one on your right. You just turned off the motion sensor. Now press the one on your left."

He did, and we heard the click, releasing the latch for the door. Then I gestured toward the parlor. We moved into that room, and his mouth dropped open when he saw part of the wall opened, much the same as Christine had when she first saw it. I grabbed the stool from the kitchen and Christine's tapestry bag and walked out the door while telling them to follow me. They did, and I set the stool under the latch to open the door and lit a lantern. Then I continued my instructions to Raoul.

"Pull right here to close the door tightly and listen to it click into place." He did and we all heard it click. "Now step up on that stool and reach up high until you can feel another spring, like the one in my music room." It took him a while to find it, but when he did, I had him push it. Again we heard a click, and I pushed the parlor door open. "Now you can get in and out of this door easily. Are you comfortable with it?"

"Yes," he said somberly.

I then pulled the door closed and led the way down to the docking room. Once there, I climbed the few steps to the window that looked out over the lake and continued my instructions to Raoul. Surprisingly, he'd been taking my orders quite well, without his usual arrogance.

"I'll leave this window open and the light on in this room. It will help you find your way back here—like a lighthouse on a shoal." As I started my descent, I also started telling him about my boat. "This is my boat that I drive with this pole. I advise you to sit as you push through the water. It can..."

"You don't need to tell me how to use a vessel," he said with a return to his arrogance.

"I'm sure you can handle the largest sea-going ship with ease, but this little dinghy can have a mind of her own and can send you into the water with nothing more than an ill-timed sneeze, so listen up, young de Chagny. I've had to take cold baths often in this lake," I said with a quick glance at Christine. "I'd hate for Christine to take one just because of your pride. So set it aside and think about her."

He didn't respond, but I continued anyway. "Now where was I? Oh, yes. Right here is the switch to open an invisible door. It's easy to see and reach, so push it."

He did, and, when what appeared to be a massive brick wall began to move out of our way, he showed more emotion than he had at any other time. His mouth dropped open, he shook his head, and his eyes became wide. He looked like a child at a circus.

"How did you do that?" he questioned. "Do you realize what an engineering feat it is to move a stone wall of that size with such ease?"

I chuckled, "Yes, I believe I do."

Until it opened completely, I stood watching him with a large smile on my lips. I'd just deceived him into thinking it was a much heavier door than what it was, but I wasn't going to tell him that. Just because I was going to the grave soon didn't mean I couldn't have some fun on my way there.

"As I was saying," I tried to start again, but he stopped me.

"No, wait a minute. You said you were showing me secrets you haven't shown anyone, is that right?" I nodded. "Well what about this door? Someone had to help you with it, so wouldn't he know about it?"

"He would, if I'd had help, but I didn't."

His eyes narrowed. "You did this alone?"

Again I nodded, and, for the first time, the expression on his face showed a hint of respect for me. I nodded again, silently acknowledging his unspoken respect.

"I'd really like to know how you did this," he said with wide-eye wonderment.

"Well, if I had more time I might be inclined to explain it to you, but I don't have that much time. However, Raoul, remember who you're talking to. I'm an illusionist, a master deceiver. I can make many things appear to be what they're not."

Raoul studied that door while I took Christine by the arm and directed her down into the bow as I had on many other occasions. Then I gestured for Raoul to sit in the stern. His eyes were still fixed on that door, but he did sit, and I handed him the tapestry satchel. After lighting another lantern and hanging it on its hook at the bow of the boat, I stepped into the boat at its middle and knelt down, preparing to keep us balanced.

"Very well, captain. We're all on board. Take us out of here," I instructed, almost jovially.

He took the pole and began moving us through the water, clumsily at first, but he got better. Although he couldn't resist the temptation of reaching out and touching the door as we slid past it. Again I had to smile at him. It was at that time that I could understand what Christine saw in him. When the arrogant exterior was stripped away, he was like a child, a playful and inquisitive child.

I told him to use the map to find the pillars, and he did. At the first one, I showed him the spring to close the docking room door, and, when he pushed it, he again watched it close with fascination. On the rest I showed him the guide marks to lead us to the wharf. As we moved through the silent water, I had a thought. I'd always known my life could have unexpected twists, but this one was bizarre. Everything I was showing Raoul I'd kept a secret for well over a decade. I hadn't even showed them to my best friend or the woman I loved, and, yet, here I was showing them to my worst enemy. Yes, weird twists indeed.

We were perhaps halfway to the dock when I gave him important information. "I have to show you what to do if something happens to your lantern, so, Christine, if you would, please turn the lantern off."

"Wait!" Raoul shouted. "Is this another trick? I don't trust you."

"Raoul, please remember, I had complete control of everyone back in my home. If I'd wanted to do you harm, I wouldn't have resurrected you. What I want to show you could make the difference in whether you and Christine make it safely to the dock or not."

He thought for a moment and then told her to turn it off. When she did, we were plunged into darkness.

"Now, wait a minute until your eyes adjust, and then start looking up. Keep looking until you see a faint light. It'll be coming from an air vent that's beyond the dock. When you spot it, head for it, but do so very, very slowly, so slowly that if you bump into a pillar or the retaining wall it won't capsize the boat. When you reach the wall, follow it until you find the dock. Are you comfortable with those instructions?"

He said he was, so I told Christine to turn the lantern back on. When she did, I looked at Raoul, and he had fear in his eyes. Hmm, I thought. This is Christine's brave naval officer? But I managed to keep my thoughts to myself for once.

He eventually got us to the wharf, coming close to capsizing us only twice, which was pretty good. Christine had been extremely quiet the entire ride, and when I held out my hand to help her out of the boat, her eyes held so much sorrow. I imagined the ride had brought back many special memories to her—as it had me. As I helped her out, she studied my face and moved close to me. I glanced at Raoul, and he had a different expression in his eyes. Here I was touching his Christine, and he didn't look as if he wanted to kill me. Perhaps we'd been able to put aside our rivalry for the time being. I could only hope as much.

Once we were out of the boat and it was tied, I told him, "I'll leave my boat on this side of the lake for you. I'll also leave a lantern. Do you have any questions about the lake crossing?"

"No," he replied. "You're a good teacher. I think I have all the information I need."

He then took Christine's arm, and I led the way to the corridor close to the well. Once there, I again began my instructions.

"You can stay here if you wish, Christine. Raoul, you follow me."

"No," she said softly. "I want to come with you."

So they both followed me to the spot I'd picked out for my burial. "This is where I'd like my final resting place to be. What better place could there be for me than in a house devoted to music? My childhood dream will become a reality, to spend eternity surrounded by music."

I heard Christine sniffle, and I tried not to look at her; instead, I continued, "The ground is soft, and it's away from the other graves."

"Other graves!" Raoul exclaimed. "You mean there are others buried down here?"

"Yes, unfortunately. They were victims from the Franco-Prussian war. I couldn't just leave them lying around my home messing it up, now could I?"

"I suppose," Raoul replied reflectively, but the look in his eyes told me he suspected I was the cause of their deaths.

"I won't ask you to dig the hole. I'll dig my own grave and put my casket inside it. All you have to do is put me in it, close the lid, and place my last blanket made of dirt over me. Then it will be over, and you can go on with your lives."

Right then, Christine broke into tears, which was why I'd wanted her to stay back on the walkway. I looked at Raoul, waiting for him to go to her and comfort her, but he didn't, so I encouraged him.

"You have a weighty responsibility on your shoulders now. She'll need your strength to lean on. Help her."

He moved toward her just in time, because I was about ready to comfort her if he didn't. I couldn't bear it when she cried. I turned my back on them and fought for a measure of my composure to return to me. My jaws ached and my eyes stung, but by the time her sobs had stopped, I was in control again, so I walked back to the path. I motioned for them to start up the stairs, and I began following them. When we reached the spot where I usually told Christine goodbye, I stopped.

"I'll say goodbye here."

Christine turned quickly, lowered her head, and broke down in tears again, while I tried to maintain my own composure. I placed my fingers under her chin and raised her beautiful face toward me. I gently kissed her bruised forehead, moved back, and then looked down into her incredible blue eyes.

"Don't cry, My Angel. In time, this will all be a faded memory. In time, you can tell your children and grandchildren the strange tale about the mysterious Paris Opera Ghost. You can tell them how the Phantom could walk through walls and make even horses disappear. You can tell them how you sang with the Angel of Music and how he kissed your voice and made it soar like an angel's voice. You can even tell them that if they're very good he'll also kiss their voices. So don't cry, my sweet. This will soon be over, and you'll be happy again."

She shook her head and lowered it again, and I turned my attention to Raoul.

"Take good care of her, Vicomte. You'll never find another jewel such as her." Then I looked into Christine's beautiful blue eyes again, lifted her left hand, and kissed the ring. "Thank you, My Angel, for allowing me the privilege of a living wife." I smiled at her. "And, Christine, thank you for my first kiss. I'll never forget it."

Abruptly, she threw herself against my chest, sobbing. "I don't know if I can do this. I can't lose you."

"Oh, Christine, my sweet Christine. Please don't cry. Please. Everything will work out, I promise."

"No," she came back. "You told me that before, and now look what's happening. You're dying, and I'll never see you again. I'll never sing with you again. You'll never read to me again. I don't want to lose you."

I swallowed hard, but it didn't prevent my eyes from tearing up. With my arms around her, I threw my head back, trying to maintain my composure. Then I glanced at Raoul, and much to my wonderment, his eyes were also filling with tears. Strangely enough, that sight helped me. It was the first soft spot I'd seen in him, and knowing it was there gave me hope that he would treat Christine with tenderness.

Still in tears, she repeated, "I can't do this. I love you, and I can't lose you."

I placed my palm on the back of her head and tried to be encouraging. "You once thought you couldn't sing center stage, but you did it. You're a strong woman, and you can do this."

"But I had you beside me at that time," she pleaded.

I looked at Raoul. "And you have a strong man beside you this time as well. Think of what he's done for you. He jumped into the darkness of the unknown just to save you from a monster. He had no thought of his own safety, only for the woman he loved. He was ready to fight to his death for you. There's never been a knight fighting a dragon who's shown more bravery than your childhood sweetheart. Not many women can say that about their husbands, but you can. Take his hand, Christine, and let him lead the way."

"Erik," she began again with sobs, but I had to stop her.

"We can't continue to prolong this torture. Sh," I said softly while placing one finger on her lips. "Sh. No more words, no more tears, only happy thoughts of the future."

I kissed her hand once more, placed it in Raoul's hand, and gave him a final nod. He nodded in return, and then held out his hand to me.

"Erik, thank you."

I was actually surprised by that gesture, but we shook hands like two normal men passing on the street. I felt he wanted to say more, but he chose not to express it, and I chose not to question it. Then, with his arm around her, they climbed the stairs. I watched them until she glanced back at me.

Then I whispered, "Goodbye, Christine. *Au revoir*, My Angel."

Fifty-Three

Before I fell to my knees in sobs, I turned and began my journey back to my home alone. That was going to be my last glimpse of the woman I cherished and my last words to her. I didn't make it far before my tears were so thick I couldn't even make out the steps in front of me. Miraculously, I managed not to trip down the stairs or run into a pillar on my way across the lake.

When I entered my parlor, I leaned back against the door and waited for it to click into place, thinking, that was one of the hardest acts I'd had to perform, but at least I managed to tell her goodbye with a measure of dignity; however, that dignity was short-lived.

Silence. I listened closely, and all I could hear was the ticking of the floor clock. Yes, I hated silence, especially the silence that filled my home at that time. It wouldn't matter if I played my music or sang, since the silence surrounding me was the absence of Christine, and nothing could change that.

I pressed my head back against the door and closed my eyes tightly, trying to prevent any further tears, but what I'd lost spoke too loudly. I slid down the door, crying out in my agony. I crumpled in a ball, threw my arms around my head, pulled at my hair, crying out in my agony. I rocked and I rocked, crying out in my agony. I screamed, cursing my very existence.

"Oh, Christine! My Angel! My Christine!"

I rocked and I cried out her name, believing my lie to her was surely going to be my truth. It felt as if my heart was rupturing, and I longed for its last beat. Unfortunately, it kept beating, forcing me to face the silence. The only saving grace was knowing it wouldn't be much longer and my heart could take its last beat. Less than 24 hours and I could finish it.

With that realization, I got to my feet and prepared for my death. I locked the two black boxes on the mantle, turned out all but one light, and poured a glass of brandy. Then I headed for a bath and hopefully relaxation. I made it into the bath but not the tub. I was surrounded by all of Christine's lavender things. The tears started again, so, before I lost my composure completely, I left her rooms and shut her door. Then, while sitting in my chair with my brandy and staring at the dead coals, I prepared my script for Oded.

It was difficult to concentrate on it, since Christine's tears kept getting in the way. Eventually, I knew I had to get out of my home and away from everything that reminded me of her before I could concentrate on anything. So I left for Oded's.

A summer storm was threatening to unleash its power when the brougham let me off at the entrance to the *Tuileries* across from Oded's flat. I walked to a bench and sat down, going over my lines one more time, just as an actor does in the wings while waiting for his cue. I also used that time to catch my breath. I was exhausted. I couldn't remember when I'd slept last, but then, my exhaustion would add to my dying script. I wouldn't have to act nearly as much to make my story believable.

When I felt I had the strength to continue, I climbed the stairs and knocked. The thick cloud cover made the night extremely dark, without even the moon to lighten the hallway where I waited. Darius finally opened the door with a look of surprise.

"I need to speak to Oded. Would you get him for me please?" I asked, while beginning my act by leaning on the doorframe.

I entered and wearily held onto the back of a chair, while he headed toward the back of the flat. He returned shortly with a sleepy Oded, who was rubbing his eyes and blinking in the candlelight.

"Erik, what are you doing here?" he questioned with a frown and in the middle of a yawn.

I wobbled and replied breathlessly, "I need to speak with you alone."

He motioned for Darius to leave us and then waved me to a seat. I removed my cloak and hat and laid them over the back of the overstuffed chair I usually sat in, and then I sank into that chair, panting for breath, while he went to the dark window and looked out. In those few moments of rest, I realized how weak I was, but I didn't fight it. I would use it to help me play the part of a dying man.

With his back to me, he questioned in an aggravated tone, "What makes you think I want to talk to you, after all you've done?"

"I know you're angry, Oded, and rightfully so, but I need you to hear me out. It might help."

"First, tell me where Christine and Raoul are. Are they still locked in your dungeon?"

"I don't know where they are."

He turned quickly and gave me a stern look. "What do you mean?"

"I mean, I sent them on their way. Christine is in Raoul's care. By now, they should be in bed, hopefully, their respective beds, but I don't know."

He turned back to the window and huffed, "What is it you want to tell me? Make it quick. I don't feel well, and I want to return to my bed."

Well, this is it, I thought. The stage is set, and the final performance of my life is about to commence. Now, if I can pull it off successfully, without stumbling over my words and raising his suspicions, I can move on. Oded was a difficult man to fool, especially when it came to our relationship. The trying times we'd spent together over the years made it extremely difficult for either of us to deceive the other, but I had to try. So, with a weak, shaky, and hesitant voice, I began.

"She kissed me! She really kissed me, Oded. After 45 years of waiting for that special kiss from a woman, I can hardly believe it. I got my first kiss. She kissed me—right here."

As he turned and looked at me, I rested my shaky finger on my forehead and watched his expression closely. Through his anger, he almost managed to smile, but sadness filled his jade eyes. With that expression, I knew he understood how I felt, so, with a sigh, I laid my head back, closed my eyes, and relaxed even more.

I heard his words, but their meaning was lost on me, since my thoughts had traveled to Christine's eyes when she'd glanced back at me for the last time. Then I thought about the first time I saw her on that stage and how she made me feel. Even though the last few days had been a living nightmare, the knowledge that she loved me and gave me that kiss soothed the ragged edges of my heart.

"Erik!—Erik!"

Oded's voice had a sense of urgency sliding between his anger, so I opened my eyes and found him holding my wrist.

"Are you all right, Erik?"

"I should be asking you that question after the horrific experience I put you through."

"I'm suffering, but I'll live. However, you look horrible. You look like you need to see a doctor." He released my wrist and stood up straight, still looking down at me with his disciplinary father expression. "I really wish you'd leave those cellars and live a normal life in the sunlight where you belong. I believe that would help your physical ailments and maybe help you monitor your sanity in the process."

His words could have caused a heated argument. I felt he should know by then that for me to live a so-called normal life among the world of mankind was unthinkable. But, rather than argue with him and perhaps leave him in an angered state, I had to reason with him and calm him somehow.

"I've lived in the cellars for well over a decade, and I've done so while in good health. The cellars have nothing to do with my current condition. There have been a few traumatic events of late that have taken their toll on me. According to an expert opinion, the Opera Populaire will be free of its ghost soon."

His daroga eyes pierced through my words with accuracy, and I feared he somehow saw through my guise.

"What are you trying to say, Erik?"

"I'm trying to tell you that it's the end of the road for my weary heart. It's been damaged beyond repair by the repeated lung infections. My last visit to the doctor confirmed that it's just too late. He believes my life, such as it is, is going to end very soon, my friend, and I'm here to ask for your help."

"Erik! What are you trying to pull?" he came back quickly. "You have to remember, I've seen you much worse than you are right now. What kind of a prank are you conjuring now? Whatever it is, I'm not amused."

Trying not to sound angered, I responded, "You have to remember, during that time in Persia I had a good reason to live, and that gave me the will to live. I had a wonderful girl waiting for me, whereas now, I have nothing, so there's no longer a will or a reason for me to continue on. I'm much older now and my body has been through much recently, and it's tired and giving out. I've done and seen more than most men do in many lifetimes. There's nothing more I want to do—except to die."

"You can take your talent to the world," he responded in defense of my life, although I didn't know why. "You can share your genius and your inventions with mankind. That's something that would be worthwhile to many and give you a reason to live."

Still trying to speak softly, I told him, "You've never really listened to me, have you? At the age of ten, I was run out of my hometown, and, shortly thereafter, I was kept in a cage and treated like an animal—all for the enjoyment of *mankind*. After escaping, I had to live alone and like an animal in order to stay ahead of *mankind's* persecution. I really tried in Venice to be a part of humanity, but I was again shunned.

"I don't need to take you on that painful path through Persia, do I? Everything that happened there was because I wanted to share my gifts and live a normal life in the sun. I've never told you about all my near-deaths while working on the opera house and living in the cellars. You haven't forgotten what happened to Dominick, have you? That was because they were after this," I said as I tapped my mask.

"I thought if I lived in its cellars, I'd be safe from persecution and others would be safe from me, but it didn't work out that way. During the war with Prussia, I received a near fatal stabbing from a man who wanted to capture me and treat me as his trophy. You might think that happened because we were in the midst of a war, but it never stopped when the war ended.

"Only a few months back, I caught a bullet in my leg from the opera's chief scene-shifter. Remember that limp you questioned? Well, I nearly died from the infection that bullet caused. The doctor had pretty much given up any hope of my surviving it. Somehow, I did survive it, but my heart didn't. The infection destroyed the biggest part of it, and what little is left is tired and giving up.

"Just a month or so back, I caught another bullet—this time in the back and from our renowned Vicomte. That one also almost killed me. This has been my life, Oded, and I'm tired of it. I'm ready to give in to their wishes, only they won't have anything to show for it. I'll take my unique head to my grave with me, so they won't get it as a trophy.

"In addition, look what I almost caused last night—a near catastrophe for Christine, Raoul, and you, not to mention an opera house full of unsuspecting spectators. No, my friend, my body and mind are tired, and I can't fight anymore. It's no longer only a matter of my sick lungs, but now I also have a sick heart of the worst kind to contend with."

There was silence in the room while I watched the candle's light cast dancing shadows across his questioning face. His eyes began to soften, but he continued searching mine for any hint that my words were only another hoax. He got up, and, after getting us two glasses of brandy, he stood at the window that was being pelted with heavy rain. I held my breath, waiting to see if he was going to nibble on the bait that was dangling precariously on my hook.

He took a healthy swallow of his brandy, and, without turning from the window, he showed he not only took the bait but also the hook, line, and sinker along with it.

"I'm sorry, Erik. I didn't realize you were having serious heart problems. But I can't bring myself to believe that there's nothing more that can be done. Are you certain about this? Is there nothing more that you can do? Is there nothing more that I can do? Perhaps you should get a second opinion from another doctor."

Knowing him the way that I did, his reaction took me by surprise, and I almost felt guilty with the ease of it all. I tried to hide my shock and answer his questions without arousing his natural suspicious nature any more than I already had.

"I can assure you, all that can be done has already been done. The doctor who's been taking care of me has consulted all the medical books and his colleagues for a solution, but there isn't one. He's actually surprised that I'm still walking around. He thought I'd be dead a long time ago."

"I see," he said softly with a nod. "We can make room for you to stay here, and we'll take care of you until the end. You may have preferred to live alone, but you shouldn't die alone in those cold and dark cellars."

"Considering your condition last night, my friend, you may not remember, but my home is neither cold nor dark, and it has everything I need there—especially my music. I want my music at hand until the end. I should at least be able to have that. You know what it means to me."

"Then I'll stay with you in your home. I can't bear the thought of you dying alone."

I took a deep breath and tried to think fast. He was checking my every move, and I couldn't allow that. So I slipped into the next stage of my plans.

"I've lived a solitary life, my friend, so it's only fitting that my death be solitary. But I really didn't come here to discuss the pros and cons of a solitary death, and I don't have the strength to dispute with you anymore. I came here to tell my friend, my only friend, what was soon to take place, as a kindness, and to ask for one last favor."

"I understand. I'll do whatever I can to help."

I took a deep breath and searched for the right words. I'd spent hours preparing my speech, but once the time had come to present it, I found my thoughts were all in disarray. They weren't making any sense to me, so how was I going to make it simple and easy for that long-time companion of mine to comprehend? I took a sip and then another of the brown liquid in my hand, trusting it would give me the courage to face him with such a ridiculous request.

Once I got him to sit back down in his chair, I again took a sip of my brandy and a deep breath before I began telling him much the same thing I'd told Raoul and Christine the night before. I told him about my pretend marriage to Christine, my gold band on her finger, and, at the risk of sounding even more insane, I tried to let him know that I felt she really loved me. Then I described how both Christine and Raoul were going to bury me in the cellar by the well.

My words were even more ridiculous when I heard them out loud than when they first appeared in my head. I sounded more like a madman than I ever had before, and that was quite often. I wished I could have taken them all back and started over again. Unfortunately, I had no choice except to play the scene out. I could tell from Oded's body language that I didn't want to give him a chance to speak until I was finished, so I continued with my most unusual appeal.

"I've arranged for a special package to be delivered to you. It will have some of Christine's things in it. When you get it, you'll know I'm dead, and all I ask is that you place an advertisement in the *Epoque*. It only needs to read, 'Erik is dead.' Raoul will be watching for it and will know it's time for his part to begin—and my part to end."

He stared across the room at me and began wagging his head back and forth. I had to force myself to remain seated and resist the temptation to throw my hands in the air and run out of his home. I watched him slowly rise to his feet, and, once again, make his way to the rain soaked window, still shaking his head. He remained there for a moment more, while I moved forward in my chair and anxiously awaited his reply. Then, abruptly, he turned on me with his hands in the air, his voice raised, and that ever so familiar look of total disagreement on his face.

"How can you do this, Erik? How can you do this to her? How can you be so selfish? Hasn't she gone through enough? Haven't you put her through enough these past months? What are you thinking? Are you mad? Do you want to make her insane? I can't believe you're really considering this outlandish scheme."

I sat back, lowered my head, and watched my brandy swirl around in my glass before trying to answer him in the calmest and softest tone I could. But as lightning and thunder flashed and rolled through the room, he stopped my words and began pacing back and forth in front of me.

"No! This is all wrong!" he blurted out. "If you love her the way you say you do, then you can't put her through this. Can't you see how much grief this will cause her? Can't you just let her go to live her life in peace? And do you really think Raoul will allow Christine to go back to your house after all that's happened?"

"Oh, yes!" I exclaimed emphatically, moving forward again and clenching my fist on the edge of the chair. "I know for a certainty that he'll not only allow it but also insist on it. Can't you see? That will be his moment of triumph, to see his monstrous opponent finally dead and buried once and for all. I imagine Christine will cry, she cries quite easily you know, but I'm certain her young lad will be jumping for joy. In fact, I can picture him now, dancing on my grave after he's pounded the earth solidly over my lifeless body."

He stopped right in front of me, his hands spread in a pleading gesture, and his jade eyes looking down at me like an angry father disciplining his wayward child.

"Your sarcasm is not appreciated, Erik. This is neither the time nor the place for it."

I leaned back, trying to rest my aching shoulders, relax my tightening jaw, and slow my rising temper. I took a long deep breath and told myself to be patient with my friend. So I looked away from him and focused on my hands, gently rubbing my naked little finger. Again my hand looked and felt strange without my father's gold band, but the warm expression in Christine's eyes when I'd placed it on her delicate finger was worth it.

Oded deliberately cleared his throat, reminding me he was still waiting for an answer. I looked back at him and tried again to satisfy his incessant need for a logical explanation.

"You need to understand, Oded, it's for Christine that I'm doing this. She needs to know for a certainty that I'm gone. She can't just be told or it will always leave a doubt in her mind—is that shadow at the end of the drive Erik? Is that man across a crowded restaurant Erik?

"You were never able to see your family buried, and I've often seen the look in your eyes when you've seen a Persian woman or child. I know you've wondered if, perhaps, just by chance, one of them might have escaped the horrors of that day. Isn't that true, my friend? I know I've hoped—wished—that even one of them could have escaped."

He didn't have to audibly answer, but I saw it in his eyes nonetheless.

"This death—this burial of mine, is the only way she'll be able to leave all of this behind and go on with her life in peace. What I want, more than anything else, is for her to have peace—complete peace without any doubts. She has to see my dead body and watch the dirt being shoveled over me until I disappear—this time, forever.

"I want her to go away with Raoul, away from this city of memories, and start a life and family with him. And I never want her to pick up a newspaper and read about some strange occurrence at the Paris Opera House that is blamed on the Opera Ghost and then wonder. I never want her to have one moment of doubt—ever.

"Believe me, I know only too well the necessity of seeing firsthand the final curtain drop before you can accept that it's over. She has to accept my death before she can put that special relationship we shared to rest. She's been torn between Raoul and me for far too long. This is the only way, Oded. I've thought this through thoroughly. This is the only way."

His hands slowly dropped at his side, and his eyes softened with his understanding. After a moment or two, he picked up our glasses, left the room, and returned with more brandy in them. I looked closely into his eyes, using what I knew of him to determine if I'd pulled off my act successfully, and if he was going to let it rest.

He held the glass toward me, and I reluctantly took the sparkling liquid from his hand, contemplating if I could afford to be any more relaxed than

I already was. After placing it on the table beside me, I knew I had to bring the conversation, the last of many, to a conclusion.

"Thank you, my friend, for your understanding. I've said all there is to say, and I'm extremely tired, so I need to return home and rest."

I managed to get to my feet, threw my cloak over my shoulders, positioned my hat, and turned to take one last look at a very good man. Our eyes managed to exchange the feelings concealed in our hearts—the ones our lips were unable to utter. We looked at each other for a moment, before I placed a finger on the brim of my hat and made a slight nod in a gesture of farewell. Then I turned and headed for the door, believing I'd played out my last act triumphantly. But I was premature in my thinking, and he was instantly in front of me, blocking my way out of his home.

"Erik, look at me!"

I quickly glanced at him, with an irritated sigh, telling myself I should have known I couldn't get away that easily, not from him.

"No! Really look at me!" he repeated, with that tone that told me he wasn't going to let it rest, not just yet.

Our eyes met one more time. Then, just as I feared, he began those questions again that he was so famous for.

"There's something you're not telling me, isn't there, Erik? You're not going to die a natural death, are you? You're planning something, aren't you? Are you planning to use some of your own expertise on yourself? Poison perhaps? Morphine? Or is it your own lasso? What is it? What are you going to do?"

Silence filled the room, and I could hear the small pings as each rain drop hit the window. The seconds ticked away, along with my supposed control of the situation. Our eyes remained fixed on each other's, and our bodies remained perfectly still, resembling two alley cats just waiting for the other to break eye contact before the final, fatal pounce.

"You talk like a crazy man, Oded. Perhaps, you've been reading too many suspense novels. Why would I take my own life? You know how my health has gone up and down. Well, right now, it's gone down and it refuses to get up."

Without a second's hesitation, he came back at me, and that time I recognized his tone all too well. He was not only on the scent, but, like a hound dog, he had his prey cornered and was sounding his triumph. Within the next second, his daroga teeth had sunk into my lie, and I knew he'd never let go. His olive brow wrinkled, his eyes narrowed, and he ruthlessly threw more questions at me.

"Is that it, Erik? Do you plan to take your own life? Answer me straight. Don't try to drown my questions in a sea of carefully placed words. They don't work on me."

I again felt so weak in the knees, and I just couldn't endure the thought of dealing with him and his infernal questioning any longer.

"Oded, please don't push me, not now. I don't want our last goodbye to be a heated one, so don't force me to leave without another word. I'm trying to accept my death with a measure of dignity. Will you please do the same?"

My tone didn't ruffle him in the least, and he showed no sign of letting up on his infuriating interrogation. I knew then that he wouldn't give it up until he received the answer he was expecting. He had that intense lock on my eyes, as if he feared I would vanish into thin air somehow if he let go of it.

"Curse you, Oded," I shouted. "I only want to live the remainder of my days in peace—can't you understand that? Can't you just let me be?"

I placed both my hands on his shoulders and tried one last time to receive his acceptance, only that time in a softer and controlled tone.

"Oded, I know your religion teaches that a suicide can be considered a righteous act if done for the right reason. Now, I admit I'm tired and want out of this cursed life, but what I'm doing is for Christine. It's right and righteous that I do this, one final, unselfish act, to atone for the multitude of wicked ones."

He motioned for me to sit back down, and at that moment my weary body was most willing to comply. He again looked intently into my eyes and continued to question me, not with his daroga mind-set, but as the friend that only he had ever been.

"Erik, do you have any idea why I risked everything I had, even my own life, so you could live? Why do you think I didn't arrest you for the death of those men the first time I met you? And all the time I spent following you around the Paris Opera House, do you think I was doing that for my own health?"

His questions went unanswered by me, but I did sigh and take a large swallow of my brandy. Then I got up again and moved to the window, leaning against its frame. The unusual rain had stopped and a large silver moon was peeking in and out from behind dark, fast-moving, and menacing clouds. I watched a mother carrying her bundled child quickly across *Rue de Rivoli*. Then I thought about all the things I'd never been able to do, nor would I ever be able to do. With all the knowledge and powers I possessed, I'd never be able to accomplish the simple things in life that so many people took for granted.

The simple things, sitting in the park on a sunny spring day with my wife by my side, watching our child play ball with a dog, or lying beside my wife on our wedding night, full of love and with our passion satisfied. Simple things—yes, simple things, but they were all as far away from me as the elusive moon I was watching.

Oded's voice broke my gaze, and I looked at him standing beside me. From the expression in his genuine eyes, I knew I owed him honest answers to his inquiries, along with whatever time he asked of me. So back to the chair I went, sat down, and took another sip of my brandy. Then I motioned for him to be seated. He responded to my gesture, sat down, and after taking a slow breath, continued with his compassionate plea.

"That morning when I first met you on the road to Mazenderan, I knew you weren't just another man, Erik. There was something different about you, and it wasn't your mask or the rumors about your mysterious ways. I saw something in your eyes that you don't see every day, and the more I learned about you the more I was sure I'd made the right decision in not taking you into custody.

"Erik, if I were to live a thousand years, I don't believe I'd ever find someone else like you. Your brilliance and genius, your music, your love and passion for life, you can't just throw all that away. You've made it clear to me on more than one occasion that you're capable of doing anything you put your mind to, and over the years I've seen that to be true.

"Remember, I was there in Persia, and I saw you singlehandedly save over a thousand men's lives and at great risk to your own. If someone else had built that palace, they all would have been killed. But because of the *impossible* you made possible, they went on to have children and grandchildren. You have so much you could give, Erik, and I know you could find a way to give it if you would only try."

He paused again and looked even more deeply into my eyes, if that were possible, before he finished his plea. "I realize your life has been far from an easy road, but, please, Erik, please think about what I've said before you do anything that can't be undone."

With that having been said, he leaned back, and with a simple movement of his hand, he let me know he was finished and waiting for my reply. I bent forward, lowered my head, and removed my mask, rubbing my face and eyes while trying to find the right words to convince him I was right.

I was beginning to feel quite ill, but I knew I had to find the strength to finish what I started before I left. I was so fatigued physically, emotionally, and mentally that I only wanted to lie down and sleep. Oh, if he would only let the conversation go and me along with it. I replaced my mask and leaned back, searching my so-called genius mind for the right words before turning my attention back to him.

"You make a sincere supplication, my friend, but, you have to remember, I have spent a lifetime trying to share *my genius,* as you call it, and where has it gotten me? No one wants *my genius,* not if it comes with this face, no one," I said as I tapped my knuckles under my chin. "Just think about it. I've been forced to live as a total recluse in the bowels of one of the most populated structures in all of Paris—no, in all of France. No one cares, Oded, no one except you. No one will miss me when I'm gone."

I hesitated a moment and glanced out of the window and then straight back at him before I continued, "No one will miss *my genius,* because they never knew it existed. No one knows about the contributions I've given to the Opera House or any other edifice for that matter. No one knows or cares about the scientific achievements I've made or could still make if given the chance. No one.

"The Opera Ghost will be gone, and there'll be a celebration because of it. When most men die, people cry and grieve, but, when I die, people will be joyous and celebrate. In fact, I can imagine the opera management might produce a special gala event in recognition of this one-time happening. What kind of a legacy will that be?"

I took a deep breath and fixed him a special look. "No, my unique friend, I'm now convinced, more than ever that it takes a very special person to be able to see beyond this mask. They are few and far between, and I'm simply too weary to search for them any longer. Is that so difficult to understand?"

He didn't answer me, at least not in audible words, but I could sense in his expression that he had to acquiesce to my final conclusions. I paused long enough to take another sip and then reflected on my past.

"In all my 45 years, there have been only a few special individuals who cared enough to see me for the person I really am, you being one of them. At this rate, I couldn't live long enough to put together a quartet, no matter how hard I tried. Therefore, this is the best thing I can do for the two people who do care about me.

"I once warned you not to befriend me, Oded, but you chose to ignore the warning, which has brought you so much unhappiness, and my remorse over that is impossible to describe even to this day. Now it's time to put an end to the suffering of all concerned, and, more importantly, to prevent any more tragedies from occurring."

We watched each other for a few moments, and, as I saw his jaws clenching, I hammered in what I hoped would be the final nail. "Oded, you do remember that I almost killed you in anger at the palace, don't you?

And I know you couldn't have forgotten what I was responsible for at the campsite—all because of my anger."

I lowered my eyes, took a deep breath, and then looked back at my friend. "Last night, I came so close to ending the lives of perhaps thousands of innocent people all in a matter of seconds, just because of my painful anger. While you and Raoul were in my mirror chamber, I couldn't have cared less about your life.

"Do you understand what I'm saying to you? I knew the two of you were going to die in there, and I didn't care. I didn't care about my best friend's life ending at my hands. I was so out of control with hurt and anger that I didn't care who I injured or killed, and unlike that time in Persia, I can remember all of it, all the anger and uncaring hatred."

Then, looking down at my hands and again running my fingers over my naked little finger, I said softly, "I was even going to let Christine die if she made the wrong decision. I just didn't care any longer about anyone's life, including my own and that of the only woman I'd ever loved."

While thinking how he was the only man, other than my father, that I'd let get that close to me, I looked back at him and added, "I didn't care about the life of the only man I'd ever let into my heart." Then with all the strength I had in me, I poured my soul out to him and pleaded, "Do you see and can you understand what I'm trying to tell you?

"I don't think you ever understood why I locked myself down in the fifth cellar. It wasn't only to spare myself from the hurtful actions and attitudes of those around me but, more importantly, it was to spare the lives I could have taken if I'd stayed among mankind. I haven't trusted myself since we left Persia, and I made the mistake of listening to my lonely heart long enough to fall in love with Christine, and, in doing so, I almost did more harm than in all the rest of my life. I can't take the chance of letting that ever happen again."

I leaned forward, placed my elbows on my knees and my face in my hands, then finished softly. "If I wasn't such a coward, I'd turn myself into the police. Then maybe they would hang me for the crimes I'm accused of, even if I didn't commit them. But I fear they would only lock me up and not bring my sorry life to an end. I don't deserve to live any longer, Oded. I'm a danger to everyone." Then, looking back up at him, I whispered, "Even you.—Please—help me end this—just let me go."

Fifty-Four

With that having been said, those caring eyes began to fill with tears. That was my cue to leave the scene before I also lost my composure and cast myself as the imbecile in my mournful tragedy. I rose and stood before him, silently willing him to let this be the last of it. He took a deep breath, and I closed my eyes, picturing him starting up again, but he merely exhaled slowly and turned his gaze to the darkness outside. I moved beside him and placed my hand on his shoulder as a gesture of farewell.

One more time he questioned, "Are you sure you want to do this?" Then he looked up at me. "I understand why you fear to live around people in general, but that doesn't necessarily mean you have to stop living to do it. You could still live in your home in the cellars, and I could visit, and we could play chess or just talk like old times. Perhaps, from time to time, we could even take a ride in the country on horses as we once did.

"And then there's your music. You've made it clear on many occasions how much it means to you. Live for your music, and let your music give you a reason to live."

I lowered my shaking head. "Perhaps in another lifetime that was true, but no more. Without Christine, my music is voiceless."

"But you had your music long before you knew Christine."

"That's true. But just because I can enjoy the marvel of a beautiful sunset doesn't mean I'll always enjoy it. If I go blind, I can no longer see it and enjoy it. Music without Christine in it isn't music, and life without music in it isn't a life worth living."

There was silence while I watched him searching for a way to change my mind, and I felt pity for him. We'd been friends for over 24 years, and to hear me talk about death the way I was had to be painful for him. I know it would be for me if he was the one talking about death. I was searching for comforting words for him when he tried again.

"Have you thoroughly thought this through? I can't help but feel there must be another way, a way for the man who saved the life of his enemy last night to also be saved. I watched you as you took such gentle care of Raoul. It's that man I saved in Persia, and it's that man you need to save this day."

I looked down at his hand that was swirling what was left of the brandy in his glass, and then I walked across the room and turned slowly to face him. My movement made the candle's flame flicker beside him and send flashes of light into his moist eyes that returned to examine mine. They were pleading for me to reconsider, and that vision stayed etched in my heart for the rest of my days and made it extremely difficult to respond to his plea. I had to take a few deep breaths and clear my throat before I had sufficient control to make a cohesive answer.

"I have thought this through, for many years actually, and, if there's another way, I don't know of it. It's not necessarily what I want to do, but it's what needs to be done. I'm exhausted, Oded, and drained of all will to fight and too full of fear to live any longer."

With one swallow, he finished his brandy and placed the empty glass on the table beside him. Then he rose to his feet, moved toward me, and placed one hand on my shoulder.

"I'll do what you ask, but, before I let you go, I have one last request. You once told me that four days was a small price to pay for a fine jewel. Do you remember that?"

With that painful reminder, I looked him squarely in the eyes, hoping he would see the sincerity in mine. "I've never been able to forget it. Your daughter was worth so much more than four days, and I would have been willing to pay whatever you asked."

"Erik, I consider you a fine jewel. So I'm asking you for four days. Wait four days and really think this through before you do anything. Can you promise me just four days?"

As usual, I found it difficult to refuse him, so I simply nodded in agreement. I paused long enough in front of the door to glance over my shoulder one last time at the kind face of a truly good confidant—my only confidant. Finally, there was nothing more he could say to change my mind and nothing more I could say to make it easier on him.

With a knot in my throat, I opened the door, but, before I could walk through it, his fingers wrapped around my arm, and one more time he spoke my name. I reluctantly turned to face him, and then he grasped my shoulders and proceeded to kiss both of my cheeks. He backed away and spoke in barely audible words.

"May Allah walk beside you in your time of need, my friend."

I looked at him and smiled. "I hope Allah is wise enough not to walk in that dangerous position."

"Erik," he scowled. "No sarcasm. Not now. Please."

The room fell silent once more, while his expression brought decades of memories surging through my bleeding heart. No more words needed to be spoken; our moist eyes said it all.

I turned again and slowly walked down the stairs, expecting to hear his voice again, but there was no voice, only the sound of my lone footfalls on the wooden steps. As I crossed *Rue de Rivoli*, I looked up at his window and the silhouette of my true friend and companion for one brief moment more. Then I lowered my head to the breeze and began my lonely walk through the *Tuileries* and to my empty home.

The cold night air whipped my cloak open and sent a shiver to my bones, almost making me reconsider my decision not to take a brougham. I wrapped my cloak around my exhausted body and reconfirmed my determination to walk the streets of my home country.

The rain had stopped and the clouds had moved on, leaving Paris dark and quiet. But there were still intermittent flashes of jagged silver daggers in the distance, serving as a reminder that great power still remained in those clouds. As I had on many occasions, I thought about the possibility of harnessing that power for the good of all mankind. I sighed. If that were only possible. Ultimately, the investigation into that idea would have to remain in the laboratory of someone who would live longer than myself.

Once I reached *Rue Scribe,* there were more people present, mostly couples, strolling hand in hand and whispering words of love. I listened to them as they passed, not caring if they saw me or if they crossed the street to avoid me. It didn't matter to me anymore, but, strangely enough, no one seemed to notice me, or, if they did, it didn't matter to them either.

Eventually, I was making my way across the dark lake. As usual, the mist swirled and parted before me, as if obeying some silent command. Once inside my home, I immediately gave into my exhaustion and passed out across the divan. When I woke, it was to the same eerie silence I'd fallen asleep in, only I woke feeling strangely uneasy and anxious. I felt as if I'd just lived through one of my horrendous nightmares—had I? Had I only dreamt those last three monstrous days or were they real?

I sat up and glanced around, hoping there would be something—anything—I could see to bring my disquieting thoughts under control. But, when I headed toward the music room, my desire for it to be nothing more than a bad dream evaporated with the sight of a small pool of water by the door to the mirror chamber. Instantly, visions of Raoul and Oded lying unconscious in that horrible room crushed my heart. It wasn't a nightmare. It was real—only too real.

I slumped against the doorframe, took off my mask, and lowered my face to my palms, repeating, "This isn't real. This can't be real."

But my agreement with Oded spoke, too loud and too clear. The thought of waiting four days before ending it all was agonizing, and I almost didn't honor my promise to him, especially since I knew it wasn't going to make a difference. It wouldn't change who I was or prevent another disaster from happening at my hands. So why did I agree to it?

Don't question it, was my final thought. I'd given my word to my friend, so I knew I needed to keep it without thinking about how difficult it was going to be for me. So I replaced my mask and took out my watch. It had stopped, but the floor clock had a few more minutes to go before it stopped, which meant I'd already completed at least one day as I'd slept. With that in mind, I focused on keeping busy so I could live through three more days with the least amount of anguish as possible.

I had a thundering headache, and my right shoulder was stiff and sending sharp pains down my arm and into my chest. Thinking I must have slept in the wrong position and perhaps needed to eat, I got a glass of wine and some food and set them on the coffee table. I took a few bites and a few sips, and then I stretched out on the divan, laid my mask on my chest, and got comfortable.

When I did, I focused on a long-legged black spider gingerly making his way across the ceiling above me. As he skillfully spun an addition to his already extensive web, I watched him and realized we weren't much different—that spider and I.

He was a solitary and silent creature, working endlessly to create something new. While working contentedly alone, with only an occasional visitor whom he quickly destroyed, he always watched for a larger creature who wanted to destroy him. Yes, we weren't much different—that spider and I.

I too worked best alone and created endlessly, with only the occasional visitor whom I usually managed to destroy in some way. I was also constantly on the lookout for those who wanted to destroy me. Luca, Pete, and their sons were the first to try, and, in their efforts, my poor father became my curse's first victim. But, regrettably, he was only the first in a long line of victims who were unfortunate enough to make my acquaintance. There were only a few exceptions who survived my presence—my curse. Yes, that spider and I were more alike than my two-legged contemporaries and I were.

As I watched him work on his masterpiece, I thought about all the things I'd built, thanks to the excellent instruction I'd received from my father. My mind wandered through my childhood, and I thought about my first introduction to music. I relived those wonderful moments when I watched and listened to my mother playing her piano.

I smiled when I thought about my father sitting by my side on the piano bench and singing our strange duet, and I remembered the proud look on his face when he found me playing the piano all by myself. Unfortunately, I also saw the horror, uncertainty, and fear on my mother's face as the weeks, months, and years passed, and I could still feel my pain and confusion with her inconsistent reaction to me and my musical genius. Our complicated relationship, filled with our love for music and our shared hatred and fears, perplexed us both.

I relived the conversations my father had with me while trying to convince me that my mother loved me. Most of those conversations took place during our trips to the sea, trips filled with his guiding words, laughter, and our tears. The visions of the sea breeze tossing his hair like spun gold and his expressive hands, gesturing as he talked, were still vividly etched in my mind.

Most of the memories about my father involved him teaching me with emphatic emotions; his facial expressions when he talked about life and death and love and hate; his body gestures when he explained how to hammer a straight nail, trowel a smooth wall, and draw a perfect angle; the sound of his deep voice when he expressed important lessons about enjoying the beauty of a sunrise, controlling my temper, believing in my own abilities, and always being optimistic about my next day of life.

Regardless of how much time had passed, my love for my father hadn't diminished one bit; in fact, it increased measurably once I realized what a weighty responsibility he had in raising such a difficult son. He was a remarkable man in every way, and I still wished I could be more like him.

As I looked at my fingers reaching for my wine glass, I pictured my father's long fingers as they followed the words in my small storybooks, and I heard his rich comforting voice as he read each word. I could feel our excitement when I learned to read on my own and when he brought home my first real book, the one on music. He instructed me well; however, he was never able to quench my thirst for knowledge, and, to this day, neither had I.

I actually felt a chuckle in my heart when I thought about the day he brought Molly into my life. That day and the day my little sister was born were wonderful days, and they both helped me fill many more days with glee. My friendship with Celeste was another bright spot in my young life. She still held a special place in my heart, and I was thankful she lived so far away so she wouldn't hear about my death. I know it would pain her if she did.

I closed my eyes and relived the time when my father took me to Venice and we saw our first opera. Even though it had been several decades since then, I could still feel the music swirling around me and my determination that someday I would live with music surrounding me all the time. I pictured the black plaque with the gold words, Box Five, carved into it and telling myself that I would be back. Great memories, all of them.

But then I could still feel the pain during the darker side of my childhood; like the night that uncovered my rampant temper. I felt pity for that child when he discovered the chicks he loved had been killed. What made that night even worse was my anger and disappointment in my father for being a party to their lifeless bodies floating in my soup. My anger frightened me terribly that night and it still did.

Another traumatic event that surfaced while I watched that spider was when my mother refused my embrace. As if it had just happened, I felt first the pain and then the anger as I chased her down the street, screaming my hatred for her. I could feel the torment in my heart as I retreated into the forest all alone, feeling so ashamed and frightened. That day began my nightmares, filled with gawking and terrified faces, and my hatred for mankind.

I took a deep breath and could feel the many scars begin to form on my heart as well as the physical pain when my mother found me playing her violin and threw me out of the house. I closed my eyes to those horrible weeks when I suffered such agony with my first lung infection. But what was even worse was when I'd listened to the account of my birth that explained why my mother feared me so much.

That began my questions and doubts regarding my existence. Was I from another planet? Was I a demon? Or was I simply a deformed and demented child genius? I looked back at the spider and realized I was going to my grave without having answers to those questions, while, at the same time, I knew I was going there with a peace that was far overdue.

I don't know how or why it happened, but, for the first time in my life, I felt a calmness float over me with the realization that I was at peace with my mother—finally. I'd always felt I hated her, but I knew then that I didn't and never really had. If for no other reason, I was glad that Oded had encouraged me to wait before ending my life. If he hadn't, I never would have had that peace with my mother.

In retrospect, I could understand what that child felt. It was frustration and hurt because of not knowing why his mother treated him so harshly. But, as I thought about Celeste's description of my mother and her death, what I felt for her was different than what I'd felt for Franco, Pete Jr., Yves, and the rest of mankind that treated me badly.

I hated them, and that's what enabled me to want to kill them, but I never wanted to kill my mother or see her dead or even see her hurt. While

I'd lost my temper with her often, I never hurt her physically, and, since I'd nearly killed Franco, I knew I'd had the physical strength to hurt her if I'd really wanted to. I believe I was shaking my head when I finally understood why it hurt so much to hear about her death.

"I didn't hate her," I whispered.

Why couldn't I have understood that I really loved her while she was still alive? If I had, our life together would have been so much different. Another tear trickled from my eye when my heart opened up and allowed me to mourn my mother's death. It was then that I made the decision to put my father's watch and my mother's locket in that green velvet bag together and have it in my vest pocket, close to my heart, when I went to my final resting place.

Death. My life was so full of it, and, when I closed my eyes again, I could see clearly that lantern being thrown at my father and then him bursting into flames. I could hear my screams and feel the heat from his body when he said his last words to me and took his last breath. As if a knife was entering my chest anew, I felt the anguish in my heart when I saw his life leave his blue eyes.

From my earliest recollections, I'd needed to control the actions of those around me to protect my heart, but, after experiencing the horrifying death of my father, I realized I couldn't control everything and everyone.

I quickly took a large swallow of my wine, trying to change the direction my thoughts were going in, but it was too late. That horrible nightmare and the sounds and sights became real, and once more my mind wouldn't be calm. Relentlessly, my thoughts swayed back and forth between two of my worst nightmares—my last hours with Christine and my last hours with my father. I could put all my horrendous nightmares in one big bag and it wouldn't weigh nearly as much as the ones I'd had to face those two nights.

Nightmares—my life was riddled with them. Some were real life events, but most were sinister nightly visitors and thankfully nothing more. Often, I couldn't tell the difference between the two. In fact, sometimes I thought I was in the midst of a nightmare and trying to wake, only to find I was already awake and the living nightmare had only begun.

That autumn day in 1846 was one of those days, and, even though logic told me I was an adult and living in Paris, my overactive emotions turned me back into that wounded child in Perros-Guirec. I grabbed my stomach with real pain, just as real as on that morning when I'd had to wake and face the truth about my greatest fear and my worst living nightmare—my father's horrible death.

As the warmth of one lone tear trailed across my temple and nestled in my hair, I could no longer see that spider through my tears. My heart still ached with the thought of never hearing my father's rich voice or seeing his warm smile again.

I took out my watch, wiped the tears from my eyes so I could look at the time, and started to set it on the table. But then I stopped and ran my fingertips over the two horse heads on the cover, now severely worn from all the times it had been caressed. How often I'd watched my father remove that watch from his pocket, look at the time, close the cover, and feel the horse heads with his fingertips. Then he'd always smile at me as he replaced it in his pocket.

How is it that an inanimate object like my watch could hold so many memories, both special and painful? But no matter how agonizing they might be, I would never give up the memories of that extraordinary man. What a unique privilege I'd had to have him as my friend and father, my mentor and inspiration. He always tried his best to give me an abundance of love and proper guidance, regardless of how difficult I was.

My chest rose with the taking in of a deep breath, and I thought, how long should a son mourn the death of his father? One year? Five years? Ten years? It had been 35 years, and I was still lamenting the loss of that incredible human being as if it had just happened. So how long was a son to lament? That was a question I'd never been able to answer, and, since my death would put an end to it all, I never would answer it.

While my excellent memory had served me well over the years, there were times when it was truly a detriment, and the time I spent watching that spider was one of those times. To me, remembering was so much more than a mere recollection of happenings, it was a reliving of events with all the joy and despair included. During those times, I cursed my ability to recall events so clearly.

I'd spent the last few days shedding so many tears and feeling so much anguish that I really didn't want any more of it; therefore, when another surge of pain streaked across my heart and another tear escaped from my eye, I stopped watching that spider, swung my legs off the divan, and angrily rose to my feet.

"Enough," I growled. "Enough!"

Then I rebuked myself. Enough of this torturous trip into my past. I won't allow myself to spend what time I have left wallowing in self-pity—I won't! I'll prepare for my death and burial. That's what needs to be done, so that's what I'll do.

I began by throwing out all the dead and dying flowers, which was a ridiculous project. Why did I care if there were dead flowers around my home when there was going to be a dead body lying in it soon? I couldn't answer that question either, so I figured it was just another one of my idiosyncrasies.

I washed all the dishes, threw away all my dirty clothes, boxed the blood-splattered wedding dress and put it under the bed. Then I spent some time cleaning my music room that I'd left in a shambles after my angry fit. When I replaced Molly on her pedestal, I ran my fingers over her nose and ears and apologized to her for my cruelty, another peculiar act.

While in there, I tried spending some time with my music, but, as I'd explained to Oded, there was no life in it without Christine. It only made my fingers blur on the black and ivory keys, so I didn't play for long.

I hadn't had a bath in days, so taking one was a logical next step, but not a good emotional step. Her bath was still filled with her lavender things, making it difficult to be in that room. I started to put her things in her armoire, but then I stopped. It hurt to be reminded about her, but then it also made me feel closer to her, so I left them where she'd left them.

While the tub was filling, I got a glass of brandy and stripped my clothes and mask off. As I slipped under the water, my eyes closed, and I tried to relax while massaging my aching neck and shoulder. I moved it around in circles and then looked at the horrible scar that was left as evidence of our love triangle. When I did, I noticed a lot of new bruising streaking down my chest, probably from my exertion in the mirror chamber, I reasoned.

I took a swallow of the brandy, a deep breath and thought again, doesn't matter now. Not much did. However, the warm bath, that scar and the other scars that came into view, brought to the fore another distressing time in my life.

There had been far too many times when I would have given anything for a warm bath, especially during the ten years after my father died and I'd left home. Again those thoughts made my chest hurt, partially because of the loss of my father and partially for the young boy who'd lost not only his father and protector but also his childhood that October eve.

During the agony of the night my father died, I remember thinking about the cliffs at our ocean property, but nothing more. I didn't think about my goal of Venice or my excitement about its nearness just minutes earlier. And when I'd needed them the most, I couldn't hear my father's words of wisdom and direction. I couldn't recall his instruction: *Never let any obstacle stand in the way of your goals.*

But then, he couldn't possibly have known it would be his own tragic death that was the first insurmountable obstacle in my path. And in his wildest imagination, he couldn't have guessed the number of obstacles that would raise their ugly heads along that path. There were numerous heads, so vile and shocking they made my deformity pale into nothingness.

If I'd known what awaited me in the days, weeks, months, and years to come, I'm sure I would have thrown myself off those cliffs that same night. But I was innocent of all the trials that awaited me.

More brandy slid past my lips, and I closed my eyes momentarily while savoring its distinctive warmth and the warmth of the water surrounding me. Opening my eyes, I watched the crystal glass sparkle as I set it on the edge of my marble tub. Then my sight focused beyond it to my mask lying on the floor where I'd dropped it. Sighing, I reached for it and ran my fingers over its details.

Closing my eyes again, I thought it was by far the best I'd made and the one Christine favored. It was also the one I'd been wearing when I felt my first kiss from the woman who owned my heart—my Christine. It wasn't difficult to see why we preferred it, even more than the one she threw into the fire. It appeared the most human, with its tan color and unique features.

I took a sip of brandy and closed my eyes again, shivering with the thought of the days that had followed my father's death—the horror of his funeral, telling him goodbye, composing and playing "Papa's Song" for him, being robbed and having the violin he gave me crushed, being kidnapped, and spending six months in that circus cage. My time alone trying to make it to Venice had been extremely hard on me, but it was a holiday compared to the time I'd spent as a circus freak—a living corpse.

Even though I was in a nice warm bath and in my own home, it made my stomach sick to remember that time. But my next vision actually made me close my eyes tightly and turn my head away, as if my bath was responsible for conjuring up the sight of my first victim's blue face—Yves' blue face. I again shuddered and took another sip of brandy.

Once again I laid my head back against the tub, remembering the crude but clever tub I'd made in a stream. Those baths were cold, but, after spending so long in that filthy cage, they were wonderful to me.

That had been one of the strangest times in my life. I remember feeling nothing, just going through the same routine day in and day out. I ate and I bathed but I never spoke, sang, or even hummed. It was as if I didn't have a mind of my own, as if I was doing whatever someone else told me to do; however, I was completely alone during that time, with the exception of Molly. But I didn't even talk to her.

I'd found my cruelest enemy while in that cage, then I had no one while at the stream, and, shortly thereafter, I found my guardian angel—Jean Luc. As a small boy traveling alone across France and Italy, I seldom had a chance for a warm bath, except for the year I spent with Jean Luc. He truly snatched me out of the grave and gave me light and hope, and the thought of him made me feel warm in a different way.

Singlehandedly, he helped me realize there were good people who shared this world with me. He was a living example of my father's guiding words: *Give them a chance to know you, Erik, and they'll have to love you.* Thoughts about Jean Luc made me think about the Gypsies, who also befriended me.

If my thoughts could have gone straight from Jean Luc to the Gypsies, that period of walking through my memories wouldn't have been too bad, but they couldn't. Between them sat horrible times, some of the worst in my life.

I tried to breathe past the sting of that memory and focus on something pleasant, but, at that time, everything around me painted a heartbreaking picture. While looking at my mask, I saw all the roads I'd traveled with it—most of them distressing. When I looked away from the mask, I saw my home beneath the Paris Opera House and those last horrible hours with Christine.

Thankfully, I also had pleasant thoughts of her, which stirred up memories filled with happiness, music, and laughter. If I could stay focused on only those occasions, then I could ward off the grief and the temptation to let the drug end my agony before the four days were up. Concentrate, I told myself. But I couldn't get past the thoughts about that poor boy traveling across Europe alone. I wanted, or perhaps needed, to mourn his loss.

I remembered going from one day being hopeful about Venice and then the next day being in so much physical pain that I turned to alcohol to control it. Then I thought about that year when I was so inebriated that I could hardly remember anything about it, and I felt repulsed. My teeth clenched and my head shook when I thought about what it took to end that year—a bullet in my back and being jailed as a thief.

I could still see the kind eyes of the doctor who took care of me while I was behind bars and who helped me get my feet back on the road leading to Venice and the conservatory. Sadly though, I could also see the disgusted eyes of the director of that conservatory when he rejected me without an audition. Such two extremes. But then, that was my life, going from good to bad to worse and back again.

Nevertheless, as I thought about that boy after he was rejected by the conservatory, I had a measure of pride in what I'd accomplished. True, I might have borrowed their Stradivarius for an extended period of time, but I'd done so with a smile on my lips and not in angered retaliation.

And even though I was shunned by the majority of those I came across in the months that followed, I'd made the decision not to let them knock me down. I was determined to travel with my devoted horses, Molly, Libre, and Big Luc, and learn about cultures, history, music, science, and everything in between.

However, my brow furrowed and my eyes closed tightly again when I recalled the reason why my plans were altered. While fighting for my life against two full grown men, I'd killed them both. At first I was beyond traumatized. I vomited repeatedly and then spent the entire night sitting by the small lake with my mind and emotions in a thick fog, but when I came out of that fog I no longer had any feelings—good or bad.

As I watched the brandy swirl around in my glass, I remembered how empty my heart felt, almost as if it wasn't there. That was the worst period in my life, even worse than the time I spent in the cage. I killed without the blink of an eye; however, I never went looking for victims, they innocently approached me, just like a fly in that spider's web, and I killed them simply because they were in my way or they looked at me the wrong way.

I took a sip of brandy, shook my head, shivered, and forced myself to think about a better time. While remembering my ability to kill so easily, I automatically turned my thoughts to my little trainer who taught me the skill of the Punjab lasso. I learned other important lessons from him, like how to control my temper. That was something my father had spent years trying to help me learn, and yet just a few months with that strange Oriental and I had the insight I needed to manage my temper, which helped me save lives instead of taking them.

All in all, by the time I was 20, I'd learned how to live among the hateful men who wanted to do me harm without harming them, and how to be self-sufficient, or, should I say, how to get what I wanted even if I had to steal it. However, I also learned how to make a good living doing what I loved the most—creating music.

I laid my head back against the tub and remembered the time I'd spent with the Gypsies. Those were good years; traveling, working on construction sites, and meeting up with the Gypsies for their carnivals. That was the beginning of my wealth. Between working for powerful people with riches to spread around and then entertaining for people who were appreciative of my art and who also lined my pocket with what riches they had, I always had everything of a physical nature that I wanted. But few of my emotional needs were met. I was hopelessly lonely and feared letting anyone get too close to me because of what I believed was my curse.

I raised my head and nodded, thinking that my trunk in my music room still held more material goods than I would need in a normal lifetime.

But then my lifetime was only going to be a matter of days, so that wouldn't take much. I decided then to leave what I had with either Christine or Oded. Even if Raoul rejected Christine for some reason, what I had in that trunk would take care of her and Oded for the rest of their lives.

I took another sip and laid my head back again, still thinking about the carnivals. I thought about Michaela who inspired my first love ballad, "Butterfly Wings." I relived my performances in my tent that was decorated to resemble an opera house, and I remembered the elation I felt from my appreciative audiences' accolades.

Then I felt a large smile on my lips when I thought about the night I'd first encountered Oded. I even chuckled aloud when I remembered the frustration in his voice. He never did handle my pranks or sarcasm well.

When I thought about Oded, I decided to do something I'd been putting off—getting a box to put Christine's things in for him. I had a particular box in mind, so, after getting out of the tub and dressing, I headed for my old trunk in my music room and knelt down beside it. I hadn't opened it in many years, and, once I did, the smell released memories of long ago.

I thought about the Shah and how pleased he was with his palace. Even when I was fighting for my life, I was also pleased. I was victorious in battling against his powerful regime and had saved a thousand lives in addition to my own. I took a deep breath and let it out slowly, feeling good about some of my stay in Persia. Out of all my designs and builds, I think I was the most proud of that palace. It accomplished what I wanted. It protected the Shah, and it was a stunning jewel on Mazenderan's landscape.

Other than the time I'd spent with my father, that period held both my highest and lowest points—the happiest and the saddest. I learned how to accept love from others, and I learned how to trust, to a degree anyway. But then, I also learned about the darkest part of my heart—the heart that should have stopped beating at my birth. If it had, many lives would have been spared. But it didn't stop at my birth or any time thereafter, so *I* had to stop it. I glanced at my watch and realized I had two more days before I could perform my last act—like it or not.

I moved my old and tattered cloak aside, feeling the jewels enclosed in its hem and thought about how I'd acquired them all. I was still a wealthy man, but what had my wealth brought me? Nothing! Absolutely nothing! My existence was sad, cold, and lonely, just as cold as all the jewels in that hem. I might have had all the physical comforts a man could want, but, as for that which makes up a true life, happiness and contentment, all my wealth had been useless—powerless to give me a truly happy life.

When I found one lone sapphire lying in the bottom of the trunk, I rolled it in my palm. Meager trinkets and nothing more. All those years they'd been lying in my trunk, and they'd been no use to me whatsoever.

"No use to me now," I muttered.

While still looking at the blue stone in my palm, I made the decision to give Oded my jewels and gold coins. He deserved them. After all, he would still be living a comfortable and respectable life in Persia if it weren't for me. My jewels were a mere token compared to what I owed my persistent Persian.

However, the one sapphire in my hand I wanted to give to Madame Geri as a token of my appreciation for the many years she'd supported me. During the time when I was all alone and fighting for my right to have Box Five for my personal use, she was the only one who'd helped me get what I wanted. She never once turned down my request to deliver a note to my managers, sometimes at a cost to her reputation and position at the opera house. Yes, that gem would suffice nicely as a farewell gift to her and support her comfortably in her retirement, so I slipped it into my pocket.

As I moved my cloak aside, I found what I was looking for, the gold and turquoise box. I lifted it out and ran my fingers over its delicate swirls and the soft velvet inlays. Winding the spring on its bottom, I opened the lid, and then I closed my eyes and listened to the melody. For a few moments, I relived the first time I'd heard it, and I felt at peace.

During those rare months in Persia, I'd had hope for a real and happy future with Vashti as my wife. But then the music brought another vision, and I closed the lid quickly before the truth and further grief surfaced, the truth about what I'd lost in Persia—Vashti. Nonetheless, that box was the perfect place to put Christine's things, and, as I again ran my fingers over the gold carvings, I honestly smiled. I pictured Oded's grin and sparkling jade eyes the first time he saw that box and understood its purpose. That was such a happy time in both our lives.

As my soft chuckle echoed through my music room, I pictured his eyes so confused and frustrated the first time he heard my voice. I remembered having to restrain my laughter that cold night to keep from giving away my location. I could remember everything about that night in Volgograd, Russia; how the cold breeze was nipping at my fingers, the sound of the leather cinch as I tightened it, the smell of the smoldering campfire, the distant cry of a small child in his wagon, the sight of a billion stars in the dark sky, and Oded's voice the first time I heard him speak my name—everything.

I looked down at the orchids embossed on the cover of the box and remembered how irritated he'd been with me long before he'd ever met me. Poor Oded. Oh, Oded, why did you have to come looking for me that night? Why did I let my curiosity get the better of me? Why? As usual, too many questions and not nearly enough answers or the time to find them.

Holding the box in my hand, I sighed and let memories, many and varied, flow freely across my heart. I'd helped many in Persia with my imagination, but I'd also hurt many with my diabolical genius. My only wish was that I could have helped more and hurt fewer.

My thoughts also meandered through the time I spent with Oded's family. I smiled when I thought about his boys and how I taught them to ride and to build. I thought about Sari, a jewel finer than the palace, and Vashti, who would have made an excellent wife just like her mother.

I still could see her beautiful jade eyes when I removed my mask in front of her. Her expression and the words she used at that time warmed my heart, but it also fractured my heart when I thought about her horrible death and my last vision of her poor burnt face.

Enough of this torture, I told myself, so I went back to searching through the trunk. But as I moved more things around in it, a musty smell met me, bringing my thoughts to the one dark spot in the palace—the mirror chamber. While it protected the Shah, it was also the predecessor for the horror in my cellar home, and that thought made my insides shiver. It also made me think about the terrors in Persia, beginning with my assassination of those generals, their retaliation against Oded's family, and my counteraction—the campfire slaughter.

With those thoughts, the same sick feeling rushed through me that I'd had the previous nights, and I couldn't let that happen, not when I still had two days to wait for my release. I looked around and felt the walls coming in on me. I lowered my head and closed my eyes, willing myself to stay in control.

But I couldn't. That irresistible urge to run filled me and stripped away my control. I was losing what little restraint I had left, and that foreboding feeling entered my gut—like something terrible was about to happen.

Fifty-Five

As a result, I jumped up with Sari's keepsake box in hand, knowing I couldn't wait the full four days. Once in Christine's room, I quickly went through her dressing table, looking for items to put in Sari's box for Oded. I found her diary, a lone shoe buckle from the production of *Juive*, and a handkerchief and placed them in the box. I hoped if Oded had a chance to read Christine's writings then he might understand how we felt about each other.

In her jewelry box, I found the first jewelry I'd given her from the gala, her pearls from the night of our first romantic dinner, the two sets of hair combs and matching necklaces, and her watch. But I didn't want to give them to Oded. I wanted her to have them, so I left them in her jewelry box, hoping she would take them with her when she left my home for the last time. Not giving myself time to think about what I was doing, I left my home and climbed the stairs to the passage behind the mirror.

Then, with my palm on her mirror, I whispered, "Christine."

If but for only a moment we could have shared our love, my life would have been worth living. If she could have given me love for but an hour, I could have made the sun hesitate and take notice. If I could have expressed to her the depth of my love, I could have changed the course of tides. But since neither of us could or would express that love properly, the sun kept moving and the tides forever rolled and my life was no longer worth living. As Henry had told me on his deathbed—life wasn't fun anymore.

I pressed the lever, and her mirror rumbled softly on its pivots and opened, releasing her fragrance. After lighting her table lamp, I leaned back against the wall and let memories of her rush through my heart. When I pictured her at her dressing table, preparing for the gala, my entire being ached to go back to that moment. If I could, our time together could have been so different and she could have expressed her love for me—I just knew it.

During those last minutes when we were together in my home, I saw her eyes speak to me that language of love, but it was too late for those words any longer. The only thoughts left to speak were words of goodbye.

I whispered, "She's all gone."

With a heavy sigh, I set Sari's box on the dressing table and then sat in the chair, telling myself not to go to that dark place but to do what I was there to do. Therefore, I opened the drawers, looking for anything I could send to Oded and found everything still where she'd left it.

My hand and thoughts went straight to her diary that had helped me to understand her and teach her. When I lifted it out, a single dried rose petal dropped to the floor, so I set her diary on my lap and reached for the petal. I held it to my face, closed my eyes, breathed deeply, and pictured her putting those petals in her diary.

Again, I whispered, "Christine."

The melody of "One Beat" floated through my heart, and I relived the day I'd composed it. While lost in that memory somewhere, I was startled by the sound of a key in the lock. Instantly on my feet, I grabbed Sari's box and was in the passage with the mirror closing when the dressing room door opened.

Remaining motionless, I watched Meg and Jammes enter. Meg stopped abruptly, looking at the lit lamp on the dressing table. Her eyes widened and she covered her nose and mouth with her shaking fingers, while I held my breath and wondered if she'd seen the mirror close.

Jammes, looking at Meg's worried face, asked, "Meg, what's wrong?"

Meg looked at the mirror and barely whispered, "Someone's been in here."

"Christine?" Jammes questioned with excitement.

"No," Meg whispered once more. Then, while leaning in closer to her companion, she added, "Not Christine."

Meg finally turned her gaze from the mirror and glanced around the room quickly. Her sight stopped when she noticed the diary on the floor. Almost cautiously, she moved across the room and picked it up.

"See," Jammes insisted, "Christine must have been here. Isn't that her diary?"

Meg only nodded and looked again at the mirror. "It wasn't Christine who was in here, Jammes. Don't you smell that musty, damp odor?"

Taking a deep breath, Jammes answered, "Yes. What is it?"

"The mirror has been opened. He's been here," Meg murmured.

Jammes frowned, looked at Meg's face, and then at the mirror before she questioned, "Who, Meg?" Then in an instant, her fingers covered her lips and a gasp. "Do you think he was really in here?"

Meg looked down at the diary in her hands, and when her eyes came back to the mirror, there were tears in them.

Jammes, still a bit concerned about her friend, asked, "What's wrong, Meg? Talk to me."

"He loved her so much," Meg responded softly, while looking back at the diary. "He loved her, and she loved him."

My eyes closed, and I sighed. I knew she loved me. My heart pounded steadily against my chest, and, when my knees became weak, I leaned against the wall. When I heard Jammes' voice again, I looked back at the two ballerinas.

"Meg," Jammes said as she shook Meg's arm, "you're trembling. We should go. We can come back for Christine's things later."

Meg shook her head. "No, this won't take but a minute." Then she quickly grabbed all of Christine's things out of the drawers, including her diary. "We can come back for her clothes later," she added.

Jammes opened the door and was gone from sight while Meg turned the lamp off and started to leave, but then she hesitated with her hand on the door. Once more, she looked at the mirror and then lowered her head and left, closing the door behind her.

I stayed for a few moments in the dark passageway, feeling the rose petal between my fingers. "Oh, Christine," I whispered. "Oh, Christine." I then slipped the rose petal into my pocket, remembering all the times I'd watched her in her dressing room.

Meg's words echoed with each beat of my heart. Christine loved me. I knew she loved me. Then, once more, varied memories floated through my mind—like morning mist through an empty park. Christine joyful and laughing—Christine terrified and sobbing. I pressed my palm on the mirror and thought, that's where it all started, our downhill plunge into the disaster of our lives.

I didn't allow myself more than a few seconds to think about the horrible monster I was, both inside and out, before I sighed disgustedly, lit my lantern, turned, and walked away—without looking back that time. Finish it quickly, was my main thought, so with one quick glance at the keepsake box in my hand, I began my journey toward my Persian friend. It wasn't the scheduled time for me to deliver the box, but I couldn't wait the four days. I wanted and needed to finish what I'd started before I turned coward and changed my mind.

Before long, I stepped out into the open and closed the last of the Opera's doors behind me. The night was clear but had a hint of a chill as I walked the deserted streets alone toward Oded's flat. I'd walked that same path so many times before, but, that night, life was missing from my steps.

Once more, I looked down at the box in my hand, reflecting the nearly full moon, and thought about my friend. The first thought that came to my mind almost brought a smile. Despite the bitter memories of our departure from Persia and that last night in my Paris home, there were good memories also, beginning with our first encounter. Well, at least they were good memories to me. Perhaps Oded had a different version of our first meeting, but, as for me, I was definitely amused.

I looked at the stars overhead, the same stars that had appeared in the Russian sky that night. They hadn't changed one bit, they were still in their assigned places, but our relationship had moved from place to place and changed dramatically.

Once I reached the *Tuileries*, I stopped when I saw a light in his window. Since I needed him to be in bed before I left the box, I took out my watch and looked at the time. It was two a.m., so he should have been asleep, but since he wasn't, I sat on a park bench, intending to wait for the light to go out. That's what I told myself, but deep inside my heart I knew I was only postponing the inevitable.

I really didn't want to end my life, but I felt it was necessary, and those two conflicting thoughts were torturing me. So much so that for the first time I could understand how someone could put a bullet through their brain without any consideration for the ones who would have to clean up the results of their action.

To this day, I fear, if I'd had a pistol on me at the time, I might have ended it right there in the park. But I didn't carry a pistol, so I sat there, bent over with my head in my hands and pulling at my hair.

With a deep breath, I sat back up, ran my fingers over the gold box in my hands again, and looked down the silent street. I might have exasperated Oded that day in Russia but not nearly as much as during the decades that followed. I lowered my eyes to the box and sighed sadly at the memory of our time in Persia. He was a worthy opponent, and he was a worthy friend.

The gold filigree shimmered in the lamplight, and my fingers followed the curves around its graceful designs. I raised my eyes to the lit window again, and my heart ached for my unfortunate friend. My head shook with the memory of his great loss, the memory of our great loss.

I watched silently as a shadow moved across the wall of his flat until the figure of a man appeared in the window—Oded—*Mon Ami*. I took a deep breath and allowed myself to feel the pain in my heart, but it was only momentary. I thought I was hidden among the trees and the shadows, but apparently not, because he abruptly turned from the window and darted toward his door.

Instantly, I jumped to my feet and took off at a run away from him, hopefully disappearing in the darkness and the scattered trees. When he reached the street, he began calling my name and continued to call as he crossed the street and entered the park.

"Erik, don't play this game with me. Come, talk to me! I need to talk to you!"

I hid behind a large tree and held my breath, but his next words made my jaw drop.

"Erik! Comte Philippe de Chagny is dead! Do you know what happened to him? Erik! I know you can hear me. Answer me!"

For only a moment, I was shocked and confused, and I almost answered him just to satisfy my curiosity, but then, as my brow furrowed, I became angry. The tone in his voice was definitely accusatory, and I ground my teeth. It would never end. I would always be blamed for all the deaths in my sphere. It would never end.

Even though I wanted to know what had happened to the Comte, I didn't dare approach Oded with the anger I was feeling, so, while he continued to call to me, I set my jaw and slithered farther away. On my way back to the opera house, different scenarios about Philippe's death came to mind.

He didn't have any enemies that I could think of. He was liked and respected by all in his circle, or at least that's what I thought. I knew Raoul had been fighting with him about Christine, but I couldn't see Raoul killing his own brother. But then I knew he was quick to pull the trigger, so perhaps in anger he could have.

When I reached the lake, I was still in deep thought about the Comte and even somewhat sad. I knew he would be missed by many. Why was I allowed to keep living when such a fine man had died? If there was a being controlling our lives, he wasn't fair.

I was starting to get in my boat, but then I couldn't do it. My curiosity had to be appeased. I had to know what had happened to him. So as I looked back toward the stairs, I thought about two avenues to answer my question. I could go back up on the streets and find a newspaper or I could eavesdrop on any who were still awake in the opera house. I felt sure their conversations would include such terrible news.

I figured two sets of people would be awake in the house, the watchmen and the stable grooms. Since I didn't know just where the watchmen were, I hid Sari's box behind a loose brick and headed for the stable. I found two grooms playing cards and talking about the girls they'd slept with recently, so I waited for a change in their conversation. It took two changes before a familiar subject came up—the Opera Ghost. Then, sure enough, Philippe's death weaved its way into the Ghost's affairs.

Supposedly, the Ghost lured him down to the fifth cellar with incantations and then drowned him in the lake. The grooms reasoned it had been several months since Joseph died, and the Ghost needed a fresh kill. I closed my eyes tightly. I would be glad when I could no longer hear such ridiculous gossip. As I turned to leave, the grooms had another thought. The Ghost lured him down there to experiment with a different type of death, something other than strangulation.

By the time I reached the lake, I had my own ideas about his death. I could see Philippe trying to prevent Raoul from crossing the lake in pursuit of Christine, an argument ensuing, and Philippe falling into the lake. But the most plausible scenario would be Philippe using my boat to find his missing brother.

I knew how easy it was to capsize my boat, especially for someone not familiar with it. I also knew how heavy dress attire was when it was wet. More than once, I'd barely escaped death in that fashion. And since I'd found my boat in the middle of the lake with a Chagny scarf in it, I felt my version of his death was the closest to the truth.

I leaned against a pillar and remembered a conversation I'd overheard in the stable about another death blamed on the Opera Ghost. While I wasn't directly responsible for Philippe's death, I was responsible for that other man's death. But that one was truly in self-defense, and I still had his dagger and the scar it left in my side as proof.

I closed my eyes and saw all the deaths that occurred within the walls of the opera house during that traumatic time for France, and Paris in particular. Considering how they used the opera house during that war, it was a wonder it was still standing. I shuddered when I thought about all the men I'd had to bury.

As I looked at the dock, I pictured being there with Dominick when he returned from the war. He was emotionally scarred, but he was alive, and I was so thankful for that. I also remembered the other times we talked on that dock, explaining to him why I chose not to fight when tormented by the other workers. Then I pictured his battered face after being beaten up by them for defending my name.

Dominick was special to me, and I felt privileged to have tutored him and known him as a friend. I might have had to bury several men during that war, but at least none of them were friends. The only thing I lost of a personal nature to that war was my beloved horses. When I allowed myself to think about the time I spent with them by the lake before I left them alone, the pain in my heart was tremendous. I could still picture them healthy and happy in that meadow and not on someone's dinner plate, so the tears I shed over them were bittersweet.

I lowered my eyes when so many memories about the construction of the opera house surfaced. I remembered how frantically I'd worked on the plans for the judging committee and the day they interviewed me and turned me and my plans down. I remembered everything about the opera house, from my first day working on it straight through its inauguration and beyond.

I even had to smile when I thought about the way I controlled my managers and the other directors in the house. That also went for how the legend of the Opera Ghost got started and all the outlandish stories told about him—or me. I thought about all the newspaper articles written about him and how those stories helped increase the popularity of the performances.

When I took everything into consideration, I felt good about my time at the opera house. I accomplished much, not only on the structure itself, but also in the lives of the people associated with it. And I felt good about others as well, like Dominick, his family, the people in their little town, and the Marseilles and the construction of their home. Those thoughts made me think about Oded and how he tried to encourage me to see all that I'd accomplished and could yet accomplish.

I took a deep breath and began walking around the lake, looking at the arches and thinking. I glanced across the lake and remembered my excitement when I began construction on my home in the fifth cellar. At that time, I thought it would solve all my problems. But then, that was before I became known as the Phantom and before all my serious problems began.

It was strange. I'd fought my entire life to keep from being locked behind bars, and yet I'd sentenced myself to a solitary life beneath the busy streets of Paris. But even if I wasn't living in the depths of the Opera House and I'd built that sought-after castle in the sky, I would still be waking in it alone. As I walked and relived my career as the Opera Ghost, my footfalls echoed through my memories.

Before long, I was also walking through the corridors and running my fingers over the banisters, walls, sets, seats, sculptures, lamps, mirrors, and more. I looked up at the grand chandelier and remembered the day it was put in place and Box Five and the many hours I spent perfecting it and the column I escaped through. As I did so, my feelings were leaning toward what Oded wanted—the preservation of my life.

I stopped on the grand staircase and looked around at all I could see, and I remembered the day when I'd stood on the grand staircase in the palace in Persia, and I felt the same pride for both. I'd accomplished good in my life, and I knew, if there was a way to control certain situations, I could accomplish much more—just as Oded had said. What I was feeling was why he wanted me to wait the four days, and, as I surveyed all I'd done, his ploy would have stopped me right then if it wasn't overshadowed by what I almost did that last horrible night in my home.

It didn't matter what I'd accomplished—or could—in a constructive way, but what did matter was what I almost did and could still do in a destructive way. I looked at the magnificent building I was in, and in one instant I could have brought her down to nothing more than a heap of rubble with broken and bloody bodies mixed in. I closed my eyes tightly to that ghastly vision.

"No," I whispered. "I'm going to win this argument with Oded. I have to stop the possibility of any more disasters happening."

With that thought, I began my walk back to my home, and, in the process, I realized something I'd never thought about before. While I knew I was always happy when I was doing the things I loved most, creating buildings and music, it was only when I was doing it for someone else, and not my sorry self, that I was the happiest.

It began with my father. When I saw how my actions cut into his heart and then made the determination that I would no longer do anything to hurt him, my life took a turn for the better. Then when I discovered why my mother was so unhappy and knew I could no longer hurt her, I became content with her negative reactions to me.

Later when I left home, the first time I felt happiness was when I began having compassionate feelings for Jean Luc and truly wanted to help him. After that, when I learned the skill of the Punjab lasso with the purpose of saving lives, I felt contentment. And when I was traveling with the gypsies, it was the happy expressions of those I entertained that made me happy.

Even when it came to Persia and building the palace, it was the thought of doing it to protect the Shah and make him happy that gave me the most pleasure. Oded's family was the same. His happy reaction when I agreed to stay with them, Sari's happiness when she saw her new kitchen and bedroom, and Vashti's happiness when she learned how to play the piano and when I agreed to marry her brought me my most memorable and happy thoughts of Persia.

And then the happiness and change in attitudes of the Marseilles when I built their home, and the gratitude and happiness in Dominick's family when I helped them, and Madame Giry and Meg and how happy they were when I helped them, those were the times that were the most important to me. All along it was about others and not my sorry self that gave me the most happiness. Helping others and making them happy is what life was about, I finally concluded.

And that went a hundredfold for Christine. When I thought back over our time together, it was when I was making her happy that I was happy. Even when she was a babe in arms and I held that necklace up to her and laid it in her small hand, what I felt in my heart was priceless. While I began our relationship with the selfish motive of being close to her, in the end, it was the happy look in her eyes when she accomplished a piece of music, when she arrived at center stage during the gala, when I read to her, when she opened a present, and when we sang together that made it all worthwhile.

I thought, if I could go back in time and change the outcome of our time together, I would do anything to prevent her tears and broken heart. Just as an artist, with one swipe of his brush, erases what he no longer wants on his canvas, I would erase that last night with Christine and Raoul in my home. Then his near-death and her fearful cries wouldn't even be a memory.

When I entered my parlor and leaned back against the door, I thought, it's all about making others happy. The majority of my life, making my father happy was what kept me going. Even after his death, I pictured him looking down at me from heaven and felt contentment when I knew my actions would make him happy.

I knew my father, Oded, and Christine wouldn't be happy with my death, but that would be the price we'd have to pay to prevent the unhappiness to the multitudes of others if my life continued. With those thoughts in mind, I knew how I was going to spend my last day on earth.

I changed into my work clothes, grabbed my tools, and then systematically went through all my passages and dismantled all the trapdoor latches, with the exception of the ones I might still need. Those I would have to dismantle when I used them for the last time.

While I was working on the one to Christine's dressing room, I couldn't prevent my memories from taking me to our time together, but I didn't allow them to go too deep before I moved on to the next latch. Once all of them were dismantled, the doors were nearly impossible for anyone other than me to open. That would prevent anyone from accidently finding my lair or my horrible mirror chamber.

That project took a big part of the day, and then I did something I'd never done before. I went to the stable and started a conversation with the grooms, after they got beyond my mask, that is. I have to admit, though, that I did lie to them. I told them I was recently hired for a certain project in one of the cellars, and that I'd heard about the great horses in the stable and wanted to see them. But first I asked them about themselves, their lives, families, likes, hobbies, and anything they wanted to tell me about. I was smiling most of the time, thinking I then understood why Christine did that same thing so often. It was actually enjoyable to hear their stories.

Then I went to all the horses, talked to them, felt them, smelled them, and listened to them. I left César for the last, and, with tears in my eyes, I ran my hands under his mane and around his ears, reliving all the times we'd spent together. When the pain became too great, I kissed his nose, looked in his eyes, told him I wouldn't be coming back, and then told him goodbye. He nickered in response and shoved his nose against my chest, making my eyes fill with tears. Without making eye contact with the grooms, I thanked them and left the stable for the last time.

My next project was a gruesome one, but I'd given my word and I had to fulfill it. It was difficult, but eventually I had my casket across the lake and up to the third cellar. Then, with a shovel in my hand, I prepared to dig my own grave. I walked the area by the well until I found the spot I'd told Raoul about, and then I started digging. As I did, I remembered the ones I'd buried there and the situations that surrounded their deaths. Deaths, I hated them, and I had to count each shovel-full of dirt to keep my sights set on my goals and not on my death.

Once I was finished, I stared down into my casket in the dark pit for only a moment, and then I began backing away from it, feeling repulsed and frightened. I shook my head. I didn't want to finish what I'd started, but I had to. So, with an angry cry, I slammed the shovel's blade down into the unearthed mound of dirt and ran away like a frightened coward.

I entered my home out of breath and knew I had to prepare for my final hours without thinking about what I was doing. So I made a plate of food, poured myself a glass of my best wine, and then took them and my journal to my chair. I ate calmly while writing some of my last thoughts in my journal and one final note to Madame Giry. I kept an eye on my tall clock, and, when it was the right time, I took a warm and leisurely bath before preparing to take in my last opera. Once arrayed in my finest attire, I made my way through one of the passages still open to me.

After entering Box Five, I took a deep breath and allowed memories to surge through my heart. I made sure the door was locked, sat down, and placed my last box of English Sweets on the ledge along with an envelope, containing my last note to Madame Giry and the sapphire. The note held my sincere appreciation for all the help she'd given me over the years and a final goodbye. I explained I'd be leaving the Opera Populaire for good, and I wished both her and Meg many years of happiness.

I didn't think Christine would be performing Marguerite that night, and I was right, which was good and bad. There was no one who could portray that character better than Christine, so it was difficult to sit through my last opera, but then it would have been extremely difficult to sit through it if I was watching my love for the last time as well.

I leaned back in my chair and surveyed the captive audience as I had so many times before. As I sat there, my thoughts went to my first visit to an opera house in Venice with my father by my side and then to all the other times I sat all alone in that box as the Opera Ghost. I looked at the empty de Chagny box and felt sad about the Comte's death, and then wondered where Raoul and Christine were at that time.

I sighed and looked at all the colorful costumes on the performers as well as the ones the spectators were wearing. They were all nothing more than actors in one form or another. Then I gasped and threw myself back farther in my chair when I saw Oded standing off to the side on the main floor. He was talking to an usher, and they were both looking up at my box. That tenacious daroga, I thought. He's not going to give up until my final breath.

Fifty-Six

Instantly, I slid out of my chair, grabbed my hat and cloak, and crept along the wall until I reached the column. Within a minute, I was in the passage and the latch clicked into place. I waited silently for a few more minutes until I heard the key in the lock. Next, I heard whispered voices.

"I shouldn't let you do this, *monsieur*. I don't think he'll be pleased; however, since you say you're his friend, I'll make an exception. But, as you can see, he's not here."

Surprisingly, that voice belonged to Madame Giry, and my jaw dropped. Oded! He could talk a wild lion into eating straw for lunch instead of him.

"Hmm," was Oded's response. "But I know I saw him."

"Many say they do," Madame Giry replied, "but no one really does. I talk to him often, and even I've never seen him. He's a ghost, *monsieur*. He can't really be seen—not the way you think."

I looked through the hole and saw Oded look at her thoughtfully and nod, and then he began looking around. When he spotted the box of sweets and note, he started asking her questions, and I thought, no, don't fall into his trap of questions.

"What is this?" he asked.

"Oh," she nearly gasped as she moved toward the ledge and picked up the box and note. "He's been here. He's left me another gift. He does that often. He's very kind."

Oded nodded again. "Yes, that he is." He hesitated a moment and then asked another question. "I don't mean to be forward, but it's important that I know what that note says. Do you mind reading it to me?"

Madame Giry huffed and looked down at the note in her hand. "Well, I don't know, *monsieur*, it might be personal, and I really don't know you."

Oded looked at her kindly, and drove home his last question.

"Then would you read it silently and tell me anything that is not of a personal nature? This is very important or I wouldn't be asking. You could say it's even a matter of life and death."

Like so many others before her, including myself, she was hooked by his savoir-faire and did as he asked. Almost cautiously, she broke the seal, opened the envelope, and pulled out the note and the sapphire. She took in a quick breath as she looked at the large stone lying in her palm, and so did Oded.

"See," she said. "He is so kind."

"Yes, I recognize his generosity," Oded replied reflectively. Then he added, "The note? What does it say?"

She began reading it, and after a few moments, her small hand covered her trembling lips, and she shook her head slowly.

"Oh, no," she whispered plaintively.

"Madame? What is it?" Oded asked while moving closer to her.

"Our Opera Ghost is leaving us. I can't believe it. This is his last performance," she replied with her hand still over her lips.

Oded took a deep breath, nodded slightly, looked around at all the walls, and began knocking quietly on them—even the column, while I held my breath. Then, abruptly, he opened the door.

"*Merci*, Madame Giry. You've been most helpful."

He then left, leaving my humble protector in tears.

"Don't cry, Madame Giry," I said softy. "You can now let the management know that I no longer need my box so they can sell it. As I stated in my note, I've always appreciated your gracious assistance, and I feel the next owner of this box will also appreciate your attentive support. The sapphire is my final gift to you. Enjoy it in good health."

She straightened her shoulders back, nodded, and said, "*Merci*. I'll miss you."

She then slowly left, and I stood there in the dark not knowing what to do next. I felt Oded was heading for my dock in an attempt to find me, so I couldn't go home by that route. But then I couldn't be sure he wasn't going to be waiting for me to appear by the trap door he'd entered that fateful night. Or, he could be outside the box door, waiting for me to leave. Those were the only ways I had left of getting home, so, at first, I felt trapped, but not for long.

I had to stop thinking and acting like a trapped rabbit and think more like the fox. I needed to be the hunter instead of the hunted. I needed to think like Oded who was trying to think like me. He knew I saw him looking at me, so he knew I was hiding. He knew I wouldn't expect him to try to use the passage in the third cellar since that one nearly got him killed; therefore, I would think that was a safe passage for me to use.

But, *au contraire*. For that very reason, and the fact that there were plenty of places for him to hide behind sets in that location, that's where I believed he would wait first for me. After that, he would check the lake. If my boat was still there, he would wait there in the dark for a while and then head home, hoping to catch me when I left the box.

Consequently, I rushed down the passage I was in that let me out in the fourth cellar. From there, I ran down the corridors toward the lake and where I'd hid Sari's box, and then, with it in hand, I ran back up to that same passage and through it to my outside door.

There were many broughams on the street, waiting for the opera to end, so I didn't have a problem hailing one. I gave the driver Oded's address and told him to hurry. Shortly, I stepped out of it on a side street close to Oded's flat and told the driver to leave quickly. I then checked Oded's window for any sign of life inside.

There was a faint light, probably coming from the kitchen in the back, so I ran up the stairs as quietly as I could. Once at his door, I opened it with my personal key, cautiously stepped inside, and set Sari's box on the small table where my wine glass usually sat when I was in his home. I then left just as quickly and quietly and ran back down the stairs and around that same corner.

I waited a moment to catch my breath, and then I peeked around the corner for any sign of a carriage before crossing the street toward the *Tuileries*. But I didn't cross right then, since I saw a carriage heading quickly toward me. I pressed myself back against the wall and waited for it to stop or pass by.

Sure enough, it stopped, and then I heard Oded run up the stairs. Again, I waited until he came rushing back down and into the street where he turned in circles, looking for me. All the while his plaintive call tore through my heart.

"Erik! Please! Please! Come talk to me! Please! Erik!"

I silently told him, no, please don't do this, and then I pressed my head back against the wall, closed my eyes tightly, and shoved my hands over my ears. I couldn't bear to hear the pain and fear in his voice. I visualized his body lying in my torture chamber, with his blue lips and nail beds, and I understood how he felt. However, I was barely holding onto my resolve to put an end to it all, and another conversation with Oded could force my king to lie down, so I couldn't be plunged into another confrontation with him.

He kept calling and I kept telling him and myself, no. I almost gave in and answered him, but then I knew there was one big difference in his pain and mine. Oded was a good and kind man who never hurt anyone, whereas I was a monster who hurt many. He didn't deserve what I did to him, but I did deserve what I was going to do to myself.

He stopped calling my name when he began whistling for a brougham. Soon I heard one approaching and Oded enter it. Then it moved around the other corner, circling the *Tuileries*, but he kept calling my name, and I again silently asked him to let it go—just let me go.

When the coach was far enough away, I entered the park and crept my way through it in the moonlight. But then I noticed that same brougham continue to circle the *Tuileries*. That didn't surprise me, but it did make it necessary that I be more cautious as I moved through the park toward the opera house.

When I reached the other end of the park, I waited for his carriage to begin another circle before I crossed the street to the next block. From there it was more difficult to stay hidden, since he continued to circle one block after another, and I didn't have the cover of the trees.

Then, what made it worse was my desire to buy two more roses, so, when I spotted a flower vender who was just closing up his stand, it took strategic timing to approach him and purchase those two red roses and disappear again. Eventually, I reached my outside door and had it opened. Then one last time I heard the faint call of my name in the distance.

I turned, looked in its direction, and whispered, "*Au revoir, Mon Ami.*"

With a deep sigh, I entered the opera house without being seen by him, which left me with mixed emotions. I almost wished he had caught me and tried again to change my mind. If he had, I would have had an excuse not to follow through with my suicide.

Once in my home, I put the two roses in a vase and set it on Christine's dressing table next to her jewelry box. I hoped she would understand that gesture was telling her that I still wanted her future to be a beautiful one. Then, without giving myself too much time to think, I grabbed my tools and headed out to disable the last of the trapdoor latches. Once I was finished, there was only one way into or out of my home and that was by way of the lake.

I'd already left my boat at the dock for Raoul to use, so I only had a few other tasks to do for him. I turned on the light in my docking room, climbed the steps to the viewing window and opened it so it could serve as a beacon leading him to my home.

I then entered my parlor, leaned up against the door, and waited for it to click, just as I'd done a thousand times before, but that would be my last time to do so. Then I checked my mental list to make certain I'd secured everything. When I knew I had, I sighed, knowing there wouldn't be any accidental deaths due to my diabolical genius, especially considering I still felt I was a curse and could always cause someone harm even after my death.

I stopped for a few minutes and gave myself the chance to enjoy the last glass of my best wine and the warmth of a fire while thinking, not many people had the opportunity of knowing exactly when they will die, and, in some respect, I felt I was strangely privileged to have that chance.

I'd been able to use those four days to see my life as a whole, the good and the bad times, the strong and the weak times, and the laughter and the tears. But that trek through my life left me with serious doubts about what I was planning to do with the rest of it, which I knew was exactly what Oded was counting on. At the heart of it all, I believe I'd healed somewhat from the trauma of that frightful last night in my home, and I didn't want to die—not yet.

The thought of Christine's eyes when she gave me my first kiss gave me hope that something could happen between us. I saw the love in her eyes, and I felt it in the air around us that night. I knew she would love me with a love that was true—as I did her. But then, at the same time, it was the thought of her traumatized eyes that made me realize I had to free her from the harmful effects of my company. But regardless of the expression in her eyes, the bottom line was clear, my death was the best thing for all concerned.

As I took a sip of my wine and watched the sparks gracefully rise from the flames, I again questioned the condition of the dead. I didn't want to believe in another life after the one I'd mutilated. If there was a life after death, it would mean my father had been watching me my entire life. It would mean he saw all that had happened to me and, worse yet, by me. He would also know what I was about to do. Without a doubt, his heart would be bleeding and would have been bleeding all my life, since my entire life had been spattered with failures.

I took a deep breath and the last swallow of my wine. Then I glanced toward my music room, knowing what I had to do next, so I got up and went to my armoire. Once there, I took out the green velvet bag and shook my mother's locket out into my palm. I looked at my scratched name inside and felt entirely different than I had the first time I'd seen it. I felt warmth and envisioned the softer side of my mother when we shared our musical journeys together. But then I made the mistake of wondering, was she also alive somewhere and watching my life? I closed my eyes tightly and clamped my jaws, not willing to let my thoughts go in that direction.

I instantly replaced the locket in the bag and set it on top of my piano. In the same fashion, without thinking about it, I took the small box that held my supply of morphine out of my armoire and laid it beside the bag. My palm was the next item to land on my piano, and I felt its smooth finish. With another sigh, I sat down and began playing.

Even though I couldn't enjoy it the same without Christine, I played several pieces. "Moonlight Sonata" was the last one, and as my fingers traveled over the familiar keys, my eyes closed. In the darkness, I saw my mother at the piano and heard that beautiful refrain fill our home and my heart. I swayed to the rhythm, both as that child and as the man. After the last note faded from my music room, I opened my eyes and looked at my outstretched fingers lying over the keys. Then I shed tears for my poor unhappy mother and her poor unhappy son.

That unplanned journey confirmed that I loved certain aspects of my life too much to put an end to them. I deeply loved and needed my music, the one constant in my life that always gave me the courage and hope to keep living. But while it helped me want to live, it didn't help me find a way to live without hurting anyone in the process. No, there was only one answer. I gazed at the black and ivory keys and then the box—my means of life and my means of death.

With another deep breath, I got up and went back to my armoire, knowing what I needed to do next. I took out my saddlebags and then knelt beside my trunk. I took out my old cloak and tore open the hem, releasing the jewels and gold coins stored inside it. Then I put them in a leather pouch and tossed it in my hand a few times.

When another surge of memories approached, I took that pouch, and all the money I'd stored in the trunk from the opera management, and put it all in my saddlebags, and then I laid them on top of my piano. I next put my bag of treasures inside my violin case along with my violin. I was ready to close the case but then stopped and ran my fingers over the shiny amber curves, releasing memories and desires. Consequently, I lifted it out of its case and, with my eyes closed, readied it under my chin. As I raised the bow, the first notes of "Papa's Song" filled the room, just as they'd filled the cemetery that tragic day. Long before the piece was finished, my tears had escaped my mask and fallen to the instrument in my hand. My father—my Papa, I still missed him so much.

I was again ready to place my violin in its case when I had one more need, so I again raised the bow and released "Anna" from the strings. As I did, I could hear my mother's talented harmony accompanying me, and, without hindrance, I let more tears flow.

Eventually, I was able to put my Stradivarius in its case, and, after one more look and one more caress from my fingers, I closed the case. But before I could leave that room of music, I had to spend some last moments with my cello. The last notes that room held came from one of my own compositions, "Cellos in the Clouds." When the music faded, I sat quietly and thought about all the compositions I'd written. The one I'd just played was my favorite for the cello.

Not letting myself think too deeply, I went to Christine's bedroom and placed my violin on her bed and the box of morphine on the small table beside her bed. Once I got the jeweled knife out of the kitchen, I put it in the saddlebags along with the rest of my wealth.

Only one last group to organize, I thought. I gathered all my writings, the many pages containing my life story and the important pieces of music I'd composed, with the exception of *Don Juan Triumphant*. I didn't want that dark piece of music remembered by anyone. Then I put them all into my old black satchel and fastened it closed. For a few moments, I ran my fingers over the tattered bag, removing layers of dust and remembering when I began chronicling my life stories at that small lake in northern Italy.

Once that journey was finished, I set the satchel beside my saddlebags on my piano, and put the green velvet bag in my pocket. Then I took one last look around my music room and all my instruments, again with pleasant memories of the endless hours spent in my private, musical world. I looked at the bust of Molly, smiled, and ran my fingers across her nose, remembering her and the man who'd given me that gift. I took a deep breath and headed toward the door, letting my fingertips slide across the top of my piano for one last caress.

I next stood in my parlor and wound my watch and then pulled the chain on the tall clock to keep it running for as long as it could. I wasn't going to be around long enough to appreciate either of those actions, so I don't know why I did them. Then, after running my fingers over the horse heads on my father's watch for one last time, I put it in the bag with my mother's locket and put them both in my vest pocket.

Then I stood in the silence, trying to think if I'd forgotten to do anything before I brought the final curtain down. I could see the bed from where I was standing, and I pictured what was shortly to take place there. When I did, I realized that, while I'd taken precautions to make certain my death was as pleasant as I could make it and that it wouldn't present too much of a disturbing sight to those who would take care of my burial, there was something I hadn't thought about.

I wanted Christine and Raoul to think I'd died of natural causes, but if I passed out before I could hide the morphine and syringe they would question what had really happened to me. Consequently, when I sat down at the dining table to write Christine a note about what to do with my things, I had to add more to make my natural death convincing. I wrote slowly, trying to use my best hand, so it wouldn't be too difficult for her to understand.

My Dearest Christine—My Angel,

I thank you for being here and taking care of my final needs. I hope and pray it won't be too difficult for you. I love you with a love that's true, and I've never wanted to hurt you in any way, so I deeply apologize for this last unusual burial request.

On my piano, you'll find my saddlebags. They hold the accumulation of a lifetime of wealth. I'd like you to keep them for three months. If, at the end of that time, everything is all right between you and Raoul, and he's taking care of you properly, I'd like you to give them to Oded. If not, I want you to have them.

Beside my saddlebags, you'll find a black satchel. It contains my thoughts I've written down throughout my life, both in music and word form. I don't know if you or Oded want them, but if someone does, they can have them. Perhaps they might help any who read them to understand why I was who I was and how hard I tried to be a good person—even if I didn't succeed.

Beside me on the bed is my violin case with my violin and some other important treasures inside. I'd like it, along with my ring that I trust you'll put back on my finger, to be buried with me. Then, except for you, I'll be taking with me all that mattered the most to me.

All your jewelry is in your jewelry box. You should take it with you, but if you don't want it or the jewels around as a reminder, then please give it to Oded. I owe him. He gave up so much to save my life in Persia, so, now that my life is over, I'd like to repay him somehow.

I'm not sure what condition you'll find me in, so I feel the need to explain what you might see. I didn't realize my heart would cause me so much pain in the last days. I thought it would merely tire out until it stopped, but that hasn't been the case. At times, such as right now, there's so much pain in my chest that I can hardly bear it. You've seen me in dire pain, but I can honestly say this is the worst I've ever experienced. So if you see a morphine bottle or syringe you'll know I took too much while trying to relieve the pain.

I love you, Christine, perhaps with an insane love, but it was the best my heart could give. From the first moment I saw you on that stage, my heart belonged to you and it will until it beats its final beat. I wish for your life with Raoul to be a happy and complete life and that in time you'll be able to think about our time together without heartache.

Whenever you see two red roses, please remember that you deserve your present and your future to be perfect. Always believe in the gifts you've been given, and pass them on to your progeny, as all good parents should.

May your home be filled with the laughter of children and music, and your heart with unbridled happiness—my dear, sweet angel.
Your Angel of Music forever, Erik.

Once I felt I'd told her all I needed to tell her, I placed the note beside the roses and her jewelry box. Then I sat on the edge of the bed and looked back at her dressing table, picturing her brushing her long, blonde hair. I saw the look in her eyes that day when she placed the combs in her hair, and I then understood that look was an expression of her desire for me. But it was all right for me to remember and then let it go, because I also believed she loved Raoul and that he would take good care of her.

Memories. So many memories. I'd heard it said that your life passes quickly in front of your eyes before you die, but what I'd experienced over the last four days was more than a quick passing. I'd lived my entire life over again, so I'd call it more a leisurely stroll than a quick passing. But then, I'd never done anything like a normal man, so why should my final memories be any different?

I'd used my memories of Christine to help me during my four-day waiting period, and I planned to use them again before my end came. I wanted thoughts of her—her singing, her fragrance, her laughter, her eyes, her movements—to be the last thoughts I ever had. I wanted my death to be as pleasant as possible, and what better way to make it pleasant than to fill it with thoughts of the only woman I ever loved?

Knowing that my time on earth was over brought sadness to my heart, since I really didn't want to die. I loved life and almost everything that went along with it. I loved music, sunsets, horses, the ocean, conversations with friends, fine food and wine, and the laughter of children. I hated heated arguments, fighting, wars, and death. But, even though I hated those things, I was somehow responsible for them happening far too often. Why did my life have to be so complicated? Why couldn't it be like any other man's life?

I suppose no man really wants to die when the time comes to say goodbye. Most men usually don't have a choice in the matter. A war or accident or illness can snuff out their lives without their having a say. I, however, while coming close to death's door many times, had always managed to escape its grip. Well, not this time, I mused.

I had to stay focused on that last night with Christine, Raoul, and Oded in my home. I'd almost killed more people in that one evening than I had in the whole of my life. I had to stay focused to prevent any more disasters caused by my hands. It was the only solution.

I'd tried everything else during my life. I'd tried living by my father's guidance. I'd tried living a solitary life. I'd tried being human and controlling my temper and living among mankind. I'd tried burying myself in the depths of the opera house. I'd tried giving my heart to a woman. But, no matter what I tried, I always caused someone to be hurt or even killed.

Since I'd almost taken down part of Paris, I feared what my next diabolical scheme would be and how many more lives I could harm. No, I couldn't trust myself any longer. I had to end it once and for all. No more waiting periods—no more four days—this was the day of reckoning.

I sat on Christine's bed for a few more minutes, looking around the room at all her things. A few more memories traveled across my heart before I took a deep breath, and thought, I'm ready. There's nothing more to do. I've done it all. So I opened the wooden box and took out the morphine and then filled the syringe to the desired level—full. After another deep breath, I watched it lying across my palm. I'd performed that act so many times in my past, but never before with the same intent, never before with a lethal dose of the drug waiting for me.

I'd perfected my plan for a peaceful, uncomplicated, and clean death, which was nothing like the life I'd led. There would be no mess for anyone to clean up after me. No blood from a dagger or gun and no harsh sounds—just blissful silence.

I took the rose petal from my pocket and held it in my closed right fist. Then I pushed up my right sleeve and readied the syringe against my vein while thinking over my plan. I would first inject the drug quickly, throw the syringe in the drawer and shut it, lie down on Christine's pillow, and take my last breath, filled with her fragrance.

With the feel of the rose petal in my hand and the memory of what it represented in my heart, my last sight would be her room, filled with her presence. One last time, I would say her name and think of her singing, leaving my last sensations filled with only her—my love—my Christine. A perfect plan.

As if I were merely watching the scene and not participating in it, I watched the needle slide into my vein, almost painlessly. All that's left is to push the drug in, I told myself. The rest will be up to the liquid to do its quiet work and bring my existence to an end—welcomed or not. I slowly pushed and watched as the soporific liquid moved down the needle and on its way to its destination—its scheduled appointment to stop my heart.

Another small push and it began to enter my blood stream, and I felt the calm start to release me from all the physical and emotional pain of the years past. Stone-faced, I watched my fingers push again, releasing the peace we all needed. No more pain and no more sorrow, neither for me nor anyone else because of me, just peace and eternal sleep.

My eyes became heavy, and I reminded myself to push the rest in quickly and get rid of the evidence before I lay down and waited for the sweet sleep to come. Then, once more, I wondered if it would be sweet sleep or torturous awareness. Of all times, I seriously started to wonder about my lifelong belief that death was the end of it all, and that, once the drug had its final fulfillment, all I'd experience was sleep. But then how could I know for sure? What if I was wrong and so many others were right?

Maybe there was a heaven and a hell. Maybe I would wake up to torment in a hellfire. Or, worse yet, if there was a God of mercy who listened to my heart full of remorse, then I might wake up in heaven and have to look down on the earth for all eternity. Maybe my hell would be watching Raoul take Christine as his wife, hold her, make love to her, laugh with her, produce children and grandchildren with her, while I would be helpless with nowhere to run away to. How could I know for sure what was going to happen to me? Could I bear only watching for eternity?

My music? No! How could I look at my piano or violin and not be able to play them. No! I can't! I can't! Eternal torment would await me either way—heaven or hell—if I couldn't play my music. No!

"No!"

My scream fractured the still silence like a crystal vase shattering on a marble floor, and I flung the syringe from my veins and watched as it fell to the floor, landing beside its counterpart. Then I threw myself off the bed and against the armoire so hard it made it bounce against the wall with a noisy crash that echoed through my home. I reached up, gripping its façade with my fingers, and I screamed, no, again. I closed my eyes tightly and growled over and over again, pressing my head against its doors.

Going to sleep and never waking up I could handle, but to live on somehow in just another sphere and not be rid of all my torment, that I couldn't fathom doing. My head was heavy as I clamped down harder on the façade with my weakening fingers. My knees began to fail me, and slowly I repeated, no. Perhaps I hadn't taken enough to do the job thoroughly, I could only hope. My fingers gave up their hold, my knees became as rubber, my entire body gave way, and I slid down the face of the armoire.

I was crumpled like a child's rag doll on the Persian carpet and against my armoire, with my open right hand lying lifeless and exposing the dried rose petal only centimeters from the means of my demise. My increasingly blurry vision was unable to tell how much morphine I'd taken, so I had no way of knowing just how far I'd gone. My eyes became heavy, and I was doubting my ability to fight the drug's effect on me, but I had to fight. I had to maintain control of my destiny.

I fought harder than I'd ever fought. No matter how bad my body wanted to sleep, I had to make my mind work and stay conscious. I couldn't give in to that overwhelming desire to sleep. But no matter how hard I tried, my eyes closed, and I didn't know if I'd ever open them again or where I'd be in the minutes ahead of me—heaven or hell.

I forced myself to think about my father's guiding words: *You never know what tomorrow will bring, tomorrow is filled with new chances, never cover your heart with your anger, and never let anyone come between you and your goals.* Sadly, I realized, I was the only person who'd successfully stood in the way of my goals.

I'm sorry, Papa, my heart whispered. I did it to myself. I was my own worst enemy, and it's now too late to change anything. For 35 years, I'd listened to my father's guiding words in my heart. They'd kept me going, kept me trying, but it would take more than his words to stop my personally designed destiny from having its fulfillment.

I thought I'd been living with an unmasked heart since I brought Christine down into my home, but I was so mistaken. I only lowered the mask at times and then quickly pulled it back into place when it was too difficult to maneuver without it. Even during those last few hours with Christine, just as soon as I saw her express what I'd been waiting to see, I replaced that mask and prevented any further emotional connection to her. What was she thinking? Why did I take her decision-making away from her? Why did I think I knew best?

My breathing slowed and became fearfully shallow, but I still fought desperately by keeping my mind working. In the interim, I begged, please forgive me, Papa. I'm sorry. I couldn't live my life the way you wanted—with an unmasked heart.

His words and Christine's voice swam slowly through my thoughts as more of my consciousness slipped out of my reach. The final look in her eyes when she left with Raoul appeared before me, taking turns with my father's eyes just moments before he died. They changed places as they floated in front of me in slow repeating successions, first in bright flashes of color and then in nothing more than gray fog.

I couldn't feel anything, not the rug under my fingers, not my head against my armoire, not my breathing, and not my heartbeat. I was numb, and yet I could still feel my thoughts as they whispered, Christine—Christine, I love you so. I heard her voice speak my name softly, and I felt her lips on my face, my horrible face. I saw her eyes, eyes that were saying what her lips couldn't speak. I saw in her eyes a heart unconcealed, and I felt what she was feeling.

When I could no longer hear my tired and lonely heart beating—I let go. For the very first time in my life, I had no control over what happened to me, and I let go. Oh, Christine, my grieving heart whispered one last time. How many twists and turns my life had taken. With the last twist, the dream of the boy was lost because of the love of one man for one woman.

My final thoughts were of my precious Juliet's angelic face as we sang that last duet. It floated with the fog in my mind, along with her beautiful deep blue eyes speaking that language of love as she walked out of my door for the last time. They swirled and mixed with the kaleidoscope of colors, forming a magnificent painting of what our life could have been like if experienced with unmasked hearts—and then they slowly faded.

Erik had his wildest dreams and fantasies so close he could nearly touch them, but, as Christine walked out of the door for the last time, they vanished like the morning mist. Left alone with a torn and bleeding heart, he struggles with the hardest decision of his life—one that will mean life or death to the remainder of his dreams.
Continue to read his story and see where that decision takes him in Volume Six, Unmasked Hearts.

Made in the USA
Middletown, DE
03 January 2015